Boys In Blue

Everyday Heroes

Sherri Hayes

Boys In Blue: Everyday Heroes

By Sherri Hayes

ISBN (ebook): 978-1-948471-03-9

ISBN (paperback): 978-1-948471-04-6

Cover Design by Miblart

ABOUT THIS BOOK

Are you looking for an alpha hero? Follow two law enforcement officers as they find love in the most unexpected places.

Crossing the Line

A widower who's still mourning the loss of his wife, Paul Daniels isn't looking for love. He's a single dad, and he's content to raise his little girl on his own. What he didn't expect was the change that would occur when Megan moved in to help him take care of his daughter. Thirteen years his junior, she's full of life. She's brought joy back into his home and has him craving things he thought had died long ago. Can he open himself up and find love again, or will the past continue to haunt him?

***

Seducing Janey

Kyle Reed left the Army to take care of his younger sister after the death of their parents. He gave up his carefree life as a bachelor and settled into a new career as a sheriff's deputy in their small town of Liberty, Indiana. When his boss asks him to show a city detective around, he wasn't expecting a blonde bombshell. He knew the moment he saw Janey there would be more to their story than solving a murder.

These two sexy Law Enforcement romances will have you wanting to curl up with these Boys in Blue.

Crossing The Line

A Daniels Brothers Romance

CHAPTER 1

"DID YOU SEE ME, Daddy? Did you see me?"

Paul Daniels bent down and lifted his five-year-old daughter, Chloe, into his arms. "I did."

He gave her his best smile, not that she noticed. Chloe was too excited to pay much attention to anything for long. Paul thought nothing could top the excess of energy his little girl displayed the day Chris and Elizabeth called to ask her if she'd be their flower girl. He'd been wrong. Three months ago, Chloe had been full of questions about the unknown—she'd never been to a wedding before. Today, she was bouncing off the walls, and her smile matched his new sister-in-law's in pure joy.

It was as if he hadn't commented at all.

"And Eliz'beth's dress is sooo pretty. Isn't it pretty, Daddy?" Chloe didn't wait for his response this time either, before she continued. "Now she's my aunt." She concentrated to make sure she got it right. Megan had been working diligently to help Chloe improve her speech before she started school in the fall.

Paul searched the crowd of people bustling into the reception hall for the woman in question, as Chloe squirmed wordlessly making her desire to be put down known. He lowered her feet to the floor, and watched as she slipped in between two wedding guests while he continued to scan for Megan.

Megan was the younger sister of his baby brother Gage's wife. Paul had met her when she'd come to Thanksgiving with her sister. Little had he known what a savior she'd turn out to be. She'd brought life back into his house. Life that he hadn't realized was missing.

She'd rescued him when he'd been in desperate need of someone to watch Chloe. Hours before he'd loaded Chloe into the car to set off for the holiday with his parents, his in-laws had announced they were moving almost two hours away. For four years, they'd lived nearby and were able to take Chloe whenever he was called in to work. His job as a homicide detective meant that he could be called out at all hours, and he couldn't leave his young daughter alone. Megan had fit the bill by offering to move to Indianapolis and into his house as a live-in nanny. She'd saved Paul from having to spend countless hours searching for an alternative.

As if knowing the direction of his thoughts, Chloe weaved through the people in her path until she was beside her nanny. Megan smiled when she caught sight of the little girl, and she circled her arms around Chloe's shoulders, lifting her off the ground, and twirling. They were both laughing—happy. The two of them had clicked from the beginning, and his chest clenched almost painfully watching the two of them together. It should have been Melissa standing there twirling Chloe, but he couldn't be upset that it was Megan. She'd put her life on hold for them—helped them out when they'd needed it most. Paul wished he could be as carefree.

His brother, Chris, wanted to give his fiancée, Elizabeth, the wedding of her dreams, right down to the ceremony being held in a quaint little church not far from where they lived in Springfield, Ohio —and it was. Elizabeth had walked down the aisle in a long white gown, his brother in a tux. Everyone who meant something in either of their lives was present. It was . . . perfect.

Unfortunately, it brought back too many memories for Paul. Memories that were raw and painful. Almost fifteen years ago, he'd been where his brother was—marrying the love of his life. He didn't begrudge Chris and Elizabeth their happiness. No, he was grateful. His brother had had a rough time of it after his first marriage fell apart. For Paul, it was a sharp reminder that he no longer had his wife at his side. She'd been taken from him by a drunk driver.

Starting to get choked up, Paul cleared his throat, and made a beeline for the bar. He didn't drink often, and never when he had to drive afterward, but tonight he didn't have to go anywhere but upstairs to his hotel room. Chloe was here, of course, so he couldn't go overboard. He just wanted to numb some of the pain.

Paul leaned his elbows on the bar as he waited for the petite blond bartender to finish with the drink she was making for another guest. He thought the guy standing patiently waiting for his drink was one of Chris' employees. Paul was also fairly certain that the guy was single by the way he was openly eyeing the young woman from head to toe. She was pretty— Paul wasn't blind, after all. Unfortunately, there was no spark. There never was. Not since his wife, Melissa.

Six months after Melissa's accident, he'd tried. He'd left Chloe with Melissa's parents and gone out to a club. It had been loud and he'd felt out of place, but he'd met a woman he found attractive and went for it. They'd ended up at her place an hour later, clothes on the floor, with him hovering over her.

He hadn't been able to go through with it, though. As he reached for a condom, he'd seen Melissa smiling up at him, her chest vibrating as she attempted to suppress her mirth while he fumbled trying to roll the rubber down his erection. It was an old memory, from when they were teenagers, but it had stung all the same. He'd gathered his clothes, dressed, and apologized, leaving the woman, whom he only knew as Karen, lying naked on her bed staring after him.

The bartender handed over the drink she'd made, and then turned to Paul without giving the other man a second glance. Looked like he wouldn't be getting that after-closing booty call.

She turned to Paul and smiled. "What can I get ya?"

"Scotch. Neat."

Her smile got wider. "Coming right up, handsome."

Paul glanced over his shoulder, and caught sight of his mom and dad. They appeared to be engrossed in a conversation with two people he didn't know. His dad looked in Paul's direction, and Paul quickly turned back around. The last thing he needed was his dad zeroing in on his less-than- festive attitude.

The bartender placed the half-full glass of scotch down in front of him. She made sure to lean in a little closer than normal. "Here you go."

"Thanks." Paul picked up the glass and took a drink. It burned as it went down his throat, which was good. Anything was better than the knife twisting in his gut.

"So how do you know the bride and groom?"

Not wanting to be rude, Paul answered her. "I'm the groom's brother."

"Older or younger?"

Paul laughed, before backing away. "Thanks again for the drink."

He made it halfway to the corner he'd scoped out as a decent hiding place, before he was waylaid by his brother, Trent. "Hey, man." Trent looked down at the drink Paul had in his hand, and raised his eyebrow.

"Something wrong?"

"I was going to ask you the same question. Since when do you drink anything but beer?"

"I like to mix it up sometimes." Paul didn't add that those "sometimes" usually involved his wedding anniversary and the anniversary of his wife's death. Chris' wedding didn't fall on either of those occasions, but Paul was making an exception.

"Since when?"

After taking another sip of his scotch, Paul narrowed his eyes at his younger brother. "Did you have a reason for coming over here other than to give me a hard time?"

Trent frowned, but let it go. For now, at least. "Megan and Chloe were looking for you. Chloe wants some pictures of you, Megan, and her together. Chris and Elizabeth don't have a problem with it, but they wanted to make sure it was okay with you before they agreed to anything."

The last thing Paul wanted to do was pose for more pictures, but there were very few things he'd deny his daughter. Pictures of the woman she'd grown extremely close to over the last four months wasn't one of them. "It's fine."

Again, he saw that look of doubt cross his brother's face. "Okay . . ."

Paul ignored Trent's curiosity. "Where?"

"Out in the lobby. The photographer has been taking some pictures in front of the fountain."

Not waiting to see if Trent would come up with more questions regarding his odd behavior, Paul took off toward the fountain.

Before entering the lobby, he took one last gulp of his scotch, feeling the heat. He could do this. For his daughter, he could do this.

Setting his now empty glass down on a nearby table, he plastered a smile on his face, and went to find Megan and Chloe.

***

Megan Carson held tight to Chloe's hand as she continued to flutter about without a care in the world. They were in the lobby waiting on Paul. At least, Megan hoped they were waiting on Paul. It hadn't escaped her notice that he'd been tense all throughout Chris and Elizabeth's vows. And a couple of times she noticed him getting a look on his face. She couldn't help but wonder if he was thinking about his wife.

He'd smiled and laughed along with everyone else, but she could tell his heart wasn't in it. She now knew him well enough to know the difference. And she'd guess his family did, too. Although, technically, Megan was his family now as well—ever since her sister married his brother.

Chloe squealed, and pulled harder on Megan's arm. "Daddy!"

Releasing the little girl's hand, Megan stood back and watched Paul scoop up his daughter. Seeing them like this gave her a warm feeling. He smiled at Chloe, and this time it didn't look fake or forced. Then again, whenever it came to Chloe, Megan didn't question Paul's

5

love or willingness to do anything for her. Chloe was the apple of his eye—a tangible reminder of his dead wife.

"I was told there's a picture that needs to be taken out here." Paul tickled his daughter's sides.

She giggled. "Yes, Daddy. I want a picture with yous, and mes, and Megan."

Paul glanced down at Megan, and she took in his warm brown eyes. She loved when they sparkled with joy, as they did in that moment. No one could do that to him but Chloe. Not his mom or his brothers. Not even her. No matter how much she wished otherwise.

The photographer approached them with his camera hanging from a strap around his neck. "Ah, good. Everyone's here, yes?"

He quickly corralled them into the correct position, with Megan and Paul flanking Chloe as the three of them sat on the edge of the fountain. To an outside observer, they'd look like a normal family. Appearances could be deceiving, though, and in this case they were way off. Megan was Chloe's nanny, nothing more. She took care of Chloe when Paul was working, making sure she had everything she needed, and that the house wasn't a disaster when he came home.

That was where it ended. Occasionally, Paul would allow Megan to cook dinner for them, but it was rare, and usually only on days when he knew he wouldn't be home until after six. Paul took taking care of his one and only child seriously. She was his responsibility, and while he allowed Megan to take over when he had to leave, he didn't take advantage of her presence in their life—although sometimes she wished that he would.

With the pictures over, Chloe ran back into the reception with an announcement that she was going to find her grandmother—Paul's mom— leaving Paul and Megan behind.

"Thank you."

She looked up at Paul. He towered over her, at just over six feet to her much shorter five foot five. "You know I'd do anything for Chloe."

He was ultra-serious again. "I know, but you don't have to. You're not working tonight."

Megan frowned. He had that melancholy look she noticed crossed his features all too frequently. "Are you all right?"

It was Paul's turn to frown. "Of course. Why wouldn't I be? It's my brother's wedding."

His answer didn't ease her concern. Paul was a good guy—the best guy she'd ever met in her twenty-three years. He put every other man who'd crossed her path to shame, with the exception of Gage and the rest of his brothers and father. The Daniels men had certainly upped her standards in the opposite sex.

"I don't know. You just don't seem like yourself tonight."

Paul waved off her observation. "It's been a long day, that's all."

Yes, it had been a long day. Megan and all the other Daniels women, including Chloe, had met at the spa a little after eight that morning. They'd all gotten their hair and nails done while the guys did whatever guys did to get ready for a wedding. Since then, they'd all been going strong. Megan didn't think that was the problem, but she let it go. For now. "It has been a long day."

In what seemed like an effort to steer her away from any further questioning, Paul held out his arm, and motioned toward the reception. She took a deep breath, and smiled, allowing him to deflect. Whatever was going on with him today, she figured it had to do with his wife. One thing she'd learned about Paul in the four months she'd known him was that he was still very much in love with Melissa. It didn't matter that she'd been dead for over four years. She was still alive in his heart.

Once back inside, Megan was hijacked by her brother-in-law, Gage. "Would you please talk to your sister?"

Megan laughed. "What's up, Becca?"

Her sister, Rebecca, gave her husband a disapproving headshake. "Nothing, except Mr. Overprotective here doesn't think I can do anything on my own."

"I'm trying to be a gentleman." Gage huffed his response, but at the same time, he wrapped his arms around Rebecca's middle, pulling her up against him. It still amused Megan to see how Gage had changed since falling in love with her sister. He'd gone from the cocky playboy to the overprotective husband and daddy-to-be.

Rebecca leaned in to him. "I do not need for you to walk me to the bathroom. I'm not a child." She paused. "And before you say it, I'm not going to get sick. I haven't had a bout of morning sickness in over a week."

Gage kissed her temple and inhaled. "I'm sorry, beautiful, but you know how much I worry about you."

Megan watched her sister—her sister who could take down a man three times her size with her bare hands—melt in her husband's arms. "I guess you two don't need me anymore, then?"

They both chuckled, and Rebecca stood to her full height. "Of course I do. You, I don't mind accompanying me to the ladies' room."

Before she knew it, Rebecca was pushing her toward the bathroom. "Hey, slow down."

Rebecca stopped and released Megan's arm. "Sorry. It's just . . ."

"He's driving you nuts?" Megan laughed.

"It's not funny. You'd think I was terminally ill or something, instead of pregnant."

Although she knew Gage's attentiveness was probably getting to her overly independent sister, she also knew that Rebecca loved the attention. It was something Megan and Rebecca had lacked growing up—Rebecca especially. "You know you love it." Megan paused. "And him."

It took a few seconds, but then a soft smile brightened Rebecca's features. "It's sad, but I do. I know I shouldn't, but to know that he'd drop everything for me and the baby, no matter what, is a pretty amazing feeling."

"Yeah, I bet. I mean, we didn't have that growing up. He's going to be a great dad."

Rebecca glanced back to where Gage was now talking to his father and Trent. "He really is."

The talk of dads sent Megan's mind drifting back to Paul, and she immediately began searching the crowd for him.

"Looking for someone?"

Megan turned back to face her sister. "Huh? What?"

"I asked if you were looking for someone." Rebecca had a strange look on her face, and Megan knew Rebecca was going into big sister mode. It was the last thing she wanted. "Not really."

Her sister frowned. "Is something going on I should know about?"

Now Megan was confused. "Like?"

"I don't know. I mean you've gone four months without chasing after a guy. That's a record for you."

Megan rolled her eyes. "Thanks."

"I didn't . . . I didn't mean it like that. I worry about you. I want you to find a nice guy—someone who will treat you well. I don't want to see you hurt again."

"I know. And when I find him, you'll be the first to know."

Rebecca reached up to brush a strand of hair away from Megan's face. It was something she'd done since Megan was little—a motherly gesture from the only real female authority figure Megan had ever known. "Come on. Let's get to the bathroom before I burst. I think I drank way too much water earlier."

Following her sister, Megan took one last look around trying to spot Paul, but she didn't see him anywhere.

CHAPTER 2

PAUL DIDN'T MANAGE to stay under the radar for as long as he would have liked. Unfortunately, there were only so many places he could hide without leaving the reception entirely. That meant his family was able to find him without too much difficulty.

After leaving Megan, he'd ambled back over to the bar and got another drink to nurse. He needed to take it easy. No matter how bad the pain got, he didn't want his daughter to see him falling down drunk.

He made it about a half hour at his lone table in the corner, sipping his second glass of scotch and nibbling on some food, when Chris and Elizabeth found him.

"Congratulations." Paul tipped his glass to the bride and groom.

"Thank you." Chris held tight to his new bride's hand, and his smile was bright enough to light up the whole room. Paul remembered that feeling. He remembered holding his new wife in his arms—their first dance—their first kiss as husband and wife. Everything.

He was going to need another drink.

Elizabeth was the one to bring Paul out of his memories this time. "So I was wondering if maybe you'd like to dance?"

"Worn your new husband out already?" Paul attempted the joke, but it felt dead to his own ears.

Chris, luckily, didn't seem to pick up on it. Paul supposed his brother was too caught up in the joy of his wedding day, which was exactly as it should be. "Pfft. Not hardly. I'd dance with her all night if that's what she wanted. Aunt Claire, however, wants a dance."

Paul smiled. He wasn't feeling it, but he could pretend. He was good at that. "Sure. I'd love to dance with my new sister."

Reluctantly, Paul left the remains of his scotch on the table, and took Elizabeth's hand. Sure, he could have downed it like he did before, but if he kept doing that he wouldn't be able to walk soon. Plus, Chris might have noticed, and that was the last thing he needed. On the whole, Paul preferred beer, but he would have to down a case of beer to get that numb feeling he was looking for tonight. Scotch was more efficient.

Elizabeth held onto his arm until they reached the dance floor. They danced in relative silence, until he saw some of the happiness drain from her features. "Something the matter?"

She tilted her head to the side. "I was going to ask you the same thing." Obviously he hadn't been hiding his emotions as well as he'd thought.

"I'm fine. Good. My little brother got married today, and I happen to think the woman he chose is perfect for him."

She smiled, but the concern didn't leave her face. "Thank you for saying that, but what about you?"

"Like I said, I'm fine."

Elizabeth seemed to think about it for a moment, and he was really hoping she would drop it. He should have known better. "Does this remind you of your wife? Of your wedding?"

Paul shrugged, not wanting her to make a big deal out of it. "Some. It is a wedding, after all." He didn't add that when Elizabeth had walked down the aisle in her white dress he'd had a flash of Melissa walking toward him on their wedding day.

"I'm sorry. I wish I could have met her."

He nodded. "She would have liked you."

Elizabeth smiled. "I'm sure I would have liked her, too."

Although he didn't mind talking about Melissa to a certain extent —he talked about her often to Chloe—given the events of the day, he didn't think he could handle a long drawn-out discussion. When the song ended, Paul politely thanked Elizabeth for the dance, and went in search of his mom. He needed a few minutes to himself . . . away from everyone . . . but he didn't want to just up and leave without telling anyone either. That would only invite more questions from his family that he didn't want to answer.

He found his mom sitting near the buffet table. Chloe sat next to her, stuffing her face with a piece of bread and some chicken. "Hey, Ma."

"Da-mee!" Chloe's words were muffled around her food.

"Don't talk with your mouth full." His daughter didn't look fazed by his reprimand, and went back to eating.

"I was looking for you earlier."

Paul pulled out a chair beside his mom, and sat down. "Elizabeth wanted a dance."

Marilyn Daniels smiled at her oldest son. "I'm so happy for Chris. He should have married Elizabeth the first time around."

"That would have been difficult since Elizabeth was still married to someone else at the time."

His mom waved the comment away. "You know what I mean. Elizabeth should have been his first."

Paul couldn't argue with that. None of the family had been crazy about Carol, Chris' first wife. That should have been a big clue right there. Unfortunately, Chris found out the hard way that she wasn't the right woman for him when he caught her in bed with his best friend. Paul counted his blessings that he'd never had to experience a betrayal like that. He and Melissa had been childhood sweethearts. She'd been his first, and he hers.

"Paul?"

Blinking, he refocused on his mom. "Sorry. What were you saying?"

She glanced over at Chloe, and then back at him. "Chloe and I were talking about her having a sleepover with Grandma and Grandpa tonight, but I told her we'd have to make sure it was okay with you first."

"Please, Daddy? Please?" This time Chloe made sure to swallow first before she began pleading.

"Sure. We aren't leaving until around noon tomorrow, anyway."

"Yay!"

His mom laughed, and Paul managed a smile. "I was actually coming to find you to see if you could watch Chloe for a bit. I need to run up to the room for something."

"Of course."

"Did you need me to bring down some clothes for her while I'm up there?"

"Nah. We're good. I've got a T-shirt with me she can wear. You just enjoy yourself tonight. I've got Chloe."

"Okay."

"Thank you, Daddy." Chloe jumped up off her chair and hugged Paul's legs.

He hugged her back. She was growing up so fast. "You be good for Grandma and Grandpa, you hear?"

She smiled up at him. "I promise."

Bending down, Paul kissed the top of his daughter's head before walking away. He knew he could have asked Megan to keep an eye on Chloe for him, but he'd told her to take the night off and enjoy herself. She deserved it with all the overtime he'd been working lately.

As Paul headed toward the entrance, he paused and looked over the crowd. Everyone was having a good time, as it should be. He narrowed his eyes a little when he saw Megan talking to that same guy who'd been trying to chat up the bartender.

Shaking it off, he moved on. Megan was a big girl. She could take care of herself.

He looked away, and his gaze honed in on the bar once more. Chloe was spending the night with his parents, so he was free for the rest of the evening.

Throwing caution to the wind, Paul turned on his heel, and

ambled toward the bar to get a bottle of scotch to keep him company up in his room. He already knew it was going to be a long night, and he was still feeling way too much. Chloe wouldn't be there, so there was no reason to hold back. He was going to get drunk. Maybe then, he could stop feeling for a while.

***

Megan saw Paul slip out of the reception hall. She was talking to a guy named Kevin. He was nice enough, but she couldn't help compare him to Paul. On top of that, she'd met plenty of guys like Kevin before. He was looking for someone to warm his bed and, for once, Megan wasn't interested.

When a half hour passed and Paul didn't return, Megan politely excused herself from the conversation she'd been having. She'd thought Paul was going to the bathroom or something, but she was starting to worry that something else was up. Knowing Paul would never leave Chloe, she went in search of the little girl.

As she began pressing her way through the crowd, Gage snuck up beside her. "Do you want to dance?"

"You mean you're willing to leave Becca's side for that long?"

Gage clutched his chest as if she'd wounded him. "I'm not that bad."

She snorted. "You really are."

"Now you sound like your sister." Gage was frowning, which only made Megan laugh more. "Okay, fine. She sort of told me not to come back for at least fifteen minutes under threat of bodily harm. Not that I'd mind exactly, but Chris might take issue if she pulls one of her self-defense moves on me in the middle of his wedding reception."

"I'm surprised she hasn't kicked your ass yet."

His eyes lit up, and he smirked. "Who says I don't like it when your sister gets a little frisky?"

"Eww!" Megan feigned revulsion. In truth, she was ecstatic that her sister had finally met her match. Gage fawned all over Rebecca, but he also didn't let her push him away. He refused to let her hide behind that wall she'd built up because of her and Megan's parents. Megan understood. She had walls of her own. That didn't mean she didn't want what Rebecca had finally found with Gage. Of course she did. Megan wanted to be loved and adored and cherished. She just didn't think it was in the cards for her.

"Come on. Please?" Gage pouted, making Megan laugh harder. He could be such a goof sometimes.

"Sure. Fine. Come on."

Gage danced with her for two songs, and then said he needed to go check on Rebecca. Megan knew her sister was more than capable of taking care of herself. But she also knew that it was useless telling Gage that. She would love to be a fly on their wall sometimes to watch her sister put the big burly football player in his place.

Shaking her head, Megan wandered over to the buffet tables. She'd eaten some of the smaller stuff earlier, but after dancing her stomach was demanding nourishment. Filling her plate, she looked around the room for some place to sit. She spotted Gage and Rebecca immediately, but they looked to be in the middle of what Megan had learned to be foreplay for them—other people called it fighting. The last thing she wanted to do was get in the middle of that. If experience was anything to go by, they'd be sneaking up to their room soon to take out their aggression in other more sexual ways. Thank goodness her room was nowhere near theirs.

The bride and groom were across the room, eating and chatting with some of their guests, while Trent and his dad, Mike, were a few feet away. The Danielses were social people, and she liked them. A lot. It was just that she didn't know them very well. The two exceptions to that were Paul— who was MIA—and Chloe, so when she spotted the little girl with her grandmother, Megan strolled over to join them. "Mind if I sit?"

"Of course not."

"Me-gan, I'm eating chicken."

Megan smiled, and picked up her fork. "Is it good?"

Chloe nodded in an exaggerated fashion as she shoved another piece of chicken in her mouth. They'd been working on eating with utensils, and Chloe was decent at using the kiddie ones, but the normal-sized forks that they had at the reception were a bit much for her tiny hands.

"How have you been, Megan? I haven't seen you since Gage and Rebecca's wedding."

Megan swallowed the bite of food she was chewing before answering. "Good. Keeping busy. Rebecca talked me into taking some online classes."

"Oh, that's a great idea. Do you have a degree in mind?"

"Not really. I've always been interested in art, so maybe something to do with that. I don't know yet."

As if Marilyn and Megan weren't in the middle of a conversation, Chloe interrupted. "Guess what, Megan? I'm going to sleep in Grandma and Grandpa's room tonight. We're having a sweepover."

Not able to hide her smile, Megan reached for her drink. "You mean a sleepover? That sounds fun."

"Yep." Chloe was nodding again. "A sleep-over."

The next five minutes or so were spent listening to Chloe tell Megan all about the sleepover she was going to have with her grandparents, including the movie they were going to watch, and how she was going to get to stay up really, really late. It was impossible not to smile. Chloe put her whole heart into everything she did, and from what Megan had observed while living with Chloe and her father, the little girl was very much like her mother.

Those thoughts led right back to Chloe's father. Paul still hadn't returned, and Megan was beginning to worry about him. Had something happened with work? Or was it the wedding in general? The look on his face earlier reminded her of the one he'd get whenever she'd pass by his bedroom and catch him holding the picture of his wife in his hands. Paul was a great guy, and she didn't like seeing him hurting.

As Megan finished her food, she chatted back and forth with Marilyn. Every now and then, Chloe would interject a comment or share a story. When Mike Daniels, the patriarch of the Daniels family, approached the table, Megan decided it was time to go in search of

Paul. She said her goodbyes, and kissed Chloe on the cheek, before going to find her sister.

Rebecca could, of course, read her like a book. "Oh no. What's wrong?"

Luckily, Gage wasn't around. "Nothing's wrong. Where's your husband?"

"He went to get me some more food. Stop deflecting."

"I'm not deflecting." It was sort of a lie, but not really. She knew that if she told her sister she was going to look for Paul, Rebecca would tell her husband and soon the entire Daniels clan would be off in search of him. Megan knew Paul wouldn't want that.

"Then why do you have that look on your face?"

"Maybe because I'm tired?"

"Uh-huh."

Not wanting to fight with her sister, Megan got to the point. "I just wanted to let you know that I'm heading up to my room. It's been a long day, and I'm ready to crash."

"Oh. Okay."

Rebecca looked torn for some reason. "What?"

"Nothing."

"Becca?"

"I saw the way you were looking at Paul earlier."

"Okay. And?"

"And . . ." She sighed. "Is something . . . you know, going on with you two?"

Megan's mouth fell open. She felt it, and she had no control of it at all. Her and Paul? Sure, he was attractive. Okay, more than attractive. But he'd never shown any interest in her that way, so even if she wanted to, which she kind of did, she wouldn't push herself on him like that. He and his family had taken Rebecca and Megan in, embracing them as part of the family. Plus, Paul wasn't over his wife. Megan knew that, above all else. "No. Why would there be? Besides, just because you're getting your freak on all over the place doesn't mean everyone else is."

Rebecca let out a relieved breath. "All right."

As if a lightbulb went off in her head, Megan narrowed her eyes at her sister. "What? You thought that just because he's a man and I live with him now that there has to be something going on?"

"I didn't say that."

"No. You didn't, but you implied it. I'm not a little kid anymore, Rebecca."

"I know. I'm so—"

Megan waved off her apology. "I'm going to my room. I'll see you tomorrow."

"Megan?"

Megan continued walking, and she was glad to hear Gage asking Rebecca what was wrong. He would keep her sister from following her. Megan knew she'd have to deal with Rebecca tomorrow, and that was fine. Right now, however, she needed some space. And to find Paul.

Something in the back of her mind told her to let it go—to leave him be. Megan pushed it aside and told herself that she just needed see that he was all right. Then she could go up to her room, find some cheesy romantic movie on television, and fall asleep.

CHAPTER 3

MEGAN LOOKED EVERYWHERE she could think of, even walking outside to see if she could spot him talking on his cell or something, but she came up empty. He was nowhere to be found, and after twenty minutes of searching, she decided to head upstairs to her room. She figured he had to come back eventually, right?

As soon as Megan stepped inside her room, she kicked off her shoes. High heels made your legs look great, but they were killer on your feet.

Next to come off was her jewelry, and then finally, her dress. She'd dressed up more than usual for Chris and Elizabeth's wedding—more sophisticated, too. The dress she'd chosen was knee length, perfectly conservative, and had cute ruffled sleeves. To be honest, she was dressed more like her sister than she was herself. On most days, Megan preferred jeans and T-shirts, although she also liked skirts that showed off her legs. She might only be five foot five, but she had nice legs. Why not flaunt them?

She padded into the bathroom in her bare feet, figuring she'd go ahead and get ready for bed. When she emerged ten minutes later, she found the kitty cat pajamas she'd brought with her—since moving in with Paul and Chloe, she'd had to make adjustments to her sleepwear—and put them on.

Megan was about to crawl into bed and see what she could find on television when she heard what sounded like something crashing to the floor next door. Jumping up, Megan went to the door connecting her room with Paul's. He'd gotten them adjoining rooms to make it easier for Chloe, but since the little girl was with her grandmother, Megan knew the noise had to be coming from Paul.

"Paul? Are you all right over there?" No answer.

"Paul?"

Still nothing.

Without stopping to think, Megan turned the handle on the door. It wasn't locked, and it opened easily.

She peeked inside, and what she saw had her scrambling across the room in a hurry. Paul was balanced—barely—against the dresser that supported the television. He looked as if he'd just come from the bathroom, and he was drunk. Not a little drunk, but can't-walk-straight-or-talk-without- slurring-his-words drunk. She'd never seen him like this.

"Meg-Meg-an." He sighed, and attempted to raise his arm toward her as she wrapped her arm around his waist. He was twice her size, and in his current condition, he was dead weight.

With little help from him, Megan moved him a few feet over to the bed. He plopped down so hard he bounced.

Once she was fairly sure he wasn't going to topple over, she glanced around the room. That was when she noticed the bottle of scotch on the coffee table. Most of the bottle appeared to be gone, and as there was no one else in the room, she had to assume he'd drunk it all himself.

"Will you be okay for a minute?"

"Su-sure." Paul smiled up at her, and she felt something flutter in the pit of her stomach.

Stop it, she told herself, as she marched back into her room to get some ibuprofen.

He was still where she left him when she returned with something for the headache he was bound to have come morning. She took one of the glasses provided by the hotel into the bathroom to fill it up with water, before returning to stand directly in front of him. "Here. Take these. If you drank as much as I think you did, then you are going to have one massive hangover in the morning."

Without comment, or protest, Paul downed the pills like they were candy. She handed him the water, and he drained that within seconds as well.

When he was done, she took the glass from him, and went to refill it. Again, he drained it when she brought it back to him. Once he polished that one off, Megan set aside the empty glass. She couldn't help but wonder what had brought this on, although she was pretty sure she knew.

Megan was lost in thought when she felt Paul's fingers brush the outside of her legs. At first, she thought it was unintentional, but then he got bolder and flattened his palms so that they were bracketing her waist. She could feel the heat of his hands through her clothes. Megan knew she should push him away—he was drunk, after all—but she couldn't. She wanted to see what he would do.

"Always wear . . . most in . . . testing . . . p . . . jamaszzz."

She swallowed. He noticed her pajamas? Since when? "I like cats."

"Mmm." Paul slipped the pads of his thumbs under her shirt, and began making circles against her belly. It was incredibly intimate—more intimate than a lot of the sex she'd had. This felt different. It was different. This was Paul. He wasn't like the guys she normally hung out with.

"Paul?" Her voice cracked. Why did she feel as if this was her first time?

Again, he ignored her, and this time he leaned forward, pulling her closer. He lifted her shirt, exposing her stomach, and pressed his lips against her skin.

Megan reacted in the only way she could, by placing her hands on his head, lacing her fingers through his hair. What was happening?

Paul continued upward with his exploration—pushing her shirt out of the way as he went—until he reached her breasts. He cupped each one, filling both his hands, and began kneading and lifting them. Her nipples hardened, and she felt her body react in other ways. She knew she should stop him, but she couldn't. Megan had dreamt about this . . . how it could happen . . . but she'd never imagined it would be like this.

He eased her left breast into his mouth and began sucking on it as though it was his life source. Megan moaned. She was a woman who liked sex, and it had been almost five months. No matter how wrong she knew this was, if he was willing, she wasn't going to say no.

Hearing her pleasure, Paul released her breast, and leaned back on the bed, pulling her down with him. He cupped the back of her head, and a second later, his mouth was covering hers—his tongue pushing against her lips—begging, demanding entrance.

She opened her mouth, and his tongue surged inside, licking and caressing. Megan could taste the alcohol on his breath, but she also tasted him—something that was uniquely him. Even with Paul being drunk, she could tell he was a good kisser. He angled her head exactly the way he wanted it as he continued his assault on her mouth.

Megan felt him snake his other hand down her body and into her pajama bottoms. He didn't waste any time going for what he wanted. She gasped as his fingers found just the right spot between her legs. Her body was overheating. She just . . . she just . . .

Suddenly, he stopped kissing her and his hand stilled. The fingers that were tangled in her hair dropped onto the bed.

She opened her eyes and looked down at the man beneath her. His eyes were closed, his mouth opened, and he was snoring softly.

Well, that's a first.

Not ready to extract herself just yet, Megan reached up and caressed his face. He'd said her name. He'd known it was her. If nothing else, he'd known who she was. If she never got another opportunity to have him, she at least knew that he wasn't completely indifferent to her. He found her attractive—at least on some level.

Leaning down, she pressed a soft kiss to his parted lips before removing his hand from her pants. Megan knew she needed to go, but she didn't want to leave him with his feet hanging off the side of the bed.

It took some time, but eventually she was able to get his feet up onto the mattress and him into a position where she was confident he wouldn't fall off in the middle of the night. His head was near the foot of the bed, and his feet at the head, but it worked nonetheless.

Satisfied she'd done the best she could, Megan debated whether or not to sleep on the couch in his room or go back to her own. It was a hard decision, but she reasoned that he probably wouldn't want to be babied come morning, so reluctantly she went back to her room. The only concession was that she left the adjoining door open.

Curling up in her bed, Megan looked toward the open door. What would have happened if Paul hadn't fallen asleep? Unfortunately, she might never know.

***

It sounded like someone was scraping their nails on a chalkboard, and what Paul wanted more than anything was for them to stop. His head was pounding, and the noise wasn't helping. He cracked open one eye and quickly closed it again, as the sun shining through the window only made things worse. How much did he have to drink last night? He couldn't remember. From how he was feeling, though, it was a lot.

As gently as he could, he sat up. The pounding in his head increased slightly. He took a few deep breaths until he was sure his head wasn't going to fall off, and then made his way into the bathroom to relieve his bladder.

After taking care of business, he took a long look in the mirror. His eyes were bloodshot and he had dark circles beneath them. He looked as if he'd been to hell and back, and he felt that way, too.

Making his way back out into the room, he shielded his eyes as best he could as he walked across the room to close the heavy curtains. Once they were pulled tight, blocking the light from outside, the pounding in his head decreased a little more. Not willing to take the chance, however, Paul went to his bag and dug out some painkillers.

Downing them easily, he glanced at the clock. It was already after nine, which meant Chloe and his mom would be calling soon. He needed to clean himself up. Paul didn't want his daughter to see him like this.

Thoughts of his mom calling brought his mind back to what woke him in the first place. He went to retrieve his phone from on top of the nightstand near the bed, and sure enough, he had one missed call. It was from his partner, Janey Davis.

Dialing into his voice mail, he listened to her message. There had been another homicide last night. The third one in six months, all with the same MO: young woman, in her late twenties/early thirties, found in her home with her throat and wrists slashed.

With the first one, they'd thought it was a possible suicide, but the cuts were too clean and the angles wrong. Add to that the difficulty of slashing both one's throat and wrists. When the second victim turned up with identical cuts along her throat and wrists, it was obvious they had a killer on their hands. With victim number three, the higher-ups were going to start wanting answers.

Knowing he needed a shower before he called Janey back, Paul tossed his phone down on the bed, and went to grab some clothes. That's when he noticed the door between his and Megan's room was open. He strolled over to the door and peeked in. Megan was still asleep, curled up in her bed with the blankets tucked under her chin, and her hair in complete disarray.

A flash of his hand cupping the back of her head, her green eyes fully dilated staring back at him, filled his vision for a split second, and then it was gone. He shook his head, not understanding where the image came from. Nonetheless, it was enough to cause a reaction below his waist.

Knowing he needed some distance, Paul scurried out of the doorway and back into his room, quietly, yet firmly, closing the door behind him. He really needed that shower, and now he knew it was going to have to be a cold one—an ice-cold one, from the looks of it. Where had that image come from, and why now?

Paul felt much better after his shower, with one exception. He couldn't seem to get that image of Megan out of his head. It made no sense to him. She'd never looked at him that way before, and he'd never touched her like that. The flash made no sense to him, but he couldn't shake it. And every time it popped up, all his efforts to calm himself were for naught.

Knowing he needed a distraction, as soon as Paul was dressed, he dialed Janey. She picked up after the first ring. "Up late partying?"

He snorted, and felt it from his head to his toes. The medicine had helped his headache, but that didn't mean it had gone away completely. "Hardly."

"Oh, man. I need to show you how to party right, then, Daniels."

Paul chuckled. "Thanks for the offer, but I think I manage just fine."

She made a noise through the phone that sounded a lot like the raspberries he blew on Chloe's stomach from time to time. "Suit yourself. You know you're always welcome to come out with us anytime, though."

His partner and some of the other detectives from the station regularly invited him to come out with them after a shift, but he'd always made the excuse that he had to get home to Chloe. He had no idea how he would dodge that once she got older, but for the moment, it worked. None of them pushed, except for Janey, and he figured that was because she knew he was only using Chloe as an excuse.

Janey and Paul had been partners for five years. She'd been there when he'd lost Melissa, so she knew all the ups and downs he'd gone through. Janey knew more than most when it came to how much he still grieved for his wife, because she was there beside him every day.

Wanting to change the subject, Paul brought up the reason she'd called him in the first place. "Another victim turned up last night?"

"Yeah. Everything was the same as the other two, right down to the angle of the cuts. This guy knows what he's doing. Doc says he's confident now that the cuts were made by someone with a medical background."

It was something the medical examiner had brought up with the other two victims they'd found, but he'd been reluctant to go on record with it. Apparently, with this third victim, he felt he had enough evidence to support his theory.

"I suppose that narrows it down some. It will give us a place to start, at least."

"Anything is better than what we've had to go on so far."

That was the truth. This was one of the more frustrating cases he'd worked on in his fifteen years with the Indianapolis police department. There were no prints at the scene and no DNA left by the killer. There were no obvious signs anyone but the victim had been in the house at the time of death.

"When are you heading back?"

There was a knock on the door that joined his room to Megan's—the one he'd closed about thirty minutes ago. "We should be back tonight." He paused. "I've got to go. I'll call you when I get back and we can talk about a game plan."

"Don't sweat it. Enjoy your family time. I'll see you bright and early tomorrow morning."

The door cracked opened, and Megan peeked through. Her hair no longer looked as if she'd had someone running their fingers through it. Paul swallowed. "Okay. Sounds good."

Janey hesitated. "You sure you're all right?"

Paul's gaze never left Megan's. For some reason, he couldn't look away. "Yeah. I'm good."

Before Janey could interrogate him any more about his strange behavior, Paul disconnected the call. He set the phone down on the nightstand, feeling strangely uncomfortable as Megan opened the door further and stepped inside his room. She'd dressed, and was wearing an outfit he'd seen her in several times before. Why, then, did seeing her bare legs peeking out from beneath her skirt bring with it a flash of having those legs bracketing his hips?

"I didn't mean to interrupt your call."

He shrugged. "It's okay. Janey was only calling to give me an update on things."

"Oh."

When Megan didn't say anything more, he turned away from her and began to gather his things in preparation for their departure. "Are you about ready to go? I figure we can meet Chloe and my parents downstairs for brunch before we head out."

She didn't respond right away. "Paul?"

"Hmm?" He didn't look up, feeling the need to concentrate on what he was doing and not on her.

"Do you remember anything from last night?"

That made him stop. He looked over at the bed, and then to the coffee table where the bottle of scotch sat, almost empty. "I guess I drank a little too much."

She didn't comment.

Paul didn't remember getting into bed last night. And, given the door had been open this morning, he figured Megan, at the very least, must have checked on him. Maybe she'd even helped him to the bed. Either way, she was clearly concerned. "Thanks for checking on me. I usually don't go that overboard."

Megan took two steps toward him and then halted. He met her gaze and there was something there—behind her eyes—something he couldn't understand. Before he could ask her, however, she turned around and headed back toward her room. "I'll get my things and meet you in the hall."

He watched her disappear through the door, closing it behind her. For some reason, he felt as if he'd done something wrong, but for the life him, he couldn't figure out what it was.

MEGAN TRIED her best to pay attention to what Chloe was saying as she sat next to her while they ate. As Megan had asked, Paul met her in the hallway outside their respective hotel rooms and they rode down in the elevator together. He didn't say anything on the way down, but she could feel him looking over at her from time to time. It was tense, and Megan knew why, even if he didn't.

They met Chloe and her grandparents downstairs in the lobby a little after ten. The little girl was wearing a new outfit Megan had never seen before. Megan guessed that Marilyn had been more prepared for last night's sleepover than she'd let on. It was cute, and very Chloe.

Paul loaded their luggage into the vehicle since he, Megan, and Chloe would be leaving immediately after brunch, and then joined the rest of the group in the hotel's restaurant. It didn't escape Megan's notice that Paul sat as far away from her as possible, even though the chair right beside her was empty. Was he remembering, or was it only in response to the obvious tension that was hanging in the air between them? She couldn't be sure.

Chloe recounted everything she could remember about the wedding, the reception and, of course, her sleepover with her grandparents, more than once. Each time, she added something she'd forgotten the time before. Concentrating on what the little girl said was difficult, though, since Megan's mind was still firmly set on what had happened with Paul the night before and what had—or hadn't—happened this morning.

She was acutely aware of Paul on the other side of the table. She knew every time he took a drink of his water, or rubbed at his temple, trying to relieve the hangover she knew he must have. It took everything in her not to say or do something, but she knew he probably wouldn't appreciate it. Especially in front of his family.

They were about halfway through their meal when Trent, Gage, and Rebecca joined them. Trent pulled out the chair beside Megan and plopped down. "Morning, sunshine."

Trent was a flirt, and normally Megan would laugh at his antics. She didn't have it in her this morning.

He, of course, noticed. "What happened, and whose ass do I need to kick?"

Luckily, he'd leaned in and said it so low that no one around them heard him. The last thing she needed was her sister picking up on her less than stellar mood. "Nothing. And no one's."

His frown told her just how much he didn't believe her.

She tried again. "Really. I just . . . didn't sleep all that well last night."

Trent looked her in the eye, still frowning. He looked over at Paul and then back to her as his frown increased. Everyone pegged Trent as the jokester of the family—he was the least serious of the four brothers, usually—but Trent was observant. He leaned in and whispered in her ear. "All right. But if you need to talk, I'm here, okay?"

Megan nodded. She tried to smile, to let him know she was really fine, but it was beyond weak.

When she glanced across the table after her brief exchange with Trent, she noticed Paul watching her. He was observant as well, but in a different way. But the look on his face wasn't that of a detached cop.

Maybe Paul remembered more about last night than he was letting on. He'd never minded Trent flirting with her before.

Seconds after that thought crossed Megan's mind, Paul's expression cleared, and he turned to engage his father in conversation. It was as if nothing had happened. Whatever Paul's reaction to Trent's private chat with her was, he seemed to have successfully tucked it away.

The rest of the meal was relatively uneventful. That is, if you discount Gage not being able to take his hands off her sister. Before Gage, she had never witnessed Rebecca giggle like a schoolgirl. Megan had no idea what Gage was doing underneath the table, but whatever it was had her sister in a very good mood. It wouldn't surprise Megan if they were late to check out of the hotel.

As everyone was saying goodbye to one another and preparing to set off, Marilyn walked over to give Megan a hug. "You take care of yourself, and if you need extra time to study, you make sure to speak up."

Megan didn't know what to say. Her mother had never been nurturing in the traditional sense—not nurturing at all, really. It had always been Rebecca who watched out for Megan—always her sister who made sure Megan had something to eat, or gave her that disapproving look when she made the wrong decision. When Megan was a teenager, she had sometimes loathed her sister for it. Okay, sometimes she still did, but after spending so much time with Chloe, Megan was beginning to understand.

"Call me when you get there?" Megan glanced over to find her sister standing next to her. Marilyn backed away, giving the sisters a moment together to say their farewells.

"Sure."

Rebecca frowned. "I'm sorry if I overstepped my bounds last night, but I always worry about you. I can't help it."

Megan had completely forgotten about what her sister had said the night before. Ever since she'd strolled into Paul's room last night to check on him, she'd had other things on her mind. "I'm good. Really."

"You know you can talk to me, right?" Rebecca paused. "And I'll try to just listen and not tell you what to do."

That made Megan chuckle.

Rebecca pursed her lips. "You're right. That's not going to happen. I can try, though."

Megan gave her sister a big hug. "I love you, Becca."

"I love you, too, Megan," Rebecca whispered as she hugged Megan back.

Gage came up beside Rebecca, and Megan released her hold on her sister. It took all of two seconds for Gage's arm to wrap firmly around his wife's waist, his hand resting on her barely visible baby bump. "Did you get some rest last night?"

Megan rolled her eyes. "Not you, too?"

He feigned innocence. "What?"

She shook her head, leaned up to give her brother-in-law a kiss on the cheek, and then turned to go. "Take care of my big sister."

"Megan?"

Megan should have known Rebecca wouldn't let her go that easily, so she glanced over her shoulder, and winked. "Don't do anything I wouldn't do."

Taking full advantage of the embarrassment she'd caused her sister, Megan walked swiftly across the room to where Paul was standing with Chloe and his parents. Before she could say anything, Paul did.

"Are you about ready to go?"

"Yep."

Paul said a quick goodbye to his parents, and allowed Chloe some last minute hugs to her grandparents, before the three of them headed for the car. He remained silent until he had Chloe buckled into the backseat, and was situated behind the wheel.

He maneuvered the car out of the parking lot and onto the road, driving toward the interstate. They had roughly a two-hour drive in front of them. Normally their trips between Ohio and his home in Indianapolis were filled with conversation. Sometimes they'd play I Spy with Chloe, if her nose wasn't in a book or playing with her

Barbies. During those periods, she and Paul would normally pass the drive chatting about whatever came to their minds. Once, they'd ended up discussing the age-old argument of which came first, the chicken or the egg. It was silly, but it passed the time.

"You okay?"

She kept her eyes forward, not looking at him, and released a frustrated sigh. "I'm fine."

He didn't ask again, and she was glad. Every now and then, she felt his gaze on her, but she ignored it and appeared to be engrossed in watching the road. Megan didn't want to lie to him, but she had no idea how to even begin to bring up what had happened between them last night, and how much he might or might not remember about it. Add to that the fact that they were going to be spending the next two hours in a vehicle with little ears that could hear anything they said and any conversations that needed to happen weren't possible at the moment.

Besides, Megan had to figure out how in the world she was going to bring up the subject. It wasn't as if she could come right out and say, 'Hey, do you remember making out with me on the bed in your hotel room last night?'

Okay, she could, but she didn't think that would go over really well. Paul was an incredibly private person. Although he was open with his daughter—and even Megan, to some degree—she was pretty sure if she confronted him with it straight out, he'd clam up. At best, he would shut her out. At worst, she'd be out of a job.

Paul was important to her, and after what had happened, Megan knew that on at least some level, he felt something for her, too. Maybe it was just physical attraction. It was possible. Megan knew that she was attractive to the opposite sex, and it might have only been that which had prompted last night's reaction from Paul.

Even as the thought crossed her mind, Megan didn't believe it. Yes, he had been trashed. No, he didn't remember what he'd done, so he probably wasn't thinking rationally.

Megan knew all of that, and she was ashamed to admit that she had personal experience with getting plastered and not remembering what you'd done the next morning. Paul wasn't like that, though, and she couldn't see him going up to some random woman and initiating something like that just because he was out of his mind drunk.

Maybe she was deluding herself, but she didn't want last night to have happened because she was convenient. She wanted him to want her for her, and she was positive that they would have had sex if he hadn't fallen asleep. Megan wanted more than just sex from Paul, however. The problem was she didn't know if he'd ever be able to give her more than that. He still loved his wife. How could Megan ever compete with that?

***

Paul tried his best to concentrate on the road and not the woman sitting beside him in the passenger seat. His hangover lingered, but he was able to ignore it for the most part. It wasn't nearly as bad as it had been a few hours ago. What he couldn't ignore was the growing feeling that something was bothering Megan, and that he'd somehow had a part in whatever it was.

The entire drive home, he tried his best to recall what had occurred the night before. He remembered going back to his room, removing the plastic covering off one of the glasses the hotel provided in the room, and sitting down on the small couch with his bottle of scotch. Gradually, as he drank, the pain had begun to dull. Memories of Melissa—their wedding, their life—flooded his vision, but he was detached from it. Seeing her face didn't bring with it the twisting in his gut.

He swallowed, and blinked several times, forcing his concentration back on the highway in front of him. The last thing he needed was to get distracted while driving.

With that in mind, Paul pushed through what he could remember of the previous night, and pressed his consciousness for what wasn't so readily available. He squinted as if that would somehow help, but all it did was serve to nudge his headache closer to the surface once more. How was it possible he couldn't remember? Not even as a teenager had he drunk enough to cause memory loss. Surely there had to be something he could do to bring what had occurred back to him.

He kept trying even though it only increased the pounding in his head. The image of Megan standing over him, her eyes full of desire, kept surfacing in his mind the harder he tried to push through the fog in his brain. For the life of him, he couldn't figure out where it had come from. Megan had never looked at him like that before. He was sure of it. But there was something about it that seemed more real than a dream. What happened last night?

By the time Paul pulled into his driveway, he wasn't any closer to solving the mystery. The last thing he could positively remember was picking up the bottle of scotch to pour himself yet another drink, and almost dropping it. At that point, he'd decided that maybe he'd better stop.

That's it. That was the last thing he remembered. What happened after that? At what point did Megan come into his room? Had she found him on the couch and helped him to the bed, or was he already there? Had he said something to her? Done something to offend her?

Or . . .

Paul didn't allow himself to finish that thought. Shaking his head as if that would somehow clear his mind, he went back to his previous contemplation. He and Megan weren't incredibly close, but he'd thought they'd become friends of sorts. They talked, were cordial to one another. She knew about Melissa, and about the drunk driver who killed her. Of course, she didn't know everything that had happened that night—why Melissa had been running to the store to get diapers at three in the morning.

Paul squeezed his eyes shut to block out the memory, and the guilt. No, Megan didn't know all the ugly details, but she knew enough.

Redirecting his thoughts back to Megan, some of the tension in his shoulders eased. There'd been a few nights he'd come home late, needing to unwind, and the two of them had sat around the kitchen table and played a few hands of poker together. Even after spending hours at a crime scene, talking to witnesses, and going over evidence, she could make him laugh. Megan was . . . fun.

"Can I get out now, Daddy?"

Paul glanced in the rearview mirror at his daughter. She was shifting impatiently in her booster seat. Although Chloe knew how to get out of her seat, he'd drilled it into her that she wasn't allowed to unbuckle herself without asking first or him telling her it was okay. It was a safety thing, and the last thing he wanted was something to happen that would cause him to lose Chloe, too. He didn't think he could bear that.

"Yes, you may get out." The second he gave his approval, Chloe had the seat belt unfastened, and was darting out the door toward the house.

Megan opened her car door and went around to the back of the vehicle to start unloading the luggage. Sighing, Paul joined her while Chloe ran around in circles in the yard, releasing her pent-up energy.

They worked together to unload the bags. Once everything was out of the trunk, Megan hitched her bag over her shoulder, and began walking toward the house. Paul thought about stopping her, but then again, what would he say? Sorry if I said something I shouldn't have last night? That didn't sound like much of an apology. Besides, he was still perplexed by the flash of her heated gaze.

He let her go, and picked up his own bag, as well as Chloe's. "Come on, Chloe. Let's get inside and I'll get us some lunch."

"But I'm not hungry!"

"Chloe." Paul was not in the mood to deal with one of her tantrums.

Her lower lip pushed forward, and she crossed her arms as she stomped toward the house. Paul shook his head and followed her inside.

Lunch was a quiet affair. Chloe was still pouting because he'd made her come inside, and Megan appeared to be completely engrossed in a book she was reading. It gave him time to think about what he needed to say to her, because he knew he had to say something.

"May I go play now, Daddy?"

Paul glanced down at Chloe's plate. Most of her food was gone, so he nodded, and opened his mouth to give her the okay. Apparently, his nod was enough, as Chloe didn't wait for him to utter the words before she took off, running up the stairs to her room.

Once Paul was confident they were alone, he turned toward Megan. Again, he opened his mouth to speak, but nothing came out. Not because Megan subverted him in any way, but because he still had no idea what he was going to say to her.

She looked up at him and caught him staring. "Something wrong?"

"No." He shook his head and stood, taking his plate to the sink. Why was this so difficult?

"Oh." She almost sounded disappointed. "Were you planning to go into work today?"

He glanced at her over his shoulder as he rinsed off his plate. "No. Why?"

Megan shrugged. "I thought maybe I'd head to the mall if you're going to be here."

Paul smiled, and it felt as if a weight was lifted off his shoulders. "Sure. Go. Have fun."

She paused as if she was going to say something, but she must have changed her mind. "All right. I'll run up and say goodbye to Chloe before I leave." At the door, she paused, and faced him. "Did you need me to pick up anything while I'm out?"

Something clenched in his chest. "No. I'm . . ." He cleared his throat. "I'm good."

"Okay. See ya in a few hours." She smiled at him as she skipped through the doorway, and bounded up the stairs.

Alone, Paul placed his hands on the counter, and looked out the window overlooking the sink into the backyard. He'd been granted a few hours, and he needed to use them wisely. He ran over the events of last night in his mind once more. But like before, everything went blank before Megan's appearance in his room.

He heard her come back downstairs, and shortly after that, the front door opened and closed. The sound brought to mind earlier that morning when he'd peeked into her room to check on her—of her lying in bed—and again he felt those same stirrings in his groin.

Where was this coming from, and why now? Megan had lived with them for months, and not once had he reacted this way. Sure, she dressed a little sexy sometimes, and of course he noticed. How could he not? But she was twenty-three and single. Wasn't that what twenty-three-year-olds did?

Paul rubbed his eyes with the palms of his hands and sighed. He had to stop thinking about it. Later, after Chloe went to bed, he'd talk to Megan. Maybe, after he got some answers, the strange reaction his body was having would go away.

Needing a distraction, Paul finished cleaning up and made his way upstairs to find Chloe. She was in her room, playing with her dolls.

He knocked on her door, and she looked up. "Mind if I join you?"

Chloe seemed to consider his offer for a second, and then picked up one of her dolls, handing it to him. "You can be Ken."

So for the next few hours, Paul sat up in Chloe's room playing dolls with her and having a tea party, all the while trying not to think about a certain conversation he needed to have with her nanny.

CHAPTER 5

Megan ran her hand along the rack of clothes until her fingers brushed against something she liked. Removing it from the rack so that she could get a better look, she held it against herself, and smiled. She'd long finished gathering the personal care items she needed. This wasn't about need at all. This was about want.

On the long drive back to Indianapolis, Megan had done a lot of thinking—both about the previous night and that morning. Paul wanted her. At least, on some level he did. She was convinced of that. He'd said her name. He'd known it was her. Not his dead wife.

Plus, that morning at breakfast—that look he gave her—when he saw Trent whispering in her ear. Had he remembered something? The vibe coming off him had been one of annoyance. It wasn't as if Trent had never flirted with her before. Usually, he laughed it off the same as she did. Trent was only being Trent. Something had changed. At least, she hoped it had.

With all the thinking she'd done, Megan decided to play to her strengths. Maybe the mature thing would be to sit down and talk to him about what happened, but she was afraid Paul would try to dismiss it. Megan couldn't take that.

During the four months Megan had known him, she'd never seen him go out on a date—never seen him take interest in any woman. From what she gathered from little things he and his family said, Paul didn't date. At all.

Of course, Megan didn't know if that extended to booty calls or not, but she had a feeling it did. Paul didn't strike her as a one-night-stand kind of guy, which was another reason she thought what happened in the hotel might mean more than just him scratching an itch.

Tossing the pajamas over her arm, Megan rifled through the racks until she found two more sets of cute pajamas that she liked, before checking out. If Paul found her attractive, she was going to use that to her advantage.

A girl had to try, right?

It was dark by the time she got home. She smiled when she saw that Paul had left the kitchen light on for her. It was amazing how little things like that could make her feel warm inside. No one but Rebecca had ever cared enough about her to leave the light on. Not even her parents.

As she reached the bottom of the stairs, she could hear voices coming from the second floor, and realized that Paul must be giving Chloe her bath. The little girl was becoming more and more independent and she wanted to bathe herself, but Paul insisted she was still too young to be left alone. As a compromise, after running the bath water to the correct temperature, Paul would sit on top of the toilet seat and read a magazine while Chloe had her bath. Megan was waiting for the day when Chloe would cease to allow that much from her father. She was growing up. It was only a matter of time before she became fully aware of the differences between boys and girls.

With extra care, Megan tiptoed up the stairs so she didn't disturb them. She should have known better than to think she could pass by the bathroom undetected. Paul glanced up, and Megan paused, waiting. For what, she didn't know. Their gazes held, and his forehead furrowed in concentration.

Her heart began to pound. Did he remember?

Chloe squealed, breaking their connection. He averted his gaze back to his daughter, and Megan took the opportunity to make her escape.

Once inside her room, Megan closed and locked the door. She rushed over to her bed and dumped out the contents of her bags. Putting everything away except for the three new pajamas, she considered her options.

The first one had a cute little T-shirt type of top and boxer short bottoms. They were blue with bunny rabbits all over them. She remembered the way Paul went right for her legs, which was why she'd gone for all shorts-type selections.

Her second pajama set was more grown-up looking than she normally went for, but she wanted to be prepared for anything. Megan had no idea what Paul liked. It was lavender and had a spaghetti-strap top that dipped low. She didn't have a lot up top, not really, but she wasn't flat either. The bottoms that came with the outfit were much shorter than the others.

Megan picked up the last outfit. The bottoms were pink, with little red and white hearts—most likely left over from Valentine's Day. It was paired with a simple light pink tank top. She'd liked it as soon as she saw it. Megan only hoped Paul didn't think it was too much, with the hearts and all.

Deciding to take a chance, Megan put on the tank top and heart shorts. Aside from the hearts, it wasn't all that unlike what she normally wore to bed. She was hoping that while he'd notice, he wouldn't immediately become suspicious. He was a cop, after all.

After taking a look in the mirror, Megan opened her bedroom door, and peeked out into the hallway just in time to see Chloe barreling toward her. Megan bent down to brace herself for impact. Even then, she had to put a hand down on the floor to keep from falling backward.

"Are you going to help Daddy read me a bedtime story?"

"I can, if you want me to."

Chloe nodded, took hold of Megan's hand, and led her down the hall to her room, leaving Paul to follow. Megan glanced over her shoulder, and found Paul smiling. She smiled back. This was the Paul she knew—the one who loved his daughter above all else.

Inside her bedroom, Chloe released Megan's hand and walked over to her bookshelf. She selected the book she wanted and then climbed into her bed. Paul sat down on one side of Chloe, and Megan on the other. They each took turns reading a page until the little girl was yawning and rubbing her eyes.

Paul closed the book, and Chloe started to whine.

"Time for bed."

"But, Daddy . . ."

He didn't say anything, but his look spoke volumes. Chloe lowered her eyes and huffed a little, before lying down and closing her eyes.

Paul leaned over and kissed her on the forehead. "Good night, sweetpea."

Chloe kept her eyes closed tight. "Good night, Daddy."

Megan followed suit, giving Chloe a kiss on the forehead, and saying good night.

The little girl yawned. "G'night, Meg-an."

Megan smiled and ambled out of the room with Paul. She was so caught up in the bedtime ritual they'd taken part in that she was completely caught off guard when Paul reached out, stopping her from continuing.

"Could we talk?"

She met his gaze, and her heart began to race. It wasn't what she saw in his eyes, it was what she didn't. He had what she called his "cop face" on. His expression was devoid of emotion, and he looked as if he were gearing up for a battle of some sort. Was that because he'd remembered what had happened between them? Megan didn't know, and she wasn't sure she was ready to find out.

Unfortunately, running wouldn't help her cause, so she answered in the only way she could. "Sure."

He nodded and turned abruptly toward the stairs. She followed him to the kitchen.

Paul didn't sit down, so Megan didn't either. Instead, she stood right inside the doorway with her back against the wall. She might even have lifted her leg a little and arched her back, to make her chest stick out a bit more.

He strolled over to the far side of the room and leaned back against the counter, facing her. For the longest time, he didn't say anything, and neither did Megan. She was tempted, but she wanted to find out what he'd say first.

After a long, drawn-out silence, Paul cleared his throat. "I wanted to talk to you about last night."

Megan nodded, afraid that if she spoke, she'd give something away.

Paul took a deep breath and looked her in the eye. "I wanted to say that I'm sorry."

She paled. "You're sorry?"

He nodded. "Yes."

Megan felt sick to her stomach, and she saw something flash across his face before he schooled his features. "You remembered?"

Paul shook his head. "No. And I'm sorry about that, too. I can't tell you the last time I blacked out like that from drinking too much. It shouldn't have happened, and I'm sorry."

The churning in Megan's belly subsided a little, but anxiety rapidly took up residence. "So you don't remember what happened?"

She said it more to herself than to him, but he answered her anyway. "No."

Megan swallowed and pushed herself off the wall, walking toward him. He watched her with an eagle eye. She knew he was wondering what she was doing, and to be honest, she was wondering the same thing herself.

When she came to a stop in front of him, she stood closer than they'd ever been before, with only one exception. He looked down at her, and she hoped he liked the view that included a nice display of the tops of her breasts. Just thinking about Paul and her breasts together brought back the memory of his hands and mouth on them. Her body heated at the memory.

Licking her lips, she searched his eyes for any recollection. "You kissed me."

His eyes grew wide with shock, and he tensed. Other than that, he didn't react in any way to her bombshell.

Megan decided to push the envelope a little by filling in the gaps for him. She wanted to touch Paul, but she was afraid it would spook him. "I heard a noise, so I went to check on you. You'd bumped into the dresser, and almost knocked the television over, so I helped you to the bed."

The vein in his throat pulsed rapidly, but he remained silent.

"You don't remember any of this?"

"No." It sounded as if it were a struggle for him to say that one word.

She sighed and reached up to touch his face. Paul leaned back, evading her hand. Megan tried to hide how much that hurt, but she knew he saw it anyway.

Before she could regain her equilibrium, Paul sidestepped her, putting some distance between them. She wanted to grab hold of his arm, and pull him back to her, but she didn't. It would have been too much to ask for him to take her in his arms and pick up where they'd left off.

****

He'd kissed her? That was impossible. But even as that thought crossed his mind, Paul knew she was telling the truth. Once again, the sight of Megan perched above him filled his mind. This time, it took on a whole new context.

Megan wasn't lying.

Paul flexed his fingers, unsure what to do with himself. He was in uncharted territory. This wasn't like the woman he'd picked up in that club four years ago. He knew Megan. She lived in his house, for crying out loud. It wasn't as if he could up and leave.

Chancing a look at Megan, he could see the hurt in her eyes. He could tell she was trying to hide it, but she wasn't doing a very good job. He felt like a cad. She'd said he'd kissed her, not the other way around. He'd initiated the kiss. He'd changed things between them. It was his fault.

He closed his eyes, and took a deep breath before opening them again. Megan looked so small as she stood there in his kitchen in her shorts and tank top. His heart was beating wildly in his chest, as he knew what he said next would hurt her. It was the last thing he wanted, but he knew it needed to be done. He still loved his wife—would always love his wife. There was no future for him with anyone else.

"I was out of line. I'm sorry." He paused. "I still love my wife, Megan. Nothing can happen between the two of us."

She was quiet for several seconds, and then he saw her press her lips together and straighten her shoulders. "Why?"

Paul looked at her with slight disbelief. "Did you miss the part about me still loving my wife?"

"No. I didn't miss it. I know you still love Melissa." Hearing his wife's name twisted the knife that seemed to be permanently lodged in his gut.

When he didn't add anything, she continued. "Why does that mean nothing can happen between us? Don't you think she'd want you to move on? Find someone else?"

"I can't." Paul met Megan's gaze and shook his head. "I'm sorry. You have no idea how sorry I am, but I just can't."

Without giving Megan time to respond, Paul said good night, and bounded up the stairs. He was running away, he knew that, but it was either that or break down in front of her—and to Paul, that would have been worse. Talking about Melissa to Chloe was one thing. Discussing her with Megan was something altogether different. Paul didn't want to think about why that was, exactly. He knew he might find answers he didn't want to know.

Paul woke up the next morning feeling as if he hadn't slept at all. It had taken him hours of tossing and turning before he'd finally drifted off, and then when he did, he was tortured by images of Melissa and Megan. In one dream, he'd been lying in bed with his wife, talking . . . kissing. It was a pleasant dream, and one he had often.

But as he leaned in to give Melissa a kiss, the dream changed and it was no longer Melissa in front of him. It was Megan. He'd woken with a start, panting, and stiff as a board.

Sleep was impossible after that.

The smell of coffee filled the kitchen as Paul pulled Melissa's mug out of the cabinet. He'd found it in the dishwasher the day after her funeral, and he'd been using it ever since for his morning cup of coffee. It made him feel close to her somehow, as if a part of her was still with him when he started his day.

Before his wife died, Paul always drank his coffee black. He figured if he was going to drink the caffeinated beverage then it shouldn't be doctored to make it taste like something else. That was before, though.

Paul opened the refrigerator and removed the milk, setting it on the counter. Once the coffee pot stopped percolating, he filled his glass three quarters of the way, and then topped it off with milk—just like Melissa used to drink it.

After putting the milk away, Paul sat down at the kitchen table and picked up the morning paper he'd snatched from the driveway as soon as he came downstairs. This was his routine, and routines were good. Unfortunately, Paul couldn't focus on the words in front of him. It was as if he were reading some foreign language instead of English.

Frustrated, he tossed the paper down on the table, and massaged his temples. What was happening to him?

The sound of footsteps on the stairs caused him to glance up. Seconds later, Megan appeared. She was still wearing her pajamas from the night before. The bottoms only covered about a quarter of her leg, which meant there was plenty left over for him to see. Megan wasn't tall, but her legs were long, and for a moment, Paul wondered what it would feel like to have them wrapped around his hips.

Startled by the direction of his thoughts, Paul shot up out of his chair and nearly spilled what was left of his coffee.

"You okay?"

Paul noted the concern in her voice. Unfortunately that wasn't helping whatever it was that seemed to be happening to him. To them. No, to him. There was no them. "Yeah, I'm fine."

She looked at him intently for a long moment, and then strolled past him to the counter to get herself some coffee. Paul clenched his eyes closed, and forced himself to breathe. He needed to get out of there.

Clearing his throat, he turned to face her, but she had her back to him. Unfortunately, that gave him a clear view of her backside. He averted his eyes quickly as his body began to betray him. "I'm going to head to work early this morning to catch up on some paperwork."

Megan turned around, holding her coffee against her chest. His eyes narrowed in on her breasts. "All right."

He knew he needed to go—get out of there, but his feet refused to move.

"Paul?"

"Yes?"

She laid her cup down on the counter, and stalked toward him. Okay, maybe stalked was too strong a word, but that was how he felt at the moment. His feet were glued to the floor by some unknown force, and she was walking toward him. His brain was telling him to run as fast as he could in the opposite direction, but his limbs weren't cooperating.

Megan came to a stop in front of him. Without pause, she placed her right hand in the center of his chest, and met his gaze. "Why are you running away from me?"

He swallowed. "I'm not."

By the look in her eyes, she knew he was lying. "Yes, you are."

"Megan . . ."

"Paul."

Wrapping his fingers around her wrist, he removed her hand from his chest, and took a step back. "I told you last night that this couldn't happen, and I meant it."

"I'm not agreeing to that." He could hear the stubborn determination in her voice.

"You're going to have to."

"Why? Give me one good reason why this can't happen."

Her eyes were fierce. He could see the fight in her. "I'm still in love with my wife. I can't . . . I can't give you anything."

Megan's eyes softened a little. "I know you still love Melissa."

"Good. Then you understand why nothing can happen between us."

She stepped closer, eating up the space he'd put between them. "No. I don't. Why does that mean you can't give me anything?"

Megan leaned forward, brushing her breasts against his chest, causing him to suck in a breath. "What are you doing?"

"Proving a point."

"Which is?"

She looked up at him. "You want me, Paul Daniels, whether you want to admit it or not."

Before he could respond, Megan leaned back, gave him a coy smile, and slid around him. She disappeared up the stairs, leaving him dumbfounded. He didn't want another relationship. Not with Megan. Not with any woman.

He did want her, though. She was right about that. Or at least, his body did. The evidence was visible if anyone happened to walk into the kitchen at that moment.

But it didn't change anything.

Leaning his head back against the wall, Paul took several deep breaths until he felt his body was back under control. Work. That was what he needed to take his mind off Megan and whatever was happening between them. There was a serial killer out there, and he knew from experience that whoever it was wouldn't stop until they were caught.

Before his thoughts were invaded once again by Megan, Paul raced up the stairs to get ready for work. Megan was young. She probably just had a crush on him or something. It would pass.

He repeated that mantra all the way to the station, trying to convince himself that it was true. Paul didn't want to think about what it would mean if it wasn't. Megan lived in his house, and he hadn't been with a woman in nearly five years. He didn't know how long he'd be able to resist her temptations. Paul didn't want to hurt her. He cared about Megan, but he also knew he could never give her anything more than his body, and she deserved so much more than that.

CHAPTER 6

PAUL BREATHED a sigh of relief when he entered the station. People were milling around, going about their tasks even at the early hour. It was familiar. Safe.

He bristled. Safe. Since when had that become what was most important to him? He used to be willing to take risks. Used to do it all the time for his job. How many people had told him and Melissa that they would never last, yet they'd been married for more than ten years when that drunk driver ran her off the road. More than that, they'd been happily married. With a newborn baby.

Chloe had changed things for them, but not in a bad way. They'd cherished the little girl who had blessed their lives. Melissa had difficulties getting pregnant, but after five years of trying, they'd brought a beautiful baby girl into the world. Unfortunately, Melissa had only been part of Chloe's life for six months before she was taken away from both of them.

Thinking about Chloe brought him back to Megan. As he sat down at his desk, Paul replayed the conversation he'd had with his daughter's nanny. He'd had women come on to him over the years— more so since becoming a widower—but none of them had sparked anything in him. This morning was different. There had been a spark, and he wouldn't lie to himself. It scared him on a deep and primal level.

After Megan sauntered out of the kitchen, it had taken a good ten minutes for his erection to go down. No woman had done that to him with such ease since Melissa. She used to be able to look at him, and he'd be up for whatever she had in mind.

"You're here early."

Paul looked up as his partner slid into the desk across from him. "I wanted to go over the new files."

Janey glanced down at his desk and raised one eyebrow. "Were you expecting those files to magically appear in front of you?"

He shrugged and reached for the stack of folders on the corner of his desk. "Very funny, Davis."

Leaning back, she gave him a once-over. "Something happen at your brother's wedding I should know about?"

"It was a wedding." He tried to concentrate on the report in front of him.

"That doesn't mean nothing happened."

Paul continued to look down at the files as if they held all the secrets in the universe.

When he didn't elaborate, Janey sighed. "You're sure?"

"I am." He looked up and gave her the best smile he could muster. "So catch me up. What's the latest on the newest victim?"

Janey spent the next hour bringing Paul up to speed on the case. He'd only been gone for four days, but there had been a lot of new developments within that time. This newest victim was twenty-eight-year-old Casey McMurphy. She was a flight attendant, newly married, and had no children.

The similarities between this victim and the first two were few. Apart from each of the women being around the same age, and all being home alone at the time of the murders, nothing else matched up. They'd been searching for a connection between the first two victims, but had come up short thus far. Paul was hoping they would be able to find something to tie the three women together. Once they knew how the killer was selecting the victims, they would have a better chance at catching him or her.

In his absence, Janey and one of the other detectives had interviewed Mr. McMurphy, but Paul wanted to see the crime scene for himself. Throughout the drive, Janey kept glancing over at him.

"What's on your mind, Davis?"

"I was going to ask you the same question, Daniels."

He pulled into the McMurphys' drive and turned off the engine. Paul opened his door and exited the vehicle without a word to his partner.

Janey sighed and unfastened her seat belt. "Fine. I get it. You don't want to talk about it."

They strolled up to the house in silence, and Paul took the time to observe his surroundings. It was a nice neighborhood. He heard dogs barking from the house next door and there was a sprinkler going a few houses down. Nothing stood out to him as being out of the ordinary.

Paul rang the doorbell, and after several minutes, a young woman answered. She looked to be around Megan's age, but she was shorter. The woman was even wearing a short skirt, showing off her trim, athletic legs.

He quickly put a stop to the direction his mind was heading. He was working, and he needed to concentrate. Whatever was going on, or not going on, with Megan and himself wasn't what he needed to be focusing on at the moment.

"Hello?"

They flashed their badges. "Is Mr. McMurphy home?"

The woman froze for a moment, and then seemed to come out of it, stepping back to allow them inside. "H-he's in the kitchen. Let me . . . let me go get him."

Without another word, she scurried out of sight. Paul gave a questioning look to his partner, and she shrugged, letting him know that she didn't know who the woman was either.

While they waited, Paul looked around. The house was simple, but nice. In fact, what stood out to him the most was the lack of clutter or anything else that made the house looked lived in. Granted the McMurphys didn't have any children, but there should still be evidence of the two people living there. If there was, he couldn't see it from where he stood.

Evan McMurphy walked into the room looking as if he hadn't slept in days. His eyes were bloodshot, and he had dark circles beneath them. "Detectives?"

Janey took the lead. "We're sorry to bother you again so soon, Mr. McMurphy, but I wanted to introduce you to my partner, Detective Daniels. He was out of town this weekend, but he and I will be handling your wife's case."

Paul extended his hand. "Hello, Mr. McMurphy."

Evan McMurphy shook Paul's hand and nodded.

"Detective Daniels wanted to get a look at the crime scene for himself. It shouldn't take more than a few minutes."

"Sure. Of course."

Janey led Paul down a long hallway to the back of the house. The sunroom remained blocked with crime scene tape. Although the forensic unit had already been through the room from top to bottom, it hadn't been cleaned yet.

As he walked around the room, Paul noted the small similarities between this murder and the others. Opening up the file, he compared the position of the victim's body with the others. The killer not only positioned each of the bodies in a similar way, but where the women were placed in the room was the same. It was almost as if the killer had used a tape measure to find the exact center, and place the body in that spot. "Whoever this person is, they are big on details."

His partner nodded. "I agree. It does look like this one may have struggled a bit more than the others, though." She pointed to a vase lying on the floor—its contents spilled out on the beige carpet. With the other two victims, nothing had been out of place. There had been no sign of a struggle at all. It was as if whoever it was walked in, did their business, and left.

Paul worked his way over to the large French doors along the back wall. There was no sign of forced entry. He opened the door, checking for any evidence that the lock had been picked. There were some scratches, but they could have come from general wear.

He shut the door, and found Janey looking over the contents on the desk. "Hopefully she fought her attacker enough for us to get some DNA."

After speaking to Mr. McMurphy again, he officially introduced them to his friend, Sarah Cartwright, although Paul got the impression there might be more there than just friendship. At least, on her part. Then again, he might be seeing things that weren't really there. The whole thing with Megan was throwing him off, and he didn't like it.

He and Janey canvassed the neighborhood, talking to anyone who was home, hoping someone had seen a stranger lurking or a car hanging around prior to the murder. As with the others, no one appeared to have seen or heard anything unusual that night or anytime leading up to it.

Returning to the car, Paul pulled out of the drive and turned toward the station. "What do we know about Mr. McMurphy?"

Janey shrugged. "Early thirties. Works as a CPA downtown, and at a local community college teaching accounting two nights a week. I didn't get any bad vibes when I spoke to him the first time. Or this time, for that matter."

Paul nodded. "What about the woman?"

She cocked her head to the side and raised her eyebrow. "My first impression?"

"Of course."

"I think she has a crush."

"So you don't think there's anything going on there?"

Instead of answering him, she countered with her own question. "Do you?"

He shrugged. "I don't know. Maybe."

They spent the rest of the drive lost in their own thoughts. Paul was beginning to get frustrated. There were three dead women and little to no evidence to lead them to the killer. He knew that sooner or later whomever it was would slip up and leave something behind that would tie them to the crimes—they always did. Paul only hoped more women didn't have to die before that happened.

***

Megan spent her day playing with Chloe and getting some general housework done. When she'd first moved in, Paul was reluctant to let her do much of anything around the house. He was fiercely independent, and for whatever reason, he felt it wasn't Megan's responsibility to do anything beyond taking care of Chloe.

Chloe was much like her father. She liked to sit in the corner and read her picture books or play on her LeapPad. It left Megan twiddling her thumbs with nothing to do. When she'd explained this to Paul one night, he admitted that it might be helpful if she could do some minor house cleaning in her downtime. He still did his own laundry, but she took care of her own and Chloe's, along with vacuuming, dusting, and cleaning all but the master suite. That was Paul's space, and she got the impression very early on that it was off-limits. It was even rare for Chloe to go in there.

Even with the added chores, it didn't always keep her busy during the hours Paul was at work. That's why she'd decided to go back to school. Two days a week, she would log on to the school's website, and download her assignments. Eventually, if she decided to pursue an arts degree, she'd have to take some classes on campus as well, but by then Chloe would be in school.

There were a lot of things Megan was starting to regret about the last five years of her life. Growing up, her sister, Rebecca, had constantly been on her case about school. When Rebecca left for college, she had called Megan every day to make sure she stayed on top of her classes and wasn't slacking off.

Back then, Megan hadn't appreciated what her sister did. In fact, she'd resented her for it most of the time, and had only done what Rebecca asked because she hadn't wanted to deal with the fallout. As soon as Megan graduated, though, she knew she had to get away. Unlike her sister, Megan had no interest in continuing her education, which is why as soon as she graduated, she took off with the first guy who offered.

For five years, she bounced from guy to guy, hoping that one of them would love her, but they never did. Not for long, anyway. No matter how sweet they were in the beginning, they always showed their true colors eventually.

When she caught her last boyfriend in his friend's garage snorting cocaine, she'd had enough. After growing up with her parents, and her dad's drug problem, she refused to be in a relationship with someone who did illegal drugs. Megan could party with the best of them, but even she had her limits.

Moving in with Paul and Chloe had changed Megan's life. It was a fresh start—one she desperately needed. She moved into the guest bedroom, stopped partying, and concentrated on herself for a while.

Megan closed the window on her computer screen, and went to check on Chloe. She found her exactly where she'd left her over an hour before— sitting on her neon pink beanbag in the corner of her room, reading. "Chloe?"

The little girl reluctantly looked up from her book.

"Are you hungry? I can make you a snack."

She appeared to consider the question for a moment. "Can I have app- ules? And teese?"

They walked . . . well, Megan walked and Chloe hopped, down the stairs to the kitchen.

Before Megan handed the food over to Chloe, she worked with the little girl on her pronunciation. Apples were easy once Megan sounded it out for her slowly. Cheese was a little more difficult.

"T-eese."

"No. Listen to the first part of the word closely. Ch. Ch. Can you do that?"

"Ch."

Megan smiled. "Good. Now add it to the rest of the word. Ch-eese."

Chloe repeated the word exactly how Megan said it. "Ch-eese."

"Great job!" Megan handed the little girl the apples and cheese, and gave her a kiss on the top of her head, before taking a seat on the other side of the kitchen island.

Chloe dug into the cheese and apples, holding one in each of her little hands. "Meg-an, why doesn't my daddy have a girlfriend?"

Megan choked on the drink of water she was swallowing. "Um. I don't know."

"Allie says that her daddy has a girlfriend. And Debbie says if there is no mommy that daddies have to have a girlfriend to take care of them."

Not knowing how to respond, Megan said nothing for several minutes.

"You take care of me and Daddy. Are you Daddy's girlfriend?"

Megan's chest clenched. "No. I'm not."

Chloe frowned. "But . . . what if I want you to be?"

Strolling over to Chloe, Megan brushed the hair back over the little girl's shoulders, tucking it behind her ears. "It doesn't work that way, honey."

"Why not?"

Megan sighed and gave Chloe a small smile. No matter how much Megan wanted to be exactly that, Paul's girlfriend, it wasn't only up to her. "It just doesn't."

Chloe opened her mouth, ready to ask another question, but luckily the phone rang, interrupting the inquisition. It was Marilyn Daniels, Chloe's grandmother. After a brief conversation with Paul's mother, Megan handed the phone over to Chloe. Within minutes, the two were involved in a conversation that revolved around summer vacation.

Giving them a little privacy, Megan busied herself cleaning up the remains of Chloe's snack. Chloe was set to spend a month this summer with her grandparents—two weeks with Paul's parents, and two weeks with her mother's parents. Paul had brought it up a couple of weeks ago, letting Megan know she'd be free to visit her sister or go on vacation herself during that time.

Megan had thought about it. She had a little money saved up since Paul paid for almost all of her living expenses. Even if she didn't have money, she knew Gage, her new brother-in-law, would pay for a plane ticket if she asked.

Money wasn't the problem. The problem was that she didn't want to leave Paul. Sure, she'd love to spend some time with Rebecca, but her sister had Gage. Megan knew he'd take care of Rebecca and make sure she had everything she needed. He practically worshipped the ground Rebecca walked on. Plus, the two of them were like a couple of animals. She wasn't sure she could take being in the same house with them for a month while they were all over each other. Especially when she was currently sex deprived herself.

Chloe hung up the phone and raced over to stand beside Megan. "Can I go play?"

"Sure." Without wasting another second, Chloe took off up the stairs, leaving Megan alone.

Tossing the rag she'd been using into the sink, she followed Chloe. Maybe come the end of May, Megan wouldn't have to worry about whether or not she should leave and give Paul his space or not. Maybe, just maybe, a certain five-year-old would get her wish and her daddy would get a girlfriend.

***

Paul pulled into his driveway a little before six. He could have worked longer. He could have worked all night, since they were no closer to solving the case than they had been this morning, but he didn't want Megan to think he was running away. Again. That, and he'd only missed tucking Chloe into bed a handful of times over the last four-and-a-half years. He wasn't willing to sacrifice precious time with his daughter because he didn't know how to deal with his sudden attraction to her nanny.

Megan was in the kitchen prepping dinner when he ambled through the door. He cleared his throat to get her attention. "Hey."

She looked up, smiling, the same as she always did when he came home from work. "Hey."

He relaxed a little when she went back to what she was doing and made no mention of what had happened that morning. Throughout the day, images of Megan had popped up in his mind. These weren't things he remembered happening, but they felt real—more real than a dream—and Paul was almost positive they were from the night of Chris and Elizabeth's wedding. That, or her declaration that morning had triggered some very vivid imagery.

Chloe ran in from the other room and hugged his legs. "Daddy!"

Paul swung her up in his arms and kissed her cheek. "Hi, sweetpea. How was your day?"

His daughter proceeded to tell him all about her day, including the phone conversation she'd had with his mother, while she helped him tear the lettuce apart for a salad. To be honest, Paul had nearly forgotten about Chloe's month-long vacation with her grandparents. Normally, he counted down the days until he had to give her up for a month to share her with the four other people who loved her almost as much as he did. Even though it was still two months away, he'd barely thought about it.

He wasn't a fool. Paul knew the reason for that had to be Megan. She'd changed things for both of them. Their house was happier with her in it. Chloe liked having her here, and so did he.

That didn't mean he wanted a relationship with her.

Dinner was filled with random conversation about nothing in particular, and as the evening wore on, Paul relaxed even more. Chloe asked several questions about Janey, which he found somewhat odd, but his daughter was very curious. Sometimes it took people a while to pick up on that because she often kept to herself, but Chloe noticed things most adults would dismiss or ignore. He wondered if she'd follow in his footsteps and become a detective, or if she'd opt for something safer.

After putting Chloe to bed, Paul lingered for several minutes before trudging back down the stairs to the living room where he knew Megan would be waiting. He refused to run away again. She'd surprised him the first time, throwing him off-kilter. This time he was prepared.

At least, he hoped he was.

Megan was curled up on the couch, wearing another pajama set that he didn't recognize, with her feet tucked up underneath her. She was watching something on television. It was casual and completely normal for Megan at this time of night, but for some reason his gaze zeroed in on the skin peeking out below her very short shorts. He could almost feel how soft and silky it would be beneath his hands.

Paul quickly averted his eyes, but not before realizing that he'd been caught staring. Megan smirked at him, as he took a seat across the room, trying discreetly to adjust himself. She knew what she was doing to him. Paul only wished that he understood it.

"Did you want to play some poker?"

He took a few moments to consider her question and if there could be a hidden meaning behind it before answering. They'd played cards—mainly poker—many times before. It was her favorite game, and while he'd never played competitively, he and some of the guys at the station used to get together on occasion and play a few hands. "All right."

Megan smiled, and it twisted something deep in his stomach.

She jumped up from the couch, and strolled across the room to get the cards. His gaze went directly to her ass as it swayed back and forth with each step she took. He had to close his eyes to keep himself from looking. Otherwise, the problem in his pants would become much more pronounced, and there would be no way he could hide it from her.

Less than a minute later, he heard her not far from him, shuffling the cards, and figured it was safe to open his eyes. Boy, was he wrong. Megan sat not two feet from him near the corner of the coffee table. She was up on her knees, her arms pressed firmly against her sides as she manipulated the cards. The position pushed her breasts up, giving him plenty to look at from his angle above her.

Coughing, Paul swiftly lowered himself to the floor, hoping that the new angle would help. It did in some ways, but didn't in others. Megan wasn't wearing a bra, and he could see the tips of her nipples pushing against her pajama top.

Looking up to the ceiling, he took a deep breath.

"You ready?" Megan asked, bringing his attention back to her.

He nodded, not trusting his voice.

They played five hands before he decided to head up to his room, and he lost every single one because he was so utterly distracted. Something had to be done. There had to be a way to reverse whatever made this happen.

As he lay down in his bed that night and closed his eyes, the flashes he'd had earlier in the day morphed into memories. Paul groaned as he relived what he knew was no longer a dream. He didn't have to imagine how soft Megan's skin was along her thighs—he knew. He'd felt it himself.

By the time everything replayed in his mind, he was hard, and knew there was no way he was going to be able to get to sleep anytime soon if he didn't do something.

Throwing off the covers, he headed into his bathroom for a very long, very cold shower.

CHAPTER 7

MEGAN PULLED her car up in front of Chloe's best friend, Debbie's house. Chloe was bouncing in her seat, barely able to contain herself, wanting out of the vehicle as soon as humanly possible. "Can I get out now, Megan?"

"Yes, you may."

By the time Megan unbuckled her seat belt and exited the vehicle, Chloe was already at the front door, ringing the bell. Debbie and Chloe had a playdate scheduled, which meant that after Megan dropped Chloe off, Megan was free for the next two hours. She was still contemplating what to do with herself.

Before she could go any farther with her thoughts, Debbie's mom, Tessa, opened the door.

"Hey." Tessa smiled down at Chloe. "Debbie's—"

A delighted squeal was heard inside the house, followed by little feet coming down hard on the tile floor. Not two seconds later, Chloe took off into the house.

Tessa and Megan looked at each other and started laughing. "I wish I had their energy."

Megan nodded, agreeing with Tessa. "I wish I had half of it."

"Oh please, you're only what? Twenty?"

"Twenty-three."

Tessa waved her hand in dismissal, as if to say the three additional years weren't important. "You're still a baby. Wait until you're my age."

Although she kept a smile on her face, Megan grimaced. She knew Tessa didn't mean anything by it. In fact, she thought Tessa might mean it as a compliment. If not for Paul, Megan might have taken it that way herself.

"I'll pick Chloe up around five, if that's okay."

There was another squeal in the background, and Tessa shifted to look over her shoulder before refocusing her attention on Megan. "That should be fine. The girls usually settle down after a few minutes and go play in Debbie's room. Hopefully, I can get some work done around the house."

"Call me if you need me to pick her up early."

Megan waved goodbye, and walked slowly back to her car. It wasn't anything fancy, but at least it was hers. When she'd first come to live with Paul and Chloe, she didn't own much of anything, and most certainly not a car. But with Paul working all day, and some nights, she needed to have a vehicle to drive both herself and Chloe around.

As she slid behind the wheel, she remembered that first weekend when Paul took her to look for a car. They'd left early in the morning, dropping Chloe off at her grandparents so she wouldn't be bored all day. It was the first time Megan and Paul had truly been alone together, and the day she began to get to know the man that he was.

Starting her car, Megan pulled away from the curb, and headed back home. She figured she'd spend her free time getting some of her schoolwork done, and relax. It was Friday night, and so there would be no dinner to prep. Paul always brought home pizza, and they all sat around the living room and watched a movie. Considering there was a five-year-old in the house, however, most of the movie selections were of the Disney variety.

As Megan was walking into the house, the phone started ringing. She rushed across the room to answer it. "Hello?"

"You sound like you're out of breath. Is everything okay?"

Megan laughed. "Hello to you, too, Becca."

"Sorry."

Shaking her head, Megan strolled over to the kitchen table, and took a seat. "That's okay. I love ya anyway."

"Thanks." She could almost see her sister rolling her eyes. "But you didn't answer my question."

Megan sighed. "Yes, I was out of breath. I was just walking through the door when you called. Chloe had a playdate this afternoon."

"Oh."

"What? You thought it was going to be something more sinister?"

"Not exactly—"

"Maybe you leaving the FBI wasn't such a good idea, sis. What? PI work not exciting enough for you?"

"Hardy har har. Laugh it up. I'm allowed to worry about you, you know."

It was Megan's turn to roll her eyes. "Yes, I know. You remind me of that fact often enough."

Rebecca was silent for a long moment. "Am I really that bad? Gage says I need to relax, that the stress isn't good for the baby."

"You should listen to him, and no, you aren't that bad. Most of the time. You're my big sister, and you've looked out for me all my life. I get it. Maybe having a baby of your own will give you someone else to focus on."

Instead of getting a snarky comeback from her sister, Rebecca remained silent.

After several minutes, Megan began to regret her comments. "I'm sorry if I hurt your feelings, Becca. You know I didn't mean anything by it, I—"

"No. It's okay. You're right. Gage tells me the same thing all the time. He says . . . he says I worry too much about you. But I can't help it."

It was then Megan realized her sister was crying. "Becca?"

Rebecca sniffed. "I'm fine. It's these crazy pregnancy hormones. I start crying, and I can't stop."

Megan didn't know what to say to that, so she said nothing.

Eventually, Rebecca seemed to get a hold of herself. "So, the reason I was calling . . ."

"Yes?"

"Gage says that Chloe always spends time with her grandparents during the summer. I was thinking maybe you could come stay with us for a while."

Megan bit the inside of her cheek, worrying it. She'd been trying to figure out what to do for the past three weeks. Chloe was set to leave in a little over a month, and yet Megan was no closer to making a decision. "I don't know. I mean, don't you want to spend time with your new husband?"

"Gage has training camp all summer. He's gone ten hours a day, five days a week."

"But you have your work."

"I work mostly from home these days. Plus, I run the Nashville office, remember? I can take time off whenever I want."

Once more, Megan didn't respond.

"You don't want to come."

"I didn't say that."

"You didn't have to." Rebecca's voice changed, and Megan knew what was coming next. "Do you have a new boyfriend?"

"No."

"What then?"

For some reason, Megan's patience went out the window. "Why does there have to be a reason? Why can't I just want to stay here? I like it here. I'm happy here. Why does there have to be some ulterior motive?"

Rebecca said nothing, and after a while, Megan thought that maybe her sister had hung up. "Becca? I'm—"

"Hello?"

"Gage?"

"Megan?"

Megan cringed. "Yeah, it's me. Is Becca okay?"

"I don't know. I'll call you back later, all right?"

"Okay."

By the time Megan hung up the phone, she felt like crap. She shouldn't have yelled at her sister. Rebecca was being . . . well, Rebecca. And it wasn't as if Megan hadn't given her reason to question her. Besides, her sister wasn't completely off target. No, Megan didn't have a boyfriend, but the reason she didn't want to go did revolve around a guy.

Sighing, Megan leaned over, resting her head on her arms.

"You should go."

She snapped her head up, and came face-to-face with Paul. "What?"

He cleared his throat. "You should go spend some time with your sister."

The look in his eyes was guarded, and she knew the real reason he wanted her to go. For the last three weeks, she'd been teasing him mercilessly. She hadn't missed the bulge in his pants every night before he headed up to bed, or the extra showers he'd been taking. If she had to guess, she would bet they were cold ones.

Megan stood and walked toward him. The muscles in his throat constricted as he swallowed. He looked nervous.

Coming to a stop a foot in front of him, Megan looked up, meeting his gaze. This was dangerous. For her, anyway. She was the nanny, and at any point, he could send her packing. The fear was there, but she pushed it aside. If that happened, she'd deal with it—she'd have to. But what was the alternative? Do nothing? Keep things as they were? She couldn't do that. Not when she thought there was a possibility for more.

She licked her lips, and she didn't miss how his gaze flickered down to take in the movement of her tongue. "You're home early."

"I'm on call this weekend, so I cut out a couple hours early."

His voice sounded rougher than usual, and she reveled in the reaction he had to her. It had gotten more pronounced in the last few weeks. She was hoping that meant she was wearing him down.

"Oh. I see."

He glanced behind her. "Where's Chloe?"

"She's over at Debbie's. I have to pick her up around five." Megan inched closer.

Paul eyed her cautiously. "What are you doing?"

Megan played innocent. "I don't know what you mean."

He swallowed. "Yes, you do. You need to stop this . . . this game."

She reached up on her tiptoes, bringing their lips within inches of each other's. "This isn't a game. Not to me."

Closing the remaining distance between them, Megan pressed her lips against his.

***

Her soft lips made contact with his, and he nearly lost it. For the last three weeks, Megan had done everything she could to tempt him. At night, she ran around the house in pajamas that gave him glimpses of what he was denying himself—parts of her that he knew he'd once touched and kissed.

If that weren't enough, she'd taken every opportunity she could find to casually touch him or brush up against him in some way. It was driving him crazy, and he found himself aroused almost constantly whenever she was near. Paul couldn't take it anymore. She was killing him. He grabbed hold of her arms, ready to push her away, but then her warm hands pressed against his sides, and she moaned as her tongue licked along the seam of his lips.

No longer thinking, Paul pulled her tight against him and took control of the kiss. It was full of frustration, lust, and a need he didn't understand. He plunged his tongue inside her mouth. The kiss was almost violent as teeth, lips, and tongues fought each other for dominance.

Megan didn't fight him. If anything, she encouraged him. She dug her fingers into his skin, anchoring herself.

Needing her closer, Paul released his hold on her forearms, and palmed her ass. The move not only brought her flush against him, but it also gave him the leverage he needed to lift and move her. Megan eagerly embraced this new position, and wrapped her legs securely around his waist.

A few steps forward and he was able to set her down on top of the kitchen table. He didn't relinquish his hold on her, however. If anything, he pressed her tighter, letting her feel what insane things she did to his body.

Paul couldn't think properly. All he knew was that Megan was in his arms, hot and willing, and he wanted her. Trailing kisses down her neck, he leaned her back, and began edging her sweater up to reveal the amazing breasts he knew she had underneath.

Once Megan realized what he was trying to do, she reached down and quickly pulled the sweater up and over her head. She tossed it behind him somewhere, seeming to care as little as he did where it landed.

He grazed his thumbs over her hardened nipples that were still shielded by her lacy bra. She arched into his touch, encouraging him.

Brushing one cup out of the way, he wasted no time sucking her breast into his mouth and licking it. Megan moaned, and he could feel the heat between her legs increase.

His heart was pounding in his chest. It was loud. And it sounded . . . not right.

Somehow, through the foggy haze of Paul's brain, he registered that the pounding wasn't, in fact, coming from him. Someone was at the door.

He froze.

Paul straightened and took a step back. His gaze never left Megan where she was sprawled out on his kitchen table, her clothes in complete disarray, and one naked breast pink and swollen from his attention. He was rock hard, his body already protesting the loss of heat and pressure.

Megan opened her eyes, searching. "Paul?"

She sat up and reached for him.

He shook his head. "Someone's at the door."

A confused look crossed her face, and whoever it was knocked again, this time on the kitchen door. Megan scrambled to her feet, and snatched her sweater up off the floor while straightening her bra. With a sly smile, she slipped the sweater back over her head. "Aren't you going to see who it is?"

Shaking his head to try and clear it, he went to answer the door.

His partner, Janey, stood on the other side of the doorway, looking somewhere between worried and irritated. "There you are. I was starting to think I'd have to send out a search party."

"Sorry. I was . . . I didn't hear you at first."

Janey pushed her way past Paul, and handed him a folder. "This came in right as I was about to walk out the door. I thought you'd want to get your hands on it ASAP. It's the DNA results from the third murder victim." Janey paused when she noticed Megan standing across the room. "Oh, hi, Megan."

"Hello, Detective Davis."

There was tension in the room, and Janey seemed to pick up on it. She looked from Paul to Megan, and then back to Paul again. For several minutes, no one said anything, and guilt began to take root. Less than five minutes before, he'd been ravishing his nanny on the kitchen table. Nope. Not a thing to feel guilty about there.

Paul cleared his throat, and rubbed the back of his neck. "I'll read through the files tonight after Chloe goes to bed."

Nodding, Janey moved back toward the door to leave. "Call me if you need anything, or if . . ." She paused, and glanced briefly over at Megan. ". . . if you want to talk."

"I will. And thanks for the file."

Janey acted as if she couldn't get out of his house quick enough, and he knew she suspected what she'd nearly walked in on. Paul shut the door firmly behind her, and turned to face Megan. She was standing with her arms wrapped protectively around her waist.

"Don't say it," she whispered.

He closed his eyes and sighed. "Okay, I won't."

"Good."

Looking over at her, his heart clenched with his next words. "But that doesn't change anything."

She shook her head. "How can you say that?"

"Megan—"

"No! You can't stand there and say that you feel nothing. You're attracted to me. Admit it."

Paul leaned back against the doorjamb, feeling as if there were a twenty- pound weight on his chest. "Yes, I'm attracted to you."

"Then why won't you give us a chance?"

Looking at her standing in his kitchen, the way she had her body positioned, she looked young—younger than twenty-three. "We would never work."

"You keep saying that, but I want to know why." He opened his mouth to reply, but she interrupted him. "And don't say it's because you still love your wife. I know you love Melissa, and you always will. I'm okay with that. And I don't see what that has to do with us. She's not here. I am."

Paul listened to Megan's speech, and watched as she squared her shoulders waiting for his response. He averted his eyes, and took several slow, deep breaths. "A part of me died that morning the patrolman came to tell me Melissa had been pronounced dead at the scene. They didn't even bother taking her to the emergency room. She went straight to the morgue."

He found Megan's eyes again, and there were tears glistening in them. "I'm sorry," she whispered.

His heart clenched painfully, seeing that he was causing her pain. It had to be done, though. She needed to understand. "You're young. You deserve to find a guy who will be able to give you what you need . . . what you deserve. I'm sorry, but I'm not him."

Before she could say anything else, Paul opened the door behind him. "I'll get Chloe, and then we'll pick up the pizza before we come home." He paused. "You should call your sister back and apologize. Tell her you're coming to visit. The last thing you want to do is leave a rift between you and the ones you love. You never know when you won't have the opportunity to take it back."

With those parting words, Paul walked out the door leaving Megan standing in the kitchen. He hated hurting her, but she'd left him no choice. There couldn't be a them. Kissing Megan had made him feel alive. She made him feel as if he deserved to be loved again.

He didn't. The last words he ever said to his wife weren't ones of love. They were ones of frustration and anger.

No. There was one thing Paul was sure of. He didn't deserve a second chance. Not after the way he'd royally screwed up the first one. If it hadn't been for him, Melissa would never have been out that time of night in the first place, and she'd still be there with him. Chloe would still have her mother. They'd be a family.

As Paul drove toward Debbie's house, he brushed away a few stray tears. He needed to pull himself together. The last thing he wanted was for Chloe to see him crying. She'd want to know why, and it wasn't something he could explain to her.

All he had to do was make it another five weeks. Then Chloe would be off with her grandparents, and Megan would be at her sister's. Maybe the distance would be good for all of them, and Megan would realize that he wasn't the right guy for her. It was his only hope, because he didn't know how much longer he would be able to resist her if she didn't.

CHAPTER 8

MEGAN STOOD STARING at the door Paul had exited minutes before. The last words he'd spoken to her echoed in her head over and over again. He didn't think he could be the man she needed . . . deserved. How was that possible? Paul was the best man she'd ever met. He loved his daughter and would do anything for her—for his family as well.

Before she could dwell on it too much, the phone rang, and she blindly answered it. "Hello?"

"Hey, Megan. It's Gage."

That brought her quickly out of her musings. "Is Becca all right?"

"Yeah, yeah. She's fine. She's lying down at the moment."

"Oh. Okay." It wasn't like her sister to take naps, but maybe that was part of the whole pregnancy thing, too. It wasn't as if Megan was used to being around pregnant women.

Gage cleared his throat. "Look, you can tell me to butt out, or whatever, but Rebecca was really hurt when you said you didn't want to visit. She thinks she . . . we've done something to make you feel as if you aren't welcome."

"No, it's not . . . that."

"Then what?"

Megan sighed. She didn't want to lie, but she couldn't exactly tell the truth. "I'm not crazy about leaving Paul alone for an entire month."

"Why?"

"No reason."

Her reply was too quick. "What's wrong?"

The tone in his voice was the same she'd heard from Paul a time or two. Luckily, those times had all involved Chloe and not her.

She decided to be vague, but honest. "I think Chris and Elizabeth's wedding affected him more than he's admitting."

"How so? Did something happen? Did he say something?"

Megan hesitated. "No. Not exactly. It's more what he hasn't said." She paused. "Maybe I'm reading too much into it. I don't know."

But she did know. Megan knew what Chris and Elizabeth's wedding had done to Paul—knew that he'd gotten himself so drunk he couldn't remember what had happened. And given what he'd admitted to her only moments before, she was betting that his grief had more of a hold on him than anyone realized.

"Maybe I should call Ma."

"No!" Megan nearly bit her own tongue. An outburst like that wasn't going to help her cause in the slightest. "No. I mean, if he wants to talk about it, he will, right? I don't think it's good to force it, and I don't think he'd appreciate it if your parents got involved."

Gage didn't respond right away, and when he did, he didn't sound happy. "I suppose you're right. Paul's always the one taking care of everyone else. He doesn't really like it when people stick their nose into his business."

She breathed a sigh of relief. "Exactly. But you see why I don't want to leave right now."

"Why didn't you just tell your sister this? I'm sure she would have understood."

Megan released an exasperated sigh. "Because I really didn't want to say anything to anyone, nosy."

He laughed. "Okay, okay. I won't pry. But your sister does want to see you. What if you come out for a week or something? Surely Paul can survive without his housekeeper for one week."

"I'm not a housekeeper. I'm the nanny."

Gage made a dismissive sound. "Tomato, tamahto." He paused. "So will you come? I'll even set up the first floor bedroom for you so you don't have to hear us."

"Pfft. That would work if you two kept it in your bedroom."

He laughed.

"Well?"

She leaned back in her chair, and picked a nonexistent piece of fuzz off her sweater. One week. Megan didn't want to leave Paul at all, but she had to admit that she did want to see her sister. "Okay. I'll come for a week."

"Great. I'll have Rebecca call and the two of you can get everything arranged. We'll pay for your plane ticket, and pick you up at the airport."

"You don't have to do that."

"We want to. You're family, remember?"

Megan hung up a few minutes later, and she instantly felt guilty. She shouldn't have said anything to Gage. It wasn't any of his business or anyone else's, but if she hadn't told him, then he and Rebecca would have thought she was intentionally avoiding them.

Glancing up at the clock, Megan realized that almost a half hour had passed since Paul walked out. He and Chloe would be back with the pizza soon, and Megan had no idea what mood he'd be in when he returned. One thing she knew for sure, however, was that she had to find some way to make Paul understand that he was the right guy for her. How she was going to do that, though, she had no idea.

***

Tessa smiled when she saw him standing on her front porch. "Oh, hi, Paul."

"Hello, Tessa. How are you?"

She chuckled, and stepped back to allow him to enter. "Same as usual. You know how it is, chasing after a five-year-old all day."

It was his turn to laugh, although it was halfhearted. He couldn't get his mind off what had happened with Megan. Of course, lately he couldn't seem to think about much else.

Paul followed Tessa as she led him down the hall to Debbie's room, where the two girls were playing. They heard the adults enter, and looked up from their dolls.

"Daddy!" Chloe trilled, jumping up and running over to greet him.

He picked her up, and hugged her tight. Chloe was the only thing in his world right now that made sense to him. She was his one constant. "Hiya, sweetpea. How was your afternoon? Did you have fun with Debbie?"

"Uh-huh. We played with her new dollhouse. It's pretty, isn't it, Daddy?"

Chloe pointed to the large, three-story dollhouse they'd been playing with when he'd walked in. "Wow. It's big."

She nodded, and then glanced behind him. "Where's Megan? I want to show her Debbie's dollhouse."

Paul set Chloe down on her feet . . . more as a distraction. "You can show her another time. We're going to pick up the pizza for tonight and meet her at home. You can tell her all about it then."

Her lower lip jutted out in a pout. "But I wanted to show her."

"You can show her next time. Go say goodbye to Debbie."

Chloe lowered her head, and trudged back over to Debbie. "Bye, Debbie."

Debbie stood, and gave Chloe a hug, which she returned.

They said their goodbyes and Paul helped Chloe into the backseat of his car. Once he was satisfied that Chloe was strapped in securely, Paul walked around to the driver's side and got in. As he pulled away from the curb, his frown deepened. He couldn't let whatever was happening with Megan affect his relationship with Chloe—he couldn't. "What do you say we order the pizza, and then go to the park across the street while we wait?"

"Yay!" Chloe kicked her legs in excitement, and a huge smile lit up her face.

He could do this. He would do this. Megan was just Chloe's nanny. Nothing more.

***

Megan was at her computer when Paul and Chloe got back with the pizza. They were almost an hour later than she'd expected them to be. She was beginning to get worried as it was growing dark outside, but Megan figured that Paul needed to put some distance between them after their heated make-out session. She knew that it had certainly thrown her for a loop. The last time he'd been drunk, and she'd been unsure of his motivations. This time it was all him, and boy, was it ever. Just thinking about it again was making her warm all over.

Chloe came bounding up the stairs to get her for dinner. The little girl was all aglow about Paul taking her to the park, telling Megan how he'd pushed her really high on the swing.

As they entered the living room where Paul had laid out the pizza, Megan skidded to a stop, and all moisture left her mouth. Paul was bent over at the waist, facing away from them, the khaki dress pants he typically wore to work pulled taut against his backside. Megan wasn't normally one to get turned on over any one part of a man's body, but as with everything else, Paul was different. Over the last few weeks, she'd fantasized about his mouth, his hands, and she was sure that his ass would be starring in a few of those fantasies in the very near future.

They ended up watching Finding Nemo. It was one of Chloe's favorites, and in the last five months, they'd watched it at least twenty times. Megan could almost quote it word for word. At one point, Chloe had her mouth around a piece of pizza and said, right along with the characters, "Remember: rip it, roll it, and punch it," before taking a large bite with a huge smile on her face. Megan and Paul had shared a look, and chuckled silently.

Those were the types of moments she loved—the ones where they were both in this bubble—sharing something between them. It usually happened around Chloe, but then again, there weren't many times when they were together and Chloe wasn't around.

Once the movie was over and the pizza demolished, Paul took Chloe upstairs to bed while Megan cleaned up downstairs. After their "moment" when Chloe quoted Squirt from the movie, Paul had studiously ignored her. Not in a rude way, but in a way that let her know that he didn't want to interact with her if it wasn't necessary. That hurt, but she'd known all along that he was fighting whatever was going on between them. She had to keep telling herself that was all it was.

With everything back to normal in the living room, Megan headed upstairs to say good night to Chloe. To her surprise, Paul stood when she entered. "I already read Chloe her story." Then he turned to his daughter. "Say good night to Megan."

"Night, Megan."

Her chest clenched painfully as she bent to kiss the little girl good night. "Good night, Chloe."

Paul strolled by Megan, leaving the room, and she moved to follow him, turning out the light as she went.

By the time she'd stepped out of the room and closed the door behind her, he was halfway down the hall. "Hey."

He stopped, and wheeled around to face her.

When he didn't comment, she squared her shoulders, and walked forward. He didn't back away, but the way he held himself didn't encourage her either. "I wanted to let you know that I decided to go visit my sister while Chloe is with her grandparents."

She watched as some of the tension left his body. "Good." He cleared his throat. "That will be good for you. And her."

Megan nodded. "I'll only be gone a week."

He opened his mouth, but she cut him off.

"They're newlyweds. Work or not, they need their time and space. Especially with the baby coming."

He released a shaky sigh, and she wondered what was going through his mind. "You should stay the whole month."

"No."

He quirked an eyebrow at her. "No? Why not?"

Megan took a step closer to him, and he paled. "You're not getting rid of me that easily, Paul Daniels. I know you think you aren't good enough for me for some insane reason, but if you think that's going to stop me, you've got another thing coming."

"Megan . . ."

She shook her head. "I don't want to hear it. I've known you for five months now and I refuse to believe that you aren't the man you appear to be."

"And what kind of man is that?" A small smile pulled at one side of his mouth, and she was happy to see at least something break through the unmovable façade he was displaying.

"A good one. You're kind, loving, and honorable. You're a good cop, and a great dad. And . . ." She hesitated.

"And?"

"And you're one hell of a kisser."

To her surprise, Paul stepped forward. He raised a hand to cup her face, and then brought his lips down to graze the side of her ear. The heat from his palm spread down her neck, and her breath caught in her throat waiting to see what he'd do.

"That doesn't mean I'd make a good mate for you. It just means I'm good at faking it."

A second later, Paul released her. She looked up at him, stunned, and unsure what to make of his declaration.

"Good night, Megan."

Before she knew it, he had slipped into his room, leaving her staring after him. Again.

Sighing in frustration, Megan marched into her room. She wanted to slam the door, but knew she couldn't because of Chloe. Instead, she threw herself on her bed and screamed into her pillow. This was one of those times when she needed a best friend or a big sister to talk to. Although she knew she could talk to Rebecca, she didn't think her sister would be all that helpful, given the situation. Rebecca would think Megan had a crush and tell her that she needed to find a hobby or something, and get over it.

Things weren't that simple. What she felt for Paul wasn't merely a crush. She'd had crushes before. Lots of them. All those guys, boys really, that she'd followed all over the country—they were crushes. She'd seen what she wanted to see in them, not who they really were.

Changing into her pajamas, Megan crawled into bed, and grabbed the book she'd started earlier in the day. The problem was she couldn't concentrate on a single word she was reading. She closed the book, and tossed it onto her nightstand.

Sinking down lower in the bed, she raised her knees and hugged them to her chest. She was tempted to go knock on Paul's door and throw herself at him, but she didn't think that would get her what she wanted. Not in the long run, anyway.

Megan didn't sleep well that night. Her thoughts were filled with Paul and how to get him to open up to her. After what he'd said the day before, she was sure something had happened between him and his wife. Something he was ashamed of, maybe?

She dressed, and headed downstairs as she usually did. Paul was sitting at the kitchen table going over the file Janey had dropped off.

"Morning."

He glanced up, and then immediately back down. "Morning."

Trying not to take it personally, Megan went to get some coffee, and then joined him at the table. "Did you have any plans for today?"

"Since the sun is shining and it's not raining, I figured I'd do some work outside in the yard. Besides, I need to stay close to home since I'm on call."

Megan nodded and took a sip of her coffee. "Maybe Chloe and I can work on the flower beds. She was talking about all the pretty flowers the last time we were at the store."

"I'm sure she'd like that." Although he was talking to her, Paul never took his eyes off the papers in front of him.

"Can't you look at me?" Her voice was soft, and it was impossible to disguise the hurt she felt.

Paul closed the folder, and faced her.

"Thank you."

They sat staring at each other for several minutes before Paul got up and refilled his coffee. He didn't return to the table. Instead, he leaned against the counter. It was clear to her that he was putting physical distance between them on purpose.

"I'm not giving up, you know."

His knuckles turned white as he gripped his coffee mug so hard she thought he might break it. With his mouth set in a hard line, he met her gaze. "I know."

PAUL WAS CALLED out late Sunday night. He knocked on Megan's bedroom door, letting her know where he was going before taking off. She'd been groggy and rumpled, and looked way sexier than she had a right to. He was positive seeing her like that would only serve to add content to his new and rather arousing dreams the next time his head hit the pillow.

The homicide that night was of the standard variety, and they had the suspect in custody before they'd finished going through the crime scene for evidence. Even still, it meant Paul didn't get home until dawn. He was coming through the door when Megan appeared at the bottom of the stairs. "Are you just getting back?"

He closed the door, and locked it behind him. "Yeah."

She yawned and stretched, raising her arms above her head and molding her top against her chest. He quickly looked away. Luckily, she wasn't awake enough to notice.

Paul cleared his throat. "Still tired?"

"Yeah."

Laughing, he walked over to start the coffee pot.

When she realized what he was doing, Megan took a seat at the kitchen table, and rested her head in her hands. "I don't know why. Besides you waking me up last night, I slept pretty good."

Neither of them said another word until Paul brought a steaming cup of coffee over to her. "This should help."

Picking it up, she took a deep breath, and then a cautious sip.

She sighed, and smiled up at him. "Thank you."

Paul smiled back. "I'm gonna check on Chloe, and then catch a few hours' sleep."

Megan took another sip of her coffee, and then nodded. "I'll keep her downstairs once she wakes up so you can get some rest."

"Thanks."

He headed toward the stairs, but she stopped him. "And Paul?"

"Yes?"

This time the smile on her face wasn't so sleepy and innocent. "Thanks again for the coffee."

Even with his desperate need for sleep, Paul couldn't help but respond to that twinkle in Megan's eye. She knew what she was doing. He'd give her that. Before he did something he would regret, he trotted up the stairs trying to remain quiet and not wake his daughter.

After a quick glance in Chloe's room, he closed her door, and headed down the hall. Once inside the privacy of the master suite, he strolled over to his bedside table. He removed his gun and holster, putting them away, and then ambled into the bathroom.

When he returned to the bedroom, he walked directly over to his nightstand, and picked up the picture of Melissa he kept there. He inhaled a shaky breath, and released it. "What's happening to me?"

She didn't answer, of course.

Paul lowered himself to sit on the edge of his mattress, clutching his wife's photograph with both hands. "Why now? Why her?"

He paused as the scene from downstairs replayed in his head. "Why?"

Kicking off his shoes and removing his tie, he lay back on the bed, his head on the pillows. For the longest time after Melissa died, his life outside of his job and Chloe didn't make sense. It had taken him years to begin to feel somewhat normal again—like he wasn't missing an arm or a leg.

People always told him that things would get better in time. He hadn't believed them. But they'd been right, in a way. Although he never went a day without thinking about his wife—missing her—the time and distance had made it easier for him to cope. It was as he'd told Megan. He was good at faking it. As the years passed, it was easier to smile and act normal even if he didn't always feel that way.

He traced the curve of Melissa's cheek with his index finger. "She's twenty-three and very persistent." Paul paused, and closed his eyes. "I don't know what to do."

Turning, Paul laid Melissa's picture on the pillow beside his head, and stared at the beautiful woman who gave birth to his daughter. A part of him wished that she was here to tell him what he should do. The logical part of his brain, however, knew that if Melissa were there with him, he would never be in this type of situation. Megan would never be part of his life. Not in the way she currently was, anyway. She'd just be his baby brother's sister-in-law—someone he saw from the outside looking in, but never had too much contact with.

His eyes began to close as he continued to gaze at Melissa's image. Deciding to give up the battle, he sighed and allowed the exhaustion to take him.

***

Megan had a huge smile on her face as she continued to sit at the table and drink her coffee. She was wearing him down. Megan knew it. She only had to have patience. Not her strong suit, but she could do it. For Paul, she would do just about anything.

A half hour later, she was in the living room watching some television when Chloe came creeping down the stairs. She was rubbing the sleep from her eyes when she spotted Megan on the couch. Without a word, Chloe padded across the room to where Megan sat, and climbed onto her lap. Wrapping her arms around the little girl, Megan kissed the top of her head, and flipped the channel to some cartoons.

Eventually, Chloe began to wake up more. "Where's Daddy?"

"He was called into work last night, so he's upstairs sleeping. That means we need to play quietly downstairs for a while and let him rest."

"Did someone die?"

Megan nodded. "Yes, I think so."

Chloe seemed to think really hard for a while. "Why?"

"Why what, honey?"

"Why did they have to die?"

Megan brushed a strand of hair away from Chloe's face. "I don't know. Sometimes bad things happen."

While Chloe considered that, Megan decided it was time to change the subject. "Why don't we go into the kitchen and get you some breakfast, and then we can play a game or something?"

"Okay."

Seeming to have completely forgotten their conversation, Chloe slid off Megan's lap and ran into the kitchen.

Four hours later, a freshly showered and shaved Paul sauntered into the living room where Megan and Chloe were playing Candyland. Megan saw him first. "Feeling better?"

Before he could answer, Chloe chimed in, "Daddy, do you want to play with us?"

Paul walked over, and knelt down beside his daughter. "I'd love to, sweetpea, but I've got to go into work for a few hours."

Chloe pouted.

He sighed. "Maybe we can play some tonight after dinner, okay?"

"Okay." She still sounded disappointed.

Megan picked up a card, looked at it briefly, and then moved her little plastic man. "Will you be home around the usual time?"

"I should be."

"Okay." She gave him a sweet smile, and gently brushed her hand along the side of his thigh. "We'll see you at dinner."

Paul cleared his throat, and stood. It took all Megan had in her not to do a happy dance when she saw how he quickly turned away from his daughter to hide any reaction he was having. "Be good for Megan, Chloe. I'll see you tonight."

"Okay, Daddy." Chloe went back to concentrating on her game.

Paul moved to the door, and after telling Chloe she'd be right back, Megan followed him. He paused with his hand on the doorknob, and by his stance, he knew she was right behind him. She waited for a moment to see if he'd turn around, and he did. The look on his face made her want to giggle. She suppressed it, though.

"I wanted to thank you again for the coffee this morning. It was a lifesaver."

"You're welcome."

Megan glanced over her shoulder, making sure Chloe was still out of sight in the other room before she stepped closer to him.

He clenched his fists, but other than that, he didn't budge.

Inside she was grinning like a Cheshire cat. "After you went upstairs this morning, I got to thinking."

Paul swallowed. "About?"

"Tessa mentioned to me a few weeks ago that Debbie's been asking if she and Chloe can have a sleepover."

"A sleepover."

She shrugged, not wanting to make too big a deal of it. Yet. "Yeah. We'd drop Chloe off in the afternoon or early evening, and then pick her up the next morning. They'd play, watch movies, eat junk food. You know, girl stuff."

He looked over her shoulder toward the room Chloe was currently occupying, before returning his gaze to Megan. "I guess that would be okay. If Chloe wants to."

This time Megan didn't hide her smile. "Great! I'll let Tessa know."

Paul nodded, and started to leave again.

Megan stopped him. "So I was thinking . . ."

"Yes?"

"Since Chloe will be gone for an entire evening, I was thinking maybe you and I could do something. Go out." As soon as the words left her mouth, Megan's nerves skyrocketed. She might appear confident, but really she was scared to death.

"Go out?"

"Yes."

He closed his eyes, and sighed. When he opened them again, he was wearing his cop face. "You're a lovely girl, Megan, but I don't think that's a good idea."

"How will you know unless you try? We try."

Paul shook his head. "Look, I need to get to work. Why don't you . . . stop by around five, and the three of us can go out tonight? Get out of the house."

It was Megan's turn to sigh. "Fine. We can do that, but the three of us going to dinner isn't what I had in mind."

"It's all I can offer you, Megan. I'm sorry."

"You keep saying that."

"Because you don't seem to be listening."

"Megan?"

She turned toward the little girl's voice for a second, but it was long enough for Paul to make his escape. Megan gritted her teeth in frustration, and went to help Chloe.

***

Paul couldn't get out of there fast enough. She'd asked him out. On a date. At least, that's what he assumed it was. He was a little rusty at those types of things, but he was pretty sure that was her intention.

Knowing Megan, he doubted his little brush-off was going to stop her for long. The woman was relentless.

It would be easier if he didn't feel anything for her, but damn it, he did. More than he wanted to admit.

That didn't change anything, however. He still wasn't right for her. Even if the thirteen-year age difference was taken off the table, they were in very different phases of their lives. Megan was going back to college, trying to find her way in the world after being sidetracked for almost six years. Although he knew she adored his daughter, that didn't mean she was ready for a long-term commitment.

Stopped at a red light, Paul realized where his thoughts had gone, and shook his head trying to clear it. He couldn't go there. It wasn't fair to her, or to Chloe.

A little voice inside his head reminded him how it had felt to kiss Megan. To hold her in his arms—feel her soft skin beneath his hands, his lips—

The car behind him honked its horn, and Paul looked up to find that the light was now green. Cursing, he pushed his foot on the gas, and continued on to the station. He was going to have to figure something out fast.

He strolled into the station about ten minutes later.

"Hey, you made it in."

Paul reached for the coffee pot before answering his partner. "Yeah. It's amazing what a few good hours of sleep can do for you."

With his coffee in hand, he followed Janey back to their desks.

"The report's in your in-box. I looked it over. Seems fairly straightforward to me."

He took a sip of his coffee. "Yeah, it was. Perp dropped his wallet trying to get away, and went straight home afterward. We had him in custody quickly."

Janey shook her head. "There are some pretty dumb criminals out there."

"Yes, there are." He couldn't disagree with her. Most cases were solved because criminals made mistakes. Some of them were small and easily missed if the detective wasn't paying attention. Others, like the one the previous night, were blatantly obvious. "Makes our jobs easier, though, when they're stupid."

She nodded. "Now if only our serial killer would lend us a helping hand and do something equally stupid."

Paul couldn't agree with her more. "At least we now have DNA. That's something."

"It is. Doesn't help, however, that the guy isn't in the database."

The DNA the coroner lifted from one of Casey McMurphy's fingernails confirmed their serial killer was a male. But what Paul wanted to know was what had made Mrs. McMurphy fight back when the other two victims had not? "Anything new come in on the case?"

"Not really. I've been combing through our three victims' backgrounds. Again. This time I'm looking at shopping patterns, routines, anything that might put all three women in the same place. We need to find out where this guy is selecting his victims."

He nodded and took another sip of coffee. "It would be nice if we got lucky and could figure it out before he set his sights on another woman."

"Unfortunately, we are probably running out of time. I'd say we're due for a new body to turn up soon."

Paul knew Janey was probably right. Their first victim had turned up two weeks before he'd gone to his parents' for Thanksgiving. The second was found almost two months later. With the discovery of yet a third victim, also found almost two months after the one previous, a pattern had been established, and their two months was nearly up. It was one of the few things that aided in the apprehension of such psychopaths. They had an order of things, and most of them meticulously stuck to those rituals—even if, in the end, it was their downfall.

For the next hour, Paul finished going over the report from the previous night. He'd been the lead detective on the scene, so it was his responsibility to make sure all the i's were dotted and the t's crossed. He was about done, when he realized he needed some clarification on a few details from the first officer on the scene.

Paul looked around the room before focusing on Janey. "Have you seen Officer Rollins?"

"Not recently, no."

Pushing away from his desk, Paul went in search of the patrol schedule. Since Rollins was working last night, there was a possibility that he was home in bed. Sure enough, Rollins had the next twenty-four hours off.

Paul sighed, and went in search of the patrolman's contact information. He wasn't going to sit on the report for almost two days until he could track Rollins down.

Ten minutes later, Paul returned to his desk and picked up his phone. It rang several times before a groggy voice picked up. "Hello?"

"Officer Rollins?"

"Yeah?" The voice sounded measurably clearer.

"It's Detective Paul Daniels down at the station."

"Oh, hi." Paul heard movement, and he figured Rollins was getting up out of bed.

"You were the first officer on the scene of last night's homicide, were you not?"

"Yeah, I was. Is something wrong?"

"I want to go over a few details of your statement with you."

There was a grunt on the other end of the line. "Ah. Yeah. Okay."

Paul glanced up at the clock. It was already after two. "I'll be here until around five. Can you make it in before then? I want to clear this off my desk today."

It took a moment for Rollins to answer. "Sure. Give me forty-five minutes, and I'll be there."

"See you then."

He hung up the phone, and noticed Janey giving him a look. "What?"

"Being a little hard on the guy, aren't you?"

"Just trying to get this dreaded paperwork done."

"Hmm. This doesn't happen to have anything to do with a certain nanny that lives at your house, does it?"

"Megan? No. Why would completing a report have anything to do with her?"

"I wasn't talking about the paperwork itself. I was talking about the tone you took with Officer Rollins. And don't think I missed the tension between you and your nanny the last time I showed up at your house."

"I don't know what you're talking about." Paul stood. "I'm going to see what I can wrestle up from the vending machine. Do you want anything?"

Janey chuckled and shook her head. "No. I think I'm good."

Paul nodded, and went in search of something to fill his rumbling stomach. He should have known better than to think Janey wouldn't have noticed something wasn't right between him and Megan. She was a detective, after all. It would be more unusual if she hadn't noticed.

As promised, Officer Jay Rollins strolled into the station forty-five minutes later. He was freshly showered and wearing street clothes. Considering what Janey had said, Paul figured he should make nice. "Thank you for coming in. I appreciate it."

Rollins pulled up a chair beside Paul's desk, and opened the file Paul handed to him. He quickly scanned over the information. "Everything looks accurate. What more did you need?"

They were minor details, granted, but Paul knew from experience how the tiniest facet could become a huge deal when a case made it before a judge. Once Paul explained the additional information he needed, Rollins went in search of a computer so that he could adjust his section of the report.

Rollins returned at a quarter till five with the file and his updated statement.

"Thanks again."

"No problem."

Officer Rollins turned to leave, and a lightbulb went off in Paul's head. "Hey, Rollins?"

"Yeah?"

"You're single, correct?"

A questioning look crossed Rollins' face. "Yes."

"No girlfriend?"

"No. Why?"

"My daughter and her nanny will be here in a few minutes, and we're going out for dinner. I was wondering if you might like to join us."

"Are you trying to set me up with your nanny, Detective?"

Paul shrugged, trying to keep it casual.

"How old is she?"

"She's . . ." The words died in his throat as he saw Megan across the room. ". . . here."

Officer Rollins turned to follow Paul's gaze. No more than two seconds passed before Paul heard Rollins mutter, "I'm in."

MEGAN WAS SERIOUSLY CONTEMPLATING violence as she sat across from Paul. When she and Chloe arrived at the police station, she'd been surprised to find out that it wouldn't only be her, Paul, and Chloe going out to dinner. A patrolman, Officer Jay Rollins, was joining them.

At first, she hadn't thought much of it. He was a colleague of Paul's, and she figured they were friends, or needed to talk shop, or whatever. That theory quickly went out the window once they were seated at their table. Paul made sure that she and Officer Rollins—Jay —were sitting beside each other. Jay even pulled out her chair for her when she went to sit down.

She was further convinced that the whole thing was a setup when Jay began asking her all about herself, and not in a casual, friendly way. He also, aside from a few interactions when they were ordering, had pretty much ignored Paul and Chloe—focusing solely on her. Megan felt as if she were on a blind date, only no one had bothered to give her a heads-up in advance.

To his credit, Jay appeared to be a nice guy. He was cute, with sandy blond hair and blue eyes, and he had an infectious smile. Six months ago, she might have been interested, but as he continued to talk, her mind would drift back to conversations she'd had with Paul. If it was a topic they'd talked about, she'd remember what he'd said or done—if he'd laughed, or taken a firm stance on the opposite side of the argument.

Jay seemed determined not to upset her. No matter what she said, what position she took on a particular subject, he smiled and nodded. Where was the fun in that? Where was the passion? She loved verbally sparring with Paul. From the beginning, he'd valued her opinion, even if he didn't always agree with it. Up until she'd made her feelings for him known, he'd never treated her as anything other than an equal.

That was why she was currently fuming. Paul had done this on purpose because she'd asked him out. Did he not understand that she didn't want to date just anyone? She wanted to date him. Truthfully, she wanted a lot more than that, but she could be patient. Really, she could. She only wanted their relationship to move forward, no matter how slow the pace.

Unfortunately, for most of the meal, Paul studiously ignored her and Jay. He spent most of dinner talking with Chloe, and helping her color the menu the hostess gave her. It didn't matter how many glares Megan sent his way. Paul appeared oblivious. It was as if he'd put on blinders and could only see what was directly in front of him. She understood him wanting to show his daughter some attention, but Megan knew that wasn't what was going on.

After dinner, Jay walked close beside her out to the parking lot— his arm occasionally brushing against hers. Paul had rushed Chloe to the car, and Megan knew it was to give her and Jay some privacy, which did nothing to quell her ire.

She was trying not to be rude to Jay, but it was proving more and more difficult with every step. The last thing she wanted to do was lead him on.

"I'd like to see you again. I have this Friday night off—maybe we could go out to dinner, just the two of us."

Megan stopped, and turned to face him. She waited until she was positive Paul and Chloe were inside the vehicle and out of earshot. "Thank you for the offer, but I can't. I'm sorry."

"Oh. All right." He sounded disappointed. Megan hadn't thought she'd given him the impression that she was interested, but apparently, she had— at least, on some level. Either that, or he'd purposefully misread her polite responses.

She looked up at the sky, and cursed Paul for putting her, and Jay, in this situation. This whole thing was his fault—him and his crazy notion that he wasn't good enough for her.

When Megan lowered her gaze back to meet Jay's, he was watching her with a note of curiosity. She'd seen a similar look from Paul many times. "You're a nice guy, Jay, and if things were different, then maybe, but . . ."

"I thought . . ." Jay cleared his throat. "Daniels said you weren't seeing anyone."

Megan sighed. "I kind of figured."

"But you are."

She had to give him credit. He caught on fast. "It's complicated."

Her body language must have given something away because Jay glanced briefly over in Paul's direction before returning to look at her. "You and Daniels? But why . . ."

"Like I said, it's complicated."

He sighed, nodded, and leaned in to give her a kiss on the cheek. "If you change your mind, you know where to find me."

Megan gave Jay a weak smile, and watched him cross the parking lot to his car. The fact that she felt guilty for having to let a perfectly nice guy down easy only fueled her anger more. She turned, marched the short distance to the car, and hopped inside, not once looking in Paul's direction.

On the ride home, Chloe was quiet—too quiet—especially considering how close it was to her bedtime. Although she was a good kid, she was still a five-year-old, and it wasn't uncommon for her to get cranky when she was off her routine. Dinner had taken longer than it should have, and on a normal night, they'd already be tucking her in bed. The one time Megan peeked over her shoulder at Chloe to check on her, she'd been holding her baby doll against her chest in one hand, and rubbing her eyes with the other. Megan decided that Chloe must have tired herself out beyond being cranky.

That was until they arrived home. Usually Chloe was the first one out of the car unless Paul told her to stay in her seat. This time, both Paul and Megan had exited the vehicle, yet Chloe hadn't moved.

Paul went to get her, and that's when the tantrum started. Chloe kicked and screamed when he carried her into the house and up to her room. Megan followed close behind in case he needed help. She might be upset with Paul, but that didn't have anything to do with Chloe.

They worked together to put Chloe's pajamas on her, and to get the little girl into bed. In the six months Megan had been Chloe's nanny, she'd never seen her act out like this. Chloe was firmly told by her father that there would be no story tonight because of her behavior. He tucked the blankets around her, kissed her forehead, and headed for the door.

Megan followed suit, kissed the little girl's forehead, and then turned to go. As she began to back away, however, Chloe grabbed hold of Megan's jacket, and clung to it as if her life depended on it.

"Chloe, what's wrong?"

"Are you gonna leave, Me-gan?"

Kneeling down so that she could be on eye level with Chloe, she brushed hair off the distressed little girl's forehead. "I'm just going downstairs, honey. It's all right. You'll see me in the morning."

"You promise?" The words were said around sobs.

"I promise."

Chloe wrapped her arms around Megan's neck. "Love you, Megan."

Megan returned the hug, and then tucked Chloe back in bed. "I love you, too, Chloe. Now get to sleep before your daddy comes back in here."

In response, Chloe closed her eyes tight, and pretended to already be asleep. Megan chuckled silently, shaking her head as she turned off the light, and strolled out of the room.

As soon as the door was closed behind her, Megan took a deep breath, and headed downstairs where she knew she'd find Paul. With each step she took, the anger, and an increasing amount of hurt, pounded through her veins. Was the idea of dating her so terrible that he'd stooped to setting her up behind her back?

She descended the stairs into the kitchen, but Paul wasn't there. After checking the living room, she confirmed that he wasn't in there either. Glancing back up the stairs, she considered that he might have gone directly to his room, but quickly dismissed the thought. His door was open. If he'd been in there, she would have seen movement . . . heard something.

Determined to find him, Megan opened the back door to see if he'd gone outside for something. She was about to close the door again when something caught her eye. Squinting, she realized it was Paul, sitting in the backyard on the wooden swing that she'd never seen him use.

Zipping up her jacket, Megan softly closed the door to the house and crept almost silently across the yard. She lowered herself into the seat beside him, and tried to gather her thoughts. As much as she wanted to yell at him for what he did, she didn't think that would get her anywhere.

***

After leaving Chloe's bedroom, Paul practically ran down the stairs and out the back door. He'd needed air, space, something, so it didn't feel as if every breath he took weighed a thousand pounds.

Somehow, he found himself on the swing in his backyard. He remembered putting it together for Melissa. She used to sit and watch him mow the lawn, an iced tea in one hand, and a huge smile on her face—her long legs tucked beneath her. He missed that smile.

Paul was deep in thought—memories—when he heard the back door open. He didn't have to look to know it was Megan. Part of him wanted to hide from her. He could easily have held perfectly still and she would have been none the wiser to his presence.

His subconscious must have had other ideas. Without thought, his knees bent just enough for the swing to rock, drawing her attention.

He stopped the swing and waited. The closer she came, the faster his heart beat in his chest. Whether he liked it or not, he was attracted to Megan, and seeing her tonight with another man hadn't changed that. If anything, it had made it all that much worse.

She sat down next to him—her thigh pressing ever so slightly against his. It took everything in him not to twist to the side and take her right then and there. He'd somehow thought that seeing her with Rollins, giving her another option, would solve all their problems. Paul couldn't have been more wrong.

Throughout dinner, he'd kept his focus on Chloe, but he'd heard every word that both Rollins and Megan had said to each other. He imagined her smiling at his jokes—Rollins touching her in subtle ways just to gauge her reaction. It was maddening on a level Paul was entirely unfamiliar with.

Although he'd been hoping they would hit it off, and Rollins would ask her out, he hadn't been prepared for what that would mean. Against his will, he'd turned his head just in time to see Rollins give Megan a kiss. Paul couldn't tell from his angle whether it was on the lips or the cheek, but either way it caused a wave of jealousy to overtake him.

Silence enveloped them as they sat motionless on the swing. Paul had so much he wanted to say to her, but he didn't know if he could, or even should, share what he was feeling. Setting her up with Rollins had been a mistake. He knew that now.

"Why?" Megan's voice cracked, drawing his attention. Her jaw was locked tight, but he couldn't tell if it was from anger or if she was trying to keep herself from crying.

Paul didn't need to ask what she was referring to. He already knew. "I'm sorry. I shouldn't have—"

"No. You shouldn't." This time her tone was clipped, and there was no disguising how upset she was.

He didn't know what to say, so he stayed quiet.

She must have realized he wasn't going to respond. "Is it because I asked you out? Is the idea of dating me so horrible . . . so outrageous . . . that you felt you needed to set me up with someone else?"

Paul closed his eyes, and sighed.

"No. You don't get to do that. You don't get to push this under the rug and act like it didn't happen. I need to know why? Why did you do it?"

Leaning forward, he clasped his hands together, and rested his arms on his knees. "I'm not right for you, Megan. I've tried . . . I've tried to tell you. I'm sorry, but I can't be what you need. Rollins . . . I thought . . . maybe . . ."

"Is this about what happened with Melissa?"

He didn't answer.

It was her turn to sigh. "Whatever happened, I know it can't be that bad."

Before he knew what was happening, Megan had her hand on his arm, and the spot where she touched him tingled. He wanted more. As much as he knew he shouldn't . . . couldn't . . . want more, he did.

When Megan spoke again, her voice was barely above a whisper. "Jay asked me to go out with him Friday night."

Paul's chest contracted almost painfully, and he lowered his head. It was what he'd wanted to happen—what was meant to happen. So why did he feel as if he was going to be sick?

"I told him no."

He snapped his head up to look at her. "Why?"

She looked him square in the eye. "You know why."

They sat staring at each other for a long time until he looked away. Even with everything going on, even with their topic of conversation, Paul wanted to kiss her. How messed up was that?

He heard her let out what sounded distinctly like a huff, and the swing jerked a little as she removed her hand from his arm. Paul knew she was frustrated. If their situations were reversed, he supposed he would be, too.

Running a hand over his face, he took a deep breath, and looked out across his backyard. "I was called out around ten o'clock."

The moment the words left his mouth, it was as if he could feel a change in the air around them. Megan stilled to the point that, for a moment, he thought maybe she'd stopped breathing. He took a chance, and glanced in her direction. Her eyes were wide, and she held her posture rigid. She was waiting.

Paul returned his gaze to the darkness of the yard, unable to look at her or anyone else as he relived the worst night of his life. "The victim had been brutally raped and murdered. It was a gruesome scene . . . the worst I'd had to deal with since becoming a cop."

He let that hang in the air for a minute before continuing. "By the time we went over the crime scene and talked to the woman's family, it was nearly three in the morning when I walked through the door. Melissa was awake. She'd just put Chloe back down after a feeding."

Closing his eyes, he tried to push back the memories—to keep them from taking over, pulling him into the past. "I wasn't in a good mood. I was grumpy, and stressed, and angry for what had been done to that young woman. She was only eighteen, and he'd nearly torn her to shreds before killing her."

He looked down at the ground although he couldn't see much. The moon hung low in the sky, casting a heavy shadow. It fit the mood of their conversation, he supposed. "When I'd left the house earlier, Melissa noticed that we were almost out of diapers, and asked if I could pick some up on the way home. With all that happened, I'd forgotten."

To her credit, Megan didn't comment. She sat quietly and listened to every word of his confession.

"When she brought it up, I exploded. I don't know if it was the exhaustion or the stress . . . either way, she didn't deserve my anger. We'd fought before, of course. We'd been together for fifteen years. But this was different. I accused her of not appreciating what I did for her and our family. I was . . . I was mean about it. I said . . . I said things I shouldn't have. Things that, to this day, I wish I could take back."

The swing moved, but Paul didn't have it in him to look in Megan's direction to see what she was doing—how she was reacting to his revelation.

He cleared his throat, and finished what he'd started. If he was going to spill his guts, then he wasn't going to hold back. "Our fight ended when I yelled at her that she should just go get the damn diapers herself. She grabbed her purse off the counter, swearing that she'd do just that, and stormed out the door."

After a long pause, he whispered, "She never made it to the store. A mile from our house, a drunk driver ran through a stop sign and broadsided her. She was pronounced dead at the scene."

"I'm sorry."

Paul snorted. "I don't deserve your sympathy, Megan. I lost my wife because of my own stupidity—I cost my daughter her mother."

"No. You didn't."

Not wanting to argue with her, Paul stood. Keeping his back to her, he took a deep breath, and uttered the words that made him feel as if he were sticking a knife into his chest and twisting. "You should go out with Officer Rollins. I don't deserve a second chance."

Before she could reply, he walked back into the house. Hopefully, now she'd see. He wasn't the man she thought he was.

CHAPTER 11

MEGAN SAT outside thinking about everything Paul had told her, until the cool night air finally drove her inside. He'd left the lights on for her, but when she went upstairs, she noticed his door was closed. Knowing he wouldn't welcome her intrusion into his private space, Megan reluctantly trudged into her room and got ready for bed.

It was only as she was drifting off to sleep that what Chloe said resurfaced in her mind, and Megan wondered what had prompted the little girl's sudden fear. So much had happened in the last five hours that it was difficult to tell what had caused the outburst. She knew she'd have to talk to Paul about what happened. No matter what was going on between them, they couldn't let it affect Chloe.

Megan didn't get much sleep that night which, considering how her evening had ended, wasn't a big surprise. Deciding she needed as much mental armor as possible, she took the time to get herself dressed and primped before going downstairs.

When Megan sauntered into the kitchen, she found Paul sitting at the table, reading the paper and drinking his morning cup of coffee. He didn't glance up or acknowledge her arrival in any way, but she knew he was aware of her by the way he hesitated for a moment as she walked behind him.

After getting her coffee, Megan pulled out a chair, and sat down to his right. She took a sip of her coffee. "Paul?"

He glanced up. From the look on his face, he appeared to be preparing for battle.

Although she knew they needed to talk about what he'd shared with her the night before, they needed to talk about Chloe more. "After you left Chloe's room last night, she said something to me. I've been thinking about it, and well, I'm worried."

This got his attention. "What did she say?"

"She asked if I was leaving."

Paul sat up straight. She had his full attention. "Why?"

"I don't know for sure, but I have to assume that it had something to do with what happened at dinner."

"Megan . . ."

She met his gaze. "Don't. We'll talk about last night, but not now. Not when Chloe is going to come downstairs at any minute. My biggest concern is that she thinks I'm going to just up and leave her."

"You don't think I'm concerned about that, too?" He stood, and took his cup to the sink. "I'll talk to her."

"I don't think that's a good idea."

He turned abruptly to face her. "Why not? I'm her father. It's my—"

"But it's me she thinks is leaving. She needs reassurance from me, Paul. Not you. Not on this."

The sound of little feet descending the stairs ended their discussion. Seconds later, a sleepy-eyed Chloe waddled into the kitchen.

Paul crossed the room, and lifted her into his arms. She clung to his neck, burying her face against his shoulder.

He carried her over to the counter, and proceeded to grab the supplies he would need for her breakfast before depositing her into a chair, and placing the items before her. She timidly glanced up at Megan, scooted her chair a little closer to where Megan was sitting, and then picked up her spoon to begin eating her cereal.

Megan looked questioningly at Chloe as she drank her coffee and nibbled on a muffin she'd snatched off the counter. Chloe stared intently at her cereal, but would pause every now and then as if she were waiting for something.

"Good morning, Chloe."

Chloe peeked up at Megan. "Morning."

Although Chloe wasn't typically a morning person, her mumbled greeting wasn't normal.

Glancing over at Paul, Megan saw him frown. At least he realized that she wasn't exaggerating the issue.

Megan turned her attention back to Chloe. "Chloe?"

She waited until she was sure she had the little girl's full attention. "Honey, last night you asked me if I was leaving. Do you remember?"

Chloe nodded, and Megan thought she saw a note of fear in Chloe's eyes.

"Can you tell me what made you think that I was leaving?"

Chloe looked toward her father.

Paul tried to reassure her. "It's okay, sweetpea."

She still looked unsure.

Megan reached out, and placed her hand over Chloe's where it lay on the table. "No one's mad at you, sweetie. We're just trying to understand."

Chloe lowered her eyes. "You were mad at Daddy."

"Just because your dad and I don't always agree, doesn't mean I'm going to leave, Chloe. Grown-ups disagree sometimes."

"But that man. He . . . he kissed you." She said the last part in a conspiratorial whisper.

Megan sighed, and slid off her chair so that she could kneel down next to Chloe. Taking both the little girl's hands in hers, Megan tried to be as honest as she could. "I can't promise you that I'll never leave, Chloe, but I don't plan on going anywhere anytime soon, okay?"

"Okay."

There was still a little uncertainty in Chloe's reply, and Megan knew the little girl needed more assurance. "Do you think I can get a hug?"

Chloe didn't hesitate. She circled her tiny arms around Megan's neck, and squeezed tight. "I love you, Megan."

Megan hugged her back. "I love you, too, Chloe."

***

Leaving for work that morning was more difficult than usual. He wanted to stay and comfort his little girl. Paul knew he wouldn't be able to protect Chloe from every emotional, or even physical, obstacle she would face, but as her father that desire was there.

As he'd said goodbye to Chloe, giving her an extra-long hug, he didn't miss the pointed stare he'd received from Megan. He knew she held him responsible for Chloe's reaction, and in all honestly, Megan was probably correct. Paul was the one who'd invited Rollins to have dinner with them. Paul was the one who'd set everything up, including what led up to the kiss Chloe witnessed. It was his fault—at least most of it.

Paul parked his car outside the station, and took a moment to compose himself. As much as he needed to figure out what was going on in his life at the moment, he also had cases to work and a serial killer to catch.

He got out of his vehicle, and was halfway across the parking lot when he caught sight of Janey striding toward him. The look on her face told him that he wasn't going to like whatever it was she was about to tell him.

"We've got another victim."

Turning on his heel, they returned to his vehicle, and drove to the crime scene. He needed to get his head in the game, and figured the best way to do that was to begin gathering the facts. "What do we know?"

"The victim is a twenty-six-year-old female named Shelly Otis. Her roommate found her about an hour ago when she came home after a night shift."

"Anything else?"

"Not much. Since we're fairly sure this is another victim courtesy of our serial killer, they're waiting on us."

It didn't take them long to arrive. The victim's house was only about ten minutes from the station, in a middle-class subdivision. Paul noted that the surroundings were eerily similar to those of the other victims. Everything about the neighborhood was normal, average. There was nothing that made this place stand out. Was that a key to how this guy chose his victims?

"It looks like the others."

He glanced over at his partner. "Yeah. I was thinking the same thing. Could be a clue."

Janey snorted. "If it is, that he's choosing his victims based on them living in nondescript subdivisions . . . that's about as helpful as knowing he likes the color yellow."

Paul smirked. "Maybe he does."

She shook her head. "So not helpful, Daniels."

He released a harsh laugh, and then exited the vehicle. Janey followed, and they showed their badges to the patrolman positioned in front of the house, before going inside.

The forensics team was still doing their thing. Paul and Janey took a brief look at the crime scene, and Paul noted that it was in line with the others. The victim was lying in the center of the room, with her wrists and throat slashed. Blood pooled on the carpet, and stained the pink polka-dot bikini she wore.

Paul glanced out the window into the backyard, looking for any sign of a pool, and noticed what looked to be a hot tub roughly five feet from the house. "Do we have time of death?"

The ME looked up from where he was positioned over the body. "More than ten hours, so I'd say last night some time."

Nodding, Paul moved toward the door. He and Janey headed down the hall to where they'd been told the victim's roommate was waiting.

Sitting on the couch in the living room was a young woman who looked to be in her mid to late twenties with long reddish brown hair. She was staring off into space, face and eyes blotchy from the tears she'd been shedding. This was the part of the job Paul hated the most. It was hard to stay detached when coming face-to-face with the victim's friends and family. It always brought back memories for him.

Since the roommate was female, Janey took the lead. It was an unspoken agreement between them. "Katherine Bates?"

The woman turned abruptly, looking almost shocked to see them standing a few feet in front of her. "Yes."

Janey smiled. "Hello, Ms. Bates. I'm Detective Davis, and this is Detective Daniels. We need to ask you a few questions."

She glanced down, toying with a tissue. "Okay."

"When was the last time you saw your roommate?"

"Last night, before I left for my shift at the hospital. Shelly was in her room."

Janey moved to sit next to her on the sofa. "I know this is difficult, but do you remember seeing anything out of place when you left the house?"

She shook her head. "No. I was . . . I was running late, and I . . ." Tears started streaming down her cheeks, and it took several minutes for her to compose herself.

The rest of the questioning went in a similar vein. She didn't know much. She hadn't seen anything. What's more, she and Shelly often worked opposite shifts, so she didn't have a lot of information on Ms. Otis' daily routine. They wrote down what she did know, and gave her their cards in case she thought of anything else.

After leaving Ms. Bates, Janey and Paul spoke to a couple of neighbors who'd been home the night before. Like the others, though, no one remembered seeing anything out of the ordinary. Paul and Janey still had no idea how this guy was getting into the homes of his victims without anyone seeing anything, or there being any sign of forced entry.

They stopped for lunch on the way back to the station. Once they'd placed their order and their server had retreated to the kitchen, Janey turned her attention on him, an amused look on her face. "So how did dinner go last night with Rollins?"

He groaned. "I don't want to talk about it."

Janey laughed. "That bad, huh?"

Paul sighed. "You could say that."

"I could've saved you the trouble and told you that before you went."

"What part of 'I don't want to talk about it' did you miss?"

This only added to Janey's mirth. "Like it or not, that nanny of yours is smitten with you. And I doubt she appreciated you trying to throw another man in her direction."

He took a sip of his soda. "Is this one of those times when I tell you to butt out and you completely ignore me?"

She leaned forward and smiled. "Yep. It is. I've known you for five years, Paul, and I've never seen you rattled by a female. Heaven knows, I've witnessed women flirting their little hearts out more times than I can remember, but you've barely registered it. Megan Carson is different, whether you like it or not."

Paul said he didn't want to talk about it, and he didn't, but if anyone would understand it would be Janey. "I'm not—"

"Do not say you're not ready. It's been five years, Paul. Don't you think it's time you got back on the horse, so to speak?"

That wasn't it, but he let her assume that it was so she'd let the subject drop. Janey didn't know about his argument with Melissa the night of her death. He'd never told her. He'd never told anyone.

Until Megan.

***

Megan made it a point to spend extra time with Chloe that day. She tried to reassure the little girl as much as she could that she was there for the foreseeable future—for as long as Paul would allow her to be.

They read a couple of books together, and even made some brownies for dinner that night. As the day progressed, Chloe seemed to relax. It was one problem Megan could cross off her list.

She was still irritated with Paul. They needed to have a long talk, but she knew that doing so with Chloe around was tricky. Sure, Megan could wait until the little girl was asleep, but there was always a chance that they'd be interrupted.

There was also a possibility things could get heated—and not in the good, take-me-to-bed-and-have-your-way-with-me kind of way. Megan had every intention of making Paul realize that he was not responsible for what had happened to Melissa. Knowing what was keeping him from pursuing a relationship with her was equal parts frustrating and incredibly sad. It was obvious that he'd been beating himself up over this for the last five years, and Megan's heart hurt for him. She wanted to fix it.

At five o'clock, Megan and Chloe headed into the kitchen to start dinner. Paul would be home soon, and Megan had no idea what kind of a mood he'd be in. He knew her well enough to know that she wasn't going to let something like this go, but Megan also wasn't naïve. She knew it wasn't going to be easy.

They heard a car pull into the driveway, and Chloe scrambled down from her stool to wait by the door. Paul sauntered in a few seconds later. He hoisted his daughter up into his arms, and hugged her tight—a little tighter than was normal. That was when Megan noticed the tension—the stress— radiating from his body. Something had happened today at work. And as much as Megan wanted to hash it out with Paul, she knew tonight wasn't the night for it. She'd have to bide her time and wait.

For his part, Paul tried to put on a good show. He kissed Chloe on the cheek, and then lowered her back to the floor. "Something smells good."

"We're making chicken fa-fa—"

Chloe scrunched up her nose. Megan knew she was trying desperately to remember the rest of the word. "Fajitas."

"Fa-heat-taas." Chloe gave Paul a huge smile before rejoining Megan. "Did you want to help us make them, Daddy?"

Paul strolled over to stand on the other side of Chloe. "Sure. What is it that you need me to do?"

For the next half hour, they worked together to chop vegetables, marinate chicken, and warm tortillas. When there was nothing more Chloe could do to help with the food, she announced that she was going to set the table. It was haphazard, and Paul ended up with two spoons and no fork, but that was okay.

Chloe was all about helping—she'd been that way from the time Megan moved in. Sometimes Megan wondered if it was Chloe's way of supporting her dad. She might not be aware of the guilt he was carrying—the hurt—but kids were very perceptive. They picked up on things that many adults dismissed. Maybe this was her way of trying to comfort her father.

When they sat down to dinner, Paul was quieter than usual. He smiled at the appropriate times, and asked Chloe about her day, but there was something off.

Megan waited until Chloe was tucked into bed before bringing it up. They were sitting downstairs watching television—or, she was watching television. Paul was staring off into space somewhere. "Paul?"

He glanced over at her, blinked, and then sat up a little straighter in his chair. "Yes?"

She could tell by his posture that he was bracing himself. "Is everything all right? I mean, you seem . . . I don't know. Worried? Stressed? Did something happen today?"

Paul released a breath, and she figured he'd been waiting for her to start in about their conversation the night before. They would talk about that, but not when he was like this. "Just work, that's all."

Megan scooted closer. She was on the couch, and he was in the recliner almost two feet away, but she needed to be closer to him. "A case?"

He nodded.

She wanted to reach out to him, but she didn't know if her touch would be welcomed. "Is it . . . I mean, I had the news on earlier. They said there was a woman found dead in her house."

Paul sighed, and closed his eyes. "I can't . . . I can't talk about the case."

Megan decided to throw caution to the wind. She reached out, spanning the distance between them, and covered his hand with hers. He jerked, but didn't pull away.

They sat like that for several minutes before he opened his eyes and looked at her. He didn't say anything at first, but some of that haunted look he'd had before was gone. "I should get some sleep."

He stood, and she retracted her hand. Paul hesitated.

"If you ever need to talk, Paul, I'll listen."

He didn't look at her. "Good night, Megan."

She watched him stroll out of the room and disappear up the stairs. Dropping her head back against the couch, Megan sighed. He'd allowed himself to take comfort from her. That was something, right? Rome wasn't built in a day, and Megan had a feeling that breaking down the walls Paul had built around himself was going to take some serious work on her part.

Pushing herself up off the couch, Megan turned off the lights, and headed up the stairs. Tomorrow was another day, and somehow she knew that once Paul got some rest, his defenses would be back up in full force.

CHAPTER 12

MEGAN COULDN'T HAVE ENVISIONED the chaos of the next few weeks if she'd tried. One of the other detectives had a death in the family, which meant Paul and all the remaining detectives had to pull extra shifts. If that weren't bad enough, as things were returning to normal, some of the officers came down with the flu. As often happens, the illness slowly spread through the department. It was only a matter of time before Paul came down with the bug.

The week before Chloe was supposed to leave for a month away with her grandparents, Paul arrived home one evening looking paler than usual. Megan knew almost immediately something was off. When Chloe ran over to greet her father, instead of picking her up, he hugged her against his leg, and ruffled her hair.

"Chloe, can you get the milk out for me?" Megan asked.

The little girl nodded, and raced across the room to get the milk.

While Chloe was busy, Megan edged closer to Paul. "You caught it, didn't you?"

"I'm fine."

"Uh-huh. Sure you are." Megan shook her head, and took the milk out of Chloe's little hands.

Paul cleared his throat, and Megan could hear the strain. "What are we having?"

"Pork chops."

"I helped season them, Daddy." A big smile stretched across Chloe's face. She was still completely unaware of her father's plight.

He smiled in response, but it didn't reach his eyes. "You're such a great helper."

Megan knew by the way Paul was acting that he had to be feeling pretty bad. "Why don't you have a seat? Dinner will be ready in a few minutes."

"I told you, I'm fine. What do you need me to do?"

Placing her hands on her hips, Megan fixed him with a hard stare. She didn't say anything, but he got the message loud and clear. He pulled out a chair and sat down.

Megan, with Chloe's help, brought everything to the table. As Megan lowered herself into a chair, she placed two painkillers down on the table near Paul's hand.

He glanced down at the pills, and then up at her. She thought maybe he would try to argue with her, but instead, he reached for the pills, and popped them in his mouth. "Thanks."

Throughout dinner, Megan made a conscious effort to keep Chloe occupied. Normally the little girl was all about filling her father in on what she'd done with her day, but Megan didn't think Paul was up for conversation at the moment. Eating seemed to be taking a considerable effort all on its own.

When they were finished, Megan asked Chloe if she'd help her put the food away and load the dishwasher. "Why don't you go upstairs and get into bed? Chloe and I will clean up."

To her surprise, Paul didn't argue.

He was halfway up the stairs when Chloe realized Paul was no longer in the kitchen. "Where did Daddy go?"

Megan bent down so she was on eye level with Chloe. "Do you remember how your daddy told you that some people at work were sick?"

"Uh-huh."

"And you know how sometimes when you're around people who are sick that you get sick, too?"

She scrunched up her nose in concentration. "Daddy's sick?"

Megan brushed a strand of hair off Chloe's face. "I think so. Which means we need to let him rest as much as possible, okay?"

"Okay."

Smiling, Megan stood. "Do you think you can help me load the dishwasher?"

Chloe nodded, eager to help.

For the rest of the evening, Megan kept Chloe downstairs so that Paul could rest. It wasn't until bedtime that things got a little dicey. Paul always tucked her in when he was home, and she couldn't understand why he couldn't that night. It took some work, and an extra story, but Megan finally got Chloe to settle down and close her eyes.

Before heading to her own room, Megan decided to check on Paul. She knocked lightly, and when he didn't answer, she cracked the door open so she could see inside. He was curled up on his side, his eyes closed, and the covers pulled up tight to his chin. The urge to go to him was strong, but she resisted.

She almost had the door closed when she heard him call her name. Reopening the door, she stepped inside. "Yeah, Paul, it's just me."

He rolled over, and sat up a little. "Chloe?"

Megan strolled closer. "She's in bed. I had to bribe her with an extra story."

A small smile pulled at the corners of Paul's mouth. "She'll do anything to get an extra story."

Megan chuckled. It was true. Chloe would do almost anything for a story. There had been times when she'd asked Megan to make one up off the top of her head. Since Megan wasn't gifted in that way, she did her best to redirect the little girl's attentions. There were times, however, when it was impossible.

Paul coughed, and Megan momentarily forgot about Chloe. "How are you feeling?"

"Like someone ran a steamroller over my body."

Megan frowned. "Let me see if we've got anything in the medicine cabinet."

Megan ambled into Paul's bathroom. She'd only been in the space once before. Not long after Megan moved in with Paul and Chloe, the little girl had caught a cold. Paul kept all the medicine in his bathroom, out of Chloe's reach.

Like the first time, Megan was almost shocked by the difference between Paul and most of the guys she'd met. In her past experience, most men were slobs when it came to their personal space, with towels littering the floor and globs of toothpaste in the sink. There was none of that in the room she was currently standing in. The towel he'd used that morning was draped across the top of the shower bar, and the sink, with the exception of a few hairs from where he'd shaved, was clean.

Although Megan was tempted to explore some more—especially since she no longer saw Paul as only her employer, but a man she desperately wanted to get closer to—she went to the medicine cabinet, and found some cough syrup. Grabbing that, along with a glass of water in case he got thirsty during the night, Megan headed back into the bedroom.

Paul hadn't moved.

"I found some cough syrup for you. I didn't see anything specifically for the flu in there, so I'll have to go to the store and pick something up."

"Not tonight."

There was an edge of panic in his voice, and Megan immediately understood why. Even though she knew his reaction was irrational, it was also telling. "I'll wait and go in the morning, if that would make you feel better."

He took a sip of the water she'd set on the nightstand. "Thank you."

Megan sat down on the edge of the bed.

"What?"

She folded her hands in her lap. It was the only way she could keep from reaching out and touching him. "Nothing."

Paul sat up a little straighter. "Come on. You can tell me. I'm not that sick."

He punctuated his comment with another cough.

Megan reached out automatically to touch his arm, right above his wrist. Instead of pushing her away, however, Paul gripped her hand and squeezed. "I'm okay. Or I will be."

She nodded, and for a few minutes, Megan sat and watched their hands pressed together. "Did you need anything? I can make you some soup."

As if the bubble had burst, Paul released her hand, and pulled the covers higher. "No, I'm good. I need some rest, that's all."

Megan stood. "I'll let you get some sleep."

She walked to the door, and stepped out into the hall.

"Megan?"

"Yes?"

"Thank you. For taking care of me, I mean."

Megan smiled at him before pulling the door closed. She headed to her room, and stripped out of her clothes before padding naked to her bathroom. If Paul was sick, she knew she'd have to be extra diligent about keeping herself and the house clean. She'd also have to try to keep Chloe away from her dad for a few days while he recovered. The last thing any of them needed was for the little girl to fall sick days before she was supposed to go off with her grandparents.

***

Paul woke up the next morning feeling worse than he had when he'd gone to bed. He hated being sick. His mouth felt as though he'd swallowed a mouthful of cotton balls, and his throat as if it were lined with sandpaper.

He took a small drink of what was left of the water Megan had given him the night before, and winced as the lukewarm liquid slid down his throat. Paul had hoped a good night's sleep would have cured him, but that was wishful thinking on his part. Most of the department had come down with it.

With a groan, he fumbled for his cell phone, and dialed his boss. Once that was out of the way, he sent a quick text to Janey. She'd picked up that he wasn't feeling well when they'd parted ways the day before. Paul didn't think she'd be all that surprised that he wouldn't be going into work. Janey had only been back to work a week herself, after being out sick for four days.

It only took a minute or two for Janey to reply.

I got it covered. Call me if you need anything.

Everyone had been pulling extra hours trying to cover for those out sick. Paul would like to say those extra hours involved trying to catch their serial killer, but sadly, that wasn't the case. One day last week, he'd even had to go out on patrol because they were stretched so thin. Things were beginning to get better, people were coming back to work, and everything was getting back to normal. He and Janey had been hoping to sit down with their files today and reassess. It looked as though she'd be doing that on her own.

Heaving himself up out of the bed, Paul stumbled into the bathroom to take care of business and splash some cold water on his face. He looked horrible. It was difficult to say whether he looked worse than he felt or if he felt worse than he looked. Deciding he was too sick to care, he turned off the bathroom light and went back to bed.

Paul figured he must have fallen asleep again because the next time he opened his eyes, the sun was a lot brighter as it streamed in through the windows. He blinked, trying to shield his eyes, as a piercing pain shot through his head.

A light tapping noise on the door caused him more anguish, but it wasn't nearly as bad as the light.

He heard someone enter his bedroom, and pried his eyelids open against the light to see who it was. As much as he wanted to see his daughter, Chloe needed to keep her distance until he beat this bug or else she'd come down with it as well. It might even keep her from being able to go on her summer vacation with her grandparents, and Paul knew how much she was looking forward to seeing them. Melissa's parents had always been a huge part of Chloe's life from the time she was born—they'd only lived three miles away. With their move two hours north, Chloe had only seen them a handful of times in the last six months. It had been an adjustment. For all of them.

"Hey."

Megan stepped forward, blocking a good portion of the light. Some of the pain eased, and he released a sigh. There might also have been something else—calm, maybe—but he wasn't going to dwell on that. "Hey."

She must have noticed him squinting, because the next thing Paul knew, she was marching over to the windows and pulling the curtains closed.

"Better?" Megan asked as she returned to stand beside his bed.

"Yes. Thank you." He tried to sit up, and without him asking, Megan readjusted the pillows behind him. "You know you shouldn't get too close. You'll catch it, too."

"Well, if I do, you'll just have to take care of me then, won't you?" She sauntered across the room, and returned with a tray that held two pieces of toast and some tea.

Although he wasn't really hungry, Paul knew he needed to eat. He hadn't eaten much for dinner the night before, and if he wanted to kick this cold, he would need his strength. Why did every inch of his body have to ache?

Megan set the tray over his lap, and Paul picked up one of the pieces of toast. He was weak, and it irritated him. Paul was used to taking care of things, including himself. "I didn't ask you to take care of me. I'm perfectly capable—"

"Stop being a baby." Megan swiped his empty water glass from the nightstand, and strolled, unperturbed, into the bathroom.

When she returned with his refilled glass, she had a rather serious look on her face. "What?"

She set the glass down and crossed her arms over her chest. Even in his less than stellar state, Paul couldn't help but notice the way the motion pushed her breasts up, making them look fuller. Megan wasn't overly endowed in that area, but he had firsthand knowledge of how well they fit into the palm of his hand.

He suppressed a groan as his body reacted in spite of his condition.

Megan's expression softened, and she rushed to get him another dose of painkillers. She'd misinterpreted his reaction. That was probably a good thing. He didn't think he could fight her off right now.

Without argument, Paul swallowed the pills. "Thanks."

"You're welcome."

She didn't cross her arms again, which sent a wave of disappointment through him.

"Something on your mind?" He figured he might as well have her get whatever it was out of her system.

Megan met his gaze. She looked weary, but determined. "Cindy called this morning. Melissa's mom. She asked for you, and I told her that you were sick."

Okay, not what he'd been expecting. He opened his mouth to ask what she wanted, but coughed instead.

Megan handed him the tea.

He took a sip. It still felt as if there were tiny nails coating his throat, but at least it suppressed his urge to cough. "Thanks."

She frowned. "I'll add cough drops to the shopping list. I wanted to see if there was anything specific you wanted before Chloe and I head to the store."

"No. I don't think so."

"Okay."

Megan shifted her weight. She was nervous about something, and he figured it had to have something to do with her conversation with his mother-in-law.

"What did Cindy say?"

"Well, when I explained that you were sick, she . . ."

Paul waited for Megan to go on, but she didn't. "Did Cindy say something to upset you?"

He didn't think Cindy would do such a thing, but he guessed it wasn't out of the realm of possibility. When he'd told his in-laws that Megan was moving in with him and Chloe six months ago, Cindy and George had both been concerned—Cindy more so than

George. To his knowledge, Cindy had never voiced those concerns to Megan.

"No. Not exactly."

Paul was trying to have patience, but given all he wanted to do was close his eyes and sleep for the foreseeable future, her stalling was grating on his nerves. "Spit it out."

Megan jerked at his tone, and of course, his gruff reply sent him into another round of coughing.

This time, she didn't hand him his tea. He guessed he deserved that. "Sorry."

"I know you aren't feeling well, and men tend to be babies of the highest order when they're sick, but that doesn't give you the right to be rude to me. I'm trying to help."

"I know, and I appreciate it. I do." Paul sighed. "What did Cindy say to you?"

"She said that since you're sick, she and George would come get Chloe early. That way, you could rest and get better faster. Plus, she said this way, hopefully Chloe wouldn't catch whatever you have."

"So when are they coming?"

Megan bit the inside of her lip. "They'll be here this afternoon."

Paul didn't know what to think. In a way he was glad they would be taking Chloe early. She was set to leave in five days, and if Janey's illness was anything to go by, it would take him nearly that long to recover, anyway. It wasn't as if he'd get to spend any real quality time with her before she left. Still, it was always difficult handing his little girl off for any extended period of time. "I guess this means you can head down to Nashville and visit your sister a little sooner."

Megan looked at him as if he'd grown two heads. "You think I'm going to go off and leave you here alone? When you're like this? Not a chance, mister. You aren't getting rid of me that easily."

"I'm a big boy, Megan. I've been sick before. I can take care of myself."

She shook her head like a disapproving parent, and strolled toward the door. "Chloe and I are going to the store. Eat your breakfast, and leave the tray by the bed. I'll come get it when I get back."

Without waiting for his response, Megan left his room, and closed the door behind her.

Paul leaned back against his headboard, and looked toward the ceiling. He was in some serious trouble. Megan's flight to Nashville didn't leave for five days. He'd been relying on Chloe being around to create a buffer between them. It had worked in the past. What was he going to do with her gone? He and Megan alone in the house together wasn't a good combination. Sure, he was sick, but unlike with Chloe, that didn't mean Megan would keep her distance—the last twelve hours had already proven that.

He took a drink of the peppermint tea Megan had brought with his breakfast, and sighed as the warmth coated his throat. Her taking care of him wasn't helping. Paul didn't get sick often. The last time it happened, his wife had still been alive, and Chloe hadn't yet been conceived. Melissa had brought him tea and juice and made sure his blankets and pillows were just so.

The memory of Megan adjusting his pillows caused a pang of longing in the pit of his stomach. There was one problem, though. He didn't know if he was longing for Melissa or Megan, and that brought him up short. The two women were so very different. How could he be having this pull toward Megan when, at the same time, he missed his wife?

It didn't make sense, but then again not much had made sense in his life for the last two months—not since Chris and Elizabeth's wedding.

THE MOMENT MEGAN told Chloe they were going to the store to pick up some medicine for her dad, the little girl began asking questions. From the sound of it, Paul had never been sick—or at least, not that Chloe could remember. Chloe only had one parent left. She didn't want him to go away, too.

It was then Megan truly understood the little girl's freak-out when she'd thought Megan was going to leave. To think that one of the two people at the center of her world was going away, especially after she was already missing her mother in her life, was a scary prospect for a five-year-old.

The questions continued in the store. "What's this for, Megan?"

"It makes it so you don't cough."

Megan moved on to the next item on her list.

"What about that?" Chloe asked when Megan placed a box of tea in the cart.

It went on like that as they weaved their way through the store.

When they arrived home, Chloe helped Megan bring the groceries inside. Chloe was still worried about her dad, and Megan knew she would have to keep the little girl's mind off things until her grandparents arrived. Megan gathered what they'd need to make several batches of cookies. Chloe loved to bake, and they'd spent many hours in the kitchen making cakes and brownies over the last few months.

When Chloe found out what they were doing, her face lit up like it was Christmas morning. She rushed into the kitchen, grabbed her apron, and stood in the middle of the floor waiting impatiently.

Megan laughed. "Did you wash your hands?"

Chloe frowned, and ran into the small bathroom down the hall where there was a stool she used to reach the sink.

Hearing the water turn on, Megan used the time to unload and separate what they'd bought. She was almost finished when Chloe ambled back into the kitchen, wiping her hands on her little apron. "Can we make the cookies now?"

Megan attempted to hide her smile. "Not quite yet. We need to find a recipe first. Can you grab that book over there on the shelf that says cookies?"

Without waiting for any further instruction, Chloe went to the bookcase Megan indicated, the one where all the cookbooks Melissa had owned were stored. A couple of minutes later, the little girl brought the blue and tan book with the word cookies in big bold lettering. "I gots it, Megan. Now what?"

Chloe's eagerness was infectious. It was one of the things Megan loved about her. "I need you to sit down here at the table and find us a recipe for chocolate chip cookies. Do you think you can find all those words?"

The little girl nodded, and quickly took a seat, opening the book.

This time Megan didn't hide her smile. "I'm going to run these things up to your dad real quick, then I'll be back down and we can start making the cookies, okay?"

"I have to stay away so I don't get sick." Chloe repeated the explanation Megan had given her both the night before and again that morning.

It was also the explanation Megan had given Chloe when she'd explained that Chloe's grandparents were coming to pick her up early. Chloe had been torn. She missed her grandparents and longed to spend more time with them, but she was also afraid for her father. After several reassurances, and letting Chloe know that she could call her daddy anytime she wanted while she was with her grandparents, she seemed more at ease with the idea. Megan wouldn't go as far as to say she was excited. She only hoped Cindy understood that she would have to keep Chloe extra occupied for the next few days.

Megan knocked lightly on Paul's bedroom door before cracking it open to peer inside. He was lying in bed with his eyes closed, but as she walked into the room, he opened them.

"You're back."

"Yeah. I brought you some things I thought you might need." She handed him the bag and he took a look inside. Going through the grocery store, Megan had picked up anything she thought he might need, from things to settle his stomach to those proclaiming to help fight the flu.

He coughed and promptly pulled out the bag of throat lozenges. "Thanks."

"Did you need anything else at the moment? Chloe and I are going to make some cookies. I figure that will keep her busy until Cindy gets here."

"Good idea." Paul coughed.

She frowned, but after he assured her that he didn't need anything else, Megan headed back downstairs.

When she strolled into the kitchen, Chloe had already dug out the mixing bowl, the flour, and several measuring cups. "Were you going to start without me?"

The little girl smiled up at her. "I's got everything ready, Megan."

Megan laughed and shook her head as she picked up the recipe book Chloe had left lying on the table. Sure enough, it was open to a recipe for old-fashioned chocolate chip cookies.

For the next three hours, Megan and Chloe worked side by side making cookies. Megan knew she and Paul would be eating cookies for weeks— even if Megan sent two to three dozen with Cindy. Baking had done the job, though. Chloe smiled and laughed freely.

There was no sign of the furrowed brow that had been present early that morning.

At twelve thirty, Megan whipped them up a quick lunch, and then marched the little girl upstairs to clean up. While Chloe was washing her face and brushing her teeth, Megan packed Chloe's suitcase. Other than clothes and the stuffed bear she slept with, there wasn't much to take. Cindy and George kept toys at their house, and Megan had no doubts that more would be added to their collection over the next three weeks. Grandparents spoiled their grandchildren—or at least, that was how it was supposed to be.

Promptly at two, there was a knock on the door. Chloe ran to answer it, not waiting for Megan. With her grandmother here, Chloe was full of energy.

She wrapped her arms around Cindy's waist. "Grandma!"

Cindy laughed. "Oh, my. Let me have a look at you. I think you've grown two inches since the last time I saw you."

Megan brought all of Chloe's things downstairs, and then asked if she wanted to say goodbye to her dad. Without giving a verbal response, the little girl took off up the stairs toward Paul's bedroom. Megan was hot on her heels, but even still, Chloe reached Paul's door first. "Chloe."

At the sound of her name, she stopped, and looked wide-eyed at Megan. "It's okay, honey, just try to remember your daddy is sick."

Chloe looked down.

Megan sighed, and knocked on the door before pushing it open.

Paul turned his head and opened his eyes. When he saw Chloe, he smiled. "Hi, sweetpea."

"Hi, Daddy." Chloe twisted her fingers together, and shifted her weight from one foot to the other.

"Cindy's downstairs, and Chloe wanted to come up and say goodbye before they leave," Megan said when she saw a crease beginning to form in Paul's brow.

"Oh." He glanced over at the clock. "I didn't realize how late it was. Did you get all your cookies made?"

"We made lots, and lots, and lots of cookies, Daddy. We's taking some to Grandpa."

"That's very nice of you. I'm sure he'll appreciate it."

Paul coughed, which led to another deeper cough.

Megan knew it was time for them to go and let Paul get back to recovering. "We need to say goodbye and let your daddy rest. Plus, I'm sure your grandma has lots of fun stuff planned for you. You don't want to miss that, do you?"

Chloe looked up at Megan, and she ran a gentle hand through the little girl's hair. There was so much in Chloe's eyes—more than there should be in someone so young. Two seconds later, Chloe practically hurled herself at her father's blanket-covered legs. She hugged him tight, and Paul reached down to brush his fingers along her forehead.

"I love you," she whispered.

"I love you, too, Chloe." She turned her head to look at him, but didn't let go. "Be good for your grandma and grandpa."

***

It nearly broke Paul's heart to watch as Megan coaxed Chloe away from him and out of the room. He could see she was torn. She wanted to go with Cindy, but she didn't want to leave him. Whether he liked it or not, Megan and Cindy were right. Chloe would be better off with her grandparents. The longer she stayed in the house, the more likely she'd get sick, too.

He must have drifted off to sleep because the next time he opened his eyes, it was dark out. His throat was dry, and he was starving. Paul figured it was a good sign that he was hungry. Maybe he would be back to work sooner than he'd thought.

Kicking the covers off him, Paul shuffled to the bathroom and then made his first trek outside his bedroom since coming home from work over twenty-four hours before.

It was after midnight and the house was quiet. Megan was asleep. She'd left her door open—something she didn't normally do—probably thinking it would be easier for her to hear him.

Paul was careful not to make too much noise as he crept down the hall, but he couldn't help but pause at her door. The room was clothed in shadow, but he could clearly see the outline of her figure lying in the bed. Megan was full of contradictions. He knew she came from a not-so-pleasant childhood, and yet she was great with his daughter.

She's great with you, too.

He closed his eyes and took a deep breath. As he inhaled, he caught Megan's scent. It was somewhere between lilac and cherry. He didn't know if it was a perfume she wore or what, but she always had a hint of it surrounding her.

Before he could get lost in memories, Paul backed away from the doorway, and continued downstairs to the kitchen. Everything was neatly put away, and he was easily able to find leftovers to warm up in the microwave. Megan was taking such good care of him, and it made what he was feeling for her that much more complicated. If it was only physical attraction, he could deal with that. But it wasn't only physical. He liked her. He enjoyed spending time with her.

As Paul sat in the darkened kitchen eating the soup he knew Megan most likely made just for him, he considered his options. He still didn't think he was good enough for her—or anyone, for that matter—but although Megan knew what he'd done, she didn't seem to agree. Could he give a relationship with her a chance? Would it work, or was he setting them both up for failure? He was thirty-six years old. She was twenty-three. Did they even want the same things?

All the questions were making his head hurt, so he decided to put off any more contemplation until he was feeling better. It wasn't as if anything could happen while he was feeling like he was, anyway.

Putting everything away, Paul trudged back up the stairs, and tumbled into his bed. He popped a few more pills and rolled over, closing his eyes against the pain. Everything else would have to wait until morning.

Over the next thirty-six hours, Paul began to feel somewhat normal again. He no longer felt as if he'd been beaten and left for dead. His muscles ached, but it was more like something one would experience after a good hard workout.

Megan took her role of caregiver seriously. She hadn't been pleased that he'd awakened the other night and gone downstairs for food. He'd been given a nice little lecture about letting people take care of him. Was that something all women learned how to do? Did they teach it in school or something? He could have sworn he'd received a similar lecture from both Melissa and his mother at various times in his life.

As it was, Paul didn't want for much of anything. Megan made sure he had food, water, cough syrup, pain medication, and anything else she thought he might need. The only problem with all her attention was that as he started to feel better, he began craving other things. She'd go to plump up his pillows and her breasts would come within inches of his face. There was a time or two when he came close to pulling her top out of the way and sucking one of her nipples into his mouth. Knowing exactly how it would feel and taste made it doubly tempting.

He'd been home for three days when his partner showed up bearing gifts. "I thought you'd be climbing the walls by now."

Paul sat up as Janey strolled across the room. "Megan brought over the TV from her room for me to watch. Not much on during the day, but it's better than staring at the ceiling."

Janey sat down on the edge of the bed and handed him a thick folder. "I have to go to court this afternoon, so I thought I'd bring the file over for you. I looked at it until my head hurt, but I'm not finding many patterns."

"But you're finding some?"

She shrugged. "Just the usual. They all lived or worked within a twenty-mile radius, so most of them went to the same stores. There is overlapping, but nothing I can find that screams it may be the place they attracted the attention of a serial killer."

He opened the folder and paged through some of Janey's notes. "A pattern is a pattern."

"True, but I'm not finding anywhere all these women went a day, a week, two weeks before they were killed. It's possible this guy is picking his victims and then watching them until the time is right. If that's the case, it's going to make him harder to track. Considering he's killing about every two months, I have to think he's picking his victims with some degree of frequency."

Paul nodded. "I agree. There has to be a pattern. We just aren't seeing it yet."

Janey let him look over the file for a few minutes before she shifted her weight, getting his attention. "So. How are things going with the nanny?"

He rolled his eyes. "None of your business."

She laughed. "That good, huh?"

Paul grunted.

"A little piece of advice—"

"I don't need any advice on my personal life."

"Oh, but I think you do. Besides, I'm going to give it to you anyway, whether you want it or not." Janey looked over her shoulder, and then back to him. "If you like her, then you should go for it. Chloe likes her, and I've seen some of those looks she gives you. What do you have to lose?"

"It's not that easy, Davis."

"Why the hell not? Don't tell me you're not attracted to her."

"It's not—"

"Exactly. So suck it up and ask the girl out. You do remember how to do that, right?"

Paul snorted. "Yeah. I'm not that old and decrepit."

She patted his leg. "I didn't think so."

Janey stood and sighed. "As much as I'd love to stay and give you more grief, I need to get to the courthouse. Call me later if you need anything. Or if you find something."

"I will."

Paul spent the next several hours going over the case file. Janey was right. Although there were patterns, they weren't ones that stood out or screamed a connection. All of the women had been to the same grocery store in the last six months, but only three went on a regular basis, and one hadn't been to the store for four months before she was killed. While they would follow up on the lead, it was most likely a dead end.

When Megan brought his dinner, Paul set the folder aside. "Smells good."

Megan smiled and sat down on the bed. He could feel the heat of her body as it pressed against his leg. As usual, he was hyperaware of her.

"Is that what Detective Davis brought over earlier?" Megan asked.

He glanced at the file, and then took a bite of his food before answering. "Yeah. She's hoping maybe I can see something she's missing. Fresh eyes and all that."

"This is the serial killer?"

Although Paul didn't discuss the details of his cases with Megan, the murders had made the news, and she knew he had been assigned to the case. "Yes."

She nodded and bit the side of her lip.

Needing to touch her, Paul reached out and took hold of her hand. "What is it?"

She met his gaze. "Did you want me to cancel my trip? I can stay here. It's not a big—"

"No. Go. You need to spend time with your sister." He saw by the scowl on her face that she was going to protest. "And I need to catch up on the work I missed. With Chloe gone, I'll probably be pulling twelve to fifteen hour days for the next week."

Megan nodded. "All right."

Paul couldn't help the pull he felt toward her, and how right it felt to hold her hand like he was. A surge of warmth raced through his body, and he wondered if maybe he was making the wrong decision. Maybe he could try . . .

No. It would never work between them. They were too different, and he was . . .

Paul looked down at their hands intertwined together, and it was hard to remember his arguments. He had to hold firm. It was for the best. He had to keep telling himself that.

CHAPTER 14

SUNDAY MORNING ARRIVED before Megan knew it, and she was packing up her things for her trip that afternoon. Paul was feeling much better, although his cough lingered. The last two days had been interesting. She wasn't sure what to make of Paul's apparent one-eighty.

Okay, so not much had changed. It wasn't as if he'd declared his undying love to her or anything, but he was different. When he'd joined her in the kitchen for dinner the night before, the wall that always seemed to separate them wasn't there. Maybe it was only the lack of Chloe's presence. Megan was trying not to read too much into it and get her hopes up.

"Are you about ready?"

Megan glanced up to see Paul's figure framed in her doorway. He'd gone into work for a few hours the day before, but was staying home this morning so that he could take her to the airport.

She smiled and made a final check of her suitcase. "I think so. If I forgot something, I'm sure Gage or Rebecca can run me to the store."

Paul strolled into the room as Megan zipped up her luggage. He picked up the suitcase and started for the door.

"I can get that, you know."

He looked back at her and smiled. "So can I."

Megan rolled her eyes. Since he'd started feeling better, Paul had been insistent that he could do for himself. She supposed this was his way at realigning the scales, so to speak.

It was nearly a half hour drive to the airport. Megan spent most of that time staring out the window and tapping her fingers against her leg.

"You all right?" Paul asked.

She turned her head to look at him. "Yeah. It's just . . . I've only flown once before. I guess I'm nervous."

Paul nodded. "It's been years since I've flown. I don't mind it, but it's not my favorite thing either."

"I was in Oklahoma. My boyfriend at the time wanted to go see one of his friends play in New York City." Megan's voice trailed off as she let that piece of information hang in the air. That time and place in her life felt like a lifetime ago.

"We took a trip to New York when I was a kid, but I don't remember much."

Megan nodded. "I don't remember much either."

Paul glanced over at her and frowned.

She shrugged. It wasn't as if she had tried to hide her past. "I remember the airport, and taking the subway to this rat-infested motel. Billy and his girlfriend were there. They'd brought booze, and . . ."

"And?"

"And . . . we partied. A lot." Megan tried to downplay it, hoping he wouldn't pick up on what could happen in a hotel room with two guys, two girls, and a whole lot of alcohol.

She should have known better. "Define partied."

His voice had an edge to it, but she couldn't tell if he was upset, hurt, or . . . well, she had no idea. Either way, she was determined to be honest with him. "We got drunk and fooled around."

"As in . . . had sex." This time she didn't miss how he gritted his teeth as he spoke.

"Yes."

Paul's knuckles turned white on the steering wheel. "Did you even use protection? What am I thinking? You don't even remember most of it. How are you going to remember if you bothered to use condoms?"

Okay, that ticked her off. She crossed her arms over her chest and stared him down. "Look, you knew about my past. I made no secret of how wild I used to be. I made some stupid mistakes. I know that. I don't need you telling me how dumb I was."

He was silent for several minutes. "You're right. I'm sorry. I have no right to make judgments. Especially on something that happened years ago."

Although she wanted to be mad, she didn't want to leave him for a week with an argument hanging between them. "Apology accepted."

They approached the exit sign for the airport, and Paul took a deep breath. "Gage and Rebecca are picking you up in Nashville?"

"Yeah. They're meeting me in baggage claim." Megan smiled. "I wonder how big Becca's tummy is now? All she had was a little bump the last time I saw her, but she's got to be bigger now."

"She's what—about six months along?"

"Yep. So she should have a belly for sure."

Paul laughed, and it was good to hear. Unfortunately, that segued into a coughing fit.

Megan dug into her purse and found a cough drop. "Here."

He took it and popped it into his mouth. His cough subsided as he pulled up to the curb at the airport. "How did you come to have cough drops in your purse?"

She smiled and shrugged. "You never know when they'll come in handy."

Paul shook his head, but he was smiling, so she knew all was good.

They both exited the vehicle, and he unloaded her suitcase from the trunk. He set it down on the curb and turned to face her. "Call me when you land?"

Megan nodded. "Take care of yourself while I'm gone, okay?"

"You do the same."

She knew she needed to go, but there was something stopping her.

Paul glanced up at something over her shoulder, and she could guess that it was the security guard coming to tell him he needed to move his vehicle.

Before she could overthink it, Megan closed the distance between them and planted a solid kiss on Paul's lips.

When she backed away, taking her suitcase with her, Megan couldn't help but revel in that little thrill she got at the stunned look on his face. "I'll see you in seven days. Don't forget me."

He chuckled. "I don't think that will be a problem."

Megan giggled, and waved as she walked through the glass doors. She would miss Paul, but more importantly, she hoped he would miss her. If he didn't, that meant he probably didn't feel as strongly for her as she did for him. It didn't mean he never would, but it would make what she wanted more difficult to achieve.

She got her ticket and made her way through security. It was a little different than she remembered. Then again, she hadn't been paying much attention to anything other than Dale the last time she'd set foot in an airport. She had been smitten with the wannabe rock star, and at the time, she would have followed him anywhere.

As she found a seat at the gate to wait on her flight, Megan mused over how much her life and her tastes had changed. Looking back, she had trouble seeing what exactly had appealed to her about the bad boys she'd followed across the country. But even as the thought crossed her mind, Megan knew. Freedom. That was what they'd offered her. Or, at least, that's what she'd thought they'd offered her.

Thinking about her past boyfriends brought Paul back to the forefront of her mind. He'd been shocked about her revelation in the car. Megan was sure there were other things about her past that would shock the pants off him as well. She had two rules: no illegal drugs and no violence. Growing up, she'd witnessed her mom being battered around a few times by her dad. It wasn't something she was willing to put up with. Thanks to her big sister, Megan never had to. Rebecca had taught Megan how to protect herself, should the need arise.

Megan snorted. She'd given her sister such a hard time over the years. Thinking back, Megan wondered how many times Rebecca had protected her and she'd been oblivious.

A woman's voice came over the intercom, announcing Megan's flight. She picked up her carry-on bag, and made her way onto the plane. Megan needed to find a way to express her gratitude for all her big sister had done for her. Considering how bratty a child Megan had been growing up, and their father's hot temper, Rebecca might have saved Megan's life.

***

After leaving the airport, Paul drove directly to the station. It was Sunday, and as a seasoned officer, he was no longer required to work weekends unless he was on call, but he needed something to do. Saying goodbye to Megan was harder than he'd thought it would be.

Paul sighed as he pulled into his assigned parking spot outside the station. He kept trying to tell himself that going on a date with Megan wasn't a good idea. Then again, if they did go out on a date, if she could see they weren't compatible, that dating him wasn't all it was cracked up to be, then maybe she'd refocus her attention on someone else—a guy closer to her age, maybe.

A nauseous feeling settled in the pit of his stomach. He didn't like that idea either. The thought of seeing her with Rollins, or someone else like him, had Paul's insides tied up in knots. "It would be for the best."

He tilted his head back and closed his eyes.

Two sharp knocks on his car window jolted him upright. He glanced over to see one of the rookie patrolmen—Paul couldn't remember his name— staring back at him.

Paul rolled down the window.

"Everything okay, Detective?" the patrolman asked.

"Yes. Everything's fine. Is there something I can do for you?"

The young man shook his head. "No, sir. I happened to be walking by and noticed you sitting in your vehicle."

"Ah." Paul rolled up the window, removed his keys from the ignition, and opened the door. He stepped out onto the pavement and pocketed his keys. "Just doing a little thinking."

The officer nodded. "You're working the serial killer case, right?"

"Yes." Although Paul recognized the officer, he didn't really know the guy.

"I thought so."

Before the rookie could ask any more questions, Paul set off toward the building.

Of course, that didn't stop the officer from following. "Are you getting close to solving the case?"

Paul didn't answer until he was right outside the station door. He paused, and then faced the other man. "Why are you so curious?"

"Um. I—um."

"Do yourself a favor. You do your job, and let me do mine." Not giving the guy a chance to respond, Paul opened the door and went inside.

Paul didn't have long to ponder his conversation in the parking lot before Janey found him.

"Hey. I thought you might be in today. Is your nanny off to visit her sister?"

"Yes, Megan is off to visit her sister. I dropped her at the airport about twenty minutes ago."

Janey turned, attempting to hide a smirk. She wasn't all that successful, however. His partner had been abundantly clear regarding her feelings on his relationship status even before Megan entered the picture.

Needing to redirect her attention, Paul unlocked his desk and retrieved the file he'd stored there the day before. "You up for some legwork today?"

"You thinking of running down some of those leads?"

He nodded. "I figured we could hit some of the overlapping locations on our list."

With the case file tucked under his arm, Paul weaved through the desks, heading toward the station entrance with Janey following close behind. Not far from the door, he spotted the officer who'd cornered him in the parking lot. The guy was talking to another patrolman, one Paul had worked with for years.

"You okay?" Janey asked. "Not getting sick again on me, are you?"

Paul opened the door, and ambled out into the parking lot toward his vehicle. "You wouldn't get that lucky, Davis. Come on, we've got a case to solve."

They were leaving their second stop—which failed to yield any new information—when his cell phone rang. "Daniels."

"Hey. It's Megan."

He glanced down at his watch, and sure enough over two hours had passed since he'd dropped her off at the airport. "How was your flight?"

"Good. I sat beside this guy who sells advertising. He's in Nashville for some kind of convention."

A spark of jealousy surged through him, and Paul quickly clamped down on it. "Sounds . . . interesting."

She laughed. "Not really. He was nice enough, though. Oh, and he invited me to stop by the convention if I had time—he even gave me two tickets in case Becca wants to tag along."

"I see." Paul closed his eyes and tried to ignore his irrational response.

"Okay, well, I'm almost to baggage claim, so I should probably go. Becca texted that they were already in the airport waiting. I'll text you later, all right?"

"Have fun." His throat clenched as he spoke those two simple words.

"I will."

The phone went silent, and he removed it from his ear.

"Everything all right with your girlfriend?"

"She's not my girlfriend."

He climbed behind the wheel of his car, and Janey slid into the passenger seat. Starting the engine, Paul maneuvered out of the parking lot and headed toward their next destination—a nail salon. About halfway there, Paul chanced a look at his partner. She wore a knowing smirk. He decided it was probably better to ignore her, so he concentrated on what lay ahead. Questioning people, looking for clues, uncovering leads—those things he understood.

The nail salon sat on a side street not far from the local community college. Since it was Sunday, there wasn't a lot of pedestrian traffic, but Paul had to imagine that on a weekday the area would be hopping. There were restaurants along the main drag, as well as a few small specialty stores. Megan had been down to the college a few times to pick up textbooks and the like. He wondered if she'd ever been to any of the stores or restaurants.

"You coming?" Janey's question brought him back to the present.

"Yeah."

They spoke to the owner of the salon. She remembered two of the women, but couldn't recall seeing the other two. It was what they'd expected, but given what they were working with, they were hoping to catch a break.

Since they were in the area, they decided to take some time to inquire in some of the surrounding shops. Most staff didn't remember any of the women, but they got lucky when they stopped in a little pizzeria. The man behind the counter was fairly sure he'd seen three of the women in his restaurant. It wasn't a positive ID, but it was something.

After finishing at the pizzeria, they decided to call it a day. It was after five and most of the stores were starting to close. Overall, it had been a productive day, and they'd be back at it on Monday morning.

Since Paul was on his own, he dropped Janey back at the station, and then stopped off at his favorite Thai restaurant to pick up some dinner.

Nom, the owner of the restaurant, greeted him as soon as he walked in. "Paul. It's been a long time. Where have you been?"

"Been staying in a lot lately."

Nom smiled and came around the counter to give him a hug. "Ah. Well, good to see you."

Before Melissa died, they had frequented the restaurant a lot. Melissa loved Thai food. They'd gotten to know Nom and several of the staff over the years. "It's good to see you, too, Nom. How have you been?"

"Good. Good. Can't complain. You here to eat?"

Paul checked his watch. Chloe usually called him before Cindy began getting her ready for bed. "I was hoping maybe I could get something to go."

"Of course. What would you like?"

He gave Nom his order, and she disappeared through the swinging wooden doors into the kitchen. Taking a seat in the corner, he waited.

The food didn't take long, and soon he was on his way home. He was pulling his car into the driveway when he heard his phone beep, letting him know he'd received a text. His stomach did a little flip in response. Given Megan's promise to text him later, he knew it was probably her.

Somehow he made himself wait until he was inside the house before checking his phone. Sure enough, it was Megan.

I'm hiding in the basement.

He smiled. **Why are you hiding in the basement?**

They r in their bedroom. It was this, or ear plugs.

Paul laughed out loud as he removed his food from the bag and laid it out on the table. **That bad huh?**

U have no idea.

Although Paul had nothing against texting, it wasn't his favorite way to have a conversation. Hitting the call button, he waited for Megan to pick up.

Her laughter echoed through the phone. "I wondered how long it would take you to give up and call me."

He rolled his eyes. "So, other than hiding in the basement, how's your visit so far?"

"Not bad. They picked me up, and then we went to get lunch. Oh my goodness, Paul, Rebecca has the cutest belly. It's not as big as I thought it would be. It looks like she has a basketball stuffed inside her but we can only see half of it."

"Rebecca's pretty fit. That's probably why."

"Yeah, I guess. I mean she still runs every morning and stuff." Paul could almost see Megan shrug.

"That would do it."

"The house has changed a little, too. Becca moved her things in, of course, and then she took over one of the rooms on the first floor and turned it into an office. Oh, and the room across from their bedroom —the one Becca stayed in before—they're turning that into a nursery. It's covered in jungle prints."

Megan sounded happy, even if she had started the conversation off with a complaint.

"Glad you went?"

She didn't answer right away. "Yeah. I mean, there is no way I could stay here long-term if the last half hour is any indication, but . . ."

"But you missed your sister."

"Yeah."

The word hung in the air, and Paul could tell she wanted to say something else. Instead, she remained silent. He let it go, and asked another question. "So do Rebecca and Gage have any plans for you tomorrow?"

"Gage has practice, so I think Becca and I are going shopping. I tell you, this baby has done something to her brain. Becca never liked to shop. Ever."

A flash of Melissa coming home loaded down with packages after a full day of shopping filled his mind. "Babies change a lot of things."

"I guess I just didn't realize how much. Not that they didn't change things, but people. I mean Becca is still my bossy, overprotective sister, but she's different, too. I guess that's a good thing." Megan sighed. "So anyway, tell me about your day. What did you do after you dropped me off at the airport?"

They talked until Chloe called, and then Paul reluctantly said goodbye to Megan. He spent another twenty minutes on the phone with his daughter as she told him all about the day she'd spent with her grandma and grandpa. When he hung up, Paul realized he'd only eaten about half his meal. He'd been so caught up in his two phone conversations that he'd forgotten to eat. Standing up, he carried his cold food to the microwave and shoved it inside. Although his stomach was rumbling, begging for food, Paul couldn't regret the way he'd spent his evening.

CHAPTER 15

Megan looked up from the stack of baby blankets she'd been perusing. Rebecca was holding a bottle with little yellow bears in her right hand, a sheepish look on her face.

"What are you apologizing for? Ditching me, or making so much noise I had to spend most of the evening in the basement?" Megan grinned to lessen the harsh impact of her words. She wasn't mad at her sister, but she hadn't relished spending three hours hiding in their basement either. It wouldn't have been so bad had she been able to talk to Paul the entire time, but she hadn't. As it was, she'd ended up watching reruns of CSI. It was the only thing decent she could find on television.

Rebecca placed the bottle back on the shelf. "Both, I guess. I mean we didn't mean . . ."

"You're still newlyweds. I get it."

Her sister rubbed a hand over her growing belly and smiled. "It's just, ever since I entered my second trimester I can't seem to control myself."

Megan snorted. "And you could control yourself before?"

"Okay, you're right. Gage has always been able to . . . well . . ." To

Megan's surprise, Rebecca giggled. It was weird, but good, too. Her sister was happy.

"Yeah, I get it." And Megan did get it. Those two make-out sessions with Paul had her craving more of his kisses. She could only imagine what it would feel like to have him inside her . . . surrounding her.

Walking over to a rack filled with little socks, Megan sighed. She missed sex. Battery-operated boyfriends had nothing on the real thing.

Her sister threw a few items in their cart and continued down the aisle. Megan followed close behind, still lost in her thoughts, and wondering what Paul was doing right then.

"So are you seeing anyone?"

Rebecca's question brought Megan up short.

"Um. Not exactly." While she wasn't ashamed of her feelings for Paul, she had no idea how her sister would react to such information. Rebecca hadn't been thrilled when Megan made the decision to move in with Paul and Chloe in the first place.

Megan should have known her sister wouldn't let a vague answer go unchallenged. "What do you mean, not exactly? Is there someone you're interested in? You're not chasing after another bad boy, are you?"

"No. I'm not chasing after another bad boy." Megan sighed, this time loud enough for her sister to hear while she played with the button on the cutest little suit she'd ever seen.

Rebecca placed her hand over Megan's and squeezed. "I just want you to find someone who will love you and make you happy. That's all."

"I know. And I'm working on it. Promise."

They stood there for a long minute before Rebecca let go of Megan's hand and started moving forward again. Rebecca didn't say anything for a long time, but Megan knew her sister well enough to know that Rebecca's silence only meant she was choosing her words carefully.

For the next half hour, the two women weaved their way through the store, picking out a variety of items Rebecca and Gage would need once their baby was born. It wasn't until they were in the car and on their way back to the house that her sister broached the subject of Megan's love life again.

"Can you do something for me?"

"Becca, you know I'd do just about anything for you."

Rebecca grimaced, which should have been Megan's first clue.

"What?" Megan asked.

"Promise me that when you figure it out with this guy, whoever he is, that you'll bring him to meet me."

"Um—"

"Look, I'm not asking because I don't trust your judgment or anything, but . . ."

"But my judgment has sucked in the past."

Rebecca laughed. "Well, when you put it that way . . ."

Megan chuckled, and turned in her seat to give Rebecca her undivided attention. "I know you're worried, but don't be."

"Says the girl who ran off with a guy that she'd known for a week, and had me worried I'd find her in a ditch somewhere."

"Hey! I was eighteen." As much as Megan knew Rebecca was justified, it burned her when her sister threw her past in her face.

"And now you're only twenty-three."

Megan tried to keep her cool. It wouldn't do any good to yell at her sister. If anything, it would only make Rebecca think she was right.

Taking a deep breath, Megan waited until she knew she could respond without anger coloring her tone. "Becca, I love you, and I know you worry about me, but things are different. I've changed. You've changed. You have a husband now to worry about. And a baby on the way that's going to need all that protective mothering you're so good at."

Rebecca swiped at a tear that rolled down her cheek. "Is that your way of telling me to butt out?"

Megan smiled. "Kinda. Yeah."

For the longest time, Rebecca didn't say anything. She drove through the streets of Nashville, letting a heavy silence linger between them. As they turned onto Gage and Rebecca's street, her sister cleared her throat. "I can't make any promises—habits are hard to break—but I'll try not to be so overbearing, okay?"

Leaning across the center console, Megan placed a quick kiss on her sister's cheek. "Thank you."

Rebecca shook her head and laughed. "I still want to meet him. I mean, if he's important to you . . ."

"I promise that if things become serious then I will let you meet him." While she could see that Rebecca wasn't entirely happy with the outcome, Megan was glad her sister seemed willing to let it go—at least, for now.

They unloaded their purchases from the car, made some lunch for themselves, and then curled up to watch a movie in the theater room Gage had set up in the basement. It felt normal, something neither Rebecca nor Megan got a lot of growing up.

Around three o'clock, Gage bounded down the stairs, announcing that he was home from practice. His hair was still damp from the shower he took, and even Megan had to admit he looked good. As soon as Rebecca laid eyes on him, she pushed herself up from the couch, and ran over to him.

The amazing thing was Megan didn't know which one was happier to see the other. They both wore matching smiles, and as soon as they were within touching distance, they were all over each other.

"Hello, Beautiful," he whispered against Rebecca's lips a moment before his tongue disappeared inside her mouth.

Megan cleared her throat and stood. "I guess that's my cue to leave."

She went to brush past them, but Gage reached out a hand to stop her. "You don't have to leave. We can control ourselves."

"It's okay, really," Megan insisted. "I wanted to check out the pool, anyway. I'll change into my swimsuit and give you two some alone time."

As she headed upstairs, she heard Gage stop Rebecca from following. There was no way Megan would begrudge her sister her happiness, or even the great sex Rebecca was obviously having. It was difficult to witness, considering the current condition of Megan's love life, or lack thereof.

Megan swiftly changed into her bikini, grabbed a large towel, and slipped through the sliding glass doors out onto the patio. Gage had a decent sized in ground pool. When she'd stayed at his house the first time, she hadn't gotten a chance to take advantage of it. She was determined not to make the same mistake this time around.

Throwing her towel onto one of the lounge chairs, Megan sat along the edge of the pool, letting her legs dangle in the water. It was warm. Not bathwater warm, but warm enough to confirm that the pool was heated.

Megan pushed off the side and jumped in. She held her breath as water surged over her head before she popped back to the surface. It had been years since she'd been swimming. Rebecca used to take her to the local YMCA whenever she could scrounge up enough money. They were some of the best memories Megan had from her childhood.

Leaning back in the water, Megan floated on the surface, letting the Tennessee sun warm her skin. Did Chloe know how to swim? Did Paul? Megan had never thought to ask, but she'd have to find out.

As typically happened when Megan began thinking about Paul, her thoughts turned to less innocent avenues. Her nipples hardened as she imagined him standing there all wet with nothing but swim trunks on.

She closed her eyes and groaned. Yes, she'd definitely have to explore that fantasy with Paul if the opportunity ever presented itself. Of course, she'd prefer if it were far away from prying eyes, and certainly from innocent ones like Chloe's. What Megan had in mind was more along the lines of X-rated.

***

Over the next four days, Paul and Janey systematically worked their way through all the leads on their list. They'd gotten several hits tying three of the four victims together, but never all four. It was frustrating, especially when the killer could already be targeting his next victim.

The one thing they were fairly certain of, however, was that the connection revolved around the campus area. Only two of the women took classes at the college, so it was a given they frequented the area. Casey McMurphy's husband worked on the campus, which would easily tie her to the area as well. The only unknown was the first victim. There was no record of her ever taking a class at the college, and the only positive ID they'd gotten on her in the area was from the man at the pizza shop.

The only hitch in this positive progress in their investigation was the vast area of the campus itself. If one included the immediate surrounding area regularly used by students and faculty, it was easily the size of a small town. There was also the consideration that more than ten thousand people passed through the area on any given day of the week. There were students, professors, campus staff, maintenance and lawn care workers . . . not to mention all the owners and employees of the various businesses. While Paul and Janey had narrowed down their search, they were no closer to finding their killer.

After a long twelve-hour day, Paul dropped Janey back at the station to get her car, and then headed home. He popped a frozen pizza in the oven, too tired to whip up something more elaborate, and downed two glasses of water. Over the last few days, he and his partner had clocked more miles than he cared to count. It wasn't as if he were out of shape, but he also wasn't twenty anymore.

The timer went off, and he took his pizza out of the oven. Slicing it into four large pieces, Paul loaded one onto a paper plate, and ambled over to the table. He quickly devoured what was in front of him, and went to grab another. Halfway through the second slice, Paul realized what he was doing. It was almost seven, which meant Chloe was due to call any minute. It also meant that shortly after that, Megan would most likely be calling as well.

With both Megan and Chloe gone, the house felt empty. The funny thing was Chloe had been doing these trips to her grandparents since she was a year old. That first year it had been hard to let her go, but being able to chat with her every night had eased his anxiety. The first couple of days were always challenging, but after that, he was fine.

This time, it was different. While he eagerly awaited his daughter's phone call every evening, he found that wasn't the only conversation he was anticipating. Since Megan had been gone, she made it a point to call him every night. She'd tell him all about her adventures in Nashville with Rebecca and Gage, including a trip to a local bar where she'd danced with a couple of Gage's friends. He was man enough to admit that he was jealous. And that he missed her.

Paul didn't know what to do anymore. He still didn't see a relationship between the two of them working out, but it was becoming harder and harder to brush under the rug. Megan made him feel things he'd thought died with Melissa.

Before he could think too much about it, Chloe called. He spent roughly ten minutes talking to his daughter before Cindy got on the phone.

"Sometimes I don't know how you do it, Paul."

He laughed. "Do what?"

"Keep up with her. It seems the only time I can get her to slow down is to put a book in her hands."

"Now you know why she has an entire bookshelf full of books in her room. She'll sit up there for hours reading."

Cindy sighed, and he heard the sadness creep into her voice. "Just like her mother."

It was true. Chloe was a lot like Melissa.

The seconds ticked by with neither of them contributing to the conversation.

His mother-in-law broke the emotion-filled silence. "Paul, I want to ask you something, but I don't want you to take it the wrong way. The last thing I want to do is sound critical, but is something going on between you and Megan?"

He took a deep breath, but didn't answer.

"Now, I know when you first told me that she was moving in with the two of you that I expressed my concern, but Chloe has said some things and—"

"What has she said?" Paul racked his brain trying to think of things Chloe could have seen or heard. Nothing came to mind.

"It's not so much what she said, more how she talks of Megan. She thinks Megan is going to be around for the long-term. She's grown attached."

"And you think that's a bad thing?"

"I think it's a cause for concern, yes. Paul, she's already lost her mother. Now she's grown attached to another woman—a woman who lives with you—how is she going to react when Megan decides to move on? She's a young woman, Paul. Eventually, she's going to want to get on with her life. What's that going to do to Chloe when she does?"

"First of all, I don't think Megan would walk out on Chloe. It's true, Megan might leave one of these days." As the words passed through Paul's lips, he felt cold inside. "If that happens, we'll deal with it. Second, Megan has no plans to leave anytime soon. Should I deprive my daughter of a loving relationship with another woman because there is a potential for heartbreak in the distant future?"

Cindy didn't respond immediately. "I guess you're right. I just . . . I just don't want to see her hurt. Losing Melissa . . ."

"I know. But Cindy, Megan has been good for Chloe." Paul didn't mention how good Megan had been for him as well. "And as much as we both want to shield Chloe from hurt and heartache, there are going to be times when we can't."

Paul heard Cindy release a shaky breath. "I'm sorry I brought it up. It's none of my business."

"Cindy, we've always been open and honest with each other. I'm grateful for everything you and George have done for Melissa and me and especially all you've done since I've been trying to navigate this parent thing on my own. But Megan's role in our lives is a given, at least for the time being. As for the future . . . who knows?"

Paul's conversation with his mother-in-law ended shortly after that. Cindy was distraught and worried. He could understand that, but he also couldn't give her the concrete reassurances she was looking for.

Needing to wind down, Paul headed upstairs to take a shower. He brought his cell into the bathroom, just in case. If Megan called, he didn't want to miss it.

That in and of itself should have given him his answer, but stubborn as he was, he fought it. As the water pelted him, Paul replayed the original question Cindy had asked him—was Megan going to be a permanent fixture in their lives? Did he want her to be?

The answer came barreling at him full speed. Yes.

But what if it didn't work? What if she realized he was just a lonely middle-aged man with nothing to offer her?

He knew she wanted more from him than what they currently had. What he didn't know was exactly how much more she wanted. That brought up the question as to what he wanted. If he gave this thing with them a shot, where did he see it leading?

The more Paul thought about him and Megan as a couple, the more questions—the more doubts—surfaced. He glanced down the length of his body. Although he was in shape for his age, there was a little more fat around his middle than there had been five years ago. He'd seen most of her and she was taut and soft and . . .

Releasing a breath, Paul flipped the handle that controlled the temperature of the water all the way around to cold. He jolted as the frigid water hit him like daggers, but it made quick work of his growing arousal.

As he stood with his eyes closed, trying to calm down, his phone rang, and a split second later his heart was pounding in his chest. Paul swiftly shut the water off and stepped out onto the towel. He wiped off his hands, and reached for the phone. "Hello?"

"Hey. You sound out of breath. What are you doing?" Megan asked.

Paul quickly ran the towel over his body, and then wrapped it around his waist. "I just got out of the shower."

Megan released a sound that went directly to his groin.

So much for the cold shower.

CHAPTER 16

PAUL DIDN'T SLEEP MUCH the remainder of the time Megan was away. He worked as much as he could, but in the end he came home to an empty house—one that felt emptier than he could ever remember it.

On Saturday, he put in another twelve-hour day, hoping to wear himself out enough so that he'd be able to get some rest. It didn't work. He tossed and turned the entire night. When he awoke on Sunday morning, he had a desperate need to see Megan. Their phone conversations weren't enough. He missed her smile, her eyes, the way her hair bounced when she laughed.

He was in trouble, and he knew it. For the last two days, he'd argued with himself as to whether or not he should take that leap of faith and ask her out. He still wasn't sure a relationship between the two of them would work. Megan was young and full of life. He . . . well . . . he was . . . not. The last thing he wanted was to bring her down—hold her back. Paul wanted her to be happy.

There was a part of him that wanted to see if he could be part of that happiness, but fear nearly choked him every time he thought of what could go wrong. What if he messed up again? He didn't know if he could survive that a second time.

But as much as he feared the possibilities, did he really have a choice anymore? Sure, he could keep things the way they were—or try to, anyway. Given their track record, he wasn't hopeful.

Paul could also ask Megan to leave. It would probably be the most logical option. He knew that. However, the thought of her not being part of their lives anymore turned his stomach.

He'd also thrown around the idea of dating someone else. Maybe what he was experiencing was a natural progression in the grieving process—his mind and body telling him it was time to move forward. Melissa had been gone for nearly five years. Although that option might discourage Megan, it didn't sit much better with him than the thought of her leaving.

The other alternative was for him to swallow his fear, ask her out, and see if it went anywhere. Maybe their connection wouldn't be as intense once he took the challenge away. Maybe, just maybe, they'd have a horrible time, and she would realize that he wasn't the man she thought he was.

As Paul drove toward the airport, he knew how unlikely a scenario that was. Megan had lived in the same house with him for seven months. She knew his habits, his likes and dislikes. She'd even seen him at his worst when he was sick in bed with the flu.

Five miles from his exit, he saw a sign advertising a twenty-four-hour market. Without giving himself time to overthink it, he took the ramp off the highway, and followed the signs until he found the small store. Inside, they had a variety of food and beverages for travelers, not much past the basics, but he was hoping they would have what he needed.

It didn't take him long to find what he was looking for. There sitting next to the front counter were three bouquets of flowers—one made up of a dozen red roses, and two with a variety of colorful flowers. It had been years since he'd asked a woman out. In reality, he hadn't formally asked a woman out since he was sixteen. He was a little rusty.

Paul eyed the roses briefly, but swiftly changed his mind. Melissa had loved roses, but they didn't feel right for Megan.

Of the two other flower options, one was primarily pink, and the other was mostly yellow. Both were pretty, but for some reason he was drawn to the yellow. They reminded him of sunshine.

After paying for the flowers, Paul drove the few remaining miles to the airport with the flowers lying beside him on the passenger seat. He parked his car in the parking garage, and headed toward baggage claim. On the way inside, he received a few stares from passersby. An older lady smiled at him, and he held tighter to the bouquet. He hoped he was doing the right thing, and that Megan would like the flowers.

The first thing he did once he was inside the airport was check to see if Megan's flight had landed. To his surprise, the board showed her plane had arrived five minutes ago. That did nothing to calm his nerves. Was he really ready for this? If she said yes, it would change things between them. What would happen if it didn't work?

Paul was still debating with himself when he saw her come down the escalator. She didn't see him at first. Her head was tilted down, and he could see her cell phone in her right hand. She furrowed her brow, and he instinctively took a step forward.

As if sensing him, she glanced up, meeting his gaze. A huge smile lit up her face, and all the worry he'd seen a moment ago vanished. She reached the bottom of the escalator, and rushed toward him. Without any hesitation, Megan dropped her bags at his feet, wrapped her arms around his neck, and hugged him.

What he felt in that moment was difficult to describe. A whiff of lilac and cherries filled his nostrils as her warm body pressed solid against his. He circled his arms around her waist and returned her embrace, enjoying the feel of her in his arms. She was home.

They stood there for several minutes, not moving. People went around them, not seeming to pay much attention to their reunion. Eventually, Megan pulled back a little so that she could see his face. "Hi."

Paul chuckled, and put some more space between them. "How was your flight?"

"Good."

Megan reached to pick up her bags, but Paul beat her to it. He hitched her backpack over his shoulder, careful not to crush the flowers. Extending his free arm, he offered them to her. "I got these for you. A kind of welcome home present."

She took them in both her hands and inhaled.

Paul held his breath, awaiting her reaction. Had he made the wrong choice? Should he have gotten the roses?

A smile tugged at her lips. "They're beautiful. Thank you."

"I'm glad you like them." Before he could say any more, a noise sounded from the baggage carousel, and they went to retrieve the rest of her luggage.

Twenty minutes later, they were in the car, and on their way home. Paul had made his decision. Buying her flowers had sealed it. He was going to ask her to go out with him on a date. One date, and then they would see how it went from there.

There was only one problem. He didn't know how to go about asking her. Should he do it now, or should it be something more romantic? Paul hated feeling so unsure of himself. He'd never felt this way with Melissa. Everything between them had been easy, especially in the beginning.

Of course, back then things had been simple. They were kids without any real responsibilities. Their first date had been to a school dance. He'd taken her out to dinner beforehand at a moderately priced restaurant, and then to the dance. After that, he'd driven her home. Simple. Uncomplicated. The exact opposite of his current situation.

"Something on your mind?" Megan asked when they were about halfway home.

He glanced over at her. She'd turned slightly to face him, and was holding her flowers gingerly in her lap. It was now or never. "I was wondering if maybe you'd like to go out with me Friday night."

Megan didn't respond right away, and he was back to paying attention to the road so he couldn't see her reaction to his question. "Are you asking me on a date?"

Paul swallowed hard. "Yes."

Again, she didn't say anything. This time he looked in her direction. She had leaned her head back against the headrest, and was staring at him intently. He'd expected her to jump at his offer, since she'd been the one to push for it in the first place. That's why her next question surprised him. "Are you sure?"

Since they were coming up on their exit, Paul waited until they were off the highway before he replied. But instead of answering her question, he asked one of his own. "What? Have you changed your mind? I thought . . ."

She shook her head. "No. I haven't changed my mind. But I'm curious as to what made you change yours."

As scared as he was, Paul figured he needed to be honest. "I did a lot of thinking while you were gone, and well . . ." He took a deep breath, and admitted something to her he hoped he wouldn't regret. "I missed you."

Megan laughed.

"What's so funny?" he asked.

"You mean, all I had to do was go away for a week? Here I've been trying to get your attention for months, and leaving is what does it?"

"Oh, trust me, you got my attention just fine."

She smirked. "Good to know."

Paul pulled into his driveway and turned off the car. "So?"

"So what?"

He tried not to let her see how anxious he was. "You never answered my question. Will you go out on a date with me Friday night?"

"Oh. That."

Paul tightened his hold on his keys, and he could feel the metal biting into his hand. "Yes. That."

Instead of answering him, Megan opened her door, and stepped out of the car. He followed, completely perplexed.

They both came around to the back of the vehicle to get her luggage, but when he reached for the handle, she stopped him. "Kiss me."

"What?" It had been a while since he'd asked a woman out on a date, but if memory served, the kiss came after the date.

"I want you to kiss me."

This time he detected a note of amusement in her tone. He wasn't sure if he should be annoyed or not, since she appeared to be having fun at his expense. "Isn't that supposed to come after the date?"

She shrugged. "Let's just say . . . this is my way of finding out if you're serious or not."

Paul stared at her for a moment, and then decided why not? It wasn't as if he didn't want to kiss her. In fact, it had been at the top of his list since the moment he'd laid eyes on her at the airport. He'd only been holding back because . . . well, he didn't know why exactly.

Stepping forward, Paul closed the distance between them, and cupped the back of her neck with his right hand. She tilted her head up and slightly to the left, leaning into his touch. Placing his left hand at her waist, he brought her closer until he could feel the heat radiating from her body. It had been over a month since he'd felt her soft and warm beneath his fingers.

Megan closed her eyes as he lowered his mouth to hers. For once, he didn't question it—didn't think about all the reasons why not. This time, he allowed the desire he'd been keeping a tight lid on to come to the surface.

***

When Megan issued her challenge, she hadn't known how Paul would react. He'd caught her off guard when he asked her out. The entire time she'd been in Nashville, she'd racked her brain as to what else she could do to try and break through the wall he'd built up around him. There was no way she could have known that her absence would be enough to push him out of his comfort zone.

As Paul's lips continued to move against hers, Megan gave in to the urge to touch him. Holding tight to the flowers with one hand, she used the other to grip the back of his head, pulling him closer. He seemed to like that. His fingers flexed on her hip, and he shifted them slightly. She moaned as he pressed her up against the car. With every second that passed, it was becoming more difficult to remember they were in public.

Paul ran his palm down her hip to cup her ass. The movement lifted her an inch or so higher, which brought her more in line with the hard length of him pressing aggressively against his jeans. She began rubbing herself against him, seeking friction.

He groaned, and ripped his mouth away from hers.

Megan didn't want their kiss to end. She tugged at his hair, trying to get him to pick up where he'd left off.

"We can't . . . do this here." His words were broken, spoken in between short, shallow breaths.

A car passed by as they stood clinging to one another, and Megan knew he was right. They were standing in his driveway in the middle of the day. Somehow she didn't think the neighbors would like it much if they began ripping each other's clothes off on the front lawn.

She buried her face in the crook of his neck, willing herself to calm down. Even though Paul had stopped the kiss, he seemed to be in no hurry to let her go. She smiled, and placed a soft kiss at the base of his neck.

He chuckled. "What was that for?"

Instead of answering that question, she answered another. "Yes."

Unfortunately, this caused Paul to pull back so that he could see her face. "Yes, what?"

Megan smiled, and ran her fingers freely through his hair. "Yes, I'll go out on a date with you."

Paul threw his head back and laughed. The motion separated them further, and Megan let her fingers fall.

To her surprise, when he realized they were no longer connected, he grasped the back of her head with both hands, and gave her a swift, hard kiss. When he separated their lips, he didn't release her. "I missed you. I really did."

Reaching up, she ran her fingers along his jaw. "I'm glad to be home."

He kissed her again, and then took a step back. They unloaded her suitcases, and brought them upstairs to her room. There was a moment of awkwardness. Things were changing between them, and it seemed as if neither knew exactly what that meant.

After a few minutes of strained silence, Paul excused himself from Megan's room. She let herself fall backward onto the bed, and grinned so wide her cheeks hurt. Paul had kissed her. Willingly. Knowingly. They were going out on a date. A real, honest-to-goodness date. And he'd gotten her flowers. No guy had ever bought her flowers before.

Megan looked over to her dresser where she'd placed the bouquet. The flowers were beautiful. They reminded her of spring, of new beginnings, which was completely appropriate given the circumstances.

As she lay there, she began to wonder where he'd take her on their date. Not that the where really mattered. Paul was finally admitting that he felt something for her—that she wasn't only his daughter's nanny. Doubt crept up in the back of her mind, wiping the smile from her face. Maybe he's just horny.

No. She didn't believe that. If sex was all Paul wanted from her, he could have had that months ago. He'd always been the one to stop their physical encounters, not her. And he'd said he missed her. Not kissing her or making out with her. Her.

Pushing herself up off the bed, Megan flipped her suitcase open and unpacked her things. It took a while. She sorted through her clothes, throwing the dirty ones in the hamper. Rebecca had offered to let her use their washer and dryer, but Megan had brought plenty of clothes with her for the week, so she'd opted to bring her laundry home instead.

Once everything was put away, Megan headed downstairs to find some food. Rebecca and Gage had taken her out for a late breakfast before dropping her off at the airport. At the time, she'd been stuffed. That was nearly five hours ago.

When she came down the stairs, Paul was riffling through the cabinets. He must have heard her enter because he turned abruptly to face her, almost as if he were a child caught with his hand in the cookie jar. "I didn't see you there."

She walked over to the refrigerator and checked to see if she could find any leftovers. It was practically empty. Even when she'd first arrived, there had been a fair amount of food in the refrigerator.

Besides the basics—milk, cheese, condiments—there were only two bottles of beer and a container that looked as if it held some sort of cake. "Where is everything?"

"Oh. I've mostly been eating takeout." He shrugged. "I've been working long hours, and since it was only me . . ."

That made sense. Needing something more than what was to be had in the refrigerator, Megan made a beeline for the pantry. She found a box of pasta and some sauce. It might not be all that creative, but spaghetti was easy to make and filling.

As she moved about the kitchen, Paul seemed out of his element. He stood leaning against the counter for a while, and then moved to sit in one of the chairs. She glanced over her shoulder to find him tapping his fingers against the table and staring out the window into the backyard.

"Everything okay?"

He snapped his head around to look at her. "Yeah. Yes. Everything's fine."

She finished making her pasta, and loaded a healthy portion onto her plate. "Did you want some?"

"No. I'm good."

She brought her plate over to the table and sat down. Paul looked uncomfortable.

After swallowing a few bites, Megan couldn't take it anymore. "Paul, what's wrong? And don't tell me nothing."

He rubbed the back of his neck and eyed her cautiously. "I guess I'm feeling a little lost."

"Lost? Why?" Megan asked, taking another bite of her food.

Paul sighed. "I'm not sure how this is supposed to work. Us."

"How do you want it to work?"

Megan could tell he was thinking about his answer, so she waited. The minutes ticked by as she finished her spaghetti and took her plate to the sink. When he still hadn't answered by the time she was done, she strolled over to him. Deciding to throw caution to the wind, Megan straddled his lap, sat down, and rested her arms over his shoulders.

"What are you doing?" he asked.

"Cutting to the chase." She brushed her lips back and forth across his. Paul's breathing began to pick up. He closed his eyes, and took control of the kiss. Less than a minute later, he was running his hands up and down her back underneath her shirt, and his tongue was caressing hers. It wasn't as desperate as some of their make-out sessions, but that didn't make it any less hot.

This time it was Megan who pulled back. "That's how it works. This. Us."

He rested his forehead against hers. "I should probably tell you something."

She scraped her nails along his scalp, and she felt him shiver. "What's that?"

"I've never—"

"Don't even try to tell me you've never had sex before. You have a daughter, remember? That one won't work with me."

Paul chuckled and pinched her.

"Ouch."

"Serves you right. That wasn't what I was going to say."

She massaged the spot he pinched. It really didn't hurt. It was more the principle of the matter. "What were you going to say then?"

He brushed a strand of hair away from her face. "My wife— Melissa—is the only woman I've ever dated."

Megan's eyes went wide with shock. "Really? As in, ever?"

Paul nodded.

"Wow." She thought about it a moment. "What about sex? Was there anyone else besides—"

"No."

"Not even . . . after?"

He shook his head.

The primary emotion Megan was feeling was disbelief. Not that she didn't think Paul was telling the truth, more that she couldn't imagine someone as passionate as him going without sex for so long. Finding out his wife had been his only lover stunned her. Wow. Five years. Megan couldn't imagine.

"So does that mean you don't want to? Have sex, I mean. Is that why you never . . ." Megan held her breath waiting for his answer.

He was quiet for what felt like a really long time. "I tried once. About six months after my wife died."

This was good, wasn't it? I mean, it meant he wasn't saving himself for marriage or anything. "And what happened?"

Paul shook his head. "It's a long story, but needless to say I didn't try again."

"But that doesn't mean you don't want to, right?"

"I didn't for a long time."

Megan searched his face, hoping she wasn't misinterpreting what he was saying. She didn't think she was.

Standing, she reached for his hand.

He hesitated for only a moment before linking his fingers through hers and following her up the stairs.

CHAPTER 17

PAUL HAD A PRETTY good idea where they were heading, and yet he couldn't figure out if he was excited about finally making his fantasies a reality, or scared out of his mind. The closer they came to her bedroom, the less distinguishable the two emotions became. It was as if the fear and the anticipation had combined.

With their hands still linked, Megan dragged him across the threshold of her bedroom, and over to the nightstand. She opened the drawer and extracted a condom. Tossing it on the bed, she turned to face him.

He swallowed, and tried not to let her see how nervous he was.

She stepped closer, releasing his hand, and placed both of hers, palms down, on his chest. "You can say no."

The thing was he didn't want to say no. He'd been dreaming about Megan for the last three months.

Knowing he needed to show her that he was in this all the way—that he wanted this—he took hold of her hips, and drew her toward him. She sucked in a breath as their lower bodies connected. He was painfully hard, and more than ready. "I don't want to say no."

Megan smiled, and ran her hands up his chest and neck until her arms rested on his shoulders. Her breasts flattened against his chest, and Paul closed his eyes. He felt her breath on his face, and turned his head to meet her lips.

"Relax," she whispered.

Their mouths met in a tender caress. It wasn't desperate need, but a slow burn. There was an energy inside him that was increasing in intensity.

She slid her tongue along the seam of his lips, and he opened his mouth, allowing her to slip her tongue inside. He dug his fingers into the flesh of her ass, increasing the friction against his groin. His eyes rolled into the back of his head at the sensation. It was at that point instinct started to take over, and he began moving them closer to the bed.

When the back of her legs hit the mattress, Megan broke the kiss, and sat down on the edge of the bed. She immediately went to work on removing his jeans. "Take off your shirt."

Without stopping to think, Paul pulled the T-shirt over his head, and threw it somewhere a few feet away. By that point, Megan had unfastened his jeans and worked them halfway down his thighs.

She glanced up at him, a wicked gleam in her eyes. "Tighty-whities, huh?"

"They're practical."

Without taking her gaze from his, she ran a finger over his erection. He thought he was going to lose it. No one had touched him like that in five years. Paul felt as if he were dangling from a cliff, hanging on for dear life.

Then she went and did something he hadn't expected. Although, knowing Megan, he should have. She took hold of both sides of his underwear, and yanked them down to join his jeans. He stood there, fully erect, with his pants bunched down around his knees.

Paul was about to kick them off and out of the way, along with his shoes, when Megan sucked his length into her warm mouth. He released a strangled moan, and tangled his fingers loosely in her hair. It had been years. He'd forgotten how good it felt to have a woman's mouth on him.

He closed his eyes and enjoyed what she was doing with her lips and tongue. All too soon he felt his orgasm building. He didn't want her to stop, but if she continued, they'd never make it to the main event.

With great reluctance, Paul pushed her back. The cool air was a stark contrast to her warmth. She smiled up at him, licking her lips.

Paul kicked off his shoes and then finished removing his jeans. Leaning forward, he lowered himself onto the bed—his hands spread wide, bracing himself. She leaned back on the mattress as he towered over her. "You're wearing too many clothes."

She lifted her arms over her head and stretched, arching her back. "So why don't you do something about it?"

Reaching for the bottom of her shirt, Paul worked it up past her breasts, and she helped him ease it over her head. She wore a pale pink bra with little blue flowers. It was cute and innocent. A direct contrast to the hard nipples he could see outlined beneath the thin fabric.

Paul remembered what Megan's breasts felt and tasted like against his tongue. Pushing the material of her bra out of the way, he quickly latched on to her nipple, and drew it into his mouth. She held his head in place, pushing her chest up, encouraging him to take what he wanted.

And take he did. No matter how much he licked and sucked, he couldn't get enough. If not for the growing need he had to be inside her, he could have spent hours—days—lavishing attention on her breasts.

Megan rotated her hips, and Paul could no longer ignore the pulsing in his groin. Reaching down between them, he unbuttoned her jeans, and then unzipped them. She helped him push the denim over her hips and down her legs, letting them fall to the floor beside the bed along with her shoes. The only things that remained between them were her bra and panties, and even those seemed too much. Megan seemed to agree, and between the two of them, the offending items were gone in a matter of seconds.

He ran his hands down the length of her body, taking in its perfection. Her curves were subtle, but they were there. Paul wondered how they'd change after she had a child of her own, and then swiftly stifled the thought. That wasn't what this was about. They hadn't—

Megan touched the side of his face. "Hey. Where did you go?"

Shaking his head, Paul kissed her. "Nowhere. It's just been a long time for me."

"Ah, yes. Well, we can take care of that easy enough."

A second later, Paul was lying on his back, and Megan was climbing on top of him. He recognized the move she'd used as one commonly taught in self-defense classes. This was the first time he'd had it executed on him outside of the gym.

"Where did you learn that?" he asked.

She straddled his waist, trapping his erection beneath her. "Becca. She was big on making sure I could take care of myself."

"I'd say she did a good job, then. That was an expert m—" The word died in his throat as Megan started rocking against him. He dug his fingers into her hips and guided her movements.

"Did you want to talk, or did you want to do something way more fun?" Her voice held a playful tone, but he heard the desire there.

Grabbing the back of her head, he pulled her face down to his. This kiss was all tongues and teeth as they moved against one another. He could feel her heat against him, and he needed to be inside her.

Reaching for the condom he knew was beside them on the bed, he snatched it up and tore open the packaging. Megan sat up, and took it from his hands, scooting back a little so that she could roll it down his length. Once it was in place, she lifted herself up onto her knees, and held him in position while she lowered herself down.

Paul held his breath as her heat enveloped him. It had been so long that he'd almost forgotten how it felt to be inside a woman, to have her surround him completely. It was indescribable.

Megan released a soft moan as he filled her, and he could see the pleasure on her face. It was an amazing sight, and he wanted to see more—he wanted to give her more. Repositioning them slightly, Paul began moving. In response, Megan leaned back, bracing her hands on his thighs, and met each thrust of his hips with one of her own. It felt good. Right.

Unfortunately, Paul hadn't been intimate with a woman for five years, and all too soon he felt his orgasm approaching. The only way to stop it would have been to halt all movement, but that wasn't something he was willing to do. "Megan?"

She met his gaze—her eyes glazed over with her own arousal.

"I'm . . ."

Before he could get another word out, she reached between them, and began pleasuring herself.

Paul groaned, and gritted his teeth. Watching her was making it that much harder to hold on, but he couldn't look away. It was the sexiest thing he'd ever seen.

With each brush of her fingers, she brought him closer and closer to the edge. He was sweating, not only with the exertion of sex, but also from trying to hold his climax at bay.

The moment he felt her spasm around him, Paul let himself go, and with only a few more thrusts, he found his own release. It left him sweaty, and spent, and feeling better than he had in years.

Megan collapsed on top of him, her breathing heavy against his neck. He wrapped his arms around her back, and buried his nose in her hair. She still smelled like lilac and cherries.

***

All Megan's limbs felt as if they'd come loose at the joints. She'd missed sex, but even she could admit this was different. It hadn't only been about having fun—which, of course, it was—but it was more than that. This was Paul. And being able to show him how she felt without having to hold back was beyond amazing.

He shifted a little as he separated himself from her. Megan felt the loss, and wanted him back. In that vein, she started kissing his neck and shoulders, anywhere in easy reach. Lazily, she threaded her fingers through his hair, and massaged his scalp with her nails.

Paul chuckled. "Easy. I'm an old man, remember? I need some time to recover."

She smiled against his neck, and then propped herself up on her elbow to look at him. "So what you're saying is that you're going to need a few minutes before we go at it again?"

He brushed the backs of his fingers down her cheek, before rubbing his thumb along the curve of her lips. "I'm afraid it will take more than a few minutes."

Paul pulled her down for a kiss. It was fairly chaste considering they were lying naked together on her bed. Still, it had her pulse racing in no time.

Before she could get carried away, Paul ended it. "I need to go clean up."

The cold air hit her as soon as he left the bed. She watched as he strolled into her bathroom and disappeared from sight.

Glancing down at their clothes on the floor, Megan wondered if she should get dressed. Normally, that's what happened after sex—well, unless she passed out drunk beforehand. That wasn't the case here. Plus, she really didn't want to get dressed. What she wanted to do was crawl into bed with Paul and stay there for the foreseeable future.

When Paul reentered the room, she was sitting up on the bed with her legs crossed Indian-style. He sat down beside her, and the awkwardness returned. She knew she needed to do something to fix it, but she wasn't sure how. They were in uncharted territory—for both of them.

She laid her palm face up on the bed between them. Paul hesitated for a moment, and then placed his hand on top of hers. He laced their fingers together, and gave them a squeeze.

They sat there not talking for several minutes until she shivered. He noticed. "Are you cold?"

Megan shrugged. "A little."

Paul stood, releasing her hand. She was regretting her confession until she realized what he was doing. He walked around to the opposite side of the bed and pulled the covers back. "Get in. I don't want you to catch cold."

She pushed herself up on her knees, and reached for the sheet and blanket. "Only if you join me."

He smiled. "That's the idea."

Megan scurried beneath the cool blankets, and her stomach did a little somersault when Paul slid into bed beside her. As soon as he was in, she snuggled against him. He held her close, and it felt natural. It was where she was meant to be.

They lay there for a long time, him tracing patterns on her back, while she played with the hair on his chest. Most of the guys she'd been with had little to no hair on their torsos. Paul's was covered with brown curls. Megan liked it. It seemed to fit him somehow.

"What are you thinking so hard about?" he asked.

She smiled, and twirled several strands of his hair around her finger. "I was thinking about the hair on your chest."

"Ah. I do have a lot, don't I?"

"You do. But I like it." Megan propped her head up to rest on her hand while she continued playing. "You know, this is the first time I've seen you without a shirt. Even when you were sick, you always wore a T-shirt."

"Habit. When Chloe was younger, there were a lot of nights I'd have to go into her room for one reason or another. It was easier to already have something on than to fumble around for clothes in the middle of the night."

"And before Chloe?"

"Um. No."

"So . . ."

He rolled onto his side to face her. "After I moved out of the college dorms, I got used to sleeping in the nude. Going back to pajamas was an adjustment, but it doesn't bother me anymore. It's all what you get used to."

"Do you think this is something you could get used to?"

Paul raised his eyebrows in question.

Megan didn't want to push, but she also remembered how unsure he'd been earlier. Had that all disappeared? "Us, I mean."

He searched her face, and then shrugged. "I don't know. This," he gestured between them, "is new to me—different."

"Because of your wife."

"Partly, yes."

She edged closer to him. "I know I said this before but I do understand that you'll always love Melissa, and I'm okay with that. But Paul, she's not here anymore, and I am. I want to be part of your life, and not just as your daughter's nanny."

Paul caressed her cheek with his thumb. "I hope you realize after this afternoon that I don't just think of you as the nanny."

Megan smiled, and closed the distance between them. "Good to know."

The kiss was teasing, and full of possibilities. She felt him growing hard against her hip. Megan was ready for another round. When Paul leaned back, she groaned.

He laughed. "You know, I wasn't joking earlier. I'm an old man. I need recovery time."

She rolled her eyes. "You're not old."

Paul raised an eyebrow.

"Okay, you're older. That doesn't make you old."

"If you say so."

Megan pushed him onto his back, placed her hands on his chest, and rested her chin on top. "I do."

He was quiet for a long moment. "Did you have somewhere you wanted to go Friday night? I haven't been on a date in over five years. I'm a little out of my element."

She tilted her head to the side. "You still want to go?"

"On a date? Sure. Why wouldn't I?"

"It's just . . ." Megan gestured to their current nakedness.

"You thought because we slept together that I'd change my mind?"

Megan shrugged and looked away.

"My word. What kind of jerks have you been dating?"

She didn't answer.

Paul tilted her chin back to where she was looking at him again. She was somewhat embarrassed. Most of the guys she'd dated in the past weren't jerks exactly, but they weren't what you'd call gentlemen. They hung out and had a good time together, which often included some down and dirty sex. She had no idea what Paul was seeing as he looked at her, but she felt almost guilty. It was new, and she wasn't sure she liked it.

Hoisting her further up his body, Paul pressed their foreheads together so he was looking her straight in the eye. "Megan, I have no idea what's going on between us. This," he mimicked her gesture from before, "is only part of it. If all I wanted was a quick roll in the hay, I could have gotten that years ago."

"Of course you could have. You're hot."

He laughed. "You're not making this easy, you know."

Megan smiled. "Sorry."

"What I'm trying to say is that there's more to what's between us than physical attraction. At least, I think there is."

"Are you trying to say that you like me?" It was so easy to tease him sometimes.

"Possibly."

She bracketed his head with her forearms, and kissed the tip of his nose. "I like you, too. But what happened to you thinking you're not good enough?"

"Oh, I still think I'm not good enough for you. I messed up before, and there's no guarantee I won't do it again."

"You didn't mess up."

"Megan—"

She cut him off with a kiss—one she refused to end until she felt the tension in his body melt away. Releasing his lips, she began working her way along his jaw, and down his neck. "Think you're ready to go again, old man?"

Megan let out a squeal as Paul rolled them over. Heat flared in her body as his mouth blazed a trail down her torso to the space between her legs. For the next thirty minutes, Megan didn't think about much of anything, which suited her just fine.

AFTER THEIR SECOND round of amazing sex, they lay holding each other until they both drifted off to sleep. Over the years, Megan had learned to sleep almost anywhere and in any position. She also trained herself to wake up at a moment's notice. That's why when Paul began to jerk and twist beside her, she was instantly alert.

His eyes were closed, so she was fairly sure he was dreaming. From the look on his face, though, it didn't look to be something pleasant. "Paul?"

There was no change.

"Paul. Wake up. You're dreaming. Paul!"

Paul's eyelids flew open in panic, and he held his body rigid. The only exception was his chest, which continued to move up and down rapidly.

Megan had no idea what was going on, but she knew better than to touch him. That was a sure fire way to end up getting slapped or punched.

She decided to wait him out. It didn't take too long before he realized that there was no immediate danger. He shifted his gaze to the side, and noticed her for the first time.

"Did I hurt you?"

"No." Megan scooted closer. She'd been in a few situations similar to this in the past—one of the hazards of sleeping next to guys she didn't know all that well. On a scale of one to ten, this situation ranked low on her fear meter.

Paul sat up and held his head in his hands. Beads of sweat glistened off his back.

"Do you want to talk about it?" she asked.

He sighed and shook his head.

"Okay." Megan was at a loss. Something had happened and he was shutting her out. She knew this thing between them was new, but it still hurt.

Without looking in her direction, Paul threw the covers off him, and began gathering his clothes. Unsure what was going on, Megan followed his lead. He was finished dressing before she had her jeans halfway up her legs.

"Are you hungry?" He didn't wait for her to answer. "I'm going to see what I can dig up downstairs. Maybe call for a pizza."

Megan stood there completely dumbfounded as Paul rushed out of her room. What the hell was going on?

She finished putting her clothes back on and headed downstairs. Paul was sitting in the living room with phone in hand, talking to the pizza shop.

"Yes, I'd like a large supreme pizza. And can you put extra black olives on half of it?"

That made her smile. No matter what was going on, Paul had remembered she liked extra black olives on her pizza.

Paul gave their address, and then hung up. He set the phone down on the coffee table without looking in her direction. "The pizza should be here in about forty minutes."

"Okay." Megan leaned back against the doorjamb observing him. If she didn't know him so well, she would have thought she'd imagined what happened in her bedroom. He sat casually on the couch with his forearms resting on his knees. The only real giveaway was the way he held his shoulders. He wasn't as relaxed as he appeared.

Megan wanted to do something to make it better, but she was at a loss. She wasn't even sure what had happened beyond he'd had a nightmare of some kind. Was it work related? Was it about his wife? Either was a distinct possibility.

He reached for the remote and turned on the television. Apparently, he was planning to ignore the elephant in the room.

Megan decided to play along for the time being. Crossing the room, she sat down beside him, and tucked her feet under her.

Paul glanced briefly in her direction, but then went back to flipping through the channels. He settled on a sitcom.

They watched in silence, sitting side by side yet not touching, until the pizza arrived. Paul got up and paid for their dinner while Megan busied herself in the kitchen getting them something to drink. He brought the pizza to the table, and they both took their usual seats.

When Paul reached for his third slice, Megan decided she couldn't take it anymore.

"Are we just going to act like nothing happened?"

He stopped mid-chew, but didn't answer her.

"Did you have a nightmare? Was it about your wife?"

Paul dropped his pizza back into the box.

"I thought we were going to try and make this work between us. How can we if you shut me out?" Megan was trying to remain calm, but the way he was acting was beginning to scare her.

"It's not a big deal. It was only a dream." He sounded defeated.

Megan reached across the space between them, and covered his hand with hers. He stared at her with a blank look on his face. "I want you to talk to me."

He shook his head.

"Please."

For a long time, he said nothing. The silence was almost deafening. "Yes, it was about Melissa."

Megan breathed a sigh of relief. He was talking. Anything else she could deal with, but if this had any hope of working between them, they had to communicate. "Okay."

Although she wanted to know more, she decided not to push. Instead, she shoved away from the table, and walked over to put her arms around his neck. It was a simple gesture, but Megan recalled many times in her life when all she had needed was a hug and her world made sense again. She was hoping maybe she could give that to Paul.

At first, he didn't react. Then something changed, and she felt him release the tension in his body. He circled his arms around her and pulled her down onto his lap. She held on tight, and reveled in this new connection between them.

"Are you sure this is what you want?" he asked. "I'm not such a catch, you know. I have a lot of baggage."

She hugged him tighter. "So do I."

He leaned back so that he could look her in the eye. "I'm serious, Megan. I don't know how to do this with you. With anyone. Melissa was . . ."

"The love of your life."

Paul hesitated. "Yes. I thought I'd be with her forever."

Megan nodded. It wasn't exactly what she wanted to hear, but it wasn't as if she hadn't known. No man remained celibate for five years after losing a woman he wasn't over the moon about.

He snorted. "I'm not doing so well, am I?"

"You're doing fine. I knew what I was getting myself into." Megan tried to comfort him.

"What I don't understand is why you would want to?"

She framed his face with her hands, and placed a chaste kiss on his lips. "Because I think you're worth it."

He sighed, and rested his forehead against hers. "So what do we do now?"

"Well . . ." Megan straddled him and brought her mouth to hover above his ear. "We could finish eating the pizza you ordered, or we could do something more . . . fun."

Paul's chest vibrated against her.

Megan gave him the most innocent look she could manage. "What?"

"You have a one-track mind."

"I don't know what you mean. I was thinking if you were full of pizza, maybe we could play a game or something. That's all." She kept a straight face, but inside she was struggling to stay composed.

"Sure you were." His tone was serious, but she could see the twinkle in his eye. He was having fun. More importantly, the haunted look that had been plaguing him since he woke up had disappeared.

Reaching behind her, Megan tore off a bite of pizza, and popped it in her mouth. She made sure to lick her fingers nice and slow, teasing him.

It worked. His brown eyes dilated, and she felt evidence of his interest against the inside of her thigh. She repeated the process, and watched as his eyes grew perceptively darker.

When she went to take her third bite, Paul stopped her. "You're a tease, do you know that?"

Megan grinned. "Only if I don't plan to put out, which I do."

"Oh you do, do you?"

"Yep."

She ran her tongue along the seam of his lips, and he groaned. "Maybe we should wait."

"Wait for what?"

He sucked in a breath. "It's . . . Chloe . . ."

That got her attention. Megan glanced up at the clock and sighed. She sat up, but remained straddling his lap. Paul was right. Chloe would be calling any minute. It wouldn't do them any good to get all hot and heavy, and then have to stop in the middle to answer the phone. There was no way Paul would miss his daughter's call, and Megan would never ask him to.

***

Paul was having a hard time remembering why he couldn't take Megan back upstairs and bury himself deep inside her—a very hard time. When he made the decision to ask her out, he never imagined that less than two hours later they'd be in her bed. She was full of sexual energy, and it was all directed solely at him.

For his part, Paul couldn't remember the last time he'd had sex twice in one day. He and Melissa had a fairly active sex life, but they'd been together for fifteen years. The days of endless hours in bed where they were doing more than sleeping died off somewhere in their twenties. Neither had seemed to miss it, but now he was wondering if maybe they should have.

Megan took another bite of her pizza. "A penny for your thoughts?"

He followed suit, and reached for the slice of pizza he'd deposited back in the box earlier. It was a little awkward to eat with Megan sitting on his lap like she was, but he had no desire for her to move. "I was trying to remember the last time I had sex more than once in a day."

Her eyes grew wide.

"Don't look so shocked. When you get older, things change."

She scrunched up her nose.

Fortunately, that was the end of the conversation for the time being, as the house phone rang. Megan reluctantly got up, and he went to answer it.

They both took turns talking to Chloe. His little girl was having fun. She'd forgotten all about him being sick, and was busy enjoying the time with her grandparents.

He slipped out of the room when Megan took the phone, to give her a little privacy. It was also the first real opportunity he had to regroup after waking up from his nightmare. It wasn't the first time he'd had that particular dream. After Melissa died, he'd had it almost every night. Over time, it happened less often, but when it did, it was intense. Once, he broke his bedside lamp. And more than a few times he'd ripped his bed sheets.

When he woke up and realized he wasn't alone, it had terrified him. What if he'd hurt Megan while dreaming? He didn't know if he could live with himself. It was one more reason not to have a relationship with her.

There was one huge obstacle arguing the other side, though, and it was Megan herself. She was smart, sexy, and she made him feel more alive than he had in years. Megan had awakened a part of him he'd thought dead and buried. He wasn't sure he wanted to give it up. He wasn't sure if he could.

Megan found him in his bedroom. "Cindy wanted me to tell you to call her if you needed anything."

He smiled. "Thanks. Sometimes I think she's having a difficult time letting go. When they lived in town, I relied on them a lot. Even after all these years."

"That's understandable, I guess."

Megan remained by the door, and he realized she was waiting for an invitation to enter. He'd been somewhat protective of his bedroom. It was his space. The only time she'd come in without waiting for permission was when he was sick. Even then, Megan had been cautious. She'd brought him food and medicine, and she would retrieve items from his bathroom when he needed them, but that was all. Paul realized that if whatever this was between them had any hope of working, he was going to have to let her in. Not only to his personal space, but to everything else as well.

Paul sat on the edge of the bed and patted the space beside him.

Megan smiled and strolled into the room. She took a seat beside him and took hold of his hand. "I wasn't sure if you'd want me in here."

"I have been a little overprotective of my bedroom, haven't I?"

She shrugged. "A little. But I get it."

He grunted. "You let me off the hook too easy, Megan."

"What would you have me do, hmm? I won't fault you for loving your wife. It's not a competition."

"No, I suppose it isn't." He couldn't deny her logic, but it was almost too rational.

"Look, I won't say I'm not a little jealous sometimes. I mean, you loved her. But it seems petty to me to get upset with you over it. At least from everything you and your family have told me about Melissa, it sounds like she loved you just as much."

Paul took a deep breath to steady himself. "Thank you for understanding. I don't think most women would."

She squeezed his hand and laid her head on his shoulder. "Yeah, well, I'm not most women."

He laughed. "No. You most certainly are not."

They sat there for several minutes staring off into space before Megan spoke. "Does me being in here bother you?"

"No. I thought maybe it would, but it doesn't."

Megan hugged his arm. "Good."

"I don't know . . ." He paused. "I don't know if I'm ready to . . . sleep with you in here yet, though."

She smiled up at him. "But you still want to sleep with me, right?"

He brushed a strand of hair away from her face. "I do. But . . ."

"But?"

As much as he didn't want to talk about his dream, he knew if they were going to continue sharing a bed, he'd have to. She needed to know what she was getting herself into. If she chose to kick him out of her bed, then that was her decision and he'd respect it.

"Sometimes I have dreams—nightmares—like I did today."

Megan's expression turned serious. "Okay."

This was harder than he thought it would be. "Most of the time they revolve around the night Melissa died. I don't want to go into the details, but sometimes when I have them I get . . . violent."

"Violent how?"

He frowned. "I broke my lamp once. If you look closely at the base, you can see the crack where I glued it back together."

She looked over his shoulder at the lamp and then back to him. "That's why you asked if you'd hurt me."

"Yes. I've always been alone when it's happened before. And the lamp hasn't been the only casualty. I've had to replace quite a few sheets as well."

When Megan didn't respond in any way, he became anxious. "I would never hurt you on purpose."

"I know that." She sounded somewhat insulted.

He sighed. "Anyway, I wanted you to know, and I'll understand if you don't want to take the risk."

Megan gave him a funny look. "Are you serious? You really

thought I wouldn't want to sleep in the same bed as you on the off chance that you have another nightmare?"

"I could hurt you, Megan, and I wouldn't even be aware of it."

She sat up and turned to face him. "Paul, how much do you know about how I grew up?"

"Only what you've told me." Granted, that wasn't much. He knew it had been far from a fairy-tale childhood, and that her older sister, Rebecca, had pretty much raised her. Paul also knew that neither Megan nor Rebecca had anything to do with their parents.

"I guess I should probably fill you in, huh?"

"You don't have to—"

"Yes, I do. If I'm asking you to be open and honest with me, then I owe you the same."

He couldn't disagree with her there, and to be honest, he was curious.

Megan straightened her shoulders and took a deep breath. "My dad wasn't around when I was born. He was in prison."

Paul blinked, but didn't say anything.

"You see, my dad had a thing for drugs. Both using and selling. It was small stuff mostly, but he wasn't very good at evading the law. He was in and out of prison my entire childhood."

"I'm sorry." Paul felt as if he should do or say something, but he was at a loss. Being a cop, he saw situations like the one she was describing. It was rough enough to see from the outside looking in.

"To be honest, things were better when he was away. Mom was depressed and drank a lot, but other than that, things weren't bad. Becca made sure there was food in the house and that the bills were paid. She helped me with my homework and made sure I got to school on time.

"Everything changed whenever Dad was home. The first few days weren't horrible. He was happy to be out of prison, and he'd hug and kiss us—tell us he loved us, and that things would be different. At first, I believed him. Becca never did, though."

Paul tugged Megan's hand into his lap, and rubbed the inside of her wrist with his thumbs. He didn't know what else to do.

"About a week would go by, and then one of his friends would stop in to see him. They'd start drinking, and then the drugs would come out."

"Your father did drugs in the house in front of you?" Anger welled up inside him.

Megan nodded. "Becca always made sure to get us out of there if she could. Or at the very least, she'd stock up on snacks and water, and we'd hide in our room. I can't tell you how many blanket forts we made during those times."

It was then Paul understood the connection between Megan and her sister. He knew they were close, but the relationship had always seemed a bit unnatural. Now he knew why. Rebecca had been Megan's protector.

"It wasn't a great childhood, but Becca got me through it. I don't know if I would have made it without her."

Paul heard what Megan didn't say. There would have been no reason to hide if there was no danger. "Megan, did your father ever . . ."

"No. He never hurt me, although he used to knock Mom around sometimes. And I think he got to Becca once or twice. She never said anything, but once I saw some bruises on her arm that looked like fingerprints."

He'd heard enough. Wrapping her in his arms, he buried his face in the crook of her neck. "I'm so sorry you had to go through that."

She circled her arms around his waist and returned his embrace. "Paul, I didn't tell you all that to make you feel sorry for me. I'm not that little girl anymore."

Paul pulled back enough to see her face. "I know that."

Megan ignored his comment. "I told you because I wanted you to understand that I know the difference. You aren't a violent man, Paul, and I'm not helpless. Nor am I defenseless. If worse comes to worst, I can always go for the family jewels. That would wake you up, for sure." She winked at him, taking some of the sting out of her threat.

"It really doesn't worry you?"

"Nope."

He smiled and let the warmth in his chest grow. Paul wasn't stupid. He recognized the feeling for what it was. He was falling for Megan, and all his reasons why they shouldn't be together—all the reasons why they couldn't work—were quickly becoming less and less important.

MEGAN WOKE up alone this time. They'd made love again before going to sleep in her bed. Paul had been restless near morning, but he didn't thrash around as he had the day before. She had taken a chance and snuggled up to him. He settled down almost instantly.

She rolled over to look at the clock. It was a little after six thirty in the morning. Paul had to be in to work at eight, so he'd probably left her to sleep while he went to his room to get ready. Tossing the covers off, Megan threw on some clothes, and went in search of coffee.

As Megan measured out the grounds and started the coffeemaker, she couldn't stop smiling. She and Paul were dating. They were going to explore what was between them. Megan was flying on cloud nine, and she didn't want to come back down to earth anytime soon.

Arms circled around her waist from behind, and she leaned back into the warm chest crushed against her back. She didn't know if it could get any better than this.

Paul ran the tip of his nose along her neck. "Good morning."

"Good morning." She tilted her head to the side to give him better access. He placed little kisses along her neck and jaw while he toyed with the skin along her belly beneath her shirt. She felt the heat grow between her legs. All he needed to do was say the word and she was ready.

His next words burst her bubble. "I need to get into the station early, since I took yesterday off."

She groaned, and he chuckled.

"You can't still be horny after last night," he said.

Megan turned in his embrace and wrapped her arms around his neck. He pulled her flush against his body, and whether he admitted it or not, she didn't think it would take much to get him going either. "I've got a newsflash for you, Detective. I have a pretty healthy sex drive."

He smiled. "Is that so?"

"Yes." She rubbed up against him seductively to drive home her point.

Paul sucked in a shaky breath. "You're going to be the death of me."

She released him, and stepped back. "Oh, but what a way to go."

He shook his head and adjusted himself.

Megan retrieved their mugs and poured them both a cup of coffee. He gave her a chaste kiss in thanks, and then they both took their places at the kitchen table.

"Do you think you'll be working late tonight?" she asked.

"I don't know. I'm waiting for some documents I requested. If they're delivered today, I'll probably stay late to work on them. Otherwise, I should be home around the usual time."

She nodded and took a sip of her coffee. "I'll go to the store today and restock the fridge. Did you have any requests for dinner?"

"You don't have to cook for me, Megan."

His statement confused her. "I cook for you all the time."

"No, you cook for us. Yourself, Chloe, and me. That's different."

Megan set her mug down. "No. It's not. Why are you so against me doing things for you? When I moved in, I had to fight you to do basic chores around the house. Now you don't want me to make dinner?"

"It's not that I don't want you to." Paul massaged his temple.

It hadn't been her intention to start their morning off with a fight.

"Then what is it? Please, help me to understand, because I don't get it."

He sighed and met her gaze. "I don't want you to feel as though you have to do things for me."

"And if I want to?"

"Why would you want to?" he countered. "You're twenty-three years old. You have your whole life ahead of you."

"Yeah. So?"

"So. I'm a middle-aged man with a five-year-old daughter."

Megan stared at him. She was starting to get angry. "Why does our age difference bother you so much?"

"Because I don't want to be the one that holds you back." With that, he pushed himself away from the table, and went to the sink to dump the rest of his coffee.

"Don't you think that should be my decision?"

He braced his hands on the counter in front of the sink and bowed his head. "Megan, do you understand what us being together means?"

"Yes."

Paul turned around to face her. "Are you sure? You're walking into a ready-made family. Once we've crossed that line, there's no going back."

"Don't you think it's a little late for that? Or are you regretting last night?"

He softened his voice. "No. I don't regret it. If anything, I want to drag you back upstairs and stay there with you for the next three weeks."

"So what's the problem?" She really wasn't understanding. If he wanted to be with her, and she wanted to be with him, what was the issue?

"In three weeks, Chloe will be back home. And she's going to realize things have changed between us."

"Of course she will. She's a smart little girl." Megan still felt as if she were missing something—something big.

Paul sighed and ran both hands over his face before letting them fall to his sides. "What I'm saying is that once Chloe finds out about us, her imagination is going to take off. She's . . ."

"She's what?"

"She's going to start thinking that we're going to get married and that . . . that you're going to be her new mommy."

Megan tried to keep the anxiety out of her voice. "And that's not what you want."

"Argh. Why does this have to be so difficult?"

"I don't know." Maybe she'd read Paul all wrong. Maybe all he was looking for was someone to warm his bed every now and then. How could she have misread him so badly?

Something akin to a growl rumbled deep in Paul's chest, and he crossed the room in two long strides to where she was sitting. He hoisted her up by her arms to stand in front of him. "Please don't look at me like that."

"Like what?"

He framed her face with his hands, and she closed her eyes. "Like I've just killed your puppy."

She opened her eyes. "I don't have a puppy."

Paul ignored her comment. "I'm going to be honest, Megan. I don't know what I want. This thing between us—how I feel about you—it's new. And shocking. And I don't know what to make of it. But if it did work between us, then yes, I would want a future with you. A permanent one."

Megan smiled and leaned into his touch. "Me, too."

"You'd be willing to accept a ready-made family and everything that goes with it?" he asked.

"Yes."

"How can you know that?"

Megan placed her hands over the top of Paul's, and brought their faces closer together. "Do you trust me?"

It was his turn to look offended. "Of course I do."

"Then trust me to make my own decisions. I know what I'm getting myself into."

"How—"

She covered his mouth with her right hand. "Paul, I've known what I want for a while now. And I know everything that comes with it—Chloe, Cindy and George, your family. I want to see where it takes us. See if what I've been imagining—you and me—is possible. It doesn't scare me."

"It scares me," he mumbled under her fingers.

Megan smiled and leaned in to give him a kiss. "Don't be scared. It's just me."

He groaned and hugged her against him. "That's what scares me."

She laughed and kissed him again. Paul didn't make it to work early that morning.

***

Two hours later, Paul sat at his desk going over paperwork. Not only had he not made it to work early, he'd been almost an hour late. Granted, with all the weird hours he'd been working, he doubted any of the other officers would even notice the anomaly. Of course, his partner was the one exception.

"About time you showed up, Daniels."

He didn't bother looking up. "Overslept."

Janey rested her hip on the edge of his desk. "Didn't your nanny come home yesterday?"

"Yes, I picked Megan up from the airport yesterday afternoon. Which you know perfectly well, because I told you that's what I was going to do." This time, he shot her a piercing glare before returning to the file. Janey was a good partner, but she could be incredibly nosy. Maybe it was because she was a cop, but he didn't remember having the same problem with his previous partner, Doug. Then again, Paul and Melissa were already married by the time he and Doug had been partnered up. Maybe that was the difference.

"Uh-huh. And you're trying to tell me she had nothing at all to do with you being late this morning?"

"I was late. That's all. Can we drop it and get to work?"

She chuckled and sauntered over to her desk. "So tell me what you've got, Oh Great One."

Paul rolled his eyes. "I was thinking we could canvass the campus area again. Drive around. Talk to some of the pedestrians."

Janey groaned. "Do you really think spending another day driving around is going to garner any new information?"

"Do you have a better suggestion?"

"What about that list of employees and students the college was supposed to send over?" Janey asked.

Paul leaned back in his chair. "Still waiting on them."

She shook her head. "There's got to be something. Maybe we should talk to the families again."

"All right. That might be a good idea. Since we're fairly sure the campus area is where our killer is choosing his victims, they might help us narrow our search area."

He stood and grabbed his jacket off the back of his chair. They made their way to his vehicle, and headed toward the first victim's parents' home. Jessica Chase was single, living alone, so her parents and her best friend were their closest connection.

Less than a minute after they left the station, his phone beeped letting him know he had a message. Since he was driving, he ignored it. Janey, however, did not. She snatched the phone from the center console where he'd placed it.

"What are you doing?"

"Being inquisitive. You never get texts. Maybe it's important."

"I'm sure it's not." Paul said, hoping Janey would take the hint and return his phone to the console.

She didn't.

With a few swipes across the touch pad, his partner pulled up his text message. "I knew it!"

Paul glanced in her direction and frowned. It didn't take a genius to figure out the text was from Megan. She and Gage were the only two people who ever sent him text messages, and the last message Gage sent him had been months ago. But what did Megan text him that had Janey looking so smug?

"Care to change your story, Detective Daniels?"

Janey turned the phone so that he could see the screen. His heart skipped a beat, and he had to concentrate to keep from losing control of his car. There, on his phone, was a picture of a woman in her bra and panties—a bra and panty set he recognized.

His partner laughed at his reaction. "No comment, Detective?"

He swallowed, and tried his best to focus on the road. "Fine. We're . . . exploring our options."

She laughed. "From the looks of it, you'll be exploring a lot when you get home tonight. I guess that means you won't be working late anymore."

Paul shot her a look. "Do you think we could stick to the case and not my love life?"

Janey smiled and returned his phone to the center console. "At least you admit that you do have a love life."

He grunted.

"I'm happy for you. Really. And from everything I've seen, I think Megan is good for you."

"Are you finished?" he asked.

"For now."

They arrived a few minutes later at Jessica Chase's parents' house. Her father was outside working in the yard. Paul and Janey exited the vehicle.

"Good morning, Mr. Chase." Janey extended her hand to the older man.

"Detectives." Devlin Chase removed his gloves and met them in the middle of his yard. "Have you found new information about our daughter's killer?"

Paul shook the man's hand. "We were wondering if you and your wife had a few minutes to talk to us."

Mr. Chase was obviously curious, but he nodded. "Sure. My wife's inside."

Janey and Paul followed Mr. Chase inside the house. The closer they got to the kitchen, the stronger the scent of cinnamon and sugar became. It reminded Paul that he'd skipped breakfast in favor of other activities. Shaking his head, he did his best to dispel the memory of Megan's legs wrapped around his head.

"Detectives." Elaine Chase wiped her hands, and stepped around the counter.

To try and stay focused, Paul decided to take the lead. "Good morning, ma'am."

Mrs. Chase reached for her husband. "Did you find something?"

For most families, the worst part of an investigation was the waiting. They wanted closure so the healing could begin. "We wanted to ask you a few more questions."

"Of course." Mr. Chase wrapped his arm around his wife.

"Do you know if your daughter frequented the area near the local community college?" Paul asked.

The couple looked at each other before Mr. Chase answered. "I think she may have tutored someone there last year, but I don't know who it was."

"Trudi would probably know, wouldn't she, Devlin? She's probably at work." Mrs. Chase clung to her husband.

They asked a few more questions, and Mrs. Chase remembered that they'd found a better picture of their daughter, if they wanted it. The one the family had originally provided was a profile shot. There wasn't anything wrong with it, but sometimes profiles were harder for people to identify.

With the picture in hand, Paul and Janey got back in his car and headed for the restaurant where Trudi Olsen worked. There was one big advantage to visiting Jessica's best friend at her place of employment—he'd have the opportunity to get some much needed food.

By the time they were seated in Trudi's section, Paul's stomach was growling.

"Didn't you eat anything this morning?"

Paul didn't bother to look up from the menu when he answered Janey. "No."

She snorted. "I wonder why."

"Hello. My name is—"

Janey smiled up at Trudi. "Hello, Ms. Olsen."

"Um. Hello. What are you doing here? I mean, did you find something?" Trudi glanced over her shoulder.

Paul laid his menu on the table. "We were hoping to order some food, and maybe chat with you a bit if you have time."

"Yeah. Sure. Um. Let me get your order in, and then I'll let my manager know I need to take a break."

The restaurant was still serving breakfast, so he ordered a stack of pancakes, three eggs, and some bacon. It was a lot of food, but he was starving. There was no telling how many calories he'd burned off in the last twenty-four hours.

Trudi disappeared into the kitchen, and then returned less than ten minutes later with his food and Janey's coffee. As he dug into his breakfast, Trudi pulled up a chair, and sat down. "So what's up? Did you find something?"

Since he was eating, Paul let Janey run with the questioning. "We were hoping you could tell us about any connections Jessica may have had to the local community college, or the area itself. Her mother thought she remembered Jessica tutoring someone there last year."

"Yeah, she did. It was last summer." Trudi's eyes grew wide with concern. "You don't think that was somehow related to her death, do you?"

Janey patted Trudi's hands reassuringly where they lay clasped together on the table. "We're just following some leads. No stone left unturned— that sort of thing."

Trudi nodded.

Paul took a sip of his coffee. "Do you happen to remember the person's name she was tutoring?"

"I think his name was Scott. He was in a fraternity, I remember that. He invited Jessica to a couple of parties."

This could be the break they needed. Jessica had been the only victim they couldn't positively link to the campus area within six months of her death. "Do you know if she ever went to any of them?"

Trudi thought about it for a long moment before answering him. "I don't think so. To be honest, I think she was kinda glad when the tutoring was over."

"And why is that?" Janey asked.

"I think he was hitting on her. She had a boyfriend at the time, so she told him no."

Paul set his fork down on his plate. "He didn't take the hint?"

Trudi shrugged. "He was . . . persistent. Jessica said he never got physical with her or anything, but he was constantly flirting."

They wrote down all the information Trudi could remember about the young man Jessica had tutored the previous summer, as well as the name of Jessica's boyfriend at the time. This was the reason why one had to go over information dozens of times. Both he and Janey had specifically asked about boyfriends more than once, yet this was the first time they were hearing about Jessica's.

Hoping they could speed things up, when they left the restaurant, they made their way to the campus admissions office. The dean was extremely helpful, especially since they'd already sent over a warrant for records. By the time they left, they had a list of all the fraternities and their members. All they had to do now was find the Scott they were looking for.

PAUL AND JANEY spent the rest of the day back at the station going through the list of fraternity brothers the dean had provided. The Internet allowed them to get background on the eight Scotts they had on their list. By the end of the day, they had pictures of each of the men, along with an idea of each one's personality. It always amazed Paul how much information people shared on social media sites. On days like this, he was grateful. It made his job that much easier.

At five o'clock, Paul shut down his computer, and slipped on his suit jacket. Janey smiled, but didn't say anything.

The drive home was full of anxious anticipation. Megan had continued to text him periodically throughout the day. None of them were as provocative as the first—mostly small reminders she was thinking about him. Paul had to admit that they were a nice pick-me-up to his day.

He pulled into his driveway and turned off the engine. It was taking all he had not to rush into the house to find her like some sort of crazed madman. He hadn't felt like this in a long time.

As calmly as he could, Paul made his way inside. He glanced around the kitchen, but didn't see Megan anywhere. Closing the door behind him, Paul called out to her. "Megan?"

Her voice floated down from the second floor. "I'm upstairs."

His heart started racing as the possibilities of why she was upstairs flitted through his mind.

All his restraint went out the window as he ran up the stairs to find her. He was out of breath by the time he reached the top, but he didn't slow down. In three strides, he was at her bedroom door.

The sight that greeted Paul had him hard in a matter of seconds. Megan lay on the bed in nothing but the bra and panty set she'd texted him that morning. It was dark blue with lace trim—a striking contrast against her skin.

Megan sat up, resting her weight on her arms behind her. "Welcome home."

He released a shaky breath. "What are you doing up here?"

"I thought maybe we could have a picnic." She waved her hand toward a wicker basket he'd yet to notice sitting on the floor beside the bed.

Paul was trying to wrap his head around what he was seeing.

When he didn't move, Megan crawled off the bed to come stand before him. She reached for the lapels of his jacket, and pushed it up and over his shoulders. It dropped unceremoniously to the floor behind him. Next she went for his tie. "You're wearing way too many clothes, Detective Daniels."

As soon as she removed his shirt, Paul removed his gun and holster, grabbed hold of her waist, and crushed her against him. She gazed up at him with a look he was becoming very familiar with. Threading his fingers through her hair, Paul lowered his mouth to hers.

Megan enthusiastically kissed him back. If he didn't know any better, he would have thought she was attempting to crawl beneath his skin the way she rubbed herself against his body. She didn't hide that she wanted him, and it had his erection protesting against the confines of his suit pants.

Completely forgetting about food, he walked them back toward her bed. Megan scraped her nails along his back, sending shivers down his spine. He needed to be inside her already. Paul kicked off his shoes, and together they made quick work of getting rid of his pants and underwear—the only thing left between them were the scraps of satin and lace she was wearing.

Before he could remedy that, Megan broke away, and crawled backward onto the mattress. She had her back arched and her legs spread. He could see the evidence of her arousal seeping through her thin panties. Paul couldn't take his eyes off it.

"Did you change your mind, Detective?" she asked.

Paul blinked and adjusted his gaze up to meet hers. She was grinning. Megan knew exactly what she was doing to him.

In response, Paul narrowed his eyes, and launched himself onto the bed. He covered her body with his, and trapped both her hands above her head.

Megan giggled. "I didn't know you liked it kinky, Detective."

He attacked her neck with vigor—licking and biting at her flesh. "I'll show you kinky."

Something snapped inside him, and Paul shifted his hold so he could grasp both of her wrists with a single hand. With the other, he covered her breast and began tweaking her nipple.

"Paul."

The way she said his name was all the encouragement he needed. Paul continued to play with her breasts, but he was getting frustrated with her bra. It was getting in his way.

He let go of her wrists, and Megan seemed to know exactly what he wanted. She twisted to the side so he could reach behind her and unclasp her bra. They worked together to remove it, and then Paul went back to worshiping her.

While his mouth was busy, he used his hands to encourage Megan to wrap her legs around his waist. As soon as her heat was pressed up against him, he nearly lost it. "Now you're the one wearing too many clothes."

She laughed and dropped her legs. Reaching between them, Megan worked her panties down her legs. As she did this, however, she began scooting herself further up the bed—away from him.

Paul waited until the offending material was gone before diving forward to catch her by the hips. He pulled her back down the bed until she was where he wanted her.

Megan circled her arms around his neck and shook her head. "So impatient."

"Says the woman who sent dirty pictures of herself to my phone."

She smiled and ran her fingers through his hair. "Only one."

He groaned. "One was enough."

Using his neck as leverage, Megan pulled herself up to whisper in his ear. "You didn't like it?"

Before he could respond, she covered his lips with her mouth. Paul didn't fight it. He could admonish her later.

Everything happened rather quickly after that. There was kissing and touching. She fumbled around for a condom, and he quickly rolled it on. Then he was pushing himself inside her. Paul was lost in the need to possess every part of her. It was as if he couldn't get enough—couldn't get close enough to her.

She met him thrust for thrust, grinding her hips against him, seeking her own pleasure. It was a heady feeling, knowing she desired him as much as he did her.

Paul felt his climax approaching, and more than anything he wanted her there with him. Reaching between them, his touch edged her closer. Megan dug her nails into his shoulders, and she threw her head back. "Paul!"

Seeing Megan orgasm had to be one of the best things he'd ever seen in his life. She embraced her sexuality completely. It was enough to send him over the edge.

Megan laughed as he collapsed on top of her.

"Sorry," he said, rolling to his side.

She turned to face him, still smiling. "I don't think you have anything to apologize for."

Her gaze roamed down his length and back up again. There was a hunger in her eyes that did nothing to stop the blood that was pounding through his veins. Ten years ago, he would probably have been ready to jump her again.

"You're insatiable."

"Is that a complaint?" she asked.

It was his turn to laugh. "No."

She smiled. "Are you hungry?"

"Famished."

Megan reached across his lap and over the side of the bed to retrieve the wicker basket he'd noticed before. She pulled it up onto the bed, and rearranged herself so she was sitting with the basket on the mattress in front of her. One by one, she began removing the items.

Paul excused himself so that he could clean up. When he came back into her bedroom, he slipped into the bed, and got comfortable against the headboard. Every few seconds Megan would cast him a sly glance, but other than that, she focused on what she was doing. The more he watched her, the more it hit him that she truly seemed to want him, and not only in the physical sense.

"Are you all right?" Megan positioned herself beside him at the top of the bed.

"Yes." He suddenly had an impulse to kiss her, so he did.

She smiled and handed him a container. "There's little sandwiches, fruit, cheese, chicken—"

He cut off her list with another kiss. "It's wonderful. Thank you."

Megan shrugged. "I know you've been stressed lately with the case and . . . well . . . with us."

Paul reached for her hand and laced their fingers together. "I'll make you a promise, okay? I'll try my best not to stress about what's going on between the two of us. We have a lot to figure out in the next three weeks, but I'm willing if you are."

***

Paul's words were music to Megan's ears. She felt as if she'd been waiting to hear him say them forever.

She tilted her head up, and placed a featherlight kiss on his lips. "That's all I want."

He smiled, and for the first time Megan thought everything

might really work out the way she hoped. Paul felt something for her—he was willing to give a relationship between the two of them a chance.

For the next several minutes, they busied themselves eating. She was biting into a chicken wing when Paul cleared his throat. "Janey knows. About us, I mean."

Megan swallowed. Did he not want his partner to know? "Okay."

"She saw your text this morning. The picture."

"Oh." Megan didn't know what to think. It was only a picture of her in her bra and panties. She wasn't naked or anything. Although taking a picture like that had crossed her mind, she knew Paul wasn't quite as adventurous as her, so she had toned it down. "Did you not want her to know, then? About us?"

He was quiet for a long minute. "I don't know. I guess I was hoping to keep it to ourselves for a while. We don't know if this is going to work, and once people start finding out—"

"It complicates things. I get it." And she did. He wasn't sure this was what he wanted. It would be easier if no one knew, in case things didn't work out.

What she was thinking must have shown on her face, and he jumped in to correct her assumption. "No. That's not what I mean."

"Then what did you mean? If you're ashamed of us, Paul, then this isn't going to work." The thought turned her appetite sour.

Paul made a frustrated noise, and laid the food he had on his lap off to the side before pulling her into his arms. "I'm not ashamed but, Megan, you have to understand that this is a big step for me. I want us to be sure that this is going somewhere before we announce it to the world. Does that make sense? Who knows, maybe you'll find out something about me that repulses you?"

Megan snorted.

He kissed the top of her hair, and she wrapped her arms around his torso. "Hey, it could happen. I'm not perfect."

She looked up at him. "I know that."

"I mean, look at this. Clearly, I could have done a better job explaining myself."

Megan shook her head. "That was my fault. I shouldn't have jumped to conclusions."

Being with Paul was a roller coaster of sorts. They had the friendship thing down, now they had to figure out if it could be more than that. He was right. It was going to take time.

"I've never been in a situation like this," Megan admitted.

She seemed to take him off guard with her comment. "What do you mean?"

"I've never been friends with a guy first."

"Never?" Paul looked somewhat horrified.

"Never."

"Well, I've already expressed my opinion of the guys you used to date." He reached once more for the food, and handed her one of the little sandwiches she'd made.

She took what he offered, and thought about what he said. "Does it bother you that I've been with so many men?"

They'd pulled the covers up around their lower halves, but other than that they were naked. Maybe it wasn't the right time to bring something like that up, but Megan had always been one to speak her mind, no matter the situation. Of course, it had gotten her into trouble more times than she could count.

"The truth?" he asked.

"Always."

Paul dropped his arms from around her, and he sat up a little straighter. Megan matched his posture. He clasped his hands together in his lap and met her gaze. "I try not to think about it."

"Because it does bother you." She knew they had to get it all out in the open.

"A little, yes."

Megan nodded, and bowed her head. Never before had she regretted the number of partners she'd had. "I figured it might. You've only been with one other person."

He sighed and reached for her again. She went willingly, needing to feel the security of his arms. "This isn't going to be easy, you know. We're very different."

"I know. I don't expect it to be easy. I've tried easy, and it's not all it's cracked up to be."

"How about we take it one step at a time? We have three weeks to see if we can make this work before Chloe comes home," Paul said.

"Right."

They went back to eating the food she'd made, but this time they kept one arm around the other. As they ate, they talked about their day. Megan had spent most of it doing laundry from her trip and going to the grocery store.

Most of the food she'd placed in the basket was gone, but neither of them seemed to have any desire to move from the bed. Megan rested her head on Paul's chest while he ran his fingers up and down her spine.

"Have you thought any more about where you'd like to go Friday night?"

Megan glanced up, and then went back to playing with the curly hairs at the base of his stomach. "Do you like to dance?"

He chuckled. "I haven't danced in years. Not since high school."

"So is that a no?" she asked.

"No. It isn't a *no*. It's an *I have no idea*. Do you?"

"I love to dance." Megan smiled.

"Do you want me to see if some of the guys at work can suggest something? I'm sure there's a club in Indianapolis where we could go."

She loved that he was willing to do something out of his comfort zone for her, but Paul wouldn't know what he was looking for. "I have a better suggestion. Why don't you let me take care of it? I've got time during the day with Chloe gone anyway, and I don't want to take time away from your case. I know it's important to you."

Paul kissed her forehead and eased them further under the covers. "I think I'm showing my age. It feels wrong for you to plan our date when I'm the one who asked you out."

Megan turned over on her belly so that her face was only inches from his. "Do you know how sweet it sounds to me that you actually care about that?"

He pushed the hair back from her face. "That's me. Sweet."

She smiled. "You are. Sweet, and sexy, and . . ."

"And?"

"And . . ." Megan trailed her palm down his chest, and wrapped her hand around his length.

"Megan? Maybe we should finish talking about this first. I mean, it's still early, we can—"

Megan cut off his protest with a bone-searing kiss. When she removed her lips from his, she went to work on his neck. She loved the way his body felt under her lips and hands. She loved his reactions. Everything about Paul was honest. He didn't pretend to be something he wasn't. No, he wasn't perfect, but she would take his imperfections over lies any day.

As Megan continued to lick and suck on the skin around his neck and shoulder, Paul threaded his fingers through her hair. She wasn't sure if he was trying to encourage her or stop her. Either way, Megan was loving it. "Go ahead. I'm listening."

He laughed, but there was no humor in it. "I can't think with you touching me like this."

She smiled against his neck, and took a section of his skin between her teeth, worrying it. "Sure you can."

Paul groaned. "What were we even talking about?"

Megan laughed and pushed herself up so that her forehead was touching his. "You were disagreeing with me finding you sweet and sexy."

"Was I?"

She nodded. "Uh-huh."

They stared at each other for several beats before Paul brought her face down to his. Megan always enjoyed kissing—mainly because it almost always led to other things. While she couldn't wait to make love to him again, she could also go on kissing him all night. It wouldn't be the same, but there was also something about it that felt as if they were connecting on a different level. Not only the kissing, but the touching—the caressing. The way he held her made her feel like she was precious to him.

Eventually, the kissing built to the point where they both needed more. Paul dug one of the condoms she kept in her bedside table out of the drawer, and they were soon connected in the most intimate way. They had a long way to go, and a lot of things to figure out, but she would take it. Paul was special. All she had to do was get him to see it, too.

CHAPTER 21

MEGAN STOOD on her tiptoes and wrapped her arms around Paul's neck to kiss him goodbye on Friday morning. The last three days had been good. Really good. They were beginning to settle in to being a couple.

"Unless something comes up, I'll be home a little after five." Paul held her close, showing no sign of wanting to let her go.

"I'll probably be upstairs getting ready."

He kissed her again, trailing one hand down her spine until he was cupping her backside.

She giggled. "You know you're going to be late if you don't leave soon."

Paul groaned and reluctantly released her. "I'll see you tonight."

Megan waved goodbye as he left. Tonight was their date, and she was beyond excited.

Once Paul was out of sight, she headed upstairs to finish getting ready for the day. She had a lot of things to do. Not to get ready for the date, but to keep herself busy so the day wouldn't feel as if it were dragging on forever. Grabbing her purse, she locked up the house and made her way to her car. Her first stop was to the nail salon. Megan wanted to look her best for their date, so she was treating herself to a manicure and pedicure. She'd also bought a new dress for the occasion.

On her way out of the salon, Megan spotted Paul and Detective Davis across the street. She debated whether or not to make her presence known, but the decision was made for her when Paul noticed her. He looked confused. She hadn't told him she was coming down to campus, but it wasn't like she normally cleared her day with him ahead of time.

She waited as Paul said something to his partner and then crossed the street. "Hey. I didn't know you'd be here."

"I didn't know you'd be here either."

Megan had to press her hands against her sides to keep from reaching for him. He was working. It wouldn't be appropriate if she threw herself at him, would it?

Paul glanced over his shoulder and nodded in his partner's direction. "We're here working a case."

Megan smiled and held up one of her hands. She'd picked vixen red as her color to match the dress she'd chosen for that night. "Getting my nails done."

He raised his eyebrows. "Interesting color choice."

She knew she probably shouldn't, but Megan couldn't resist. Taking a step forward, she got close enough to whisper so only he could hear. "I thought it would look good later tonight as I'm running my hands all over your body."

Paul sucked in a breath and averted his gaze. "Tease."

Megan laughed.

"Are you on your way home, then?" He tried to discreetly adjust himself and divert her attention.

This only made her smile wider. "Not yet. I'm taking a summer class, and I need to stop by the bookstore to pick up a couple of textbooks."

He furrowed his brow. "Be careful, okay?"

"All right. Is there something going on?" she asked.

Paul hesitated, and she knew he was debating how much to tell her. She also realized that because he was choosing his words carefully, the answer to her question was yes.

"It's okay. I get it. You can't talk about it. I'll be extra careful. Promise."

He took a deep breath and released it. "Thank you."

Megan smiled, trying to ease the tension the subject matter had created. "I'll let you get back to work."

Paul seemed reluctant to leave, but then he nodded. "I'll see you at home."

She watched as Paul jogged back across the street to rejoin his partner. He waved to her and Megan waved back before she walked the short distance to her car. Slipping inside, she started the engine, and pulled away from the curb.

A few minutes later, Megan pulled into the small parking lot outside the campus bookstore and library. The two buildings were connected, which she loved. It meant that she could pick up her textbooks and any research materials she needed, all in the same stop. A win-win in her opinion.

On her way inside, Megan spotted Jay—the patrol officer Paul had tried to set her up with. He wasn't in his uniform, so she had to assume he was off duty. "Jay!"

He smiled when he saw her. "Megan."

Now that he wasn't being thrown at her as a possible suitor, Megan was genuinely happy to see him. "How have you been?"

"Good. You?"

Megan smiled. "I'm good."

Jay looked behind him at the library, and then back at her. "So are you a student here?"

"Yeah. I've been taking some classes online. I still prefer textbooks to the online manuals. There's something about being able to flip through the pages and highlight what I'm needing." Considering how much she loved technology, using electronic textbooks had never appealed to her. She had tried it with her first online class, but had ended up breaking down and buying the book anyway. This time, she decided she wasn't even going to bother with the online version.

"Ah. A woman after my own heart."

They both laughed.

"So what about you? Are you a student here, too?" Megan asked.

To her surprise, Jay blushed. "Yeah. I'm taking some classes in criminal psychology."

"That's great." Megan was truly happy for him.

"Do me a favor, though, will you?"

She was thrown for a minute by the change in his demeanor.

"Don't tell anyone that you saw me here, all right? I-I don't want anyone at the station finding out."

Megan didn't understand why he wouldn't want anyone to know he was taking classes, but she figured that was his business. "Sure. I won't say anything."

He smiled. "Great. Thanks. Well, I'll let you get back to whatever. It was great seeing you again, Megan."

"You, too."

Jay breezed past her, and she resumed her way into the bookstore.

Inside the building, Megan located the classic art section, and began browsing through the textbooks. She knew what she was looking for, so it was only a matter of finding it.

A man wearing a red apron with the school logo on it approached her. "May I help you?"

She smiled and handed him the list of books she needed.

"Ah, yes. We've got those right over here." He walked farther down the aisle and stopped in front of a large display. One by one, he plucked the books she needed off the shelf.

"Thanks."

He smiled back at her. "That's everything except for the one on Da Vinci. It's in our library section. Would you like me to show you?"

The man's help was saving her a lot of time, so she nodded. "That would be great."

Megan followed him into the connecting building and up a flight of stairs. She was learning that most places tucked their arts sections into a corner, and the campus library was no different. She followed the man across the room to the back corner. It was a place Megan imagined she'd be spending a lot of time in over the next few years if she hoped to finish her degree.

It took a few minutes, but the man was able to locate the book on DaVinci Megan was seeking.

"Thank you, so much. You just saved me an hour of searching."

"No problem. It's my job."

She smiled as she flipped through the book.

When she closed it and looked up, she'd expected the man to be gone. Most employees disappeared quickly once they were no longer needed— off to help someone else or get back to their regular work. He remained standing roughly three feet away from her, shifting his weight from side to side.

He noticed her staring at him, and cleared his throat. "Um. I . . ."

The man cleared his throat again. He appeared nervous. "I was wondering if . . . if maybe you'd . . . you'd like to . . . go out sometime."

Megan was completely caught off guard. "You're asking me out?" He nodded.

Although the man was cute in a nerdish sort of way, her heart already belonged to another. "I'm sorry. I can't. I'm seeing someone."

He sagged his shoulders in defeat. "Oh. I understand."

Before she could utter another word, he was striding away from her. Megan was left feeling as though she'd done something wrong, when of course she hadn't. He'd asked her out, and she'd said no. So why did she feel so bad about it?

Trying to push what had happened to the back of her mind, Megan took her items to the front desk so she could check out. She had a date to get ready for. Tonight was to be about her and Paul, and having fun together. In many ways, this would be a first for both of them, and she wanted it to be special.

Taking her bag of books, she headed to her car. With every step, she became more confident about tonight and what she had planned. She couldn't wait to get their date started.

✳

Paul was more unnerved by the sight of Megan than he should have been. He knew she took classes through the college, and he knew she'd been on campus before. For some reason, it had never crossed his mind to warn her to take extra precautions. Because of that, he spent the rest of the afternoon cursing himself. That, and as his date drew closer, the butterflies in his stomach were turning into something much more violent.

"Something bothering you, Daniels?" Janey asked when they finished talking with the president of the last fraternity house on their list.

He waited until they were in the car to answer her. "I just have a lot on my mind."

Paul pulled out into traffic and started toward the station. It was already after four thirty. He was going to be late. The good news was they were fairly sure they had found their Scott. He'd graduated the year before, thanks to some tutoring he received for a required math class. No one at the fraternity could remember the woman's name who had tutored Scott, but the timing fit. Their next move would be to track Scott down. According to his social media profile, he was still in the area.

Janey twisted in her seat. "About the case?"

"No." Paul debated whether or not to continue, but decided why not? "I have a date with Megan tonight."

"That's great. Where are you taking her?"

He shouldn't have been surprised at his partner's curiosity or her support. "I don't know. She offered to plan everything."

"Wow. I'm impressed. Somehow, I always pictured you as a take control kind of guy."

Paul grunted. "Normally I am. With Melissa I always planned our dates—even after we were married."

Janey nodded. "But with Megan, it's different?"

"Yeah. It is."

"That can be a good thing. As long as it's what you want." Janey leaned back in her seat and scanned their surroundings. They were passing through a residential area where there had been some recent break-ins. Although burglary cases didn't usually fall in their laps, keeping your eyes opened was a cop thing.

He was quiet until they turned onto the road that led to the station. "I like being with her. She . . . she makes me feel alive again."

His partner chuckled. "And for that reason alone, I would like her. Paul, you've grieved for Melissa long enough. It's time to move on. It's okay to move on. Don't you think that's what your wife would have wanted? For you to be happy?"

Paul nodded. It was the only response he could give since his throat constricted with the overwhelming emotion he felt.

As soon as the car was parked in its spot, Janey was out of the vehicle, and on her way inside the station. "Come on. Let's go get this paperwork done so you can get home to your hot date."

It took them over a half hour to log the necessary reports. Paul sent Megan a message to let her know he'd be late, and she responded with a quick, I'll be waiting. For some reason, Paul was expecting her to be agitated. She'd made plans, and his job was getting in the way.

Paul pulled up in front of his home at five forty-two. He was twenty-two minutes late.

Megan was coming down the stairs when he strolled through the door. "Hey. You're home."

She was dressed in a deep red dress that cut off around mid-thigh. It was fitted, and left very little to the imagination. He felt his lower half react almost instantly.

"You look amazing."

The smile that graced her features only made her more beautiful. She walked over to him, and gave him a soft, lingering kiss. "Thank you."

Seeing her like this made it easy to forget they had plans—plans that didn't include him ripping that dress off her. Paul had to remind himself that there would be time for that later. "Just let me go upstairs and change. Then we can go."

Megan showed no signs of being in a hurry. "Don't you want to shower? I don't mind waiting if you do."

"Yeah, I would. Are you sure you don't mind?" he asked.

She gave him another chaste kiss, and then walked over to the other side of the kitchen. "Not at all. We've got time."

"I'll be quick." Before he could be tempted any further, Paul raced up the stairs to his room.

It didn't take him long to shed his work clothes and hop in the shower. He did take some extra time shaving to make sure he didn't miss any unwanted hair. It was strange how much he felt like a teenager again. When you're with someone for so many years, you fall into a routine. They know you. You know them. The mystery fades. What's left is a level of companionship that can stand up to whatever the world throws at you. He missed that. But what he also found he missed was this—this edge of excitement, the unknown possibilities.

Finished grooming, Paul went to his closet to find something to wear. He opted for a dark gray dress shirt and a pair of light gray slacks. Paul debated on adding a tie, but decided against it. If they were going dancing, he wanted to be comfortable.

When he walked back downstairs, Megan whistled.

He laughed. "Thanks. Are you ready to go?"

"Yep. Ready when you are."

Paul offered her his arm. He led her to his car and opened the door for her. She pecked him on the cheek and then slid inside.

Once he was behind the wheel, Paul turned on the engine, and began backing out of the driveway. "Where to?"

She gave him directions, and they ended up about twenty minutes from his house at a little Japanese restaurant. After waiting in the lobby about fifteen minutes, they were escorted to their table and given menus. It had been a while since Paul had been to a place like this. Having a small child often meant steering restaurant selections to places that served more kid- friendly items. He didn't see many of those items on this restaurant's menu.

"I thought this would be good. Different," she said.

He looked up at her and nodded. "I don't see many things on here Chloe would be thrilled about."

Megan chuckled. "I know. Could you imagine how she'd react to sushi?"

Paul snorted. "We'd probably draw a lot of unwanted attention."

The server came to take their drink orders. They decided to order some sushi as well for an appetizer. Paul had never had it before, but Megan said she loved it when it was done right. He was willing to give it a try.

"How in the world did you go through thirty-six years of life and not eat sushi?" Megan asked as their food started to arrive.

He shrugged. "Never had it growing up, and once I was an adult, the opportunity never presented itself, I guess."

She picked up one of the pieces of sushi and held it up to him. "It's tuna." Paul opened his mouth and bit into the raw tuna and rice.

Megan waited for several seconds while he chewed. "What do you think?"

"It's different. Not bad. Just different."

Before she popped the remaining bit of tuna into her mouth, she pointed to the butterflied shrimp. "Give that one a try. If you like steamed shrimp, you'll like that one."

He did as instructed, and she was right. It was very similar to steamed shrimp, which he'd eaten numerous times at parties, dipped in cocktail sauce.

They finished off the sushi Megan ordered—some he liked more than others. The best part, though, was when she wanted him to try a new one and would feed it to him. He wasn't sure why he found that appealing, but he did. Maybe it was how her face lit up, or how she'd bounce slightly in her seat as she waited for his reaction.

By the end of dinner, Paul had to admit he was enjoying himself. The food was good and the company was even better. He and Megan had always been able to talk. Paul had feared that maybe changing the parameters of their relationship would alter that, but thus far, it hadn't. If anything, it had opened the conversation up more.

"You ready to go dancing, old man?" Megan teased as they ambled out of the restaurant.

He pulled her against him, and walked her backward until she was pressed against the cool metal of the car. At first their age difference had truly concerned him, but the more they were together, the more he realized that it wasn't an issue. Not for her and not for him.

"I'll show you old," he whispered a moment before his lips crashed over hers.

By the time they broke apart, they were both panting. He raised his eyebrow, waiting for her to retract her original statement.

Instead, Megan sidestepped him, running her palm over his crotch as she moved to the passenger side of the vehicle. "It's a good start. Let's see how you do on the dance floor."

CHAPTER 22

PAUL WAS STILL SHAKING his head as he steered his car toward the club.

"You all right over there? Something wrong with your head?" Megan asked.

"My head is fine, you vixen. Other parts of my body—well, I'm not so sure."

She laughed. "You'll be fine. Besides, we're just warming up for later."

"Is that so?"

Before he could say anything else, his cell phone rang. It was after seven thirty, which meant it was most likely Chloe. He hadn't told his daughter, or Cindy, of his date with Megan. No one knew except his partner. It was easier that way.

"Can you answer it and put it on speaker since I'm driving?" he asked. Megan reached for the phone and hit the necessary buttons. She propped her elbow on the center console, and held the phone up where it would pickup his voice. "Hello, sweetpea."

His daughter's voice resonated in the close confines of the car. "Hi, Daddy."

The conversation lasted for several minutes as Paul weaved through Friday night traffic. Megan sat stoically silent in the passenger seat, holding his phone. He saw her smile a couple of times as Chloe talked, but she kept her comments to herself.

When Chloe was finished, she passed the phone over to Cindy as per usual. Paul had told his mother-in-law that he most likely wouldn't be home when it was time for Chloe to call, so to phone his cell instead. Cindy hadn't asked, and he hadn't gone into detail as to why.

"How are things?" Cindy asked.

He glanced over at Megan. She was busying herself looking out the window at the passing buildings.

Paul came up to a traffic light and made a left before answering. "Things are good here. Work is keeping me busy."

She paused. "And how's Megan?"

Megan glanced over and met his gaze. "She's good, too."

"Paul, please tell me you aren't fooling around . . . with that girl." Cindy lowered her voice for the last part, presumably to keep Chloe from overhearing.

He watched as Megan's eyes widened in shock at the obvious disapproval. "Cindy, my relationship with Megan—whatever it may be—is between me and her. I know you're concerned, and I appreciate it, but I'm asking you to please butt out."

Cindy was quiet for longer than was natural. "What if—"

"There will always be what ifs, Cindy."

He heard sniffling from the other end of the line. "I have to go give Chloe her bath. Good night, Paul. Stay safe."

"Cindy?"

His question was met with dead air.

Megan lowered the phone and placed it back in the center console where Paul always kept it while driving. "Well, that was interesting."

"I'm sorry about that. I thought she and I had already had this discussion. I didn't realize she'd bring it up again."

"So you knew she disapproved of us?" Megan asked.

Paul glanced over at her. He didn't like that Megan was frowning. They'd been enjoying themselves. He wanted to see her smiling again, but he figured it was best to get it out in the open. They'd agreed to be honest with each other, after all. "It's not that she disapproves. She's worried."

"About what?"

There was no easy way to say it, so he decided to spit it out. "Chloe. Cindy is afraid that you'll . . . get bored."

Megan turned in her seat. "Bored? With what? You? Chloe? Having a place to call home? Someone I can trust won't walk out on me as soon as things get tough?"

He knew she was upset, and it wasn't what he wanted. They were supposed to be on a date. Having fun. "Yes. She's worried about all those things."

"Are you?" He heard the challenge in her voice.

"Not as much as I used to be."

Anger turned to hurt. "That means you still are. At least, some part of you is."

Paul reached out and took hold of one of Megan's hands. She pulled it out of his reach.

Frustrated because driving limited his actions, he found the closest parking spot, and pulled over. Once his hands and attention were free, he released both their seat belts, and reached for her.

She resisted a little, but after he persisted, she allowed him to pull her into his arms. It was awkward, given they were in his car, but he had to do something. Ten minutes ago, they had been laughing and teasing, and then one phone call with his mother-in-law and her feelings were hurt.

"I'm sorry. Cindy didn't say those things to hurt you," he whispered.

Megan shook her head against his shoulder. "I don't care about what Cindy says or thinks. I care about what you think—how you feel."

He sighed. "I'm not going to lie and say I don't have doubts. I do. But every day we're together, they get quieter. I'm starting to believe this can work."

She sat up so that he could see her face. "Really? You're not just telling me what I want to hear?"

Paul brushed the hair away from her face. "Really."

A second later, Megan's lips were covering his, and her tongue was inside his mouth. He kissed her soundly for several minutes, and then forced them apart. They were both breathing hard again, and the semi-erection he'd been sporting since the restaurant was tenting his pants.

"We should get going." He had no idea how he managed to get the words out or sound so rational.

Megan licked her lips and lowered herself back into her seat. She was smiling once more.

When he continued to sit there, she smirked, and ran her hand from his knee to his thigh. "Were you planning to get to the club at some point tonight, or did you want to go straight home?"

He removed her hand to a safe distance and took a deep breath. "Behave."

She pouted. "Where's the fun in that?"

Paul laughed and started driving again. "You don't make it easy, you know."

"Easy is boring."

It was his turn to frown.

"Oh, stop looking like that. You are anything but easy, and neither am I. We both have baggage out the wazoo."

Megan was right. He was still dealing with the loss of his wife, and she had a rocky past that tainted her outlook on life and relationships. "I think we're doing pretty good so far. Don't you?"

She didn't answer right away, but he felt her gaze on him. "Yeah, I do."

Paul laced their fingers together, and brought the back of her hand up to press against his lips. "Good. Now, where exactly is this club?"

***

Megan was trying her best to let what Cindy said roll off her back, but it was nagging at her. Was Paul right? Was Cindy only worried about Chloe? Or was it more than that?

They drove by the club and found a place to park a few blocks away. Paul walked around the car and helped her out of the vehicle.

He must have realized something was still bothering her. "Hey, are you all right?"

"Yeah, I'm good." She gave him the best smile she could manage.

Paul wasn't buying it. "You're still upset by what Cindy said."

She nodded.

He crushed her against his chest and brushed the side of his cheek against hers. It was completely smooth—smoother than she'd ever felt it. And he smelled divine. She'd have to ask him sometime what cologne he was wearing so she could stock up.

His voice vibrated against her ear. "Don't be. What she thinks doesn't matter. This is about us."

Megan held on tight, not wanting to let him go. "You don't care that she doesn't approve?"

Paul shrugged. "She didn't approve of me at one point, so no."

She leaned back and quirked an eyebrow at him. "Cindy didn't approve of you?"

"Neither did George. Although, I don't think it was me, specifically. I think it was more they didn't like the fact that their sixteen-year-old daughter was dating. Since having Chloe, I'm beginning to understand. I'm fairly certain I'm not going to enjoy her teenage years."

Paul grimaced, and Megan laughed.

They began walking hand in hand toward the entrance to the club.

"I'm sure you'll do fine. Somehow, I imagine you being a cop will make any of Chloe's suitors think twice about doing anything stupid."

He kissed the top of her head as they approached the door. "I hope you're right."

Megan had done a lot of research to find a club she thought they would both enjoy. This one was a little more subdued than some she'd found, but she didn't think Paul would be able to relax and have a good time at one of the more trendy locations.

As they made their way inside, she recognized various parts of the club from the online pictures. The walls were painted a dark blue, but there were lighter accents throughout. To their right was a long bar that stretched almost the entire length of the wall. On the left there were tables and booths—most of which were occupied. The center of the room was dedicated to a large dance floor with a stage at the back. An all-male band was currently playing an upbeat dance track she recognized from about five years ago.

"Come on, let's see what kind of dance moves you have."

She dragged him by the hand through several groups of people until they were near the center of the dance floor. Ignoring convention, Megan rested her arms on Paul's shoulders, and began swaying her hips to the beat.

Following her lead, Paul placed his hands on her hips, and matched her movements.

By the end of the song, Megan was no longer worrying about Cindy. "You're not bad."

He laughed. "I never said I was bad, only that it had been a while."

The next song was a little slower, so Megan took the opportunity to press their bodies together. It was still a dance beat, but it almost reminded her of the steady rhythm of lovemaking. She took advantage and ground her pelvis into his.

Paul looked around frantically, but when he realized that no one was paying the least bit of attention to them, he dug his fingers into her ass and mimicked the motion. They danced like this for several songs, adjusting the timing of their movements to the beat. It was one of the sexiest things she'd ever done.

By the time the band finished their set, Megan was about to crawl out of her skin for want of him. The more they danced, the less it became about dancing and more about touching and rubbing against one another. All that was left was to shed their clothes and they would have been going at it like two rabbits in the middle of the dance floor.

Paul guided her over toward the bar. "I need something to drink."

Megan couldn't agree more. She was parched. Problem was she didn't think anything at the bar was going to quench her thirst—not entirely, anyway.

Since he was driving, Paul ordered himself a coke. Megan got a margarita. They took their drinks across the room and found a table.

The club was noisy, but not so much that you couldn't hear the person next to you. It was another reason she'd chosen this particular club. It seemed classier than some of the others. That, and it wasn't marketed to college students. Most of the people present were in their twenties and early thirties, but the club didn't give off that sorority/fraternity vibe.

"Are you having a good time?" Megan asked.

He took a drink of his coke and leaned in close to whisper in her ear. "I can't believe you're asking me that."

She ran a hand along his thigh, and this time he didn't stop her. "Well, I didn't want to assume . . ."

Paul shocked her when he grabbed hold of her wrist and placed her hand over his crotch. He was hard and pulsing against her palm.

Megan swallowed and met his heated gaze. "I'll be back."

Removing her hand from his lap, she stood, and made a beeline for the bathroom. Once inside, Megan splashed some water on her neck so as not to ruin her makeup. She needed to cool down. The whole point of tonight was for them to get out and have some fun. In public. To see if they could be a couple outside the confines of Paul's house.

She took a deep breath and waltzed back out into the main room of the club. Halfway back to their table, Megan caught sight of Paul. He looked somewhat lost sitting there all alone. She knew exactly how to remedy that.

"You ready to take another go at the dance floor?"

"Don't you want to finish your drink first?" he asked.

Megan picked up her margarita, took a long sip, and then reached for his hand. "I can multitask."

The floor was more crowded this time, so Megan and Paul stuck to the outside of the designated dance floor. They swayed their hips to the music, commenting every now and then on the song or the original artist. She was having fun, and he was, too.

After a second full set from the band, Megan was ready to call it a night. They'd been teasing each other for almost two hours. All she wanted was to find a flat surface, lift up her skirt, and have him buried deep inside her. Paul was a cop, though, so she knew better than to suggest they find a dark corner to slake their lust.

It took almost forty minutes for them to get home. By then, Megan was rubbing her legs together in an attempt to stave off the need to jump him. As it was, as soon as he'd parked the car in the driveway, Megan popped the button on her seat belt, and crawled across the console into Paul's lap.

Her ass hit the steering wheel, beeping the horn. She shifted a little, and then she heard Paul release his own seat belt and felt him slide the seat back as far as it would go.

"I want you," she murmured against his lips. His response was a strangled moan.

Paul snaked his hands beneath her skirt, pushing it up around her waist. With the newfound freedom of movement, Megan parted her legs, and straddled him. He took hold of her hips and rotated his pelvis, giving her the friction she desired.

"W-we should go inside." His voice was strained as Megan continued to move against him. Her dress was up around her waist, and one of her breasts was exposed. They were making out like teenagers.

But they weren't teenagers, and what Megan wanted to do to him was anything but childish.

After a long kiss, Megan reluctantly removed herself from Paul's lap. His hair was sticking up in spots, and half his shirt was unbuttoned. She also thought she saw a wet spot on his slacks.

He moved first. "Come on. Let's get inside before I forget all common sense and take you here, despite the consequences."

Megan would have laughed, but she felt the same way. She needed him, and she was past caring about their surroundings.

They made it as far as the kitchen. He shut the door, flipped the lock, and then reached for her.

Clothes disappeared quickly after that. They were inside their home with no one else around. All that mattered was her and Paul.

He laid her flat out on the kitchen table and spread her legs. She was naked and more than ready for him. Paul had the patience of a saint, though. No matter how much she tried to hurry him along, he was determined to pleasure her first.

Megan threaded her fingers through his hair as he knelt between her legs. She closed her eyes and let the feelings overwhelm her. *I love you.*

Her world shattered, and her heart beat with every bit of love she felt for him. As he moved up her body, covering her, Megan wanted more than anything to tell him how she felt. But she wasn't sure he was ready for that yet.

So instead of declaring her love for him, Megan let her body do the talking. She plunged her tongue inside his mouth, tasting herself on him. Paul hummed in response, meeting every thrust of her tongue with one of his own.

"Upstairs," he said in between kisses. "No condoms . . . down here."

The last thing on Megan's mind was condoms. She wanted him, and she wanted him now. "I'm on birth control. And I'm . . . I'm clean."

He stopped, and she groaned. "Are you sure?" he asked.

Megan ran her fingers along his face and met his gaze. "I'm sure."

Paul appeared to debate with himself for half a second. Then he reached between them and positioned himself at her entrance. She pushed her hips forward, encouraging him.

As he slid inside her for the first time without protection, Megan had to bite her lip not to scream out. It was the best feeling.

"You okay?" Beads of sweat dotted Paul's forehead.

She raised up to lick his lips with the tip of her tongue. "I'm more than okay. You?"

He closed his eyes and started to move. "You feel amazing. I want . . ."

Megan was trying not to get lost in how good everything felt. "You want what?"

"I don't want to stop. Ever."

Paul picked up his pace, and she knew he wouldn't be able to hold on much longer. They'd been teasing each other all night. It was one of the things she loved about dancing. When done right, it was the perfect aphrodisiac.

Suddenly, he was pulling out of her, and she felt bereft. "What—"

Without saying anything, Paul led her up the stairs. She had no idea what was going on. Maybe he'd changed his mind about the condom, although she really hoped that wasn't the case. Megan had gotten a taste of what making love to him was like without anything between them, and she wasn't sure she ever wanted to go back.

He surprised her when he bypassed her room and continued on to his.

She looked at him with a startled expression. "Paul, we don't—"

"Shh," he said as he pulled her flush against him once more.

Paul kissed her thoroughly until she was barely able to remember her own name, let alone whatever it was she was going to say.

He guided her over to the bed and eased her down onto the mattress. As he hovered over her, Megan saw something change in him. For the first time, she believed that Paul might actually be able to love her.

MEGAN LAY SPRAWLED out on her back, trying to catch her breath. She'd had great sex before, but the last few hours had completely blown her previous experiences out of the water. And that didn't even count the added sensation of him not wearing a condom.

Once Paul brought them to his bedroom, it was as if he'd wiped the slate clean, and they'd started from scratch. She couldn't remember how many times she'd climaxed. Six times? Maybe it was seven. The amount really didn't matter. What did matter was how attentive he'd been. By the time he found his own release, her entire body was vibrating with pleasure, and it felt as if all her bones had been liquefied. Maybe it was because he was older, but it seemed he knew exactly where to touch her to make her body sing.

She felt the mattress move beside her, and then the next thing Megan knew Paul's arm wrapped around her stomach. He pulled her flush against his chest, and she rolled over so that he could spoon her from behind. Megan knew things would be different with Paul—she loved him. What she hadn't expected was how overwhelming it would feel. If something happened and she lost him, she didn't know what she would do.

The deep rise and fall of Paul's chest told her he'd fallen sleep. It took much longer for sleep to claim Megan. Before, she hadn't fully understood what he must have gone through when he lost his wife, but she did now. She wondered how he'd survived it.

But she knew the answer to that, too. Chloe. She had been his reason for living—what kept him going for so long.

Megan's heart broke for all the pain he must have endured. More than anything, she wanted Paul to be happy, and she wanted to be part of that happiness.

Eventually sleep claimed her, and she woke up to something tickling her cheek. Blinking open her eyes, Megan turned to see Paul propped up behind her, smiling. He had a tiny feather—most likely gleaned from one of the pillows—pinched between two fingers.

He leaned down to give her a brief kiss. "I was wondering if you were going to sleep the day away."

She craned her neck to the side and stretched. Her muscles ached in a very good way. "What time is it?"

"After ten."

That surprised her. "Aren't you going in to work today?"

Paul shrugged. "I need to go in at some point for a few hours. It can wait, though."

He kissed her again, but this time there was nothing quick about it. When he tried to deepen the kiss, however, she turned her head. "I should go brush my teeth."

"I don't care about that," he grunted into her neck.

She laughed. "Yes, well, I do."

He sighed and released her. "Fine. Go brush your teeth and get dressed. I'm taking you out for breakfast. Or I guess it might be lunch by the time we get there."

Megan punched him lightly on the arm before hopping out of bed. "I'll meet you downstairs in fifteen minutes."

The sound of his laughter echoed down the hall after her as she dashed into her room to get ready. She gathered her hair up into a ponytail and took one of the quickest showers of her life. Throwing on some underwear, a pair of jeans, and a fitted T-shirt, Megan added a pair of flats and she was set. She arrived downstairs with a minute to spare.

Paul was already in the kitchen. His eyes nearly bugged out of his head when he saw her.

"What?" she asked, thinking maybe she'd forgotten something important.

He shook his head. "You look about sixteen with your hair pulled up like that."

Megan grinned. "Afraid someone will think you're robbing the cradle, Detective?"

She was expecting him to come back with some sort of an affirmative, but he didn't. Instead, Paul backed her up against the wall, and kissed the daylights out of her.

When he released her, he had a smug look on his face. "There. I've been waiting to do that since I woke up this morning."

Megan was still trying to get her bearings when they climbed into his car. "Our age difference doesn't bother you anymore?"

She had to ask. In the past, it had bothered him a great deal.

"No." He shot her a glance as he pulled into the restaurant parking lot. Paul turned off the engine, but neither made any move to go inside.

"What changed?" she asked.

She felt something shift in the atmosphere around them.

He reached for her hand and met her gaze. "I realized that you were right. We're both adults, and as long as it's what we both want, then the rest shouldn't matter."

"Wow."

Paul cupped the back of her head with his free hand, and brought her mouth to meet his. The kiss was slow, and it reminded her of the night before when he'd all but worshipped her body from head to toe.

She held tight to him, not wanting to let go. Her thoughts from the night before came back to the forefront, and she wanted so badly to tell him how she felt.

He rested his forehead against hers. "Let's go eat. Something tells me I'm going to need my energy later."

Megan laughed and scraped a manicured nail down the back of his neck. "I think you might be psychic."

They ended up sitting side by side in a back corner booth. The food was good, but it was made better when Paul started feeding her bites of his Belgian waffle. He always made sure his aim was slightly off so she'd get whipped cream on her face. She couldn't really complain, since he was right there to lick it off for her. Megan had never imagined Paul with a playful side, but she loved every minute of it.

Nearly two hours later, they were on their way home. She knew he would be leaving for work soon, but the selfish part of her didn't want him to go.

"Something wrong?" he asked as he pulled into the driveway.

She shook her head. "Not really. I'm just enjoying our time together so much I don't want it to end."

He entwined their hands, and squeezed. "I'll be gone three . . . four hours at most."

"I know. Don't mind me. I'm being silly."

Paul was quiet for a long moment. "You're not being silly. It's different now."

She knew he was talking about them. "Yeah, it is."

They sat there holding hands until Paul broke the silence. "I'm not sure how things will be once Chloe comes home. I don't know how she'll react. To us being together, I mean."

"I think she'll be fine. She was worried about you having a girlfriend, after all."

"What? When?" Paul demanded.

Megan laughed. "Don't look so shocked. Chloe picks up on things like how all her friends' parents are either married or they have girlfriends or boyfriends."

"She asked you about this?" He sounded as if she'd knocked his legs out from under him.

"She did."

Paul shook his head. "Why didn't you tell me?"

"Would it have changed anything? She asked me months ago, and I explained it to her the best way I could."

"I still should have known." He was upset.

"Paul, you can't know everything." He started to interrupt her, but she pushed on, cutting him off. "Are you more upset that I didn't tell you or that she asked in the first place?"

He opened his mouth and then closed it. "I don't know."

Megan leaned her head on his shoulder, and he rested his cheek against her hair. "You don't have to have all the answers, you know."

"Then why does it feel like I should?" he asked.

She tilted her head so she could look up into his face. Megan's eyes drifted to his lips, and she pulled his mouth down to hers. "You don't have to do it all on your own anymore."

They kissed until his phone started vibrating. He seemed reluctant to burst the bubble they were floating in. "I should get that."

"You should," Megan said, putting some distance between them. He picked up the phone and answered it. "Daniels."

After a few seconds, Megan realized it was his partner.

"I'll be leaving the house in a few minutes. Yes, I know. Can it, Davis. I'll see you when I get there."

When he hung up the phone, Megan could have sworn he was blushing. "Everything okay?"

He sighed. "Everything's fine. Janey's just giving me a hard time because I told her we had a date last night. She's letting her imagination run wild."

Megan perked up. "You told her about our date?"

"Yeah. Although now I'm rethinking the wisdom of that decision."

She ran her fingers along his jaw before letting her hand fall. "Don't be. She wouldn't be giving you a hard time if she didn't care. I'll let you get to work."

Paul caught her hand as she was stepping out of the car. He didn't say anything—just met her gaze and held it for a long moment before letting her go.

***

As Paul drove toward the station to meet Janey, he couldn't get what Megan had said out of his head. *You don't have to do it all on your own anymore.* He'd been doing it on his own for a long time. But then he realized that ever since Megan entered their lives, that had begun to change. She was so much more than a nanny—she always had been. Even from the beginning.

Her revelation about Chloe asking about him having a girlfriend was eye-opening. It hadn't crossed his mind that his daughter would worry whether or not he had a woman in his life. What else didn't he know about?

Janey was waiting outside for him when he pulled into the parking lot. She opened his passenger side door and got in. No words were spoken, but he could tell she was dying to say something.

"Spit it out already."

"I think you're getting paranoid. I wasn't going to say anything," Janey said, acting all innocent.

Paul eyed her skeptically. "Sure you weren't."

"I'll just say this—"

"There it is."

She stuck her tongue out at him.

He laughed.

"As I was saying, before I was so rudely interrupted." Janey tilted her head forward, giving him one of those you-better-listen-if-you-know- what's-good-for-you stares. "You'd better not let her get away."

Paul flexed his fingers against the steering wheel. Something had occurred to him that morning as he and Megan were lying in his bed. He was in love. It had hit him out of the blue as he watched the sunlight dance across her face.

Something had prompted him to take her to his bed the night before. He hadn't understood it then, but when he'd woken up and felt her warm and soft beside him, he'd known. All his crazy arguments were gone. For whatever reason, Megan wanted to be with him, and he wanted that, too.

"Earth to Paul?"

He blinked and glanced over at his partner. "What?"

She smiled knowingly. "I asked you if Chloe's having a good time with her grandparents."

"Oh. Yeah. She's loving it. Ma's going to have her hands full, I think. Cindy and George are spoiling her rotten."

Janey laughed. "I'm sure she'll be fine. Your mom can always call your brothers if she gets desperate. Chloe's always been a sucker for her uncles."

"True," Paul said as he pulled up in front of Scott Parker's apartment. They'd debated on whether or not to show up at his place of employment, but decided maybe a one-on-one visit without an audience would be best.

Paul and Janey exited the vehicle and strolled up the short path to Parker's apartment. It was in a decent neighborhood—completely average. It was a direct contrast to the flashy persona their suspect presented online.

Janey knocked and they waited patiently for Parker to answer the door.

When the door was opened, however, they came face-to-face with a young woman with a baby on her hip. Although it was an unexpected development, he and Janey didn't react outwardly.

Paul showed the woman his badge. "Hello, ma'am. Is Scott home?"

The woman adjusted the baby, turned her back on them, and walked into the apartment. She left the door cracked open, and they could hear voices coming from inside.

Janey glanced in his direction, and he shrugged. Paul had no idea what was going on. After ten years on the force, not much surprised him anymore. That's also why he made sure not to let down his guard. People did weird things like run, jump out two-story windows . . . you name it, and he'd probably seen it.

Luckily, the only thing they got this time was a groggy-looking man in his mid-twenties who looked as if he'd had one too many the night before.

"Scott Parker?" Janey asked.

"Yeah. Who wants to know?"

They both flashed their badges this time, and he squinted like he was looking into the sun. "What did I do?"

"May we come inside?"

Parker shifted his gaze to Paul, and backed into the apartment. It appeared neither Parker nor the woman were overly talkative.

When Paul and Janey entered the apartment, the first thing they noticed were the toys scattered around the living room floor. It was obvious from what he could see that the baby lived in the apartment, or had at least been there for an extended period of time.

Once they were all seated, Janey started in on the questioning. "Mr. Parker, last year you received some tutoring for a math class, is that correct?"

Parker rubbed his eyes and blinked. "Yeah. That's right."

"Was your tutor's name Jessica Chase?" Paul asked.

The young woman hovered in the background, curious, but not participating. Parker didn't seem bothered by her presence. "Yeah. She helped me get through my class. Why?"

They ignored his question. "And how long did you meet with Ms. Chase?"

Parker appeared to do some calculations in his head before he answered Janey. "About two months."

"So you stopped meeting with her in . . ."

"August? Yeah. It was August."

"Do you remember when exactly in August? Janey prompted.

"Hmm. I'm not sure. It was hot. I remember that. She wore this white tank top that showed off her tits."

"Thank you for that detailed description of Ms. Chase, Mr. Parker. Could you tell us where you used to meet Ms. Chase?" Paul was hoping it was somewhere on campus. That would positively put her in the same location as the other victims.

"In the library. I tried to get her to meet somewhere a little more . . . romantic, you know. I mean, the library?" His revulsion was evident. "Hey. Why are you asking all these questions about Jessica?"

Paul and Janey looked at each other, and then Paul shrugged.

Letting the cat out of the bag wasn't likely to hurt anything at this point. "Jessica Chase was murdered."

That sobered him some.

"Is there anything else—besides Ms. Chase's physical appearance—that you can remember about your last few meetings?" Paul asked.

"Oh, there was this dude. Yeah."

"What dude?"

Parker leaned forward in his seat to answer Paul's question. "Didn't get his name. He was some book nerd. I think he worked at the library or something."

"And what was it about this guy that makes you think we should talk to him?"

"Because he was weird. I mean he would hang around all the time. And I think he even asked her out." Parker's nose scrunched up in distaste.

Janey took down a description—or what Parker could remember, at least—of the man in question. They would have to take a trip to the library and see if they could locate him. As it was, they'd gathered as much information as they could from Scott Parker.

Twenty minutes after leaving Parker's apartment, they arrived back at the station. They both went inside to make a report of their activities.

It didn't take long for Paul to finish his paperwork. There wasn't all that much to report, after all. Parker had been moved way down on their suspect list, and the information they had on this library employee was sketchy at best.

Paul logged off his computer, and made sure he had both his cell phone and his keys. His mind was already on ways he and Megan could spend their evening.

Janey looked up from the report she was still working on. "Tell Megan I said hi."

Paul paused for a second before reaching for his jacket. "I will. See you Monday, Janey."

"You're not coming in tomorrow?" she asked. Then she shook her head. "Of course you're not. Go enjoy your new girlfriend. I'll be thinking of you while I'm sitting at home all alone eating bonbons."

He laughed and patted her on the shoulder as he went by. His partner had a very active social life. It was the main reason she always gave him such a hard time about his lack of one. "Enjoy your bonbons."

By the time Paul made it home, he was almost giddy. It was a strange way to describe a grown man, but that was how he felt. He was in love— something he never thought would happen to him a second time. It scared him to death, but he was through fighting it. He had a second chance at happiness, and he was going to take it.

PAUL STEPPED out of the shower on Monday morning with a smile on his face. Of course, that probably had a lot to do with how he'd been awakened. Not by an alarm clock, but by Megan. He'd opened his eyes to find her poised between his legs. It was one of those things wet dreams were made of, and he hadn't been dreaming.

When he arrived home late Saturday afternoon, they'd worked side by side in the kitchen to make dinner, and then spent the rest of the evening curled up on the couch watching a movie. It was a stark contrast to the high energy of the dance club, but that hadn't seemed to matter to either of them.

That night they once again slept in his bedroom—as they did Sunday night. Megan hadn't asked him about the change in venue, but he hoped she understood the significance. It was a big step for him, letting her into his personal space.

He was also trying to open up more and let her into his life. Although the thought of messing up again still haunted him, Paul was determined to give this relationship a go. Megan made him feel alive. When he saw that teasing glint in her eye, his heart skipped a beat. He was, beyond a shadow of a doubt, in love.

As Paul continued getting ready for work, he mused over the rest of their weekend. They'd spent Sunday working outside in the backyard. Megan and Chloe had started a flower garden along the back of the house, so Megan worked on that while he did the mowing and trimming. It was incredibly normal, and yet in some ways it felt extremely intimate to him.

After a long day outside, they'd ended up in his shower together. Megan had introduced him to shower sex. It might sound strange, but he and Melissa had never showered together, with the exception of her last two weeks of pregnancy. She'd had difficulty washing, and so he'd stepped in and helped. There hadn't been anything sexual about it, however. His wife had been miserable at the time as she counted down the days until Chloe was born.

Lifting his shirt collar, Paul situated his tie, and secured it around his neck. He flipped the collar down, and reached for his belt and holster.

Sometimes it felt odd to compare Melissa and Megan. They were complete opposites. But Paul supposed it was natural. Melissa had been the only other woman in his life. Outside of his parents, his relationship with her was the only thing he could use as a guide.

Although Megan was night and day different in personality to Melissa, there were similarities. He and Melissa used to stay up late into the night talking. It didn't matter the subject. More than once they'd both gotten in trouble with their parents for staying up well after midnight chatting on the phone when they were supposed to be asleep. Obviously with Megan, it was different—he was no longer a teenager sneaking around to talk to his girlfriend, but conversation came as easily with Megan as it had with Melissa.

There was also the chemistry. With Melissa, it had been a slow burning fire that would consume him. Megan drew from that same fire, but it was more of a flash flame. Every time he touched her, he wanted everything she had to offer and then some.

Slipping his jacket on, Paul made his way downstairs. When he strolled into the kitchen, Megan was flipping eggs, and humming to herself. She turned to smile at him when she heard him enter the room. "Did you enjoy your shower?"

That glint in her eye was back, and it had his body reacting despite the recent release it had. He walked over to where she was standing in front of the stove, and pulled her back against him with more force than necessary. "Yes, I enjoyed my shower. But not nearly as much as my wake-up call."

She giggled, and pushed him away with her hips. "Go pour yourself some coffee. Breakfast will be ready soon."

Normally he grabbed a muffin or some cereal before heading out to work, but he wasn't going to turn down a hot breakfast.

Doing as he was told, he went to retrieve his mug from the dishwasher. His hand covered the mug, and he froze.

Megan noticed. "Is something wrong?"

He shook his head and removed his hand. "No. Nothing's wrong."

Closing his eyes, he took a moment to let the conflicting emotions flow through him, and then searched in the cabinets for another mug for his coffee.

She didn't comment until she brought their food to the table and sat down beside him. "You're not using your regular coffee mug. Was there something wrong with it? Did the dishwasher not get it clean or something?"

Paul breathed deep and took a sip of his black coffee. It was bitter. He'd gotten used to having it doctored up with sugar and cream. He didn't look at Megan as he spoke. "It was Melissa's mug. She used it every morning for her coffee. I-I found it in the dishwasher the morning after the funeral."

Megan placed her hand over his. It was the only reaction she made to the information he shared.

"I don't know why, but I took it out and started using it. I even made my coffee the way she used to—three quarters coffee, two sugars, and fill the rest of the mug with milk. It was strangely comforting, so I kept doing it."

He looked up to find moisture in Megan's eyes. It wasn't the reaction he'd been expecting. But then again, Megan usually surprised him.

She blinked. "It made you feel close to her."

Paul nodded.

Their eggs were getting cold, but neither of them seemed to care.

They stared at each other for what felt like an eternity before Megan broke the silence. "You don't have to stop. Not because of me."

He glanced down at their hands—now clasped together on the table between them. "Yes, I do. This morning I realized that I was holding on to the past. Melissa isn't ever coming back, and no matter what I do, or how I drink my coffee, there is nothing I can do to change that. I can't give Chloe her mother back."

There was a catch in his voice as he said that last part. It was what he'd felt guilty about more than anything. His choices five years ago had stolen Chloe's mother away from her. That was something he would never forgive himself for.

"Paul, you didn't kill Melissa." Megan's voice was soft and soothing. She was more than he deserved.

"I did."

Megan opened her mouth again to contradict him, but he cut her off. "That's why I want you to know that I'm going to try my best not to make the same mistake again."

He looked her in the eye and took a deep breath. "I love you, Megan. I don't deserve this second chance, but for some reason you think I'm worth it, and I'm tired of fighting. You make me feel whole again."

Tears ran freely down her cheeks, and Megan didn't bother brushing them away. "You love me?"

Paul scooted his chair away from the table and knelt down beside her. He took her hands in between both of his and gazed up at her. "I'm sorry I pushed you away for so long. I know I must have hurt you."

She sniffed. "Say it again, please."

He rose up on his knees, bringing their faces level, and brushed her lips with his. "I love you."

Megan made a sound somewhere between a laugh and a cry. "I love you, too."

Their lips met in a heartfelt kiss.

"I don't deserve you," he mumbled.

She pressed her lips to his again. "Yes, you do."

***

He'd said it. Paul had told her he loved her. Megan had no idea what it would mean for their future, but she did know it meant Paul wanted one—a future—with her. He wouldn't have said it otherwise.

They had to warm up their breakfast in the microwave, but it was worth it. She kissed him goodbye, and started in on some housework. With Chloe gone, there wasn't much to do. Paul was surprisingly neat for a bachelor.

Megan was practically skipping as she got into her car around midday and drove into town. Since Chloe wasn't with her, she stopped off at the mall to pick up a few non-food items at her favorite department store. One could never have too many bra and panty sets, especially when there was someone to show them off to.

It turned out the store was having a sale, so Megan took her time going through all the items and picking out the ones she liked the best. She couldn't wait to see Paul's face when he saw them. One set was made of a very thin see-through material. She'd tried the bra on in the fitting room, and delighted at how it left very little to the imagination. It almost reminded her of those wet T-shirt contests, without the need for water.

As Megan was checking out, she had the distinct feeling that someone was watching her. She glanced behind her, but didn't see anyone looking in her direction. Everyone in her line of sight was busy shopping.

Taking her purchases, Megan walked back out into the main area of the mall. She didn't need anything else, but since it was rare she had the time to shop without a five-year-old in tow, she decided to browse. The whole time she felt as if something was off, but when she couldn't spot any valid reason for it, Megan pawned it off as paranoia.

After a relaxing lunch in one of the mall restaurants, she headed back to her car. She still had grocery shopping to do, and she wanted to make sure she had plenty of time to get home and cook dinner.

The grocery store was a little more crowded than she was used to. That was probably because it was later in the day. When she brought Chloe along with her, they typically came early in the morning. It was already after two.

Driving home was another exercise in patience. There was an accident and one of the main roads had been closed off. They were detouring everyone five miles out of their way in order to get around it. Megan was hoping the ice cream she'd bought wouldn't melt, considering it was nearly eighty degrees out. Air conditioning helped, but there was little she could do about the sun beating down in the backseat.

Eventually, she made it on the other side of the detour. The rest of the drive was, thankfully, uneventful.

She brought the food into the house and got it all put away before starting on dinner. There was a recipe she'd found online that she wanted to try, but it meant marinating the meat for at least two hours.

With that task completed, Megan grabbed her shopping bags, and started upstairs to put her new lingerie away. As she reached the top of the stairs, the phone rang. Not knowing who it was, but hoping it was Paul, Megan ran the few remaining feet into her room, and snatched the receiver out of its cradle. "Hello?"

"You sound like you're out of breath." Her sister's voice held a note of concern.

Megan felt a bit of disappointment that it wasn't Paul. "I just got back from the store."

"Get anything good?" Rebecca asked.

Setting her bags down on her bed, Megan began removing the items and laying them out on the mattress. She'd need to wash them before she could wear any of them. They'd all been in a large bin for people to sort through. It was hard to tell how many hands had been on them. "Just some new undies."

Her sister was too quiet.

"What?" Megan asked.

"You went to the store specifically to buy underwear?"

Megan wasn't getting what the big deal was. "Yeah."

She heard Rebecca release a heavy sigh.

"Would you just spit it out already?" Her sister didn't normally beat around the bush like this.

"Your shopping trip wouldn't have anything to do with that guy you were telling me about, would it?" Rebecca asked.

Why was it that her sister could make her feel as if she were twelve years old again and getting in trouble for eating a cookie before dinner? "Not entirely."

"Oh, Megan."

She could hear Rebecca's disappointment, but Megan refused to act ashamed of her relationship with Paul. Even though her sister had no idea Paul was the guy in question. "Don't say it like that. You can't tell me you've never bought sexy underwear to wear for Gage."

"That's different."

"How's it different?" Megan demanded.

"He's my husband."

"So you didn't dress sexy for him until after you married him? Please. You may be a stick in the mud sometimes, Becca, but even I know better than that." She hated fighting with her sister, but she wasn't going to back down on this. Rebecca needed to stop treating her like a child.

Her sister didn't answer immediately, and Megan was beginning to fear that Rebecca had run off in tears again.

"I don't want to see you get hurt again."

Megan sighed and sat down on the edge of the bed. "He won't hurt me. Not intentionally, anyway. You don't have to worry."

"So does that mean you and he are . . ."

"Yes." Megan smiled thinking back to earlier that morning when Paul told her he loved her.

"I see. So does that mean I get to meet him?" Rebecca asked.

"It's still new, but yeah. I think maybe we can arrange something soon." Although she and Paul hadn't talked about it in detail, they both knew that once Chloe returned home there would be no keeping their relationship secret. Given how their family was already connected, it would probably be better to come clean to everyone sooner rather than later.

"What's he like? Tell me about him."

Megan chuckled. "So the interrogation is about to start?"

"No interrogation. I promise. I'm just curious."

This was going to be tricky. Her sister was a private investigator. Megan knew Paul wanted to keep things quiet to their families for a little while longer, but she also knew that if she didn't give Rebecca something, her sister had the resources to start digging up info on her own. That wasn't how she wanted Rebecca or the rest of Paul's family to find out.

"Well, he's a lot different from the other guys I've dated. He has a job, for one thing."

Rebecca laughed. "That's a good start. What does he do?"

"I thought you said this wasn't an interrogation?"

"What? I can't even ask a question?" Megan could almost hear her sister rolling her eyes.

"No. You can't."

"All right. Fine. Go ahead. I'll try not to ask you anything," Rebecca said.

"Thank you."

Megan waited for several moments to see if her sister was going to keep her end of the deal before she continued. "He's good to me. And he can be really sweet. Friday night we went to a Japanese restaurant and I got him to try sushi for the first time. I don't think he liked all of it, but he tried everything because I asked him to."

"You're right. He does sound different from the others." Her sister almost sounded impressed. Or shocked. Either way, it meant that maybe Rebecca would cut her some slack.

"After that, we went dancing. It was a great date." Megan tried to keep the dreaminess out of her voice.

"You love him." Rebecca didn't ask it as a question. It was her sister's job to read between the lines.

Megan didn't bother to deny it. "Yeah. I do."

"And he feels the same way?" The worry was back.

"He does."

"Okay."

Megan's eyes widened with shock. "Okay? That's all you're going to say?"

"I'm going to try and trust you, all right? That's what you want, isn't it?" Rebecca asked.

"Thank you." Megan couldn't express how grateful she was to her sister. Rebecca had always been there for her, no matter how screwed up Megan's life got.

Figuring it was time to redirect the conversation, Megan brought up the one subject sure to get her sister talking. "So tell me about the nursery. Have you finished decorating yet?"

Sure enough, Rebecca began telling Megan about all the new additions to the nursery they'd made since she left. Even though it had only been a week, her sister described each new item, along with several other ideas she had for the baby's room. Apparently, Rebecca had found the perfect rocking chair at a flea market but hadn't been able to fit it in her car, so she'd sent Gage to pick it up in his SUV after practice.

In many ways, Gage and Rebecca were a lot like her and Paul. Not that Megan was anything like her sister, or even that Paul was remotely similar to Gage. It was more that Gage and Rebecca were very much opposites, and the same could be said for her and Paul. On the outside, they didn't seem to fit. But in reality, they were each other's perfect balance.

Megan and Rebecca continued to talk about babies and nursery decorations until Gage arrived home around four. Rebecca said goodbye with a reminder that she couldn't wait to meet Megan's mystery guy. Megan had no idea how her sister would react when she found out Paul was the guy, but she was hoping it would be a good thing. Paul was a good man. Rebecca knew that. Megan only hoped all that knowledge didn't go out the window when the truth came out into the open.

After hanging up with her sister, Megan took the time to wash her new acquisitions before going back downstairs to start dinner. She'd just put the chicken in the oven when there was a knock on the front door.

Wrinkling her nose, Megan wiped off her hands, and went to see who it was. She wasn't expecting anyone. Maybe it was one of the neighbor kids.

She rounded the corner and came face-to-face with the last person she thought she'd see on the other side of her door. Walking the few remaining steps, Megan pulled open the door, and smiled. "Jay. What are you doing here?"

CHAPTER 25

PAUL AND JANEY spent Monday morning going through the list of students and faculty the college finally sent over to them. Given the information they'd gotten from Scott Parker, they focused on the male library employees and student volunteers. It was a longer list than they would have liked, but by the time they left for the college, they were armed with some basic knowledge about each of their suspects.

It was after one by the time they arrived at the library. The college was currently in between sessions. Paul was hoping that didn't mean their killer had taken some time off due to the break.

When they walked inside the building, they split up. Janey went to take a look around—get a lay of the land—while Paul strolled over to the main desk. "Hello."

The young woman behind the desk glanced up from her computer. "May I help you find something?"

He smiled, attempting to put the young woman at ease. If she sensed something was wrong, she might attempt to alert the other members of the library staff, and that would only make his job harder. "I was wondering if you could point me in the direction of Mr. Chaney."

240

"The library director?"

"Yes. I was told I could find him here?" Again, Paul tried to keep his tone light and conversational.

"Um. He should be up in his office."

"And where is that exactly?" he asked.

"Oh. Up the stairs and to your right, there's a hallway. Follow that, and his office is the last door on the left. Did you want me to call up and see if he can come down to meet you?"

Paul shook his head. "No, that's all right. I'm sure I can find it."

As he headed toward the staircase, Paul locked eyes with his partner, and nodded toward the second floor. Janey tilted her head in assent and held her position. If the killer was on the premises, they might spook him. Having Janey remain near the entrance was a precaution. If someone suddenly made a beeline for the door, she'd be in a better position to intercept him.

Finding the director's office wasn't difficult. The hallway only had a total of six doors—three on each side—all with nameplates. Paul stood in front of Phillip Chaney's door and knocked.

A few seconds later a man not much older than Paul himself opened the door. "May I help you?"

"Mr. Chaney?" Paul asked.

"Yes?"

Paul showed the man his badge. "May I come in?"

The library director's eyes widened at the sight of Paul's badge, and he quickly motioned him inside. Mr. Chaney took a seat behind his desk, and Paul lowered himself into the chair nearest the door.

"Thank you for your time, Mr. Chaney. My name is Detective Paul Daniels."

It was always good to be polite in situations like these. Phillip Chaney, while not completely off their list of suspects, was a good way down the list. He was married with three kids, and he'd been the director at the college library for nearly ten years. There was nothing in his background that screamed "serial killer". He did, however, have direct contact with all the other library staff, and could be valuable in helping them narrow down their focus. It had already been a month since the last victim was found. If the killer held to his pattern, they had less than a month left before he killed again.

"What can I help you with, Detective?"

"Sir, I'm looking for a person of interest in a case I'm working on, and I believe he either works or volunteers here."

Shock crossed Mr. Chaney's features. "Who?"

"Well, Mr. Chaney, that's where I need your assistance. All I have is a description."

Mr. Chaney swallowed nervously. "And you want me to tell you who I think it is?"

"Exactly."

"But . . . but what if I get it wrong? I wouldn't want to point the finger at someone who's innocent," Phillip Chaney said.

"I only wish to ask this person some questions. He may have information on a murder investigation I've been working on."

"Murder?" Chaney's eyebrows disappeared above his hairline.

Paul kept his tone even and polite. "Yes. So will you help me?"

"Y-yes. Of course."

After giving Mr. Chaney the description Scott Parker had provided, Paul could tell the library director had a specific person in mind.

"Do you know who this might be, Mr. Chaney?"

"I-I think so."

Paul leaned back in his chair, feigning nonchalance. "Who, Mr. Chaney?"

The library director reached up to straighten his tie, almost as if it were suddenly too tight. "Adam Stalz."

"And is Mr. Stalz working today?"

Mr. Chaney turned to his computer, and after a few keystrokes, he nodded. "He's scheduled to work from three to nine."

Paul looked at his watch. It was almost two. They had an hour to kill before Adam Stalz made his appearance, so Paul decided to use the time wisely. "What can you tell me about Adam?"

By the time he left Mr. Chaney's office forty-five minutes later, Paul had a much better understanding of his suspect. Adam Stalz was a sophomore at the college. He'd gotten a job at the library roughly ten months ago to help pay for tuition. The timeline fit.

As Paul made his way downstairs to the main floor, he spotted his partner loitering in front of a bookcase not far from the library entrance. She met his gaze.

"I was beginning to think I'd have to send a search party in after you."

He smirked and shook his head. "Just getting some intel."

"A productive meeting, then, with the library director?"

"Very." Paul tilted his head, motioning toward a more isolated corner of the library.

Instead of saying the suspect's name, Paul found it on the list they'd been provided, and pointed it out to Janey. The chances they would be overheard were minimal, but he wasn't taking any chances. "Three o'clock."

Janey glanced down at her watch and nodded.

"I'm going to take up a position in the store, in case he enters from that end. I'll call if I spot him first. The director was kind enough to offer us his office if we need it," Paul said.

"Very generous of him." His partner never took her eyes off the door.

"Yes. Very."

Once everything was in place, Paul walked over to the other side of the building. It was more crowded than the library, but he supposed that made sense.

At two fifty-six, a young man meeting the description they'd been given entered the bookstore. Paul double-checked the picture they'd found off the Internet, and with the exception of his glasses and a slightly different hair color, it matched. He dialed Janey's number to let her know as he continued to follow the young man.

Stalz stepped behind the counter and retrieved what looked to be one of the aprons all the library staff wore, and then he crossed the room, walking right past Paul, and disappearing into a side room marked *Staff*.

Janey appeared from the adjoining building, and they closed in on the door their suspect walked through. No one seemed to be paying them any attention, which was good. The fewer people who knew what was going on, the better.

They were two feet away when Stalz reappeared. He noticed them, and although Paul could tell he was startled, Stalz grinned, and greeted them.

"Is there something I can help you with today?"

"Are you Adam Stalz?" Janey asked.

A look of apprehension crossed Stalz face. "Y-yes. That's me."

"We were wondering if we could speak to you in private. Maybe a manager's office? We wanted to ask you a few questions about a few of your library patrons that we wouldn't want overheard." His partner used her most nonthreatening voice. Janey could be menacing when she chose to be. Right now, that wouldn't get them what they wanted.

Stalz swallowed, and Paul could see the vein at his neck pulsing wildly. The guy was nervous. "Is something wrong?"

This was the tricky part. Not to lie, but not give anything away at the same time. Paul continued to remain silent and allow Janey to do what she did best. "We're hoping you can help us with something we're working on. Do you think you could spare a few minutes?"

Stalz looked around, unsure. "I-I guess. I mean I'm supposed to be working now, helping customers."

"I'm sure it will be fine. Maybe your boss' office, that way you could clear it with him?"

The suspect still looked torn. "I guess so."

"Great. Which way?"

"Um. Upstairs . . ."

Not giving Stalz time to change his mind, Janey turned on her heel, and headed back into the library.

The man hesitated for a moment, glancing over at Paul.

"After you," Paul said.

***

Once the three of them were in Mr. Chaney's office, Paul offered

244

Stalz a chair and took up position to the left of the door. Janey pulled up another chair that had been against the wall, and positioned it a couple of feet in front of the suspect.

"Adam, my name is Detective Davis, and this is Detective Daniels. Do you have any idea why we wanted to talk to you today?"

Stalz shook his head. "No, ma'am."

Polite. That was a point in Stalz's favor. They'd see if it held once they began questioning him in earnest.

Paul opened the folder he had tucked under his arm, and pulled out the pictures of the four victims. "Do you recognize any of these women?"

Adam Stalz looked intently over each picture. "I-I don't know. Maybe."

"Come now, Adam. We know you asked at least one of these young women out several times while you were working. Does Mr. Chaney know you've been harassing the library's patrons?"

"No. I haven't been harassing anyone. No. That's not true." Stalz was getting agitated. "Okay, I asked them out, but when they said no, that was it. I would never do that."

"So you asked all of these women out?"

He didn't answer right away.

"I'm sure we could find other women you've harassed to come forward, Adam. All we have to do is ask around, and—"

"No! I mean, yes, I ask a lot of girls out. But like I said, when they say no, that's it. I leave them alone. Honest."

Paul continued to scowl at the suspect while Janey leaned forward. "We'd like to believe you, Adam, but you see, we have a problem. All of these women, they were found dead in their homes after they refused to go out with you."

It wasn't a lie.

"Did you follow them home, Adam? Did you stalk them, waiting for the right time, and then kill them?" Paul demanded.

Stalz shook his head violently. "No. No. I wouldn't do that. I couldn't kill anyone. I faint at the sight of blood."

"And why should we believe you?" Paul asked.

"Ask any of my friends. They'll tell you." Stalz turned to Janey. "Please. You have to believe me. I didn't kill anyone."

Paul took a step forward.

Stalz sat up straighter in his chair, pushing against the back, trying to put distance between him and Paul.

"Don't you think it's a bit of a coincidence that all of these women wound up dead after they turned you down? Why do you think that is?"

"I don't know. A lot of pretty women come to the library."

"And do you ask all of them out?" Janey asked.

His eyes flickered to her and then back to Paul. "Yeah. Most of them."

Paul crossed his arms. "So you only kill the ones that say no."

"I told you. I didn't kill anyone."

Janey jumped in, redirecting Stalz's attention to her. The two of them had done this song and dance routine many times since they'd become partners. Paul's size made it easy for him to play the gruff bad cop role, while his partner would turn on the charm—a direct contrast to what Paul was projecting. Suspects would often begin pleading their case to Janey and let something valuable slip.

"Maybe he's telling the truth. Maybe he was just being friendly. The women are pretty," Janey said to Paul before turning to their suspect. "Adam, you have to understand that we're trying to find out who did this, don't you?"

He nodded.

"So were you maybe watching them? Before you asked them out?" she asked.

Adam lowered his head, broadcasting his guilt.

Janey softened her voice. "Adam? You watched them, didn't you?"

"Sometimes. It wasn't anything, though. I promise. I just paid attention when they came into the library. Offered to help them find stuff. I didn't do anything wrong," he insisted.

His partner glanced up at him, and Paul nodded. Stalz's responses were consistent. Other than his initial response when asked about the women, and that could be chalked up to embarrassment or fearing for his job, he reeked more of desperation than anything else. Serial killers usually had huge egos. Paul wasn't getting that impression from Stalz.

"Is there anything you could tell us about these women that might help us find out who killed them? Maybe you saw something that would help us. Was there something they had in common?" Janey asked.

They were grasping at straws, but considering their best lead had dried up, it was worth a shot.

Stalz was quiet for an extended period of time. Although Paul was tempted to break the silence with another question, he remained patient. It paid off.

"There was this guy," Stalz said.

He was looking at Paul when he said it, but Janey was the one who responded. "What guy, Adam?"

Stalz shrugged. "I don't know his name. He hangs out at the library sometimes."

"And why do you think this guy may have something to do with these women?" Paul asked.

"Because I see him hanging around talking to girls all the time."

Stalz had their complete attention. "What can you tell us about him? Do you remember what the guy looked like?" Janey asked.

"Tall. Not as tall as you, though," he said to Paul. "And he has blond hair."

Paul opened the folder to make notes. "Bleach blond or more of a sandy blond?"

"Sandy."

"Anything else about him you can remember?" Paul asked.

"I think he might be campus security or something."

Paul jotted that down. "Why do you think that?"

"Because sometimes he'd come in wearing a uniform."

"Anything else?" Paul asked.

Stalz shook his head. "No. But he was here last Friday."

Janey stood. "Do you know if he spoke to anyone?"

"I didn't see anyone, but I was helping someone at the time so I wasn't paying close attention."

Paul and Janey glanced at each other, and he knew they were both thinking the same thing. There had been a thief at the store two years ago. The detective that usually handled burglaries was on vacation, so he and Janey had drawn the case. It turned out to be some sort of prank, but after that, the library put in security cameras. Hopefully, their mystery man had been caught on camera.

Janey thanked Adam Stalz and walked him out. When she reentered the room, Paul was leaning against Chaney's desk facing the door.

"We've got to get our hands on those security tapes."

He pushed himself away from the desk and joined her at the door. "Agreed. Let's just hope Mr. Chaney is in a giving mood and doesn't require we get a warrant first."

His partner chuckled as they strolled out the door. "Well, maybe if we ask real nice."

***

It took a little while to find Mr. Chaney. Since Paul and Janey had taken over the library director's office, he'd gone down to the basement to get some archival work done. One of the library volunteers eventually remembered seeing him head toward the stairs, and had gone down to search.

They got lucky, and after calling the dean, Mr. Chaney agreed to pull the security footage from Friday. The catch was they couldn't remove it from the premises without a warrant.

As a compromise, the three of them set up shop in Mr. Chaney's office to go through the footage. It was a long process, since they didn't exactly know who they were looking for.

Roughly an hour in, something caught Paul's eye. "Go back."

"What? What did you see?" Janey asked.

Paul didn't answer until he had what he was looking for on the screen. "Is that who I think it is?"

Janey stood and walked closer to the monitor. "Is that Officer Rollins?"

"You know this man?" Mr. Chaney asked.

Both Paul and Janey ignored him.

"Is his name on the student list?" Janey asked. "I don't remember seeing it."

Flipping through the folder with the list of student and faculty names the dean had sent over, Paul confirmed that Rollins was not on the list. "We need to get Stalz back in here to see if this is the guy he saw."

Before Janey could comment, Paul was out the door in search of Stalz. There was no sign of him on the second floor, so Paul bounded down the stairs as quickly as he could. If Rollins was the man Stalz saw, there was a very real possibility that he was their killer. They'd been racking their brains trying to figure out how the man managed to get into the victims' houses without any sign of forced entry. It was all beginning to make sense. Rollins could have used his badge and most likely preyed on the women's fears.

Paul found Stalz in the connecting building. He was with a customer. "I'm sorry to interrupt, but we need to speak to you again."

Stalz paled slightly. After the grilling Paul had given him earlier, he supposed he couldn't blame the young man for being a little skittish. "Can it wait until I'm finished helping her—"

"No. I'm sorry. It can't. Maybe another one of the staff could be of assistance?" Paul was trying really hard not to drag Stalz kicking and screaming up the stairs. They were close to solving the case. He could feel it. Paul only needed Stalz's positive ID.

It took a little longer than Paul had hoped, but less than five minutes after finding Stalz, they were on their way back up the stairs.

As soon as Stalz saw the footage, Paul knew by his reaction they had their man. "Yeah. Th-that's him. That's the guy."

Knowing they would need a warrant not only for the footage they'd reviewed, but also all the library's security surveillance for the last twelve months, Paul put in a call to get the process started. "Mr.

Chaney, the warrant should be here in a few hours. We're going to need everything you have for the last twelve months."

"Everything?"

"Yes. I'm afraid so," Janey said.

"When do you think you could have it to us?"

"Most of our footage is stored digitally off-site. I'd have to make a request to have it pulled. Maybe a week? A few days, if I pull a few strings."

Janey placed a reassuring hand on Mr. Chaney's shoulder. "Pull a few strings, please. Someone else's life could be in danger."

After leaving Mr. Chaney with a few more details, Paul and Janey practically ran to the car. While Paul started toward Rollins' house, his partner put a call in to the captain to let him know what was going on.

Rollins was off duty until midnight, which meant he could be anywhere.

JAY SAT at the kitchen table while Megan poured both of them a cup of freshly made coffee. She wasn't averse to him stopping by, but she was slightly thrown by it. Sure, they'd agreed to be friends, but other than running into him outside the campus library, she hadn't spoken to him since Paul had tried to set them up. Had Jay ever been to Paul's house before? Megan didn't think so.

She brought the steaming coffee over to the table and took a seat opposite him. "Are you sure you don't want cream or sugar?"

He shook his head. "No. Black's fine. So how have you been?"

"Good. You?"

"Keeping busy. You know how it is," Jay said.

"And you're going to school, too. I can't imagine how tough that would be on top of a full-time job."

Jay lifted his coffee to his mouth, but lowered it back to the table before taking a drink. Maybe it was still too hot for him. "You're taking classes, too, though, you said. That can't be easy with a child running around."

Megan shrugged and sipped her coffee. It was the perfect temperature for her, but then again she'd added some cream. "Chloe's great. All I've got to do is sit her down with a book and she's content. If that wasn't the case, then I don't think I could do it."

He glanced around the room. "Is she in her room or something?"

"No. She's with her grandparents. It's just me and Paul at the moment."

"So did he ever get his head out of his ass?" Jay grinned and wiggled his eyebrows.

She laughed. "Maybe."

"Ah. So the great Detective Daniels isn't above chasing a pretty girl."

Megan grinned, but otherwise remained silent, tilting her head down toward her drink.

Jay cleared his throat. "Speaking of the good detective, you didn't tell him about the other day, did you? That you saw me, I mean."

"No. You asked me not to. Although, I don't really understand what the big deal is. I mean, Paul wouldn't begrudge you an education. He's been really supportive of me going back to school."

"That might be the case, but you don't know how it is at the station. Guys can be brutal if stuff like that gets out." Again, he raised the cup to his lips but didn't drink. Megan wondered if maybe he really didn't like coffee but had only accepted to be polite.

She shook her head. "Men. I will never understand the lot of you."

He laughed with her, but for some reason Megan felt it wasn't genuine. Had she offended him?

Before she could think it through too much, her cell phone rang. Knowing it might be Paul, she set her mug on the table, and stood. "Excuse me."

Unfortunately, she only made it halfway across the room before an arm wrapped around her waist, and a hand covered her mouth. "I'm sorry, Megan. You're a sweet girl—not like the others—but I can't take a chance on you blabbing your mouth."

Megan's eyes widened in horror. What was going on? Why was Jay . . .

"Don't struggle, and I'll make it quick. I promise," he whispered.

Her heart was pounding in her ears, but Megan knew she had to stay focused—look for an opportunity.

Jay began moving them back toward the table. She had no idea why, other than it put more distance between her and her phone—her phone that had quieted for only a few seconds before it started ringing again.

Knowing she needed to get him to let his guard down, Megan didn't fight him. She didn't help him move her, but she didn't prevent him either.

Breathing in and out as evenly as she could, she waited. Hoping, praying he made a mistake.

Her opportunity came a few seconds later when he let go of her waist and reached for something on the table. She stepped forward with her left foot, and with all the energy she could muster, Megan bent at the waist, pulling Jay over her shoulder.

She didn't quite manage to completely flip him—he was a big guy, after all—but her move landed him on his back.

Not giving him time to recover, Megan made a beeline for the back door. Unfortunately, he caught up to her before she was able to step outside.

Jay pulled her kicking and screaming by the ankles back into the main part of the kitchen. She no longer had the element of surprise, so she knew anything she tried he would be anticipating. Megan couldn't stop fighting, however. It wasn't in her nature.

Once he got her back near the table, Megan saw what she'd missed before. A knife. It was small, maybe six or seven inches in total. The small metal blade reflected the sunlight, almost as if taunting her.

The wheels began turning in Megan's head, and she remembered the bits and pieces she'd seen on the news about the serial killer—how the women's throats and wrists had been cut.

And then there was what Jay had said before about the other women. "You're him. The serial killer."

He grinned, and it sent a chill up her spine.

She swallowed. Jay had pulled her arms above her head and held her wrists captive with a single hand. He straddled her waist, putting pressure on her hipbones, making it almost impossible to move. Her only hope was to get him talking. Megan had to either reason with him or get him to drop his guard again. Given he'd killed four women already, she didn't put much stock in the former, so she was hoping for the latter.

"Figured that out, did you?" he asked.

He picked up the knife and held it mere inches from her neck. She tried not to move. "I don't understand. Why? I mean . . . you're a cop."

To her dismay, Jay pressed the blade against her throat. He didn't puncture the skin, but she got the message loud and clear.

"Sometimes people need to be punished. And if the law won't do it, then someone has to."

Every word coming out of his mouth was making her skin crawl. How could she have missed this side of his personality? Surely there had to have been a sign. Something.

All she knew was she had to keep him talking. That's what Rebecca always told her. Even if there was no way to talk the person down, buying time was always the best option. Megan only hoped it was Paul who'd tried to call her and he'd realize something was wrong when she didn't answer.

"What did the other women do wrong, then?" Her voice was shaking. She couldn't help it.

"Ah, ah, ah. No more questions. I promised to make things quick if you didn't struggle. Now I'm going to have to make you pay."

She gasped as he ran the knife blade along the width of her neck. It cut into her skin, and a few moments later she felt blood trickling down to stain her shirt.

He chuckled as she struggled against his hold. She opened her mouth and was surprised she was still able to speak. The cut must not be that deep. He was toying with her. "Please, don't do this, Jay. Please."

With the back of his hand, he slapped her across the face. "I said be quiet!"

His eyes were blazing with fury, and Megan knew the end was

coming. There was nothing she could do to stop him, and talking only seemed to make it worse.

He ran his nose along the edge of her face. In another circumstance, it would have been rather intimate. As it was, bile rose in Megan's throat. She closed her eyes and prepared herself to die.

She yelled out in pain as the knife sliced through one of her wrists.

***

Paul and Janey drove straight from the library to Rollins' house. Neither he nor his vehicle was there. Normally, Paul would begin tracking down the suspect's friends in an attempt to narrow down his whereabouts. That didn't sit well with him as an option. If he was right, Rollins was their serial killer. He was also a cop, which meant he had advantages above that of the average criminal.

When Paul was unable to reach Megan, he began to get a sickening feeling in his gut. Megan always answered her phone when he called. He'd known her to climb out of the shower when her phone rang. This wasn't like her. He wanted to warn her about Rollins. Although Paul knew that wasn't standard protocol, he didn't care. Megan had become extremely important to him, and he didn't know if he'd be able to stand it if something happened to her.

Especially since it would be all his fault. He'd introduced her to Rollins, after all.

"Do you want me to keep trying?" Janey asked, sensing his worry.

Paul shook his head. "If she hasn't answered by now, she isn't going to."

"You don't think . . ."

"I don't know. Do you mind if we—"

"Of course not. Let's go."

Turning around in the nearest driveway, Paul worked his way through traffic as quickly as he could to get to his neighborhood. Rollins only lived about ten minutes from Paul's house. Paul made it there in six.

The minute they turned onto Paul's street, they spotted Rollins' car. It wasn't parked in front of the house, but it was well within easy walking distance. Any optimism Paul had felt before went out the window. If Megan was hurt . . .

He didn't even want to think of the other possibility.

Paul pulled up along the curb. He jumped out, not bothering to turn off the engine, and sprinted toward the house.

He was almost to the garage when he heard Megan scream. If there'd been any doubt Rollins was inside the house before then, it was entirely gone. Releasing his gun from its holster, Paul raced toward the back of the house where he'd heard her scream originate.

Janey was hot on his heels. He knew she'd heard Megan as well.

The scene that greeted them when they burst through the back door turned his stomach. Megan was laid out on the floor with Rollins on top of her. There was blood coming from her wrist, and from her neck.

Without thinking, Paul launched himself across the room, and knocked Rollins back. They both went tumbling and hit the tile floor hard. Paul's gun went flying, but that was the least of his worries. Rollins recovered quickly from the unexpected hit, and Paul felt something sharp puncture his leg. Without seeing what it was, he knew it had to be whatever Rollins had used on Megan and the other women he'd killed.

The struggle seemed to last forever, but in reality it was probably only a few minutes. Rollins was younger, and stronger, but Paul was driven by rage. He hadn't been able to take out his anger on the drunk driver who'd killed Melissa, but Rollins was there in the flesh in front of him.

Somewhere along the line, Rollins wiggled his way free, and Paul had to tackle him again. They ended up in the hallway, rolling around on the floor grasping for the knife. Rollins managed to get the blade between them, and Paul used all the strength he had to kick Rollins away. If he was able to stab something vital, Paul knew it would be all over for him.

Rollins hit the wall, jarring the knife from his hand. Paul went for it. So did Rollins.

One minute they were fighting over the knife, and then the next, Rollins gasped and went limp. Paul pushed him away, and saw the blade of the knife sticking out of Rollins chest.

Before he could check to see if Rollins was still alive, Janey yelled from the other room. "Paul, you need to get in here."

Scrambling to his feet, Paul ran back into the kitchen. Janey was sitting at Megan's head with a kitchen towel wrapped tight around her wrist.

"I called for backup and an ambulance. She's losing a lot of blood. He only got one wrist, but it's deep and right along the vein," Janey said.

Paul lifted Megan onto his lap, and took over holding her wrist above her head to slow down the blood loss while Janey went out to meet the paramedics.

The cut along her neck didn't look deep. He wasn't a doctor, but he could tell there wasn't any immediate danger there. Her wrist, however, was another matter. The towel was drenched in blood, and if they didn't get it to stop soon, Megan would die.

He brushed his lips along her hairline. Megan was pale, and her eyes were closed. "Hold on, all right? You're going to be okay."

A minute later, Janey clamored back through the door followed by two paramedics. He knew he should move out of the way and allow them to do their job, but he couldn't let Megan go.

Janey put a hand on his shoulder and whispered in his ear. "It's okay, Paul. Let them do their job. They'll take care of her."

Reluctantly, he surrendered her to the paramedics, and let them load her onto a stretcher.

"I'm going with her," he said to no one in particular.

Janey answered him. "Go. I'll take care of things here, and keep you informed."

Paul was grateful the paramedics didn't give him a hard time about riding in the ambulance with Megan. He and Megan weren't family—not in the way that would normally make any difference to medical personnel. Whether it was because he was a cop, or because they knew him, he couldn't say, but either way he would owe them. Letting Megan out of his sight wasn't an option.

The ambulance ride was short. On the way to the hospital, they'd been able to stop most of the bleeding at her wrist. They'd cleaned up the cut on her neck as well. It would need to be bandaged, but Paul thought it would eventually heal completely. He didn't even think there would be a scar.

When they arrived at the ER, it was a slightly different story. At first, they weren't going to allow him to go with her, but the paramedic said something to the nurse and she waved Paul back.

He stood off to the side while the nurses worked to hook Megan up to all the necessary monitors. It was almost comforting when he saw her steady heartbeat on the screen.

They gave her an IV and took a sample of her blood. Everything happened extremely fast.

As the nurses were finishing up, a doctor appeared and began taking stock of her injuries. He asked Paul a few questions, and he answered them. At least, he thought he did. There was only one other time in his life when he'd felt this helpless. He'd hoped he'd never feel that way again, but here he was.

Before the doctor finished bandaging up her wrist, a nurse he'd seen before reentered the room, this time with a pint of blood. She hung it behind Megan's hospital bed and attached it to the IV tubes already in the uninjured arm.

The doctor turned to Paul. "She's lost at least a couple pints of blood, so we're giving her some O negative until we get the test results back on her blood type."

"Will she be all right?" Megan still hadn't regained consciousness, but her heartbeat was steady. He knew that was a good sign, but Paul needed reassurance.

"She's stable, and after we get some blood back into her system, she should wake up. After that, we'll have a better gauge of her condition."

Paul nodded.

"Is there someone you can call for her? Family?"

He blinked several times, staring at the doctor as if he were speaking a foreign language.

"Mr. Daniels?"

The doctor clearly thought Paul was losing his mind. Maybe he was. "Yeah. Her sister. I-I'll call her as soon as she wakes up."

"Mr. Daniels, we really like to have . . ."

Paul looked the doctor in the eye and lowered his voice. "I'm not leaving her side until she wakes up."

Sighing, the doctor lowered his gaze to Paul's leg. "We should probably take a look at that."

He looked down at the dark stain on his pants. Paul had completely forgotten about being stabbed. "I'm fine."

The doctor ignored him and waved one of the nurses over.

The wound wasn't deep and it was clean. They disinfected and cleaned the area, and the doctor sewed him up with five stitches before he backed out of the room. The nurse finished bandaging Paul up and then left him alone with Megan.

He scooted his chair closer and took hold of her hand. It was tricky with the IV and all the other tubes, but he worked around them. Paul needed to touch her. He needed that connection.

"I'm so sorry, Megan. I would never have introduced the two of you if I . . . if I . . ." A sob caught in his throat. He'd warned her that he feared he'd mess up again—that he didn't deserve her.

Paul rested his head beside her on the mattress, stroking her fingers. He would make sure she was okay and then send her back to Nashville with her sister. It was the only way. The only way to keep her safe.

He didn't know how he'd make it no longer having her in his life, but he didn't have a choice. There was no way he could lose her like he had Melissa. He'd rather she lived a long and happy life without him than have her life end prematurely. Rebecca would help Megan move on and see that she was taken care of.

It was the only way.

CHAPTER 27

MEGAN'S HEAD WAS POUNDING. There was also this buzzing sound that wouldn't seem to go away. Her arm felt unusually heavy, and it ached.

She tried to lift it, but a hand stopped her.

"You need to lie still." The voice was firm, yet gentle—and one Megan recognized immediately.

"Paul?"

He squeezed the fingers of her other hand. "I'm right here."

"My arm . . ."

"Is it hurting you? I can ask them to get you some medicine." There was something in Paul's voice she didn't understand.

Forcing her lids open, Megan turned her head to the side. The first thing she noticed were Paul's eyes. They were bloodshot and puffy as if he'd been crying.

Everything was coming back to her as the fog of sleep left her brain. "What happened?"

He frowned. "You don't remember?"

"Yes. I meant what happened to Jay?" The last thing she remembered was the searing pain of him cutting her wrist, and then a loud bang. After that, things started getting fuzzy.

"He can't hurt you anymore."

She could have asked Paul to clarify, but the hard set of his jaw told her what he meant. Twisting her wrist slightly, she cupped the side of his face. He leaned into it for a second and then pulled back. It was her turn to frown. "What's wrong?"

Paul stood, and her arm fell onto the mattress. "I need to call your sister. Will you be okay alone for a few minutes?"

"Of course, but—"

"I'll be right back."

Megan watched as he disappeared through the hospital curtain. What the hell just happened?

She was still mulling it over when a nurse pushed aside the curtain. "It's good to see you awake. How are you feeling, Miss Carson?"

"All right."

The nurse looked at something over Megan's shoulder. "Your vitals look good. How's the pain?"

Megan glanced down at her wrist. It hurt but she figured, given the circumstances, it could be worse. "It's tolerable."

"Well, everything is looking good so far. You lost a decent amount of blood, though, so we're going to want to keep you hooked up to an IV." The nurse patted Megan's shoulder. "If all goes well, we should be able to send you home in a few hours."

After checking the bandage on Megan's arm, the nurse exited the room, pulling the curtain closed behind her. With a few minutes alone, Megan's thoughts drifted back to Paul and his strange reaction to her gesture. It was the first time since she'd returned from visiting her sister that he'd shied away from her touch.

Was he repulsed by her injuries? Megan didn't think so. She knew he saw far worse on a regular basis being a homicide detective.

Maybe he was attempting to remain professional. Jay had admitted to being the serial killer, and that was Paul's case.

But even that didn't make sense. They were alone. If anyone had walked in on them, it would most likely have been one of the nurses. She couldn't imagine the hospital staff would have said anything. It wasn't as if he were crawling into bed with her in the middle of the ER.

She was still trying to figure things out when a hand poked through the fabric, and Paul slipped back inside the confined area. He smiled, but it looked forced.

"Rebecca will be here in the morning. I'm not sure if Gage is coming with her or not. He was going to call his coach and see if he could skip tomorrow's practice."

"What? Why?"

He lowered himself back into the chair he'd been sitting in earlier, but unlike before, he kept space between him and the bed. "She couldn't get a flight out until then."

Megan shook her head. "No. I meant, why is she coming? I'm fine."

"Megan, you could have . . . died."

Paul averted his gaze as he said that last word, and something clicked in her brain.

"Why did you pull away from me earlier?"

To his credit, he didn't deny it. "I think once you're feeling better, you should go home with your sister. With the baby coming, I'm sure she'd love to have some help."

She couldn't believe what she was hearing. Okay, she could. That didn't mean she had to like it. "I'm not going to go live with Rebecca."

He met her gaze, and his mask was back. All the tenderness she'd seen in his eyes over the past week was gone. "I want you to go."

"Why?" she demanded. If he thought she was going to pack her bags and go willingly, then he sorely underestimated her. She'd gotten a glimpse of what they could have, and she wanted it.

Paul tilted his head down, no longer looking at her. "It's the right thing. The best thing."

"For who?"

"You." He still wasn't looking at her.

The urge to scream made her head ache worse. She probably should have accepted the nurse's offer for pain medication. It was too late for that, however, and there was no way she wanted anyone interrupting their conversation. "You're what's best for me."

"I'm not."

She released a heavy sigh, trying to keep her temper in check. "Is this about Melissa again? About you not feeling good enough? I thought we'd gotten past that."

Paul looked up, but he kept his shoulders hunched over. "You could have died."

Was that it? Did the fear of losing someone else he cared about spark some sort of buried trauma? "But I didn't. I'm going to be fine."

He stood abruptly and began pacing in the small space next to her bed. "Don't you understand? You could have died, and it would have been my fault. This is why I knew a relationship would be a bad idea. I'm not good for you, Megan. I'm not good for any woman."

At that moment, Megan really wished she could shake him. "What in the world are you talking about?"

Paul stopped moving and stared several feet above her head. "If I hadn't introduced you to Rollins, he never would have known who you were."

"That's absurd."

He lowered his gaze to meet hers. "Is it?"

"Yes. The whole reason Jay came to the house was because I ran into him outside the library Friday, and he wanted to make sure I hadn't said anything to you about it. Me running into him had nothing to do with you."

Paul seemed to consider that. "But if you'd never met, he might have walked right on by you."

"Might."

He shook his head. "It doesn't matter. Your sister is going to need you, and—"

"And I'm not going. First of all, I won't leave Chloe like that. I promised her I had no plans to leave anytime soon, and I won't have her thinking I lied to her."

"Chloe will get over it," he said, interrupting her.

She ignored him. "Second, Rebecca and Gage will be fine on their own. If she needs my help for a couple of weeks after the baby's born, I can go then. But honestly, I'm guessing your mom is probably going to be all over that. She hasn't had a new grandchild in five years."

Paul didn't have a rebuff for that one.

Megan decided to press forward. "And third. I love you."

He began shaking his head. "You don't. It's just a crush. It's just . . ."

"Paul, I've been in love with you for a while now. So the question is how do you feel about me?"

"Megan, I . . ." He looked torn.

Pushing through the pain, she reached for him. The move nearly ripped the IV out of her hand, but she didn't care. This was important. "I don't care about the past. This isn't about Melissa, or Chloe, or anything else besides you and me."

He gazed down at where she was gripping his wrist. "I want you to have a long and happy life."

She smiled. "I want that, too. With you."

"That's not possible." Paul was shaking his head again. She really wished he would stop that.

"Paul, just answer the question. Do you love me?"

He took her hand in his and began playing with her fingers. As much as she wanted him to get on with it—to answer her question already—she tried to be patient and give him time.

Before he could answer, the nurse returned. She made a clicking sound with her tongue when she saw how Megan was putting strain on her IV leads. Without a word, the nurse retracted Megan's arm, and Paul released her. It felt as if any ground they'd gained had been lost with the physical separation.

"There. Everything looks to be in working order. How's the pain?" Although the nurse was speaking to Megan, she sent several reproachful looks in Paul's direction.

"I'm fine," Megan answered, not taking her eyes off Paul.

"All right. I'll be back to check in on you in a bit." The nurse sounded doubtful.

Megan waited until they were alone again. "Paul?"

He closed his eyes. "Please, don't ask me that."

"Why not?"

"Because I don't want to lie to you."

She swallowed. "I just want the truth. Please."

***

Why was she doing this? He was trying to do the right thing.

Megan shifted, and he realized she was going to reach for him again. He couldn't have that. Stepping closer, he placed a stilling hand on her forearm.

She wouldn't let it go otherwise—he knew she wouldn't.

There was noise all round them in the ER. The only thing that separated it from them was a thin layer of fabric. Even still, it seemed as if the world around them faded away.

He looked into her young, beautiful face. "Yes. I love you."

She smiled.

"Which is exactly why you need to go with your sister. Megan, I can't lose you like I did Melissa. I'd rather you live your life away from me than have it cut short. I wouldn't survive it." He sounded desperate, and he was. Paul had to get her to understand. He was doing this for her.

Megan's eyes filled with moisture. "Paul, you didn't kill Melissa. Should you have picked up the diapers on your way home like you said you were going to? Probably. But you'd just come from a murder scene. No one expects you to be unaffected by that. You are human."

"That doesn't excuse—"

"Shut up and listen to me," she snapped.

If the situation weren't so serious, Paul would have laughed.

"Melissa is the one who made the choice to go out that night, not you. She could have waited until morning. I'm sure Chloe would have survived a few hours with a wet diaper."

This was the first time Megan had said anything negative about Melissa, and Paul wasn't sure he liked it.

"And what about the drunk driver? Does he not have any responsibility in her death? He chose to drink and then get behind the wheel. They made those choices, Paul, not you." Megan's voice trailed off.

What she said made sense, but that didn't change the guilt he felt.

Before he could say anything, she continued. "I know you think you should have somehow been able to foresee what would happen and save her, but you're not perfect, Paul. None of us are. I love how protective you are of those you love, but I don't need you pushing me away because you somehow think that's what's best for me. I'm a grown woman. I will make my own decisions on who I want, where I want to live, and anything else. Clear enough for you?"

Despite their surroundings and the fact that he knew she had to be weak from her recent blood loss, Megan looked as fierce as a mother lion defending her cub. If he didn't know any better, he would think she was ready to pounce at any second.

"Well?"

"Well, what?" He'd been so caught up in studying her reactions, he must have missed something she said.

"I love you, and you love me, too. I'm not letting you get away that easily."

"I never should have told you."

"Why?" she asked.

Paul took a step back and lowered himself into the chair once more. "Because it doesn't change anything. I'm still bad for you, Megan."

She scowled at him. "And what about Chloe? Are you going to send her away, too?"

That surprised him. "What are you talking about?"

"Well, if people being in close proximity to you is such a bad thing, then I'd think you'd want your daughter as far away from you as you can get her. It's only logical, after all."

He blinked. "You think I should send Chloe away?"

"No. That's my point."

Paul sighed, and leaned forward, resting his forearms on his knees. "I see what you're trying to do, but it's different. Chloe is my daughter

—my responsibility. She already lost her mother. It wouldn't be fair for her to lose me as well."

"You realize how crazy that sounds, don't you?"

He shrugged, not really sure what she wanted him to say. The situation with Chloe was different. Making sure she was taken care of and loved was the last thing he could give Melissa.

"Will you do me a favor?"

He looked up at Megan, afraid of what she might say next. "What?"

"Stop trying to do what you think is best for me."

"I don't know if I can do that." It was the truth. Paul had always been the protector—for as long as he could remember.

"Try."

Neither of them said anything for several minutes.

"You really aren't going to leave, are you?" He wasn't sure if he was happy about that or not. It would be better for her to go, but selfishly he wanted her to stay.

"No."

Resigned, Paul leaned back in his chair. Despite everything, he felt himself grin.

"Care to share what's so funny?" she asked.

"I honestly don't know."

Megan smiled. "Will you come closer? I want to be able to touch you, and I don't think the nurse will like it much if I try to tear the needle out of my hand again."

He hesitated and then scooted his chair closer. Taking hold of her hand, he laced their fingers together. Even something as simple as touching her made him feel better. He was still scared for her, although he wasn't sure anything would ever take that away completely.

"So Becca's coming tomorrow."

Paul nodded. "Yeah. She was pretty hysterical on the phone when I first told her. Once she knew you were going to be all right, she calmed down."

Megan rolled her eyes. "That isn't surprising. My sister has a tendency to overreact. Especially when it comes to me."

"You almost died, Megan. If I hadn't gotten there when I did . . ."

She squeezed his fingers. "But you did."

He didn't argue with her. What would be the point?

Deciding to redirect the topic of conversation a little, he shared what he hoped she'd consider good news. "I spoke to the doctor before I called your sister. He says you should be able to go home in a few hours."

"That's what the nurse told me, too. So did you tell Becca to come to the house, then?" she asked.

"Yes. That helped to calm her as well. I'm sure she figured you really were going to be okay if they were sending you home." Paul lifted her hand and placed a light kiss in the center of her palm.

"She's asked about you."

He raised his eyebrows in question.

"Becca's curious about the guy I'm seeing."

"Oh." For some reason that made him nervous.

"Paul?"

He must have lowered his gaze involuntarily, because he had to force himself to look up to see her. She had a serious expression on her face.

"Do you want to be with me? I know you're afraid of what might happen, but aside from that, what is it you want?" she asked.

That was easy. He wanted her. Megan brought a joy into his life he never thought he'd experience again after Melissa was taken from him.

When he didn't answer, she placed her hand on the side of his face like she had earlier. This time, he didn't pull away. "Do you want to be with me?"

"Yes." He couldn't deny it.

She smiled, and it stirred something in the pit of his stomach. "Forever?"

He closed his eyes and nodded. "Heaven help me, but yes."

"Good. I'm glad."

When he opened his eyes again, she was grinning from ear to ear. "Megan, I—"

"Paul, I want to ask you something."

She stroked her fingers along the line of his jaw, making it difficult for him to concentrate on anything else. She had his full and undivided attention.

"I love you. I love being with you. This past week, I've been happier than I can ever remember being. Even before then, when we were only friends, you brought things into my life I'd never had before. You accepted me into your home—into your family. I'd never had that. Becca has always been the only one I could count on, and then there you were. After knowing me for a day, you brought me home with you to start a new life. I will never be able to thank you enough for that."

He wasn't sure what to say, so he said nothing.

"I know you think my life would be better without you in it, but I know for a fact it wouldn't. I've been there before. I know what it's like. I don't want that again. Every morning, I wake up excited to find out what cute thing Chloe will do that day. Plus, who would I get to play poker with me?"

He chuckled, remembering their late night poker games.

"You make me feel part of something, Paul. I don't want to ever give that up. I want to stay with you and Chloe. Forever."

She took a deep breath, and he knew something big was coming. "Will you marry me?"

Paul sat there stunned for a long moment. "You-you want to marry me?"

"Yes."

He sat there unmoving.

"But the question is do you want me to be your wife?" she asked.

All the reasons why he wasn't right for Megan swirled through his mind. Was she being serious? Had she lost more blood than they'd thought?

Looking at her, he knew the answer. She was completely serious. "This is really what you want?" He had to be sure.

"You're not supposed to answer a question with a question, Detective, but yes, it's what I want. I wouldn't have asked, otherwise."

He removed her hand from his face—her left hand—and rubbed his thumb over her ring finger. "The guy is supposed to be the one who asks, you know."

She snorted. "Well, you know me. I'm not exactly traditional."

Paul laughed. "No. That you're not."

"Well?" She was still waiting on an answer.

"Only if you agree that I'm the one that gets to buy you an engagement ring. We have to stick to some traditions."

Megan beamed. "So is that a yes?"

He smiled back. "Yes."

CHAPTER 28

It was after four in the morning before Megan was released from the emergency room. They were both exhausted, and all Paul could think about was getting her home. He knew they wouldn't get more than a few hours' sleep with Rebecca coming, but some was better than none.

The doctor told Megan to get as much rest as possible over the next few days so her body could heal. She was supposed to follow up with her family doctor in two days. The cut along her neck wasn't more than a scratch, and Rollins had only cut one of her wrists. She'd more than likely have a scar for the rest of her life, but all things considered, she'd been lucky.

Janey stopped by the hospital a little after midnight to drop off his car and to let him know that the forensic unit had released the house, and Rollins' body had been removed. She'd called in a favor and had a bio unit come do a quick cleanup of the area. They would only have removed any visible signs of blood, but he was glad Megan wouldn't have to see it.

They were also getting more information filtering in regarding Rollins. He'd served as an army medic for four years after high school, before joining the police force. It explained the precise cuts on the women. He'd known exactly how and where to cut in order to inflict the damage he wanted. They still weren't sure why he'd targeted them.

Paul pulled into the driveway and glanced over at Megan. She was asleep. As much as he didn't want to wake her, he doubted he'd be able to pick her up and carry her upstairs to bed.

"Megan? We're home, sweetheart. Do you think you can walk? We need to get you into bed."

She fluttered her eyes open. "Paul?"

He limped around to the passenger side and opened the door for her. "Come on, let's get you inside so you can rest."

It took some effort, but he managed to help her out of the car and into the house through the front door. He was glad she was out of it because they had to walk through the small hallway that connected the living room to the kitchen. The same area where Rollins took his last breath.

Paul had a momentary stab of indecision when they reached the top of the stairs. Should he take her to her bedroom, or his?

Megan sagged against him, and he decided to throw caution to the wind. She was his fiancée, after all. Of course, that was assuming she didn't change her mind once she was feeling better. He didn't think she would, though. Megan was never fickle. Once she made up her mind about something, she didn't back down.

Bypassing Megan's bedroom, he walked the extra steps to his. Everything was exactly as they'd left it earlier that morning, including the lingering scent of sex in the air.

Guiding her to the bed, Paul sat her on the mattress, and bent to take off the slippers the hospital had provided. She smiled down at him. The doctor had given her some pain medication before they left. It wasn't terribly strong, he said, but whatever it was, it had knocked her out almost as soon as they got into his car.

When Paul had her slippers removed, he began working on the rest of her clothes. Along with the footwear, the hospital had supplied a pair of scrubs for both of them. Given they'd both come into direct contact with Rollins, their clothing had been taken as evidence.

The top was easy enough to lift over her head. The bottoms,

however, were another matter. He had to help her lie back on the bed, shimmy them over her hips, and then down her legs. It might sound simple, but Megan was dead weight in her current condition.

Leaving her side for a minute, Paul rushed into her bedroom to grab one of her more chaste nighties. The last thing he needed was to be more tempted than he already was.

When he reentered his bedroom, he found Megan sitting up and trying to unclasp her bra.

"What are you doing?"

She looked up at his approach. "I can't get it off."

"Here. Let me help." He brushed her hands away and released the hooks holding her bra in place.

Megan sighed.

Paul snatched up the nightie he'd brought from the other room and slipped it over her head. The sooner he got her covered up, the less distracted he would be.

Getting her under the covers proved to be another challenge. Even after she was tucked securely under the blankets, he wasn't sure how they'd accomplished it. There had been rolling and lifting and pulling. If he hadn't already been ready to pass out, that would have done it.

Shedding his own borrowed scrubs, Paul checked the clock beside his bed, and set the alarm for ten. Rebecca wasn't due to arrive until sometime after ten thirty, and he wanted to have time to wake up and shower.

Rolling onto his side, Paul wrapped his arm loosely around Megan's waist. Although he knew he should keep his hands to himself, he needed to feel her near him. It was the only way he could convince himself she was safe.

It hadn't taken him long to fall asleep. With Megan's warmth pressed against his chest, he'd sunk into a deep slumber. Unfortunately, it was short-lived. Paul woke up a few hours later in a cold sweat. It was the same dream he always had from the night Melissa died—with one exception. When he'd been called over to identify the body, it wasn't Melissa's face he'd seen. It was Megan's.

He sat up, holding his head in his hands, trying to breathe through the nightmare. His heart was pounding a mile a minute in his chest.

"Are you okay?" a sleepy voice mumbled beside him.

Paul glanced over and saw Megan gazing up at him. He tried to smile. "I'm all right. Go back to sleep."

"Not until you talk to me."

He tried to calm his thundering heart.

"Come here."

Paul shook his head. "Your arm."

She inched closer. "My arm's fine. Just be careful you don't bump my wrist."

He debated for a long moment, but decided not only was it not worth the effort arguing with her, he also needed her comfort.

Resting his head gently on Megan's shoulder, he let her warmth penetrate all the way down to his soul.

"Do you want to tell me about it?" she asked.

Did he? Outside of the department psychologist, he'd never told anyone about his nightmares. Even then, he'd downplayed them. "It's the same nightmare I always have. Sort of."

She laid her cheek against his head, drawing him closer.

"The night she died. The state highway patrolman knocked on my door to tell me what had happened and that they needed me to come down to the morgue to identify the body."

He heard Megan suck in a breath, but other than that, she didn't react.

"I couldn't leave Chloe alone, so I packed her up and drove her the few miles to George and Cindy's house. Of course, I had to explain why I was there. Cindy fell to the floor and began sobbing uncontrollably. George didn't fare much better, but he kept it together enough to comfort his wife.

"Once she calmed down a little, I promised them I'd be back as soon as I could, and left Chloe with them while I drove to the morgue. It was the longest drive of my life. I'd driven back and forth to my in-laws' house many times over the years, but this felt ten times as long, even though it took me no more than ten minutes. Me going to identify the body was a technicality. The woman driving matched Melissa's description, and she'd been driving her car. Her purse and ID were in the vehicle as well. There wasn't likely to be a mix-up."

Although talking about it was hard, this was the first time he'd been able to do so without going into a panic. "In the dream, I'm walking down to the morgue. I pass my colleagues—their faces full of pity. Then I step into the viewing room, and the coroner pulls the sheet down."

He was quiet for several moments. "Usually I see Melissa's face staring back at me. This morning, it was yours."

She hugged him, and he wondered if it was putting too much pressure on her wrist. He went to pull away.

"Don't. Please," she begged.

Unable to deny her, he settled back down against her warmth. "I can't lose you like that, Megan. I can't."

"You won't."

"How can you be so sure?" he asked.

Paul felt her smile against his forehead. "Because if you haven't figured it out, I'm pretty stubborn. You can't get rid of me that easily."

He grinned and tilted his head up to look into her eyes. "Were you serious about being my wife?"

"You better believe it."

Reaching up, he ran his thumb along her cheek, down across her lips. "I love you."

***

Their moment was interrupted by his alarm. Paul groaned. "I need to get up and shower before your sister gets here."

Megan reluctantly let him go. "Are you picking her up?"

"No. I offered, but she insisted she could grab a cab."

She nodded and tried to get up.

Paul rushed to her side to help her. "You really should stay in bed and rest."

"I know they cleaned me up some at the hospital, but it still feels like I have a layer of . . . something on me. Do you think you could help me shower? There should be some plastic wrap downstairs to cover my bandage." If need be, Megan could manage a shower on her own, but it would be easier with his help. Plus, she was always up for opportunities to see Paul naked.

"Sit down on the bed, and I'll see what I can find." She could tell he wasn't keen on the idea, but at least he wasn't going to fight her.

He returned a few minutes later with the roll of plastic wrap. They wound the clingy material around her wrist until everything was covered completely.

The shower was uneventful, for the most part. Paul and Megan shared some kisses, but that was where it ended. Although she would have been up for a little more, he was firmly in caregiver mode. Megan accepted it, and was content to know he was no longer pushing her away.

Paul helped her to dry off and get dressed. Megan didn't want to greet her sister lying in bed, so she asked him if he'd help her downstairs. He got her set up on the couch, and after giving her a soft kiss, he headed into the kitchen to make them something to eat.

He was still in the other room when Rebecca and Gage arrived. As soon as he let them in the door, her sister pushed him aside to join Megan on the couch. Rebecca surveyed Megan's injuries, and fawned over her like a mother hen.

"What happened?"

Megan wrinkled her brow. "Paul didn't tell you?"

Rebecca waved her hand dismissively. "He told me, but I want to hear it from you. Megan, why did you let that man in the house? How many times have I told you—"

"Maybe you should go easy on her, Rebecca. She did just get out of the hospital," Gage said.

Her sister looked at her husband and then back to Megan. Rebecca reached up to brush Megan's hair back behind her shoulders. "You scared me, you know that, don't you?"

"I know. But I'm fine. Honestly. The doctor said all I need is to rest for a few days." Megan hoped that would pacify her sister.

"Well, I'm going to stay and take care of you. Gage has to fly back tonight, but I'm here for as long as you need me." Rebecca hadn't stopped touching her since she sat down.

Paul cleared his throat. "I'm going to go finish getting our lunch ready. Gage, did you want to join me?"

"Yeah. Sure. We'll leave you two alone for a few minutes."

Megan watched Paul and Gage disappear into the kitchen. There must have been something that gave her away because when she turned back to her sister, Rebecca had a "deer in the headlights" look. "Becca? Are you feeling all right?"

Rebecca's expression went from shock to anger in a matter of seconds. "Something you want to tell me?"

"About?" Megan asked.

"Paul's your mystery man, isn't he?"

Megan refused to lie. "Yes."

"Oh, Megan." By the look on Rebecca's face, Megan would have thought someone had died, not that she'd confessed to being in a relationship with the man she'd been living with for the last seven-and-a-half months.

"Please don't do that," Megan pleaded.

"He's going to break your heart." Rebecca said it as if it were a foregone conclusion.

"No, he won't."

Before her sister could berate her some more, Paul strolled into the room with a tray of food. Rebecca waited until he set it down on the coffee table before laying into him.

"I thought I could trust you. Gage assured me you weren't the type to take advantage of a woman, and I believed him."

Paul met Megan's gaze, and she knew he realized the gig was up. Instead of retreating, or getting defensive, he shifted her a little to the side, and sat down behind her. He pulled her against his chest, and wrapped his arm protectively around her. His solid form behind her gave Megan strength.

"Becca, he didn't take advantage of me."

Her sister wasn't listening to her. Rebecca was staring Paul down. But he didn't seem bothered by her disapproval.

"Paul?" There was a note of disbelief and confusion in Gage's voice. He'd ambled into the room to find Paul and Megan cuddled together on the couch and Rebecca shooting daggers at his brother with her eyes.

Paul never took his eyes off Rebecca. "Let's get this all out in the open, shall we?"

Gage moved to stand behind his wife. "Would someone please tell me what's going on?"

"Paul is Megan's mystery man," Rebecca said through gritted teeth.

"What?" Gage's loud voice reverberated off the walls of the living room.

If there'd been any doubts, they were dashed when Paul tilted Megan's head back and placed a chaste kiss on her lips. She smiled up at him. Megan knew her sister would be upset with the news, but knowing Paul was there beside her, supporting her, she knew she could tackle anything. Including Rebecca.

After giving Paul another quick kiss, Megan turned back to face her sister. "Becca, I love you, but you need to get over it. Paul loves me, and . . ."

Megan glanced up at Paul, and he nodded.

She took a deep breath, and met her sister's furious gaze. "We're getting married."

Both Gage and Rebecca's mouths dropped open.

"Married?" Rebecca asked once she regained the ability to speak.

Paul jumped in. "That's right. We're getting married. I love your sister, Rebecca, and I hope you can learn to accept us. You're the only family Megan has, and I know she'll want you to be part of everything."

There were no words to describe the look on Rebecca's face.

Gage noticed his wife's distress. "Why don't we go get some air?"

Rebecca went with him reluctantly.

Alone again, Paul reached for the sandwich he'd made, and handed it to her.

"Thank you."

He smiled and kissed her forehead. "You're welcome. Now, eat. You need your strength."

Megan took a bite, chewed, and swallowed. It was her favorite—baloney, cheese, and mustard. "I'm sorry it came out like that. Becca's always been able to pick up on subtle things. I guess I must have been ogling you or something when you left the room."

Paul chuckled. "It's fine. We would have had to tell her soon, anyway. If she's going to be staying here for the next few days, I doubt we would have been able to hide it from her for long."

"You're not upset?"

He shook his head. "Why should I be?"

"I don't know. I guess I assumed you might want to keep it quiet until we talked to Chloe. You know, to make sure she approves and all." It wasn't that Megan was having doubts exactly, but Chloe's endorsement meant more to Megan than anyone else's.

"I don't think you have to worry about Chloe. Something tells me as long as it means you aren't going anywhere, she'll be all for it."

Megan forgot about her sandwich and pulled his head toward her for a kiss. "Nope. Not going anywhere."

He kissed her back and smiled. "Good."

A throat cleared, and they looked up to find Gage and Rebecca standing across the room right inside the doorway. Rebecca appeared calmer, but her eyes still held uncertainty.

"May we come in?" Gage asked.

Megan dropped her hand from around Paul's neck. "Sure."

Rebecca took a seat in the high-backed chair a foot or so away from where Paul and Megan were sitting. Gage retook his position behind his wife, resting his hands on her shoulders. As anxious as Megan was to find out what her sister had to say, she held her tongue and waited.

"You two are really getting married?" Rebecca asked.

Megan nodded. "We are."

Her sister turned her attention to Paul. "You really love her?"

"Yes, I love her."

Rebecca released a deep breath. "Okay."

"Okay?" Megan asked.

Her sister shook her head. "I don't understand it, but Gage reminded me how odd a match we appeared to be at first."

Megan smiled. "This is true. Trent thought I was Gage's girlfriend instead of you."

They both laughed, and Rebecca nodded. "He did."

Everyone was quiet for a long moment.

"So are we good?" Megan asked.

"Yeah. As long as he treats you right, we're good."

Megan wrapped her arm around Paul's waist and rested her head on his shoulder. "I don't think you have to worry about that."

Paul brushed his lips over her hair. "No, you don't. I plan on doing everything I can to make sure Megan is happy. That's a promise."

With the tension resolved, Gage rubbed his hands together. "Do you have any champagne around here, big brother? This is cause for a celebration."

Paul laughed. "No, but I think I've got some beers in the fridge."

Gage strolled into the kitchen and returned with three bottles of beer and a glass of water for Rebecca. He handed them all out and proposed a toast. "To my brother and my sister-in-law."

They all tipped their beverages and drank. "So when is the big day?" Gage asked.

Megan looked to Paul. "We hadn't really discussed it."

"Ah. Well, I recommend you do it soon. When Mom gets wind of this, you aren't going to be able to contain her."

"We want to tell Chloe first," Megan said.

Gage smiled. "Somehow, I don't think she'll object."

EPILOGUE

A KNOCK on his bedroom door caused Paul to jump. He wasn't normally so on edge, but it wasn't a run-of-the-mill kind of day.

"Are you decent?" Chris called from the hallway.

Paul chuckled. "I guess it depends on what you consider decent."

The door opened, and all three of his brothers walked in. Trent whistled when he got a good look at Paul in his new suit. "You clean up pretty well, big brother. I'd almost forgotten."

"I was in a suit for Chris' wedding. And Gage's. It hasn't been that long," Paul said.

Trent laughed.

Gage stepped forward and placed a hand on Paul's shoulder. "Since Megan and Rebecca's father isn't a part of their life, I figure it falls to me to lay down the law and tell you that you better treat her right, or else."

Although he knew Gage said it in jest, he also knew his little brother meant every word. The Daniels family had embraced both Rebecca and Megan from the beginning. They were part of the family, and the devil help any person who hurt them.

"Hey, stop giving Paul a hard time. He'll do right by Megan. Won't you?" Chris prompted.

281

Their father strolled through the door with a small box. "Stop giving your brother grief. How are you holding up, son?"

Paul ignored his brothers and concentrated on his dad. "I'm good. Is everything ready?"

"Yep, we're all set. You ready?" he asked, handing Paul the ring he'd asked his dad to pick up at the jewelers that morning.

Tucking the ring in the inside pocket of his jacket, Paul nodded.

He and his brothers followed their father downstairs and out to the backyard. Paul and Megan had discussed it, and decided on a simple wedding in their backyard at the end of July. She didn't want anything overly fancy, although Paul was more than willing to have a church wedding. Plus, Megan insisted she didn't want to wait the months it would take to organize such a thing.

The biggest unknown had been Chloe's reaction. They shouldn't have been worried, though. When they explained that he and Megan getting married would mean Megan would be Chloe's stepmom, she began jumping up and down screaming "Megan's going to be my mommy" over and over again.

After that, it was time to tell the rest of the family. His mom and dad didn't sound all that surprised. Neither did Chris, Elizabeth, or Trent. Maybe Paul and Megan's feelings for each other had been more obvious at Chris and Elizabeth's wedding than Paul thought.

The hardest sell, of course, had been Cindy. Because of her earlier comments, they decided to deliver the news face-to-face. He was extremely proud of Megan. She could have laid in to Cindy for what she'd said, but Megan took the high road and tried to reassure Cindy she loved Paul and Chloe, and was committed to both of them. By the end, both Cindy and Megan were crying and hugging each other.

To prove how much Cindy's feelings had changed regarding his and Megan's relationship, Cindy and George were in attendance for the wedding. The only other people were his family, her sister, and his partner, Janey. Small, but in their opinion, perfect. They didn't need, or want, anything flashy.

Paul said hi to each of them as he made his way up to the front of the makeshift aisle. So much had happened in the last month and a half. Megan had moved all her things into the master bedroom the day after they told Chloe the good news.

He'd also been busy at work tying up the loose ends on the serial killer case. It turned out there'd been an incident with a young woman overseas a few months prior to Rollins being discharged. The woman had ended up dead, her murder unsolved. It now appeared that Rollins had killed her, and whatever had prompted her murder had followed him home. The powers that be were blaming it on PTSD.

The minister waited underneath a cluster of trees along the fence that surrounded the yard. Paul pushed the thoughts of Rollins and work out of his mind. This wasn't the day for those thoughts. In a few minutes, his bride would be walking toward him. Megan had kept her dress hidden from him, but he knew it was white. He couldn't wait to see it. To see her in it. And then to peel it off her later that night.

Paul took his place beside the minister and turned to face the house where Megan would make her entrance. Everyone took their seats and waited.

In addition to keeping the guest list small, Paul and Megan had also decided not to have anyone other than Chloe stand up with them. As if in tune with his thoughts, the back door opened, and his daughter tiptoed outside in her fancy white dress. She made it about halfway across the yard before she lost all sense of decorum and ran toward him with her little basket of flowers.

He caught her and swung her up into his arms.

"Did I do it right, Daddy?" she asked.

Paul laughed. "You did perfect, sweetpea."

Giving her a kiss on the cheek, he set Chloe on her feet, and positioned her in front of him.

Everyone stood as Megan entered the backyard. She wore a simple white dress that flared a little at the waist. It only came down to her knees, which showed off her legs—a definite plus in his opinion.

The closer she got, the bigger her smile seemed to get. Paul was sure his expression mirrored hers. His cheeks ached with how much he was grinning.

"Hi," he said when she finally stood in front of him.

She giggled. "Hi."

Their vows were simple and traditional. Chloe stood in front of the minister while they exchanged their rings and as the minister pronounced them husband and wife.

Threading his fingers through her hair, Paul kissed his new bride. "I love you, Mrs. Daniels."

"And I love you, Mr. Daniels. Forever."

"Forever."

Seducing Janey

A Liberty Crossroads Romance

CHAPTER 1

Janey Davis turned her head in the direction of Captain Lane's voice. He was motioning for her and her partner, Paul Daniels, to come into his office.

Paul stood and grabbed his jacket from the back of his chair. "Uh-oh. What did you do now?"

Rolling her eyes, Janey pushed away from her desk. At twenty-nine, she was one of the youngest detectives, and she'd worked hard to gain the others' respect. For the most part she had. Then she'd gone and lost her temper with a suspect about a month ago. The rate things were going, Paul was never going to let her live it down. "Marrying Megan has made you a comedian."

Her partner smirked, not even bothering to deny it.

"Besides," Janey said as they made their way across the room, "who's to say you're not the one that's going to be in the hot seat? He wants to see you, too, remember?"

Paul chuckled, but didn't comment.

When they strolled into Captain Lane's office, he pointed to the chairs in front of his desk. She lowered herself onto the pleather cushion that had seen better days and waited to see what had caused the deep crease in her boss's brow.

"I got a call from the Warren County sheriff. Last night they discovered the body of a man who'd been tased and then beaten to death with some kind of metal pipe or bat."

That got her attention. Before she could speak up, Paul did. "You think it's connected to our case?"

Her boss stood and paced behind his desk several times before stopping to fix them both with a look that said he meant business. "I think it's a possibility. So does Sheriff Jenkins, which is why I want you to head up there and check it out. If it's the same perp, we need to know."

Paul shifted in his seat. She knew what was going through his mind. It was Friday afternoon and this weekend was his parents' fortieth wedding anniversary. They were having a big party in Cincinnati to celebrate. He, Megan, and his daughter, Chloe, were supposed to hit the road as soon as he got home from work.

Captain Lane noticed Paul's reaction. "Something wrong, Daniels?"

"No, sir. I just had plans with my family this weekend. It's my parents' anniversary." He hesitated and then pulled his shoulders back. "But if it's the same person, we need to find that out. I'll call my mom. I'm sure she'll understand."

Janey was sure she wouldn't. She'd met Marilyn Daniels on several occasions. The woman was a great mother, very understanding from what Janey had observed, but she wouldn't be happy if her oldest son wasn't there for such an important event. "How about I go and check things out? It may be nothing, right? And I'm sure the captain wouldn't want you to miss your parents' anniversary party if it's just a coincidence. Right, Captain?"

Paul and Captain Lane both stared at her for several moments before the captain cleared his throat. "I suppose that would work."

"Great." Janey jumped up before anyone else could get a word in edgewise. "Do you have all the information I'll need?"

Captain Lane handed her a piece of paper. "Ask for Deputy Kyle Reed. He's expecting you."

She took the paper and went to leave.

"Oh, and Davis?"

"Yes, Captain?"

"Remember you're in their jurisdiction. Sheriff Jenkins's father was a good friend of mine, which is why he called me." Captain Lane narrowed his eyes a little in warning. "Got it?"

Janey grinned. "Of course. I'll be the model of professionalism."

Captain Lane shook his head. "Fine. Now get out of here, both of you. And Daniels?"

"Yes?" Paul asked.

"Enjoy your weekend."

"Thank you, sir." Paul followed Janey back to their desks before saying anything. "You didn't have to do that, you know. My mom would have understood."

"She so wouldn't have." He looked as if he were about to argue, but she didn't give him a chance. "Doesn't matter now anyway. I'm going up north to check out the body and the crime scene and you're going to Cincinnati to spend the weekend with your family."

After a moment, Paul sighed. "Thank you. I owe you one."

Janey chuckled and retrieved her purse from the drawer. "You owe me way more than one, but who's counting?"

After stopping by her apartment to pack a bag, Janey headed two hours north to the small town of Liberty where the Warren County Sheriff's Office was located. She could have gone first thing in the morning, but she'd never been good at waiting. It was one of her many quirks that drove her partner crazy sometimes.

The drive through the country was refreshing. It wasn't often she made it out of Indianapolis these days—she had no reason to. Her life was there. Her job was there.

It was after eight by the time she pulled up in front of the large stone building that housed the Warren County Sheriff's Office. She had no idea if Deputy Reed would still be around or not, but at the very least she figured she'd introduce herself and see if they could recommend a place to stay. That was one of the downsides to small towns. They rarely had hotel chains.

Several people looked her way as she walked inside, their gazes following her every movement. It was a good thing she wasn't overly self-conscious.

A young man who looked barely out of high school stepped forward as she approached the glass. He wore a uniform, so she had to assume he was old enough to be a deputy at least. "Good evening, ma'am. Can I help you?"

Janey showed her badge. "I'm Detective Janey Davis from the Indianapolis PD."

She opened her mouth to say more, but the young deputy interrupted her. "You're here about the murder, right?" He didn't wait for her to answer before picking up the phone and dialing. "The detective from Indy's here. Uh-huh. Okay. Will do." The deputy hung up the phone, walked around the desk, and opened the door to allow her back into the station area. "Can I get you some water or coffee, Detective?"

"No, thank you," Janey said, remaining where she was. "If Deputy Reed has already gone home, I can come back in the morning—"

"That won't be necessary," a deep voice said from behind her.

Janey spun around to face the newcomer, surprised at how he'd been able to sneak up on her. He looked to be in his mid-thirties and had sandy blond hair in need of a trim. He was also tall with broad shoulders that pulled at the worn T-shirt he was wearing. At five foot six inches, Janey was used to most men towering over her, but standing next to this man she felt smaller than usual. He had to be at least six two. "Hello."

The man stepped forward and extended his hand to her. She took it automatically.

"My apologies. When you weren't here by eight I decided to head home," he said.

It took a second or two for her brain to catch up, but eventually she registered what he'd said. "I take it you're Deputy Reed?"

He grinned and she felt her chest clench a little in response. "I am."

Janey tried to ignore her body's reaction and pulled her hand out of his firm grip. "I didn't mean to drag you back in after you'd gone home for the evening."

"It's not a problem. I was still in the parking lot when Deputy Sims called. Are you Detective Daniels or Detective Davis?"

She realized then she hadn't introduced herself. "Davis. Detective Janey Davis."

Deputy Reed smiled wider if that were possible, and Janey felt all the moisture leave her mouth.

He held her gaze for a long moment and then glanced around as if searching for something. "Is your partner with you?"

"No. It's just me." She swallowed. "Detective Daniels had a family obligation this weekend."

"So you came alone?"

"Yes." Was it her or did he act as if he liked that her partner wasn't there? She tried not to examine it too closely. "Look, if you're already done for the night we can touch base in the morning. I was just anxious to get up here and take a look at things while they're fresh. If you can point me in the direction of the nearest motel..."

He shrugged, letting her know it wasn't a big deal. "I'm used to getting called out at all hours. It's part of being a deputy in a rural county."

When he took a step toward her, Janey felt her internal temperature rise. What the hell was wrong with her? "Still—"

"It's no trouble. Really." A woman came through the front doors and waved to Deputy Reed as she walked past. He nodded in her direction, and then returned his attention to Janey. "It's too late to head out to the crime scene, but the body is downstairs if you'd like to take a look."

"Yes. Please." Her palms were sweating and her heart was beating at a faster-than-normal pace. She needed to get it together. Hopefully looking over the body would settle her hormones.

Deputy Reed strolled over to a door on her left and opened it.

"Once we're finished, I'll take you to this little place I know where you can bunk for the night."

Not trusting her voice, Janey nodded and followed him through the door. They walked down a single flight of stairs that opened up into a long hallway. It was empty, but considering the late hour, she had to imagine that most of the staff had gone home.

Halfway down the hall, Deputy Reed stopped and gave two sharp raps on a gray door.

"Come in if you dare," said a voice on the other side.

Deputy Reed chuckled before pushing the door open and going inside.

The first thing Janey noticed upon entering the room was the color. There was color everywhere—a stark contrast to the gunmetal gray of the hallway. It was also unlike any other morgue she'd ever seen.

A woman around Janey's age pushed a pair of magnifying glasses onto her forehead and looked up from the body she was examining. Her gaze went directly to Deputy Reed. "I thought you'd gone home for the night." The way she grinned at him made Janey wonder if there wasn't something going on between the two of them.

He closed the door and moved closer to the woman. "I did, but duty calls, so I'm back."

That was when the woman seemed to notice Janey. She looked at Deputy Reed and raised an eyebrow in question.

"Dr. Mackenzie Mallory, I'd like you to meet Detective Janey Davis from the Indianapolis PD. She's here about our John Doe."

Dr. Mallory removed her gloves and offered her hand to Janey. "Welcome. And you can call me Mac. Everyone around here does."

The doctor's warm smile immediately put Janey at ease. "Thank you. And please call me Janey."

***

Kyle had been on patrol at dawn when the call had come in about an unconscious man lying in a ditch along the side of a country road.

When he'd arrived on scene, it didn't take him long to realize this wasn't someone who'd gotten drunk and passed out trying to walk home. It was a dead body.

He'd called it in to dispatch and then promptly dialed his boss. Noah was one of his best friends. They'd both grown up around Liberty and he'd want to know about a possible murder in his jurisdiction. In a rural county like Warren it was rare for someone to die of anything other than natural causes or an automobile accident. Most of what they dealt with involved DUIs, domestic violence calls, and some vandalism from bored teenagers.

It had taken several hours for Mac and her assistant, Brandon, to gather all the evidence and load the body into the van. Kyle had stayed on scene along with another deputy while Mac and Brandon did their thing to make sure none of the locals decided to stop and take a closer look.

By the time Kyle had strolled back into the station hours later, he'd planned to check in with Mac then head home to crash. His plans had been waylaid when Noah spotted him in the hall. He'd been pulled into Noah's office and told that two homicide detectives from Indianapolis would be coming to take a look at the body and the crime scene.

He wasn't given a whole lot of information other than the John Doe he'd found earlier that morning might be linked to another homicide case in Indianapolis. And the icing on the cake? Noah informed Kyle that he was to be the two detectives' tour guide. He was to make sure they were shown around and had access to everything they needed.

At first, Kyle wasn't thrilled with his new assignment, but things were looking up. The pretty blond detective standing beside him talking to Mac was a benefit he hadn't been expecting. She was of average height, probably around five five or five six, and had long dark eyelashes that framed her gray eyes.

He let his gaze linger over her curves as she spoke to Mac about the John Doe. Janey Davis had long legs that led up to a nice round ass.

"Kyle's the one who found him," Mac said, pulling him out of his daydream.

Janey Davis looked at him as if waiting for something. Of course, he hadn't been paying attention. His mind had been on other things. "Sorry. I must have missed the question."

Mac rolled her eyes. "Janey was asking how the body was found."

"A call came in through dispatch about someone passed out along the side of the road. When I went to check it out, I found our John Doe here."

"Did you notice any footprints at the scene?" Janey asked.

Kyle shook his head. "It's been pretty dry around here lately. Aside from the body itself, everything else appeared to be undisturbed. Not even the corn a few feet away had any damage. No signs of a struggle."

"So the body was most likely dumped there."

"That would be my guess," Kyle said, agreeing with her assessment.

Mac pointed to marks on the victim's arms. "Given the guy's size, I would have expected him to put up more of a fight if he'd seen his attacker coming, but I haven't been able to find any defensive wounds. There was some dirt under his nails. I sent a sample off to a lab that specializes in soil samples."

Janey nodded and leaned in to take a closer look at the bruise the Taser left on John Doe's abdomen. "Might be able to help us narrow down where he was killed."

They spent a few more minutes looking over the body before saying good night to Mac and going upstairs. It was almost dark by the time he escorted Janey out to the parking lot. She halted beside a silver SUV, which seemed to suit her.

"You mentioned knowing somewhere I could crash for the night?" she asked after unlocking her vehicle.

"I did." He smiled, hoping it had the effect on her he wanted it to. "It's a little outside of town. You can follow me there."

She opened her door, not looking him. "That isn't necessary. I'm sure I can find it if you give me directions."

"I have no doubt about that, but considering I'm going to be dumping you on my sister's doorstep, I figure I owe her a bit of an explanation." Janey's eyes went wide as she met his gaze. He couldn't help but laugh. "It's not as horrible as it sounds. Ava runs a bed and breakfast, and I happen to know she has a free room."

"I don't want to cause trouble between you and your sister."

"You won't. Besides, the closest motel is over a half hour away and I wouldn't recommend it."

He waited for several moments while she weighed her options. "All right. If you're sure she won't mind."

Kyle stifled a chuckle. He was sure his sister *would* mind, but she'd get over it. "I'll pull my truck around."

The drive to his sister's place didn't take long. Ava only lived about ten minutes outside Liberty. His sister must have heard them pull up because by the time they exited their vehicles she was standing on her front porch. "I didn't expect to see you tonight."

"Can't I just drop by and see my little sister?" Kyle asked, bounding up the stairs. He pulled her into a hug and kissed her on the cheek.

She batted him away. "Of course you can, but you usually don't. At least, not at this time of night. Shouldn't you be at home getting ready for your shift?"

"Normally, yes, but plans change." He nodded at Janey who was walking toward them, a backpack slung over one shoulder. "Ava, I'd like for you to meet Detective Janey Davis. She's here consulting on a case and needs a place to stay for a night or two."

His sister raised an eyebrow. "And you figured you'd bring her to me."

"Of course."

Ava shook her head then looked at Janey. "It's not that I mind having you. It's just that I wish my brother would've given me a heads-up."

"If it's a problem, I'm sure I can find somewhere else," Janey said.

"Not without driving a ways. Besides, I do have room."

She motioned Janey to follow her inside, and Kyle trailed after them. He knew he should leave and let Janey get settled, but he didn't want to. Not yet.

Ava led them down the short hallway to the kitchen. "Are you hungry? I'm sure I can dig something up for you."

"Thank you, but I ate a sandwich on the drive up."

His sister nodded. "Make yourself at home. Kyle knows where everything is if you need something and don't see it. I'm going to run upstairs and get a room ready for you."

Janey placed her purse and backpack on the large farm table that took up almost half his sister's kitchen. "I don't want you to go to any trouble."

Ava ignored her protest. "I'll be right back."

When they were alone, Kyle went to the cabinet and began making tea. He'd rather have coffee, but considering it was after nine and he actually needed to sleep tonight he figured tea would be the better option.

Once the kettle was on the stove, he returned his attention to Janey. She hadn't moved from her position beside the table. "You can sit down, you know."

She met his gaze and then looked at the table as if she were seeing it for the first time. "I'm debating whether or not I should go."

"If you go now, my sister will be insulted."

"And whose fault would that be? You never should have brought me here." Her eyes lit up with her annoyance.

Kyle leaned against the counter and crossed his arms over his chest. He would have loved to move closer, but something told him he might regret it. "Would you rather have spent the night at my house?"

She straightened her shoulders and jutted out her chin. "That's not what I meant, and you know it."

"That's not a no." He was enjoying pushing her buttons.

Janey snorted. "Are you always this arrogant?"

He chuckled. "Only when I have a beautiful woman standing in front of me."

It took her a moment to respond. "I'm here to do a job, Deputy Reed."

"So am I." He paused and lowered his voice a little. "And it's Kyle. We are going to be working together, after all."

She swallowed, her gaze never wavering.

He stared back at her, wondering what she saw there. She was a detective. It was her job to look beyond the surface.

They stood unmoving and locked in each other's gaze until Kyle heard his sister at the top of the stairs. He turned, breaking the connection, and removed the kettle from the burner. "Do you take milk or sugar in your tea?"

"Sugar." Her voice sounded a little strained, which made him grin. Having her around was going to be fun.

CHAPTER 2

Janey had set her alarm for six the next morning. She wanted to get up and moving before things in the house got too hectic. The night before she'd run into another couple who were staying at the bed and breakfast with their two young children. While she liked kids well enough, she knew what breakfast could be like when there were children involved and she wanted to avoid that. More than anything, she needed to stay focused on why she was there and not get distracted.

She finished getting dressed and headed downstairs to see if there was something quick she could grab to eat or if Ava could recommend a local restaurant. When she rounded the corner, Janey did a double take. Ava stood at the counter rolling out dough while her brother, Deputy Kyle Reed, stood next to her holding a little boy who didn't look to be more than two. Unlike the night before, Deputy Reed was wearing his uniform.

A few seconds passed before he noticed her standing there. "Good morning, Detective."

Ava looked over her shoulder. "I'm making cinnamon rolls but they won't be ready for another hour. I could make you something else if you don't want to wait."

"Thank you, but if you could point me in the direction of some coffee I'll be good," Janey said. She'd worry about food later.

"It's by the sink. Kyle started it about fifteen minutes ago, so it should be ready. And there are mugs in that cabinet." She motioned toward the one to the right of the sink, directly above the coffee maker.

"Thanks." Janey took her time selecting a mug, pouring her coffee, and adding the sugar. It was something she could have easily done in less than a minute, but she needed the distraction. A good night's sleep hadn't lessened her reaction to Deputy Reed... Kyle. If anything, it was worse.

When she turned back around, coffee in hand, he was no longer standing at the counter with his sister. He'd moved to the large wooden table, the boy on his lap, playing with sugar packets. They were lining them up to form a train. She felt her heart clench again.

"Are you sure I can't make you something? Surely you need more than coffee before you and Kyle head out." Ava's voice was almost like an electric shock to her system.

Before she could answer, Kyle did. "We'll grab something in town. Noah wants to meet Detective Davis before she and I head out to Butler Road."

"Noah?" Janey asked.

Kyle grinned up at her, and she felt her heart rate pick up. "Sheriff Jenkins. He called this morning and asked if I could bring you by. He wants to meet you."

"Oh. Well, I guess that makes sense. I am in his jurisdiction, after all." Janey took another sip of her coffee and placed it down on the counter next to the sink. "We should probably get going, then."

He shook his head. "There's no rush. Finish your coffee. Besides, Noah's probably at the diner having breakfast right now. If we go to the station this early, we'll just be hanging around waiting."

Janey picked her coffee back up and rested against the counter as she watched Kyle and the little boy push the packets of sugar around and make little choo-choo sounds. He looked up at her a couple of times, but for the most part he focused on the child on his lap. It was a complete contradiction to how he'd been the night before when they'd been alone.

Ava kissed the top of the little boy's head before walking to the sink to wash her hands. Janey stepped to the side to give her room. "He comes over in the mornings when he can to watch Cole for me so I can cook. I don't ask him to. He just does it."

"That's what family's for, right?" Not that Janey would know. The only family she had were the people she worked with—Paul in particular. He, his wife, Megan, and daughter, Chloe, had sort of adopted her.

"It wasn't always like this. Kyle's ten years older than me. But after my husband was killed..." Ava paused. She cleared her throat and reached for a towel to dry her hands. "Sorry. I didn't mean to—"

"There's no need to apologize."

Ava met Janey's gaze, a look of sad resignation in her eyes. "He was killed in the line of duty. A sixteen-year-old kid who'd robbed a liquor store."

"I'm sorry."

"Thank you." Ava took a deep breath. "It's been almost two years. Cole was just a baby. Which is why I decided to move back home." She looked over at her brother and her son. "There's no way I could have done it on my own, and luckily I didn't have to."

Janey was glad Ava had a strong support system, but hearing how great her brother had been wasn't helping Janey's attraction to him.

"Let me pop these in the oven," Ava said, "and then I'll make us all some eggs and toast."

"Really, that isn't necessary. I'm..."

The look Ava gave Janey had the words dying in her throat. Apparently she'd be having breakfast this morning whether she liked it or not.

A half hour later, belly full of not only eggs and toast but bacon and fresh fruit, Janey and Kyle made their way into town. All along the main street there were little shops. Most of their signs still read closed, but she could see people moving around inside, getting ready to open.

"Is this your first time in Liberty?" Kyle asked as they turned down the street that led to the station.

Janey nodded. "I don't get out of Indy very often."

"That's too bad."

She raised an eyebrow in question as he pulled into the parking lot and found a spot. "Why's that? I happen to like Indianapolis."

"Because you're missing out. Sure, the big city has a lot to offer, but so do places like Liberty."

"Like?"

"Like... I bet you all don't have hog roasts in the big city."

Janey laughed. "Hog roasts? We do eat pork in Indianapolis, you know."

He smiled and turned to face her. His knee grazed her leg when he changed positions, reminding her how tall he was. "Eating pork in a restaurant isn't the same thing at all."

"Really? And how is it different?" Her heart was pounding in her chest and it had nothing to do with their conversation.

Kyle rested his arm on the back of the seat and leaned in. "You'd have to see for yourself."

"And how would I do that?" She knew it was the wrong question to ask the moment the words slipped from her lips.

"Ethan's family is having a roast tonight. Come with me and I'll show you."

"I don't know if that's a good idea." Janey knew she wasn't misinterpreting the signals Kyle was sending out. She'd promised her captain she'd be the model of professionalism. Somehow, she didn't think going on what would essentially amount to a date with one of Sheriff Jenkins's deputies would qualify.

"I think it's a great idea. And besides, most of the town will be there." One side of his mouth turned up in a smirk. "You'd be perfectly safe."

"I can take care of myself. Maybe it's you who should be worried about your safety."

His smile grew. "I think I'll take my chances."

He swiftly got out of the vehicle, leaving her sitting there wondering what had just happened. She had no idea what she'd agreed to. Well, not exactly agreed to, but she sure hadn't said no. Maybe the country air was getting to her.

Kyle was still grinning when she joined him in front of the building.

"You can wipe that smile off your face. I didn't agree to go with you."

Instead of responding to her comment, he asked, "Ready to meet Sheriff Jenkins?"

Janey narrowed her eyes a little but nodded.

The station was busier than it had been the night before. It still wasn't anything like where she worked, but there were several people moving about. One woman had on a headset. Janey figured she had to be their dispatcher.

"Noah's office is this way," Kyle said.

"After you." That smile of his got bigger again. Janey could only imagine what was going through his head at that moment. "You call your boss by his first name? Is that a small-town thing?"

"Maybe. But in this case, it's that we've known each other most of our lives. His brother and I played football together in school."

"So you're friends."

It wasn't really a question, but he answered anyway. "Yep."

Not much chance the sheriff would help keep Kyle from crossing professional boundaries, then. If anything, they'd probably be giving each other pats on the back.

Kyle walked to the far side of the room. He stopped in front of a big door with the word SHERIFF embossed on the glass. "I think you'll like Noah. He's a lot like me."

Great.

***

Kyle knocked twice before entering Noah's office. The room had wall-to-wall bookshelves which Kyle had always found a little confining, but Noah seemed to like it. He said it gave him places to

301

put things. The only contrast to all the wood was a single window at the back. It wasn't enough, in Kyle's opinion.

"Perfect timing," Noah said.

"I figured you'd just be getting in." Kyle motioned toward Janey. "Noah, I'd like for you to meet Detective Janey Davis."

Noah stood and extended his hand to her. "It's a pleasure to meet you, Detective Davis. Your captain speaks highly of you and your partner."

"Thank you. I appreciate you allowing me to come take a look at things. We've run into a dead end on our case back home. If this is related, it could provide the lead we need to locate the suspect."

"We don't get many murders around here, so when Kyle discovered the body I did a little research. That's how I found out about your victim in Indianapolis. The similarities were too close for me to pass them off as coincidence without doing some more investigation." Noah sat down and leaned back in his chair. "I trust Kyle is taking good care of you... showing you around?"

Janey glanced over at Kyle and then turned her attention back to Noah. For a moment, he wondered if she'd object to him being her liaison. "Yes. He is. We stopped by the morgue last night to have a look at your John Doe. There was a similar bruise on the body. Not exactly like the one on our victim in Indy, but close enough," she said.

"Murdering someone can be unpredictable."

"Exactly. From what I've seen so far, I'm not willing to say they're not related." Again, she glanced over at Kyle then back to Noah. "I'm looking forward to visiting the crime scene."

"Well, I won't keep you. Just let me or Kyle know if there is anything you need." Noah looked down at some papers on his desk before glancing up again. "Do you mind giving me a minute with Deputy Reed? There are some things I need to go over with him."

"Of course." Janey exited the room, and the door closed with a click behind her.

As soon as they were alone, Noah leaned forward, clasping his hands on his desk in front of him. "I heard you dropped her off at your sister's last night."

"Ava had an open room. It made more sense than having her drive to a motel out by the highway."

He nodded in understanding. "And Ava was okay with it?"

Kyle wondered if there was more to Noah's question than there seemed. Why would he care if Ava was upset? "She wasn't thrilled I didn't give her a heads-up, but you know my sister. She doesn't turn anyone away if she can help it."

"No, she doesn't. Which is why you shouldn't take advantage of her good nature." This wasn't the lecture Kyle had been anticipating.

He debated voicing what was going through his head. If something was going on between his sister and Noah, Kyle wasn't sure he wanted to know about it. Noah was two years older than Kyle, which meant he was almost twelve years older than Ava. "I'll make it up to her. I always do."

Noah nodded again and picked up his phone. "Let me know if you two find anything. If this looks like the same person killed both these men, we need to know. I don't want a murderer running around Warren County."

"I'll call you."

Kyle found Janey standing a few feet from Noah's office, talking to Hayden, one of their dispatchers. Or maybe *talking* wasn't the most accurate term. Listening to Hayden ramble on was more like it.

When Hayden saw Kyle her eyes glazed over a little. He knew she had a bit of a crush on him, but as far as he was concerned she was off limits. She'd turned eighteen last summer and applied for the dispatcher's job. He liked her well enough, but she still had a lot of growing up to do. Kyle was thirty-five years old. He was interested in women who knew what they wanted out of life, not ones who'd barely graduated high school and were only beginning to figure out their path.

"Morning, Hayden."

She blushed. "Good morning, Kyle."

"Are we ready?" Janey asked.

"Yep. I need to grab the report, and then we can be on our way."

Hayden's eyes widened and she shifted her weight forward some.

"You're going to the crime scene, right? The guy Kyle found is big news around here, but you probably see stuff like this all the time in the city."

Janey met his gaze for a brief moment, and a type of silent communication passed between them. He went to retrieve the file while she responded to Hayden's question. "Yes, we see quite a few murders, unfortunately."

"What's it like?" he heard Hayden ask. "I've never seen a dead body before." She paused. "Well, except at a funeral, but it has to be different, right?"

He didn't give Janey time to answer. "Got it. We should probably get going."

"It was nice meeting you, Hayden."

"Sure. Maybe I'll see you tonight at the hog roast," Hayden called as they left.

Once they were outside, he heard Janey chuckle.

"Sorry about that. Hayden's lived here all her life and she's a little starstruck about the big city."

"I could tell," Janey said as they reached his county-issued SUV. It was what they would be taking to the scene. "Crazy thing is, I remember when that was me."

Kyle stopped and stared at her. "Which part?"

Janey climbed into the passenger seat without answering.

He waited until they were on their way and tried a different approach. "Somehow I can't see you being like Hayden."

A smile pulled at the corners of Janey's mouth. He hadn't fooled her. She knew exactly what he was doing. "You'd be surprised."

"Hmm. Now you have me curious."

"Curiosity killed the cat, you know."

It was his turn to laugh. "You're a hard nut to crack, Janey Davis."

She didn't say any more until he'd pulled up behind another deputy's SUV. Noah had posted someone overnight to be sure nothing was messed with. He was taking it personally that a murder had happened on his turf.

They both got out and walked over to where Ethan stood leaning against the hood of his vehicle. He straightened when he realized Kyle wasn't alone. "Morning, ma'am."

"Janey Davis, I'd like you to meet Deputy Ethan Price. Ethan, this is Detective Davis from the Indianapolis PD," Kyle said.

Ethan removed his hat and gave a little bow. "It's a pleasure to meet you, Detective."

"Thank you." Janey seemed pleased with Ethan's southern manners. For some reason that irritated him.

"Anything new overnight?" Kyle asked.

Ethan shrugged and resituated his hat on his head. "A few cars slowed down to get a better look, but no one stopped."

"Where did you find the body exactly?" Janey asked, not wasting any time.

"Over here." He took her to the spot in the ditch where John Doe had been lying. "His leg was extended out toward the road, which is most likely what drew someone's attention and prompted them to call it in."

She nodded and knelt down. "Mac said the guy had been dead for at least twelve hours before you found the body."

It didn't feel right to stand over her, so he bent down, balancing his weight on the balls of his feet. "That doesn't narrow it down much."

"No. But it does tell us that whoever dumped the body is most likely familiar with the area."

"Why do you say that?" he asked.

Janey met his gaze and stood. He followed suit.

She turned in a circle, taking in their surroundings. "How far is the highway from here?"

"At least twenty minutes. And that's if you're not entirely paying attention to speed limits."

"This isn't exactly a well-traveled road, correct?"

No, it wasn't. It was one of those back-country roads that didn't even have a center line painted on it. There was no need since ninety-nine percent of the people who used it were local. "You think whoever it was had to know where they were going."

"I'd almost guarantee it. This is too remote to be random. If it were off a main road, I could see it being a convenience thing, but not here."

Before he could formulate another question, Janey was striding away from him. She halted a foot or so from the edge of the cornfield, looked to both sides, and then turned to her right and began walking. He jogged to catch up. "What are you looking for?"

"I'm not sure."

Kyle remained silent, letting her do whatever it was she was doing. After fifty paces, she spun around and headed back in the opposite direction. They were about thirty feet on the other side of the crime scene when she stopped.

"What is it?" he asked.

She reached into her pocket and pulled out a pair of gloves. After slipping them on, she pushed a few of the cornstalks out of the way.

A second later, a huge grin spread across her face. She looked up at him. "We may be in luck."

He moved to see what she'd found. There, a few feet inside the cornfield, was a pile of empty beer bottles. "I doubt it's related. Probably a bunch of high school kids."

"Exactly." She released the cornstalks and faced him. "And if they come here often, which from the looks of it they do, then they may have been here the other night." She paused. "We may have witnesses."

CHAPTER 3

JANEY WORKED with Ethan to take pictures of the area and put the beer bottles in plastic evidence bags while Kyle called Sheriff Jenkins. There had to be at least twenty bottles that appeared to have been recently discarded. It was wishful thinking that the kids had been around when the body was dumped, but at the moment it was the best lead they had.

She'd dropped another glass bottle into a clear plastic bag when her phone began to vibrate. She held her bag out to Ethan. "Can you take this?"

"Yes, ma'am."

His formal reply had her grinning. She removed her gloves and dug her phone out of her pocket. Paul's name flashed across the screen. "Miss me already, huh?"

Paul laughed. "Something like that. Have you found anything?"

"Well, I'm standing in a cornfield surrounded by empty beer bottles. Does that count?"

He was quiet for a long moment. "Okay, I'll bite. Why are you standing in a cornfield surrounded by empty beer bottles?"

"They're about thirty feet from where Kyle found the body,

probably left by some teenagers. I'm hoping we can get an ID off the prints and that one of them saw something."

"Kyle?" he asked, and she could hear the wheels turning in his head.

"Deputy Reed."

"I see."

Janey made her way out of the cornfield and walked another ten feet or so away from the vehicles to get a little privacy. "It's a small town. Things are laid back here. You know how it is."

"If you say so." She knew he didn't believe her.

"Aren't you supposed to be celebrating your parents' anniversary today?" she asked, trying to change the subject.

"We're heading over to the reception hall in about half an hour. Ma wants to look over everything and make sure the caterers didn't screw something up. She's not used to other people doing the cooking."

"I'm sure it'll be fine." Janey looked across the two-lane road at the wide expanse of soybeans that went all the way back to a row of trees about a mile away. Then her gaze fell on Kyle. He was still on the phone, nodding at whatever was being said. She couldn't read the expression on his face. He looked somewhere between frustrated and resigned.

"Janey? Did you hear me?" Paul asked.

She averted her eyes from the distracting deputy. "Sorry. I was thinking about the case. I don't know if this is the same person or not. I mean why dump one victim behind a dumpster in an alley and the next in the middle of nowhere two hours away?"

Paul didn't respond right away. "Maybe they knew it would be another jurisdiction and were hoping no one connected the dots."

"Maybe."

"You don't think so?" he asked. Paul had taught her to trust her instincts.

"I don't know. Something feels off. The change in location bothers me. Why here?"

"He or she is familiar with the area?"

"I thought about that," Janey said. "It's possible. Especially given how far it is from the main road."

She heard a muffled voice in the background and then the sound of Paul sucking in a lungful of air. "Janey, I need to go. I'll call you later."

"No, he won't," Megan said in the background.

Janey chuckled. "I'll see you on Monday." She slipped the phone back into her pocket and went to see what, if anything, the sheriff had to say about what they'd found.

Kyle and Ethan were loading the bagged evidence into the back of Ethan's SUV when she approached the vehicles. "Everything all right?" Kyle asked.

"Yep." She ignored the question in his eyes.

Ethan closed the back and locked it. "I think that's everything. I'll get it back to the station so they can start pulling the prints." Without waiting for a response, he walked to the driver's side of his vehicle and opened the door. "Hope to see you at the hog roast tonight, Detective Davis." He climbed inside the SUV and was off before she had a chance to answer him.

Janey couldn't help but laugh. In less than four hours she'd been asked if she was going to this pig roast—hog roast—whatever they wanted to call it, by three different people. What was so special about cooking a pig that had everyone in this little town so fixated on it as if it were some huge, not-to-be-missed event?

She felt Kyle come up behind her, and her amusement swiftly turned to something else entirely. "We should stop by the diner and grab some lunch."

"I'm not hungry." Her words came out as not much more than a whisper.

He stepped closer and her body went on alert. Not from fear, but from anticipation. "Neither am I, but it's a good place to ask around to see if anyone knows who might have been in that field the night before last."

"All right." She took a deep breath and turned to face him, trying to shake off the torrent of emotions swirling around inside her. "Let's go."

She managed to take two steps before he put his hand on her arm to stop her. Sure, she could have pulled away, but the feeling of his warm hand on her bare skin had her temperature rising.

Kyle came up behind her again, but this time he stood close enough that his chest was touching her back. He leaned in so his mouth hovered right above her ear. "Don't run away from me, Janey."

"I'm not."

"Aren't you?" He didn't move an inch.

"We have a job to do. I'm trying to catch a killer." Again, she could have easily walked away—his grip wasn't all that tight—but she didn't. Something was keeping her rooted to the spot.

"Don't try and change the subject." He skimmed the palms of his hands down her arms, leaving tingles in their wake. "We have plenty of time to get to the diner, and the fingerprints will take a while. This is about you and me."

She swallowed. "There is no you and me."

Her words hung in the air for a long moment before he spoke. "Come with me tonight. Let me show you a good time."

"And then what?" She had no idea what prompted her to ask or even what kind of a response she was hoping to get.

"And if, after that, you don't want anything to do with me, I'll back off."

They stood there for what felt like forever, not moving. She closed her eyes in an attempt to get her bearings. What would it hurt to go on a date with him? Chances were good that after this weekend she'd never see him again. His life was here in Liberty. Hers was two hours south in Indianapolis.

Janey turned around to face him. They were standing so close she had to tilt her head back in order to look him in the eye. "One date."

He smiled. "That's all I'm asking."

She held his gaze, searching for any deception. She didn't find any. "Deal."

"You won't regret it. I promise."

"I'll hold you to that."

He snorted, which broke some of the tension. "I'm sure you will. Now, let's see if anyone at the diner knows anything."

As they drove into town, Kyle gave her what he called the nickel tour. He pointed out the local hardware store, the library, and some of the little shops they passed.

"Have you lived here all your life?"

Kyle nodded. "I own the house where Ava and I grew up. It's about a half mile from here."

"You never wanted to leave? See what the outside world had to offer?" Janey asked.

"I spent four years in the Army. That was enough for me."

He turned down a side street and pulled into a parking lot. There were a few other vehicles, but if not for them she wouldn't have pegged it for a parking lot at all. There were no signs—no lines dividing the places for cars. It was just an empty piece of pavement.

She climbed out of the SUV and followed Kyle down a walkway that ran between two buildings. It led to the main street they'd been on moments before. He made a right and pulled open a door, motioning that she should go inside.

"This is it?" she asked, looking for a sign.

"This is it." He pointed toward a little sign in the window that she'd missed. The sign looked like it had seen better days. It was faded, but the words *Liberty Diner* were still there.

Janey figured it must be one of those hole-in-the-wall places that only the locals knew about. Hopefully the food was decent and she wouldn't get sick from it.

***

Kyle waited for Janey to enter the diner and then followed her inside. At the sound of the bell over the doorway, Claire Lawrence, the owner, looked up to see who the new arrivals were. She grinned when she saw them. "Find a seat wherever. I'll be with you in a minute."

He and Janey made their way to an open booth and sat down across from each other. Kyle did a quick scan of the area and noticed Janey doing the same. It was almost noon and the lunch rush would be flooding in soon. The other waitress, Kennedy, was behind the counter, stocking the pies.

Claire came over to their table and handed them both a menu even though he didn't need one. "I didn't expect to see you in today, Kyle."

"Plans changed," he said.

"I heard you were the one to find that man yesterday. It's terrible to think of something like that happening so close to home." Claire turned her attention to Janey. "You must be the detective from Indy."

"Word travels fast."

Claire shrugged. "It's a small town and this is big news."

"Not much happens around here, huh?" Janey asked.

"Not like this." Claire visibly shuddered. "They can keep the crime in the big cities. I like it here in our quiet little town."

Kyle figured this was as good a time as any to question Claire and see if she'd heard anything that might help them. "The major crimes anyway. We still have plenty to keep us busy, including bored teenagers that like to get into mischief."

Claire nodded. "That's true. Just last week some kids spray-painted the high school parking lot."

"At least it was spray paint and not something worse," Janey said.

"That's true. I hadn't thought of it that way."

Kyle laid his menu on the table. "You haven't heard of any kids partying in some of the cornfields, have you? I'm looking into some complaints we've received."

"Sorry, I haven't. But if I do, I'll let you know."

"Thanks, Claire. I'd appreciate it," he said.

"Do you two need a few minutes, or do you know what you want?"

Kyle glanced at Janey, but she was still looking over the menu. "I think we might need a few minutes."

"I'll go grab you some waters and be back." Claire scurried away to greet another table. Things were going to start getting hectic, but that was what he wanted. Sometimes observing people was the best way to the next lead.

"How busy does this place get during lunch?" Janey asked, her focus still on her menu.

"There are only a few places to eat in town, so most of the locals come here at least a couple of days a week."

Janey nodded. "Do *you* come here a lot?"

"Probably more than I should, but I'm not a great cook and I try not to take advantage of my sister any more than necessary."

"So that's a yes, then." Janey met his gaze and there was a spark of amusement in her eyes.

He grinned back at her.

"Here you go," Claire said, placing a glass of water in front of each of them. "Do you still need some more time?"

Kyle let Janey answer since he'd known what he wanted the moment he sat down. "I'll have the roast chicken, please."

Claire jotted it down on her pad. "Anything to drink besides the water?"

"No. I'm good. Thanks."

"And you?" Claire asked, looking to Kyle.

"I'll take my usual."

Janey quirked her eyebrow up at his answer.

Claire made another note. "Burger and fries it is."

Once they were alone again, or as alone as they were going to be in a public place like the diner, Kyle relaxed back in his seat and focused on Janey. "I told you a little about me, so I think it's only fair you share, too. Have you always lived in Indianapolis?"

"No," she said after taking a long drink of her water. "I moved there after I graduated high school."

"And where were you before that?" he asked, curious.

She hesitated, which he found interesting. Why wouldn't she want him to know where she grew up? "Outside of Fort Wayne."

"Fort Wayne is a decent-sized town."

"It is."

He sat forward, placing his forearms on the table. "Why does my asking about where you grew up make you uncomfortable?"

"It doesn't." At his skeptical look, she clarified. "I just don't like to talk about it, that's all."

For a moment he thought about pushing the issue. It was in his nature to get to the truth, but Janey wasn't a suspect. He was going to have to be patient. "All right."

"Thank you." She averted her gaze and took another look around the room. "There's a restaurant not far from Paul and Megan's house that's a little like this."

"Paul Daniels, your partner?" If she didn't want to talk about the past, he'd take information about her present.

Janey nodded but offered nothing more on the subject. "So what's your plan? Are we going to talk to all these people before we leave?"

"Nope."

"No?"

He shook his head. "I told Claire I was looking for information. She knows who the farmers in the area are. She'll make sure to mention something about it to each of them and see if she gets any hits. If she does, she'll let me know."

"You're counting on her gossip?"

"Not exactly," he said. "Claire overhears a lot of things she doesn't share, but she's in a unique position to help us out from time to time. That's why Noah comes here every morning. If she's gotten wind of anything, she can let him know discreetly. She's been a great source of information since she moved to town."

"She didn't grow up here?"

"No. She moved to Liberty about four years ago after her divorce. I'm not sure what all happened, but she got a large settlement out of it and she used it to buy the diner."

Janey tucked a loose strand of hair behind her ear. "Sounds like there's a story there."

"I'm sure there is, but I don't like to pry."

She released one hard laugh. "You could have fooled me."

Kyle smiled and leaned forward again. "I'm not interested in Claire. You, on the other hand…"

Janey sobered. "Why me?"

"Why not you?"

Claire arrived with their food, silencing any response Janey might have made. They spent the next several minutes eating and listening to what was going on around them. Most of the chatter was about the weather. It hadn't rained in over a week and the farmers were beginning to worry about their crops.

No one mentioned the dead body that was found the previous day, which Kyle found a bit odd. The only reason he could come up with was that they were unsure of Janey. Everyone else in the diner was local. She was an outsider.

They were finishing up when Claire came by with a slice of pie for each of them and the check. "Gerald said Fred Mitchel mentioned that he ran off some kids from one of his fields a week or so ago. You just never know about kids these days."

He nodded and thanked her for the information. "No, you don't."

To her credit, Janey waited until they were back in his SUV before commenting on what Claire had said. "I'm impressed. That's quite a system you all have worked out."

Kyle grinned as he put the key in the ignition and started the engine. "Let's go pay a visit to Mr. Mitchel and see if he got a look at any of the kids he ran off."

Mitchel's farm was a good twenty minutes from town in the opposite direction from where he'd found John Doe's body. That didn't mean anything, though. Most sixteen-year-olds in the county had a driver's license, since not having one severely limited one's mobility. There was no public transportation in Warren County.

Janey stared out the window as he drove. She appeared to be deep in thought about something.

"Penny for your thoughts?" he asked.

She turned her head to look at him then went back to watching the fields. "I was thinking about the case. My case. In Indianapolis. He was found behind a dumpster in an alley. It's a heavily trafficked area, and yet no one saw anything."

"Were you able to identify the victim?"

"Yes. Travis Merrick. He was a construction worker. Clean record. Nothing out of the ordinary that would explain how he would wind up dead in an alley behind a dumpster. His wife said he'd called to say he was running late after work, but then he never came home."

Kyle realized then why she kept looking at the fields. "Why would whoever it is change the dump site so drastically if it was the same person that killed both guys?"

Janey nodded.

"Do you think it's a copycat, then?"

"Too early to say, but I'm not ruling it out."

Kyle slowed as Mitchel's farm came into view. He was hoping the aging farmer had some information for them. Not only could it provide them with a lead that would catch the killer, but it also meant Janey would have an excuse to stay a little longer.

He turned onto the dirt driveway and followed it to the old farmhouse. Two golden retrievers ran out to greet them, barking and wagging their tails. A few seconds later, the screen door at the side of the house opened and out stepped Fred Mitchel.

"He doesn't look pleased to see us," Janey said, noting the scowl on the old farmer's face.

"Don't take it personally. He's not a fan of visitors in general, which is probably why he complained about the kids being in his field."

"Do you want me to wait here, then?" Janey asked. "If he's not fond of visitors, I doubt my presence will help loosen his tongue."

CHAPTER 4

JANEY WASN'T SO sure about Kyle's assessment of Fred Mitchel. As they crossed the lawn, the irritation on his face didn't lessen. He wasn't happy to see them.

"Afternoon, Fred," Kyle said when they reached the edge of the porch. "I was hoping we could talk to you about the kids you ran off a couple of weeks ago."

Fred Mitchel's gaze shifted from Kyle to her, then he turned his head and spat over the porch rail. "Who's she?"

"This is Detective Davis. She's visiting from Indianapolis." Kyle didn't seem bothered by Fred Mitchel's attitude.

The farmer looked her up and down. "She here about the body you found?"

Janey stayed quiet, letting Kyle decide how much to share. "Among other things."

"Humph." Mitchel took a step forward. "And what does that have to do with me and the kids I chased off my property?"

Kyle shrugged. "Probably nothing."

"And yet you're here harassing me." Mitchel huffed again and crossed his arms over his chest. "Well, on with it. What do you want to know? I've got work to do."

"Where were the kids when you discovered them?"

"Cornfield." Short and to the point.

"How many were there?" Kyle asked.

"Don't know. Maybe ten. Fifteen." Mitchel shrugged. "Was gettin' dark."

Kyle nodded. "Did you happen to recognize any of them?"

"No." Disappointment settled in Janey's gut. Unless they got a hit on those fingerprints, they'd struck a dead end again.

"Thank you for your time, Fred. We'll let you get back to work." Kyle headed toward his SUV and she followed.

"That was a waste," she said once they were inside the vehicle.

He nodded. "It was worth a shot."

"Now what?"

"Now…" The look Kyle gave her had her heart rate picking up. "I drop you off at my sister's so you can rest up for our date tonight."

Janey bit the inside of her cheek. She had no idea if going to this shindig with him was a good idea or not, but if she was being honest with herself, she had to admit she wanted to go. It had been a while since a guy had piqued her interest the way Kyle did. "I was talking about the case."

"We cross our fingers and hope the lab gets a hit on one of those fingerprints."

It was close to three by the time he dropped her off at Ava's with a promise to be back to pick her up around six. Ava was in the living room folding laundry. She glanced behind Janey expectantly, and then frowned. "Kyle isn't coming in?"

"He'll be back later." Janey wasn't sure how much he'd want his sister to know, but figured she'd find out eventually. "Apparently there's some sort of pig roast tonight."

A sly smile crossed Ava's face as she took a towel from the basket.

"What?"

"Nothing." When Janey continued to wait, Ava sighed. "It's just been a while since Kyle showed any real interest in anyone. It's good to see. I want him to find someone. Settle down. He deserves to be happy."

Curiosity nagged her, but she wasn't sure she wanted to know. Kyle lived here in Liberty. Her life was in Indianapolis. Granted, it wasn't a huge distance, but it was far enough.

Realizing how absurd her train of thought was, Janey excused herself and went to grab a shower. She told herself nothing was going to happen tonight, but even she didn't believe it. Besides, it was better to be prepared. If nothing happened, it wouldn't hurt to make sure everything was shaved and neatly trimmed.

It was as she was standing at the end of her bed in nothing but a towel that Janey realized she had a problem. The only clothes she'd brought with her were khaki pants and shirts—her work attire. Somehow she didn't think that would help her to fit in at what sounded more like a community barbecue.

Janey threw on some clean clothes and headed back downstairs. Ava was roughly the same size. Hopefully, she wouldn't mind letting her borrow something. Janey didn't think she had time to make it to the nearest mall and back before Kyle returned to pick her up.

"Ava?" Janey called out when she didn't find her in the living room or the kitchen, the only two rooms she'd been in on the first floor.

"In here."

Janey followed Ava's voice to what had to be the master bedroom.

"Hey. Come in," Ava said, setting aside the book she was reading.

"I didn't mean to bother you in your personal space."

Ava waved her comment away. "It's fine. I was just enjoying some peace and quiet while I can. What did you need?"

For a moment Janey reconsidered. It didn't feel right asking Ava, Kyle's sister or not, if she could borrow an outfit. She didn't even know the woman. "Nothing. Never mind."

"Janey, just spit it out."

"I was wondering if maybe you had something I could wear tonight. All I brought with me were work clothes. I wasn't planning on going out."

Before she'd even finished her sentence, Ava was up and moving toward her closet. "I'm sure I have a dress that would fit you. Let me see..." She rooted around in her closet, pushing hangers to one side until she found what she was looking for. "What do you think?"

The dress was navy blue with a white belt at the waist. It was simple but cute. "As long as it fits, I think it will work."

Ava held it out to her. "Go try it on. You can use my bathroom if you want. And if it doesn't work, we can find something else."

"Thanks, Ava. I really appreciate this."

Janey hurried into the bathroom and stripped out of the clothes she'd put on a few minutes earlier. Since the dress had wider straps, she was still able to wear her bra, which was a good thing. She wasn't exactly small on top. It was a little loose around the middle, but the belt took care of that. Otherwise, it was a pretty good fit. On the downside, there was no way she'd be able to carry her gun. Considering her options, it was a sacrifice she was going to have to make.

"What do you think?" Janey asked when she stepped out of the bathroom. She did a little twirl and loved how the skirt flared up slightly.

Ava moved in for a closer look. "Wow. I think it looks much better on you than me."

"Thanks, but I doubt that." Kyle's sister had one of those hourglass figures, and a dress like this would only highlight that.

A sad smile crossed Ava's face, and Janey wondered if the other woman was thinking about her late husband. "I'm glad it fits. Now you can go out and have a good time tonight."

The way she said it gave Janey the impression that Ava wouldn't be attending. "Aren't you going? Your brother said most of the people in the area would be there."

"Oh, they will be. The Price family does this every year. It's a big deal around here."

"But you're not going." It wasn't a question.

Ava shook her head. "I have lots to do here. Besides, I need to get Cole to bed by eight or he'll be cranky all day tomorrow."

Janey chose to keep her mouth shut. She didn't know Ava well enough. "Well, I should probably go upstairs and finish getting ready."

"Let me know if you need anything else." Ava smiled and lifted Cole from his playpen. "I'm going to go make this little guy some dinner."

It didn't take Janey long to finish getting ready. She was a minimalist when it came to makeup. A little bit of eye shadow, some mascara, and a touch of lip gloss. That was it. Anything more had her feeling as if she had goop slathered all over her face.

With five minutes to spare, she descended the stairs, but Kyle was already standing near the front door waiting for her. He wore a pair of faded jeans and a burgundy shirt with the top two buttons undone. She had the urge to run her hand down the front of his chest and slowly release each button.

His gaze moved down her body, and then back up to her face as she walked toward him. "You look amazing."

"Thanks," Janey said, trying to ignore the butterflies tumbling around in her stomach. "I borrowed the dress from your sister."

He offered her a hand. "We should get going. They'll be pulling the hog out of the pit soon. I don't want you to miss it."

Janey had no idea what the big deal was, but she was willing to give him the benefit of the doubt. "Let me just say goodbye to Ava."

The words had barely left her mouth when Kyle's sister poked her head out of the kitchen. "You two have a good time. I won't wait up." She winked.

Heat rushed to Janey's cheeks. Of course Kyle noticed. "We'll see you later, sis."

Ava waved as they walked out the door, Kyle's hand resting on Janey's lower back.

"That wasn't awkward at all," Janey mumbled.

"You want to talk about awkward? Try walking in on your little sister going at it with her husband on the couch." He shuddered as he pulled open the passenger door of his truck for her.

Janey giggled and brushed past him to climb inside the cab. "Got an eyeful, did you?"

"Oh yeah. There is no amount of brain bleach that'll get rid of that memory."

***

The best part of the Prices' annual hog roast was that the family farm had plenty of space for everyone. A large farmhouse sat in the center of the property, surrounded by more than one thousand acres of farmland. There were four barns, and all of them served a purpose. Tonight one had been converted into a dance hall of sorts.

Kyle parked his truck along the long driveway, hopped out, and went to help Janey. He hadn't even thought about her not having something to wear when he'd asked her to come with him tonight. Then again, he wouldn't have cared if she'd stayed in what she'd worn earlier.

They had to walk a ways to reach the roasting pit where everyone was gathered. It was situated on the back side of the barn to keep the smoke away from the other festivities.

"What's everyone waiting for?" Janey asked as they approached the crowd.

"You'll see."

A few minutes later, Ethan, his brother Evan, and their father emerged from one of the other barns, all three of them with shovels. They made a beeline for the mound of fresh dirt covering the pit and began digging. After a few minutes three other men stepped up and took turns removing the dirt. This back and forth went on until they reached the sheet metal underneath. Ethan and Evan pried the metal back while their father, wearing heavy gloves, pulled out burlap sacks.

"Are those the pigs?" Janey asked in a low whisper.

Kyle nodded. "Best pork you've ever tasted. Trust me."

"It doesn't look all that appetizing at the moment."

A few of the guys stayed behind to cover the pit up again so no one accidently fell in, while everyone else moved into the barn. Kyle guided Janey over to a long table set up with drinks. "What would you like? They've got everything from water and Kool-Aid for the kids to beer."

Janey glanced around, looking slightly uncomfortable. "I think I'll just stick to water."

"Two waters," Kyle told Elena, Ethan and Evan's sister, who was manning the table.

She opened a cooler to her left, dug two bottles of water from the ice, and placed them on the table.

He picked up the drinks. "Thanks, Elena."

"Enjoy your evening."

Kyle handed Janey one of the waters and guided her over to a less crowded area of the barn. It would take ten minutes or so for the meat to be ready, and the band was still getting set up. For the moment, there wasn't much to do besides wait. Wait and try to get to know his date a little more.

"How long have you been a detective?" he asked. Work seemed to be a safer subject with her than her past.

She sat down on a nearby chair, and he lowered himself into the seat next to her. "Almost six years. I worked patrol for a couple of years before that."

"Why did you decide to change?"

"I always wanted to be a detective. That was always the goal. So at the first opportunity, I took the test." The look on her face told him all he needed to know. Janey loved her job. He knew the feeling. Being a deputy made him feel connected to the community. He didn't want to be anywhere else.

"I know what you mean. As soon as I got my discharge papers from the Army, I applied to the sheriff's department."

"Did you ever think about working in a bigger city?"

Kyle tried not to read more into her question than there really was. "Not really. Ava was still in school and I wanted to be here for her last years of high school." He took a drink of his water. "I think I can do more good here. People... they care about each other. Even Fred Mitchel, who acts like everyone and everything annoys him. I've seen him pitch in and help a neighbor whose crop was about to go bad because he couldn't get it in fast enough."

Janey rolled her bottle of water between her fingers. "That's hard to imagine."

"People can surprise you."

She met his gaze and whispered, "Yes, they can."

Kyle had an undeniable urge to kiss her in that moment. The only thing that stopped him was where they were. Not that he had any problem kissing Janey in public; more that he wanted a little privacy the first time it happened.

He stood, needing to move. "Why don't we see if the food's ready? I'm starving."

There was already a line at the food table. Several people stopped to introduce themselves to Janey. Most already knew who she was.

With their plates piled high, Kyle and Janey headed outside to one of the picnic tables. He should have known they wouldn't be alone for long. Within minutes of sitting down, Avery Richards and Mac joined them, both with full plates of their own.

"Mind if we join you?" Avery asked after she'd already begun sitting down.

Kyle figured he should probably make introductions. "Janey, this is Avery Richards. She's the town pharmacist."

"Nice to meet you," Janey said.

Mac picked up her fork and stabbed a chunk of pork. It was almost violent, which made Kyle think something was up. "Bad day?" he asked.

"Just disappointing, that's all." He knew she had to be talking about their John Doe. Unfortunately, with Avery at the table, they couldn't talk in detail.

"It'll work itself out. It always does," Janey said. Her optimism surprised him. She'd been the frustrated one earlier when they had come away from Fred Mitchel's without a name.

He took a chance and placed his free hand on her leg. She tensed for a moment and then relaxed. Her reaction gave him confidence that he wasn't misreading things. Janey felt the same pull he did.

Avery began asking Janey about life in Indianapolis. He was only half paying attention since most of what they were saying had to do with stores and restaurants. His focus was on the feel of Janey's soft skin under his fingers. He gradually pushed the hem of her skirt out of his way, giving her time to stop him, but she didn't.

There was a break in the conversation when Mac and Avery turned to watch two of the Johnson boys try to see how many pieces of watermelon they could shove down their throats in sixty seconds. Janey took the opportunity to lean over and whisper in his ear. "You're making it very hard to concentrate."

He inched his fingers up a little higher on her thigh. "Do you want me to stop?"

She hesitated, and for a moment he thought she was going to say yes. He nearly jumped out of his seat when he felt her nails scratch along the inside seam of his jeans. If she kept it up, he wasn't going to be able to leave the table for a while.

Kyle placed his hand over hers, stopping her movement. "Would you like to dance?"

A small crease formed in Janey's forehead.

"Don't tell me you don't like to dance," he said, linking their fingers.

"It's not that. I just figured..."

There was a hint of insecurity in her tone, which threw him for a minute. Janey didn't strike him as the insecure type.

He glanced over to see that Mac and Avery were still otherwise occupied before leaning in closer to Janey. "If we leave now, everyone is going to assume we're going back to my place."

Her gaze searched his. "And that's not what you want."

Kyle chuckled. "Oh, it's definitely what I want." He brought her fingers up to his lips and placed a soft kiss on her knuckles.

"Then..."

"This is a small town. Like it or not, people gossip."

She broke eye contact, looked over his shoulder, and then met his gaze again. "I get it."

Her tone of voice told him she didn't. "There are going to be people who will speculate no matter what, but we don't need to add fuel to the fire. I'd rather keep them guessing. They don't need to know what's going on in my personal life."

Janey took a deep breath and got up from the table. "Didn't you mention something about a dance?"

In less than a minute she'd gone from flirty to hurt, and he had no idea why. Didn't she understand how small towns worked? He had every intention of taking her home with him tonight if she was willing, but the rest of Warren County didn't need to know that.

He picked up their empty plates and tossed them in a nearby trash can then led her back into the barn where the makeshift dance floor was set up. Several couples were already dancing, so he pulled her against him and started to move with the music. She followed his lead, swaying her hips to the music, but he could tell something wasn't quite right. He wanted the playfulness of five minutes ago back.

"Are you going to tell me what I did wrong?"

She blinked. "You didn't do anything wrong. I'm just being overly sensitive, that's all."

"I'm just trying to protect you."

Janey smiled. "I know. Thank you for that." She scratched her nails along the back of his neck right below his hairline, and the sensation went straight to his groin. "How long do we have to stay before it's safe to leave?"

It was his turn to blink. "You still want to?"

She tilted her hips forward, brushing the part of him that was already sitting up to take notice. "Does that answer your question?"

JANEY WAS IRRITATED WITH HERSELF. Here she was with a man she really liked, and she was being stupid. Logically she knew he was telling the truth. She'd grown up in a neighborhood that wasn't all that different from Liberty. If she and Kyle ran out of here pawing at each other, it would be all anyone wanted to talk about.

Granted, she was most likely on her way back to Indianapolis soon unless new information turned up, but that didn't mean she'd never return. If there was a connection between the two cases, she might have to come back. There was no sense making the investigation harder because she couldn't keep her hormones under control... or her insecurities.

They ended up dancing for another hour. Some of the families with younger children began to filter out as the sun sank lower in the sky, leaving an older crowd inside the barn. The teenagers gathered outside near the fire pit and she was tempted to go out and talk to them—see if any of them would admit to being in the cornfield—but she let it go. Even if some or all of them were there that night, they would likely close ranks.

"You ready to go?" Kyle asked, pulling her from her thoughts. Another song had ended and the band was taking a break.

Butterflies filled her stomach again and she nodded.

Kyle was careful to keep a respectable distance as they made their way out of the barn and down the driveway. A few people waved goodbye as they passed, wishing them a good night. Once they were both settled inside his truck, he reached for her hand. "Do you want me to drop you off at Ava's or would you rather go back to my place?"

She knew what he was asking, and she appreciated it. All too often guys assumed that a date meant she'd be putting out. More than once she'd had to set them straight. But tonight she wanted to be with Kyle. As crazy as it sounded, she wanted time alone with him when all the barriers of professionalism and propriety were gone. "I'd love to see your place."

That hung in the air for a moment before he put the vehicle in gear and headed toward town. The air in the cab was thick with tension as they drove past fields full of crops not quite ready to harvest. Kyle rubbed his thumb along the inside of her wrist as the sun continued to set. She closed her eyes, letting the sensations take over.

Janey felt his gaze on her and turned to look at him. Concern marred his features. She smiled, letting him know she hadn't changed her mind.

A few minutes later, he pulled up to an old Victorian-style house. She couldn't see much detail since it was now almost completely dark, but she thought it had brown or black shutters on the windows.

"This is it," he said, then got out and came around to get her door. "Thanks."

Once her feet were on the ground, Kyle crowded closer, pressing her back against the edge of the seat. There was heat in his eyes—heat Janey desperately wanted to tap. She slid her palms up his chest and cupped the back of his neck with her right hand.

That was all he needed. He grabbed hold of her hips with so much force it took her breath away. Then his lips were covering hers and the thought of breathing went out the window altogether.

Kyle molded her body to his as much as their clothing would allow and wasted no time darting his tongue between her parted lips. He ran his hands up the length of her back and then down over her ass. She wanted his hands everywhere.

He was breathing hard when he finally broke the kiss. "I've wanted to do that all day."

Before she could respond, he kissed her again.

"Janey?" he asked, not bothering to remove his mouth from hers this time.

"Yes?" It was hard to talk or even think at that moment.

"I want to take you inside." He peppered kisses along her jaw and down her neck. "Tear off all your clothes." She felt his hand slide up the back of her thigh. He paused right below her backside for a moment before tracing the edge of her panties. "And then, once I have you naked, I want to learn every inch of you."

She sucked in a breath, hoping her next words came out as confident as she hoped. "What are you waiting for?"

Janey expected him to rush them into the house, but he didn't. He covered her mouth with his again and lifted her back onto the seat, this time positioning himself between her legs. Even then he still wasn't close enough for her liking.

"We need to go inside. Too many clothes," she said between kisses.

Kyle's chest vibrated, but he didn't stop kissing her. He'd said he wanted to get her naked, and given they were both law enforcement, she doubted he'd risk getting down and dirty in his driveway. She wrapped her legs around his waist, needing more friction, hoping he'd get the message. If he didn't get it soon, she was going to spell it out for him.

Then she felt his thumb glide up and down the front of her panties. A moan erupted from her throat and she didn't even try to stop it. Luckily, there was some distance between Kyle and his neighbors. Although she wasn't sure at that moment if she would have cared even if someone did happen to overhear them.

She dug her fingers into his shoulders and neck as he continued to touch her. Their mouths were fused together, tongues exploring and tasting. She felt as if she were going to catch on fire from the inside out if she didn't come soon.

"Kyle?"

"Hmm." He cupped the back of her head with his free hand and met her gaze. "Do you want me to keep touching you, Janey?"

She lifted her hips. "If you stop now, I'll never forgive you."

He laughed and gave her a hard kiss. The pleasure between her legs went up another notch as he increased the pressure of his thumb exactly where she needed it.

Janey tilted her hips up to meet every downward motion of his hand, driving her toward her orgasm. She was close. So close.

And then she was soaring. Her breath caught in her throat and her entire body shook. Kyle took her in his arms and held on tight, letting her ride out her climax.

She rested her forehead on his shoulder as she caught her breath. "That was unexpected."

"You've never had an orgasm before?" His tone was full of shocked disbelief.

She gave him a gentle shove, which did nothing to move his solid form. "That's not what I meant, and you know it."

Kyle angled her chin up and brushed his lips against hers. Unable to resist, she pulled his mouth closer and took what she wanted.

Seconds later they were moving. He placed her feet on the ground, moved her away from the truck, and slammed the door. She giggled as he guided her along the side of the house, and then proceeded to fumble with his keys trying to get inside.

They'd barely made it over the threshold before he was on her again. He pushed her back against the wall and hiked her dress up around her waist. She couldn't keep track of his hands. They were constantly moving, touching her everywhere.

"We need to get you out of this dress," he mumbled as he placed open-mouthed kisses on her collarbone.

She couldn't remember the last time she was this turned on. "You have on more clothing than I do."

To her surprise, he stepped back and removed his shirt. A light brown sprinkling of hair covered his torso. And beneath that were the muscles she'd only gotten hints of before.

Unable to resist, Janey placed both hands on his chest, letting the fine hairs tickle her palms, being careful to avoid the top of his gun where it peeked out of his waistband. She looked up, meeting his gaze. "Not bad, Deputy Reed."

He closed the distance between them again, tangling his fingers in her hair with one hand while he removed his gun and holster with the other, tucking them into a nearby drawer. "I promise it only gets better from here."

"Rather confident, aren't you?"

"Uh-huh." With that he crushed his mouth over hers and went to work proving his point. Their clothing fell to the floor—first her dress, then his pants. He reached behind her to unhook her bra. Once she felt it give, Janey shrugged out of it, wanting to feel his bare chest against hers.

But as soon as her bra was out of the way, Kyle cupped her ass and lifted her feet off the ground. The move happened so fast she let out a squeal of surprise and grasped at his shoulders to stabilize herself.

"Sorry," he whispered against her lips as he helped her wrap her legs around his waist.

Janey ran her fingers through his hair as he headed toward the stairs, presumably taking her to his bedroom. "No complaints here. Just maybe give me a little warning next time."

He chuckled. "I'll keep that in mind."

***

Kyle hadn't planned on getting Janey off in his driveway, but when she'd responded to his kiss the way she had, he'd needed to touch her... and keep touching her. Hearing her moan and gasp at what he was doing had been addicting and he hadn't wanted to stop.

He still didn't want to stop. She clung to him as he climbed the stairs to his bedroom. It would have been easier to have her walk, but he hadn't wanted to release her even for that short amount of time.

She'd be leaving soon enough. Going back to her home, her life, in Indianapolis. He wasn't sure how he felt about that.

All thoughts of anything but the gorgeous woman he held in his arms left his brain when she leaned down and scraped her teeth along his neck. His erection throbbed and he almost tripped over his own feet. He landed a firm swat to her backside. "Behave."

She did it again and then laughed. "Nope."

He picked up his pace, which only amused her more.

As soon as Kyle reached the bedroom, he walked over to the bed and dumped her on top of the sheets. "I'm going to make you pay for that, woman."

Janey scooted back on the bed and propped herself up on her elbows, not seeming the least bit worried about his threat. She lifted her leg and rubbed the ball of her foot along the part of him that was trying to burst through his boxer briefs. If he wasn't careful, he was going to embarrass himself.

Taking hold of her ankle, he placed her foot flat on the bed and climbed on top of her. "You like playing with fire, don't you?"

"I don't know what you mean," she said, a look of feigned innocence on her face.

In response, he took one of her nipples into his mouth and sucked hard. Janey let out a shriek followed by a sound that told him it wasn't going to take much to get her there a second time. She arched her back and held his head to her chest. He was more than happy to oblige her silent request. Sucking on Janey Davis's breasts was something he could do for hours. He alternated sucking and licking, even taking a page out of her book and scraping his teeth along the sensitive flesh. Once her left nipple was nice and hard, he turned his attention on the other one.

Janey brought her feet up to the waistband of his boxer briefs and tried to push them down his hips, but they were giving her trouble. She growled in frustration.

"Getting a little impatient?"

"Yes." She huffed. "I want these off."

He released her breast, placed a soft kiss on her lips, and leaned back on his heels. "Your wish is my command."

She snorted. "I highly doubt that."

Kyle smirked down at her while he worked his underwear the rest of the way off. He dropped them onto the floor beside the bed and retook his position between her legs. This time, though, he brought his face level with hers. He brushed the back of his fingers along the side of her face. "You might be surprised."

The atmosphere around them shifted. All playfulness dissipated.

Needing to prove his point, Kyle rolled over, lying next to her on the bed. "I'm all yours."

She turned her head to meet his gaze as if trying to gauge if he was serious or not. After a long moment, she pushed her panties down her legs and kicked them off the end of the bed. "Condom?"

He grinned and nodded toward the stand next to his bed. "In the top drawer."

Janey crawled over him, her derriere conveniently up in the air less than a foot above his face. He took advantage of the situation and gave her a playful bite on her right butt cheek. She collapsed over his lap, laughing.

All laughter ceased when he slipped two fingers between her legs. She gasped and fisted the sheets. "Lower."

He did as she requested. It wasn't hard to know he'd found the right spot. Janey pushed herself back against his fingers. "Is this what you were wanting me to do?"

That seemed to bring her out of her fog. She scrambled to sit up.

"Not exactly." She held up a single foil square and ripped it open. When she began to roll it down his length, he had to press his hands into the mattress to keep from reaching for her. However, the moment she was finished, he pulled her down on top of him, flipped them over, and used his weight to press her into the mattress.

Janey grinned up at him. "That didn't last long."

"Next time." He tangled his fingers in her hair and kissed her with everything he had. She met him stroke for stroke and hooked her knee around his hip, urging him closer.

Propping himself up on one elbow, he reached between them and lined himself up. Kyle held Janey's gaze as he pushed inside. As he began to move, she met each one of his thrusts with one of her own. She was there with him in the moment, taking what she needed.

He kept up a steady rhythm, enjoying the friction and the way her breasts bounced each time he surged forward. Janey looked down, watching their bodies as they came together. It was incredibly erotic. And it was making it difficult to keep his climax at bay.

She scraped her nails along his scalp, sending shots of electricity down his spine. He closed his eyes, trying to concentrate on anything other than how good she felt. Then she snaked her hand between them. The moment he registered what she was doing, he almost came right then and there.

"Janey," he said through gritted teeth.

"I know."

If he'd been ten years younger, he might not have been able to hold on, but by some miracle he managed. Her breath came faster, harder, and her hand moved at an almost fevered pace, driving her toward her goal.

A gasp escaped her lips a moment before he felt her muscles tighten around him. She dug her nails into his neck so hard they probably broke the skin. It flipped a switch in him. Kyle let himself go and allowed all the sensations he'd been keeping in check overtake him. He felt the energy surging and leaned forward to capture her lips as he thrust one last time.

They lay there, him still inside her, as their breathing slowed. He felt her fingers graze over the spot on his neck where her nails had dug into his skin. "I didn't mean to mark you with my nails like that."

He snorted and kissed the tip of her nose. "I'll take the exchange any day."

"Still, we should probably clean it. I don't want it to get infec—"

His kiss effectively silenced her. Janey kissed him back, but he could tell she was still concerned. "I'll let you look at it in a little while, okay? But I just finished making love to a beautiful woman, who I still happen to have in my arms, and I'd like to focus on that right now."

Kyle thought she was going to argue with him, but she didn't. Maybe he wasn't the only one who didn't want to break the connection quite yet.

He didn't want to move, but eventually he had to. After rolling off her, he removed the condom and threw it in the trash can beside his bed. He'd had every intention of pulling her into his arms again, but when he turned back around, Janey was sitting up. The look on her face had him worried. "What's wrong?"

She shot him a weak smile. "I was just wondering what your sister's going to say when I come home tonight."

"I hadn't planned on you going back to my sister's tonight." He scooted closer, circled his arm around her middle, and tugged her back down until she was lying beside him again.

"I thought you didn't want people in town to know."

He shrugged. "It would be easier if they didn't, but I'm not going to sneak you off in the middle of the night just to be sure my neighbors don't figure out I brought a woman home with me. Besides, my sister doesn't count."

Janey frowned, which wasn't what he wanted. He wanted her smiling again, laughing.

"If you go back to my sister's tonight, who's going to make sure the marks you gave me aren't getting infected? Hayden?" he asked.

It worked. Janey rolled her eyes at him. "Fine. I'll stay. But I'm letting you handle your sister. I'm not going near that one. If she asks, I'm going to tell her she has to talk to you. Got it?"

Kyle grinned. "Yes, ma'am."

They lay there for a while, her head resting on his chest. It was peaceful, something he hadn't felt in a while, especially not with a woman. It made him want to hold on to that feeling for as long as possible.

"Janey?" he asked, making sure she hadn't fallen asleep.

"Yeah?"

"When do you have to head back to Indy?"

She moved so she could see his face. "I have to be at work at eight o'clock Monday morning, so I was planning to head back in the morning unless something came up."

He combed his fingers through her hair and tried to keep his voice even. He didn't want her to feel any pressure. "Push your plans back a few hours and spend the day with me tomorrow."

CHAPTER 6

IT WASN'T Janey's alarm that woke her on Sunday morning. Kyle gently roused her from sleep with barely-there kisses followed by what she was beginning to think were magical fingers. He brought her to yet another orgasm thanks to those talented digits before reaching for another condom.

After her fourth climax in less than twelve hours, she lay there trying to catch her breath while Kyle cleaned up in the bathroom. Janey wished she'd thought to bring her bag with her last night or had Kyle swing by his sister's house to pick it up. All she had to wear were the clothes she'd worn the night before, and the thought of putting her dirty panties back on wasn't appealing.

Janey was still lying on the bed when Kyle strolled out of the bathroom with nothing but a towel wrapped around his waist. She could still see drops of water clinging to his chest and had the urge to lick each and every one of them.

"If you keep looking at me like that, we're not going to make it out of the bedroom today." His husky voice had the muscles in her belly clenching in remembrance.

"You're the one who decided to walk out of the bathroom in nothing but a towel," she said, getting up.

He raised one eyebrow. "Would you rather have me walk out naked? That can still be arranged."

She held his gaze as she left the bed and passed by him on her way to the bathroom. "I'm sure it could be, but since someone got me all dirty last night, I'm in need of a shower."

"Want some company?" he asked, placing a hand on her hip to stop her.

As tempting as that was, Janey needed a few minutes to herself. She shook her head. "Maybe you could go downstairs and get my clothes instead."

His eyes darkened and he pulled her against him. He gazed down the length of her body, and then placed a lingering kiss on her lips. "Enjoy your shower."

By the time she opened her eyes, he'd stepped out into the hall. She tried to clear the cobwebs out of her head. It amazed her how he could do that to her so easily.

Janey headed into the bathroom to start her shower. He'd laid a couple of towels on the counter for her, which she thought was rather sweet. She tried not to take it for anything other than what it was. Given she'd never been in his house before, she wouldn't have had a clue where the towels were and she would have felt weird rummaging through his closets trying to find some.

Then she noticed the toothbrush lying next to the towels. It was brand new—still in the package. Her heart rate sped a little and she felt warmth bloom in her chest.

"It's nothing, Janey," she mumbled to herself. "He just has good manners. That's all."

After turning the water on, she tested it to make sure it was the right temperature and stepped into the tub. From what she'd seen of Kyle's house, which admittedly wasn't much, it was old but well taken care of. She wondered how long it had been in his family.

There was shampoo and conditioner along the back edge of the bathtub. When she opened the body wash, a sigh left her before she could stop it. Janey knew every time she smelled that scent she would think of Kyle.

The mirror over the sink was steamed up by the time she pulled back the shower curtain. She stepped out onto the fluffy bath mat and reached for one of the towels. Realization that she didn't even have a brush for her hair had her going over her options. She thought she might have a ponytail holder in her purse. It wouldn't be pretty, but she'd have to make it work until she could get her things.

Kyle was sitting on the end of the bed waiting for her when she walked out. Her blue dress—the one she'd borrowed from his sister—was draped over his lap. He held it out to her and she took it. "Thanks."

"Your bra and panties are on top of the dresser. I figured you'd want the bra. I wasn't sure about the panties." His smirk said it all.

Janey wasn't one to go around without panties on, especially in a dress, but this might have to be an exception to the rule. She recalled them being rather damp when she'd stripped them off the night before. Just thinking about putting them back on was making her feel dirty again. "I need to get my things from Ava's anyway. I'm sure she'll want to get the room ready for someone else."

"So is that a no on the panties?" he asked with a light in his eyes.

She had the yearning to push him back on the bed and wipe that smug grin off his face, but she didn't. "As long as we go there first, I think I'll survive."

"I might be willing to test that assumption."

Reaching for her bra, Janey dropped the towel and began getting dressed... or at least as dressed as she could be without panties or clean clothes. She knew she needed a diversion or they were going to end up right back where they started the day—in his bed. "I thought you wanted us to spend the day together."

"Oh, we would be." There was no mistaking his meaning.

She shot him an incredulous look. "Outside of your bedroom."

Kyle chuckled and stood, slapping his hands on his thighs. "In that case, I'm going to go see what I can throw together in the kitchen."

He paused for a moment at the door, taking a long look at her once more. She saw the conflict in his eyes, but after several long moments he turned on his heel and disappeared into the hallway.

A deep sense of feminine pleasure filled her. Her body wasn't perfect. What woman's was? But when Kyle looked at her she felt like the most beautiful woman in the world. It was clear he liked what he saw.

It only took a few minutes to put her bra on and slip into her dress. Pulling her hair up into a ponytail took a little longer. Every time she thought she'd gotten all her hair gathered together and twisted the band in place, a section wasn't lying flat so she had to take it out and start again. After the fifth try, she gave up. She figured she'd fix it once they got to Ava's and her things.

On her way downstairs, Janey paid more attention to her surroundings than she had going up the night before. There were six doors on the top floor. She assumed at least one of the other doors was a bathroom, which meant the house likely had five bedrooms. It was a lot bigger than she'd thought it was.

When she reached the bottom of the stairs, a muffled curse pointed her in the direction of the kitchen. She followed the sound and found Kyle frantically waving his hand in the air. "Did you burn yourself?"

"I hate cooking. Did I mention that?" He removed two pieces of bread from the toaster and threw them onto a nearby plate with more force than necessary.

"I'm not sure making toast qualifies as cooking."

He narrowed his eyes at her.

Janey laughed and sashayed over to stand in front of him. It had been a while since she'd had this much fun with a guy. She picked up the hand he'd been shaking when she'd entered the room. "Would you like me to kiss it and make it better?"

His eyes darkened. "No. But I'm sure I can find something else you can kiss and that would definitely make me feel better."

She went up on her tiptoes and gave him a quick peck on the cheek. "There. Did that make it better?"

Without warning, Kyle picked her up and set her on top of the counter next to him. One of the plates went crashing into the sink. He ignored it and set about getting the type of kiss he'd wanted—one that was far from the innocent peck she'd given him.

He held her exactly where he wanted her, much like he had outside the night before. She couldn't have moved far even if she'd wanted to. Not that she did.

Her head was spinning when he pulled back, his chest heaving with his labored breaths. He retrieved the plate from the sink, placed two pieces of toast on it, and set it on the table. Then he put another two pieces of bread in the toaster. Aside from his breathing, one would never have known he'd just kissed the living daylights out of her.

Janey hopped off the counter and straightened her dress, making sure everything was covered. "Do you have any coffee?"

"I'll get it," he said.

"That's okay—"

He cut her off with another kiss and slowly walked her backward until her knees hit the chair.

She sighed and sat down at the table. "Fine."

***

Stopping at his sister's went about as well as could be expected. Ava was all smiles until Janey was out of sight. "Is this a one-time thing, or do you plan to see her again?"

Kyle leaned against the back of the couch, his stance casual. "I don't know. We haven't discussed it."

His sister snorted then mumbled something under her breath that sounded a lot like "*Men,*" and then headed into the kitchen, Cole on her hip. She was gone all of two seconds before she marched back into the room. He'd known she wouldn't let it go. "Why haven't you discussed it?"

Luckily, he was saved from answering by the sound of Janey's footsteps on the stairs. He pushed away from the couch and went to meet her. "Got everything?"

"Yep," Janey said, and then looked at Ava. "Thank you so much for letting me stay here. I appreciate it. How much do I owe you for the room?"

"Anytime. And don't worry about it. I'm sure Kyle will figure out some way to make it up to me."

He reached for Janey's suitcase. "We should get going."

She gave it up without a fight, which surprised him. "Thanks."

"Call me later," his sister called as they walked out the door.

Kyle put Janey's suitcase in the trunk of her SUV and held her door open for her. Over breakfast they'd decided she'd drive her vehicle back to his place and leave it there while they were gone. He insisted it would be better that way since his place was closer to town and the road she'd need to take back to Indianapolis.

"You going to tell me where it is we're going?" she asked after she'd parked her vehicle in his driveway and climbed into the cab of his truck.

He'd considered his options carefully. They only had a few hours, so they couldn't go too far. "Have you ever been horseback riding?"

It took her a moment. "Yes."

"Good."

Silence filled the cab.

"Is that a problem?" Kyle asked.

"No. Just... unexpected, I guess."

He glanced over at her and winked. "I'll take that as a compliment."

It took them almost a half hour to reach their destination and another twenty minutes to get their horses saddled and ready to go. She hoisted herself onto her horse, showing she did know what she was doing, and pointed it toward the trail.

The forest closed in around them, sheltering them. It was what he loved about coming here.

Janey tightened her grip on the reins as the trail sloped downward. "Do you do this often?"

"Every now and then." He let that hang in the air for a while before adding, "Sometimes it's nice to get out here by myself. Gives me the opportunity to think." There was no one but the two of them for as far as the eye could see. They were completely surrounded by nature. It was perfect as far as he was concerned.

"I've never been here before. It's nice." She paused. "Quiet."

Kyle grinned. "A lot different from the city."

"Yes," she agreed.

The trail they were on gradually led down to the river. He'd taken it many times over the years, first as a boy and then as an adult. Kyle picked up his pace a little, pulling ahead when the ground beneath them leveled out some.

Janey was right behind him. She was comfortable on a horse, more so than he'd expected. It made him even more curious about her.

When he reached the water's edge, Kyle loosened his hold on his mount's reins, allowing him to drink. He reached into his saddlebag, removed the bag of trail mix they'd been given, and sat back in his saddle. The river was fairly calm here, but he could hear more rapidly moving water not far downstream.

Coming up beside him, Janey followed his lead, allowing her horse to drink. He offered her some of his snack and she lifted herself in her saddle to grab a handful. "Thanks."

They sat there for several minutes watching the water go by and listening to the sounds around them. As much as he loved coming up here by himself, he found that having Janey with him made it better rather than taking something away.

His sister's question this morning popped into his mind. He hadn't answered her, but even then he'd known. Yes, he wanted to see Janey again. But was that what Janey wanted? He had no idea.

Uncertainty gripped him. He'd dated his fair share of women in his thirty-five years, but for some reason asking Janey if she wanted to make this more than a one-night stand, or weekend fling or whatever, had him sweating.

The situation struck him as amusing. Or maybe ironic was a better word. He was a police officer. Over the years he'd had to talk down more than one out-of-control drunk or jealous husband. This should have been cake.

But it wasn't.

"Want to share what's so funny?" Janey asked when she noticed the goofy grin on his face.

Kyle reached for her hand and was pleased when she laced their fingers together. "I've been thinking."

She waited for him to continue.

"I'd like to see you again."

The seconds ticked by as they sat there, the sounds around them suddenly seeming louder than they had a few moments before. It was one of those times when he really wished he had the ability to read her mind. "I thought..."

"What did you think?" he asked, curious.

When she didn't move away from him, he took that as a good sign. She looked down at their linked hands. "I wasn't thinking it was going to be anything more than last night. And today."

"Is that all you want?" He held his breath waiting for her answer.

"I live two hours away."

Kyle dropped her hand and shifted in his saddle so he could touch her face. He tilted her chin up until she was looking at him. "That doesn't answer my question, Detective."

She smiled at his use of her title. "I know, but I'm trying to think rationally."

"Does that mean you do want to see me again?"

Janey removed his hand from her face but didn't release it. "I've tried the long-distance thing before and it doesn't work."

He opened his mouth to argue, but she cut him off.

"We both have unsolved cases. Cases that might very well be connected. I don't want it to be awkward if we have to work together again."

"You're worried we couldn't work together professionally if things didn't work out between us?"

"Aren't you?" she asked.

One of his best friends was his boss and they'd figured it out. Even if he and Janey couldn't, Kyle thought it was worth the risk. "No. I'm not. I like you, Janey."

"I like you, too."

All his anxiety fell away. Janey wanted this, too. She was just scared. He didn't quite understand her fear, but he wouldn't dismiss it either. "What are you so afraid of?"

Instead of answering his question, she asked one of her own. "What about the women around here? Claire, for example."

"Claire isn't my type." He squeezed her hand and grinned. "And you didn't answer the question."

Janey sighed and looked toward the river. "I don't want to get attached and then you decide it isn't worth it."

Kyle knew in that moment that she was speaking from experience. "What if I get attached and you decide I'm not worth it?" He rubbed his thumb along the inside of her wrist. Her pulse was beating rapidly under her skin. "You know as well as I do that there are no guarantees in life."

She held his gaze for a long moment before rising up and pressing her mouth to his. It was completely unexpected, but not unwelcome. Kyle cupped the back of her head and held her to him for as long as possible, enjoying the feel of her lips.

"You make it very hard to say no to you," she whispered, lowering herself back into the saddle.

Kyle smiled and traced the outline of her lips with his index finger. "Then say yes."

She held his hand in place against her cheek. "Just promise me something, okay?"

"I'd promise you just about anything if you agree to see me again."

"Somehow I doubt that." She grinned and lowered their hands to rest on her leg. "Promise me that if you change your mind, you'll tell me."

Another puzzle piece fell into place. "I promise."

She looked down for several minutes, seeming fascinated with their hands. When she met his gaze once more there was determination and something else that had him wishing for more room in his pants. He was mentally doing the calculations of how quickly they could get to the stables, return the horses, and make it back to his house when Janey picked up her reins and began moving away.

"Wha—"

She had a serious look on her face, but the heat was still there. "I think I might have forgotten something at your place."

"Really?" he asked, catching on to her line of thinking.

Janey nodded and turned her horse in the direction of the trail. "Yeah. I think we should head back. I wouldn't want to leave it behind."

"We wouldn't want that, now, would we?"

"Certainly not."

CHAPTER 7

Eight hours later, Janey let herself into her apartment, kicked off her shoes, and carried her suitcase into the bedroom. As she removed each item and tossed it into the hamper, she couldn't help but smile. Nearly every article of clothing she'd brought with her now had a memory of Kyle associated with it.

"You really shouldn't get yourself too attached, Janey," she said to herself. She'd learned the hard lesson years ago that most people didn't stick around for long.

But try as she might, the happy feeling she got whenever she thought of him wouldn't go away. Especially not after their goodbye. He'd walked her out to her vehicle, placed her suitcase in the back seat, and put his arms around her waist, his left hand cupping her ass.

Then he'd kissed her. It wasn't the passion-filled kiss they'd shared earlier, but one that left her wanting more. His lips and tongue had teased her to the point where she wanted to say "screw it" and drag him back into the house. But right as she was about to do exactly that, he'd released her. The smug grin on his face had told her he'd known exactly what he was doing.

Once she'd been able to think again, she'd promised to text him when she got home, and climbed in her vehicle. He'd leaned in to give her one more brush of his lips across hers before she drove away.

The entire scene occupied her thoughts the entire way home.

Without overthinking it, Janey picked up her phone and sent Kyle a quick text.

Janey: I'm home.

It didn't take long for the reply to come through.

Kyle: I'm sitting on the side of the highway with a thermos full of coffee. It's going to be a long night. Someone kept me from getting much sleep last night. 😴

She didn't even hesitate.

Janey: Who kept who up last night?

Kyle: What can I say? Having you in my bed was just too tempting.

She sat down on the edge of the bed and typed her response.

Janey: Sorry I was such a temptation for you.

Kyle: I'm not.

She bit the inside of her cheek and type her response.

Janey: Neither am I.

He didn't respond right away and she began to wonder if she'd been too forward. She tried not to psych herself out too much, though. He was working, and more than likely he'd tagged a speeder or gotten sent on a call. Still, the insecure part of her kept whispering in her ear that she shouldn't have said that. She should have played coy or hard to get or whatever. Then again, that ship had already sailed. There wasn't much more of her for him to get that he hadn't already gotten.

Janey set her phone down on the bed and finished putting her things away. By the time she threw a load of laundry into the washer and tucked her suitcase into the closet, she'd almost given up hope of hearing from him again that night. It was getting late and she had to be up early the next morning. Her captain would want to be briefed on what had happened over the weekend.

She'd just closed her eyes when her phone dinged, alerting her to a new message.

Kyle: Still awake?

Janey: Maybe.

Kyle: LOL. Does that mean you're already in bed?

Janey: Yes.

She paused for a brief second before she continued typing.

Janey: I have this nice big bed all to myself.

Kyle: *groans* You're killing me.

A bubble of laughter erupted from deep in her chest.

Janey: I think you'll survive.

Kyle: Maybe not. I still have eight hours left on my shift. Sitting here thinking of you lying in that bed. Naked.

Janey: Who says I'm naked? Maybe I'm a flannel pajamas type of girl.

Kyle: Hmm. That just means I can imagine getting you out of them.

The visual image that created in her mind made her nipples harden. It was crazy how easily he could get a reaction from her body with only a few words. Then again, she could vividly remember how he could make good on those words of his. She had whisker burn on her inner thighs from earlier.

She was still off in fantasy land when her phone dinged once more.

Kyle: I'll let you get to sleep. I'll call you tomorrow night before my shift. Sweet dreams.

He knew exactly where her mind had gone. It should bother her that he could read her so well, but it didn't. Of course, that might have something to do with the fact that all she could think about was buying a pair of flannel pajamas so he could peel them off her one button at a time.

Knowing she needed to get to sleep and he had work to do, she typed her response.

Janey: Good night. Stay safe.

Returning her phone to the nightstand, she leaned back into her pillow and sighed. She had no idea if this long-distance relationship with Kyle would work. The last time she'd tried such a relationship it had ended with her heart being broken after she'd found out her boyfriend of two years had been cheating on her. According to him, no man could go more than a week without sex.

At the time, Janey had believed him and blamed herself. After all, it hadn't been the first time she hadn't been good enough to hold onto someone she cared about. Then she'd met her partner, Paul. His wife had been killed by a drunk driver, leaving him to raise their young daughter by himself. He'd dedicated his entire life to taking care of his daughter. Although he didn't talk about it, she knew he hadn't slept around with random women after his wife died and he hadn't dated either. There had been no one serious in his life until he met Megan.

He was the best man Janey knew and it had given her hope. Hope that there was a decent guy out there for her. She had no idea if Kyle was that guy, but as scary as it was, she was willing to give him a chance. If she'd learned anything from watching Paul and Megan's relationship unfold, it was that sometimes you had to follow your heart.

Janey closed her eyes, ready to drift off to sleep, when her phone rang. She snatched it up and glanced at the caller ID. Paul.

"Hey. I didn't expect to hear from you tonight."

She heard a lot of movement in the background. "Are you back in town?"

"Yeah. I got back about two hours ago."

"Good. We got a case."

She sat up, threw the covers off her, and made a beeline for her closet. Her thoughts immediately went to the case she'd been working on all weekend. Or at least part of the weekend. "The same MO?"

"No. This one looks like a robbery gone bad from the initial reports, but there were at least a dozen witnesses."

Janey knew what that meant. Each one of the witnesses would have to be interviewed. "Give me the address and I'll meet you there as soon as I throw on some clothes."

It took her twenty minutes to dress and make her way to the crime scene. She parked her vehicle two blocks away from all the flashing lights and went to find her partner.

One of the patrol officers gave her a curt nod as she ducked under the crime scene tape. He'd asked her out once not long after she'd made detective, but she hadn't wanted to mix work with pleasure. It was a good thing she'd turned him down, too, since a few weeks later he'd ended up meeting his wife. They now had two little ones with a third on the way.

She shook her head. It was strange how life worked sometimes.

Paul was standing next to the coroner with a notepad in his hand. He looked up as she approached. "Sorry to drag you out as soon as you got back in town, but it will go a lot faster with two of us."

"You said there were a dozen witnesses?"

He tilted his head toward a group of people who were being guarded by two patrol officers. "At least. Those are the people who stuck around. Given the area, though, I'd guess there are more. Tomorrow morning we'll probably have to come back and go door to door."

"Sounds like fun." Janey pulled out her notepad and pen. "I guess I should get started."

It was four in the morning by the time they finished interviewing their last witness, a young mother who'd recently moved into the area and was now questioning whether or not it was a good neighborhood in which to raise her family. Janey was exhausted. Between all the exercise she'd got and the two-hour drive back to Indianapolis, she'd been ready to get some much-needed sleep. As it was, she could barely keep her eyes open and she still had to go back to the station and file her report.

"You got everything?" Paul asked.

"Yeah." She could feel the bags forming under her eyes, but sleep was going to have to wait. They'd divided and conquered, which meant they needed to compile all their notes and look for similarities. Going through witness statements was a lot like trying to put together a puzzle that had a lot of wrong or irrelevant pieces mixed in.

"Why don't we head over to the truck stop? I need some food before we head to the station."

As soon as he mentioned food, her stomach growled. "Food sounds great."

Paul opened the door to his car and climbed behind the wheel. "I'll meet you there."

Fifteen minutes later they were sitting in a corner booth, cradling mugs of coffee. The diner at the truck stop wasn't fancy, but it was open twenty-four hours a day, which came in handy when they had to pull an all-nighter.

"What ended up happening with the beer bottles?"

She took a sip of her coffee. "Unless they found something after I left, nothing so far. Apparently, it's not uncommon for the local teens to party in the cornfields. Even if we track down whoever the beer belonged to, it doesn't mean they were there Thursday night."

"Any other leads?"

Janey shook her head. "Not really. We don't have the full autopsy report yet. Maybe that will turn up something."

"I'm not getting my hopes up. If it is the same person who's behind this, they didn't leave much the first time around."

"If it is the first time," Janey said.

Paul raised his eyebrows as he peeked up at her from over his coffee cup. "You think there are more victims?"

"I don't know, but it seems too clean for a first timer. This person either has had practice or knowledge of forensics." No DNA on the first body. The only visible marks were from a Taser and the blunt force trauma of the fatal blow. These didn't feel like rash killings to her. These were planned out. Or, at least, that's what it seemed to her.

He nodded. "I was thinking the same thing over the weekend. It's too clean. If it were a heat-of-the-moment type killing then it would be sloppier."

Their waitress, a young woman who didn't look to be much past eighteen, strolled up to their table with their food. Paul's plate was piled high with eggs, bacon, and home fries. Janey had gone for something a bit healthier. "Can I get you two anything else? More coffee?"

"Yes, please," Janey said, knowing they'd both need more caffeine.

Paul picked up his fork and dug in before their waitress had left the table.

"What would Megan say if she saw you eating that?" Paul had his yearly physical last month and his blood pressure was slightly elevated. Nothing major, but his doctor recommended that he eat more fruits and vegetables and less meat and potatoes. Since then, Paul's wife had completely revamped their diet, sending him to work with a packed lunch full of things like carrot sticks and hummus.

"I eat the rabbit food most of the time, but I've been up all night and I need my protein."

Janey chuckled. "I'll remember to mention that the next time I see her."

"You wouldn't."

She just shrugged. No, she wouldn't, but he didn't need to know that.

They finished eating their breakfast but neither seemed to be in any hurry to leave. They had a pile of paperwork waiting for them at the station, let alone the debriefing about her trip to Liberty. It was going to be a very long day.

***

Kyle parked his patrol vehicle and headed into the station. It had been a slow night for the most part. He'd tagged Brad Napper, owner of the local hardware store, going seventy in a fifty-five. Brad was well known for having a lead foot. Especially on the country roads where there wasn't a lot of traffic.

The rest of his shift had been quiet. He'd made his rounds, checked on the local businesses to make sure they were locked up tight, and patrolled some of the lesser-used roads for any signs of suspicious activity, but nothing looked out of place. The most excitement he got was when he was driving past the diner, saw some movement, and then a second later realized it was a raccoon raiding their dumpster.

All that non-activity had given Kyle a lot of time to think about the weekend he'd spent with Janey. Every time he closed his eyes he could see her laid out on his bed, her blond hair fanned across his pillow as she smiled up at him. Those lips of hers begged him to kiss them. It was as if he were addicted to the taste of her mouth. Crazy, but he couldn't deny it. He'd spent hours kissing Janey as they'd lain in his bed Sunday afternoon, and he couldn't wait for a repeat performance.

There was only one problem with his fantasy. She lived two hours away.

Granted, two hours wasn't the other side of the world. He could drive down and back in one day if he wanted to, but given both their jobs, it wasn't something they could do on a whim. Being a deputy meant he had a fairly set schedule. Yes, he could get called out for something special or pick up extra shifts from time to time, but it wasn't the same for Janey. She was a detective, which meant she was almost always on call.

Mac waved to him as he climbed the stairs, hurrying to catch up. "Morning."

"You're here early," he said, opening the door and motioning for her to go first.

"I was hoping to go over the body one last time before it's released to the family. They're supposed to be in to sign the release forms at noon."

"Do you really think you missed something?" Knowing Mac, that was unlikely.

She heaved a sigh. "No. But considering I haven't found much, I'm holding out for a miracle, I guess."

"Still no hits on the fingerprints or DNA, I take it?"

"The fingerprints were a bust and the DNA won't be back for at least a week." She sounded frustrated, which he could completely understand. There was a murderer on the loose—maybe a serial killer if their John Doe turned out to be related to Janey's victim in Indianapolis. No evidence meant no suspect.

"Hopefully we'll get lucky and get a hit on the DNA, then."

"Maybe. But I'm not holding my breath. I did get some material from under John Doe's nails, but it looked like dirt to me." She hugged the binder she'd been holding to her chest and worried the bottom of her lip with her teeth.

"What is it?" he asked, not liking her hesitation.

"There's just something about this case. I don't like it."

"You and me both. Janey and I searched the area where the body was dumped but didn't find anything new that would point us in the direction of the killer. I was really hoping we'd get a hit on the fingerprints. At least we could talk to the kids and find out if they saw anything. Right now there are too many unanswered questions."

She nodded, and then did a complete one-eighty. "Speaking of Detective Davis, I heard she spent the night at your house after the hog roast."

That was one thing about small towns. It was really hard to keep a secret. "I didn't think you were one to listen to gossip."

"It's not gossip if it's true. Besides, I drove by your house on the way into town on Sunday and saw her vehicle parked outside. It doesn't take a rocket scientist to put two and two together."

There was no reason to deny it, especially not to Mac. He liked Janey, and if he had his way, it wouldn't be the last time she spent the night at his house. "Yeah. She spent the night."

Mac glanced down and then over to the door that led to the stairwell before looking at him. "Are you going to see her again? Unofficially, I mean."

Kyle always knew Mac had a bit of a crush on him, but she'd never pushed the issue. They'd known each other since they were kids, and to be honest he'd never seen her as more than a friend. Growing up, she'd been a tomboy, right there beside him and the other guys climbing trees and playing with bugs. Even though he'd seen her growing up into a beautiful and incredibly smart woman, he'd never really thought of dating her. He could laugh and joke with Mac for hours, but that was all it had ever been for him. "Yes."

"I thought maybe you might. When she was here"—he saw her swallow and she averted her eyes again—"you two had chemistry."

He knew he needed to be honest, even if it hurt. "I like her."

Mac nodded. "I like her, too. She'll be good for you, I think."

"Mac—"

"I should get going. Twelve o'clock will be here before I know it." She crossed the room and reached for the door handle. "I'll catch up with you later."

Before he could respond, she'd opened the door and disappeared. He could hear her footsteps as she descended the stairs to the basement.

Kyle debated going after her but decided against it. What would he say to her, in any case? He'd never lied to her. He'd never given her false hope. None of which made him feel any better.

Taking a deep breath, he signaled to the desk attendant to buzz him in. He'd give Mac a little time. For now, he had a report to finish and some sleep to catch up on.

CHAPTER 8

JANEY DOWNED what had to be her tenth cup of coffee. It was the only thing keeping her going. After breakfast, she and Paul had driven to the station to begin typing up their reports. Halfway through they'd gotten a tip for one of their other cases, so as soon as they'd finished filing their report they had to head out. She was close to thirty-four hours with no sleep, and she was feeling it. If not for the coffee, she'd have been conked out on her desk. All she wanted was her bed. Instead, her eyes glazed over from staring at the passing buildings as Paul drove them to the station after chasing another dead end.

"You still awake over there, Davis?" Paul asked.

"Yeah. It's just been a long couple of days, that's all. My bed is calling my name."

"I'm with you there."

When they got back, Janey planned to get in her vehicle, swing by a drive-through on the way home because there was no way she had the energy to make dinner for herself, and then go home and crash. She was having daydreams of her nice comfy bed when Paul's phone rang. He answered it and put it on speaker since he was driving. "Daniels."

"I missed you this morning."

He glanced at Janey before clearing his throat. "Um, I'm driving so I have you on speaker. Janey's with me."

"Hi, Janey."

Janey chuckled. "Hello, Megan. Sorry I kept him out all night."

"Are you guys on your way home?" Megan asked.

Paul made a right and moved into the left lane. "Turning in to the station parking lot now."

"Any idea when you'll be home?"

He parked the car and shot Janey a look. Paperwork was the last thing either of them wanted to do, but it was part of the job. "We probably have about a half hour of paperwork to do and then I can head out."

"Good. That will give me time to finish the ribs and bake the mac and cheese," Megan said. "Janey, you should come, too. I'm making plenty."

It was tempting. She loved ribs.

"Come on. You've got to eat. Besides, Chloe would love to see you."

Megan wasn't going to make this easy. And apparently, neither was Paul. "She's right. You do have to eat."

Janey rolled her eyes at her partner. "All right."

"Yay. I'll see you in a bit." Megan paused. "And Paul?"

"Yes?"

"Don't take too long." Megan's flirty goodbye to her husband had him swiftly grabbing for the phone.

Sure enough, a second later his phone dinged, letting him know he had a text message. Janey didn't see it, but whatever it was had her partner sweating under the collar. Knowing Megan, it was probably a picture of her wearing very little.

Janey opened the door and stepped out. When she noticed he wasn't doing the same, she poked her head back into the vehicle. "You coming, Daniels?"

He looked up at her, then back down at his phone before reaching for the door handle. "Yeah."

Shaking her head, she walked inside, knowing he was right behind her.

Less than forty minutes later, she was pulling into Paul and Megan's driveway. Paul climbed out of his vehicle ahead of her, and she followed him up the driveway to the side of the house.

Their home was in a small subdivision with lots of other young families. It was the exact opposite of the condo where Janey lived. Then again, she didn't have kids. Or even a dog. So there was no need for a yard.

Plus, there were definite perks to living in a condo. One of those was the close proximity to nightlife. Janey loved to dance, and she frequented a couple of clubs that were within walking distance of her home. That wasn't something one would find in the suburbs.

It wasn't something you'd find in a small town like Liberty either.

Before going inside, Janey checked her phone. Kyle said he'd call her tonight, but she had no idea when. And that little voice inside her head kept telling her not to get her hopes up.

She tucked her phone into her pocket and went inside. Either he'd call or he wouldn't. She would have to deal with it either way. There was no point in stressing about it.

"Janey!" Chloe saw her before she'd stepped over the threshold. The little girl hopped off her chair and ran toward Janey at full speed.

Bending down, she embraced the little girl.

"I haven't seen you in soooo long," Chloe said as she continued to hug her.

Janey laughed. "It's only been two weeks."

Chloe removed her arms from around Janey's neck and reached for her hand. She led her to the table and resumed her seat before handing Janey a piece of paper. "I started the first grade."

The paper had the letter *D* at the top and the rest was lines. Chloe had begun making her uppercase D's to match the example. She was already halfway done filling the page.

Janey pretended to examine the paper, nodded, and handed it back to Chloe. "Do you like your teacher?"

"Yes! Mrs. Simon is really nice." Chloe leaned in as if she were going to confide something to Janey. "Daddy and Mommy are in the other room."

Pressing her lips together to keep from spoiling what Chloe felt was a serious moment, Janey asked, "What do you suppose they're doing in there?"

"Kissing," she whispered.

"You think so?"

Chloe nodded. "I think Daddy likes kissing Mommy. He does it *a lot.*"

Luckily, she was saved from answering when the couple in question strolled back into the room. Megan's hair looked slightly out of place and her shirt wasn't quite sitting right. Paul, on the other hand, had a rather smug look on his face.

"Everything is pretty much ready. We just need to finish the ribs off on the grill and carry the rest of the food outside."

Two hours later, she was sitting in Paul and Megan's backyard, belly full, and with no desire to move. Paul was helping Chloe build a sandcastle in her sandbox while Janey and Megan watched on from the sidelines.

"How was your trip to… where was it again?" Megan asked.

"Liberty. It's a small town about two hours north of here." Janey contemplated whether to say anything about Kyle to Megan. Although Megan was younger than her by several years, she was the only close girlfriend Janey had. The downside was that if she told Megan, Megan would tell Paul. For that reason, she decided to keep it to herself. At least for the time being.

"I've never heard of it. What's it like?"

"It was nice," Janey said. "Small, but quaint." Trying to think of things she could say without giving too much away or revealing things about the case, she added, "I went to a hog roast."

"A what?" The look on Megan's face was priceless.

"They roast a pig in the ground all day, and then dig it out and serve it at a big party in the evening. They had a band, dancing, and a bonfire."

"Sounds... interesting."

Janey shrugged. "It was fun."

Megan looked doubtful.

"Hey," Paul said, coming up to them and wiping the sand from his hands. "I'm going to take Chloe inside so we can finish her homework and get her ready for bed."

Janey stood. "I should probably go."

"You don't have to," Megan said.

"I know, but I should head home before I'm too tired to drive. It's been a very long day."

She said her goodbyes and made her way home. With every mile she drove, her exhaustion began to catch up with her. By the time she reached her front door, Janey felt as if she had weights on her eyelids. All she wanted to do was fall into her bed and sleep for the next twelve hours.

***

Janey had no idea how long she'd been asleep, but something was making a noise and it wouldn't stop. She groaned and forced her eyes open.

To her surprise, it was light out and the insistent noise was coming from her phone.

Forcing her feet to the floor, she went to get her phone from the dresser. The incoming call was from Paul. "What's up?"

"Did I wake you up, Davis?"

She rubbed the sleep from her eyes and stretched. "Yeah. I guess I forgot to set my alarm."

He released a loud sigh. "You realize you were supposed to be at work over an hour ago, right?"

Glancing at the clock confirmed what he'd told her. It was after nine in the morning. She was an hour late for her shift. "Shit. I'll be there as soon as I can shower and change."

It had been a while since Janey had gotten ready in such a mad dash. Even still, it was pushing ten by the time she ran into the station.

"About time, Davis," her captain said as she rushed by him on her way to her desk. He didn't look amused.

"Morning, Captain."

She slid into her seat at her desk across from Paul. He raised his eyebrows in question. "You sure you're okay?"

"I'm fine. I was just exhausted. I thought I'd set my alarm before I nodded off, but I guess not. Knowing my luck, it'll go off at six tonight."

He gave her a long look and then nodded. "You ready to get started, then?"

The bulk of their day was spent on paperwork and searching through records. They went over their cold cases to see if anything new jumped out at them. Most of the time it didn't, but sometimes they got lucky, like today when there'd been a break in a case they'd been working on for well over a year.

Janey was climbing into Paul's car when it hit her that she hadn't heard from Kyle. Or, at least, she didn't think she had. Truth be told, she hadn't looked at her phone other than to take Paul's abrupt wake-up call.

Sure enough, a check of her phone showed that she had a missed call from last night. Based on the time stamp, Kyle had probably called her right before his shift.

Paul was still talking to the store clerk, so she sent a quick text.

Janey: Sorry I missed your call. I fell asleep early last night. Call you later?

A response came about a minute later, right as Paul was getting into the vehicle.

Kyle: I'll be waiting.

The corners of her mouth lifted in a tiny smile.

"Something you want to share, Davis?" It was only then she realized Paul hadn't started the car. Instead, he was looking at her, waiting.

She put the phone away and reached for her seat belt. "Nope. Just checking to see if I had any messages, that's all."

Paul looked doubtful but didn't push it. Starting the engine, he maneuvered them into traffic.

Luckily, there were no new cases sitting on their desks when they returned to the station, so they were able to write up their report on the lead they'd pursued and call it a day. She was eager to get home, not only because she had plans to call Kyle but because she wanted some downtime. It felt as if she'd been going nonstop since she got back to Indianapolis. A nice bubble bath and a glass of wine sounded close to perfect.

***

Kyle had just woken up when he got the text from Janey. He'd been getting a little worried when she hadn't answered his call last night, but he figured she might be at a crime scene or something. Then she hadn't messaged him back either. He knew they were still feeling things out and that it would take time, especially with their schedules, but it had made him nervous. He cared about Janey more than he probably should given they'd known each other for a few days. That didn't change the fact that his heart rate increased every time her name popped up on his caller ID.

Removing his French bread pizza from the microwave, he checked the clock for what had to be the twentieth time in less than an hour, and then carried his dinner to the table. It was crazy how nervous he was waiting for her to call. Janey wasn't his first girlfriend. Hell, he'd been in a war zone and hadn't been this anxious.

His pizza almost slipped from his fingers when his phone rang. He didn't even bother to look to see who it was before answering. "Hello."

"Hi," Janey said.

He leaned back in his chair, his pizza forgotten. "You called."

"I told you I would, didn't I?" Her voice filtered through the line, easing the tension that had been building.

"You did."

The line was quiet for a long moment before Janey spoke. "Sorry about last night. After we talked Sunday evening, I got called out to a major crime scene. We were there all night, and then I worked straight through the day. By the time I got home, I was drained. I didn't even hear the phone ring when you called."

"Sounds exhausting."

She released a half laugh/half snort type sound that had him grinning. "It really was."

"I'm sure it didn't help that I'd kept you up for most of the previous night either."

Janey released a soft sigh, one that had him needing to adjust himself. "Yes, you did."

"I didn't hear any complaints at the time." He loved flirting with her.

Instead of stroking his ego, she gave him sass. "Confident, aren't you?"

"Very."

"You might have to work on that cockiness, Deputy Reed."

"You were quite fond of that part of my anatomy, if I recall."

He could almost see her rolling her eyes at him through the phone. "I said cockiness. Not cock."

Kyle laughed. "Is there a difference?"

"I'm beginning to wonder."

He didn't think he could grin any wider if he tried. "How was your day?"

"Boring. Yours?"

"About the same. I did run into Mac this morning at the station. She wanted me to tell you hi."

There was a long silence on the other end of the phone.

"Janey? Everything okay? You didn't fall asleep on me again, did you?"

She chuckled. "No. I'm still here."

"Okay. So why did you get quiet on me?"

"Mac likes you." Then she hurried to add, "Not just as a friend."

He released a loud breath. "I know."

"And..."

If this wasn't such a serious conversation, Kyle would be amused by the way she was trying to get him to tell her his feelings for Mac. "And I don't feel the same way."

"You live in the same town. You work together. You're friends. A relationship between you two would be easy."

"Who are you trying to convince?" He sat up and began picking the pepperoni off his pizza. "It's you I want, Janey. Not Mac."

She didn't say anything.

"Is this about the long-distance thing again?"

"It's only been two days and we're already having trouble."

He raised an eyebrow. "This is trouble?"

"You know what I mean."

"No. I don't think I do."

Janey exhaled. "Right now things are new and it doesn't bother you that I missed your call, but eventually you're going to get tired of it. Eventually, you're going to decide it's not worth it."

A few things clicked into place in his head. He might not be a detective, but as a police officer he'd learned to read people pretty well. She wasn't talking in the hypothetical here. She was speaking from experience. "Who was he?"

"What?"

He didn't beat around the bush. "Who was the guy who broke your heart?"

It took her a while to answer, so long in fact that he didn't think she was going to. "His name was Ted." She hesitated. "It was a long time ago."

Apparently, it wasn't long enough if she was still letting it affect her relationships. "What happened?"

"It's not important."

"Janey?"

"Yes?" When they were teasing each other, she was all confidence. At the moment, she sounded anything but.

"I want to understand why you're so hesitant about us giving this a shot, and I can't do that if I don't know what happened between you and Ted to make you feel this way."

Again there was a long pause. It took everything in him to sit there and wait her out. "I was seventeen. He was nineteen. We started dating when I was a freshman and he was a junior. Everything was great until he went off to college in Ohio."

He could already see where this was going, but he kept his thoughts to himself.

"At first, things were the same as they always were. We talked on the phone almost every day, and he'd come home on breaks. Then things started to change. He still came home, but we didn't do all that much talking when he was there. All we really did was fool around."

She stopped talking.

He waited, but after several minutes he grew concerned. "You all right?"

"Yeah." He thought he heard a sniffle, but he couldn't be sure. "Then the summer between my junior and senior year, things changed."

He was trying not to push, but he also wanted to understand. "What happened?"

"A lot of things." It came out in a whisper, but in a firmer voice she went on. "When he went back to school in the fall, he was distant. I didn't hear from him for two weeks. Then one Saturday night he called me to say he couldn't do it anymore, that this long-distance thing was too much for him to try and balance with school and everything."

A long silence filled the air and he got the distinct impression that she was leaving something out, but he didn't want to push. As she'd mentioned before, their relationship was new. Trust was something that came with time, and he was willing to earn hers.

"I found out a few weeks later that he had a girlfriend at college and that they'd been dating for several months." Janey released a heavy sigh. "It took me a long time to move on. I almost failed the first quarter of my senior year. I probably would have flunked out entirely if not for my grandmother. She sat me down after seeing my grades and told me I needed to get my act together and not let what happened destroy my future."

He was at a loss for words. "She sounds like a smart lady."

"She was." The love for her grandmother came through the phone. "I miss her."

"I'm sorry." Kyle wished he could be there to hold her. He didn't like having these types of conversations over the phone.

"Like I said, it was a long time ago."

She might be trying to brush it off, but he knew better. "He was an ass."

That got a weak chuckle out of her. "Yes. Yes, he was."

JANEY COULDN'T BELIEVE she'd told him all that. Or that she'd almost told him about her daughter. She never talked about that. Paul knew about Ted, but she'd never told him about the baby. It wasn't something she liked to relive, and yet tonight it had been on the tip of her tongue.

Reaching for the glass of wine she'd brought into the bathroom with her, she took a long drink. "Sorry. I didn't mean to dump all that on you."

"That's what boyfriends are for, right?"

The sides of her mouth tilted up in a smile. "Is that what you are? My boyfriend?"

"I guess that's up to you, now isn't it?" The teasing lilt was back.

When she didn't answer, he cleared his throat and got all serious. "Janey Davis, will you be my girlfriend?"

She shook her head and giggled. "You're insane."

"Maybe." He waited until her laughter died down. "You didn't answer the question, though."

Leaning her head back against the cool porcelain of her tub, she closed her eyes. It was crazy... insane. They hadn't known each other for that long. They didn't even live in the same town. Agreeing to be his girlfriend made no logical sense, and yet her instinct was to say yes. "Don't you want to date other people?"

His answer was simple and direct. "No."

She took another sip of her wine, hesitating before giving her response. Not because she didn't want to be his girlfriend, but because she knew what it would mean. At least, to her. "Okay."

"Okay?"

"Yes. Okay. I'll be your girlfriend."

"Good." She could picture him on the other end smiling from ear to ear. "When can I see you again?"

Janey sat up, sloshing the water and sending some over the side of the tub. "Um. I don't know."

"I have next weekend off. What if I come down to visit?"

"Come here?" She wasn't sure why, but she'd always thought she'd be the one traveling to see him all the time.

"Why not?" He paused. "Unless you don't want me to come to your place."

"No. It's not that." She hurried to clarify. "I just didn't think you'd want to come to Indy."

"I'm down that way at least a few times a year. Now I have a reason to go more often."

Her belly did a little flip when his voice dipped low. It was as if he were right there beside her, whispering it in her ear instead of two hours away.

"I'm on call Saturday night, but we could do something during the day." She was already mentally going through a list of the other detectives to see if maybe she could trade with someone. Paul would do it if she asked, but then she'd have to tell him why she needed to switch.

"I'll have to hope everyone behaves themselves Saturday night so you don't get called out, then."

The water was beginning to cool, so she drained the rest of her wine and placed the empty glass on the floor. "Can you hold on for a minute?"

"Sure. Everything all right?"

"Yeah. I just need to get out of the bathtub and dry off, and I can't do that holding the phone."

He gasped. "You were naked the whole time and you didn't tell me?"

Janey rolled her eyes. "Yes. Naked. Wet. And covered in bubbles. Hold on."

Right as she pulled the phone away from her ear, he groaned. She couldn't help but chuckle. Men. They were so predictable.

She took her time drying off and putting lotion all over her body. As her hands skimmed over her skin, she imagined what it would be like having him in her space. Her condo was much smaller than his family home, but it was big enough for her.

After wrapping a towel around herself, she picked up the phone again, and strolled into her bedroom. "Miss me?"

"You're killing me."

She chuckled. "Nah. I think you'll survive."

"Doubtful. My cock is about ready to bust out of my pants thinking about you wet and naked. I don't know if I can wait till next weekend."

His voice dropped low again, causing her body to warm. It remembered every detail of their time together. "It'll be a very long two weeks."

"Ten days."

Her mouth was suddenly dry. Ten days until they saw each other again. Ten days until he was in her bed.

It was her turn to clear her throat. She needed to change the subject. Pronto. "What time does your shift start?"

There was a long silence, and then she heard him sigh. "I should probably head out. I want to check on a few things before I start on patrol tonight."

"Everything all right?" Liberty was a small town, but that didn't mean it was crime free.

"Yeah, it's fine. Ava wanted me to swing by and check on her chickens. She thinks a fox or a raccoon has been sniffing around, and she wants to make sure they can't get in the coop. I told her I'd stop by before my shift."

Janey opened her top drawer and selected a pair of dark blue panties. Tossing her towel in the hamper, she cradled the phone against her shoulder and shimmied her clean underwear up her legs. "Such a good brother."

He laughed. "I'll call you tomorrow. Sweet dreams."

"Good night."

She was smiling by the time he disconnected.

After throwing on one of her favorite old T-shirts, Janey made herself some herbal tea and climbed into bed. She wasn't on call tonight, so unless there was a break in one of their cases, she had the evening to herself.

There was absolutely nothing on television, so she popped in a movie. By the time the credits rolled, she was barely able to keep her eyes open.

She stopped the movie and was about to turn the television off when something on the news caught her eye.

"The body of a man was discovered today in the alley behind me," a reporter was saying. "Police say it's too early to speculate on the cause of death, but that the man appeared to have been hit over the head with a blunt object and that a Taser may have been used to subdue him."

Without even thinking about it, Janey reached for her phone.

A few seconds later, Paul answered, his voice groggy. "Hello?"

"There's been another one."

It took him a second to answer. "Another what?"

"Blunt force trauma to the head and a Taser used. This one was on the eastern side of the city. It was on the news. They found the body today in an alley."

"Guess we know what we'll be doing tomorrow."

"Yeah."

Paul sighed. "Get some sleep. It's probably going to be a long day tomorrow."

She knew he was right. "I'll see you in the morning. Good night."

"Good night."

Janey looked down at her phone and bit her bottom lip. Kyle would be on patrol. She shouldn't bother him. But if it were her, she'd want to know. Especially since it could be tied to the case in Liberty. She thought it was a stretch that there'd be two bodies with similar markings, but three? That wasn't a coincidence.

Janey: They found another body. Taser. Blunt force trauma.

His response came back almost immediately.

Kyle: Where?

Janey: East side of the city.

Kyle: Male?

Janey: Yes.

Kyle: Can't be random.

Janey: I don't think so either.

Kyle: I'll let Noah know in the morning.

She knew she needed to let him go. Not only did he need to focus on work, but she needed to get some sleep. Paul was right. Tomorrow would be a long day. Given there were now three victims, the higher-ups would no doubt want to be involved. There was going to be red tape up the wazoo. Just what they didn't need.

Janey: If we find out anything else, I'll let you know.

Kyle: Thanks.

She was about to put her phone down when it pinged again to let her know she had another message. It was a picture of Kyle in his uniform, sitting in his patrol car.

Kyle: Wishing you sexy dreams.

He knew just what to say to get her mind off the case and onto something a lot more pleasant.

Plugging her phone in beside her bed, Janey snuggled under the covers. She let her thoughts drift to Kyle. He'd be there in ten days. With her. In her home. In her bed.

She rolled over and spread her fingers over the empty space beside her. Running the tips of her fingers up and down the cool sheets, she imagined him there—his large body next to hers. The feel of his arms, his legs, his chest. Then he'd look at her with those blue eyes of his and that confident smile on his face and her heart would skip a beat.

Sighing, Janey retracted her hand and turned over on her back. It was going to be a long ten days.

***

Kyle strolled into the diner the next morning, removed his cap, and quickly located Noah. His friend had his nose in the morning paper.

"I'll be with you in a minute," Claire said as she carried three plates to a nearby table.

"That's okay. I'm here to see Noah."

She set the plates down on the table in front of her. "I'll be by with some coffee, then."

Nodding, he made his way down the aisle to where Noah was sitting.

His friend folded the paper he'd been reading and set it aside. "Wasn't expecting you this morning. Did you tick your sister off or something?"

Kyle sat down, and before he could get a word out, Claire was there with the coffee. "Your usual?" she asked him.

"Yes, please."

With that she was gone, leaving the two men alone.

"Ja—" He caught himself. "Detective Davis contacted me last night. Apparently there's been another victim."

"Same MO?" Noah asked.

"Looks that way. Detective Davis and her partner are going to check it out today. She said she'd let me know once they had more information."

Noah frowned. He glanced around. The diner was full of locals—the same as it usually was at this time of day. Luckily for them and their current conversation, none of them were close. "I don't like the idea that there may have been a serial killer in our town." He paused. "Or heaven forbid, is still here."

"I know. If this third victim turns out to be connected to the others..."

His friend took a sip of his coffee. An outside observer would think the two of them were talking about nothing more serious than the weather. "I want you to stay on top of this."

Kyle blinked. "You don't want to call in a detective from the state patrol?"

"No." Noah met his gaze with hard determination. "I know we don't have a full-time detective right now and that you've only been filling in when needed, but at the moment you know more about this case than anyone else here." Without so much as a pause, he added, "Plus, you're nailing the pretty detective from the city."

Almost choking on his coffee, Kyle forced the liquid down his throat.

"Can't say I blame you. She's easy on the eyes."

"Thanks. I think."

Noah chuckled. "Did you really think I wouldn't find out? Hell, I'm pretty sure half the town knows she spent the night at your house."

"Guess we weren't as stealthy as we thought."

"Yes, well, I'm not sure I'd call making out in your driveway stealthy."

"Who—"

"Your neighbor, Mr. Thompson, called me. He wanted to make sure I knew just what kind of officers I had working for me." Noah's amusement was clear. He was grinning from ear to ear like the Cheshire cat.

Kyle grunted. "I should have known."

"Yes, you should have. You grew up around here. You know how it works in a small town."

Claire walked up to the table, two plates in her hands, and placed them in front of Kyle and Noah.

"Thanks," they both said.

"Can I get you anything else at the moment?"

They both looked at each other, and Noah answered her with a smile. "I think we're good."

"Holler if you need anything," she said, already backing away.

They ate in silence for a few minutes, each one too focused on their food for conversation. Kennedy refilled their coffee and gave Noah a wink before heading back behind the counter.

"I think she likes you," Kyle said to Noah.

His friend shot him a confused look. "She flirts with everyone."

It was true. Kennedy did flirt with most of the male diners, but that wasn't the point. "You should ask her out."

"Why would I do that?"

"She's single. You're single."

"So?"

"Don't you like her?" Kyle had no idea why he was pushing so hard. Okay, he did. While he loved Noah like a brother, he wasn't sure how he felt about Noah and Ava. Not that there was a Noah and Ava.

Noah polished off the rest of his eggs and bacon before responding. "I like her just fine, but that doesn't mean I'm going to date her." He pushed his plate aside and reached for his coffee. "Why don't you ask her?"

"Can't."

He raised an eyebrow in question. "Seeing the pretty detective again?"

Kyle raised his coffee cup to his lips and grinned. "Next weekend. I'm driving down to Indy."

"Good. You can find out what's going on with the case."

"That isn't exactly my motivation for going," Kyle said.

"I'm sure you can find some time in between your bouts of sex to acquire a bit of information." Noah finished his coffee. "I meant what I said. I want you to stay on this. I don't like the idea of a killer running around in my town."

Kyle didn't either. He gave his friend a curt nod.

After saying goodbye to Noah, Kyle drove to Ava's. He was a little later than usual, but his sister knew not to count on him showing up at a specific time. Given his job, the end of his shift didn't always line up with what it said on a clock.

"Anybody home?"

Ava was at the stove. She turned to look at him. "I was starting to think you weren't coming this morning."

"Sorry. I had to swing by the diner and talk to Noah." He pulled out the chair next to Cole's and ruffled his nephew's hair as he sat down.

"Something happen last night when you were out on patrol?" She finished stirring whatever was in the pot and removed it from the stove.

"No." He hesitated, knowing as soon as he brought up Janey's name his sister would latch on like a dog with a bone. "Janey contacted me last night with an update on the case, and I needed to fill him in."

Seeming to forget completely about why he and Janey were thrown together in the first place, she focused instead on the fact that she'd made contact with him. "How is Janey?"

"Fine." That, of course, was an understatement of epic proportions. Janey was way beyond fine.

His sister busied herself pouring what looked to be pie filling into several containers. She liked to make big batches when she could get the ingredients on sale at the local farmers' market and freeze it so she could use it later. "Hopefully they aren't keeping her too busy in the city."

Kyle knew what she was doing. His little sister was fishing to see if he and Janey were still seeing each other. "Considering they found another victim last night that looks to be connected to the case she's been working on and the man I found out by Sherman's place..."

"Oh no!" His sister's shoulders dropped and sadness for this stranger she'd never met filled her face.

Cole took that moment to drop a grape. It rolled across the floor and landed a few feet away from Ava. She reached down to pick it up without missing a beat.

"It's the same person, do you think?" she asked as she walked over to wash the grape before placing it once again in front of Cole.

"We don't know." They didn't, but his sister was smart. She knew, the same as they all did, that the probability was high.

Ava wiped her hands off and sat down across from him. She picked up a piece of cereal and rolled it along the tips of her fingers for several moments before meeting his gaze. "You'll be careful, won't you?"

He opened his mouth to speak, but she cut him off.

"I know what you're going to say. You don't know yet why these men are being targeted. But that's all the more reason for you to be careful. I already lost my parents and a husband. I don't know if I could take it if I lost you, too."

Kyle covered her hand with his. He and Ava hadn't always been close, but since they'd both moved back to Liberty they'd gotten to know each other as adults. She was still his little sister and he was still the big brother—that wasn't ever going to change, but she was right. They were each other's only family. They were all each other had. "I'll be careful. I promise."

Ava stood and walked around next to him. She leaned down and hugged him. "I love you."

He wrapped his arms around her waist and returned the hug. "Love you, too."

They broke apart when Cole squealed. He apparently wanted in on the affection.

Kyle reached over, plucked him out of his booster seat, and stood him on his lap. "I think someone's jealous," Kyle said to Ava.

She smiled and ran a hand over her son's head and down his back. "Family hug?"

He stood, resting Cole on his hip, and brought Ava in for another hug. Cole let out a joyous giggle as Kyle and Ava both circled their arms around him.

This was why he'd moved back to Liberty.

THE CAPTAIN WAS WAITING for them when Janey and Paul arrived at the station. He ushered them both into his office and closed the door. The look on his face was grim, and she braced herself.

"I spent an hour last night on the phone with the commissioner. He's not happy; nor am I."

Janey and Paul shot each other a look.

Their captain didn't seem to notice or didn't care. He crossed his arms in front of him. "I'm assuming you've both heard they found another dead body yesterday?"

"Yes, sir," Paul said. "Janey saw it on the news last night and called me. We figured we'd take a ride out to the crime scene today and drop by the coroner's office."

Captain Lane looked straight at her. "Where are you at with this case? Have you found anything new? Did they turn up any DNA or fingerprints in Liberty?"

"Mac—" She stopped and started again. "Their coroner, Dr. Mallory, found something under the victim's nails and sent it off to the lab. To my knowledge, they're still waiting on the results."

Paul chimed in. "We've been going through the evidence again, but there isn't much there. Whoever it is doing this is really good at cleaning up the evidence."

"Well, you need to find something. The commissioner already had a reporter call him yesterday asking if the cases were related. All bets will be off if they find out about the third victim in Liberty. We'll have a shitstorm on our hands, and I don't need to tell you what that means."

"No, sir," they both said in unison.

"Good." Captain Lane waved his hand, dismissing them. "Now get out of my office and find some evidence."

Janey and Paul hurried out of the captain's office, grabbed the file they needed, and headed out. The captain was right. They needed to find a lead somewhere and fast. If not, the press was going to descend and that was never a good thing.

The drive to the east side of town was slow. There was an accident, and as they were in an unmarked car and it wasn't an emergency, there wasn't much they could do except wait it out like everyone else.

It was almost ten by the time they pulled up to the crime scene. There was still yellow tape blocking the alley, and a patrol officer was standing guard. They both flashed their badges and he nodded for them to pass.

Janey had a sense of déjà vu. The alley was flanked by brick walls. It was roughly two car lengths wide, but some of that space was filled by three dumpsters that were positioned randomly along the right side of the alley.

As they approached the second dumpster, they could see the chalk outline of the body. Paul turned three hundred and sixty degrees, taking in their surroundings from the vantage point of their victim. "Off the beaten path and unlikely to be seen from the main road."

"Same as the other one," she said, agreeing with his assessment. She walked around to the side of the dumpster. "I don't see any signs of a struggle and minimal blood splatter."

Paul was scanning the area. He was looking for anything that might be a clue, the same as she was. They'd worked together long enough to trust the other's process. It was one of the advantages of working with the same partner for so long.

She knelt down to get a different perspective. It wasn't an overly sanitary place. Janey was still trying to come up with a way the attacker was convincing their victims to follow them down an alley.

Of course, the obvious answer was sex, which meant the suspect they were most likely looking for was a woman. The only potential problem with that theory was that none of the victims had been so hard up for cash they couldn't afford a decent hotel. It could be a prostitute, but that theory didn't feel right. They had to be missing something.

Janey was about to stand up when something caught her eye. "Daniels."

He turned to face her, lifting one eyebrow in question.

She pointed to what had caught her eye under the dumpster. It looked like a ring, but it was too far away for her to be sure.

"I'll get a blanket from the car," Paul said.

Since it was still an active crime scene, they didn't want to contaminate any potential evidence. Especially now.

Paul returned a few minutes later with a blanket and camera. He took a picture of the dumpster, then spread out the blanket and lowered himself down onto it so he could reach underneath.

Before he disturbed anything, he took several more pictures. With a pencil, he picked up the item. She was ready with an evidence bag when he held it up.

"You were right. It's a ring."

She examined it through the plastic. "Looks like a class ring."

"I don't recognize the school, though, so maybe a high school?" he asked, thinking out loud.

"Probably. And definitely a woman's ring." As excited as she was with this find, Janey tried to rein it in. The ring could have been there for weeks or months.

"Might not have anything to do with the murder, but at the very least maybe we can find its owner and return it to her. Do our good deed for the day."

Janey nodded, sealed the evidence bag, and tucked it into her pocket.

They took another look around, making sure they didn't miss anything else, and then headed for the coroner's office.

When they arrived, the coroner was not in a pleasant mood. "I'll tell you the same thing I told the other detectives. I don't have anything for you yet and won't for several more days."

"All we need are the basics. Do you have a cause of death?" Paul asked.

"Blunt force trauma to the skull. A first-year med student could have told you that."

"And there was evidence a Taser was used?" Janey prompted.

"Yes. The poor guy probably never saw the blow to the head coming."

Paul nodded at the body lying on the exam table. "Any idea what was used to hit him over the head?"

"Appears to have been made of metal. My best guess? A bat, most likely, given the shape of the wound. Once I get the lab results back, I should be able to tell you more."

Janey took a step closer to the body. "Anything else that you noticed? Were you able to pull any skin from under the nails?"

The coroner huffed. "No. And if you'll excuse me, I do have work to do."

"Of course," Paul said, nodding that Janey should follow him out. "We'll look forward to reading your report."

Janey waited until they were out in the hall to speak. "Someone woke up on the wrong side of the bed this morning."

"I'm sure the brass are breathing down his neck as much as they are ours." Paul checked his phone and returned it to his pocket. "Let's get that ring over to the lab so they can swab it for prints and DNA. It's a long shot, but right now it's the best lead we have."

Things went much smoother at the lab. Amy, one of the lab techs, had the ring logged and back to them in less than thirty minutes. Unfortunately, there were no usable fingerprints. "I'll give you a call once we have the DNA results."

"Much appreciated."

Amy grinned up at Paul, a dreamy look in her eyes. "Anytime, detective."

Janey had no doubt that Amy would be the one calling Paul personally with the results. No wonder they'd gotten such friendly service. "I thought maybe women would stop flirting with you so much once you had a ring on your finger."

They'd left the building and were almost to his car. He stopped and looked at her with confusion.

She tilted her head down and raised her eyebrows. "Please don't tell me you didn't notice."

He continued walking. "She was just being friendly."

Janey snorted. "Sure. You keep telling yourself that. Wanna bet Amy will make sure to call you directly with the lab results?"

"I'm the lead detective on the case. It would make sense for her to call me."

"Uh-huh."

They reached the vehicle and Janey climbed in.

Paul got behind the wheel and started the engine. He glanced over at Janey. "Should I have done something differently? Megan has always said I'm oblivious to stuff like that."

Chuckling, Janey put on her seat belt. "You can't help how charming you are, Daniels. Besides, sometimes it comes in handy. And if it means Amy will get the results to us that much faster, then I'm not going to complain too much."

***

The first thing Kyle did when he woke up was check his phone. He'd been secretly hoping there'd be a message from Janey. It didn't matter if it was about the case or just a quick hi.

He shook his head and threw the covers off his naked body before heading into the bathroom. After taking care of business, he jumped in the shower, shaved, and got dressed in a pair of jeans and a T-shirt.

He didn't have to be at the station for a few hours and he wanted to get in some target practice.

Grabbing his range bag, several boxes of ammo, and his service pistol, he locked up his house and drove to the range. He waved to a couple of guys he knew on his way in. Living in such a small town, it was almost impossible to leave one's house and not run into someone you knew.

Kyle blew through two hundred rounds of ammo before calling it quits for the day. He packed up his things and was headed out when he ran into an old buddy of his from the Army. "Austin? Is that you?"

"Hey, man." His old friend smiled and embraced him in a firm hug. "How've you been?"

"Good. You?"

"Can't complain. Wouldn't matter if I did anyway."

Kyle stepped back and took a good look at Austin. He had a few gray hairs around his temples, but other than that he hadn't changed much since the last time Kyle saw him. "What are you doing in Liberty?"

"I needed to get out of the city, so I took a job as a park ranger. I figure communing with nature has to be better than people screaming about how unfair their life is because someone took their parking space."

They'd served two tours together and they'd seen a lot of shit. After Kyle's second tour, he got out of the Army and came home. For several reasons. One was that he'd seen what being in a war zone had done to guys who'd been deployed over and over again. He didn't want to end up like that. "So you're here permanently?"

Austin shrugged. "We'll see how it goes. For now I'm renting a cabin not too far from here."

"Well, if you ever want to get a beer sometime, give me a call." Kyle took out one of his cards, scribbled his cell number on the back, and handed it to Austin.

"You ended up in law enforcement, huh? Couldn't get enough of the insanity?" Austin asked, nodding toward the insignia on Kyle's range bag.

"Something like that." Kyle's gaze fell on the clock that hung above the counter. "Look, I need to run. Give me a call and we'll get that beer."

"Will do." He slipped Kyle's card in his bag. "It was good to see you."

"You, too." Kyle walked toward the door but stopped a few feet from the exit. "Don't be a stranger."

Austin held up his arm in acknowledgement, and then disappeared behind the door that led to the shooting lanes.

Once outside, Kyle made a beeline for his car, threw his range bag behind the seat, and drove home. He needed to get changed, eat, and call his girlfriend.

Recalling their conversation the night before brought a smile to his face. He knew he'd thrown her off guard, but that had been his intention.

Kyle pulled into his driveaway fifteen minutes later. He had enough time to change and pop the leftovers Ava had sent home with him in the microwave before calling Janey. He snatched his range bag from behind the seat and jogged inside.

It took him less than five minutes to put on his uniform and attach his sidearm. With one last check to make sure he wasn't forgetting anything, he grabbed his cell and headed downstairs. He was already dialing Janey's number as he was putting his dinner in the microwave.

She picked up on the second ring. "Hey, handsome."

"Please tell me you're taking another bath tonight." His imagination hadn't stopped creating vivid imagines of her naked, wet, and covered in bubbles, as she'd so eloquently put it.

Janey's laugh was deep and sultry. "Not tonight. Tonight I was thinking of doing some yoga."

Thoughts of her ass in the air had him shifting to make more room in his pants. A common occurrence around Janey. "Tease."

"I promise to make it up to you when you get here."

The microwave dinged. He removed his food and carried it to the table. "I don't know. Between last night and tonight.. . and then no doubt all the teasing between now and when I get there…" He blew out a loud breath. "That's a lot to make up for."

"You'll just have to trust me."

He paused, pretending to think about it, and let out a defeated sigh. "All right."

"You're crazy," she said, chuckling.

"You know it." Kyle stabbed a piece of meat with his fork. "So how was your day?"

"Long. I walked in the door about five minutes before you called."

He looked at the clock. "Did you get stuck at a crime scene?"

"No. Daniels and I were going through all the evidence again trying to find some connection between our victims."

"Any luck?" He didn't want to make this all about work, but if he didn't ask, Noah would be up his ass.

"Not so far. The body they found yesterday has all the same markings as the other two. We're going on the assumption they're connected for now."

"Anything I can do to help?" he asked. It wasn't as if he didn't have connections.

"Not at the moment. We're still waiting on lab results and combing through paperwork." She paused. "We did find a ring at the crime scene today. No idea if it's connected to our killer, though. People throw lots of things in alleys."

"I know. You should see some of the things I find in the alleys here."

"Come across a lot of strange things in that small town of yours, do you?" The conversation turned more lighthearted after that, which was what he'd wanted. He was calling his girlfriend, not Detective Davis.

They talked until he reluctantly had to go or risk being late for the start of his shift. "I'll call you tomorrow night around the same time?"

"I look forward to it."

Kyle disconnected the call and took his dishes to the sink. After a swift rinse, he loaded everything into the dishwasher, swiped his keys from where he'd left them on the counter, and dashed out the door.

Given how late it was, the parking lot only had about ten cars in it and he recognized all of them. He climbed out of his vehicle and jogged up the stairs. Halfway up, he ran into Ethan heading in the opposite direction. He looked to be in a hurry. "Heading out?"

"Some of the cows got loose and Dad needs some help getting them rounded up. I'll have my radio with me if you need anything."

"Let's hope for a quiet night, then."

Ethan nodded and raced down the stairs toward his vehicle. He pulled out of the parking lot as Kyle reached for the door to go inside.

One of the nice things about working the night shift was that things were quieter at the station. Sure, there was still activity—a police station never completely stopped—but there was next to no civilian traffic this time of day. Everyone there worked for the department or the county.

Hayden waved as he passed by dispatch on the way to his desk. He waved back, and he could have sworn he saw her blush.

"There you are." Kyle looked up at the sound of Noah's voice.

"Hey," Kyle said. "What are you doing here so late?"

"Waiting on you."

Noah motioned for Kyle to come into his office, so he changed direction and headed in to talk to his boss.

"Close the door."

Kyle did as instructed.

"Did you find out anything more about the victim they found yesterday in Indianapolis?"

That's what this was about? Kyle lowered himself into a chair. "It looks to be the same as the others. Janey said they found a ring at the scene, but they don't know if it's connected yet."

"A ring? What kind of ring?"

Kyle shook his head. "I don't know. They're still looking into it."

Noah frowned. "You didn't ask?"

"No." He leaned forward and met his friend's gaze. "If you want me to find out information from her in an official capacity, that's fine, but if so, I need to do it on official time—hers and mine. Our conversation was off hours and I didn't want to make it seem like an interrogation."

They stared at each other for a long moment, before Noah sighed. "You're right. I don't like it, but you're right. Tomorrow I'll file the paperwork to get official copies of all the files on the other two murder victims. Maybe if you and I put our heads together, we can come up with a link between the victims. I don't doubt that Detective Davis and her partner are good at their jobs, but they don't know Liberty the way we do."

They sat for a minute not speaking before Noah dismissed him.

"Is it all right with you if I let Janey know you'll be making the request? I don't want her to think we're trying to step on their toes."

"Go ahead." Noah leaned back in his chair and folded his arms across his chest. "I wouldn't want to be responsible for causing problems in your relationship."

Kyle resisted the urge to roll his eyes. "Thanks. I appreciate it."

"Sure." His friend stood and reached for his keys. "Be safe out there tonight."

"Always am." Kyle opened the door and strode out into the main part of the station. After a brief stop at his desk to check his messages, he made his way out to his patrol vehicle to start his shift. Nothing like a talk with the boss to get the evening off on the right foot.

CHAPTER 11

EVERY EVENING KYLE would call Janey around six o'clock. She'd begun to anticipate it. So much so that Paul was beginning to get suspicious.

It all came to a head two days before Kyle was scheduled to come visit. Paul and Janey had been called to a hit and run. The victim was a teenager who'd been walking home from school. The young woman hadn't survived. It was heartbreaking seeing her lying there on the side of the road—even for someone who'd seen her fair share of dead bodies. It always hit hard when a child was involved.

Her phone rang as they were taking statements from witnesses. Janey had known who it was right away, so she didn't bother to look at the caller ID. She sent it straight to voice mail and went on with her interview.

Her partner noticed.

They were leaving the scene when he confronted her. "Something going on I should know about?"

She swallowed, nervous. "Like?"

"You've been acting... strange lately."

"In what way?" She should have known he'd catch on sooner or later. It wasn't as if she typically walked around all melancholy, but even she noticed a difference in her demeanor. Paul had worked with her for going on six years. He was bound to figure it out sooner or later.

He furrowed his forehead, deep in thought. "You seem"—he paused and glanced in her direction before turning his attention back to the road—"overly cheerful lately."

"Do I?" She looked out the window, hoping he'd let it go.

She should have known better. "Who called you when we were talking to that witness?"

"I forwarded it to voice mail."

"Yes." He drew out the word. "And you didn't bother to look to see who it was first. That tells me that you already knew who it was... that you were expecting the call."

Janey considered her options. She could lie to him. It was a personal matter, so it wasn't as if he needed to know who she was talking to and why.

Even thinking that had her feeling guilty. Especially after how she'd encouraged him to explore things with Megan. So she decide to be honest, albeit vague. "It was Officer Reed. I've been giving him updates on the case."

While that was true, it wasn't as if that was all they'd talked about during their nightly conversations. In fact, it'd only come up once or twice. More often than not, their talks steered clear of work-related topics.

Paul twisted his mouth to one side. "I didn't know you were still in contact with him. I guess that makes sense considering one of the victims was found in their jurisdiction."

She didn't comment.

They drove for several minutes before he broke the silence again. "Why is Officer Reed your contact, though? Don't they have a detective up there that should be handling the investigation?"

Janey was beginning to understand how he'd felt when she kept asking him how things were going with Megan. "I don't know. I wasn't introduced to a detective while I was there."

"So you were with Officer Reed the entire time?"

She saw the trap clear as day, but she had no idea how to avoid it. "Most of the time. Yes."

Again, Paul grew quiet. He didn't say anything until they reached the station. "When are you seeing him again?"

Not if, but when. "Umm."

He cut the engine and removed the keys from the ignition. "I knew something was going on after I caught you humming at your desk the other day. That, and you've done your best for the last week to leave exactly at five. I'm usually the one anxious to get home these days."

The gig was up. It wasn't as if she were trying to hide her relationship with Kyle. Not really, anyway. "He's driving down on Friday afternoon."

Paul nodded. "Staying for the weekend?"

"Till Sunday. He has to work Sunday night."

Her partner opened his door and got out. She followed suit.

They walked side by side across the parking lot to the station entrance. Right as they were about to go inside, Paul spoke up. "You two should come by on Sunday. I'll fire up the grill."

"I don't—"

He raised his eyebrows in question.

"I'll think about it."

Paul chuckled. "Don't feel so good when the shoe is on the other foot, now does it?"

He walked inside, leaving her standing there with her mouth hanging open.

It was after eight o'clock before she strolled into her condo. Kyle had left a message earlier saying he was sorry he'd missed her and that he'd talk to her soon. So far things had been great between them. The distance, while frustrating, didn't seem to trouble him. Instead, he'd said he couldn't wait to see her again.

It was a far cry from her previous experience.

Janey moved around her kitchen, gathering items to make a quick stir fry for dinner. It was late and she was starving.

As her food cooked, she picked up her phone and sent Kyle a quick text.

Janey: Sorry I missed your call tonight. We were at a crime scene.

A few seconds later came his reply.

Kyle: I figured you might be. Are you just now getting home?

Janey: Got home a few minutes ago. I'm making dinner. I was starving.

Kyle: What are you having?

Janey: Stir fry. I'm too tired to make anything else.

Kyle: Sounds more appetizing than my dinner. Hot dogs.

Janey filled her plate with the stir fry she'd made and retrieved a fork from the drawer. She was too hungry to bother carrying it over to the table.

Janey: Ava didn't send you home with leftovers today?

Kyle: She took Cole to visit his grandparents. She'll be back Thursday.

Janey knew Kyle and Ava's parents were deceased, so she had to assume he was talking about Ava's late husband's parents.

Janey: Where do they live?

Kyle: Kentucky. It's about a four-hour drive from here.

That had to be a long drive with such a young child.

Janey: So you're fending for yourself until she gets back?

Kyle: Something like that. I'll grab something at the diner in the morning, and then I have some frozen pizzas I can warm up. I'll survive.

She chuckled.

Janey: I'm sure you will.

Kyle: I've got to go. I'll call you tomorrow. Sweet dreams, baby. I miss you.

Janey grinned. And before she could second-guess herself, she typed her response.

Janey: I miss you, too.

She finished eating and cleaned up the small mess she'd made in the kitchen. It wasn't much—she'd kept her meal simple—but it still took almost fifteen minutes to put everything back in its place and load the dishwasher.

Satisfied her kitchen was in order, she switched off the lights and headed for the living room to see if there was anything on television. It was still early, but she didn't feel like going out. In fact, she hadn't been out clubbing since she got back from Liberty. Carla had asked Friday afternoon if she'd wanted to go out for drinks, but Janey had turned her down in favor of going home and waiting for Kyle's call. It was very unlike her.

Janey glanced at her phone, and then at the television. She was becoming a hermit. It wasn't healthy. Besides, she doubted Kyle was rearranging his life so he could talk to her. He had his sister and his friends. She'd just have to figure it out.

Balance. That's what she needed. She couldn't get completely swept up in Kyle and forget her friends.

Her hand was inches from the phone when she remembered how

Paul had realized she was seeing someone. Carla was the type of person who easily picked up on subtle changes in people's behavior. It's what made her a good police officer.

While Paul might tease her about her new relationship, he would drop it if she asked him to. Carla? Not so much. Her friend was a diehard romantic. She was always trying to set Janey up with guys they ran into in the bar, pushing them together, hoping sparks would fly. Most of the time, however, Janey was looking for a way to get the guys to leave.

Carla's heart was in the right place, but she tended to go toward guys who liked to party. Janey loved to dance, but that was pretty much where it ended. She was too old for binge drinking and body shots.

Sighing, she settled back on the couch and flipped through the channels until she found something decent to watch. She'd call Carla tomorrow.

***

Kyle's Thursday night shift felt as if it was moving at a snail's pace. Other than tagging a speeder about ten miles outside town, it had been a quiet night. He'd had a lot of time to think about his upcoming weekend with Janey. While he'd enjoyed their phone calls and texts over the last two weeks, he couldn't wait to see her again.

He needed to get home and get some sleep, but first he had to swing by Ava's. She'd sent him a text the day before to let him know she and Cole were home, and he'd told her he'd see her in the morning.

It was a little after eight when he pulled up to Ava's bed and breakfast. The house seemed quiet, but then again Ava hadn't scheduled any guests since she knew she'd be out of town. He took the steps two at a time and let himself in, not bothering to knock.

"Anybody home?"

"In the bedroom," she called back.

He found Ava curled up in bed, Cole tucked beside her, watching the morning news.

This wasn't like her. He couldn't remember the last time his sister was still in bed at eight o'clock in the morning. She was an early riser. Always had been. "Are you feeling okay, sis?"

"I'm fine." When he gave her a skeptical look, she added, "I just thought I'd take the morning off, that's all."

If he didn't know her well enough, he probably would have let it go. He did know her, though. "Did something happen at Andy's parents'?"

Ava pressed her lips together and avoided his gaze.

Kyle crossed the room and took a seat on the end of the bed. "What happened?"

She shook her head. "It's nothing really."

He waited.

"Molly just said she thinks I work too much. That I'm not spending enough time with Cole because I'm too focused on the B&B."

"Does she not expect you to work so you can provide for you and Cole?" Kyle didn't understand where this was coming from. Granted, he'd only met Molly and her husband, Jacob, a few times, but they seemed to be practical people. Surely they understood that, being a single mom, Ava had to work, and the bed and breakfast allowed her to work from home.

Again, she hesitated. "I don't think it's the work, exactly. I don't think she likes the fact that Cole is exposed to so many strangers."

"I see."

"I explained to her that I make sure he's never alone with them, but.. ."

"But what?" he prompted when she didn't continue.

"She implied that one of these days I'd have my back turned and something would happen to him." Ava met her brother's gaze, a pleading look in her eye. "Do you think that's true? Am I putting Cole at risk by running the B&B?"

"No, I don't." He took her hand in his and squeezed. "You're a great mom and you're careful about who you let stay here. Molly is overreacting. Maybe she's missing her son and doesn't like the fact that you and Cole live so far away."

"I told her they should come visit," Ava said.

"That's a good idea."

"I thought so. But she said Jake's too busy with work."

Kyle didn't like the way Molly had been trying to guilt trip his sister. "Their loss, then." He scooted closer and made sure she was looking at him. "Anything I can do to help?"

She gave him a tiny smile. "Want to help me make some cinnamon rolls?"

"Sure," he said, standing. "And then I need to talk to you about this weekend."

Ava lifted Cole from her lap and got out of bed. "What's this weekend?"

It was his turn to feel guilty, especially knowing how her visit with her in-laws had gone. "I'm off this weekend, so I was going to drive down to Indy."

The smile on his sister's face got bigger. "You're spending the weekend with Janey."

It wasn't really a question, but he answered it anyway. "Yes." Then he hurried to add, "But if you need me to stay here—"

"Don't be ridiculous. I'll survive. It's not the first time I've met with their disapproval, and I doubt it'll be the last." She picked up Cole and brushed past Kyle on her way to the kitchen. "You just have to promise me one thing."

"What's that?" he asked.

"I want you to ask her if she'll come for Labor Day weekend. You can say I invited her if that makes it easier."

He opened his mouth to respond, but she cut him off and reached into the cabinet for her rolling pin.

"I know what you're going to say. You don't know if she has to work, yada, yada, yada." She waved the rolling pin around in time with her last three words.

"You know me so well."

It was as if he hadn't said a word. "She won't be working the entire weekend, surely, which means she can come here for a day or two. Right?"

Ava finally came up for air as she placed the rolling pin down on the counter and pulled out her mixing bowl.

"I don't know."

She gave him a look that said she didn't like that answer.

"I'll ask, okay? That's all I can do. Happy?"

"Yes." She continued moving around the kitchen, Cole still on her hip.

He reached for his nephew, and the little boy came to him willingly. "Why are you so eager for her to come for Labor Day weekend?"

"I just want to get to know her better, is all. It's been a while since I've seen you this interested in a woman and, well, we really didn't have much chance to talk when she was here the last time."

"She stayed in your house." From his perspective, Janey and Ava had spent plenty of time getting to know each other already. Wasn't there some unspoken girlfriend bond or something that happened when borrowing each other's clothes?

"We had two real conversations. Two. And even then I don't know all that much about her. Where's she from? What's her family like? Does she have any siblings?"

"She's from Fort Wayne. I believe all her family is dead. And no, she doesn't have any siblings."

"Okay, smart ass."

He shrugged. "You asked."

Ava began putting ingredients into the bowl. "I like her, okay. I think she'd be good for you. But I know that long-distance relationships aren't sustainable forever. Eventually, one of you is going to have to move. I want her to feel... welcome."

"In other words, you're trying to bribe her into moving to Liberty."

"Joke all you want, big brother, but it's scary moving to a new town, even if you're doing it for love. I want her to know she has a friend. Friends. Here."

He thought about that for a moment and realized she was right. While he liked Indianapolis well enough, it wasn't home. He was a small-town guy. Not to mention, his sister was here. "Thank you."

She stopped what she was doing and gave him a questioning look.

"For wanting to make Janey feel comfortable here."

It was Ava's turn to shrug. "Like I said, I like her."

Kyle set Cole down on the floor and handed him a toy from the basket Ava kept in the corner. Then he walked over and gave his sister a hug from behind. "Thanks, sis."

She bumped him with her hip, and he stepped back. "You're welcome. Now grab me the eggs from the refrigerator."

For the next hour he helped her make the cinnamon rolls. Well, she made them for the most part while he kept Cole entertained. He hadn't spent much time around children since Ava was little, but he loved spending time with his nephew. He'd seen a lot of horrific things when he was overseas and even some pretty terrible ones as a deputy. There were a lot of good people in the world, but he saw a good number of them at their worst. It was amazing the joy he felt when Cole would look up at him with those big eyes of his and give him a toothy smile.

"So when are you leaving?" she asked as she slid a batch in the oven, interrupting his thoughts.

"I'll go home and catch a few hours' sleep, and then I'll head out this afternoon." He didn't need more than a few since he planned to be spending the night in Janey's bed.

Ava nodded. "You don't want to fall asleep behind the wheel."

"That wasn't quite my concern, but sure, let's go with that."

She rolled her eyes at him again. "You're such a guy."

He laughed. "Thank you?"

"You know what I mean. All you think about is sex."

"That's not true. I think about other things. Food, for example. How long until those rolls are done?"

"Ten minutes. Think you can last that long?" She finished dividing and wrapping the remaining dough and put it in the freezer.

He sighed. "It'll be hard, but I suppose I'll manage."

"Good for you. Now, why don't you wash the dishes for me while I get dressed?"

Kyle stood to attention and saluted his sister. "Yes, ma'am."

She lifted Cole from the floor and shook her head. As she was leaving the room, he could have sworn he heard her mumble "smart ass" under her breath.

CHAPTER 12

KYLE LEFT his house around two in the afternoon and headed south toward Indianapolis. The drive was fairly uneventful until he was about ten minutes outside the city. Traffic slowed until it was inching along. He tried to be patient, and normally it wouldn't have bothered him, but he was anxious to get to his destination. Janey's condo was not far from downtown and he wanted to be there when she got home from work.

After almost a half hour of stop and go, traffic began to move a little. It was still slow going, given it was close to five o'clock on a Friday evening, but at least he wasn't hitting the brakes every two seconds.

His heart rate picked up when he saw the sign saying Janey's exit was one mile ahead. He was almost there. According to the GPS, he'd arrive at his destination in seven minutes.

Once he was off the highway, he weaved through several residential streets, making note of his surroundings. It was a cop thing. He was getting a lay of the land, so to speak. In this case, it would also help him know Janey better. This was where she lived and worked.

"You've arrived," his GPS announced.

He followed the instructions Janey had given him and located the parking garage to her building. It was smaller than what he'd imagined. When she'd said she lived in a condo building, for some reason he pictured a high-rise with twenty-plus floors, but in reality it was no taller than any other building in the area and consisted of only five floors.

Parking his car wasn't difficult. Visitor spaces were clearly marked. He removed his bag from the back seat and went in search of her unit.

Janey had given him her pass code so he didn't have to wait in the garage for her to get home. He used it to get inside the building and then to her floor. They appeared to have a decent amount of security, which he could appreciate. It made him feel better knowing her building was secure and not just anyone could show up at her door unannounced.

While she'd given him her code to get to her condo, she had no way of giving him a key to get in, so he parked himself outside her door and waited.

At five thirty-seven, the elevator dinged, drawing his attention. The doors opened and Janey strode into the hallway. She spotted him immediately, and a radiant smile spread across her face.

"You made it."

Kyle pushed himself up off the floor and stood. "Did you think I wouldn't?"

"Some people have trouble finding the parking garage," she said. "I was expecting a phone call saying you were lost."

When she was within a few feet of him, he opened his arms, inviting her closer.

She walked into his embrace, and he wrapped his arms around her, letting her soft warmth seep into him. It felt wonderful to hold her again. Even better than it had felt the first time he'd stepped foot on American soil after his first deployment. Having her in his arms felt right.

Before he could wax sentimental, Janey pulled back. "Come inside."

She removed her key from her pocket and unlocked the door.

The inside of her condo had an industrial flair to it. There was exposed duct work along the ceiling and the same brick surrounding the windows as was on the outside of the building.

"What do you think?" she asked.

He thought he might have detected a hint of nervousness in her question—like she wanted him to like it but wasn't sure if he would or not. It was quite different from his home, but he hadn't expected it to be exactly the same. Even with the industrial elements, it had a certain amount of charm. "I like it. Did this used to be a factory or something?" He knew a lot of old manufacturing buildings were repurposed into housing.

"A shoe factory." Janey made her way into the kitchen. "Hungry?"

"I could eat."

Janey nodded. "I wasn't sure what you'd like, so I thought we could order in. There are several restaurants that will deliver." He'd thought her nerves were regarding what he thought of her condo, but she still sounded anxious. Or maybe *jittery* was a better word.

He walked over, took hold of her hands, and turned her to face him. "I'm not a picky eater. Whatever you want is fine."

She gave him a shaky smile and reached for a stack of what he assumed were takeout menus. "Okay. How about Italian? There's a little place—"

Kyle cut off her words with a kiss.

She froze for a second and then melted into him exactly as he'd hoped she would. Her arms circled his neck and she pulled his body closer to hers.

"That's better," he mumbled against her lips.

"Hmm," was her only response before she fused their mouths together again.

Before long he had her pressed up against the counter and her hands were dangerously close to the erection straining in his jeans to get out. "I thought you were hungry."

"I am." She kissed his jaw and down his neck.

He chuckled as he tilted his head to the side to give her better access. "I meant for food."

She popped the button on his jeans, relieving some of the pressure. A moment later he felt her hand dip inside and palm his cock.

What was he saying again?

Taking her face in his hands, he crashed his lips over hers and plunged his tongue inside her mouth. Janey moaned and flexed her fingers around his erection.

"Bedroom."

She ignored him, pushing his jeans down his hips and dropping to her knees. Her face was level with his very hard cock, and the only thing covering it was the thin layer of his underwear.

Leaning in, she gave his cock a very wet kiss, soaking the fabric. When she sat back on her heels again, she took hold of either side of his boxer briefs and yanked them down. His erection bobbed eagerly in her face.

Janey placed her hand at the base of his cock and guided him to her mouth. All he could do was hold on. She'd done this to him once before, but he couldn't remember it feeling this good. Then again, maybe it was just the fact that it was happening here and now, and the feel of her mouth was all that mattered. The world could blow up around them and he'd be oblivious.

As good as it felt, though, he didn't want to come like that. Call him crazy, but he wanted to be inside her. He'd driven for two hours to see her again, to feel her, and that's exactly what he wanted to do.

Lifting her from the floor, Kyle set her back on her feet. "Either you tell me where your bedroom is, or I'm going to take you right here on your kitchen counter."

She licked her lips, sending his pulse racing. Did the thought of them having sex on her kitchen counter turn her on?

Going up on her tiptoes, she gave him a hard kiss. She took his hand and led him out of the kitchen and through the living room.

Kyle barely noticed Janey's bedroom because the moment they stepped over the threshold she began stripping. First came her shirt, then her bra, then she was removing her pants. "Are you waiting for an engraved invitation, Deputy?"

He smirked and finished removing what was left of his clothes.

Janey sauntered toward him, her hips swaying, calling to him. He pulled her flush against him, their naked bodies aligning perfectly.

Wasting no time, he picked her up, wrapping her legs around his waist, and carried her to the bed. Her mattress gave way as he lowered them both down on it, fitting her beneath him, cradling himself between her legs. She felt just as good as he remembered.

Now that he had his hands on her, he didn't want to stop touching. His fingers explored her body, moving top to bottom and back up again.

Janey seemed to be doing the same, relearning, remembering what he felt like. He bucked his hips when she cupped his ass, her fingertips skimming along his cheeks. He wanted to be inside her, but he didn't want to rush either.

"It feels like it's been longer than two weeks," he said as he kissed down her neck on his way to her breasts.

She gasped as he took one of her nipples into his mouth. "It does."

As he licked and sucked, enjoying the feel and taste of her, Janey laced her fingers through his hair, holding him to her chest. Her breasts were perfect. They weren't huge, but they fit nicely in his mouth and hands with a little to spare. Not to mention how sensitive they were. Every time he scraped his teeth against her nipple a little moan escaped her throat. It had his cock ready to burst solely from the sound of her pleasure.

One of her hands left his head, and he heard a drawer opening.

He released her nipple and glanced up, although he had a pretty good idea of what she was doing.

Janey shoved a condom in his face. "I want you inside me. Now."

Kyle chuckled and took the condom from her. He leaned back on his heels and ripped the package open. "Impatient tonight?"

"You're not?"

He rolled the condom down his length and lowered himself on top of her again. "I was trying to go slow. Savor the moment."

She circled her legs around his waist, digging her heels into his ass, urging him forward. "Later."

***

Thirty minutes later, Janey had her head tucked into the crook of Kyle's shoulder, listening to his heartbeat. He had his arm around her, running his fingers through her hair. It was strangely hypnotic. Or maybe it was the postorgasmic endorphins.

She must have hummed or something because he asked, "Happy?"

"Very." Janey glanced up at him. "You?"

He smiled down at her. "I have a beautiful woman lying naked in my arms. What's not to be happy about?"

"So that's all it takes?" she asked, teasing. "A naked woman?"

Shifting his weight, he brought them face to face. He leaned closer, bringing their lips a breath apart. "Not quite."

Janey's heart was racing. It was like this every time with him. "I forgot *beautiful*, right?"

He nodded and gave her a soft kiss. "Right."

The sound of his stomach growling caused them both to chuckle.

"I should probably order us some food." Janey inched her way out of bed and went to find a long T-shirt.

"Not bad." Kyle propped himself up on one arm. "But I think I still prefer you naked."

She ignored his comment. "Italian still good or did you want something else?"

"Italian's fine. I think I'm gonna need the carbs."

He gave her that sexy smile of his, and it did something to her insides. "I'll get the menu."

It took almost an hour for their food to be delivered. Janey had returned to the bed and they'd spent the time talking. He told her about Ava's visit with her in-laws. Janey had never had in-laws before, but she'd heard horror stories from some of her coworkers.

They sat in her bed, surrounded by takeout containers full of spaghetti and meatballs, lasagna, and fettuccini alfredo. It had been a long time since Janey had eaten in her bed, but neither one had seemed anxious to leave.

"What's Ava going to do?" Janey asked once they started to eat.

"Nothing." He stabbed one of the meatballs and added it to his plate. "Or at least, she's not going to change what she's doing now. Ava screens all the families before she books them. Molly and Jacob are overreacting. It's happened a lot since Andy died."

"I'm sorry. That has to be horrible for Ava."

He paused for a long moment. "My sister wanted me to invite you to Liberty for Labor Day weekend. I promised her I'd ask."

"Okay." Janey was caught off guard a little at the invitation. She knew she'd be visiting Liberty again, especially if she and Kyle continued their relationship, but she hadn't planned on it being so soon.

"Okay, you'll come, or okay, you'll think about it?" Kyle asked as he twirled some pasta onto his fork.

"I'd have to check my work schedule." That anxious feeling returned and settled in the pit of her stomach. She didn't understand it, though. Everyone in Liberty had been friendly. But maybe that was the point. She felt comfortable there, and on some level that frightened her. She still didn't know if this thing between her and Kyle was going to last.

"I'll have to work, at least to help out during the parade, but you could hang out with Ava. She says she wants to get to know you better."

"Why?" Janey regretted the question the moment it left her mouth.

"She likes you. Besides," he said, giving her a wink, "you are dating her brother."

She froze with the fork halfway to her mouth. Things with her and Kyle felt like they were getting serious fast, and she wasn't sure how she felt about that.

"Hey, what's wrong?" He must have noticed she'd stopped eating.

"Nothing." When he gave her a look that said he wasn't buying it, she clarified. "I was just thinking that it feels like this thing between us is moving really fast. I mean we've only known each other for a few weeks."

"Is that a bad thing?"

Janey took a moment to think about it. Was it a bad thing? She liked him. A lot. Things between them, despite the distance, had been really good. In some ways, she felt closer to him already than she ever had to any of the other guys she'd dated. Even Ted, and she'd dated him for three years.

She decided to be honest. "I don't know."

"If it helps, it's a little scary for me, too."

"Really?" She was surprised by his admission. He didn't seem to have an issue with the pace of their relationship.

"I think about you all the time. You're the last thing I think about before I fall asleep and usually the first thought I have when I wake up. Not to mention the fact that most nights you star in my dreams as well."

She lowered her head as she felt heat rush to her cheeks.

Kyle lifted her chin so she would look at him again. "I've never felt this way about a woman, Janey, and yes, that scares me a little."

"Thanks."

He brushed his thumb along her lower lip and grinned. "Anytime."

They finished eating and put the leftovers away in the refrigerator. Once everything was cleaned up, it was still early, so they decided to get dressed and go for a walk. It was tempting to spend his entire visit in bed, but she didn't want their time together to be all about sex. She'd been there and done that before. She liked him. Really liked him. And despite her trepidation regarding the long-distance thing, she was going to give this thing between them an honest try.

"Got your keys?" he asked as they headed out the door.

"Keys, gun, phone. I'm all set."

He held open the door and motioned for her to go first.

It was a nice evening. It was warm, but there was a gentle breeze. Several people were out walking their dogs. She waved to a jogger they passed as they rounded the corner.

"A friend of yours?"

"Not really," Janey said. "We've passed each other jogging a few times. I don't think we've ever said more than 'hi' or 'good morning.'"

"You don't get that kind of anonymity in Liberty. Everybody knows everybody, or at least they know their mom or their cousin or... you get the idea."

Janey steered him into a little shop that sold the best cupcakes. "Isn't that weird? Everyone knowing everyone's business?"

"Sometimes," he said. "But you get used to it. Besides, when push comes to shove, the community pulls together, and I like that."

While she could see the appeal, Janey couldn't imagine that happening in a city as big as Indianapolis. Or even Fort Wayne, for that matter.

Before she could stop it, the question slipped out of her mouth. "Do you ever think about living somewhere else?"

They were standing in the bakery, looking at the menu, but he stopped and turned to face her. The look on his face was serious. "I traveled a lot in my early twenties. I've seen a lot of places, but nowhere but Liberty has ever felt like home."

"Oh." Well, she guessed she got her answer.

"But," he added, "I've also learned that home has a lot more to do with people than it does with a place."

The way he was staring at her had all the moisture leaving her mouth. "We should... probably order."

He held her gaze for a moment longer, nodded, and turned his attention to the menu again.

They ended up getting a chocolate cupcake and a red velvet cupcake. Finding a table by the window, they split the treats in half and each took a piece.

"These are really good." He downed his half of the chocolate cupcake in two bites.

"I know," Janey said. "I eat way more of them than I should. Every time I pass by this place, I can't resist stopping in."

She was still working on her first half when he finished his red velvet cupcake. "Going to finish that?"

Janey pulled her cupcakes closer when he pretended to snatch them from her plate. "These are mine. If you want more, go order yourself more."

He chuckled but didn't make any move to get up and order another.

They sat watching the people pass by as she finished her cupcakes. "Have you ever thought about getting a dog?"

She polished off her last bite and began gathering up her trash.

He did the same.

"Not really. My schedule is too crazy." She waited for him to dispose of his trash as well before they headed back out onto the street.

"Makes sense." They began walking back toward her condo. "I've thought about getting a dog, and then I talk myself out of it. Like you said, crazy schedules and dogs don't mix. While mine might not be as crazy as yours, I work long hours and sometimes pick up shifts during the day."

"You could get a cat." He shot her an 'are you kidding me?' look, which made her giggle. "I'm serious. I've thought about getting one myself, but the timing never felt right. Cats are a lot more independent than dogs, you know."

"I've heard."

"You don't like cats?" she asked, picking up on his mood.

"I've never had a cat. But I've heard stories."

"We had a pair of cats when I was growing up. They weren't so bad. One of them loved to lie in your lap. She'd curl up into a ball and fall asleep."

They were approaching the front of her condo when someone called her name. She looked up to find Paul striding toward them. Her heart sank. If he was here, there must have been a break in one of their cases, which meant she wasn't going to be spending the rest of her evening snuggled up to the man next to her. Instead, she'd most likely be combing through files and evidence.

Janey plastered on a fake smile and braced herself for a long night.

CHAPTER 13

A MAN APPROACHED THEM. He was tall, around six foot, with dark brown hair. If Kyle had to guess, he was in his mid to late thirties.

Janey stiffened beside him, and he immediately went on alert. Was this an ex? He'd called her by name, so the man knew her.

"I called your cell, but you didn't answer," the man said.

"I left my phone upstairs."

The new arrival turned his attention to Kyle. He gave him a once-over and offered his hand. "You must be the new man in Janey's life."

Kyle shook the man's hand, trying to remain neutral, but it was proving to be difficult. "I am. And you are?"

It was Janey who spoke. "Kyle, this is my partner, Paul Daniels. Paul, this is Kyle Reed."

Now that he knew who the man was, he relaxed a little. Paul's face said he was here on business, which Kyle figured explained Janey's reaction. "I've heard a lot about you."

Paul glanced in Janey's direction, and then back to Kyle. "I can't say the same. She's been rather tight-lipped about you." He looked at Janey again. "Megan wants to talk to you about that, by the way."

Janey grimaced. Again, he had no idea who Megan was. He vaguely recalled her mentioning someone by that name before, but he couldn't recall who she was. A friend, he assumed. Maybe Paul's girlfriend or wife?

"Anyway, I don't want to take up your entire evening, but the lab called with the results on that ring, and I didn't want to wait until Monday to go over them with you."

The three of them made their way upstairs to Janey's condo. She unlocked the door and they all filed inside. "Did you want something to drink? I've got iced tea, lemonade, or I can make some coffee."

"I'm good, thanks," Paul said, making himself at home on her sofa. He removed a file folder from his jacket and laid out its contents on the coffee table.

Janey took the seat across from him.

"They found small traces of the victim's blood on the inside of the ring. Based on where we found it, I say there's a good chance it belonged to the killer."

"Have we gotten any hits yet on the ring itself?"

"No. It's taking a while to run down possible school matches when all we have is LBHS."

"Liberty-Bass High School." They both stared at him. "It's the local school district. It goes about ten miles south of Liberty all the way to Bass."

"I guess it's a good thing you're here," Paul said. "We could have spent another few weeks trying to figure that out."

"Do you have a picture of the ring?" Kyle asked.

Paul picked up one of the papers and handed it to him. "Looks like one of our class rings. Would have been someone in Ava's class, too. I wonder if she'd recognize it."

"Ava?" Paul asked.

"Kyle's sister."

Paul returned the picture to the file. "Do you think she'd be willing to take a look?"

"Sure. Let me see if I can get her on a video chat."

It took a few minutes to get everything arranged. Kyle called her first, knowing she'd be furious with him if he initiated a video call with her and expected her to converse not only with him but with

Janey and a man she'd never met. It wouldn't matter if the man was a detective and they were calling about a police matter.

"Of course, I'll help if I can. Do you have the ring?" Ava asked.

"We have a picture of the ring. The actual ring is locked up in evidence." Janey held the picture up to the phone so Ava could see it.

His sister concentrated hard on the picture. "It definitely looks like one of our class rings. I don't know who it belonged to, though." She paused. "You might want to contact Kelly's. They're the ones we all bought our class rings from. They should have a list of everyone who purchased a class ring and what all the specifications were for them. At the very least, it would narrow down your search."

"Thanks, Ava," Kyle said, turning the phone back around so he could see his sister.

"Anytime." She lowered her voice a little, but not enough considering he was only a few feet away from Janey and Paul. "How's your weekend with Janey going so far?"

Kyle rushed out of the room to get some privacy, but he didn't miss the smirk on Janey's partner's face.

Once he was alone in Janey's bedroom with the door closed, he addressed his sister. "The weekend was going fine. Better than fine, really, until her partner showed up with new evidence in the case."

"Are you pouting?" His sister was finding amusement in his plight.

"I'm not pouting. I understand the importance of looking at the new evidence as soon as it's available."

"But..."

"You know what? I'm not talking to you about this. You're my baby sister. You're not even supposed to know about sex."

Ava laughed. "You do remember I have a son, right? Cole. Your nephew?"

"I prefer to think about that as a onetime deal."

His sister snorted. "Do I need to remind you of the time you walked in on me and Andy?"

Kyle really needed to move the conversation away from sex—his sex life and Ava's—something he really didn't want to think about. "Are you feeling better?"

"I'm fine. Or I will be. You're right. I can't let her get to me. I'm a good mom. I know that. It's just easy to forget that when I'm there listening to her tell me all the things she thinks I'm doing wrong."

"Isn't that kind of what mothers-in-law are supposed to do?"

She cracked a smile. "Yeah."

"If you need me, call me. I'm only two hours away."

Ava dismissed his offer. "Don't worry about me. You have fun with Janey. I'll make sure not to disturb you. I wouldn't want to interrupt your sexy times."

With that, she waved to the camera and disconnected the call.

Kyle shook his head and returned to the living room. Paul appeared to be leaving. "I'll make some calls in the morning and see if I can get a printout of all the class rings purchased through Kelly's for that year. Being the weekend, I'm not holding out much hope we'll have anything before Monday."

"Probably not." Janey's gaze drifted to Kyle. There was a look in her eye he'd seen before, and it had him itching for them to be alone.

Paul walked over to the door, folder in hand. "I'll see you two Sunday, then. Megan's anxious to meet you," he said to Kyle.

"Sunday?"

Janey glanced at him, a nervous expression on her face. "Sorry. I hadn't had a chance to tell you yet. We've been invited over for a cookout at Paul and Megan's house on Sunday."

Not exactly what he'd expected to be doing right before he headed home, but these were Janey's friends. There were worse ways to spend an afternoon. "I guess we'll see you Sunday, then."

Once Paul was gone, Janey locked up. She kept her back to him for an extended period of time, took a deep breath, and turned to face him. "Sorry I didn't tell you about the cookout. I meant to earlier, but we got a little sidetracked."

Kyle pulled her into his arms and gave her a kiss. "Yes, we did."

She circled her arms around his neck, resting her elbows on his shoulders. "So you're not upset?"

"Why would I be upset?" He rubbed his thumb back and forth

along the small of her back. It was so nice being able to touch her like this.

"I know you came down to spend the weekend with me. You probably figured it'd be just the two of us."

He chuckled. "I wasn't expecting for us to be locked away in your condo all weekend. I figured we'd have to come up for air sooner or later."

Janey smacked his shoulder. "You know what I mean. I didn't want you to feel like you had to hang out with my friends. Megan can be a little pushy."

"You have met my sister, right? Or did you forget that she wanted me to invite you to spend Labor Day weekend in Liberty?" He didn't bother to mention he and Ava's phone conversation. His sister could be a royal pain in the ass when she wanted something.

"So you're okay spending your last few hours here on Sunday over at Paul and Megan's?" She still seemed a bit unsure.

"Positive."

She bit the inside of her lip, appearing to be deep in thought. Then she looked up at him. "Thank you."

"Why are you thanking me? It's not a big deal. We'll have other weekends together."

"That's not what I mean." She paused. "Well, not exactly anyway. I'm not used to guys being so... accommodating."

"That's me," he said, lifting her feet off the ground and bringing their faces level. Her lips were right there, calling to him. "Accommodating."

She took the hint and closed the distance between them. Her mouth covered his and she wrapped her legs around his waist, bringing her center in line with his groin. "Very accommodating."

Janey loved kissing him. His lips and tongue were so sure against hers. He knew what he wanted and he wasn't afraid to go after it.

Kyle palmed her ass, holding her body in place. His fingers massaged the flesh of her cheeks, sending her arousal up a notch. The man knew how to kiss… and other things.

Kyle backed them up against the door, using it for support so he could free one of his hands to release the snap on her shorts. Once they were unsnapped, the zipper pulled apart and he slipped his fingers inside her waistband. It didn't take him long to find what he was looking for.

She moaned, grinding herself against his hand.

"Feel good?"

"Yes," she said. "Don't. Stop."

He released her mouth and kissed a line from her jaw to her ear. "Yes, ma'am."

Janey didn't even care that she was being bossy. She was so close and all she cared about in that moment was her impending orgasm.

"Come for me, baby."

He scraped his teeth along her neck, and that was all it took. She gasped as her orgasm rippled through her.

"You okay?" he asked a few moments later. She was still trying to catch her breath.

"That was…" Words really couldn't describe it. "Wow."

"Glad you enjoyed it."

She lifted her head from where she'd been resting it on his shoulder. They were still up against the door. And he was still very aroused. The evidence was right there against the inside of her thigh. "Did you want to take this into the bedroom?"

Kyle shook his head.

"No?"

"No." She'd seen that look in his eyes before. Several times. "I have this fantasy of taking you up against a door, and I figure this is the perfect time to make that a reality."

"You want to have sex against my door?" She'd never done that before, but the more she thought about it, the more she wanted to try it.

"Think your neighbors will mind?"

At that moment, she didn't much care what the neighbors thought. If they had a problem with it, she'd deal with it later.

Janey reached for the hem of her shirt and began working it up her torso.

Kyle laughed and used his free hand—the one that had brought her only a few moments ago to a powerful orgasm—to help her get the shirt over her head.

"Now you," she said, going for his T-shirt.

It took a little maneuvering, but soon it joined hers on the floor.

She reached behind her to unclip her bra, but before she could get it undone, Kyle had his mouth covering her nipple. She tried to concentrate, but all she could think about was him sucking on her breast.

"Having trouble?" he asked. "Need some help?"

"I can't concentrate with you doing that."

He looked up at her, a twinkle in his eye. He knew exactly what he was doing. "Would you like me to stop?"

"No."

A deep rumble came from his chest as he redoubled the assault on her nipple.

It took her several attempts, but eventually she felt the clasp of her bra come loose.

Kyle didn't miss a beat. He took hold of the middle of her bra, pulled it down, and tossed it somewhere behind him. Then he went right back to what he'd been doing before. Only this time there was no fabric between him and the object of his attention.

Tilting her head back against the door, Janey let the sensations roll over her. The way he would alternate between licking and nibbling on her sensitive flesh had her squirming against hm. She didn't want him to stop, but she needed more at the same time.

"Kyle?"

"Yes?" he asked as he worried her nipple between his teeth.

"I need you inside me." She tugged at his hair, trying to get his attention. "Now."

"Well, since you asked so nicely." He gave her a hard kiss and lifted her higher, making sure to hold above the waistband of her shorts. "Get rid of your shorts, Janey."

Reaching down, she pushed her shorts down her legs. Before she could get them past her knees, though, he latched onto her nipple again and sucked. Hard.

Janey gasped. "Kyle."

"Can't help it. You taste too good."

She grunted as she kicked the last of her clothes onto the floor. As soon as she was free, she returned her legs around his torso and dragged his mouth away from her breast, making him look at her. "Your turn."

His smile had her heart skipping a beat and her pulse racing. He held her gaze as he reached into his back pocket, removed his wallet, and extracted a condom. "Hold this for me."

She took the condom from him, and he went to work removing his jeans. Once they were on the floor, he kicked them out of the way and plucked the condom from her fingers. He swiftly rolled it down his erection and lowered her into position, lining himself up with her entrance. "Ready for me?"

"More than ready." She'd been ready the moment he'd pushed her up against the door.

He eased inside her, taking his time and driving her crazy. Janey used the little bit of leverage she had to try and make him go faster.

It didn't work. If anything, he went slower.

"More. I need more."

"You need more?" he asked.

"Yes. You're going too slow."

Without any warning, he plunged the rest of the way inside. Her muscles flexed around the intrusion, welcoming him. She covered his lips with hers and sighed. "Much, much better."

His chest vibrated with his amusement as he began to move. Every time he thrust inside, a zing of pleasure radiated from her sex throughout her body.

They moved and kissed and touched, letting their bodies communicate in the most primitive way. She didn't have to think about anything except him... them. Everything outside them in that moment disappeared, and all she could do was feel.

She slowly felt her climax building. It was as if she were climbing a mountain, waiting to tumble over the other side. She dug her nails into his shoulders, feeling it getting closer and closer.

As if he knew she was almost there, he adjusted his hand so his thumb was directly over her clit. She bucked her hips and moaned into his mouth.

"That's it, baby. Come for me. Let me feel you."

He increased the pressure on her clit, and she couldn't hold it back any longer. Her world exploded. She had to bite into the side of his neck to keep from screaming out.

Kyle let her ride out her orgasm, continuing to move inside her. When she lifted her head, he had a smug look on his face. "Ready?"

He didn't give her a chance to respond before picking up his pace. Where before it had been all about going slow and feeling every inch of him as he filled her, this was hard and fast and unrelenting. He pounded into her over and over again, her back slapping against the door.

It was rough. It was primal. And her body loved it. She could already feel another orgasm building.

His lips captured hers in an almost brutal kiss and he plunged his tongue inside her mouth. She met him thrust for thrust, needing to be closer. It was unlike anything she'd ever experienced before during sex.

One of his hands cupped her breast, massaging it. His touch was surprisingly gentle, a direct contrast to how he was pounding into her. It sent her head spinning and her body craving more.

She needed...

Kyle seemed to sense exactly what she needed. He shifted them so that with every thrust of his hips, he was brushing against her clit.

Her eyes rolled back in her head as her entire body caught fire. She felt the skin on his back give under her nails. She felt as if she were falling and she was desperately trying to find something to hold onto.

This time her climax snuck up on her. Her entire body began to shake and then it shattered.

She heard Kyle grunt and let out a loud gush of air before collapsing against her.

"You okay?" he asked, his voice barely above a whisper.

Janey nodded, unable to speak. She was all right. At least, she thought she was. Then again, she still felt as if she were floating.

"Think you can walk?"

She took several deep breaths before speaking. "Don't know."

He chuckled and leaned back so he could look at her. "I'll take that as a compliment."

"You really should."

Kyle set her on her feet, making sure to keep hold of her until he was sure she wasn't going to fall. "I need to go clean up."

She nodded. "I'll meet you in the bedroom."

He cupped the side of her face and gave her a long, lingering kiss before heading for the bathroom.

Janey leaned back against the door and sighed. She was never going to be able to look at her front door again and not think of what they'd just done.

Gathering up their clothes, she carried them into the bedroom. She threw her clothes into the hamper, laid his on a chair, and climbed into bed to wait for him.

CHAPTER 14

THEY LAY in bed Saturday evening, Janey with her head on his shoulder. They'd made love several times since waking up that morning, but it didn't feel rushed. They were just enjoying their time together. It was one of the most relaxing weekends he'd had in a long while. Maybe ever.

Janey had gotten a call from another detective about an hour before, but luckily she didn't have to leave. Aside from the brief interruption the night before, the odds had definitely been working in their favor.

In between bouts of sex, they talked. He'd shared with her a little of his time in the Army, and she'd told him more about her grandmother. She sounded like an amazing woman. He would have loved to have met her.

What Janey had been vaguer about was how she'd ended up with her grandmother. He was trying not to pry, to let her share what she was comfortable with, but he had to admit he was curious. Then again, he was curious about everything that had to do with the woman in his arms.

"How old were you when you started living with your grandmother?"

Janey ran the tip of her finger down the inside of his arm. "Four."

Younger than he'd thought. Kyle couldn't imagine how confusing that must have been for her at that age. At any age, really. Hell, it was confusing to him.

He was trying to figure out how to ask what happened to her mother, when she went on.

"My mom threw my clothes and a couple of toys in a bag one morning and took me to Grandma's. I thought we were going to visit, but then my mother left. She didn't come back."

He was starting to understand Janey's issues with abandonment. First her mother, then Ted. And Kyle still didn't know what had happened to her father. She'd never mentioned him. "Ever?"

Janey shrugged. "She showed up one night when I was ten. It was late and I was already in bed. Someone knocked on the door, and I remember hearing Grandpa arguing with someone. I sneaked downstairs to see who it was." She paused and he waited. "I'm sorry. You don't want to hear this."

Kyle rolled them onto their sides so they could face each other. "I do. I want to learn everything there is to know about you, Janey."

"Why?" She seemed genuinely confused why he wanted to know about her family.

"Why not?" He brushed the hair away from her face and looked deep into her eyes. "You're my girlfriend and I care about you."

She searched his face, no doubt trying to determine if he really meant it. "My mom is a drug addict. Or she was. I haven't seen her since she showed up that night when I was ten. I don't even know if she's still alive."

There was a blank look on her face, almost as if she were bracing herself for his reaction. Kyle had to wonder if there was a story there as well. He let it go, however. "Did you ever think of using your resources to try and find her?"

"I seriously thought about it a couple of years ago. Paul said he'd help me if I wanted him to, but..."

"But?"

Janey flipped onto her back, looking up at the ceiling. "I thought over all the different scenarios and decided that maybe it was best if I didn't know." She turned her head to look at him. "What if I found her and she's clean, living a great life, yet never attempted to contact me? Or what if she's still strung out on cocaine or meth or heroin?" Sighing, she refocused on the ceiling again. "No, it's better not knowing, I think."

Reaching for her, Kyle tucked her against his side once more. She came willingly, snuggling into him. "I understand. Sometimes not knowing is better."

She nodded against his chest. "Not everyone understands. Carla thinks I'm crazy for not wanting to know."

Kyle hadn't met Carla yet, but Janey had mentioned her several times. He knew they were friends and that they went out to clubs together, but he didn't get the impression that they hung out beyond that.

Clearing his throat, he dove into territory that he usually avoided at all costs. She'd shared something deeply personal with him and he felt the need to do the same. "When my parents died, I was the one who found them."

Janey reared back to look at him. "You said they died in a car accident."

He nodded. "I was six months out of the police academy. It was late and I got a call on the radio that there'd been an accident out on Collins Road." Kyle felt the emotions of that night bubbling to the surface. He did his best to breathe. "They were already dead when I found them. There was nothing I could do."

She wrapped her arms around him and buried her face in his neck. He held tight, soaking in her warmth. Given her job, he didn't have to tell her the graphic nature of what he'd seen. She could no doubt picture it. He wished he could unsee his parents lying there in their car, blood caked on their faces, but he couldn't. Until the day he died, he'd remember.

"We're quite a pair, aren't we?" she mumbled against his neck.

Kyle kissed the top of her head, breathing in the scent of her shampoo. It was oddly comforting. "I'll be paired with you anytime."

She brushed her lips along his neck, sending a chill down his spine. He shivered and she noticed. "Cold?"

"Not at all." He trailed his fingers down the length of her spine then flattened out his palm to cup her ass. Her skin was so soft, so feminine.

He moved his hand lower, lifting her leg so it wrapped around his waist. She was still so wet from their last round of sex. He dipped his hand between her legs, touching her heat.

Janey gasped and pushed against his fingers as he slipped them inside her. She reached up, pulling his mouth down to hers. Their tongues mingled as he moved his fingers in and out.

Kyle was about to reach for another condom when her phone rang.

She whimpered. "I have to get that."

Reluctantly, he removed his fingers and let her go. He was as hard as a rock, and seeing her roll over to get her phone, her bare ass facing him, wasn't helping his predicament.

"Sure. I'll be right there," he heard her say before disconnecting the call.

Janey turned to face him, but he already knew what she was going to say.

"You have to go to a crime scene."

She sat up and crawled out of bed, leaving the sheet behind. "It sounds like a domestic dispute gone bad. Hopefully I won't be gone too long."

He put his feet on the floor and began gathering his clothes.

Janey finished dressing, making sure to grab her gun and her badge. "The remote is on the coffee table if you want to watch some TV. Or I have some books you could read if you like mysteries. There's also—"

"Go. I'll be fine. I'm sure I can find something to keep myself busy for a few hours."

She closed the distance between them, rose onto her tiptoes, and placed a long lingering kiss on his lips.

His erection was still protesting the fact that it wasn't going to be getting what it wanted anytime soon. He took hold of her hips and pulled her against him, letting her feel every hard inch of him through his jeans. "Hurry back."

Her breathing was labored when she stepped away. She was flushed and her eyes were still dilated with arousal. He was glad he wasn't the only one who was fighting the urge to forget the outside world and go back to bed.

She took a deep breath. "I'll leave a key on the kitchen counter. In case you need to go out while I'm gone."

He shoved his hands in his pockets and nodded.

Turning on her heel, she took two steps out of the room, and then ran back in to give him another hard kiss on the lips. "I'll be back as soon as I can."

She raced out of the room, and a few seconds later he heard the front door open and close.

Kyle ran a frustrated hand over his face and head. He knew how this worked. He had at least two hours to kill before Janey would be back.

Heading into the living room, he found the remote and made himself comfortable on her couch. Hopefully there was at least something decent on he could watch while he waited. Otherwise it was going to be a very long two hours.

***

Janey didn't get home until after midnight. What she'd hoped would be an open-and-shut case had turned out to be more complicated. A man had shot his estranged wife and child in their family home. Then he'd turned the gun on himself.

The complication was that not only did the wife have a restraining order against her husband but the man was a felon, which meant he hadn't gotten the firearm legally. That caused a lot of red tape and got the ATF involved. Not exactly the way she'd hoped her night would play out.

Kyle was waiting in the living room, surfing through channels, when she'd walked in the door. He'd taken one look at her, turned off the television, and carried her to the bedroom.

She was feeling better the next morning, more like herself. Getting called out to a crime scene that involved a child was always emotional, but it was even worse when it was a family. Janey would never understand how a father—or mother, for that matter—could kill their own child.

"Feeling better?" He nuzzled his nose against her neck.

"Yeah."

He pulled her against him, her back to his front. "Want to talk about it?"

Last night things had been too raw. She could still see the bodies lying there. It wasn't an easy image to forget.

"She had a restraining order and the husband was a convicted felon. Armed robbery."

"Black market?" His voice was calm and even. Exactly what she needed.

Janey shook her head. "I don't think so. The firearm was purchased legally five days ago."

"So you're thinking straw purchase."

"Yeah." At least there would be someone to hold responsible. Still, it didn't seem quite enough. They should be made to walk though that crime scene as she had and understand what their actions had caused.

Kyle sighed. "We don't see that kind of stuff that often in Liberty. Everyone knows everyone else and their business. It can be a pain sometimes, but it does tend to keep people honest. It's hard to hide anything when you have nosy neighbors."

She could see the benefits of that. Although, it wasn't as if the family had been isolated. They'd lived in a neighborhood, too. The closest house was only about thirty feet away. The neighbors were the ones who'd heard the gunshots and called it in. "I can't get the image of that little girl out of my head. The neighbors said she was supposed to start kindergarten in a couple of weeks."

He held her tighter and she leaned into him. It had been a long time since she'd felt she could lean on anyone. "Anything I can do to help?"

Janey turned in his arms, facing him. "No. But thank you." She glanced at the clock and back to him. "We should probably get up and start getting ready. Paul wanted us there at one, and it's already after eleven."

"Maybe we should save some time and take a shower together."

He raised and lowered both eyebrows several times, causing Janey to laugh. "Somehow I don't think that would speed things up at all."

"Maybe not, but it would certainly be more fun."

She scraped her teeth over her bottom lip as she thought about having him in the shower with her. Maybe what she needed was to get her mind off the crime scene and onto something a lot more pleasant. The idea definitely had appeal.

Before she could change her mind, Janey hurried out of bed and began making her way toward the shower. At the doorway, she stopped, turned, and gave him her most flirtatious look. "Do you promise to wash my back?"

A slow smile spread across his face as he scrambled out of bed.

Two hundred pounds of naked man barreled toward her. He picked her up, fireman style, giving her the perfect view of his ass.

She sunk her teeth into his backside, and he landed a swat to her rear. "Behave."

Janey giggled. "Or what?"

"Or I might have to wash more than just your back."

"Promises, promises."

***

Somehow, they made it to Paul and Megan's with a few minutes to spare. They used all the hot water in her shower before finally taking their activities back to the bed. Janey had been able to forget about the crime scene and focus on Kyle for over an hour.

Chloe was the first to see them. Janey was starting to think the little girl had a sixth sense or something. Even if Chloe was upstairs in her room, she'd race down the stairs within seconds of Janey walking through the door. It was uncanny.

"Who's this?" Chloe asked, looking up at Kyle.

Kyle knelt down and offered Chloe his hand. "I'm Kyle. And you must be Chloe."

She shook his hand and nodded. "Are you Janey's boyfriend?"

He grinned. "Yes, I am."

Chloe gave him a good once-over. "What's your job?"

"I'm a police officer." He didn't seem to have an issue answering Chloe's questions.

"Like Daddy and Janey?"

Paul cleared his throat and stepped forward. He extended his hand to Kyle.

Kyle stood and took it.

Looking down at his daughter, Paul explained. "Janey and I investigate crimes after they've happened. Kyle here tries to prevent the crime from happening so Janey and I don't have to deal with it."

It was a very simplistic way of explaining the differences between their jobs, but as it turned out, it made sense to a six-year-old.

Megan approached with a huge smile on her face. "Hi, I'm Megan. Paul's wife."

"Nice to meet you," Kyle said. "And thank you for inviting me."

They moved into the backyard and Paul fired up the grill. "I heard you got called out last night," he said to Janey.

Most of the time she and Paul worked together, but that wasn't always the case, especially on the weekends. Given her partner had been a detective for more than ten years, he got most of his weekends off. She, however, was still paying her dues. "Yeah. Domestic dispute."

Paul nodded. They'd both been called out to their fair share of domestic issues, both as detectives and even more so as patrol officers. She didn't need to tell him how bad the scene had been. He would know.

Not wanting to talk about last night anymore, she steered the conversation toward something more productive. "Did you make any progress on the ring?"

"I spoke to the manager at Kelly's. She's going to send over a list of all the rings purchased that year. Hopefully we'll be able to find a match."

"If you need any help, let me know. We'll assist you in any way we can," Kyle said.

Paul placed the meat Megan had brought out onto the grill. "We might take you up on that. If the person is somehow connected to Liberty, you'll know the territory a lot better than we do."

"The high school is small. My graduating class had sixty-seven students. I think Ava's had seventy-something. If who you're looking for is female, that will cut your list of suspects in half."

"Does your sister have a yearbook we could borrow?" Janey asked.

"I'm sure she does. I can mail it to you this week."

Paul came to sit down across from Janey and Kyle. "I'm thinking we might need to take a drive up to Liberty."

Janey stared at him, not sure where he was going with this.

"Right now the connection to Liberty is our only lead. I'd actually like to talk to Kyle's sister ourselves. I'd like her to look at the ring in person and see if it jogs any memories."

"I'm sure she'll be happy to help, although that was eight years ago. I'm not sure how much she'll remember."

Janey stood and went to get herself a pop out of the cooler while Paul and Kyle continued to talk about the case.

Megan strolled up to her and got herself a water. "He's cute."

Janey smiled.

"I'm a little hurt you didn't tell me about him, though."

"Sorry. It's just that it's still so new. I wanted to feel things out first."

Megan twisted the cap off her water. "You sound like Paul."

Janey chuckled. "Maybe after all these years of being his partner he's rubbing off on me."

Paul got up and flipped the meat before returning to talk to Kyle. Janey stayed where she was, keeping Megan company. After last night, she really wasn't in the mood for shop talk.

"His sister wants me to spend Labor Day weekend in Liberty."

"That's great." Megan frowned. "Isn't it? I mean his sister must like you if she's inviting you to come visit them, right?"

"Ava's great. She's been very supportive of a relationship between Kyle and me from the beginning."

"But?" Megan asked.

"But nothing, I guess. I'm just nervous. I mean we live two hours apart. We both have dangerous jobs. What if—"

"You really are starting to sound like Paul." Megan placed a hand on Janey's shoulder. "Sometimes you have to live in the moment and go after what you want, even if on paper it doesn't make sense." She looked over at her husband, a smile pulling at the edges of her mouth. "Things have a way of working themselves out."

CHAPTER 15

"Hopefully you'll come back to see Janey soon and we can do this again."

Kyle grinned at Megan. "I would like that. Thank you."

He and Paul shook hands. "We'll give you a call and make arrangements to bring the ring up so your sister can take a look."

"Just let me know. I'm sure Noah would like to see it as well. He doesn't like a murderer roaming around in his backyard."

Paul nodded.

After saying their goodbyes, they drove back to Janey's condo. It was after four o'clock, which meant he would need to leave soon. As much as he'd loved to stay, he had to work tonight.

"What time do you have to leave?" Janey asked as she neared her place. She must have been reading his mind.

"I need to be on the road by five so I have enough time to swing by my house and change before I go to the station."

Janey pressed her lips together and nodded. She kept her eyes on the road, not saying anything.

"I wish I could stay longer. My bed's going to feel very lonely when I get home."

She glanced over at him. "I know what you mean."

Kyle reached over and took her hand, lacing their fingers together and bringing them to rest on his leg. "If you and Paul come to Liberty this week, then we'll see each other again sooner than we thought."

"True. But I doubt we'll be staying for more than a few hours."

He gave her hand a little squeeze and then released it so she could pull into the parking garage.

As they were exiting her vehicle, a feeling of melancholy surrounded them. He'd been there for such a short time and he was having to leave.

They held hands as they made their way into the building and climbed into the elevator that would take them to her floor. He waited until the doors closed before backing her up against the wall and capturing her mouth with his.

Janey responded immediately. She held him to her as if she wanted to ensure he wouldn't back away.

The elevator dinged and the doors opened. Someone cleared their throat.

They both looked up to find an older gentleman staring at them with a smirk on his face. "Hello, Detective Davis."

Janey dropped her arms and straightened her shoulders. "Hello, Mr. Ellison. How are you today?"

He stepped into the elevator as they exited, his smile even wider than it had been before. "Oh, I'm just fine. Not as good as you, apparently."

She didn't get a chance to respond before the doors closed again and Mr. Ellison disappeared.

A low groan escaped Janey's throat as she unlocked the door to her condo. "Of course the biggest gossip in our building has to be the one to catch me making out with my boyfriend in the elevator."

"Could have been worse," Kyle said, shrugging. As soon as they were inside her condo, he reached for her, pulling her flush against him once more. "We were only kissing."

Janey raised an eyebrow at him. "We were practically dry humping each other in a public place."

He chuckled. "I'm not sure I'd go that far. Although, if you'd like, we could try it again and you can show me what you mean."

She gave him a playful push on his shoulder, which only make him laugh harder. "Not funny. No more elevator make-out sessions."

"Now that I can't promise." He lowered his head and brushed his lips against hers. "I kept my hands to myself all afternoon. Once we were alone—" She opened her mouth to protest, so he altered his statement a bit. "Once there was no one else around, I took advantage of the situation."

"And we got caught. By my neighbor."

Kyle moved his lips to her neck and suckled right below her ear. He felt her pulse kick up a notch.

She tilted her head to the side to give him better access. "How do you always do this to me?"

"Do what?" he whispered against her skin.

Her only response was to cup the back of his head, encouraging him to keep going.

"Janey?"

"Hmm?"

"Tell me what I always do to you," he whispered in her ear.

Kyle felt her shiver.

She still didn't answer his question.

"Do you want me to stop?"

"No."

He smiled against her neck and went back to what he'd been doing. "Then tell me. I want to know what I do to you."

"You know what."

"No, I don't. Tell me." To add a little extra persuasion, he pulled her hips against him, letting her feel exactly what she did to him. Every. Damn. Time.

"Every time you touch me, you make me forget about everything but you."

He lifted his head to look at her. Janey's eyes were dark with arousal. She was feeling all the same things he was, and it wasn't only about sex. Yes, she could turn him on like no one else, but it was more than that. Knowing he had to leave her here in the city was near torture.

Without words, he lifted her up, wrapping her legs around his middle, and carried her into the bedroom. He knew they really didn't have time, but for the first time in his life he didn't much care if he was late. Kyle needed to connect with Janey on the most basic level. He needed to feel her surrounding him one more time before he went weeks without. Sure, they could fool around over the phone, but it wouldn't be the same as her fingers in his hair or her nails on his back.

He lowered her onto the mattress and began to remove her clothes.

"Don't you have to leave?" she asked, staring up at him.

"I need to be with you one more time before I go." He smiled down at her. "One more for the road."

Janey didn't even laugh at his corny joke. She reached up and pulled him down, her mouth dancing across his as she teased him with the most powerful drug. It was on the tip of his tongue to tell her how he felt, but he held back. As much as he wanted to put voice to his feelings, he knew she wasn't ready.

As they continued to kiss, their clothes slowly made their way to the floor. Neither of them spoke. Everything they needed to say was done with their bodies. When he came, it felt as if he were giving over part of his soul to her. And maybe he was. He'd never felt a connection like this with another person. Janey was special, and he was going to do everything in his power to make sure she knew that.

He just had to make sure he didn't scare her away in the process.

They lay tangled in each other's arms until time forced him to get dressed. The sleepy look of contentment as he leaned down to kiss her goodbye had his heart aching. He'd never had a long-distance relationship with anyone before, but he was beginning to understand how difficult they really were. Not because of the distance itself, but because it was so hard to leave once their short time together had ended.

Kyle knew he'd see her again. Knew it wouldn't be long. But in the moment, all he wanted to do was crawl back into the bed with her and forget about the outside world.

He brushed a strand of her hair away from her face. "I'll text you when I get home."

Janey covered his hand with hers, and then let it fall to the mattress when he backed away.

Stopping at the door to her bedroom, he took one last look at her in bed, rumpled from their lovemaking. Then he commanded he legs to move and headed back to his life in Liberty.

***

Janey and Paul spent most of Monday going through the list the jewelry store had sent over. There were forty names on it. By the time they called it a day, they'd narrowed it down to seven based on the symbols on the ring.

Paul had also called Sheriff Jenkins and made arrangements for them to drive up to Liberty Tuesday morning and go over what they'd found so far. He was anxious to hear any updates they had and was very curious about the ring.

At six o'clock Tuesday morning, Paul picked Janey up outside her condo. She thought maybe she'd be anxious about the trip to Liberty, but she was more excited than anything else, and it had nothing to do with the case.

She'd spoken to Kyle the night before and he'd told her he'd see her at the station. The sheriff wanted him to join them for their meeting. Then he was going to take them to Ava's so she could have a look at the ring.

"Nervous?" Paul asked about an hour into their trip.

"No. Why?" She'd been quiet for the most part, mainly because it was early. That, and she was gathering her thoughts. Janey had been doing that a lot lately. Thinking about her life. Her future. It was something she hadn't allowed herself to do in a long time. Her focus had been on living in the moment.

"You're awfully quiet this morning. That's not like you. Normally you're talking my head off."

Janey rolled her eyes. "I'm just thinking about some things."

"I see. And would those things happen to revolve around a certain deputy we'll be seeing this morning?"

"Some of them."

Paul chuckled but didn't go on.

"What?"

He shook his head. "Nothing. I'm happy for you. He seems like a good guy."

She nodded and went back to looking at the scenery.

"What is Liberty like?" Paul asked, apparently not done with the conversation. "I've never been there."

"It's your typical small town. The courthouse is in the center of town. There's a diner and a small hardware store."

"You said Kyle's sister owns a bed and breakfast?"

"Yeah. It's a few miles outside of town. Megan would love it." Janey grinned thinking about it. Paul's wife was taking art classes at the local community college. Ava's house was built in the early 1900s and was full of fun architecture. There were also a few paintings hanging around the house Janey thought would interest Megan. They might not be along the lines of Monet or Picasso, but Megan had developed a taste for the whimsical and Ava's place would be right up her alley.

"Maybe I'll have to bring her up here for a weekend or something. It's been a while since we've gotten away, just us."

Janey smiled. "I'm sure she'd like that."

It was a few minutes after eight when they turned onto Main Street. Nothing had changed since the last time she was there. In fact, as they passed the diner, she noticed the exact same specials sign in the window.

The courthouse was easy to locate, and on the back side was the sheriff's station. They found a place to park and went inside.

Janey couldn't stop herself from looking around as they climbed the steps. There were several patrol vehicles in the parking lot, and she wondered if one of them belonged to Kyle or if he was still out on the road. His shift was technically over at seven, but she remembered from her own patrol days that she rarely made it back to the station on time. A call always seemed to come in at the last minute.

They were buzzed in and escorted to Sheriff Jenkins's office. He stood when they entered. "Come in and have a seat."

Janey and Paul lowered themselves into the two chairs directly in front of Sheriff Jenkins's desk.

"It's good to see you again, Detective Davis." There was a sparkle in the sheriff's eye, and Janey knew that he was aware of her relationship with Kyle. Not that she figured they'd be able to keep it a secret. Small towns didn't work that way.

"Thank you, Sheriff. It's good to be back."

He turned his attention to Paul. "This your first time in Liberty, Detective Daniels?"

"Yes, although Davis was telling me about the bed and breakfast Kyle's sister owns. My wife and I might have to schedule a visit."

"I'm sure Ava would love to have you."

There was a knock on the door, and they all turned their attention to the new arrival.

Kyle stood in the doorway, still in his uniform. Her heart skipped a beat as he strolled into the room. His gaze lingered on her for a long moment before he addressed the room as a whole.

"Sorry, I'm late," he said. "I caught someone doing eighty in a fifty-five this morning."

Sheriff Jenkins waved him in. "That's all right. We were just getting started."

Kyle shut the door behind him and moved to take up a position a few feet from Janey. He leaned against the wall, crossing his arms in front of him. The material of his uniform stretched across his chest, and she felt her body warming. She had to make herself look away.

Needing a distraction, Janey removed the bag containing the ring from her pocket and handed it to Sheriff Jenkins.

He examined it closely before handing it back to Janey. "It does look like one of our class rings."

She took it and placed it back in her pocket. It was the best lead they had at the moment, and she was guarding it with her life.

"The ring came from a place called Kelly's. Apparently, they do most of the class rings around here," Paul said. "They provided us with a list of every ring that was purchased with that graduating year and the engravings selected. We've been able to narrow it down to seven individuals. Unfortunately, ring sizes aren't listed on the document, or we'd be able to narrow it down even more."

Paul handed the paper to Sheriff Jenkins and he looked it over. "Betsy Canfield died a few years ago. Cancer. So you can mark her name off your list. The others? I know most of them. Can't see them committing murder, let alone three murders."

"Sometimes it's the people you least suspect."

There was a tone in Paul's voice when he said it. Even the sheriff seemed to pick up on it. But Janey knew Paul wouldn't elaborate. He'd made the mistake of misjudging someone once and he was still blaming himself for it.

Janey knew she needed to move things along. "Maybe Ava can help us knock a few more names off that list."

"Yes," Sheriff Jenkins said. "Ava's eager to help if she can."

Kyle shifted. "We should probably get going."

Janey and Paul stood.

"Let me know if there's anything we can do to help. I want to catch this person as much as you do. Maybe more."

Paul extended his hand to Sheriff Jenkins. "We appreciate your help, Sheriff."

"Anytime."

It had started sprinkling by the time they made their way back outside, and Janey was mourning the sunshine that had provided a beautiful sunrise less than two hours ago. Kyle didn't seem to be bothered by the change in the weather. "I figured we could take my SUV over to Ava's, and then I can drop you both back here."

Paul already had his keys out and was moving away from them. "Why don't you two head over and I'll follow you?"

Janey opened her mouth to say something, but Kyle interrupted her. "Sounds good. We'll see you there."

Paul jogged the rest of the way down the steps toward his vehicle, leaving Janey and Kyle alone.

"Did you two have this planned or something?" Janey asked.

Kyle laughed. "Not at all." He motioned toward his truck. "Since Paul isn't riding with us, there's no need to take the SUV.

She followed him to his pickup truck. He unlocked the passenger door and held it open for her. "Thank you."

Once she was seated, he closed the door and made his way over to the driver's side. A minute later, they were heading out of town toward his sister's.

"You didn't have to do that, you know."

He looked over at her, and then back at the road. "Do what?"

"Open the door for me. We're here on official police business. I'm not your girlfriend right now."

Kyle frowned. "You breaking up with me?"

"What? No." Janey turned in her seat to look at him. Or she tried to, with the seat belt fighting her every step of the way. "Why would you think I'm breaking up with you?"

"You said you're not my girlfriend right now."

"What I meant was that Paul and I are here in an official capacity, so we should conduct ourselves in that manner." She paused and sat up a little straighter. "Would you hold the passenger door open for Hayden?"

Instead of confirming that he wouldn't, he asked a question of his own. "Why would I be driving Hayden to my sister's place?"

Janey sighed. "You're missing my point."

Kyle reached for her hand.

She jerked, but he held firm, bringing the back of her hand up to his lips. "Janey, no matter what's going on, you're still my girlfriend and I'm going to treat you that way. My feelings for you don't switch off once I'm on duty or you are."

"People will think we're unprofessional." She'd worked hard to get where she was in her professional life. Being one of the youngest detectives in the Indianapolis Police Department meant she'd had to deal with her share of challenges. She wanted people to have confidence in her as a detective, not disregard her or her opinions because she was Kyle's girlfriend.

He lowered their hands but didn't let go. "That might be the case in the city. Around here, everyone already knows we're seeing each other, so they'd be surprised if I didn't hold doors open for you."

"Everyone knows?" Her heart sank a little. She'd gotten the vibe from Sheriff Jenkins that he was aware of their relationship, but she knew he and Kyle were friends. Now she was wondering if some of the looks they got as they'd exited the building were less about having detectives from the city in Liberty and more about Kyle's girlfriend being there.

"Maybe not everyone, but I'd say more than half."

She groaned.

"What's wrong?" he asked as they turned into Ava's driveway.

"What if we have to interview suspects? It's going to completely diminish my authority. I need them to respect my position and take me seriously."

He put the truck in park and turned off the engine. "Things are different around here. If anything, people will be more likely to open up to you because we're dating. Not the other way around." The look on her face must have told him how much she questioned his way of looking at things because he continued. "Remember Mr. Mitchel? The first thing he did was ask who you were. People around here, they trust the people they know—the people they've known for years. It takes time to gain their trust and get them to open up. Being my girlfriend, you now have an inside ticket, so to speak."

"I don't know." What he said made sense. Sort of. But she was still doubtful.

"Trust me." Movement from the front of the house caught their attention. His sister was standing on the porch with Cole on her hip. "Come on. Let's go talk to my sister."

CHAPTER 16

JANEY SLID out of the truck and made her way up the steps to where Kyle's sister was standing, hair pulled back in a ponytail and wearing an apron that looked as if it had seen better days. No doubt she'd come from the kitchen. Janey even thought she saw a smudge of flour on her cheek.

Ava's smile grew wider the closer Janey came. She lowered Cole to the ground and embraced Janey. "It's good to see you again."

"Thanks for helping us out." Janey hugged Ava back, and then stepped away to introduce her partner who'd made his way up the steps. "Ava, this is my partner, Detective Paul Daniels."

"It's nice to meet you, Detective." She grabbed Cole's hand and tilted her head toward the house. "I made some coffee and banana bread if you're hungry." Ava didn't wait for anyone to respond. She turned on her heel and walked inside, leaving them all to follow.

"I can see what you mean," Paul said seconds after they entered the house. "Megan would love this place."

"Is Megan your wife?" Ava asked.

Paul nodded. "She's working toward her art degree, and while she appreciates the classical artists, she loves all types of art."

"Most of the pictures on the wall came with the house, as did a few pieces of furniture. The rest I found at antique shops." She removed four mugs from the kitchen cabinet and placed them on the counter next to the coffeepot. "Cream or sugar?"

"Black for me, thank you," Paul said.

Janey took a seat at the kitchen table next to Kyle. "Both, please."

Ava fixed them each coffee, made sure Cole was occupied in the corner with his toys, and joined them at the table with several slices of banana bread. "Did you bring the ring?"

Removing it from her pocket, Janey placed the bag with the ring on the table in front of Ava.

Kyle's sister picked up the bag and turned it over in her hand. "You think the person this ring belongs to is the one who killed those men?"

"We don't know. But it's a lead and we have to follow it."

Ava nodded and looked closer at the ring. "Looks almost identical to mine except for the stone in the middle."

Paul handed her the list of names. "We're hoping you can help us narrow down our list of suspects."

With a solemn expression, Ava looked over the list.

Kyle took a slice of the banana bread. "We already know about Betsy."

Ava took a deep breath but didn't say anything. Janey helped herself to some of the banana bread, and Paul followed suit.

Janey closed her eyes in pure enjoyment as she bit into the bread. It was moist and flavorful. The only thing that would have made it better was a smear of butter on top. Ava knew how to bake. There was no doubt about that.

When Janey opened her eyes again, she found Kyle staring at her. The look in his eyes said he wasn't thinking about the case or food.

She swallowed the banana bread she'd been chewing and swiftly turned her attention back to Ava. "Do any of these people jump out at you?"

Ava scrunched up her nose. "It's not Carrie. And I don't think it's Melissa either."

"What makes you say that?" Paul was still firmly in detective mode.

He either completely missed the vibe between Kyle and Janey, or he was ignoring it. Janey was hoping for the former, but it was more likely the latter. Paul was a good detective. And when he was paying attention, not much got past him.

"Carrie's..." Ava paused. "The ring would never fit Carrie. Not even in high school. It's too small."

"What about Melissa?" Paul asked.

"The same. She's lost quite a bit of weight since high school, but back then... there's no way this ring would have fit her."

Janey could still feel Kyle's gaze on her, but she tried to focus on what Ava was saying. She cleared her throat. "You're sure?"

Ava nodded. "It's smaller than my class ring. I'd say it's probably a size five or six. No way Melissa or Carrie would have worn that size back then."

That still left them with four names.

Paul took a sip of his coffee, appearing relaxed. Janey knew better. "Any of the other names stand out to you as possible owners of the ring?"

"No. I'm sorry. I mean, I know all of them, but I know that's not what you're asking."

"That's all right," Paul said. "You helped remove two more names from our list."

Ava gave the list of names back to Paul. "Can I get anyone some more coffee?"

Paul tucked the paper back into his jacket. "Thank you, but no. I'd like to see where your brother found the victim's body. I know Janey has already looked things over, but I'd like to get the lay of the land myself. See how it compares to the other locations."

"Of course," Kyle said. "You can follow me over. It's not too far from here."

They all stood, including Ava. She placed a hand on Janey's arm as she turned to leave. "Did Kyle say anything to you about coming for Labor Day weekend?" She shifted her weight. "It's kind of a big deal around here and I was hoping you could come."

"He mentioned something along those lines."

"Does that mean you'll come?" she asked. "I can keep a room open for you here if you want, but I kind of figured you'd want to stay at Kyle's."

"I'm on call most Saturday nights." Being that she was still one of the younger detectives, she got stuck being on call when the older detectives wanted time off to spend with their families. Since she was single, she didn't mind. She could go out on Friday night or Sunday night as easily as she could Saturday night.

"So come down Sunday morning. We have a festival that runs from Saturday through Monday." She leaned in as if confiding some big secret. "They're going to roast another hog."

Janey chuckled. "I'll keep that in mind."

When Janey exited the house, Paul and Kyle were talking beside Kyle's pickup truck. They both looked up at her approach, but their expressions were quite different. Paul quirked one eyebrow up in question, probably wondering what had kept her. In contrast, Kyle had an amused look on his face. No doubt he knew exactly what his sister was doing. They were both pushing her in their own ways, and she didn't know if she liked it.

"Ready to go?" Janey asked, already reaching for the passenger side door of Kyle's truck.

The two men exchanged a look before Paul strolled over to his vehicle.

Kyle eased himself behind the wheel. "Did you have a nice chat with Ava?"

Janey fastened her seat belt. "You knew she was going to waylay me and ask about Labor Day."

He shrugged and started the engine. "I had a pretty good feeling."

They drove for several miles down country roads, many of which didn't have dividing lines on them. There was nothing around except for fields full corn and soybeans.

Kyle turned right onto another road, and Janey realized they were almost there. Despite the fact that everything looked so similar—at least to her—she remembered the electrical lines in the distance.

Sure enough, a few seconds later Kyle pulled off the road.

The cornstalks rattled in the breeze as they left their vehicles and followed Kyle to where he'd found the body.

"Right here." Kyle pointed to the area where he'd discovered John Doe.

Paul looked up and down the roadway and then at both fields. "I see what you meant, Davis. This really is a great place to dump a body. No cameras. No lights. No houses."

"Over here is where we found the empty beer bottles." Janey crossed the ditch into the cornfield. The stalks that had been broken were still lying on the ground.

Kyle kicked at one of the fallen stalks. "Doesn't look as if they've been back since we were here last."

"I'm sure they heard about the dead body," Paul said.

Janey moved to the other side of the makeshift circle of destroyed cornstalks. "That wouldn't deter some kids."

A noise had all three of them freezing. They looked at each other, confirming they'd all heard something.

Kyle motioned he would go left. Paul slinked off to the right, leaving Janey to take the center position.

She moved with as much stealth as she could through the corn, hand on her firearm. It could have been a deer they'd heard, or a coyote. Or it could be a person. And if it was a person, what were they doing hanging out in a cornfield in the middle of the day?

"Let go of me!"

Janey rushed toward the sound, no longer caring if she made a noise. She guessed it was safe to say what they'd heard wasn't a coyote.

***

Kyle didn't loosen his hold until he saw Janey and Paul appear through the tall corn. Even then, he made sure the young man he'd caught wasn't going to take off at the first opportunity.

"Let me go. I didn't do anything." Johnny Vanhoose. A local boy.

Sixteen years old. Which meant he should have been in school at this time of day.

"Why are you sneaking around in a cornfield?" Kyle asked.

"None of your business." The young man struggled against Kyle's hold, but it was useless. Kyle had at least eighty pounds on the boy and a lot more muscle. That didn't stop him, though. Not until Paul took a step toward them. Johnny saw the movement and stopped fighting. He decided to change tactics. "Come on, Kyle. I ain't done nothing. Let me go."

Kyle didn't miss the use of his given name. Johnny's dad coached football at the high school, and Kyle helped run drills from time to time. The kid's attempt at manipulation didn't go unnoticed.

Steering them out of the cornfield, Kyle hauled Johnny toward his pickup truck. "No can do."

"Why not?" There was a hint of panic in the young man's voice as he continued to struggle. Kyle didn't know if that was because he'd got caught skipping school or because he knew something about the dead body that had been dumped there.

Once they emerged from the tall stalks, Kyle released Johnny with a warning. "If you try to run, I'll put you in cuffs. Understand?"

Johnny opened his mouth, no doubt to say something sarcastic, but then he seemed to catch himself. "Yeah. Okay."

"Good. I'm glad we have an understanding."

The young man snorted and stuffed his hands in his pockets.

Paul and Janey stood off to the side, neither saying anything. They both seemed to realize Kyle would have a better chance of getting information out of the kid than they would.

Kyle crossed his arms and leveled a hard stare at the kid. It helped that he was still in his uniform. Even though he wasn't officially on duty, Johnny didn't know that. "Now, let's try this again. Why aren't you in school?"

Nothing.

"Do we need to take this down to the station?"

"You can't do that!" The panic was back. That was good. Maybe the kid would think twice next time before he decided to wander around a cornfield in the middle of the day.

"I can and I will if we can't get this sorted out here."

Johnny kicked at a clump of dirt in front of him. "I decided to skip, okay?"

"Why'd you come here?" Kyle would deal with the young man ditching school later. Right now he needed to find out if he was there by chance or if he'd come to that area of the cornfield deliberately.

Again he was met with silence. Kyle was about to escort Johnny to his truck and follow through on his threat to bring him into the station when the boy finally answered. "A few of us come here to hang out sometimes."

"You mean you come here to party." Considering the amount of empty beer bottles they'd found, it was more than a few.

Johnny lifted one shoulder in a half shrug.

"You know there was a dead body discovered out here a few weeks ago, right?"

The young man nodded.

"Were you here partying the night before?" No sense in beating around the bush.

It was as if a light bulb went off in the kid's head. His eyes went wide. He brought his hands up in front of him and took a step back. "We didn't have anything to do with that, Kyle. I swear. You have to believe me. We didn't kill anyone."

"But you were here the night the body was dumped," Kyle said.

Johnny began shaking his head. "We didn't see anything. We just..."

"You just what?"

The young man's gaze darted around, looking for allies and finding none, before landing back on Kyle. "We heard a car, and we were afraid we'd get caught, so we ran."

"Did you see the car? Did you see who it was?"

He shook his head. "After we saw the lights and heard the car door open, we got outta there."

Now they were getting somewhere. "What time was this?"

His answer came quick. "Around midnight."

"You're sure?" Kyle asked.

"Yeah. I'm sure. I ran straight home, and when I climbed in my bedroom window the clock said it was twelve eleven." Johnny paused. "Am I in trouble?"

Kyle relaxed his stance a little. If nothing else, they had a time when the body was dumped. The road they were on didn't get much traffic, so the chances of another random car stopping the same night was slim. First things first, however. He met Johnny's gaze. "For skipping school? Yes."

"You can't just let me go? Come on, Kyle. My mom will kill me if she finds out." The panicked look was back. Kyle's mom was a teacher. He was right. She wouldn't be happy if her son got busted for truancy.

"Tell you what," Kyle said. "I want to talk to everyone who was here that night." Johnny started to say something, but Kyle cut him off. "If you can get them to meet me at the park near the statue today at three thirty—all of them"—Kyle made sure to stress that point —"I might be willing to forget about you not being in school today."

The young man still looked nervous, but he didn't hold his shoulders as stiff as before. He was probably considering the likelihood of being able to get all his friends to show up. "Thanks."

"But"—Kyle pointed a finger at him—"if I catch you skipping school again, not only will I be telling your parents, I'll also have to turn you over to the truancy officer."

Johnny nodded in quick agreement.

"I'm glad we understand each other." Kyle looked up and down the road, and then back at Johnny. "Do you need a ride home?"

"If I go home, Mom'll find out I skipped. Mrs. Epps is nosy."

Mrs. Epps was Johnny's neighbor. And he was right. She was nosy. In fact, she was one of the biggest gossips in the county. Kyle tried hard to hide his amusement. He'd been where Johnny was. Exactly where Johnny was, actually. Except he hadn't had the bargaining chip of possibly having overheard a murderer dumping a body. "You make a good point."

Johnny looked around him, taking in where Paul and Janey were standing. They'd been patiently watching the exchange, strategically placing themselves between Johnny and the cornfield. "Can I go now?"

Nodding, Kyle made sure to remind him of their appointment one last time. "Don't forget about this afternoon."

"Three thirty at the statue in the park. Got it." Johnny was already backing away. Once he was clear of the vehicles, he crossed the road and started toward the cornfield on the opposite side.

"Don't be late," Kyle yelled right before Johnny's figure was engulfed by the swaying corn.

Paul walked to stand beside Kyle. "I guess we're going to be sticking around here longer than we thought."

"Let's just hope they show up," Janey said, moving to stand beside her partner.

"They will," Paul and Kyle said in unison.

Janey sent them both a questioning look but let it go. "Well, it looks as if we've got a few hours to kill. Paul and I can hang out at the station if you want to get some sleep. We can meet you at the park at three."

Sleep? He had no idea how he was going to sleep knowing Janey was so close, but he knew he would have to try. There wouldn't be much time after the meeting for him to sleep before he had to be on patrol again. "Why don't you guys come back to my house and hang out for a while? I have an internet connection and a laptop. Maybe you can start looking into the four remaining women on your list."

Paul and Janey looked at each other, and Paul nodded. "Sounds like a good way to kill some time. Lead the way."

They climbed into their vehicles and made a U-turn back toward town. Kyle had to admit he had ulterior motives for getting Janey back to his place. Although they wouldn't be alone, he was hoping he might be able to steal her away for a few minutes. He hadn't been able to kiss her yet, and it was driving him crazy.

Janey sat in the seat next to him, looking out the window, deep in thought. Her hair, even though she had it pulled back, whipped in the wind and swirled around her face. She looked almost angelic.

He covered her hand with his and laced their fingers together as they drew closer to his house. She turned to look at him, a tiny smile pulling at her face. Was she thinking along the same lines he was? It had only been two days, but it felt as if it had been weeks since he'd felt her body next to his.

"I need to use your bathroom once we get to your house."

Not what he was expecting. "Okay."

Then he noticed a sparkle in her eyes. "I don't think I remember where it is. Think you can show me?"

"Yeah," he said, meeting her gaze. "I can definitely show you."

The ten-minute drive to his house felt like an eternity.

KYLE UNLOCKED the door to his house and motioned for Paul and Janey to go inside. He turned on the lights and strolled over to the refrigerator. "Can I get you something to drink?"

"Some water would be great," Paul said.

Kyle grabbed a glass out of the cabinet. "Janey?"

"That sounds good."

He handed them both a glass of ice water and directed them into the living room. "Let me grab my laptop."

Without another word, he ascended the stairs two at a time, retrieved his laptop, and rejoined Paul and Janey in the living room. He handed the laptop to Paul.

"Thanks," Paul said, placing it on the coffee table in front of hm.

Janey set her glass down on a coaster and stood. "Can you show me where your bathroom is again?"

Anticipation curled low in his stomach. "Sure."

He turned, knowing she would follow. The only bathroom on the main floor was a half bath on the other side of the kitchen. It wasn't ideal, given Paul was only a room away in the living room, but it would be too obvious if they went upstairs. Then again, Paul was a smart guy. He probably knew what they were up to.

Not that Kyle cared. He doubted that if the roles were reversed Paul wouldn't be doing the same thing with Megan. Especially since he was pretty sure the two of them had done something similar on Sunday when he and Janey were there. It didn't take ten minutes to cut and serve cake, did it?

As soon as they reached the bathroom, Kyle tugged Janey inside and closed the door. His mouth was on hers a second later.

She molded her body to his, pressing her sweet curves into him. He was eternally grateful in that moment that he'd had the forethought to remove his gun belt while he was upstairs. It was impossible to keep his hands to himself, so he didn't even try.

Lifting her onto the counter, he stepped between her legs, letting her feel what she did to him. Janey responded by dipping her tongue into his mouth and deepening the kiss.

"Hmm. I've been wanting to do this all day," she whispered against his lips.

"Me, too."

"We can't stay in here long," Janey said. "He'll know what we're doing. He probably already knows what we're doing."

"Well then, we shouldn't waste any time, should we?" He quickly removed her sidearm from her waist and went to work on removing her pants.

She didn't comment until he had unzipped them. "What are you doing?"

He grinned up at her. "Having a snack before bed. Raise your hips."

A blush colored her cheeks, but she did as he requested. In less than twenty seconds, he had her naked from the waist down.

Kyle eased her bottom close to the edge of the counter and knelt between her legs. At the first lick, Janey's head tilted back. She tangled her fingers in his hair as he continued to worship her with his tongue.

It didn't take long for her breathing to become labored, and he enjoyed watching her chest rise and fall with each inhale and exhale.

He inserted two fingers inside her, adding to her pleasure. "Come for me, baby."

"I... I.. ."

He redoubled his efforts, determined to send her over the edge.

Janey gasped, and then he felt her nails dig into his skull as she let go.

Removing his fingers, he placed a final kiss between her legs before getting to his feet again.

She rested her head on his chest, still trying to catch her breath. "Did I hurt you?"

He chuckled. "Totally worth it seeing you come apart like that. I'm going to have very sweet dreams."

A low moan vibrated through her chest and she pulled his mouth down to hers. She kissed him slow and deep. "I wish we had more time."

"Me, too. But if you don't get back out there soon, your partner is going to come looking for you." And as much as he hated to admit it, he did need to get some sleep. It was already after ten and he would need to be up by two if he was going to have to be at the park by three thirty.

She ran her hands down the front of his uniform. "I like seeing you in your uniform."

"Yeah?"

"Yeah. You're very sexy, Deputy Reed."

He groaned. "If you keep that up, I'm not going to care if your partner is in the other room or not."

Janey laughed and kissed him again. "Go on, then. I'll get myself cleaned up, and then Paul and I can spend the afternoon researching."

Kyle hated to leave her, especially when she made such a pretty picture sitting there half naked on his bathroom counter. He cupped his hand beside her neck and gave her another hard kiss. "I'll see you in a few hours."

The flirty grin she sent him did nothing to help the problem in his trousers. "Sweet dreams."

Before he could talk himself out of it, he opened the bathroom door and left her sitting with her legs spread, still wet from her orgasm. The image itself made his cock pulse. It knew what it wanted. Too bad it wasn't going to get it. At least, not anytime soon.

Kyle didn't miss Janey's giggle as he closed the door behind him and marched up the stairs to his bedroom. He needed to get to bed, but there was something he had to take care of first or he was never going to be able to fall asleep.

***

It took Janey a few minutes to clean up and get dressed. She tried to wipe the smile off her face, but it was impossible. Especially when her cheeks still had that postcoital flush.

As a last resort she splashed some cold water on her face, and rejoined Paul in the living room. He glanced up when she entered the room, and then went back to what he was doing. "Feel better?"

Heat crawled up her neck to her cheeks. He hadn't been fooled. He'd known exactly what they'd been doing in there. Okay, maybe not exactly what they'd been doing, but he knew they were fooling around.

Instead of responding to his question, she asked one of her own. "How's the search coming?"

"I'm looking through Cindy Fisher's social media. So far nothing out of the ordinary." He scrolled down through some more of her posts. "I called the captain to let him know what was going on and that we'd be here for the rest of day."

They spent the next few hours going through the social media accounts of each of the four remaining names. Two of the women still lived locally. One had moved to Indianapolis. And the fourth didn't have a location listed but appeared to travel a lot. Nothing they'd come across sent up any red flags.

She wouldn't call it a useless afternoon. They knew more about the women on their list, their lives, their hobbies. One never knew what small piece of information would lead to the next. It was always good to know as much as possible and then filter out what was helpful and what wasn't.

The sound of movement upstairs pulled their attention away from the screen. Kyle was awake.

Janey had been trying not to think about him so she could concentrate on her job. She'd be okay until she'd lean back against the couch and get a whiff of his scent. Then everything would come rushing back to her, his touch, the taste of him on her tongue. She'd had to get up more than once and refill her water.

Paul shut down the computer and closed the lid. "I'm gonna step outside and call Megan. I need to let her know I won't be home tonight in time for dinner."

Waiting until she heard the door open and shut, Janey headed for the stairs. It didn't take a genius to realize that Paul was giving her some time alone with her man. He really was a great partner.

Kyle wasn't in his room. She stopped to listen and heard the shower running.

Janey bit the inside of her cheek as she considered her options. She'd love to join him, but they didn't have time for that.

The shower shut off and her heart rate kicked up half a dozen notches. She could already feel her body softening, getting wetter, readying itself for him.

Glancing around the room for something to do, she settled on looking out the window. That wouldn't seem weird, right?

She heard the door open but kept her back to him. The sound of his footsteps echoed and then stopped. He'd seen her.

Silence filled her ears for what felt like forever before she heard him moving toward her. His chest brushed against her back, the heat from his body seeping into her pores and his presence making her a little dizzy. He leaned in, his breath teasing her ear. "I had some very pleasant dreams."

Janey released a shaky breath and turned.

He circled his arms around her, spreading his palms along her back. His heart beat a steady rhythm against her hand where it rested against his bare chest. He was naked except for the towel that was wrapped around his waist, and it wasn't doing a good job of hiding his pleasure at finding her in his bedroom.

She tried to swallow, but all the moisture in her body seemed to have gone south. "Daniels stepped outside to call Megan."

His eyes darkened and he lowered his head until his lips were an inch away from hers. "Good."

After that, all thought went out the window. His mouth covered hers and he pulled her in for a kiss that was bone deep. Her body didn't care if there was a murder to solve or even if her partner was downstairs waiting on them. All it knew was that it wanted Kyle.

She reached for his towel, but he covered her hand with his own. "Baby, we can't. As much as I want to, we can't."

He kissed her again, and then put some space between them.

It took her a few moments to calm herself down. No guy had ever got her motor running as quickly as Kyle did. She always needed a little warm-up, but with him all he had to do was touch her and she was ready to give herself to him in any way he wanted.

That was a scary thought, and one she wasn't willing to examine too closely. They were dating. That was all. It was a good thing that she wanted him. And that he wanted her. That's the way it was supposed to be.

Only it didn't feel like what she was feeling was normal. When she'd dated Ted, granted she was still a teenager at the time, but it was different. She'd been attracted to him and she liked him, or at least she had at first. But he'd never been able to get her heart racing with a single word or touch. There used to be a lot of foreplay first, and even then it sometimes wasn't enough for her. With Kyle, she didn't seem to have a problem. Ever. Even with the other men she'd dated over the years, it had taken work to get her there.

And it wasn't only the sex. She missed Kyle when he wasn't around. Their nightly phone conversations had become something she looked forward to.

"Penny for your thoughts?" While she mused about her feelings for Kyle, he'd gotten dressed in a clean uniform. He stood in front of his closet, buttoning his shirt.

No way was she going to let him in on the direction her mind had taken. Janey sauntered over to him, making sure to put a little extra sway in her hips. "I can't get over how sexy you look in your uniform. It's a wonder the women around here can keep their hands to themselves."

Kyle chuckled and placed his hands on her hips. "Maybe you should stay here and fight them off for me."

"No can do. I have a killer to catch."

Sighing, he gave her a soft kiss. "I guess I'll have to do my best on my own, then."

Janey rolled her eyes. "We should get downstairs."

He picked up his belt, secured it around his waist, and checked his sidearm before holstering it. Seeing him do that shouldn't have made her hot, but it did.

She headed for the door and followed him out. They walked side by side down the stairs to find Paul waiting for them in the living room.

"Is Megan upset you're gonna be late?" Janey asked, trying to direct the conversation so it didn't end up on her and Kyle.

"She's a little disappointed, but she's used to my crazy hours." They all made their way into the kitchen. "Besides, she knows I'll make it up to her."

Janey shook her head, and Kyle laughed. "You guys hungry?" he asked, opening the refrigerator. "I think I have a pizza in the freezer I can heat up."

She liked pizza. Really, she did, but she avoided frozen pizza like the plague. "What about the diner? Would we have time to swing by there and grab something before we have to be at the park?"

Checking his watch, Kyle nodded. "We have about forty-five minutes. Should be plenty of time."

"Great." Janey smiled.

"Since we're going to be cutting it short on time," Kyle asked Paul, "do you think you could follow me to the station? I want to pick up my patrol vehicle. Figure it will make my questioning of the kids look more official."

Paul removed his keys from his pocket, ready to go. "Always a good idea, in my opinion."

The drive to the station was short. This time, however, Janey rode in Paul's vehicle. She sat beside him while Kyle ran inside the station.

"I don't know how you two do it," Paul said as they sat there waiting.

"Do what?" She had no idea what he was talking about since they currently weren't doing anything.

Her partner tilted his head at Kyle, who was striding toward the SUV he used on patrol. "The long-distance thing. I don't know how you do it. I'm not sure I could. I'd be driving to see Megan every chance I got."

She didn't want to lie. "I don't know. We just do, I guess. I mean, it's not like we have a choice. He has his job and I have mine."

"And how long is that going to work?" Paul asked.

"What do you mean?" Janey didn't know where he was going with this.

Paul maneuvered out of the parking lot, following Kyle to the diner. "It means I think I'll be breaking in a new partner in the not-too-distant future."

"You planning on requesting a transfer?" she asked, even though she knew that's not what he meant.

"I see the way you two look at each other." He glanced over at her, then back at the road. They were almost there. "Mark my words, sooner or later you'll be moving to Liberty to be with him."

His certainty irritated her a little. Even if he was probably right. "Maybe he'll move to Indy. Or maybe it won't work out. We haven't known each other that long."

Paul didn't comment. He parked along the curb, right behind Kyle's patrol vehicle.

She watched Kyle get out of his SUV and wave to someone on the other side of the street. Paul was right. If she and Kyle stayed together, he wouldn't be the one moving. She didn't know how she felt about that either. When it came to her relationship with Kyle, everything seemed to be all or nothing, and that scared her more than anything had in a long time.

Kyle met them at the front of Paul's vehicle, and they all went into the diner together. As they ate their food, Janey thought about what Paul had said. The more she thought about it, the more she knew he was right. Kyle fit here in Liberty. More than she had ever fit in Indianapolis. If they stayed together, she would be the one to move, and there was a part of her—the independent part—that fought against that idea. Why shouldn't he move in order for them to be together?

But even as the question crossed her mind, she realized how ridiculous she was being. They'd been dating for less than a month.

"You okay?" Kyle asked when Paul excused himself to use the restroom.

Janey needed to shake it off. They had an interrogation to do in less than thirty minutes. She needed to have her head on straight. "Yeah. Just have a lot of things on my mind, that's all."

"I know what you mean. I'm hoping one of Johnny's friends stuck around and saw something. Even if they got a glimpse of the car, that would be something."

He was wrong about the direction of her thoughts, but she went with it. "That would be helpful, but I'm not getting my hopes up. I still think the ring is our best chance of finding the person behind this."

Kyle checked to make sure Paul wasn't on his way back before leaning in closer to her. He lowered his voice to a whisper. "I'm kind of hoping the kids have some useful bit of information we have to track down and it'll keep you here another day."

"I can't stay here forever." Her voice sounded really breathy, but she couldn't help it. Not when he looked at her like that.

"A man can wish."

Paul slid into the booth across from them, and Kyle sat back in his seat. "You two ready to get going?" Her partner was trying to hide his amusement, but he was failing miserably.

Kyle signaled for the check. He insisted on paying, even though

Paul tried to tell him they could expense it since they were on official business. It didn't matter, and eventually Paul relented.

Less than ten minutes later, they arrived at the park. It was three twenty-five and there were already a handful of kids hanging around the statue. They all stared at the two vehicles as they entered, looking nervous.

They'd talked about how this would go at the diner, and like before, it was decided that Kyle would lead the interrogation. He might not be a detective, but this was his turf. He knew these kids and they trusted him. At least, that was the hope. The fact that they showed up was a good start.

Kyle exited his SUV. Paul and Janey did the same. It was showtime.

BY THE TIME they'd parked their vehicles, every one of the kids was staring in their direction. That was good. He wanted them to be paying attention.

Kyle exited his vehicle and strode toward them, taking in who was present. All the boys were members of the football team, most of them juniors or seniors, but there were a few underclassmen. Some of the girls he knew, but two were unfamiliar to him. Either they were new in town or from a school outside the county.

He stopped a few feet away from the group and addressed Johnny. "Is this everyone that was there that night?"

Johnny looked around. "Yeah."

Kyle nodded and spoke loud enough for everyone to hear. "I'm willing to bet that no one here is over twenty-one. I know most of you aren't. However, I'm willing to forget about the underage drinking if you all help me out with the case we're working on."

They looked from one to another. No one spoke aloud, but he knew they were deciding whether to help him or take their chances.

He could have hauled them all in and called their parents. Since he knew most of their mothers and fathers, he doubted he'd have a problem getting permission to fingerprint them. It would confirm the bottles of beer they found in the cornfield belonged to them.

Several moments passed before Jeremy Collins spoke up. "And you won't tell our parents?"

"I think we can keep this to ourselves." Kyle paused. "This time. However, if I catch you again..."

The threat was clear, and again they all looked at each other, deciding.

Jeremy was the one who answered. It was obvious he was the leader of the group. Kyle would have to remember that for future reference. "What do you want to know?"

He cut to the chase. "A few weeks ago, a vehicle interrupted your party. Did any of you see the vehicle?"

Everyone remained silent.

Kyle was about to move on when one of the girls he didn't know lifted her hand ever so slightly. "Yes?"

"I didn't.. ." She glanced around at the others again before returning to look at him. "I didn't see the car, but I heard a woman talking."

This was better than he could have hoped for. "Could you hear what she was saying?"

The young woman bit her bottom lip. "She said 'piece of shit.'"

He schooled his features, careful not to react. "Are you sure that's what she said?"

She nodded.

"What's your name?" Kyle asked.

"Becky." When he continued to wait, she realized he wanted her last name as well. "Becky Morris."

"I don't think I know your family, Becky. Are you new to the area?"

"Her family moved in this summer." Jeremy again. Kyle really was going to have to watch that young man.

Nodding, he looked over the group again. "Did anyone else hear or see anything?"

One by one they shook their head.

Well, it wasn't much, but it confirmed what they'd suspected. They were looking for a woman.

"You can go now. And lay off the partying. You want to have a few brain cells left for college."

Within seconds everyone had scattered, including Johnny, leaving Kyle, Paul, and Janey alone in the park. Paul and Janey joined him near the statue.

"What do you think?" Kyle asked, eager to hear their opinions.

Janey stood with her hands on her hips, all business. "Sounds personal. And if I had to go with my gut, I'd say this was revenge." Janey twisted her mouth. It shouldn't have been cute, but it was. "Although, either this woman offends easily, or she's had some really bad luck with men."

"So, what, you think it's more than one person doing this? A team?" Kyle asked. It was bad enough when they thought they were looking for one person.

"Maybe." Paul pulled out a notebook and jotted something down. "But serial killers have been known to have peculiar temperaments. It doesn't always take much to set them off."

This was true. Still, more than one person would explain the difference in location. Killers tended to stick to a pattern—and while the methods of all three murders were consistent, the where was not. "So what do we do now?"

"I still think the ring is our best lead at the moment. We need to find out who it belongs to," Janey said.

"Agreed." Paul pulled out his phone. "I need to call the captain and give him an update. The brass are chomping at his heels on this one."

Paul walked several yards away to make his call.

Kyle and Janey stood in awkward silence for several minutes before Kyle whispered, "You have no idea how much I want to kiss you right now."

Janey snorted. "You have a one-track mind."

"Only around you."

She rolled her eyes. "We're supposed to be focusing on the case."

"I can do both."

Janey didn't get a chance to respond. Paul walked toward them as he put his phone away. "The captain wants you to stay in Liberty for a few more days. He wants you to see if you can find out any more information and interview the women on our list who are local. I'm to head back to Indy and see if I can dig anything up on that end. I'll track down the woman on the list who's now in Indy and see if I can locate our traveler."

She narrowed her eyes at her partner. "You're the senior partner. Shouldn't you be the one staying here to follow the hotter lead while I go back home and start on a wild goose chase?"

Paul smiled. "I figured you might like to be the one to stay behind, so I recommended you for the job."

Images of Janey in his bed again filled his mind. It was difficult to concentrate on anything else, but somehow he managed.

"I didn't bring a change of clothes," Janey said.

"I'm sure Ava has some clothes you could borrow." The look Janey gave Kyle wasn't exactly what he'd hoped. Was she not happy about getting to spend a few extra days with him?

"I'll ride back to Indy with you tonight and drive back up tomorrow morning. There isn't much I can do tonight anyway."

Okay, so maybe her concerns were more of the practical variety. He'd been around his sister long enough to know that women tended to need things men just didn't care about.

Paul looked at his partner, seeming to consider his options. "That should work."

Janey's shoulders relaxed. "We should probably get on the road, then. I need to have time to pack tonight so I can hit the road first thing in the morning."

"I'll give you two a minute." Paul walked back to his vehicle and climbed inside, shutting the door behind him, giving them the illusion of privacy.

Kyle closed the distance between them but didn't touch her. "You'll stay with me while you're here?"

"I don't know." She bit the inside of her cheek. He noticed she did that when she was thinking really hard about something. "Maybe I should stay at Ava's. I don't know if I'd be able to concentrate on work if I stayed at your place."

"What if I promise to be on my best behavior while you're working on the case?"

She was tempted. He could see it in her eyes.

He lifted three fingers on his right hand. "Scout's honor."

"Were you a Scout?"

"Yep," he said with pride.

Janey hesitated, and then sighed. "Why can't I resist you?"

He chuckled and leaned in to give her a gentle kiss. "You shouldn't try."

Her eyes fluttered back open and she stared up at him for a long moment. "I should go."

Kyle ran the backs of his fingers along her cheek, reveling in the softness of her skin. She was so beautiful. "Text me when you get home?"

"I will."

Janey backed away from him, and he let his arm fall to his side. She stopped before getting in the vehicle and looked at him. A flirty smile played at her lips before she opened the passenger door and slid inside.

He couldn't help but chuckle. She'd be in his arms again in less than twenty-four hours and he couldn't wait.

***

It was after seven by the time Paul dropped Janey off at her condo. She'd sent Kyle a text as promised, and then went about packing for an indefinite amount of time.

Good thing she didn't have that pet they were talking about or else she'd have a whole other problem to deal with.

As it was, it took her until after eleven to get everything she needed washed, packed, and ready to go. By the time her head hit the pillow, she felt as if she'd run a marathon.

The next morning, Janey carried her suitcase to her car and set off toward Liberty. It was early. The first rays of the sun were peeking out from the horizon. She was hoping to get to Kyle's house before he got home from his shift so she could surprise him.

When Paul had told her she was staying behind the previous day, her first thought was to wonder what her captain had thought about Paul's recommendation. Captain Lane didn't know about her relationship with Kyle. If he did, Janey was sure he wouldn't have agreed to have her stay behind and work the case from Liberty.

Then there was Kyle. Her pulse kicked up every time she thought of him. His soft plea, asking her to stay with him, had pulled at her heart strings. She'd so badly wanted to say yes as soon as he'd asked, but her years of fighting for her place as a detective had made her reluctant to agree to his suggestion.

But she couldn't resist him. She never could. There was something about him that had her always wanting to say yes. It was dangerous. In her mind she knew that, but her heart wouldn't listen.

She pulled up in front of Kyle's house a little before seven thirty. His shift ended at seven, but she knew he'd have to stop at the station first before coming home.

Leaving her suitcase in her vehicle for now, she went to wait on the step for him. If she'd had a key, she would have gone inside and perhaps prepared a slightly different surprise.

About fifteen minutes later, Kyle turned into his driveway. Her heart pounded in her chest and anticipation curled in her belly.

He spotted her before he killed the engine. With a calm far removed from what she was feeling, he strolled toward her.

Janey stood and wiped her sweaty palms on the side of her pants. She opened her mouth to say hi, but before she could get the words out, he picked her up off her feet and planted a solid kiss on her lips.

"You're early," he said, not letting her go.

"I wanted to surprise you." She smiled. "Surprise."

He captured her mouth again in a searing kiss. "You can surprise me like this anytime you want."

She hummed as he went back in for another taste.

The sound of her phone ringing broke them apart. He set her feet back on the ground. "Luggage in your car?"

"Yeah. I—"

"I'll get it. Answer your phone."

Janey took out her cell and nearly had a heart attack when she saw the number on her screen. "Morning, Captain."

"Are you on your way to Liberty, Davis?" Paul must have told him that she'd come home to pack a few things.

"I just got here, sir."

"Good." There was some rumbling in the background. "I don't need to tell you how important this case is. We need a suspect and we need them yesterday."

"Yes, sir. I'm going to begin tracking down the women on the list the jeweler sent to us."

"Good, good. Keep me informed. And Davis?"

"Yes?" Kyle was walking back toward her, suitcases in hand, but she made herself look away. She couldn't afford to get distracted while talking to her boss.

"Watch your back. One of these women could be a cold-blooded killer. Don't do anything stupid."

"I won't, sir. And I'll call you with regular updates."

He huffed and then disconnected the call.

"Everything all right?" Kyle asked as he approached her.

His hair was a little wild from their kissing, and all she wanted to do was mess it up some more. Man, she could jump him right there. Unfortunately, she had work to do.

"Yeah. It was my captain. He wanted to remind me how important it is that we solve the case."

Kyle eased around her and unlocked the door to the house. He motioned for her to go inside. "Don't worry. We'll figure it out."

She set her purse down on the table and turned to face him. "We?"

"Noah wants me to tag along with you while you interview the local women on your list." He put her luggage along the wall and made a beeline for the coffee maker.

Janey wasn't sure how she felt about that. Not that she minded having Kyle's help, but did Sheriff Jenkins not trust in her abilities as a detective? Or was this a jurisdiction thing, like he didn't want her interviewing his citizens without one of his people present?

As if reading her thoughts, Kyle went on. "It's not that he doesn't think you can do it on your own, but he's taking this one personally. We don't get a lot of murders up here, and he wants this person caught as soon as possible."

How could she argue with that? Besides, if Sheriff Jenkins wanted, he could send her packing. The only reason the case hadn't been turned over to the state police was because her captain had gone to bat for her and Paul. They'd been on this case for more than two months and knew it inside and out.

Janey watched as Kyle made a fresh pot of coffee. "How are you going to help me and patrol?"

He looked over his shoulder at her and grinned. "I'm all yours for as long as you need me."

The way he said that made it sound like a lot more than him tagging along with her to conduct interviews. "So who's going to cover your shifts if you're with me?"

"Noah."

"Sheriff Jenkins is going to patrol for you?" she asked.

Kyle readied two mugs and got out the milk and sugar. "Yep."

She didn't say anything more while he finished making the coffee. Once it was ready, hers made exactly how she liked it, he brought it over and handed it to her. "Thanks."

He took a sip. "I'm not gonna lie. I'm kind of hoping this takes at least a week. That way you'll be here for the Labor Day weekend festivities."

"Did you and Paul concoct a plan so I'd be here for Labor Day?" She was trying to remember if the two of them had time to conspire.

Kyle chuckled. "No, but I like that you think we would. I kind of got the impression that Paul was a pretty straitlaced kind of guy, but it's good to know he has a devious streak in there somewhere."

Paul was a straitlaced kind of guy. Or at least he was most of the time. Megan had sort of rubbed off on him, though.

Deciding not to go down that rabbit hole, she moved the conversation in a more relevant direction. "Did you want to get a few hours' sleep before we head out to the first address?"

"Nah, I'm good. This cup of coffee will get me through till lunchtime at least."

She wasn't going to argue with him. "Okay. I was thinking we could try Cindy Fisher. She's the first one on my list. Any idea where she lives around here?"

"Not exactly," Kyle said. "But we can find out. Mary Fisher lives out on Mason Road, north of town. Cindy's her youngest."

"You think they'll tell us where we can find Cindy?" Janey was thinking more along the lines of looking Cindy up in the BMV records. She would have done that yesterday if they'd been at the station instead of using a laptop in Kyle's living room.

"I wouldn't see why not."

Janey looked at him over her mug. "We're conducting a murder investigation. It's been my experience that family members usually don't hand over information on their relatives' whereabouts all that often."

"This isn't the city. Things are a little different around here."

"So you've said."

Kyle downed the rest of his coffee and rinsed his mug out in the sink. "Besides, Mary likes me."

Janey raised an eyebrow in question.

"She was stranded on the side of the road a few months back and I stopped to help."

Instead of disagreeing with his assertion that Mary would gladly give up the whereabouts of her offspring, Janey finished her coffee. "So when can we head over there?"

He glanced at the clock. "Mary works the evening shift at the truck stop out near the highway, so she probably won't be up and about quite yet. Let's get your things upstairs and then we can head into the station. I think Noah wants to talk with us before we head out anyway."

"Maybe I should stay down here," Janey said when Kyle picked up her bags to take them to his room.

That seemed to amuse him. "Don't trust yourself to be alone with me, do you?"

"Something like that."

He shook his head and laughed. "Fine. I'll run these upstairs, freshen up a little, and then we can go. The remote is on the coffee table if you want to watch TV."

"Thanks."

His shoulders were still vibrating as he climbed the stairs.

Maybe she was being overly cautious, but she knew how she was around him—she lost all sense of logic and reason—and she needed her wits about her. She had a killer to catch. It was going to be hard enough to concentrate on interviewing potential suspects with him. The last thing she needed was to have fresh memories of sex lingering in her mind.

Deciding to take his suggestion, she sat on the couch and turned on the television. Janey flipped through the channels trying to find something to watch. She wasn't really paying attention—how could she when she knew Kyle was upstairs? He really was quite the distraction.

CHAPTER 19

AFTER KYLE SHOWERED and changed into a clean uniform, he drove Janey to the station. They walked inside and he caught sight of Mac. She'd been MIA every time he'd come into the station this week. He was beginning to think she was avoiding him. "Hey, Mac."

She stopped and turned to face them. Her gaze immediately went to Janey standing beside him. She clutched the folder against her chest and straightened her shoulders. "Are you just getting in from patrol?"

"No. My shift ended a couple of hours ago." He nodded in Janey's direction. "Noah wants me to tag along with Janey while she's here running down some leads."

Mac smiled, but he could tell it was forced. He hated that she was so uncomfortable around him these days. It made him feel as if he'd done something wrong by leading her on, but he hadn't.

"Good luck." She extracted some papers from her folder. "I was going to drop these off at your desk later. The lab reports came back. No DNA was found other than that of our victim. The only things under his nails were some dirt that matched the field where he was found and salt."

"Salt?" Janey asked.

"Yes. Common table salt." Mac shrugged. "Maybe he was eating not long before he was killed."

That meant they might be looking at a bar or restaurant as the last place their victim was seen alive. Again, it wasn't much, but he was hoping maybe all the little clues would add up to something big.

Janey accepted the lab reports from Mac and flipped through them. "The first victim didn't have any DNA evidence either. It would have been too much to hope that there'd be any on your John Doe."

"Any idea when the dental records will be back?" Kyle knew dental records took time, but they typically came in quicker or around the same time as DNA. It would be nice not to have to call the guy *John Doe* anymore.

"It should be any day now. I wasn't expecting the DNA results back this soon, but I'm guessing someone pulled a few strings and got it bumped up on the schedule." Mac made a point of looking at her watch. "I need to get going." A smile firmly in place, she said to Janey, "It was good seeing you again."

"You, too," Janey said as Mac disappeared into the stairwell.

Kyle guided Janey to the door that led to the offices and dispatch. The day shift was in full swing. He knew everyone there, but he rarely worked with them since they were typically coming on shift when he was going home.

Noah walked out of the break room and spotted them as he was taking a sip of his coffee. He lowered his mug and grinned. "I see you made it back to Liberty in one piece, Detective."

"Yes, sir."

The three of them weaved their way through the rows of desks to Noah's office.

"How was the drive? It's a beautiful morning. I'm betting the sunrise was quite stunning."

"It was beautiful watching the sun come up over the fields," Janey agreed.

Noah motioned for Kyle and Janey to take a seat. He shut the door behind them and sat down behind his desk. "I won't bore you with pleasantries, but I'm trying to keep the buzz in the office down to a minimum."

"I understand," Janey said. "I'd rather keep the details of the case isolated to the people who need to know for the time being."

"Agreed." Noah rested his forearms on his desk and leaned forward. "While you're here, I'd like you and Kyle to stop by my office every morning around this time for a briefing. I want to keep tabs on what's going on in my county."

"Understood, sir."

"So what are your plans for today?" Noah asked, leaning back in his chair.

Kyle glanced over at Janey before answering his boss. "We're heading out this morning to Mary Fisher's place. I figure she'll know where we can find Cindy. From there the plan is to work our way down the list of suspects."

Noah nodded. "Let me know if you need anything."

"We will," Janey said. "Thank you."

"Anytime." Noah stood, effectively dismissing them.

They exited Noah's office, and Kyle steered her toward his desk at the back of the room. He shared it with another patrol officer since the only time he used it was to fill out his reports.

Kyle grabbed a chair from a nearby empty desk and offered it to Janey. "I want to see if we have anything on Cindy in our database before we head over to see Mary."

Janey sat down and scooted closer. "Are you hoping to find anything specific?"

"Not really. I see Cindy around town from time to time, but we don't exactly hang out in the same circles." He typed her name into the search bar and waited for the results. "I just like to have all the information I can before going in."

"Always a good idea." Janey appeared pleased he was taking the initiative.

She scanned the large room, and he wondered how it all looked to her. They might be a small-town sheriff's office, but this wasn't Mayberry. The office was bigger than most big city stations. The difference was the square miles they covered. A station in the city might be responsible for a five or ten square mile radius. They patrolled an entire county.

"So why don't you guys have a detective?" Janey asked, pulling him out of his thoughts.

It was a valid question. He was surprised she'd waited until now to ask. "We had one up until about three months ago. Jerry met a woman online and moved to Texas. Noah's interviewed a few people for the job, but he hasn't found a good fit yet."

They sat in silence for several minutes while the computer completed its search. Other than the basic information from her BMV record, which was three years old, only one hit came up. "Looks like Mike pulled her over for speeding last year. Other than that she's clean. I remember she got caught drinking a few times back in high school, but that was a long time ago and, of course, she was a minor so those records are sealed."

"What about Heather Sanders, Candy Wilson, Melissa James, Carrie Madison, and Angel Bryant?"

"I thought we'd ruled out Melissa and Carrie?" He vaguely remembered Melissa James. While he hadn't seen her in years, not since Ava was in school, he agreed with his sister. The ring that was found wouldn't have fit her. Not to mention he doubted her family would have been able to afford something as frivolous as a class ring. Carrie was another story. He wasn't sure he'd ever met her.

"I know they're both unlikely suspects, but I'm not ready to cross them off the list just yet."

Kyle nodded. He'd thought about all the women on the list last night while he'd been on patrol. "Let's see what we can find." Kyle typed Heather's name in first. "Heather is Hayden's sister, so I doubt there's anything in here on her. At least, nothing recent. She got picked up for a drunk and disorderly once, but that was at least three years ago."

Nothing new came up when he searched for Heather, so he moved on to Melissa. Her listed address was the same house where she'd grown up. Kyle wondered if that meant she'd never married.

He moved on to Candy. The address that came up for her placed her in a town about thirty minutes outside Indianapolis.

"Her social media was full of pictures from all over the world. Either she has a job where she travels a lot, or she's come into a considerable amount of wealth."

"She's a flight attendant."

They both turned toward the new arrival.

Patty Camp, one of the file clerks, was standing a foot or so behind them. "Sorry. I heard you mention Candy's name. She's my cousin."

Janey seemed to handle the intrusion better than he did. She smiled up at Patty. "Thanks. That helps."

Patty worried her bottom lip with her teeth. "Is Candy in some sort of trouble?"

Again, it was Janey who answered. But instead of responding to Patty's question, she asked one of her own. "Do you happen to know if she's still living in Greenville? There something on the case I'm working on that I think she could help with."

"Yeah," Patty said. "I mean she's usually home when she's not working."

"Thank you. We appreciate the help." Janey glanced over at him, raising her eyebrow.

He took the hint and stood. "Yes. We really appreciate it." He eased Patty away from his desk, asking her about a report he'd turned in the week before, leaving Janey to finish up the remaining searches on Angel Bryant and Carrie Madison.

When he returned from distracting Patty, Janey had already powered down his computer. "Anything?"

"Not so much as a parking ticket for either of them."

He knew it would be a long shot for them to find something on any of the women that would throw up a red flag, but it was better to check, especially if they were going to be interviewing them.

They began gathering their things. "Does Hayden typically work the night shift?" Janey asked.

Kyle returned the chair he'd borrowed for Janey to the desk beside his, and they headed out. "Yeah. She's a good kid."

Janey chuckled. "I wouldn't let her hear you calling her a kid. She has a crush on you, remember?"

"I'll try to keep that in mind."

The drive to Mary Fisher's house only took a few minutes. He parked beside a sedan that had to be at least ten years old. He knew it belonged to Mary since it was the car she'd been driving when he'd changed her tire. There was also a red pickup truck that was newer parked alongside. He'd lay odds it belonged to Mary's boyfriend, Clyde.

Kyle knocked on the door while Janey scanned the area. He hadn't been to the Fisher house in years. Not since Mary's husband died.

A minute or so later, the door opened and Clyde stood there looking half asleep in a pair of jeans. "Yeah?"

"Sorry to bother you so early, but we were hoping we could talk to Mary. Is she around?" Kyle asked.

Clyde ran a hand over the top of his head, sending what little hair he had pointing in all different directions. "Yeah. She's here." He looked behind him, and then back at them standing on the porch. "Come on in and I'll get her."

"Thanks."

The house was clean, although most of the furnishings were older. Clyde led them into the living room and indicated they should have a seat on the couch. "She'll need a few minutes to put herself together. Um, can I get you coffee or anything?"

Kyle lowered himself onto the couch. "Sure. That'd be great."

It ended up taking almost twenty minutes before Mary joined them in the living room. She was fully dressed with her hair and makeup in order. Clyde took up a post behind her.

"Sorry to disturb you this early, Mary, but we were hoping you could tell us where we could find Cindy," Kyle asked.

Mary released a loud breath. "Thank the Lord. I thought you were here to tell me something happened to one of my babies." She paused. "Is Cindy in trouble?"

"No, ma'am," Janey said. "We just wanted to ask her a few questions."

Mary really looked at Janey for the first time. "Are you Deputy Reed's girlfriend? The one from Indianapolis?"

He felt Janey stiffen beside him. "Yes. I'm also a detective with the Indianapolis PD."

"You're very pretty." Mary turned to look at Clyde. "Clyde, isn't she pretty?"

He nodded.

"Thank you, ma'am." Janey shifted. She was clearly uncomfortable with the direction the conversation had taken.

Kyle cleared his throat, hoping to get them back on topic. "Do you happen to know where we could find Cindy?"

Mary rattled off the address. "And if you can't find her there, she'll be at work in a few hours over at the feed store."

He and Janey stood. "Thank you. We're sorry again for dragging you out of bed so early."

She waved off his comment. "I needed to get up anyway. Always so much to do. You know how it goes."

The address Mary had given them was on the opposite side of town. Even still, it didn't take them long to get there.

They parked in front of a traditional ranch house. The shutters on the windows needed a fresh coat of paint, but the lawn was freshly cut and the flower beds well maintained.

Voices from inside greeted them as they approached the front door. A child squealed with delight somewhere inside, causing Kyle to smile automatically.

They knocked, and a somewhat frazzled woman came to the door. She had a smile on her face until she saw Kyle. "Can I help you?"

"Cindy Fisher?" Kyle asked.

"Yes."

"I'm Deputy Reed and this is Detective Davis. We were wondering if we could come in and ask you a few questions about a case we're working on."

A little girl about three years old threw herself around Cindy's leg. Her eyes got big when she saw Kyle. "You's a police officer."

"I am." Kyle knelt down to the little girl's level. "My name's Deputy Reed. What's your name?"

She pressed her face against Cindy's thigh, and then turned her head to look at Kyle again. "Sadie."

"It's nice to meet you, Sadie."

"We could talk out here if you'd prefer," Janey said.

Cindy looked past them, nervous, and then opened the door to let them in.

***

Janey was trying not to think about the interaction Kyle had with Sadie. When he'd knelt to talk to the little girl, it had done something to Janey's insides. She hadn't thought about having children in years... not since she'd given her daughter up for adoption.

"Sorry about the mess," Cindy said. Toys were scattered everywhere in the room they walked through. The kitchen, however, wasn't quite as chaotic.

"You've lived in Liberty all your life?" Janey asked Cindy as the three of them sat at the table. Sadie had stayed in the living room to play.

"Yep. Born and raised." Cindy brushed a strand of hair out of her face. "I always wanted to move to a big city, but things didn't work out that way."

"How old is Sadie?"

Kyle sat back and let Janey do the questioning. This was her rodeo. He was just along for the ride.

"She'll be four next month." Cindy played with a paper towel that was on the table. "Can I get you anything to drink? Water? Coffee?"

"No, thank you," Janey said. "We don't want to take up too much of your time. You graduated high school the same year as Kyle's sister, Ava, right?"

"Ava Reed. Yeah." Cindy rubbed the back of her neck. She was anxious, but Janey couldn't tell if it was because she had something to hide or solely because of who her visitors were. "Ava was one of the popular kids."

"Lots of guys asking her out?" Janey asked.

Kyle groaned. "Don't remind me."

Cindy chuckled.

"Such a big-brother response."

"Yeah," Cindy agreed.

"High school seems like another time, but it always seems to stick with you, doesn't it? No matter how many years pass."

A shy smile graced Cindy's lips even as she looked down at the table.

It was the type of opening Janey was looking for. "Did you get one of those class rings? Ava said they're really big around here. You wouldn't still have yours, would you?"

Cindy scrunched up her nose, slightly thrown by the question. "I think so."

Janey's tone was relaxed. She could have been asking Cindy about the weather. "Could I see it?" Figuring since everyone seemed to know she was Kyle's girlfriend, she asked, "Things are so different in these small-town high schools. I don't even recall if I got a class ring my senior year."

"Sure. I guess." Cindy stood. "I'll just... let me go see if I can find it."

"Thanks." Janey smiled. "That'd be great."

Cindy checked on Sadie and left them to go in search of the ring.

Janey caught the look in Kyle's eye. He was impressed, as he should be. She was a professional. She knew what she was doing.

Cindy returned five minutes later with the ring. It was in a small velvet pouch. Without pretense, Cindy removed it from the pouch and handed it to Janey. It looked exactly like the ring they had in their possession, with one exception. The stone didn't match. It confirmed what Ava had said. The ring they'd found was from Liberty-Bass High School.

"I haven't worn it in years. It just sits in my jewelry box."

"It's a nice ring," Janey said. "I like the dog on the side here."

"The Liberty-Bass High School Bulldogs."

They both looked at Kyle.

"What?" he asked.

Janey shook her head and grinned. Now that she was fairly sure Cindy wasn't the one they were looking for, she could relax a little. "I'm trying to picture you all decked out in your school colors, spreading school spirit."

"Oh, Kyle spread a lot of school spirit. Especially when he would come home on leave from the Army." Cindy's smile lit up her face. She was a completely different person from when they'd first sat down.

"Mommy, Mommy! Daddy's home! Daddy's home!" Sadie came running into the kitchen, excitement in her voice. She took off toward the front door.

Janey handed Cindy back her ring. "We'll get out of your hair."

"Sure." The nervous woman was back, and Janey realized instantly what was causing Cindy's unease.

Quickly, before the new arrival could interrupt them, Janey handed Cindy one of her business cards. "If you ever want to get together and chat, about high school or whatever, give me a call. I'll be in town for a few days."

At the sound of the front door opening, Cindy took the card from Janey and shoved it in the front pocket of her jeans.

"Cindy?" A loud booming voice vibrated through the house.

"In here," she called back, her voice sounding half as strong as it had five minutes ago.

A large man, close to six feet tall and with a chest as wide as Janey's torso was long, strolled into the room. He was at least fifty pounds overweight and swayed a little when he walked. He took one look at Janey and Kyle and narrowed his eyes. "What are you doing here?"

Kyle took the lead and Janey let him. If what she suspected was true, she knew that Kyle had a better chance of defusing the situation than she did. "Hey, Keith. How've you been?"

"Busy. Some of us work for a living. Unlike people like you who harass people for a living."

Ignoring the jibe, Kyle motioned to Janey. "Detective Davis is here from the Indianapolis PD working on a case. She wanted to ask Cindy some questions about her high school experience."

He looked Janey up and down. "What's so special about Cindy's high school experience?"

Janey knew for Cindy's sake she was going to have to give up some information she'd been hoping to keep under wraps. "We think someone Cindy went to high school with may be involved in a murder investigation I'm working on."

"Murder, huh?"

"Yes," Janey said, leaving it at that and hoping it was enough.

Apparently, it was. He turned his attention to Cindy. "You got my lunch ready?"

Cindy went to the oven, removed a dish, and set it on the stove. She scooped several large helpings onto a plate.

Kyle placed a hand on the small of Janey's back. "We'll leave you to your lunch. Have a good afternoon."

They made their way down the walkway to Kyle's SUV in silence, both no doubt hoping they were reading the situation wrong.

"You did good," Kyle said as he started the vehicle and pulled away from the curb.

She knew he wasn't talking about questioning Cindy regarding the ring. "It's not the first time I've been in that type of situation, unfortunately." The house faded away in the background. "Hopefully she'll call me."

He placed a comforting hand on her knee. "You did what you could. Now it's up to her."

Janey nodded. He was right, of course, but that didn't help the knot forming in her gut. This was a part of her job she hated. A part of her wished she had enough evidence to bring Cindy in for questioning. Not that she hoped she was the murderer, but to give the woman time to consider her options.

Then Janey remembered the little girl, Sadie. Leaving a situation like that was always harder when there was a child involved.

She took a deep breath. "Where to next?"

"It's still early. I figured we could grab some lunch at the diner and then head out to the Sanders farm."

Leaning back in her seat, Janey placed her hand over Kyle's where it still rested on her knee. Even though she wasn't really hungry, she needed some time to collect herself before they met with Heather Sanders. Hopefully, they wouldn't run into any more surprises.

CHAPTER 20

KYLE FINISHED his sandwich and pushed his plate away. "I wonder if Claire has any of her apple pie."

Janey was still eating. She'd picked at her lunch, taking small bites in between staring out the window.

He knew what was bothering her and he understood. Half his calls were domestic issues in one form or another. It was tough no matter how many times you encountered it. "I can make a few calls. See if anything's been reported."

She met his gaze. "I'm not sure it will do any good."

"You never know. Something could be sitting on someone's desk and they just haven't gotten to it yet."

"Can I get you two anything else?" Kennedy strolled up to the table.

"I'll take a slice of apple pie if you have any and a coffee." He winked at her.

"You big flirt," she said, giving him a playful push on the shoulder. "And in front of your girlfriend." She turned her attention to Janey. "What about you?"

Janey shook her head. "I'm good. Thanks."

"One slice of apple pie and a coffee coming right up." Kennedy hurried behind the counter, leaving them alone once more.

"You should finish eating." Kyle pointed to the half sandwich still on Janey's plate. "No telling how this afternoon will go."

She rolled her eyes at him, picked up her sandwich, and took a bite. "Happy?"

"Getting there." Especially since her response sounded more like the Janey he knew.

Kennedy returned with his slice of pie and his coffee. She also left the check. "Holler if you need anything else."

Janey pulled out her phone after Kennedy went to wait on another table. "I should give Paul a call. Check in."

Kyle dug into his pie while she made her call. From what he overheard, Paul had gotten an address for Angel Bryant, but he hadn't spoken to her yet. Janey had kept her update to him vague since they were in a public place but told him she'd text the information they'd found for Candy. Besides, it wasn't as if they had much else to share at this point. Nothing that had to do with the case anyway.

By the time Janey was finished with her call, he'd scarfed down his pie and polished off his coffee. He'd been in desperate need of a caffeine boost because he'd been up for almost twenty-four hours. "Ready to head out?"

They paid the cashier, and he swiped two lollipops from the bowl next to the counter. Once they were outside, he held both up in front of her. "Grape or cherry?"

"Those go straight to your hips, you know."

He grinned at her, determined to take her mind off how their morning had ended. "That's okay. I happen to like your hips."

Janey snorted and swiped the cherry one from his hand.

Kyle chuckled. He removed the wrapper from the grape candy and popped it in his mouth. It had been a while since he'd had a lollipop and the rush of sugar hit his tongue and filled his mouth. "I forgot how sweet these are."

Janey sucked on hers, pushing it to one side of her mouth. "I used to love these growing up."

He opened the door for her. "I preferred Tootsie Rolls."

"I never would have pegged you for a Tootsie Roll kind of guy," she said, climbing into the passenger seat.

"What can I say? I'm full of surprises."

The drive to the Sanders farm took about twenty minutes. Pete and Mae Sanders had lived there for close to forty years. They had four daughters: Hannah, Heather, Helen, and Hayden. Both Hannah and Helen were married, but Hayden, and as far as he knew, Heather, still lived at home with both their parents.

A dog barked inside, but other than that there were no signs of anyone around as they made their way up to the house.

"Let's check the barn," Kyle said.

Unfortunately, there was no one in the barn either.

Janey looked around, hands on her hips. He had to resist the urge to kiss her. "Any ideas?"

"I have a few."

She met his gaze, waiting. Then her mood shifted and she seemed to realize he wasn't talking about the case at all. Janey sucked in a breath and let it out slowly. "We're working."

"I know."

The energy in the barn began to change, and he knew if they stayed there much longer he was going to forget why he shouldn't drag her into an empty stall. For the life of him, though, he couldn't get his feet to move.

Luckily, there was a noise from the front of the barn. They both turned to see a horse being led into the stables. Hayden held the reins. She smiled when she saw him. "Kyle."

"Hey."

She shifted her weight and blushed. "Hey." Then she seemed to notice Janey standing beside him and she sobered a little.

He took the reprieve he'd been given. "Were you out riding?"

"Yeah. It helps to clear my head." She walked her horse over to the far wall and began removing his saddle. "Plus, it's fun."

He waited for a beat and asked, "Are your folks home?"

Hayden reached for the horse's bridle. "No. They'll be back

tomorrow, though. They went to visit Aunt Jenny and Uncle Bob in Terre Haute."

"Did Heather go with them?" He was hoping she wouldn't read too much into him asking about her sister since he'd asked about her parents first.

"Nah," Hayden said, removing a brush from the shelf. "I think she went shopping or something."

"Any idea when she'll be back? I was hoping to talk to her about something."

She frowned but continued to brush her horse.

"I could swing by later tonight if that works better."

Hayden stopped her movements. "Heather has a boyfriend."

Her assumption left him scrambling for a response. When he'd asked about her sister, it had never crossed his mind that she'd think he was interested in dating her. Especially since it was fairly common knowledge that he was dating Janey.

Stepping forward, Janey tried to salvage the conversation. "I didn't realize you had a sister. Is she older or younger?"

Hayden stared at Janey for several moments, then continued to brush her horse. "I have three sisters. They're all older."

"Do they all still live at home?" Of course, Janey already knew the answer, but Hayden didn't know that.

"No. Just me and Heather." The horse let out an impatient huff.

Janey walked closer. "You two must be pretty close, then."

Hayden shrugged.

"I always wanted a sister," Janey said. "One of the downsides of growing up an only child."

"It's okay. Most of the time." Hayden didn't sound all that thrilled about having siblings.

Janey ran a gentle hand along the horse. "I'd love to meet her. Maybe the two of you could meet us for dinner at the diner tonight. Do you think she'd be home by then?"

Hayden looked at Kyle before returning her gaze to Janey. "Sure. I guess. What time?"

"Let's say six thirty? Our treat."

Again, Hayden shifted her gaze to him. It lingered too long on a certain part of his anatomy before returning to his face. "All right."

"Great," Janey said. "We'll let you get back to your horse. He's beautiful, by the way."

The look of pride shone on Hayden's face. "Thanks."

Kyle and Janey took their time heading back to his vehicle. "Thanks for stepping in back there," he said, starting the engine.

Janey laughed. "I have a bit more experience with subterfuge than you do. Besides, it was fun seeing you squirm a little."

He turned the vehicle around and drove down the gravel driveway that led back to the road. "Do I need to be worried? About the subterfuge, I mean. Hayden I can handle."

"I've no doubt you can handle Hayden. She's a young girl with a crush. Eventually she'll get over it."

He nodded as he maneuvered the SUV back onto the main road.

"Got something to hide, Deputy?"

"What?" he asked, not understanding what she was asking.

"You were concerned with me being better at subterfuge than you are, so I asked if you had anything to hide. Do I need to do some digging on you? Do you have a secret past I should know about?"

Kyle chuckled. "I have plenty to hide, but for you I'm an open book. Ask me anything."

She contemplated that for a moment. "Would you ever consider moving to Indianapolis?"

That wasn't what he'd been expecting. "I don't know. I haven't really thought about it."

"But you love living here in Liberty." It wasn't a question.

"Yeah, I do. And Ava and Cole are here." Was she thinking about them? Their future? Was she trying to tell him that she'd never move away from the city? "What brought this up?"

Janey shrugged. "Something Paul said before he left."

Now he was really curious. "What did he say?"

"It's not important."

"Janey—"

She shook her head. "Let's just focus on the case. We have a few hours to kill before dinner."

He knew how they could kill a few hours.

As if reading his mind, she added, "We're not going back to your house."

Kyle laughed. "What did you have in mind, then?"

"Let's head back to the station. I want to talk to Mac again. Paul emailed me the file for the third victim. I'd like to see if she has any further insights."

Spending the afternoon with Mac wasn't exactly what he wanted to do. Then again, nothing was going to sound as appealing as spending a few hours in bed with Janey.

"I know what you're thinking," she said, a smirk on her face.

He raised an eyebrow. "Do you?"

"You're thinking you'd rather have me naked in your bed." She knew him too well.

"I'm a guy. That's pretty much a given."

She giggled. "Work first. There'll be time for fun later."

Kyle brushed his fingers down her arm. "Promise?"

He heard her suck in a breath.

When he glanced at her, Janey was staring at him. He waited for her response. "I promise."

***

Janey leaned against a file cabinet in Mac's office while she looked over the coroner's report on the third victim. The two of them were alone. Kyle had gone in search of coffee. He'd been awake for more than twenty-four hours and he was beginning to feel it.

Liberty's coroner chewed on the end of her thumb as she scrutinized the file.

"What do you think?" Janey asked.

Mac glanced up from her reading. "It looks very similar to our John Doe."

The look on Mac's face told Janey there was more. "But?"

"It may be nothing, but the Taser marks on this third victim, they're higher than on the other two."

Janey crossed over to the desk, and Mac pointed to the diagram in the file where it indicated the markings.

"On the first two victims, the Taser marks were down here, right above the pelvic bone. But on this victim, the marks are about six inches higher."

She was right. Although, there could have been several reasons for that. "Maybe the victim saw the attack coming and deflected it. Could also be the victims were different heights."

They flipped through all three files. Victim number one was five foot eleven inches. Victim number two was six foot. And their newest victim was six foot one. If anything, the marks should have been lower, not higher.

Janey leaned forward, resting her hands on the desk. "What do you think it means?"

"I don't know. But either the killer was standing on something when they tased the third victim—"

"Or we have more than one killer out there."

The two women were pondering that scenario when Kyle came back into the room nursing a cup of coffee. "What'd I miss?"

Janey and Mac shared a look but didn't say anything.

"What?" Kyle asked when he noticed the vibe in the room.

It was Janey who answered. "Mac thinks we might be looking at more than one killer."

He seemed to carefully consider the new possibility. "What makes you say that?"

The question was directed to Mac. "The Taser marks don't match on the third victim. They're a good six inches higher than on the other two."

"Maybe the third victim was on the ground when he was tased."

Mac was shaking her head before he finished his sentence. "I don't think so. If he'd been on the ground with the killer standing over him, the Taser marks would have come straight down. These were at an upward angle, exactly like the other two."

"Whoever tased the third victim was taller, standing on something, or wearing extremely high heels," Janey said. "I think we need to consider the possibility that we're looking for multiple suspects. They could be working together, and it just so happens that one of them tased the first two victims and the other took care of the third."

"Do we have any idea how the killer—or killers—are choosing their victims?" Kyle crossed the room and picked up one of the files that were on Mac's desk.

He stood so close Janey could feel the heat radiating off his body. It made it difficult to concentrate, but she forced herself to focus on the conversation and not her hormones. "Not yet. We should have the background check on the third victim, Luke Mayfield, any day now. Maybe we can find a common connection. That doesn't help us with your John Doe, however." She turned to Mac. "Any word on the dental records?"

"I was promised I'd have them tomorrow."

"Can you let me know as soon as they come in?" Janey asked. She hated waiting on lab results.

"You'll be the first to know."

Kyle closed the folder he'd been looking over and handed it back to Mac. "We should get going. I want to swing by the house and change before dinner. I think it might go a little better if I'm not in uniform. We don't want to give her any reason to be on guard."

Janey chose to stay outside in Kyle's pickup while he went in to change. She knew if she went inside with him, they'd most likely end up making out at the very least. They'd been working side by side all day, and other than a few intimate touches, they'd behaved themselves.

She filled the time by calling Paul again. Even though she enjoyed working with Kyle, it was weird not having her partner with her while she conducted interviews. Paul's experience meant he often picked up on subtle things she'd miss. "You got a minute?"

"Yeah. I'm on my way home. What's up?" Paul asked.

"I sent a copy of the file for the third victim to the local coroner here and had her take a look. She noticed something."

"She found evidence our coroner missed?" He didn't sound happy about that idea.

"Not exactly. She noticed that the Taser marks on the third victim were higher than on the other two victims. Given the third victim was the tallest of the three, it suggests the killer was also taller."

Paul immediately came to the same conclusion as Mac had. "There's more than one killer."

"That's what Mac thinks." Janey bit the inside of her lip as her gaze strayed toward the house. "I'm not sure what it means, though. I mean we have three victims, all with the same MO but with two different killers? Mac wondered if they were maybe working together."

"It's possible." She could tell he was thinking through the new information.

"Did you have any luck with Angel Bryant?" He'd mentioned he was going to try and track her down today.

"She wasn't home, but a neighbor said she works at a local bar. I was going to swing by there tonight after dinner."

"Just be careful, all right? I know you're a big tough guy, but you should have backup, too."

Paul chuckled. "I've got it covered. Reece is going to meet me there at seven."

Calvin Reece was another detective. He was close to retirement, but at least Paul wouldn't be going alone. "Call me if you find out anything."

"Always, partner."

Right as Janey disconnected the call, Kyle emerged from his house, dressed in dark jeans and a rust-colored T-shirt that hung loose. She should probably also have gone in to change, at least to move her sidearm to somewhere on her person that was less visible, but her current outfit would have to do.

When Kyle slid in beside her, he surprised her by reaching across the seat and pulling her closer. She let out a little squeal at the sudden movement, but it was quickly squashed when he covered her mouth with his.

"That's better," he whispered.

Her eyes fluttered open and she met his gaze. The way he was staring at her had her chest filling as if it were going to burst with emotion. She was falling in love with him. Giving her heart over to this man—any man—scared her, but she wasn't sure there was anything she could do about it. Sure, she could walk away, but even thinking about doing that hurt her deep in her soul.

Kyle rubbed his thumb along her jaw, making her feel as if she was precious to him. It was a feeling she hadn't experienced since she was little when she was with her grandmother.

Out of nowhere, the words came bursting out of her. "I had a baby. A little girl."

A look of confusion crossed his face.

Maybe it was seeing Sadie today and how he'd interacted with the little girl, but something made her want to tell him about her daughter. "You remember when I told you about Ted?"

He narrowed his eyes. "Yes."

Janey never talked about this, but the words kept coming anyway. "That's why he ended things with me. I got pregnant, and he didn't want to be a father."

Even though Kyle never stopped rubbing her jaw, she felt his muscles tighten and release. He was quiet for several long moments before he asked, "What happened to your daughter?"

"A nice couple adopted her." It was the one thing she hadn't regretted about the whole situation. A couple in their mid-thirties who couldn't have children of their own had adopted her baby. He was an accountant and she was a nurse. Janey knew, if nothing else, her little girl would have a good life. She'd be loved.

The muscles in his jaw clenched as silence filled the truck once more. She'd never told anyone about her baby or why Ted had left. No one knew except her grandmother and the social worker who'd helped with the adoption. "I want to punch him."

She didn't pretend not to know who he was referring to. And while his response was somewhat sweet, it was unnecessary. "He's not worth it."

"Maybe not, but you are." Kyle rested his forehead against hers. He opened his mouth to say something but stopped himself.

"We should get going. We don't want to be late."

Instead of releasing her, he placed a soft kiss on her lips. "Thank you for telling me."

The air around them changed again. She reached behind his head and brought their lips together once more.

Janey packed this kiss with everything she was feeling—even the things she wasn't ready to admit out loud. He took everything she gave and then some. By the time they separated, it took both of them a few minutes to get their breathing under control again.

He clenched the steering wheel several times before starting the engine. "Tell me about your grandma."

"What?" His question completely threw her.

Kyle kept his eyes on the road as he backed out of his driveway. "What was she like? Did she look like you?"

That was when Janey understood. He was trying to distract himself.

Janey glanced at his crotch, and sure enough he had a large bulge straining beneath his jeans. She pressed her lips together, trying not to laugh. From his point of view, she doubted it was funny. They had work to do, and it wouldn't look good if he showed up to the diner with a hard-on, so she tamped down her amusement and answered his question.

CHAPTER 21

HEATHER AND HAYDEN were already there waiting for them when Kyle and Janey walked into the diner. They were sitting in a booth about halfway back. He plastered a friendly smile on his face, hoping to give the impression to Heather that this was a casual get-together and not an interrogation.

Both women noticed them around the same time. Hayden focused solely on him, her eyes sparkling with excitement. She didn't seem as bothered about Janey's presence as she had been earlier. He was hoping that meant she was getting over her crush, but given the way she was looking at him, he was pretty sure that was wishful thinking on his part.

Heather, on the other hand, appeared to be a little more reserved. That could have been for a lot of reasons. Or that could have been her natural way of being. He didn't know her all that well.

Kyle let Janey into the booth first so she was opposite Heather, and he took the seat across from Hayden. Janey wasted no time. She extended her hand to Heather. "You must be Hayden's sister, Heather. I'm Janey."

Heather took the offered hand reluctantly. "Nice to meet you."

"Didn't I see you two earlier today?" Claire said with a smile as she brought menus over to the table.

Kyle took two of the menus and handed one to Janey. "We gotta eat, and I figured it would be better than poisoning Janey with my cooking."

Claire laughed and pulled out her notepad. "What can I get you all started on to drink?"

Once they placed their drink orders, Janey took control of the conversation again. He loved watching her work. She really was good at getting information from people without them realizing what she was doing. Before their food was on the table, she'd found out what Heather did for a living, where she'd gone to college, and that she'd recently broken up with her boyfriend.

"You and your sister both grew up around here, right?" Janey asked, even though she already knew the answer to that question.

Heather stabbed a piece of chicken onto her fork. "Yeah. We've lived here all our lives."

"Heather went to school with Kyle's sister," Hayden said in between bites. "They weren't really friends, though."

"You're the same age as Ava?" Janey asked.

Heather nodded.

"High school seems to be a big deal around here. Kyle was telling me how he helps out with the football team, and Ava was showing me her class ring." He liked how Janey segued to what she really wanted to ask. "Class rings weren't really a big thing in my high school."

Heather took another bite of her chicken, this one much larger. "Yeah."

"Do you still have yours? Ava said every student's was different depending on what extracurricular activities they were in."

Hayden was the one who answered. "Mine had a person playing the clarinet since I was in the marching band."

"Really? That's cool." Janey addressed Heather again. "What did yours have on it?"

Heather finished chewing, and then took a large drink of her pop. "I don't remember. It was a long time ago."

"Heather wasn't in the band like me. She was too cool for that." Hayden seemed to be oblivious to the tension radiating from her sister.

Kyle schooled his features so as not to give any indication he'd picked up on Heather's unease. Could she be their killer?

Heather shot her sister a look, but Hayden either didn't notice or ignored it. "She was a cheerleader. Always hanging out with the football team."

There was a cheerleader on the ring they had in their possession. Of course, they already knew the ring Heather purchased had a cheerleader on it. That was why she was on their list of suspects.

Janey didn't seem bothered by the sisters' exchange. "Well, I'd love to see it if you still have it. Seems like a big deal around here."

Silence fell over the table, and Kyle decided it was time for him to pull his weight in the conversation. "Hayden was out riding today when we stopped by. Do you do a lot of riding as well, Heather?"

The goal was to get her mind off the previous questioning and, apparently, he'd picked the right topic. Heather's eyes lit up, the first time he'd seen her perk up since they'd sat down. "I've been showing horses since I was eight."

"That's impressive," Janey said.

Heather blushed. "Thanks."

The topic transitioned from there to Heather's job, and then back to her college classes. In less than an hour, they'd found out several valuable pieces of information.

"Do you think she's one of our murderers?" Kyle asked once they were in his truck again.

Janey reached for her seat belt and secured it in place. "I'm not ruling her out."

"She seemed nervous. Both when we first sat down and when you were asking about the ring." He drove toward home, eager to get Janey back to his house.

"I agree. The big bite of chicken was a good cover, but it stood out, giving her away. She definitely seemed like she had something to hide. We just don't know what yet."

"I can't see her as a murderer," Kyle said. "Maybe it's because she's Hayden's sister, but it's hard to picture her bashing a guy's head in."

Janey didn't respond right away. "You'd be surprised what some people are capable of when given the right motivation."

He'd never been happier to see his house come into view. Pulling into his driveway, he parked his truck and hopped out. He was at Janey's door in two seconds, helping her down. As tired as he was, there was no way he was going to miss the opportunity to be with Janey. She was here. She was staying in his house, in his bed, and he was going to savor every moment of it.

After unlocking the door to his house, he went inside and turned on the lights. Janey closed the door behind them and flipped the lock. He raised an eyebrow in question. Not that he didn't normally lock his doors at night, but her action was rather abrupt. "We're interviewing murder suspects. I don't want any surprises."

He couldn't argue with that logic. Anyone who was capable of luring a man down an alley and hitting him over the head until he was dead was surely able to sneak into a house and try to harm the people who were attempting to bring them to justice.

Crossing the room, he pulled her into his arms and leaned down for a kiss. "I think we should call it an early night."

"Do you now?" She circled her arms around his neck, letting her fingers tangle in the hair above the collar of his shirt.

Kyle skimmed his nose along her neck before taking her earlobe between his teeth. "Uh-huh."

She tilted her head to the side to give him better access.

The sound of Janey's phone ringing caused Kyle to groan in frustration.

"I need to get that."

"I know," he mumbled against her throat.

Without losing contact, she retrieved her phone and put it to her ear. "Davis."

"I was expecting you to call me and give me an update." The sound of her captain's voice had her pulling away from Kyle's embrace. She couldn't be wrapped in her lover's arms while talking to her boss.

"I'm sorry, sir. I just called it a night. I was questioning one of our suspects."

"And?" Captain Lane wasn't in a talkative mood tonight. Then again, he rarely ever was.

"She seemed nervous and vague about her class ring. Her sister did confirm that her class ring had the image of a cheerleader on it, which matches the one we found. I told her I'd love to see hers but didn't really get a yes or a no out of her."

Kyle walked out of the room, leaving her alone in the kitchen.

"What are you planning to do now?"

"I might see if I can get any more information out of her younger sister. She has a crush on one of the deputies here. I might be able to use that to our advantage." Janey paused, gathering her thoughts. "I got the feeling Heather Sanders is hiding something. I just don't know what yet."

Before he could ask anything else, she filled him in on the rest of her discoveries. He was glad they were making progress, although it still wasn't fast enough, of course. He and the higher-ups wanted this case solved yesterday.

Janey disconnected the call and went in search of Kyle. He wasn't anywhere on the main floor, so she climbed the stairs to the second story.

As she neared his bedroom, she thought she heard a noise. It took her a moment to realize what it was, but her suspicions were confirmed once she reached his doorway.

Kyle lay on his bed, snoring away. He'd removed his shirt and his shoes, but that was it. Even his gun was still in its holster at his waist.

She stood there, taking in the scene. It almost looked as if he'd been sitting on the bed and just fell over on his side. One arm was draped over his head and the other hung off the side of the mattress. To be honest, the position didn't look all that comfortable.

Chuckling to herself, she creeped across the room as quietly as she could. Janey lifted his legs and placed them on the bed. Next, she removed his gun and holster, not wanting him to wake up with his gun grinding into his side. Moving down to his feet, she slipped off his shoes and put them in his closet. She considered attempting to remove his pants, but she didn't want to wake him.

After she was satisfied that she'd gotten him as comfortable as was possible, she went to her suitcase and extracted her toiletries. It didn't look as if her evening was going to end quite the way she thought it would, but that was surprisingly okay.

****

Kyle woke up the next morning with something digging into his stomach. He reached down to see what it was and discovered he was still wearing his belt. Peeling his eyes open one at a time, he glanced down to find that his pants and even his socks were still in place.

It only took a few moments for his sleep-addled brain to wake up enough to not only remember taking off his shirt and sitting down on the bed but to figure out that he must have fallen asleep and Janey had finished undressing him. He looked over to find her sleeping next to him in the bed. She was on her side, facing him, with the covers pulled up to her chin. Kyle's heart swelled as he took in her presence beside him. He knew he wanted to repeat this morning over and over. Although, hopefully without his belt buckle digging into his flesh.

Careful not to disturb her, Kyle padded into the bathroom to take care of business and grab a shower. His alarm clock said it was only six thirty in the morning and they didn't have to meet with Noah until nine, so he decided to let her sleep. There wasn't really any reason for her to be awake yet.

Okay, there was a reason. The erection he was sporting was hard to ignore, but she'd let him sleep last night when he'd needed it, and he was going to allow the same courtesy to her. He'd just have to deal with things himself for the time being.

Janey was still fast asleep when he strolled into the bedroom after his shower. He threw on a pair of jeans and a T-shirt, and snuck downstairs to begin making breakfast.

That was a bit of an exaggeration. He was going to pull out from the freezer some muffins his sister had made and unthaw them. It worked, right?

While the muffins were defrosting, he grabbed his laptop and checked his email. Yesterday when they'd stopped home before dinner so he could change, he'd sent an email to a friend of his in social services to see if Cindy or Sadie Fisher were on their radar. He'd been vague about why he was inquiring, wanting to see what she had first.

Karen's email was at the top of his in-box. He opened it and read through her response. The ER in the next county over had filed a report about a suspicious broken arm eleven months ago. Cindy had said it was from a fall, but the doctor had noticed some bruising that didn't match her story. The local police had come to talk to her, but no charges were filed.

That was all she had on record, which wasn't much. Either Clyde had only recently begun to get violent, or things were escalating over time. He was betting on the later. Abuse tended to get worse the longer it was allowed to go on. It rarely ever got better. And by rarely, he meant never. Kyle had never seen an abuser mend his ways. They tended to stick to a pattern, and it was never a good end for the person they chose to focus their energy on.

Kyle sent a quick email of thanks to Karen and asked her to let him know if she came across anything else. The sad part was that there wasn't much they could do at the moment. He only hoped Cindy would reach out to Janey for help. Then they could do something.

"Why didn't you wake me?"

Janey stood on the stairs in a gray nightshirt with a cat face across her chest. The material hung loose, but it gave hints at what lay underneath. He raked his gaze over her from head to toe before he answered. "I figured I'd let you sleep. We don't have to be at the station until nine."

He couldn't take his eyes off her as she came down the stairs. It was obvious she wasn't wearing a bra, and his brain immediately wanted to know if she had on panties. The possibility she was naked underneath that thin shirt of hers turned his brain to mush.

A knowing smirk from her told him she had a good idea what he was thinking. He should probably care that this woman had so completely enthralled him, but he didn't. As far as he was concerned, she could have him wrapped around her finger forever.

She strolled over to the couch and positioned herself between him and his computer. Instinctively, he sat back on the couch, and she took that as an invitation to straddle his lap. His hands gripped her thighs, staking their claim on her. It was as if they had a mind of their own. Then again, his brain was having difficulty forming a coherent thought at that moment.

He closed his eyes at the feel of her fingers threading through the hair at the base of his neck. She brushed her lips against his. "I thought you'd to wake me up this morning."

"We had a long day yesterday. I wanted to let you sleep."

Janey moaned as he moved his hands to cup her ass and bring her center in line with the bulge straining the front of his pants. He was right. She wasn't wearing panties.

"Sorry I fell asleep last night. I'm not sure what happened."

She kissed her way down his jaw to the curve of his neck. He tilted his head, enjoying the feel of her mouth on his skin. "You were tired."

He dug his fingers into her flesh as she scraped her teeth along his skin.

Before he could say anything, she went on. "So what have you been doing down here while I was sleeping in?"

It took a moment for her question to register. "I was checking my email."

"I see."

While he didn't want to ruin the moment, he also wanted Janey to know he hadn't been joking yesterday about doing a little digging on Cindy and her boyfriend. "I sent an email yesterday to a social worker friend of mine."

That brought Janey's head up as she abandoned her assault on his neck to focus on what he was saying. "And?"

"And there was an incident last year in the next county over. Cindy came in with a broken arm and some bruising that was inconsistent with her story."

The sexy vixen of a few minutes ago was gone, replaced by Janey the cop. The horny part of him wasn't thrilled with the new direction, but the more mature, rational part of his brain understood. What he'd found in no way dispelled their suspicions from the day before.

"She'll let us know if anything else comes across her desk about Cindy or Sadie."

Janey appeared to be deep in thought. She didn't move from his lap, which meant he was still very much aware of the scantily clad woman he had in his arms.

"What's going on in that head of yours?" he asked after several minutes had passed and she remained quiet.

"I'm trying to come up with a way to bring her in for questioning so I can talk to her and maybe convince her to press charges. But I don't want to put her or Sadie in any more danger."

"It's tough," he said. "I see it way too often around here. Murders may be uncommon, but domestic issues we encounter all the time. You'd probably be surprised at how many calls I get a month from neighbors complaining they hear fighting."

"It happens a lot at home, too, but I haven't had to deal with it as much since I've been a detective."

He nodded.

"I hate this," she said, sliding off his lap to sit next to him on the couch.

"I know. I'm not happy about it either. But all we can do is hope she calls you." Kyle reached for her hand and brought it up to his lips for a kiss. He knew he needed to get her mind off Cindy. "Are you hungry?"

Janey gave him a tentative smile. "What did you have in mind?"

He ignored the way his body responded and stood, offering her a hand up. "Muffins."

She blinked.

"My sister's muffins, to be exact."

"Well, why didn't you say so?" Janey began backing away from him toward the kitchen. "Your sister's muffins always trump sex."

The gleam in her eye told him she knew what she was doing.

He caught up with her in two seconds flat, picking her up and throwing her over his shoulder.

She squealed and started laughing. That was until he snaked his hand under her shirt.

His sister's muffins would have to wait.

CHAPTER 22

As it happened, Janey and Kyle barely made it to the station by nine o'clock. Janey wasn't complaining, though. No way was she going to complain about the three very intense orgasms Kyle had given her that morning. He'd seemed determined to make up for falling asleep the previous evening.

She'd rushed through a shower while he got dressed and got them coffee and muffins to go. It was crazy, but she felt a little like a teenager again. Not in the 'I don't have a clue what I'm doing' sort of way, but more that 'everything feels new and fresh and fun.'

Janey realized she was enjoying her time with Kyle. When she was with him, she could forget about the gruesome things she'd seen in her job, and all the baggage from her childhood didn't exist.

That was until she had time to think about it.

As she'd been getting dressed that morning, Janey realized again how comfortable she felt. She'd never lived with a guy before, but she'd always thought there would be a major learning curve. This was his space and she was invading it.

Granted, she wasn't actually living with him in the traditional sense. Even though he'd offered her a drawer for her stuff, she'd kept her things in her luggage. Janey didn't know how long she'd be there and there was no sense in getting too comfortable.

As much as it pained her to admit, she was scared. Kyle had the ability to hurt her. She didn't know when it had happened or how, but Janey knew if things didn't work out with him she'd be spending days, if not weeks, mending her broken heart in front of the television with a bucket of bonbons.

It wasn't a pleasant image. She hadn't cried over a boy since she was a teenager, and the prospect of sitting in her darkened living room, crying her eyes out over Kyle wasn't a pleasant one. There was a voice in her head that told her to run. To protect herself as much as she could—that maybe it wouldn't hurt as much if she was the one to leave him.

But even she knew that was a lie. Besides, she wasn't a teenager anymore. She didn't run away from her problems.

No matter how much they frightened her.

Sitting in Sheriff Jenkins's office later that morning, she tried to push her concerns out of her mind and focus on the case. On the agenda for the day was for them to go see Melissa James. She lived about thirty minutes away on the far edge of the county, almost to the small town of Bass. Even though, according to Ava, there was no way the ring would have fit Melissa, Janey thought she would feel better if she met the woman herself and was able to get a feel for her.

"You all right over there?" Kyle asked as they drove north toward Melissa's address.

"Yeah, I'm fine. Just thinking about the case." That wasn't a lie. She was thinking about the case.. . among other things. What Janey needed was to focus. "Take me through the call you got the morning you found John Doe again."

He glanced over at her but laid out the details once more. "It was around six forty-five when I got the call. I was already on my way back to the station when I got the call from dispatch. A passerby had spotted someone lying along the side of Butler Rd. I immediately turned around and headed in that direction."

"How far away were you?" Janey asked.

"Not far. Maybe five minutes." Kyle turned left onto a two-lane highway and almost immediately made a right onto another road with no center dividing line. "Dispatch had let me know it was between Monroe and Ada roads." He glanced over at her. "There's not much in the way of landmarks to reference on that stretch of Butler."

Janey nodded and waited for him to continue.

"It took me a few minutes of searching before I saw what looked like an arm poking up from the ditch. Once I got close enough, it became obvious the person wasn't alive. There was blood in his hair and on the collar of his shirt. I bent down to checked for a pulse, and the guy was already cold. I called it in and waited for the EMTs and then Mac to arrive."

"Did the person who reported it see anything else?

Kyle took a moment to answer. "I don't believe the caller gave their name. There wasn't one on the report that I recall."

She pondered that for a few minutes, and he let her have her thoughts while he concentrated on the road. The other two victims had been found next to a dumpster by employees taking out the trash. Janey had talked to each of them personally. They'd been eager to provide whatever information they could.

"So whoever called it in could potentially be our killer."

"What?" he asked, eyes wide, and he looked from her to the road.

"Sorry. I was just thinking out loud." She gave him a tight smile.

Instead of responding right away, he seemed to consider her assertion. "You may be right."

It was her turn to be shocked. "What do you mean?"

He shook his head. "When I pulled up to the scene, the only thing I could see was an arm, and I was looking. If I hadn't known it was there, I probably would've driven right past it."

"Maybe whoever called it in was just really observant," Janey said, playing devil's advocate.

"It was early. The sun was only beginning to rise above the horizon. Twenty minutes before that, it would have been too dark to see anything."

"Headlights?"

Again, he shook his head, understanding what she was asking. "I don't think so. As I said, it was difficult for me to see in the dim light, and I knew what I was looking for."

Janey pressed her lips together as she looked out the window. "I'd like to listen to the call when we get back to the station. Maybe there'll be something in there to give us a clue who it was."

"I'll call Noah when we get to Melissa's and have him retrieve the file so it'll be waiting for us when we get back."

As they pulled into Melissa's driveway, Janey got a text from Paul.

Paul: Talked to AB last night. Didn't have the ring on her, but I don't think she's our perp.

Kyle noticed her looking down at her phone. "Paul?"

"Yeah," she said, not taking her eyes off her phone. "He went to see Angel Bryant last night. He doesn't think she's the one we're looking for."

"Why's that?" Kyle turned the engine off and shifted in his seat to face her.

Janey shrugged. "Paul's pretty good at reading people. If he doesn't think she's involved, she's probably not."

Still, she was curious herself as to why he was willing to dismiss her so quickly as a suspect.

Janey: Why not?

His response was instant, which meant he was probably at the station.

Paul: She has an alibi for all three murders. She was working until close.

Solid reasoning, then.

Before she could come up with a reply, he sent another text.

Paul: I'm heading out to Greenville this afternoon. Will let you know how it goes.

Janey: We're at Melissa James's house. Will let you know how it goes.

He didn't respond, and Janey figured that was just as well. She and Kyle couldn't stay parked in Melissa's driveway all day.

She tucked her phone into her pocket and reached for the door handle. Kyle had gotten out of the SUV already to make a call to Sheriff Jenkins and to give her some privacy. Janey met him at the front of the vehicle. "Let's go see what Melissa can tell us."

***

Kyle hadn't seen Melissa James in years. He wasn't sure what he expected, but it wasn't the woman standing in front of him. She was at least thirty pounds thinner than the last time he'd seen her, and she wore enough makeup to stock an entire cosmetics store. Her clothes hugged her body and not in a good way. She wasn't unattractive, but the makeup caked on her face made her less appealing, at least from Kyle's perspective.

The cat must have had his tongue because after standing there for several long moments, Janey spoke up. "Are you Melissa James?"

"Yes." She was looking at Kyle, clearly wondering what a cop was doing on her doorstep.

Clearing his throat, he forced himself to get with the program. "I'm Deputy Reed and this is Detective Davis from the Indianapolis Police Department. We were wondering if we could come in and ask you a few questions."

She thought about it for a moment. "Sure, I guess."

Kyle let Janey go first. It wasn't as if they were expecting trouble. Melissa wasn't a prime suspect.

One of the things he noticed right away when they entered the house was the knickknacks. The house appeared to be well taken care of, but there were little figurines everywhere he looked. He didn't think there was a horizonal surface in sight that wasn't covered.

They were led down a short hallway to the kitchen. It was much like the rest of the house, except the counters were empty of the clutter that seemed to plague the other rooms.

Melissa sat down at the table, and Janey and Kyle followed suit.

"How long have you lived here?" Janey asked.

The woman across from them glanced around the kitchen before answering. "It was my grandma's house. When she died, she left it to me."

"It's quite a ways from town."

Melissa nodded at Janey's observation. "I know. I don't mind. Actually, I love that I don't have neighbors on top of me."

Kyle knew that was a reference to her childhood. Melissa had lived in the poor part of town where not much more than a driveway separated one house from the next. That certainly wasn't a problem here. Melissa's nearest neighbor was separated from her by at least ten acres of soybean fields.

"You're lucky. I live in a condo. The only thing that separates me from my neighbors is a wall." Since Melissa seemed comfortable with Janey, Kyle sat back and let the two women talk. Hopefully Janey would be able to put her at ease enough that she would open up.

They went on discussing nothing in particular for the next few minutes until Janey decided Melissa was sufficiently relaxed. "We don't want to take up your entire morning, but we wanted to ask you a few questions about a case we're working on."

"All right." Melissa glanced over at Kyle as if she'd forgotten he was there, and then back to Janey.

"I know it's been a while since high school, but I'm told that around here it's a big deal to get a class ring your senior year."

"Yeah. It is." The woman sitting across from them frowned.

Janey cut to the chase. "Did you get one?"

Melissa's frown deepened. "Yes. We didn't have much money growing up. I mean we never went hungry, but there wasn't much extra for things beyond the necessities. I had to save up money from babysitting in order to afford it. Looking back, it was silly. I mean, it was just a ring, but back then it was a big deal. Or it seemed like it was at the time."

Janey reached into her pocket and removed the ring—still in the evidence bag—and laid it on the table in front of Melissa. "This was found at a crime scene. We're hoping whoever it belongs to saw something and can help us solve the case."

Kyle was stunned Janey had shown Melissa the ring. She hadn't done that with either of the other two women they'd spoken with. Then again, their talk with Cindy had been cut short, and Heather... well, he was still making up his mind about her. Yes, she was Hayden's sister, but that didn't mean she was innocent.

At first, Melissa just stared at the bag as if it might jump off the table and bite her. Then she leaned in to take a closer look.

"Does it look like it's from your high school?" Janey asked.

Melissa looked up from the ring, meeting Janey's gaze. "Yeah."

Janey let her look at the ring for a little longer before asking her next question. "Any idea who this one might belong to? Does it look familiar to you?"

She narrowed her eyes, looking closer. "Looks like it belonged to a cheerleader."

Given the little cheerleader with the pom-poms on the ring, this wasn't new information. Unfortunately, all of their suspects had been on the cheerleading squad at some point during high school. Including Melissa James. "Anything else?" Kyle asked.

"Not really." Melissa stood and walked over to the coffee maker. She retrieved a mug from the cabinet. "I haven't had nearly enough coffee this morning. Would you like some?"

Janey got to her feet, removed the evidence bag from the table, and returned it to her pocket. "We're good. Thank you."

Kyle followed Janey's lead and stood as well. "Is there anything else you noticed about the ring?"

After taking a long sip of her coffee, Melissa shook her head. "I'm sorry I couldn't be more help. High school was just such a long time ago."

"Well, we won't take up any more of your time." Janey began moving toward the door.

He placed one of his cards on the table. "Give us a call if you happen to think of anything else."

Melissa nodded.

Janey was already sitting in his patrol vehicle by the time he exited the house. She waited until they were on the road before saying anything. "She's hiding something."

"I got that impression as well." Kyle drove for another five minutes before he asked the question that had been on his mind since they left Melissa's house. "Do you think she knows who the ring belongs to?"

"Maybe. Or she thinks she might." Janey blew out a frustrated breath. "I knew this interview was a long shot, but instead of crossing Melissa off our list of suspects, she's worked her way to the top."

"We've eliminated two of the six so far. At least that's progress. Hopefully listening to the call will give us something else to go on." He turned onto the main road that led back to town. "Noah said he'd have it ready for us when we got back."

"I need to call Daniels. Let him know about Melissa."

Kyle listened to the one-sided conversation. Janey filled Paul in on the details of their meeting with Melissa James. It was interesting watching her work. She might have seemed completely relaxed during the interview, but she'd taken in bits of information he would have completely dismissed. Like the fact that Melissa kept glancing to her right. Kyle had chalked it up as nerves, but when Janey relayed the information to her partner, she pointed out that Melissa's cell phone had been sitting on the counter. Exactly where she'd been looking.

His girlfriend was good at her job and that was an incredible turn-on. He really wished they weren't on the hunt for a killer. He would have liked to take her home and keep her in his bed for a few days.

Unfortunately, that wasn't an option. They had a killer—or two—to catch.

She disconnected the call as they neared the edge of town. "Paul's on his way to Greenville now with Rollins. He did some more research on Candy Wilson this morning and confirmed she works for an airline, which is why she's constantly traveling."

"Do we know if she was out of town when the murders happened?" Kyle asked.

"Not yet. He's been trying to track her movements via social media since she likes to post pictures from her travels."

Kyle maneuvered into a parking spot in front of the station and turned off the engine. He covered Janey's hand with his and gave it a comforting squeeze. It wasn't what he really wanted to do, but that would require them being alone, preferably with a nice comfy bed nearby. Since that wasn't an option at the moment, he settled for touching her hand.

Janey met his gaze and smiled.

They were so lost in the moment they didn't see or hear Mac walk up to the SUV until she rapped on the glass.

Both Kyle and Janey jerked away from each other at the sound and turned toward the noise. Mac's face stared back at them.

He opened the door and climbed out of the vehicle. "What's up?"

Mac waited to answer until Janey joined them. "The DNA results came back on our John Doe this morning. His name's Martin Clawson. He was twenty-six years old and lived about forty-five minutes from here." She handed Janey a folder. "I figured you'd want the information as soon as possible."

"Thanks." Janey took the folder and immediately began scanning through it.

"Any progress?" Mac asked as they moved toward the building.

He opened his mouth to answer, but Janey cut him off. "Some. There are still quite a few pieces of the puzzle that aren't adding up yet."

Kyle held the door open for Janey and Mac while they went inside.

"Well, let me know if there's anything else I can do."

"We will," Janey said. "And thanks again."

Mac grinned and crossed to the stairwell.

Once they were alone again, Kyle leaned in a little closer. He could smell the scent of her shampoo. "Seeing anything interesting in there that could help us solve the case?"

Janey took a step forward, putting some distance between them. "I don't know. I want to compare it to the other two files. See if there are any similarities."

She started to walk away, but he grabbed her arm and pulled her off to the side. It wasn't completely private, but it was better than standing out in the middle of the foyer. "What's wrong?"

"Nothing."

He held her gaze, waiting.

Janey sighed. "We shouldn't be... touching like that when we're working. It's unprofessional. Mac—"

"Mac knows you're my girlfriend."

"That's not the point." Janey looked around, surveying their surroundings. "I just... I can't think when you touch me like that, okay?"

A slow smile crossed his lips.

He didn't get to process his thought any further, though. Right as he opened his mouth to respond, Noah marched into the foyer toward them. "I need you two in my office. Now."

CHAPTER 23

Janey's heart raced. What had happened? Had there been another murder?

The sheriff ushered them into his office and closed the door firmly behind them. He didn't mince words. "I can't find any record of the call to dispatch."

He didn't need to explain what call he was talking about. They all knew what he was referring to.

"The record's missing?" Kyle leaned against one of the bookcases lining the wall, but he looked anything but relaxed. The muscle in his jaw flexed as he waited for his boss's answer.

Noah Jenkins walked over to the window. "I went to find it right after we hung up, but it wasn't there. I thought maybe in the craziness of that morning that somehow it hadn't been logged right, so I went through all the calls an hour before and an hour after you discovered the body." He looked at Kyle, deep lines creasing his forehead. "All the internal calls dispatching additional deputies were there, but nothing external. It's as if it didn't exist."

"That's impossible," Kyle said.

Janey took a step forward. "Could they have been moved somewhere else?"

"No." The sheriff shook his head. "All the files are recorded by the system and immediately archived. It's all automatic. As soon as the call comes in, it starts recording."

Janey knew this, of course. Incoming calls to dispatch could be used as evidence in court, so making sure they were not only recorded but kept secure was imperative.

None of them spoke for several moments, each mulling over what this could mean. Janey was the first to speak up. "Is it possible someone hacked into the system and deleted it?"

Sheriff Jenkins answered. "I suppose it's possible. It is a computer system, after all, but who around here has that kind of skill?" He paused for a moment. "And access."

"Brent?" Kyle asked.

Tension radiated from the sheriff as he considered that for a few seconds. "He could probably do it, but what would be his motive?"

"A woman?"

The sheriff seemed to consider the question for a moment. "I've never seen him with anyone or heard any rumors."

"Who's Brent?" Janey had met quite a few people since coming to Liberty, but she didn't recall being introduced to anyone named Brent.

"He works next door at the courthouse. You haven't met him, but he's a wiz at computers. If you ever need help finding something, he's your guy."

Kyle seemed to be as worried about the new development as Noah was, and Janey couldn't say she disagreed. It made her think that maybe she was correct. Maybe there was something on the recording that pointed to the killer. "Hayden was the one working dispatch that morning, right? Maybe we should talk to her. See if she remembers anything out of the ordinary."

"It's worth a shot." Kyle moved to stand beside Janey—a little too close considering they were in his boss's office talking about a case. But she was beginning to realize that no one here seemed bothered by her and Kyle's personal relationship. The more laid-back attitude of a small town was going to take some getting used to.

"Agreed." Noah crossed his arms over his chest. "I'll make a call to a buddy of mine who's good with computers. Maybe he can tell if the file's been tampered with."

Kyle placed his hand at the small of Janey's back. "Did Mac show you the DNA results on our victim?"

"Martin Clawson. I've got a call into the local sheriff to see if he has any information." Noah turned his attention to Janey. "I already put a call into your partner. He's running a background check as we speak. Hopefully we'll find a common denominator between the three victims."

Janey was a little shocked he'd called Paul, but it was his decision. "There's always something. We just have to find it."

Noah nodded and crossed to his desk. "How did the interview go with Melissa James?"

"She was nervous when we showed her the ring." It was hard to concentrate with Kyle touching her, but somehow she managed. "She said she didn't know who it belonged to, but I'm guessing she either knows who the rings owner is or she thinks she does."

"Do you think she's involved?" Noah asked.

Kyle and Janey shared a look before he answered. "We don't think so. While she was curious when we showed up on her doorstep, it wasn't until Janey pulled out the ring that she showed any signs of unease."

"Before you head over to see Hayden, why don't you swing by your sister's." Noah took a seat behind his desk. "See if she remembers who Melissa hung out with in high school. If she recognizes the ring, chances are it belongs to someone she was close to."

Nodding, Kyle began moving them both toward the door. Janey guessed they were done.

Kyle's hand was on the doorknob before Noah spoke again. "Watch your back. Both of you. We're ruffling some feathers here, and if whoever's involved in this is local, then they most likely own a firearm or have access to one. I don't want the next call I receive to be that one of my officers has been shot."

The drive to Ava's was quiet. Janey was mulling over the newest development and figured Kyle was doing the same. That and the possibility that somehow the audio files had been tampered with. And if those had been tampered with, had others? The implications were huge. Past cases could be called into question. Convictions could be appealed. The whole thing could snowball quickly.

They were each still deep in thought as they walked into Ava's house. A loud squeal greeted their ears, causing them both to grin for the first time since leaving the station. Cole's joy at whatever held his attention lifted their mood.

"Oh. Hey," Ava said as she came around the corner. Cole was in her arms, stuffing his face with a cookie.

Kyle extended his arms toward his nephew. The little boy didn't hesitate. He nearly leaped into his uncle's arms. "How're you doing, buddy?"

"Yummy cookie."

They all chuckled.

Securing Cole on his hip, Kyle addressed his sister. "We need your help with something. Do you remember who Melissa James used to hang around with in high school?"

Ava motioned for them to go into the living room. Kyle took a seat with Cole in the high-backed chair while Janey and Ava sat on the couch.

"Mommy, juice," Cole said.

Before Ava could get up, Kyle was already on his feet. "Is his sippy cup on the counter?"

She sent him a grateful smile. "Yes. Thank you."

Once the women were alone, Janey got back to why they were there in the first place. "We think Melissa may know who the ring belongs to. That makes us think it may be someone she's close to. Or was."

Ava walked over to a cabinet along the far wall. "Even though Melissa's family wasn't wealthy, she had a lot of friends."

"Any that stand out to you?"

She removed a book from the bottom shelf and brought it back with her. Ava set it on her lap and began flipping through the pages. It was a yearbook from Liberty-Bass High School. "Not really. I mean she hung out with a group of girls, but I don't recall her being closer to one more than the other."

Once Ava had found the page she wanted, she handed the book to Janey. It was group of five girls, all of them smiling. Three of them were in cheerleader uniforms.

"That's Melissa," Ava said, pointing to the girl on the far left. She was slightly heavier than the woman Janey had met earlier that morning and she wore a lot less makeup. "The other girls are Cali Mitchel, Riley Brennen, Heather Sanders, and Angel Bryant."

Janey had recognized Heather immediately. She hadn't changed much since high school. "What do you know about Heather and Angel? What were they like back then?"

Both were on her suspects list and both were wearing cheerleading outfits in the picture. Given Melissa's reaction, there was a good chance Melissa thought the ring belonged to one of them. Now all Janey had to do was figure out which one.

"I didn't really hang with either of them, but they seemed nice enough. Heather was really involved in showing horses. She would occasionally miss school to drive to shows and stuff. Angel was more of a bookworm. If she wasn't cheering or hanging out with her friends, she was reading. I think she missed out on being valedictorian by like a half percentage point or something."

"Either one of them show any violent tendencies?" Janey asked.

"Not that I remember."

Janey ran her fingers over the picture.

"I can tell by your frown I didn't help much, did I?"

"It's okay," Janey said, handing the yearbook back to Ava. "Every bit of information helps, even if it doesn't always appear to at first."

Ava bit her bottom lip and glanced over Janey's shoulder toward where Kyle had disappeared with Cole. "Can I be nosy and ask how it's going with my brother? You two seem to be getting along pretty well."

Much to her dismay, Janey felt her cheeks heat. She wasn't expecting quite such a personal turn in the conversation, but she guessed she shouldn't have been surprised. Of course Ava would want to know where Janey's relationship with Kyle was going. She was his sister after all, and Janey knew Kyle was the only family Ava had left. Still, it was awkward. "We're fine."

"Just fine?" Ava raised her eyebrows, eager for her to share.

Janey's gaze danced around the room before looking Kyle's sister in the eye. She didn't really know what to say. She wasn't used to sharing these things with anyone. "Things are... good."

The smirk on Ava's face said she wasn't fooled. "Well, I'm glad. I think you two make a cute couple. And Kyle seems really happy."

Not sure how to respond, Janey remained silent.

"Maybe we should go check on the boys." Ava stood and waited for Janey to join her.

Glad to be moving away from the discussion of her personal life, Janey let Ava lead her into the kitchen. They found Kyle and Cole sitting at the kitchen table. The sight of him with his nephew hit her harder than it had the first time she'd seen them together. He'd be a great father someday. And instinctively Janey knew he wouldn't shy away from his responsibilities.

Her breath caught in her throat as Kyle looked up and met her gaze. Their eyes were only locked for a moment, but it was enough to send her pulse racing. Every inch of her skin heated. She needed some air. Or maybe a cold shower.

"And what have we here?" Ava asked.

Kyle shifted his attention to his sister, a guilty expression crossing his face. It was then Janey noticed the cookie crumbs covering the table in front of Kyle and Cole... along with an empty plate.

Kyle swallowed and turned on that charming smile of his that always made her melt. "You ladies finished?"

Ava shook her head and sighed, not appearing to be affected by his smile in the least. "How many cookies did you let him have?"

"Just a couple."

"Uh-huh." Ava grabbed a cloth out of the drawer, ran it under some water, and began cleaning the mess from her son's face and hands. Then she moved on to the table itself.

In an effort to help with the cleanup, or maybe to make up for allowing Cole to eat an unknown number of cookies, Kyle carried the now empty plate to the sink and rinsed it off. "Did you need me to stop by later? We're heading out to the Sanders farm, but we could swing by on our way back if you need us to."

Ava finished wiping the table and dumped the crumbs in the trash. "You two have enough on your plate right now. Don't worry about me and Cole. We're just gonna hang around the house."

He pulled his sister in for a hug and placed a kiss on top of Cole's head. "Call me if you need anything."

Janey said goodbye to Ava and they headed out.

"Did my sister have any information that could help us?" Kyle asked as soon as they were outside.

She glanced down at the yearbook she held in her arms. "Maybe. There's a picture in here of Melissa with two of our other suspects. Both of them are wearing cheerleader uniforms."

"Let me guess," he said, opening the door to his SUV. "One of them is Heather Sanders."

"Yep."

He settled behind the wheel and put the key in the ignition. "And the other?"

"Angel Bryant."

Seeing as how Paul didn't think Angel was involved, that left Heather. Of course, that didn't mean she was actually involved. It did, however, mean she was now their prime suspect.

Kyle seemed to be thinking along the same lines as she was. "Maybe we'll get lucky and both Heather and Hayden will be home. Suddenly I feel the need to have another chat with Heather."

***

The minute they pulled up in front of the Sanderses' home, Kyle knew their visit was going to be a bust. The horse trailer was gone. Most likely the entire family had headed out of town for a show or rodeo.

"I don't think they're home."

Janey had already unbuckled her seat belt. "Why's that?"

He nodded toward the side of the barn where the trailer had been parked. "The horse trailer is gone and all the windows in the house are closed. So is the barn."

After several moments, Janey snapped her seat belt back in place. "Let's head back into town and grab some lunch. Maybe someone at the diner knows where they went."

Kyle grinned at his companion. "Now you're starting to talk like a local."

Janey ignored his comment. "Does the diner have WiFi?"

Her question caught him off guard. "Yeah."

"Good. Let's stop by your house on the way and pick up your laptop. I want to log into the files of the other two victims now that we know who John Doe is and see if we can spot any similarities."

He had to admit he was anxious to go over the files himself. Not that he had a clue what exactly they were looking for. Chasing bad guys he knew how to do. And interviewing suspects wasn't all that different from his usually job either. All too often he'd find himself talking someone down. Sifting through files, however, wasn't something he was used to. "Anything in particular we should be looking for in the files?"

She shrugged. "Anything that pops up for more than one of the victims."

"Not all three because it might have been missed."

"Exactly." Janey turned to look at him. Or she tried. The seat belt restricted her movement considerably. "After lunch, we should check in with Sheriff Jenkins and see if his tech guy was able to find anything. If not, maybe we should pay a visit to this computer wiz of yours. If he's not in on it, then maybe he can help us. If he is in on it, maybe we can get some idea of motive."

Kyle chuckled. "When are you going to start calling him by his name?"

"What? Who?"

"Noah. You always call him Sheriff Jenkins."

Janey shrugged. "I don't know. It doesn't feel right."

"You've got to lose that city way of thinking. We're a lot more laid back around here."

She didn't answer right away. "Does that mean this thing with us is just casual to you?"

Her question came from out of the blue. "No. Not at all. Why would you ask that?"

Again, she shrugged. "Just wondering, that's all."

He wasn't going to let her off the hook that easily, though. "Have I given you the impression that I'm not taking our relationship seriously?"

She pressed her lips together and stared straight ahead. "No."

"Then what brought this up?" When she didn't answer, he reached out and took her hand in his. "Talk to me."

"I'm just.. ." Her voice trailed off, leaving the thought unfinished.

He gave her hand a comforting squeeze and waited for her to continue.

Janey took a deep breath and released it. "I think I'm falling in love with you."

Kyle parked his vehicle in front of his house but left the motor running. "And you're afraid I don't feel the same way."

"Yeah." She gave him a sideways glance.

Given what she'd shared with him about her relationship history, he understood where her fear was coming from. He also knew he'd been holding back on telling her how he felt because he was afraid it would scare her away.

He removed his seat belt and cupped her cheek, bringing her gaze to meet his. Once he was positive he had her complete attention, he laid it all out for her in three simple words. "I've already fallen."

She stiffened and then her eyes opened wider. "Are you saying what I think you're saying?"

The look on her face was a cross between amazement and fear. He was hoping the fear was because she was hoping it was true and was afraid she was misinterpreting what he was saying and not that she didn't want him to have fallen in love with her.

"I love you, Janey Davis. Head over heels. Swept off my feet." He rubbed the pad of his thumb along her skin and watched her reaction. "You get the idea."

He was starting to get nervous when she didn't say anything. Or move. It was as if she were a deer in the headlights.

"You love me?" Her voice was barely above a whisper.

"I do." He didn't want her to doubt his sincerity. "Are you okay with that?"

It took her another handful of moments to answer. "Yeah. I'm okay with that."

"Good." He closed the distance between them and covered her mouth with his. The kiss was soft and gentle, reverent.

When they broke apart, he ran his thumb along her bottom lip, wondering if the kiss had felt half as wonderful for her as it had for him. "We should go inside and grab my laptop."

Janey released a shaky breath and leaned back in her seat. "I think it's better if you run in and get it. I'll wait here."

He couldn't help but smile. "Afraid you won't be able to control yourself if we're alone?"

She let out a sound somewhere between a laugh and a snort. "Something like that."

CHAPTER 24

KYLE WAS STILL SMILING when they strolled into the restaurant fifteen minutes later. He'd decided to test his theory about Janey not being able to control herself before he'd gone in the house to grab his laptop. The cute half snort/half laugh she'd emitted had seemed like a challenge, and he'd accepted it with gusto.

Without warning, he'd cupped the back of her head and fused their mouths together in a heated kiss. He didn't hold back, letting her feel every ounce of passion coursing through his veins. She melted against him within seconds, tangling her fingers in his hair and trying to climb across the center console to get closer.

With the half a brain he had left, he'd broken the kiss. They were both breathing as if they'd run a marathon.

His point proven, he'd shot her a satisfied grin, announced he'd be right back, and hopped out of the truck. When he'd returned, she still looked a little flustered, although she was doing her best to cover it up.

"You all right?" He couldn't wipe the satisfied look off his face as they slid into a booth in the back corner of the diner.

"Fine. You?" Her tone was defiant.

"Peachy."

She rolled her eyes at him.

He picked up his menu and looked over the specials. "You know, you didn't have to kiss me back."

Claire came to take their order, so he let it go. They had work to do anyway.

"Been busy today?" Kyle asked Claire. It was late for lunch, so there were only two other tables with customers besides them.

"Breakfast was crazy as usual. Lunch was a little slow, though."

"Oh? Is there an event or something out of town this weekend? I noticed the Sanderses were away."

Claire paused for a moment. She knew what he was asking. "Yeah, they drove up to Huntington. Should be back before the parade on Monday, though."

He thanked her for the information with a nod and gave her his order. Janey did the same, and Claire hurried away to check on her other customers before putting their order in.

Once they were alone again, waiting on their food, Janey logged onto her department's website and pulled up the files she was looking for. Kyle switched to sit beside her so he could read over the files as well. Two sets of eyes were better than one, after all. Plus, it didn't suck sitting this close to her. The scent of her shampoo teased his senses, but he forced himself to focus. There'd be time for fun later.

Their food came and they ate while scanning over the pages of reports on each victim, including the coroner's reports and background checks, along with any other information they'd been able to find.

"There." They'd been scrolling through documents for over two hours when Janey's enthusiastic pronouncement caused him to jerk. He'd been staring at the screen so long he was going cross-eyed.

"What'd you find?"

She pointed at the screen.

He got a glimpse of the name of a college about an hour away from Liberty before she switched to another screen, bringing up the file of the second victim. The same college was listed.

"And here." Janey flipped to his email where Mac had sent him a copy of the third victim's file. Sure enough, all three victims attended the same college.

"Could be a coincidence," he said. "A lot of people go to college."

"True. But I've learned not to dismiss details like this. It's the first connection to all three we've found. The thing is I don't remember seeing a college listed for the first victim when I looked over his file the last time."

"Maybe Paul updated it. He's been working on the case, too."

As if they'd called Paul's name, Janey's phone rang and her partner's name came up on the caller ID. "Are your ears burning?"

He could hear Paul chuckle through the phone since he was still sitting right next to Janey. She filled him in on what they'd found, being as vague as possible given they were in a public place. As suspected, he'd been the one to enter the information after interviewing a friend of the first victim, Travis Merrick, earlier that morning.

"How'd it go in Greenville?" Janey held the phone so Kyle could hear his answer as well.

"She was home. I got the impression she doesn't like cops, though. She wouldn't let us in, and we were only able to ask her five questions before she told us she had to go. I'm not sure if she's hiding something or if she just has an aversion to law enforcement."

Janey frowned. "So we can't mark her off our list."

"The last question I asked her was if she'd been a cheerleader in high school. That was when she informed us she had better things to do and slammed the door in our face." Paul paused. "As frustrating as it was getting shut down, it isn't enough reason to haul her into the station for questioning."

"We need to see if any of our suspects went to the same college," Janey said.

"Heather did." It was the first time Kyle contributed to the conversation. "I think Candy and Angel did as well. Not sure about the others. We could probably find out, though." Janey raised her eyebrows in question. "It's a small town."

Janey shook her head. "We'll start looking into it."

"Meanwhile, I'll look into the college careers of our three victims. See if anything stands out. Maybe they have more in common than their choice of alma mater."

After the call ended with Paul, Kyle and Janey packed up their things and headed out. Their first stop was to Noah's. Kyle had texted him before they left the diner and found out he'd run home to grab some food and a nap after covering some of Kyle's shifts.

Noah met them at the door and ushered them inside. He was still in his uniform, so he couldn't have been home long.

They filled him in on what they'd found. "Do you know if Cindy or Melissa went to the school as well?"

"I don't recall Cindy going off to college. I do think she took a few courses at the community college a few years back, though." He stood deep in thought for a minute or two. "Melissa left for a year or so after high school, but then she came back. If she went to college, she didn't stay."

"Any idea who in town might know for sure?" Janey asked.

Kyle and Noah looked at each other for a long moment before they both answered. "Mrs. Wheatman."

"Who's Mrs. Wheatman?"

Kyle filled her in. "She's the high school guidance counselor. Or at least she was. She retired about three years ago."

"Okay. So we go see her. Does she live around here?"

Noah scribbled an address down on a piece of paper. "She lives about forty-five minutes from here in a retirement community."

Both Kyle and Janey looked at him, wondering how he knew where to find her without having to look it up.

He shrugged. "She was one of my favorite teachers. I visit her from time to time."

Kyle took the paper, glanced at it, and tucked it into his shirt pocket. "Any word from your contact about the missing recordings?"

"No." Noah placed his hands on his hips. "He's doing a little more digging, but according to him the file was never there."

"As in nothing was deleted because it never existed?" Janey voiced the question that had been swirling in his brain.

"That's what he says." Noah shook his head. "I'm not sure what this means. I mean, on the one hand, I'm happy Brent seems to be in the clear, but then how did it land in dispatch? I can't imagine someone walked into the station and left an anonymous note. That would have been in the file."

"Hayden was the one to send you out to the scene, right?" Janey asked Kyle.

The wheels started turning in his head and he didn't like where they were spinning. "You think Hayden was somehow involved? That she knew where the body was and directed me to it?"

"I don't know, but right now all arrows seem to be pointing toward Heather Sanders. There've been too many clues that keep leading back to her."

"But we know, or at least believe, there's more than one person involved. Heather had a boyfriend at the time of the murders." Kyle paused as another thought crossed his mind. "Or could Hayden be involved in the murders as well?"

"Let's not jump to conclusions," Noah said. "All we have is conjecture at this point. We need proof. If I'm going to accuse a member of the community of murder, I need to be one hundred percent confident we have the right person."

Janey checked her phone before slipping it back in her pocket. "Let's go talk to this Mrs. Wheatman."

"Call me if you need anything. I know the sheriff over there and can call in a favor if I need to."

"Do you need me to patrol tonight?" Kyle asked, knowing Noah had to be burning the candle at both ends. He kind of felt bad for his friend.

"No. I want you to focus on finding whoever did this. I can manage with a couple less hours' sleep for a few days."

***

"What are you thinking so hard about over there?" Kyle asked as they drove down the highway.

"The case. We're missing a motive. Based on what the teen overheard, this wasn't a random killing, and we have to assume the others weren't either. If it was Heather Sanders, what prompted her to commit three murders?"

"Good question."

The rest of the drive was spent bouncing ideas off each other as to what motivation the killer might have. It was something she and Paul did on a regular basis. It helped to put them in the head of the perp and could sometimes point them in a direction they hadn't considered before.

Mrs. Wheatman's neighborhood was quaint. The streets were lined with small white homes and all the lawns were manicured. Some had flowerbeds or tiny gardens along the front.

They located the address the sheriff had given them and parked along the curb.

"Think she'll remember you?" Janey asked as they headed up the walkway.

"I guess we'll soon find out."

Kyle rang the doorbell and they waited.

Less than a minute later, they heard shuffling inside. Not long after that, the door opened to reveal a woman almost as tall as Janey with salt and pepper hair. She took one look at Kyle, smiled, and opened the door wide, inviting them inside.

"Kyle Reed. It's been a few years since I've seen you, young man. What have you been up to?" She glanced over at Janey. "And who is this lovely young lady you've brought with you?"

He ignored the first question and answered the second. "This is Janey. She's a detective from Indianapolis."

"A detective." Mrs. Wheatman looked Janey over once more. "Vice?"

It was a popular misconception. When she'd first joined the force, she'd been encouraged to work vice because of her looks. Apparently they thought she would be a good stand-in for a prostitute. Janey, however, had avoided those duties whenever possible. And once she'd passed her detective's exam, she'd pushed for homicide, not vice. She wanted to catch killers, not case drug dealers or pimps. "No, ma'am. I work homicide."

"Murder." Mrs. Wheatman shook her head as if trying to clear it. "That's a gruesome business."

Janey found she liked Mrs. Wheatman. The woman was direct, but not obnoxious. "Yes, it is."

"My brother spent twenty-five years as a patrol officer in St. Louis. He used to tell me stories." She led them into the living room. "Can I get you anything? I have coffee, tea, water…"

They both declined her offer and got down to business. Since this was someone Kyle knew from his school days, Janey sat back and allowed him to ask the questions. She was learning he was a pretty good detective. If he wanted the job, she was sure he could step into the open position at the sheriff's department with no problem. "I wish I could say we were here to visit, but we need your help."

Her brow furrowed and she tilted her head to the side as if considering a question he had yet to ask. She looked at Janey. "If you're a homicide detective, then that must mean you're here about a murder."

Janey didn't feel there was any reason to keep the information from her. "Three, actually."

Mrs. Wheatman's eyes widened. "There've been three murders? In Warren County?"

"No," Kyle assured her. "One in Warren County and two in Indianapolis. Which is why Detective Davis is here."

"Oh my." Mrs. Wheatman placed a hand over her heart.

Kyle gave her a minute to digest that information before he went on. "We have reason to believe someone that graduated from Liberty-Bass High School might be involved."

"You think one of my students is a murderer?" Her voice went up slightly on the last word. Janey understood. It was hard to wrap your head around the thought you might know someone who had taken a human life.

"Or might know who the murderer is." Again, Janey was proud of

Kyle. He was trying to ease her fears without lying. They didn't know for certain if the ring belonged to the murderer.

She nodded.

"I know it's been a while, but we have reason to believe the person we're looking for was in the same graduating class as my sister, Ava, and went to Bailon College. Do you recall which students applied to that college?"

"Let me see." She listed off several names, including the ones they already knew. "I'm sorry, but that's all I can remember. They should have a complete list at the school, though."

"Records requests take time, especially on minors, which is why we came directly to you." Janey grinned at Kyle, then turned her attention back to Mrs. Wheatman. "Sheriff Jenkins spoke very highly of you."

A proud, almost motherly glow came over her. "He comes by to see me every once and a while. I'm so pleased to see him doing well. Now all he needs is to find a good woman to settle down with."

Kyle shifted beside her and stood. "We won't take up any more of your time."

"It was no problem, dear. You stop by anytime."

"Thanks."

Mrs. Wheatman held out her hand to Janey. "It was very nice to meet you, Detective."

"You, too. And thank you again for the information."

They were on their way back to the vehicle when Janey's phone rang. It was Paul. "Davis," she said as she climbed into the SUV.

"Kyle with you? I found out some information I think you both should hear."

Janey glanced at Kyle. "He's here." She put the phone on speaker and placed it in the center console. "You're on speaker. Go ahead."

"I called Bailon College and spoke with someone in the administration office. She wouldn't tell me anything other than the men went to the school and were all part of the same fraternity." Kyle and Janey looked at each other as they digested this new bit of information. "When I pressed her on whether or not there had been any incidents with the fraternity during the years the victims were there, she got really nervous and said I'd have to put in an official records request."

"Do we know anyone in the police department up there?" Janey asked.

Kyle piped in. "If you don't, Noah probably does."

"I didn't, but Rollins does. He used to go to high school with one of the local deputies." The sound of papers being shuffled filled the air for a few seconds before Paul continued. "The fraternity in question is known for hosting rather large parties. Lots of beer, music. Typical frat stuff." He paused. "There've also been some rumors that some girls have been drugged."

"How is this not public record? These guys would've been adults." Kyle asked the exact question that was on the tip of Janey's tongue.

"No charges were ever filed." She could almost see Paul rubbing the back of his head through the phone. "I'm driving up there this afternoon to see if I can find out any more information."

"We'll meet you there."

Kyle wasted no time getting on the road. "You thinking what I'm thinking?"

"That these guys did something to whoever our murderer or murderers are back in college and they're now seeking revenge?"

He met her gaze for a long moment before turning his attention back to the road. "Yeah."

"It would make sense. If they really were drugging women and doing who knows what else, that would explain the brutal nature of the deaths."

Kyle's hands tightened on the wheel. "Why didn't they file charges?"

Janey shrugged. "It's hard to say. Some women don't feel like they can come forward. Or maybe they tried and something or someone stopped them from filing a formal complaint."

"You're right. The woman Paul talked to at the college knew something had happened, which means it's most likely known to the locals." He blew out a frustrated breath. "Is it always like this?"

"What?" she asked, not sure what he meant.

He thought about it for a minute. "I feel... conflicted. The cop in me says murdering someone is wrong and the person who did it needs to be brought to justice, but the man in me understands the need to do violence against these guys if they really did hurt who knows how many women. If someone had hurt Ava..."

Janey understood exactly what he was saying, and she was right there with him. "No. They aren't always like this. In fact, I've only had one other case in the last seven years that has left me wondering if catching the perpetrator was the right thing to do." She let her thoughts drift to one of the first cases she'd handled as a detective. "I'd been a detective for less than two months when Daniels and I were assigned to investigate a shooting outside a bar. The guy had been about to get into his car when he was shot five times and killed."

Kyle kept his eyes on the road, but she knew he was listening.

"It didn't take us long to track down who the shooter was." Janey swallowed as the memory of the arrest hit her as clear as if she was still standing in the woman's living room. "The man had been beating his wife. He'd get drunk and then come home and take out whatever his frustrations were on her. She didn't see another way out, so she drove to the bar, knowing what time he usually left, waited in the shadows, and while he was fumbling with his keys she shot him in the back."

"He never saw it coming," Kyle said.

Janey shook her head. "No. And since it was premeditated, it wasn't considered an act of self-defense. At least, as far as the law was concerned." The case still got to her. Even after all these years. "It was one of the hardest arrests I've ever made."

Kyle let out a loud breath, reached for her hand, and didn't let go for the rest of the drive.

CHAPTER 25

KYLE DROVE around the campus until he found a place to park. They were meeting Paul in the common area. It was a small college—only about five thousand students—so someone had to know something. Five years wasn't that long ago.

As they made their way across campus, he couldn't stop thinking about what Janey had told him. He'd been in several domestic situations and they were never easy. Emotions ran high and could get out of hand fast.

After hearing Janey's experience, he understood her deep desire to help Cindy Fisher. Janey had gone on to explain to him that the woman who'd killed her husband had been too poor to hire an attorney and ended up with a public defender. He'd had no sympathy for her situation and had pretty much let the defense eat her for lunch. She'd gotten the book thrown at her and was now serving a life sentence for first degree murder.

He'd heard the emotion in her voice as she talked. Janey wouldn't want the same fate to befall Cindy. Especially given there was a child involved as well. A child who would have to grow up without a mother if she was convicted of murder.

Kyle didn't want to think about the parallels there with Janey's upbringing. Granted, her mother hadn't been convicted of murder—at least as far as he knew—but that didn't change the fact that she hadn't been part of Janey's life. Luckily, Janey's grandmother had stepped in and raised her, as Kyle was sure Cindy's mother would do as well, but a child needed its mother. He was an adult by the time he lost his parents, but it still stung. He couldn't imagine being Sadie's age and faced with never seeing his parents again.

Paul and another man were waiting for them when they arrived. He was wearing a uniform similar to Kyle's, so he was guessing this was the local friend Paul had told them about. If he was here officially, hopefully that meant the local department was on board as well.

"You got here fast," Janey said to Paul.

"I was already on my way when I called." He offered his hand to Kyle. "Good to see you again."

"You, too."

"Janey, Kyle, I'd like to you to meet Kevin Berkley. He's lived around here his entire life and knows a lot of the locals, including a lot of the staff here."

They all shook hands.

"It's nice to meet you," Kevin said.

Kyle looked around the area. It was almost three o'clock and most of the students had disappeared inside the various buildings. "So what's the game plan?"

"I figured we could split up into two groups. We have a lot of ground to cover. Kevin and I are going to head over to the fraternity house and see what we can find. Janey and Kyle, why don't you start in the cafeteria? Kevin said there are several ladies there who've worked for the school over twenty years. Maybe they've heard something."

"We're probably more likely to get them to open up than we would someone in the administration office," Janey said.

Paul nodded. "Exactly."

Once their game plan was in place with the agreement to meet back there in one hour, Kyle and Janey walked the short distance to the cafeteria. They tried the door, but it was locked.

"Let's go around back. Maybe one of them is out taking a smoke break or something." Janey didn't wait for him to comment before she turned on her heels and marched toward the rear of the large brick building.

As soon as they turned the corner, he could smell the stink of rotting garbage and the sound of women talking. It looked as if they were in luck.

Three women were perched on crates in a semicircle. They all stopped talking when Kyle and Janey came closer.

"Hello, ladies," Janey said.

All they did was nod. Not exactly the friendly greeting they were hoping for.

Their cool demeanor didn't seem to bother Janey. "We were wondering if you ladies could help us with something."

No response. Not even a twitch.

Janey went on. "We're trying to find out about a fraternity. Delta Theta?"

One of the women snorted. "Aren't you a little old to be chasing fraternity boys?"

Another woman, this one a little younger than the first, maybe in her forties, chuckled. "Never too old to be doing that."

Janey grinned and pushed on with her questioning, not allowing the women to get sidetracked. "I've heard they throw some pretty wild parties."

"You could say that again," the first woman said. "Some of those boys could drink me under the table, and that's saying something."

"Lots of alcohol is usually a given at frat parties. Any drugs?" Janey asked.

The women sobered a little, taking in Kyle's uniform. He was wondering if maybe he should have changed before they came. "What are you two looking for?"

Janey waved her hand dismissively. "Just some rumors we're trying to clear up. Do you know anything that may have happened at that fraternity roughly five or six years ago?"

They were all quiet for a few moments as if contemplating what they should say. Finally, the oldest of the three women spoke up. She'd stayed silent up until then, letting her younger counterparts do the talking. "There's always talk."

The younger woman flashed a shocked look in the other woman's direction.

"Any idea who was involved?" Janey asked.

The oldest woman stood, kicking the crate she'd been using to the side. "We're just cooks. If you want information on that kind of stuff, you'll need to be talking to the people up at the main office." She turned to the other women. "Come on, ladies. We have dinner to prepare."

As the three women walked back into the building, the youngest one, the one who'd said there'd been some talk about the Delta Theta fraternity and drugs, hesitated for a second before following the other two into the building.

Once they were gone, Janey turned to Kyle. "We need to talk to her alone. She has something to say but is afraid to in front of the others."

He completely agreed. "What do you suggest?"

"Let's see if we can talk to a few other people and then meet up with Paul and Kevin. I have a feeling we're going to be hanging out here until after dinner, and then maybe we can catch her on her way home. Preferably without her entourage."

They spent the next half hour roaming the campus asking random people they ran into about Delta Theta. For the most part it was a waste of time. However, one of the students they'd spoken with happened to be a member of the fraternity. He'd been reluctant to talk to them at first until Kyle decided to take a different approach. He started talking to the guy as if he were one of his Army buddies, asking about the parties and the girls.

After that, the guy couldn't stop talking. They'd learned there was a party at the house at least once a week and that they tended to include binge drinking and lots of sex. He'd added that the parties were way tamer than they used to be, but they were still the best parties on campus. Unfortunately, he didn't know the reason behind the change.

By the time they parted ways with the guy, they were confident they were headed in the right direction with their original assumption. The fraternity was the link they'd been looking for. Now all they had to do was find out what incident had driven someone to murder years later.

Paul and Kevin hadn't arrived yet when Kyle and Janey returned to the designated meeting area, so they sat on a nearby bench to wait and do a little people watching. He was watching a couple of guys throwing a Frisbee when Janey cleared her throat. "You seem to know quite a bit about frat parties. Been to a lot of them?"

He turned his body so she had his complete attention, somewhat amused by her question. Was she jealous or merely curious? "Not a single one."

"Then how—"

Kyle chuckled. "Get a bunch of college-aged guys together, add a significant amount of alcohol, and you'll end up with a similar result." He rested his arm on the back of the bench. The urge to touch her was strong when she was so close, but he resisted. "Also, I've watched movies like *Animal House*."

"So you just made it up?"

"I didn't say that." He leaned in as if imparting a secret. "I never said I was a saint during my time in the Army."

A sly grin spread across her face. "Anything I should know about?"

He skimmed his fingers along her shoulder, unable to stop himself. "That depends."

"On?"

A throat cleared behind them. Kyle knew who it was without looking. He sat up, putting some space between them once more, and faced the new arrivals.

***

"Are we interrupting?" Paul stood a few feet away with a knowing smirk on his face. Janey couldn't believe she hadn't heard him and

Kevin approach. She was off her game. That wasn't good considering they were investigating a case.

She did her best to cover up her embarrassment. "Just waiting on you. Did you get anywhere with the fraternity?"

"Nothing concrete. A couple of the guys mentioned there'd been a crackdown by the dean several years ago after some of the parties had gotten too out of control. They didn't know the details—or said they didn't," Kevin said.

"What about you? Have any luck?" Paul still had a knowing grin on his face that Janey wished she could wipe off. The only thing that made her feel better was that the shoe had been on the other foot a time or two. Still, she needed to stay focused.

Janey recounted their conversation with the three women. "Kyle and I are going to hang around here for a few more hours and see if we can catch her before she heads home."

Paul nodded. "I want to stop by the dean's office before I head back to Indy. I doubt he'll tell us anything, but you never know." He checked his phone, probably to see the time. "I'll call the captain and give him an update on the way back."

"We'll let you know if we get anywhere with the cook," Janey said.

Kevin had been standing off to the side during the exchange. He handed Kyle one of his cards. "I'll be around tonight if you need some backup."

Kyle tucked the card into his shirt pocket. "Thanks."

They watched as Paul and Kevin walked toward the admissions building. Janey was hoping the woman tonight would be able to give them a name. She knew it was a long shot considering how long ago the incident would have happened, but this was a small town. People talked. She'd learned that much from Kyle. Hopefully, that meant their memories were long as well.

"Hungry?"

"What?" His question pulled her back to the present.

"Food. We have a couple of hours to kill. Might as well get some grub."

He was right. It was only four o'clock and dinner on campus was from five to six. Other than wandering around the campus, there wasn't much they could do until they closed the mess hall. "Know any local restaurants?"

Kyle held up his phone. "That's what the internet is for."

They ended up at a pizza place a few blocks from campus. It was small—only eight tables in the entire place—but the food was good. She'd had a lot worse during stakeouts.

"You ever go to college?" he asked before taking a bite of pizza.

Janey nodded. "I have a bachelor's degree in criminal justice." She reached for another piece of pizza. "What about you?"

"Nope. The Army was my education. I took a few classes at the local community college after getting back, but it wasn't for me. I get too antsy sitting in a classroom for hours on end. I'm more of a hands-on kind of guy."

"Yes, you are." She flashed him a flirty grin.

Kyle chuckled. "You're lucky we're in a public place right now or I'd give you a demonstration of just how hands-on I am."

Some of the uncertainty that had been nagging at her eased. She liked being with Kyle. He was fun and genuine and good at his job. In some ways he reminded her of Paul, and that wasn't a bad thing. Her partner was the best guy she knew. Until him, she didn't think there were men like that still out there. Lucky for her, Kyle was one of them.

After finishing their dinner, they moved their vehicle so it was parked in the closest lot to the dining hall. The spaces were marked 'reserved for staff,' but given it was after five a lot of the spaces had been vacated. They positioned themselves along the tree line so they'd have a good view of anyone entering or exiting the back of the building.

"So what do you and Paul normally do when you're on a stakeout?" Kyle asked after a few minutes of staring at the back of the building.

Janey shrugged. "Not much. We just talk and watch our surroundings. It isn't that exciting. In fact, most of the time it's downright boring."

"What's the longest one you've ever done?"

She thought back. "I think it was about ten hours."

"That's a long time to sit in a car," he said.

"You're telling me. My butt went numb."

Kyle laughed.

"I'm serious. It wasn't a pleasant experience."

He cleared his throat, trying to stop himself from laughing. "Well, if your ass goes numb on this stakeout, I'll do all I can to help make it better."

Without her permission, her sex clenched at thoughts of all the ways he could make it better.

She opened her mouth to give him a snarky reply when movement caught her eye. Two women emerged from the back of the building. A few seconds later, the door opened again and the third woman walked out.

The three women chatted as they made their way toward the parking lot. Two of them walked toward where Kyle and Janey were parked. The other, the one they needed to talk to, went in the other direction.

They waited until the other two women were in their vehicles before pulling out. Janey wondered if it would have been better to take an unmarked car since Kyle's patrol SUV stood out like a sore thumb, but it was too late to do anything about it.

By the time they made it to the other woman, she was behind the wheel of her car, and she didn't look happy to see them.

"Do you remember us from earlier?"

The woman looked at Janey as if she'd lost her mind. "I'm not senile. Of course I remember you."

"We were hoping to ask you a few more questions."

She looked around, probably wondering where her friends were. "I don't want any trouble."

"Why would there be trouble?" Janey asked. When the woman didn't answer, Janey decided to try a different tactic. "Is there somewhere else you'd rather talk?"

With that, the woman relaxed a little. "Can you follow me home? I only live about ten minutes from here."

"Lead the way," Kyle said, not hesitating. By the way this woman was acting, she knew something. Janey just hoped it was something that could actually help them.

They ended up following the woman to a two-story house about five miles outside town. She invited them in and hurried down the hall, leaving them to follow.

She stopped when they reached the dining room and flipped on the light. "Have a seat."

The room was packed with furniture and random boxes. Either the woman was in the process of moving, or she was a bit of a hoarder.

Janey and Kyle each pulled out chairs and sat down. "Thank you for agreeing to talk to us." Janey paused. "I'm sorry. We didn't get your name before."

"Paula," the woman said. "My name's Paula."

"It's nice to meet you, Paula," Kyle said, turning on the charm. "You have a lovely home."

"Thanks."

"How long have you worked at the college?" Janey asked.

Paula thought about it for a minute. "It'll be fourteen years in January."

"That's a long time. You must enjoy your job." Even though she wasn't a suspect, it was always good to get the person you were questioning comfortable, in Janey's experience.

"It's a job and the pay's good."

Janey smiled again, trying to put her at ease. "We were wondering if you could tell us about something that happened roughly five years ago."

Paula frowned. "This is about the fraternity."

"Yes," Janey said. "Do you remember anything involving the fraternity?"

Standing, Paula walked over to hutch along the wall and knelt to dig through the bottom of the cabinet. After a minute or so, she pulled out a stack of papers and brought them to the table. Paula flipped through half the stack before she pulled out the page she'd been searching for. "Is this what you're looking for?"

Janey's eyes scanned over the page. It was a printout of the school newspaper dated nearly six years ago. The headline read *Members of Delta Theta Accused*. The article went on to say that three female students had claimed they'd been drugged and sexually assaulted after attending a party at the Delta Theta house. The article was very vague and didn't give many details. The female students weren't named and neither were the fraternity members involved.

"Are there any other mentions of the incident in future issues of the paper?" Kyle asked. He'd been reading the article over Janey's shoulder.

Paula shook her head. "No. There were rumors flying around campus for a month or so after, but then everything sort of went away."

"Do you mind if we take this with us?" Janey asked. Things were starting to fall into place, and she didn't like where it was going. They needed to find out who the accusers were, who the men involved were, and why there was no other mention of it after this.

CHAPTER 26

It was a long drive back to Liberty. Janey called Paul and her captain to fill them in on the new information. Paul said he'd call Kevin in the morning and see if he could dig up anything more. Surely someone in law enforcement was contacted back then. Now that they had the timeframe pinpointed, they could narrow down who was involved and why it was apparently brushed under the rug.

Kyle unlocked the door to his house. He was glad to be home. More importantly, he was glad to be home with Janey at his side. While detective work wasn't really his thing, he was enjoying working with her. And he really liked having her in his bed at night.

"You hungry?" he asked.

Janey plopped down on the nearest chair. It had been a long day. "Starving."

"Pizza? Subs? Or I could pull something out of the freezer."

"I could do subs."

Not wasting time, he dialed Cap's Pizza and put their order in. "It'll be here in about forty minutes," he said after hanging up the phone.

She tilted her head to the side to stretch her neck muscles and rolled her shoulders. The latter move pulled her shirt tight against her breasts, causing his cock to pulse. It didn't matter that he was as tired as she was.

Moving to stand behind her, he placed his hands on her shoulders and began to massage her tight muscles. Her head fell forward and she hummed. "I could get used to this."

He knew her comment was in relation to being pampered, but he couldn't let it go. "I hope so."

Several seconds ticked by. He could feel the tension in her neck increase beneath his fingers. "What are you saying?"

This wasn't a time to mince words, so he didn't. "I think you should talk to Noah about the detective position here in Liberty." He paused, letting that sink in for a moment before he continued. "And I think you should move in here with me."

Janey stood and he let his arms fall to his sides. "You want us to move in together?"

No room for doubts. Not that he had any. "Yes, I do."

"We don't.. . I mean we haven't..." She stared at him as though he'd suggested she go join the circus.

He was prepared for this. She'd brought up the short time they'd known each other several times before. That didn't matter to him. When something was right, it was right. Time didn't change that. "You're concerned our relationship is too new."

"Yes." She said the word so fast he had to keep himself from laughing. "What if I give up my job, move my entire life up here, and you decide it isn't what you want?"

Kyle didn't miss that she'd said he would decide it wasn't what he wanted. He wished he could make her understand how he felt about her, but only time would do that. "Not gonna happen."

"How do you know that?" Before he could get a word in edgewise, she continued. "Things change. People change."

He closed the distance between them, placing his hands on her forearms. "I'm thirty-five years old, Janey. I'm not a teenager who doesn't know what he wants." Raising one hand, he traced his fingers along the line of her jaw. "I love you, Janey Davis. I know you're scared. I am, too, a little, but I know what I want—what I need in my life—and that's you."

The sound of her cell ringing broke through the intense emotions surrounding them. "I should get that."

As much as he hated it, she was right. He nodded and took a step back.

"Davis." Janey's voice wasn't quite as confident as it usually was.

A woman's voice came through the phone. He couldn't hear what she was saying, but he could hear the emotion and she sounded scared.

"Are you somewhere safe?" Janey asked.

That got his attention.

"Okay, where are you?"

Without being asked, he handed her a pen and paper he kept on the refrigerator.

Janey scribbled down the address. "I'll be there as soon as I can. You stay put, all right?"

There was a look of anger and determination in Janey's eyes when she hung up the phone. It only took a moment for him to put two and two together. "Cindy?"

She nodded. "This is the address she gave me." She handed him the paper. "Do you know where it is?"

"Yeah. Let's go."

They were halfway down the road before he remembered the subs. "Shit!"

Janey turned toward him. "What?"

Instead of answering her, he dialed Cap's. Luckily, he had the number in his phone. He was a frequent customer. "Hey, this is Kyle Reed."

"Hi, Kyle. Your subs are almost ready. Should be on their way soon."

"That's why I'm calling. I won't be there to get the delivery. I've been called out on police business." While it wasn't official, it still fell under police business. He was helping a woman being abused by her boyfriend.

"Did you want to cancel the order?"

"No." He shook his head even though he knew the man couldn't see him. "You've got my card on file. Go ahead and charge me for the subs, then you all enjoy them. I don't know how long I'll be."

"Are you sure?"

"Positive." He tossed his phone in one of the cup holders and continued driving toward the address Janey had written on the paper. It wasn't far, about twenty miles outside town.

"I'd completely forgotten about the food."

Kyle glanced over to Janey, who wore a grim expression. He knew she was worried about Cindy. She'd said her boyfriend had slapped her around. That could be anything from a few bruises to some broken bones. He knew all the scenarios were going through Janey's mind. They were going through his.

If she was ready to get out, though, they would help her. She needed somewhere safe to stay. Her mom's house wasn't an option. That would be the first place Keith would look.

They pulled up to the gas station ten minutes later. Cindy and Sadie were standing near the ice cooler, keeping to the shadows. When they exited his vehicle and moved closer, Kyle noticed Cindy's lip was busted and the area around her left eye was beginning to swell. She was going to have a black eye by morning.

Sadie was clinging to her mom's legs. Her eyes were wide as she huddled as close to her mother as possible. The fear on the little girl's face tore at his soul.

Cindy ran a comforting hand over her daughter's head. "Thank you. I didn't know who else to call."

"I'm glad you called me," Janey said, looking Cindy over and making her own assessment. "Are both of you all right?"

Cindy nodded even as tears began to form in her eyes.

Kyle made a split-second decision. He knelt so he was eye level with Sadie. "Do you like ice cream?"

Sadie nodded.

"Why don't you and me go inside and see if we can find some?"

He held out his hand, offering it to her, but she didn't budge.

"What's your favorite kind?" he asked, hoping if he got her thinking about it she'd be more willing to go with him.

"Strawberry." There was a slight tremble in her voice as she spoke.

Kyle rubbed his chin, pretending to be deep in thought. "Hmm. Strawberry's pretty good, but I'm not sure it beats out chocolate."

"Mommy likes chocolate." Sadie glanced up at her mom.

Cindy smiled at her daughter, the action pulling the skin around her busted lip. "That's right. I do."

Seeing his opening, he went for it. "Maybe we can find her some chocolate ice cream, too. I know when I'm having a bad day, ice cream always makes it better."

The little girl seemed torn. She wanted the ice cream, but she didn't want to leave her mom.

"It's okay," Cindy said. "Go get us some ice cream with Officer Reed. I'll wait for you right here."

Kyle stood and extended his hand again to Sadie.

This time she took it.

"We'll be back in a few minutes with the ice cream." As he strolled into the store with Sadie, he was already figuring out ways he could distract the little girl and keep her in the store as long as possible. Janey would need to get the whole story of what happened from Cindy, and he wanted to make sure she had plenty of time. Lucky for him, this convenience store had its own ice cream parlor with thirty flavors to choose from. He made it his mission to get Sadie to try each and every one.

***

Janey pushed all the emotions she was feeling to the back of her mind and went into detective mode. "Why don't we have a seat?"

There really wasn't a place to sit other than the curb, so they made do.

As soon as they were seated, Janey addressed the most pressing question. "Do you need medical attention?"

Cindy pressed her fingers to her lip. "No. I'll.. . I'll be okay."

Since Janey didn't see any other injuries besides the cut on Cindy's lip and her black eye, she let it go. They'd have to take photos for evidence later, but for now she wanted to get Cindy talking. "Can you tell me what happened?"

"Keith came home. He'd been over at one of his friends' houses and they'd been drinking." She paused. "He's not a bad guy, you know. I mean, when he's not drinking, he can be really sweet."

Janey had heard the story a million times. It didn't change anything. "What happened when he came home?"

"I was getting ready for bed. Sadie was asleep, and I was going to do a little reading." Cindy was quiet for a few moments. "I heard him come in the house. He was loud, and I was afraid he'd wake Sadie, so I whispered down the stairs that she was asleep so he'd know to be quiet."

The dread of what came next churned in the pit of Janey's stomach.

"When I saw his face, I knew I shouldn't have said anything. I tried to calm him down. Apologize. But..."

"But it didn't matter," Janey said.

Cindy shook her head.

Reaching out, Janey took hold of Cindy's hand. "What happened next?"

"He told me I needed to learn my place. That he worked hard to provide for me and Sadie." She gripped Janey's hand hard as she continued. "He slapped me across the face so hard I fell into the wall. He said that would teach me to talk back to him." Cindy sucked in a deep breath. "Then he dragged me into the bedroom, threw me down on the bed, and..."

Janey closed her eyes, steeling her own resolve before she asked her next question. "Did he rape you, Cindy?"

A muffled sob escaped her throat. "Yes. No. I mean, he's Sadie's father. My boyfriend. He—"

"That doesn't mean he can't rape you. If he forced you to have sex with him, then it was rape. It doesn't matter if you've willingly had sex with him in the past."

This time the tears flowed freely. Cindy hunched over and hugged her knees, and she let go.

All Janey could do was rub a hand along her back, trying to provide a little comfort. "We should get you to a hospital and have them do a rape kit."

Cindy shook her head. "No. I just... I feel like such a terrible mother." She wiped the tears from her cheeks.

"You're not a terrible mother."

Cindy didn't seem to believe her. "What am I going to do now?"

"Do you have a place to stay for a day or two?" Janey asked. "A friend or family?"

"Not really."

"What about your mom?" They'd met Cindy's mom a couple of days ago and she seemed nice enough.

"No. I don't want her to know. Not yet."

While Janey didn't completely agree with that, it wasn't her call. If Cindy didn't want to go to her mom's, maybe Kyle would have some ideas. He was always telling her how great small towns were.

The two women sat in silence for several minutes as the world went on around them. It was getting late, so there weren't that many people around, but every now and then someone would look their way. Janey ignored them. "Do you think they found the ice cream?"

Cindy glanced toward the entrance to the store and a tiny smile tugged at her lips. "I hope so. I could really use some chocolate ice cream right about now. Maybe an entire half gallon."

Janey chuckled. "You know, I worked in an ice cream shop in high school. My grandma told me I'd get sick of ice cream working around it all the time, but I still love it."

"I'm not sure it's possible to get sick of ice cream."

"Me either."

A few moments later, Kyle and Sadie came out of the store. Sadie was holding a round dish of ice cream with both hands, careful not to drop it. Kyle had a large container of what looked to be chocolate ice cream in one hand and a cone with two scoops of chocolate in the other. He handed the overflowing bowl to Cindy. "Two extra-large scoops of chocolate. Sadie insisted."

She stared down at the bowl for several moments before lifting the spoon to her mouth. "Thanks."

Kyle turned to Janey. "I figured we could share."

Janey raised her eyebrows in question. He just shrugged and held out the cone for her to take a bite. The whole thing felt out of place given why they were there.

She glanced over at Cindy and Sadie who were sitting on the curb, eating their ice cream. Sadie was filling her mom in on all the different flavors she and Kyle had tried.

"They need somewhere to go tonight," Janey said, taking the cone from Kyle.

He nodded. "Let me make a call."

Janey waited while he walked several feet away and took out his phone. She could hear him talking but didn't get more than bits and pieces of the conversation.

The ice cream was almost gone by the time he returned to her side. He bent down and took a large bite.

"Everything good?" she asked when he didn't say anything.

"Yeah. All's good." He took another bite of the cone. "Did you get what you needed from Cindy?"

"For the most part." Janey moved them farther away from Cindy and Sadie, not wanting the little girl to overhear. Once she was confident they were out of earshot, she filled him in on the details of her conversation with Cindy.

"I need to call Noah." Kyle looked over at the mother and daughter. "Do you think she's willing to press charges?"

"I think so. I didn't get the impression she wants to go back. Tonight scared her. Hopefully, it scared her enough for her to realize he's never going to change."

He popped the last of the cone into his mouth. "I'll get the paperwork rolling. Why don't you get them loaded up into the SUV so we can get going?"

It took a good ten minutes to get Cindy and Sadie, along with the stuff they'd brought with them, into Kyle's patrol vehicle. Kyle didn't want to bring Cindy's vehicle with them in case Clyde came looking for them. It was doubtful he would, at least tonight, but Janey agreed they didn't need to take any chances.

Shortly after they got back on the road, Sadie drifted off to sleep. She was still out when they pulled up in front of a log cabin in the woods.

"Wait here." Kyle got out and jogged up to the front door. After a few seconds, the door opened. A man stood in the entryway but Janey couldn't make out who he was from inside the vehicle. He and Kyle spoke briefly before Kyle returned to the SUV. "Let me help you get Sadie inside."

Cindy didn't argue. She was no doubt as exhausted as her daughter.

Kyle carried a sleeping Sadie into the cabin, and Janey and Cindy followed. The cabin was larger than it appeared on the outside. The main room was about the same size as her condo in Indianapolis.

Standing to the left of the large stone fireplace that dominated the living area was the man Janey had seen in the doorway. The first thing she noticed about him was the scar on one of his cheeks. It was about three inches long and curved, almost following the line of his jaw. The second thing she noticed was the look in his eyes. They were guarded as if he were gearing up to go into battle.

Kyle shifted the little girl in his arms, pulling her tighter against his chest. "Cindy, I'd like you to meet Austin Hughes. He and I served in the Army together."

Janey guessed that answered her question on how Kyle knew him. It most likely explained the scar as well. And the look in his eyes. She'd worked with officers who'd served in the military. Some brought the battle back home with them.

"The extra bedroom is all made up." Austin motioned toward the door behind him.

"I'll lay her down, and then we can go over everything." Kyle disappeared into the next room, leaving Janey, Cindy, and Austin standing in the living room.

Figuring this was as good a time as any, she motioned for Cindy to join her on the couch. "Are you sure you don't want to see a doctor?"

"I'm sure."

As if noticing Cindy's injuries for the first time, Austin jumped into action. He went to the freezer, pulled out a bag of frozen peas, and brought them wrapped in a dishtowel over to Cindy. "It'll help with the swelling."

"Thanks," she said, taking the bag and pressing it against the side of her face.

Janey waited until Kyle returned to the room, and then got down to business. "Cindy, we need to talk about pressing charges and what happens next."

Cindy winced as she touched her lip with the bag of peas. At least it wasn't bleeding anymore. "I don't want Sadie to grow up seeing her mom like this." She lifted her gaze to meet Janey's. "What do I need to do?"

CHAPTER 27

JANEY COULD BARELY KEEP her eyes open. It was well after midnight by the time they left Austin's house. They'd taken pictures of all Cindy's injuries and got her official statement. Given the hour and that she and her daughter were safe for the night, Noah had decided to wait until morning to make the arrest.

"Didn't you need to turn back there?" Janey asked.

Kyle glanced over at her and then back to the road. "I don't know about you, but I'm starving, and the only places open at this time of night are out by the truck stop."

Her stomach voiced its agreement. The ice cream cone they'd shared hadn't filled her up for long. "What are our options?"

"We can go into the truck stop and get something, or there's Taco Bell."

She wasn't sure she could stay awake long enough to sit through an actual meal. "Taco Bell works."

Five minutes later, Kyle maneuvered them into the drive-through and placed their order. Once they had their food, he pulled into a parking space.

Neither said much as they scarfed down their dinners. She wasn't even sure how much of hers she tasted. It was all about a means to an end. She was hungry and so she ate. But the fuller she got, the more the need for sleep took over.

"I'm hoping I can make it up the stairs to bed. I might just pass out on the couch," Kyle said.

Janey was too tired to laugh. "I know what you mean. I feel like I need toothpicks to keep my eyes open."

"It's been a long day."

She sighed. "Yeah, it has. But a productive one. We confirmed something happened at the fraternity." Their visit to the college felt like days ago, even though it was mere hours.

"Noah knows a lot of the county sheriffs. I'm sure someone knows something about it."

Darkness surrounded them as they drove down the two-lane road toward Liberty. "I wonder what triggered it?"

"Triggered what?"

It was difficult to form her thoughts into words, but she tried. For some reason, her mind wouldn't shut off even though her body was more than ready. "It's been years. Why now?"

He seemed to think about it for a moment, and she wondered if he was having the same problem she was. "I don't know. People get triggered by different things."

As they came into town, Janey noticed a large banner suspended above the street. She leaned forward to get a better look.

"It's for the Labor Day festival."

She sat back in her seat and looked around for any more additions to the downtown décor but didn't see anything. It was dark apart from the few streetlamps. The moon was hiding behind a blanket of clouds.

"The banner's the first thing that goes up," he said, turning onto the street that led to his house. "Tomorrow they'll add banners to the light posts for the parade. Everything else takes place in the park."

He pulled into his driveway and turned off the engine. "I didn't think we'd be gone this long or I would have turned the porch light on before we left."

It took a lot more effort than it should have to climb out of the vehicle. She yawned as they made their way toward the side door that led to his kitchen. Kyle's bed was calling her name.

His hand was on the doorknob when Janey saw something out of the corner of her eye. If she hadn't been so tired, her reaction time would have been much faster.

Janey felt the sting of the Taser graze her arm, jolting her awake. She rolled in the opposite direction of the threat, needing to put some distance between her and whoever her attacker was.

As soon as she was on her feet again, she reached for her weapon. The only things she could see were shadows, but that was enough. Three petite figures stood less than four feet away from her. Two of them held what she assumed were Tasers.

The third figure held something long and slender over their head as they stood above Kyle, who was lying unmoving on the ground.

Janey's adrenaline kicked up as she pointed her gun at the most immediate threat. Understanding of the situation and who'd been waiting for them crystalized in her brain. "Drop the weapons. All of you."

They all froze, but none of them followed her command.

"Drop your weapons," Janey demanded again as she stood.

She needed backup, but there was no way she was dividing her attention with three armed suspects standing in front of her and the man she loved on the ground.

The two with the Tasers let them fall to the ground.

Two down. One to go.

Janey focused her attention on the suspect still holding their weapon, keeping the other two in her peripheral vision. "I won't tell you again. Drop the weapon."

Instead of following Janey's orders, the shadowy figure followed through with her original goal. With as much force as they could muster, they lowered the object toward Kyle's head.

Visions of the three victims' skulls being cracked open filled Janey's mind. She took aim at the suspect and moved her finger to the trigger, ready to take her shot.

***

Kyle had been aware of the scene going on above him from the moment he heard Janey yell her first command for their attackers to drop their weapons. His head was spinning a little, but he wasn't completely out of it. Not anymore anyway. The initial jolt had knocked him on his ass for a few seconds, but with each moment that passed he was feeling more like himself.

He tilted his head up so he could get a better look at the person above him. It was a woman. He could tell that much. And by the set of her shoulders and the way she was gripping the bat in her hands, she was thoroughly pissed off.

Yeah, well, he wasn't feeling all that happy-go-lucky himself.

When Janey gave her third order to the woman standing above him to drop her weapon, he knew he was going to have to act. He saw the bat come toward his head and took evasive action.

Swinging his legs out, he hit the side of the woman's knee with as much force as he could muster, knocking her off balance. She let out a squeal as she fell backward and landed on the ground with a muffled thump.

Kyle scrambled to his feet and lunged for the woman.

"You got her?" Janey yelled from several feet away.

"Yeah." It was then Kyle realized that the other two suspects had taken off. Janey raced after them.

"Get off me!" She was fighting him. Normally it wouldn't be an issue. She was no match for him physically. However, she hadn't just endured being tased.

It took a little more effort than it should, but he flipped her onto her stomach and reached for his handcuffs. "Stop resisting."

"Never, you pig."

Once he had her secured in cuffs, he reached for his radio. "This is Deputy Reed. I need all available units to my home. I have one in custody, and Detective Davis is in pursuit of two others on foot."

"Copy. Units are being dispatched to your location."

Kyle shook his head, trying to clear it, before rocking back on his heels and flipping the woman over. He kept one hand on her and reached for the flashlight on his belt. She turned her head away from the bright light, but it didn't matter. Even with her black clothing and her hair tucked under a baseball cap, there was no hiding it was Heather Sanders.

"Get up." He went to grab one of her arms and she tried to pull away from him. "It's over, Heather. Roll onto your side and let's get you on your feet."

He clipped his flashlight back to his belt as he helped her up. Even still, he could feel the daggers she was shooting his way. Her demeanor was a far cry from how she'd acted at the diner.

Once she was on her feet, Kyle stopped to listen for any signs that Janey was nearby, but he couldn't hear anything but sirens in the background. He knew Janey could handle herself, but that didn't make it any easier for him to stay with Heather while his girlfriend was out chasing two other suspects through his neighbors' backyards. The only thing that made him feel a little better was that the two Tasers they'd used were still lying on the ground where they'd dropped them. That didn't mean they didn't have other weapons on them, though, and that's what weighed on his mind as he waited for backup to arrive.

Kyle had just gotten Heather situated into the back of his patrol vehicle when another deputy pulled up in front of his house. Ethan had barely gotten out of his vehicle before Kyle ordered him to stay with Heather while he went in search of Janey and the two other suspects. He knew at least one more deputy was on their way, and most likely Noah, but he wasn't waiting for them to arrive. He jumped the fence behind his house and took off through his neighbor's backyard, keeping an eye out for any signs of Janey or the suspects.

***

Janey had no idea how far they'd come or whose yard they were in. She'd followed the two suspects through several backyards and across a road. She was pretty sure the sheriff's office had a K-9 unit and she was hoping they were on their way. It would make a search like this go faster.

And it would be a lot safer. The danger of tracking two suspects in the dark through a residential area was at the forefront of her mind. She had to be alert. Even though they'd left their Tasers behind, that didn't mean they didn't have any other weapons. Besides, she'd passed more than a few shovels that could easily bash someone's head in.

The sound of a dog barking in the next yard over drew her attention and she headed in that direction. Her heart was racing both from the adrenaline and the distance they'd traveled in a short amount of time. She needed to find her suspects.

"Shh." The female voice stood out in the quiet of the night.

Janey crept in that direction, her weapon drawn, making sure not to get tunnel vision. She needed to protect her back since there was no one else to do it at that moment.

As she drew closer, Janey could make out a small figure huddled under a wooden deck. She scanned the nearby bushes for the second suspect but didn't see any movement. The situation made her uneasy, but there wasn't anything she could do about it.

She pointed her firearm under the deck, straight at the person trying to make themselves as small as possible. "Come out and keep your hands where I can see them."

Silence.

"Now!"

A branch snapped under the deck as the suspect crawled out. "Please, don't shoot me."

It was a woman's voice. One she didn't recognize. As curious as Janey was, the person's identity wasn't important right now. "Lay face down on the ground and place your hands on your head."

The woman lowered herself onto her stomach and followed the instructions she'd been given. Janey wasted no time taking her into custody and reading the woman her rights. She helped her to stand and turned her around so Janey could get a look at her.

The woman looked to be in her mid-twenties. She wore no makeup and had her sandy blond hair tucked into a knitted cap. Her wide eyes looked innocent enough. No doubt they had gotten her out of a lot of trouble in the past. That was unlikely to happen this time around. Assaulting a police officer was a serious offence, and if the three turned out to be the ones who'd murdered those three men, it was likely they'd be looking at attempted murder as well.

Janey took one look around the immediate area and was about to walk her suspect out front to the street when she heard someone running toward them. She placed her hand on her sidearm and waited to see who emerged from the bushes.

It was Kyle. A rush of happiness flooded through her at seeing him. She'd taken off after the two suspects before she could be sure he was really okay.

As much as she wanted to run into his arms, she knew they had a job to do. There'd be time later to express her feelings for him. "I've got this one."

Kyle seemed as torn as she was, but eventually he nodded. "I'll keep searching. The K-9 unit is on its way."

He took off through the bushes into the next yard while Janey walked the woman she had in custody to the street in front of the house. "Sit down and cross your ankles in front of you."

The woman sat on the curb as instructed. Janey counted her blessings that the woman was cooperating.

Keeping an eye on her suspect, she pulled out her cell and dialed Sheriff Jenkins's number. It was the only local one besides Kyle's she had in her phone.

"Where are you?" He'd obviously been briefed on the situation, either by dispatch or by Kyle.

Luckily, the house the woman had chosen as a hiding place was near a crossroads. She rattled the names on the street signs to the sheriff. "I have one in custody. Deputy Reed is still in pursuit of the third suspect."

"I'll be there in two."

He disconnected and Janey had no choice but to stand in the middle of the street waiting for the cavalry.

***

Kyle was about to give up when he heard a mumbled "ouch" coming from a couple of houses over. It was almost two in the morning, so the odds were pretty good it was his suspect.

He rounded the corner to see a petite figure bent over, looking at their leg. Moving into position, he drew his weapon. "Put your hands where I can see them."

The suspect's head whipped around to stare at him for a split second before they took off. Even as tired as he was and after having been tased, he caught up to them easily. He closed in on them and pounced, tackling them to the ground.

"No."

He ignored the woman's muffled protest and swiftly got her cuffed. Rolling her over, he took his first good look at who he'd been chasing—who'd tried to kill him and Janey.

Nothing could have prepared him for who he saw staring back at him.

Hayden.

The young woman who'd smiled and flirted with him for the past year.

He wanted to tell himself that it was all Heather's fault. That she had to have put Hayden up to it, but it didn't matter. Even if it had been her sister's idea, Hayden had gone along with it. She'd willingly participated.

"Come on," he said, getting them both to their feet.

"Please. I didn't want to hurt you. Heather said we had to."

Knowing what he had to do, Kyle blocked out her pleas and read Hayden her rights as they made their way to the street.

Backup, including Breaker, one of the county's K-9's, arrived a few minutes later. Breaker's handler, Seth Russell, took possession of Hayden, patted her down, and placed her in the back of his vehicle until another unit showed up.

"You need a medic?" Seth asked. "You're looking a little pale."

Kyle shook his head. "Nothing a little sleep won't cure. It's been a long day."

"Missing patrol, are you?" Now that the danger was over, they could all relax a little.

"Something like that."

Two more patrol vehicles, Noah in his personal vehicle, and EMS pulled onto the street, their lights flashing. Lights had been turned on in some of the nearby houses, and a few people were gazing out their windows. With the additional vehicles, there was little doubt people would be venturing outside soon to get a closer look.

His boss and longtime friend marched toward him with a frown on his face. "You okay?"

"Yeah, I'm good." Kyle looked over Noah's shoulder. "Where's Janey?"

"She's at the crime scene with Ethan watching our other two suspects." The last word trailed off as he noticed who was sitting in the back of Seth's patrol vehicle.

Kyle knew what he was feeling. Or at least, he could relate to what he was feeling. "I'm guessing she knows why we couldn't find a phone record of the call she took." He paused. "If there ever was one."

"Nothing would surprise me at this point." Noah took in the entire scene. "Russell, you got this under control?"

"Yes, sir."

Noah nodded and turned his attention back to Kyle. "Let's get you back to your place. We need a statement from both you and Detective Davis."

Now that the surge of adrenaline was leaving him, all Kyle wanted to do was sleep. Correction: What he wanted to do was curl up in his bed with his arms wrapped around Janey.

He knew that wasn't going to happen, though, for at least another hour. Statements had to be taken while they were fresh, and the crime scene needed to be processed. They'd be lucky if they made it to sleep before sunrise.

CHAPTER 28

IT WAS WELL after sunrise before Janey and Kyle made it back home and into bed. After all the evidence was collected from the scene, they'd gone to the station, wanting to be there when Heather, Hayden, and the other suspect, who turned out to be a woman by the name of Christy Manning, were interrogated.

Heather had refused to answer any questions, demanding a lawyer almost immediately. Hayden, on the other hand, sang like a bird. She'd confirmed that there'd never been a call to dispatch the morning Kyle discovered the body along Butler Road. According to her, the whole thing had been orchestrated by Heather as a means of revenge. Hayden even showed Noah a text she'd received from her sister telling her where she'd dumped the body and to send a deputy out. Hayden swore, however, that tonight was the first time she'd helped her sister try to hurt anyone.

The woman neither of them had known before tonight, Christy Manning, spent most of the time crying. It had taken quite a while to get her to calm down enough to get anything out of her. When they did, though, the entire story unfolded.

She'd been Heather's roommate at college. They'd become best friends and did everything together. Everything except go to a party at the Delta Theta house the night Heather was gang raped by three guys.

Christy said she hadn't been feeling well that night, so she'd stayed in her dorm. She, or maybe it was Heather, convinced herself that if she had gone that night Heather wouldn't have been raped. The guilt was what had led her to participating in the murders of the three men Heather claimed had assaulted her.

Once all three women had been booked, Janey and Kyle had decided to tag along with Noah and Ethan as they went to arrest Keith. They wanted to be there early, hoping to catch him before he was fully awake and had come to the realization that Cindy and Sadie were gone.

By the time all that was finished and Janey had called both Paul and her captain to give them an update of the situation, Kyle had driven them back to his house and they'd crawled into bed utterly exhausted. Janey didn't even remember taking off her shoes, although when she woke up several hours later they weren't on her feet.

As she became aware of her surroundings, she heard movement in the hall and sat up. A second later, Kyle strolled into the bedroom wearing nothing but a pair of jeans slung low on his hips. Her sleep-addled brain warred with the ache in the pit of her stomach as she took in how sexy he was.

"I thought you might need some coffee." It was only then she noticed the two mugs in his hands and the tempting aroma coming out of them.

Janey hummed and reached for the steaming cup of liquid caffeine.

He took a seat next to her on the bed, the mattress dipping beneath his weight. "I called Noah. The judge denied bail."

Her brain was slowly waking up. "I'm not surprised given the seriousness of the crime and that they tried to murder two police officers."

They sat sipping their coffee for several minutes, letting the caffeine do its thing. She'd pulled a few all-nighters as a detective, but she'd never felt quite as drained as she did this morning. Or was it this afternoon?

Glancing at the clock beside his bed, the numbers read four twelve. Since the sun was still high in the sky, she had to assume that meant it was four o'clock in the afternoon. She'd slept longer than she'd thought.

"Paul called about an hour ago. I didn't want to wake you, so I answered it."

She was surprised to realize that his answering her phone didn't bother her. If any guy she'd dated in the past had done that, she wouldn't have been happy and would have made it clear that next time he should let it go to voice mail. "Did he need something?"

"Not really. He just wanted to let you know he, Megan, and Chloe were driving up tomorrow for the Labor Day festival."

Janey quirked an eyebrow at him. "They're coming up for the festival?"

He shrugged. "That, and I think he wants to get a look at Heather, Hayden, and Christy himself." Kyle took a slow sip of his coffee and met her gaze with a glint in his eye. "Is your partner a bit of a control freak?"

She nearly spat out her coffee. "Just a bit."

Kyle smiled. He took another drink of his coffee before focusing on some unknown object across the room. "I'd like for you to move in with me."

While she knew they'd visit this subject again, she'd hoped she'd have more time. She wasn't sure why. Maybe because it would be a huge change. But after what had happened last night, how she'd felt seeing him on the ground and knowing he was about to be hit over the head with a baseball bat, had made her realize how much she wanted him in her life. The question she really had to ask herself was if she was ready to leave her life, her job, in Indianapolis and move to Liberty.

She set her mug on the nightstand and placed a hand on his cheek.

He turned to face her. His eyes were guarded as if he was bracing himself for her rejection. Her heart squeezed in her chest as if there was a vise grip surrounding it. He was putting himself out there, leaving himself vulnerable. No man had ever done that for her. Not even close.

"I love you," she whispered.

He covered her hand with his, leaning into it. "But?"

Janey smiled and scooted closer. "No buts. You're right. If we want to try and make this relationship work, one of us has to move, and I doubt you'd be happy in a big city like Indianapolis."

Lowering their hands, he rested them on his leg, playing with her fingers. Little sparks of energy raced up her arm. She was awake now, which meant her libido was waking up as well. They'd been so busy the last couple of days that they hadn't been intimate. She missed that connection as they came together.

The direction of her thoughts almost made her miss what he said next. "I understand this would be a big step for you, and I don't want you to do it if you're not ready, but I didn't want there to be any misunderstanding. I want you with me. Whether that's here or in Indianapolis."

Closing the distance between them, Janey pressed her lips to his, giving him a soft kiss before meeting his gaze. "I'll talk to Sheriff Jenkins."

She didn't need to elaborate on what she meant. He knew.

A slow grin tugged at his lips until it was a full-blown smile. "He'll hire you in a heartbeat."

Although he was probably right, nothing was set in stone. She wasn't sure the fact she and Kyle had almost died the night before would be a glowing mark on her resume. "I'm sure my captain won't be happy. And even if I do get hired, I'll have to give notice, so it won't be right away."

He threaded his fingers in her hair. "I'll try to be patient."

Her chuckle was cut off by his kiss. She melted into it. Kyle dipped his tongue between her lips and tangled it with her own, tasting and teasing. She gripped his shoulders, pulling him closer, needing to feel more of him.

As their kiss grew more intense, he shifted, and she realized he was putting his coffee on the nightstand next to hers. A second later, his other hand was on her hip, lifting her higher on the bed.

He followed, his body covering hers as they continued to kiss. She ran her hands over the muscles in his back and shoulders, feeling them flex has he hovered over her.

Suddenly he stopped and held himself above her.

She blinked. "What is it?"

"Maybe you should call him now. Why wait?"

It took her lust-filled mind a moment to realize what he was talking about. "Because," she said as she pulled his mouth back down to hers, "I'm a little busy at the moment and I don't plan on us leaving this bed anytime soon."

As if to drive home her point, she slid her hand down to cup his erection. A low moan rumbled from deep in his chest. "You're right. It can wait."

***

They did make it out of bed later that evening. Noah stopped by to check on them and to give them an update. Heather and Hayden's father had almost gotten himself arrested when he'd stormed into the station earlier, demanding his daughters be released.

Now that they knew who had committed the murders, it was just a matter of filling in all the pieces of the puzzle. The judge had issued a search warrant for the Sanderses' home, barn, and the horse trailers, considering both Heather and Hayden's love of horses and the hours they spent around them. They'd also gotten a search warrant for Christy's residence in Indianapolis, even though they didn't really expect to find anything.

All the evidence pointed to Heather and it was only confirmed by what they'd found on her computer. From the looks of it, she'd stalked the three men for at least six months, tracking their movements, finding out the places they frequented. They were pulling her bank records to see if they could place her in proximity of the crimes on the dates in question, but Kyle had little doubt they'd find the evidence they needed. It was only a matter of time.

Janey sauntered into the living room and plopped herself onto the couch beside him. Kyle raised his arm and tucked her into his side. They'd taken a shower not long before Noah had shown up. Luckily, he'd called to give them a heads-up he was coming. Otherwise, Kyle wasn't sure what his friend would have interrupted.

It was a nice shower, too. For once, neither of them had anywhere they needed to be, and they took advantage of it. He still had the image fresh in his mind of the water sliding down her breasts and belly before it disappeared between her legs. Just thinking about it had him needing to adjust himself.

"You comfortable?"

He kissed the top of her head. "Nowhere else I'd rather be."

Janey laughed. "You're so cheesy sometimes."

"You like cheese," he said as he brushed his lips along her ear.

He heard her suck in a breath a moment before she turned her head and met his gaze. "Yeah, I do."

Accepting the invitation. Kyle pulled her lips to his, cradling the back of her head.

She wasted no time climbing onto his lap, straddling him. "I asked Noah about the job while he was here."

Kyle's heart rate increased as he waited to hear more. It almost felt as if his entire future hung in the balance. "And?"

Janey threaded her fingers through his hair, sending tingles down his spine and straight to his groin. They'd already made love twice since waking up, but that didn't matter. He wanted her again. He would always want her.

The look on her face was somber and serious. Had Noah told her he didn't think she'd be a good fit for the position?

He was already running through all the arguments in his head to try and convince his friend that hiring Janey to be their detective was a good idea. Great, even.

"Well..."

The suspense was killing him.

"He said he'd need to talk to my captain, but the job is mine if I want it."

"You little minx." Kyle reached for her sides and started tickling her.

She cracked up laughing, trying to get away from him.

"You enjoyed torturing me, didn't you?"

"Yes," she choked out between bouts of laughter. "You should... have seen... your face."

Flipping her over, he pinned her beneath him, her arms stretched overhead. The position lifted her breasts higher, drawing his attention.

Janey felt the shift in his mood and arched her back, tempting him more. He adjusted his grip so he could hold both her wrists in one of his hands. The sweetest sound left her lips as he rubbed his thumb over her nipple. His cock jumped in response.

"I'm going to make love to you now." He continued to run teasing circles over her nipple but made no move to take things further.

"Touch me."

A wicked grin crossed Kyle's face. "I am touching you."

She made a frustrated sound. "I need more. Touch me more."

"Like this?" He trailed his hand down her torso to her hip, and then ground his pelvis against her.

"Yes. More."

Kyle chuckled as he pushed her shirt up, exposing her stomach, and lowered his mouth to the skin right above her waistband. "You're so sexy."

She twisted in his hold, but he held firm. "I want to touch you."

He shook his head, letting the tips of his hair tickle and tease her belly. "Not yet."

Her frustrated sigh changed to one of longing when he popped the button on her shorts and slipped his hand inside. It was a sound he'd never get tired of hearing from her. He couldn't wait to have her here with him every day.

The way her breath hitched as she climbed higher toward her

climax had his cock straining for release. He ignored it, though, and concentrated on getting her there.

It didn't take long before Janey's eyes rolled back in her head a moment before she fell over the edge. Her face and neck were flushed and her chest was heaving as she tried to catch her breath. It was a beautiful sight to see.

She met his gaze and he couldn't keep the smug look off his face. "Is it your turn now?"

He released her hands and brought his face down to an inch above hers. She combed her fingers through his hair, holding him to her.

Kyle shook his head and brushed his lips against her mouth. "Tonight's about you, baby. I know moving here is going to be a big step for you, so I want you to have plenty of"—he dug his fingers into her ass and ground her against his erection—"*incentives* to remember when you go back to Indy."

She snaked an arm around his waist and lowered her hand to his backside. Without any pretense, Janey sunk her nails into his ass and pulled his lips down to hers. The mix of pain and pleasure went right to his cock. Then again, just about anything she did had that effect on him.

Her breath ghosted against his lips as she pressed her mouth to his in the barest of touches. A complete contrast to her nails digging into his flesh.

Janey held his gaze, a look of wicked promise in her eyes. "Something tells me I'm going to like Liberty just fine."

Kyle knew she would love Liberty. He'd make sure of it.

EPILOGUE

"That's the last one," Kyle said, walking into the house, carrying another box.

"I can't believe this is all mine." Janey had lived in her condo for a little over five years. She didn't think she'd accumulated a lot of stuff, but the stacks of boxes sitting in Kyle's living room said different. "It's gonna take me weeks to go through all this."

He came up behind her and wrapped his arms around her waist, pulling her flush against him. "It's a big house and we have plenty of time."

"True." She twisted in his embrace and circled her arms around his neck. The feel of his mouth against hers as their lips met in a slow kiss still sent tingles all the way down to her toes.

"Knock, knock." Ava's voice rang out, announcing her arrival. "Are you both decent?"

Kyle rolled his eyes at his sister.

Janey chuckled, gave him another peck on the lips, and dropped her arms. "We're in here."

Ava entered the room a moment later carrying a plate piled high with goodies. Cole trailed behind her with a toy truck in his hand. "I brought you some cookies. I figured you might like a little treat for when you're unpacking boxes. I remember how tedious that can be."

"Thanks, Ava." Janey took the offering and placed the plate of cookies on the coffee table next to a bowl she'd unpacked earlier.

"I wanted to make sure you were still coming to dinner tomorrow."

"Of course," Kyle said, lifting Cole into his arms. "There's no way I'd turn down one of your Thanksgiving dinners."

Janey's heart did a little flip every time she saw Kyle with his nephew. The longer they were together, the more she'd been thinking about them having a family one day. She knew it wouldn't be easy, not with both of them being law enforcement.

"I'm gonna see if we have some milk to go with those cookies," Kyle said before disappearing into the kitchen with Cole on his hip.

"You two thinking about having one of your own?" Ava asked once she and Janey were alone.

"Not really." Janey shot Ava a nervous grin. "I mean, maybe. Eventually."

Ava nodded. "He'll make a wonderful father."

Of that Janey had no doubt. "I know."

She cleared some space for her and Ava on the couch, and they sat and talked while Kyle and Cole were in the kitchen.

"Did you get everything finalized with your condo?"

Janey had spent almost every waking hour she wasn't working for the last month showing her condo to potential buyers. It was exhausting, but eventually the hard work had paid off. "Yep. All the paperwork's signed. Paul is going to meet them later today to hand over the keys."

"I'm glad it all worked out. I know you were worried you'd have trouble selling it."

It had caused her a few sleepless nights. "Everything worked out the way it was supposed to."

"Yes, it did." Ava smiled. "Oh, I ran into Cindy Fisher at the store the other day. She said she and her daughter are settling into their new apartment."

"Yeah, Kyle stopped by to check on her the other day. He said she seemed to be doing well."

Ava nodded. "I'm just glad the trial's over and her boyfriend's going to be spending some time behind bars."

Not enough, in Janey's opinion. He got three years—less with good behavior.

"She mentioned her mom was out of town visiting her sister, so I invited her and Sadie to join us for Thanksgiving dinner tomorrow."

"That was really nice of you." Janey wasn't surprised Ava had extended an invitation to Cindy. That was the type of person Ava was.

From there the conversation turned to Christmas. They were making plans to go shopping together when Kyle and Cole returned to the living room.

"Everything all right?" Ava asked when both of them remained unusually quiet.

"Yep." Kyle had a shit-eating grin on his face that told her he was up to something.

Cole giggled and climbed on his mom's lap.

"What are you two up to?" Ava asked.

"Remember what we talked about," Kyle said to Cole.

His nephew pressed his lips together and nodded.

Janey raised her eyebrows, but Kyle either didn't see or he ignored her silent question.

"You need us to bring anything for tomorrow, sis? I can swing by the store and pick up some pop or wine."

"Just yourselves. I've got everything prepped. The turkey will go into the oven tonight and I'll finish everything else off tomorrow."

Janey felt as if she should be doing more to help. Ava had done so much to help with her transition to Liberty, including driving down to Indianapolis with Kyle to help them clean her condo from top to bottom before she put it up for sale. "Did you need us to come early to help with anything? I may not be a great cook, but I can chop and mix with the best of 'em."

Ava chuckled. "It's fine. Really. I made all the casseroles and pies this morning. All that's left to do is pop the casseroles in the oven to bake and add the dressing to the salads."

"You're so organized. I don't know how you do it," Janey said.

"Baking's easy." Ava shifted Cole so he was standing on her legs in front of her. He was getting restless. "I don't know how you two do what you do."

They sat and talked for several more minutes until Ava decided she'd better go before Cole had a meltdown.

Ava hugged her brother goodbye before turning to Janey. "I'm so glad you're finally here. Officially." Then she pulled Janey in as well. Kyle's sister was a hugger and it was taking Janey some time to get used to it.

Alone once more, Kyle and Janey began working through the mountain of boxes she'd brought with her. The sad part was she'd slowly been bringing items to his house over the last few months and she still had at least thirty boxes worth of stuff to find homes for. It was going to take a while.

***

The next morning, Janey woke up to Kyle kissing his way up her spine. It tickled a little, but more than that, it had all her female parts sitting up and taking notice.

"Good morning," he mumbled against her skin.

"Hmm. Morning." She stretched her arms out in front of her, not wanting to do anything to divert his current trajectory. "What time do we have to be at your sister's?"

"Not for a few hours yet."

Janey yawned, making sure to exaggerate it for effect. "Good. That means I can catch up on my beauty sleep."

He slid his arm around her waist and inched his hand up her torso until he zeroed in on her breast. "I had something else besides sleep in mind."

She couldn't stop the moan that escaped her throat when his fingers began massaging her flesh in the most delicious way. He'd gotten to know her body well and knew what she liked. It didn't help, of course, that neither one of them was wearing a stitch of clothing.

Still, she wasn't going to make this easy on him. "I suppose we could cuddle."

Kyle responded by pinching her nipple at the same time as he grazed his teeth along the sensitive skin of her neck.

Her eyes rolled back in her head and she felt the space between her legs warm.

"This is our last day off before we both head back to work. I plan on making the most of it." Kyle rolled her onto her back and hovered over her. "Any objections, Detective?"

Without any conscious thought on her part, Janey's legs parted, making room for him between them. She pulled his face down to hers. "Not a single one."

***

Somehow, they managed to make it to his sister's on time. Kyle was ridiculously happy. He was sporting a goofy grin and he didn't even care.

That smile slipped a little when they walked into Ava's kitchen to find Noah seated at the table, playing with Cole. He hadn't noticed his friend's vehicle out front.

"Hey," Noah said when he noticed them. "I came over to see if your sister needed any help with dinner, but she insists she's got it taken care of, so I offered to keep Cole out of her hair."

Kyle glanced over at his sister but didn't say anything.

Janey must have picked up on his discomfort. She gave his hand a squeeze before going to take a seat across from Noah and Cole. "We offered to help, too, but she insisted she had it all under control."

"*She's* right here," Ava said, sending a glare in their direction over her shoulder as she continued chopping carrots.

In an effort to change the subject and to get his mind off the reasons why Noah was there more than an hour before dinner was supposed to be on the table, he ambled over to stand next to his sister and plucked a carrot from her pile.

She batted his hand away.

He popped the carrot in his mouth and gave her a kiss on the cheek. "Are you sure we can't do anything to help?"

"I'm sure." She glanced over again at her son. "Cole wanted to go out and see the chickens earlier, but I haven't had time."

"Say no more." Kyle pushed himself away from the counter. "Want to go check on the chickens?"

Cole practically jumped off Noah's lap. "Chickens!"

They call chuckled.

Janey joined Kyle and Cole as they headed out to the chicken coop. The basic structure was there when his sister had bought the place, but she'd made quite a few improvements. While Janey and Cole watched the chickens, Kyle did a quick inspection of the rainwater collection system his sister had designed. It was quite impressive and seemed to be working well.

They hung out at the chicken coop for a while, and then walked over to the barn where Ava kept all her gardening supplies. Janey had never been out there, and she was fascinated by his sister's extensive collection of all things gardening related. He honestly wasn't sure there was a tool she didn't own.

Eventually, though, it was time to go back inside. "You ready to go in?" he asked Cole. "Your mom will have dinner on the table soon. Are you ready to eat some turkey?"

After getting detoured by a wildflower that caught his nephew's attention halfway to the house, they made their way inside. The smells that greeted them had his mouth watering. His mom had been a good cook, but he was pretty sure his sister was better.

"Oh, good. You guys are back," she said upon their arrival. "Could you help bring everything to the table?"

They were setting the last of the food out when there was a knock on the door. "I'll get it."

Kyle jogged to open it.

On the other side stood Cindy and Sadie.

He smiled. "You're right on time."

Dinner went off without a hitch. It took a while for Cindy to relax, but eventually she joined in on the conversation.

Throughout the meal, Janey kept putting a hand on his thigh. It was distracting, but then he realized why she was doing it and it wasn't to get his libido going. Noah was sitting next to Ava, and every now and then his friend and his sister would share a look that made Kyle distinctly uncomfortable. He kept trying to tell himself there wasn't anything beyond friendship between Noah and Ava, but if he was honest with himself, he wasn't so sure of that. Still, he wasn't ready to think about it.

Apparently, he wasn't as good at keeping his feelings to himself as he thought because Janey leaned over and whispered in his ear. "Your sister could do worse."

She was right. Ava could do worse. A lot worse.

Kyle took her hand under the table and laced their fingers together. He brought her hand up to his mouth and placed a kiss along her knuckles. She really was the best thing that had ever happened to him.

They finished eating and Ava brought out the pies. Even though he was stuffed, there was no way he was passing up some of his sister's pie.

"You ready to get back to work tomorrow?" Noah asked Janey as he tucked into a slice of pumpkin pie piled high with whipped cream.

"More than ready."

Noah grinned around his mouthful of pie.

As they were finishing up, Kyle got his nephew's attention. He whispered a reminder to Cole, and then sat back and waited.

The little boy ran out of the room. Less than a minute later, he returned carrying Janey's purse.

He took it to Janey, handing it to her.

"Thank you," she said, confused as to why Cole brought her purse to her.

"Look. Inside." His little voice was confident.

Janey glanced around the table at all the adults. Kyle was doing his best to keep a straight face. Ava shrugged.

Cole stood there waiting while she opened her purse, and then took off to go play again as if nothing had happened.

As soon as she slid the zipper open, he heard her suck in a breath. "What's this?"

Inside her purse was a note and a small box. She removed the note first.

"What is it?" his sister asked.

"A note."

Everyone was paying attention. Even Cindy. "What's it say?"

Janey cleared her throat and began reading the note.

Janey,

The first time I saw you, I knew you were someone special, but even I didn't know how special. You've changed my life for the better and now I can't imagine it without you.

You moved your entire life here to be with me and I want you to know how much that means to me. I want to share everything with you. My life. My love. My future.

Kyle

She met his gaze, moisture glistening in her eyes.

"Open the box," he whispered.

Janey removed the small box from her purse and flipped the lid open. She sucked in a breath as she stared at the ring.

His chair scraped against the floor as he got down on one knee and took her hand. "Janey Davis, will you marry me?"

She blinked several times before her lips pulled up into a smile and she nodded.

Kyle released a shaky breath. "You had me worried for a minute there."

Janey chuckled. "Had to make you work for it."

He snorted and then crushed his mouth to hers for a hard kiss. "I love you."

"I love you, too."

Removing the ring from the box, he slipped it onto her finger. Janey looked at it for a moment, and then back to him. "This is what you and Cole were conspiring about yesterday?"

He just smiled.

"Sneaky."

Ava rushed over to hug Janey and get a closer look the ring. He'd kept it simple, wanting her to be able to wear it when she was working.

It didn't matter, though. His sister oohed and aahed over it while Noah came over to pat him on the back. "I was wondering how long it would be until you popped the question."

Cindy joined Ava and Janey, commenting on how lovely the ring was. Every now and then Janey would glance his way, a huge smile on her face. His chest felt as if it might explode with the joy he felt seeing her so happy. They had forever in front of them and he couldn't wait to see what came next.

***

Make sure you don't miss any of Sherri's new releases. Sign up HERE to be added to Sherri's email list.

READY FOR MORE EVERYDAY HEROES? Click HERE to purchase your copy of BURNING FOR HER KISS and start reading today!

CAN'T WAIT FOR SHERRI HAYES' NEXT BOOK?

Let her know by leaving a review and telling her what you liked about
BOYS IN BLUE: EVERYDAY HEROES

Beth Davenport has no interest in getting involved with another man for the foreseeable future. To say her last relationship ended in disaster would be a colossal understatement. The only reason she agrees to put in an appearance at Serpent's Kiss, a private kink club in downtown St. Louis, is because her best friend, Nicole, won't quit nagging her. When she walks in the door that night, the last thing she expects to do is meet a man who will have her reconsidering her ban on men.

As a captain with the St. Louis Fire Department, Drew Parker is used to being in charge. His crew relies on him to make sure they know what they're doing and return home to their families after every shift. It isn't, however, what he wants in a relationship. Drew decides to join Serpent's Kiss to see if what appeals to him in fantasy is something he wants to explore in the real world. He's also hoping that he'll be lucky enough to meet a woman with whom he can explore his desires. The night Beth walks into the club, he is intrigued. Drew has to get to know her better.

After what happened to her, Beth is reluctant to get involved with Drew. It doesn't matter that he is sweet and charming. She's been burned before and Beth doesn't think she can survive having her heart crushed again. Drew, however, won't take no for an answer. He wants a relationship and is determined to chip away at her defenses until she relents. Will she give him a chance, or did her ex leave her with scars too deep to heal?

Click HERE to purchase your copy and start reading today!

Drew Parker had finally drummed up the courage to come to Serpent's Kiss by himself four weeks ago. He'd been anxious about walking into a kink club. The idea of going alone terrified him. In the end, after a lot of internal arguments, he'd done it. He'd made the leap into the unknown.

In the months leading up to his first trip to the club, Drew attended a few local munches. That had been daunting in and of itself. He hadn't known what to expect, but the people were more welcoming than he'd thought they'd be—especially John and his mistress, Allison. They seemed to sense his need for guidance and had taken him under their wing, so to speak.

It was through John and Allison that Drew found out about the club. Serpent's Kiss was a private club in the heart of downtown St. Louis. On the outside, it appeared to be an old warehouse. No one would know it was a BDSM club unless they paid close attention to the people who came and went on Friday and Saturday nights.

With the help of his new friends, he was introduced to the club and its owner, Mistress Katrina. Drew was a little surprised a woman owned and ran a kink club. He wasn't sure why, but he'd just assumed a man would be in charge. The joke was on him, however. If he'd ever been in doubt as to his submissive tendencies, they'd disappeared after his interview with Mistress Katrina. The moment she began questioning him from behind that big wooden desk, her tone of voice changed and he felt his heart pick up its pace. She seemed to get a kick out of his reaction, and after a few more questions, she'd shown him around the club.

While Mistress Katrina's dominant nature got his blood pumping, that was where his reaction to her ended. There was no physical attraction. He was confident part of that was because the dungeon mistress was a busty blonde. He preferred leggy brunettes with a little extra cushion in the back end.

Thinking of his first meeting with the club's mistress made him squirm in his seat. She was certainly nothing like he'd expected her to be. Then again, most of the Dommes he'd met weren't what he'd expected. Allison was a perfect example. The Dommes he'd seen in online videos barked orders at their submissives, and seemed to take pleasure in humiliating them at every turn. Allison was nice. Drew had no doubt that, if pushed, she could be hard as nails, but she'd been nothing but pleasant to him. She'd even offered to do a scene with Drew if he wanted. Although it was tempting, he wasn't sure if he was ready for that step yet. For the time being, he was content to watch. Everything was still so new to him.

To be honest, Drew was relieved to discover not all Dommes were like the ones he'd seen online. While he wanted his lover to be in control in the bedroom, public humiliation wasn't on his list of desires. He wanted to serve his partner—to worship her body and mind. Meeting Allison and John gave him hope.

As Drew glanced around the main room, he spotted some familiar faces. It was a typical night. The main room was scattered with people talking and sipping on drinks. Submissives were in various stages of undress. Some were on leashes kneeling on the floor next to their masters or mistresses. Others were sitting beside or on top of their master's or mistress' laps. Mistress Katrina was near the bar talking to a male Dom and his female sub. Drew recognized both of them, but he didn't know their names.

There were also a handful of people Drew had met at the munches he'd attended. While he'd met a few others since coming to the club, the atmosphere was different. Munches were for socializing. Serpent's Kiss was for playing.

The club was divided into sections, which was one of the things Drew liked the most. There were plenty of seating areas scattered around the main floor, as well as a bar along one wall, a small dance floor, and a raised platform. He'd been told the platform was used for demonstrations, but he'd yet to witness one of those since he'd been a member. As for kinky play, very little beyond the occasional spanking or some other light impact play occurred in the main room. Everything else took place upstairs.

A couple of weeks ago, he'd drummed up the courage to climb the stairs and take a look around. The upstairs rooms looked completely different with people in them than they had when Mistress Katrina had shown him around during the club's off hours. The sounds alone charged the atmosphere.

Although Drew didn't consider himself a voyeur, he couldn't help himself. He was drawn into watching some of the scenes. Most of the items in the rooms were things he'd seen online in his initial research into the lifestyle. Some of them appealed to him. Some of them didn't.

Drew had the desire to submit to a mistress, but he wasn't looking for just the physical aspects of submission. Maybe that sounded cheesy, but he'd done the whole sex-only thing in the vanilla world. There was physical gratification, yes, but he'd never truly felt connected to a woman before. Drew knew part of that was his desire to give up control to his partner. He was twenty-eight, and he wanted someone he could share his life with.

As a firefighter, he saw death and tragedy on a regular basis. He didn't want to wake up ten years into the future and still be searching for someone who could give him what he needed. That was why he'd decided to plunge headfirst into this new lifestyle instead of dragging his feet in the regular dating pool. Even still, Drew knew it was going to be an uphill battle. There were more male subs than there were female dominants. Even at the club, there were five male Doms to every one Domme. But as his new friend John had reminded him on multiple occasions, if Drew didn't put himself out there, he'd never find the woman he was searching for.

Drew watched as John sat at his mistress' feet with his head in her lap. It wasn't demeaning in any way. It was affectionate, and Drew wanted that for himself.

Allison moved, getting John's attention. "Get me a drink, my boy."

John was swiftly on his feet. "What would you like, Mistress?"

That was the last of their exchange Drew heard because his attention had shifted to the door. He vaguely registered John leaving the cozy sitting area, but Drew was too focused on the woman who'd walked through the club's main entrance.

The new arrival surveyed the room. From the way she was carrying herself, Drew was almost positive she was a Domme. If he was being honest with himself, he was hoping she was a Domme. Whether she was or not remained to be seen.

She looked to be about five foot six or seven, but the black heels she had on added a good three to four inches to her stature. Her long hair was pulled up into a high ponytail and looked almost black in the dim club lighting. The black corset and jeans she wore accented her curves to the point where Drew was afraid he might be drooling.

Only a few seconds passed before the woman strolled with confidence over to the bar and ordered a drink. Drew continued to stare. She chatted with the bartender for several minutes, even after he'd handed the woman her drink. Drew didn't recognize the woman as anyone who'd been to the club since he'd joined, but the bartender seemed to know her. Of course, that didn't mean anything. For all Drew knew, the mystery woman and the bartender lived next door to each other. Then again, this was a private club. In order to be here, she had to be a member. Especially since she'd come alone.

Drew's eyes followed the woman as she headed to a booth across the room. She sat down with another group of people similar to the one he was with. He recognized most of them. They were all regulars.

Abruptly, John sat down next to him on the couch having returned with his mistress' drink. "I wouldn't get your hopes up."

Drew reluctantly pulled his gaze away from the woman. "What?"

"Don't *what* me. You're staring at Lady Beth."

Then what John said registered. "What do you mean I shouldn't get my hopes up? She is a Domme, right?"

"Oh yes, definitely a Domme."

"She doesn't like male subs?"

"She does." John drew out the two words, and Drew knew there was a 'but' coming.

He sighed, frustrated. "Then what's the issue?"

John lowered his voice to a whisper so no one around them could hear the information he was about to disclose. Drew doubted his friend would tell him anything ninety percent of the club didn't already know, but he decided to play along. One of the first things Drew learned was that word traveled fast in the small community—especially if it was something bad. "She used to come here all the time with her sub, Ben. They'd been together for years, from what I heard, before Mistress and I began getting involved in local events. Then, three months ago, they both suddenly stopped coming. To the club. To munches. Everything."

Drew couldn't help himself. He was intrigued. "What happened?"

"Ben traveled a lot for his business. Sometimes he was out of town for weeks at a time going to all sorts of places. Apparently, his trips weren't business related. At least, not completely. Lady Beth found out he had a wife and daughter in Florida."

"That's insane. It's like something you hear on TV." Drew shook his head, trying to digest the information he'd received.

"I know. He'd lied to her the entire time."

Drew's gaze drifted back to Lady Beth. He couldn't imagine what it would be like to have trust broken in such a way.

John's voice pulled Drew out of his musings. "I don't know if she's ready to dive back into a relationship, man, and I know that's what you want."

It was true. Drew did want a relationship, but he was willing to work for it. One step at a time, right? So the first thing he had to do was find a way to introduce himself.

***

Beth Davenport tried to ignore all the stares she received when she entered the club. It had been three months since she'd stepped foot inside Serpent's Kiss. She knew showing up would mean she'd be the hot topic of gossip for the evening. Her best friend and fellow Domme, Nicole, had warned her about the rumors floating around. They were surprisingly accurate as far as rumors went except no one knew how Beth had come to find out about Ben's lies. Only Nicole knew the whole truth, and Beth wanted to keep it that way.

Domme or not, finding out a large portion of the life you'd been living for the last three years was a lie left Beth broken in a lot of ways. She wasn't even sure why she'd come to the club. Oh, that's right. It was Nicole's hounding over the last two weeks. Nicole had insisted three months was enough moping.

Every Friday afternoon for the last month, Nicole had called Beth asking if she was going to put in an appearance at Serpent's Kiss. Each time, Beth had weaseled out of it. Her friend had even enlisted Katrina's help more than once.

The club mistress was a formidable woman in her late forties. She'd been married to a man who wanted no part in her kinky ways. Beth didn't know her back then, but the way the story went was that at forty-four, her husband was diagnosed with a rare form of cancer. He'd died within two months. The sudden change in Katrina's life prompted her to take stock. Six months later, she opened Serpent's Kiss.

While Beth admired Katrina and her take-the-bull-by-the-horns attitude, Beth wasn't sure she was ready to be back at the club. Unfortunately, when Katrina had put her on the spot, Beth hadn't been able to say no. Both Katrina and Nicole had been incredibly supportive after what had happened with Ben. While Beth had no desire to put herself back out into the dating world—it was the last thing she wanted at the moment—Nicole and Katrina had convinced her that she needed to get out and mingle. She had friends here, and it wasn't right for her to turn her back on them because Ben had been a class-A jerk.

So here she was, sitting with Nicole and a group of their friends. Beth was the only Dominant in their group without a sub. It was a little awkward, but she tried to ignore it and have a good time. Nicole was right about one thing, Beth had missed her friends. She wasn't going to let what Ben did tarnish that.

"I think you have an admirer," Nicole whispered in Beth's ear, jarring her from her thoughts.

"What?"

Nicole scooted closer to her. "There's a guy across the room that hasn't been able to take his eyes off you for the last fifteen minutes. I'd say he's interested."

Beth didn't even bother to look. "I'm not."

"Oh, come on. He's hot, and I happen to know he's a sub."

"That doesn't change anything. I'm not ready to get back into the dating pool again."

Her friend rolled her eyes. "Well, you don't have to date him, you know."

She shook her head. "I'm not into playing with random subs and you know it. Even if I was, I don't think I could even do that after everything."

Nicole frowned. "You have to get back on the horse sometime."

Beth sighed in defeat. "I know. Maybe in a month or so—"

Her friend placed a hand on her arm, stopping Beth mid-sentence. "I don't think he's going to wait a month or so. He's coming over."

"What do you mean he's coming over? Here?"

Nicole nodded and turned back to their group, effectively leaving Beth to fend for herself. Taking a deep breath, Beth prepared herself for whatever line this guy was going to try to sell her.

Her heart pounded as she felt him drawing closer, but Beth refused to show any outward signs that she was aware of the man. It would only encourage him.

To her surprise, instead of coming over and trying to sweet-talk her, the guy sat down in the chair to her right and said nothing. It was odd to be sure, but since she wasn't interested in the slightest anyway, Beth decided to ignore him and refocus on her friends' conversation. Maybe he'd eventually get the idea and go away. Or maybe she was only being paranoid and he didn't walk across the room for her at all.

Ignoring him turned out to be more difficult than Beth originally thought. Although he didn't attempt to engage her in conversation, she felt his presence beside her. Even with her eyes purposely averted, Beth knew he wasn't a small man. She'd seen enough in her peripheral vision to know he was tall and nicely proportioned.

No matter how aware she was of his presence, Beth outwardly ignored him. That was until she finished off her drink. She scooted forward in her seat, preparing to head to the bar for a refill, but he moved, too, inevitably drawing her attention. "May I, ma'am?"

Beth tilted her head to look at him for the first time, and all the moisture seemed to disappear from her throat. Cute did not begin to describe the man sitting next to her. He was tall and lean, but she wouldn't call him lanky with his broad shoulders and muscled arms. His hair was a light brown and he was clean-shaven, but it was his eyes that drew her in. They were the most amazing baby blue.

When she didn't respond, he repeated his question. "May I get you a refill on your drink, ma'am?"

"Y-yes." Then, catching herself, she spoke again with more confidence. "Um. No. Thank you. I don't know you from Adam."

He extended his hand. "Drew Parker."

She raised an eyebrow.

"Allison and John will vouch for me. No funny business. I promise." He tilted his head toward another Femdom, Allison, and her longtime boyfriend and sub, John. Beth knew them both, although not well.

Beth waited until Allison looked in her direction, and gave her a questioning look. Allison smiled and nodded.

Reluctantly, Beth handed her glass to the man sitting beside her.

"What would you like?" he asked.

"The bartender knows. Just tell him it's for Beth." Her answer came out more clipped than usual. She wanted him to take his leave as quickly as possible before she went and did something stupid. Beth kept her gaze on him as he walked away. Her stomach was doing flip-flops and she didn't like it one bit.

He returned a few minutes later and handed her a small glass filled with half Coke and half Sprite. Beth rarely drank alcohol, and never at the club. Whenever she came to Serpent's Kiss, she was either playing with Ben or she was alone where she'd have to drive home. Either way, she didn't drink.

After taking the glass from Drew, she turned back to her friends, effectively ignoring her unwanted admirer once more. Nicole had a knowing smirk on her face that Beth desperately wished she could wipe off. Maybe she could borrow one of the club's floggers. It had been a while since she'd thrown one, and she had to admit the thought of having the leather in her hands again was appealing.

For the next hour, Drew continued to sit beside her in silence as she chatted with her friends. Everyone in their small group brought Beth up to date on what was going on in their lives. Meanwhile, her new admirer said nothing. And although he did little more than sit there, he was making her uneasy. Every one of her nerve endings seemed to be aware of him.

Finally, Beth couldn't take it any longer and turned to face him. "I don't know what you're looking for, but let me spell out exactly what I'm *not* looking for. I'm not looking for a submissive and I don't play with random partners."

"I understand." His voice was smooth, and it sent tingles down her spine. This was not good.

She quirked an eyebrow at him. "You understand?"

"Yes, ma'am."

Beth waited for him to leave, but he remained where he was. "So if you know I'm not looking for a relationship or a play partner then why are you sitting here?"

"I'd like to get to know you, if you're agreeable." He sounded sincere.

"You want to be friends?" she asked.

"Yes, ma'am."

"Why?"

He shrugged. "You seem interesting."

Beth gave him a hard look trying to decide if he was telling the truth or not. She never used to question her judgment, but after Ben, everything was different. "Do you have a mistress?"

"No, ma'am. I'm pretty new to the lifestyle."

"How new?"

"A few months." His gaze never left hers.

"Have you ever played with a Femdom before?" Why she was asking was beyond her. It wasn't as if she ever planned on playing with him.

"No, ma'am."

Again, she had no idea why she was pressing for information, but the questions kept coming to the forefront of her mind and she kept asking them. "No vanilla girl out there for you?"

"I've tried vanilla relationships and they don't work for me. I want a woman to take control."

The image of him tied to a bench completely at her mercy flashed in her mind before she squashed it. No. She would not go down that path.

If he wanted to be friends, she could try, she supposed. But there would have to be ground rules—no seeing him outside the club being the number one. She had no idea if he frequented the local munches or not. If so, she would have to be careful. Munches were more laid back. That could open up a whole new set of problems—especially since she was already having a physical reaction to him.

Theirs would have to be a lifestyle friendship only. If Drew had questions about BDSM or needed help finding a Domme, she could maybe give him advice. That was it, though. Beth wasn't ready to get tangled up in another web of emotional attachment.

Taking a deep breath, she offered her hand, and introduced herself. "I'm Beth. Beth Davenport."

He wrapped his fingers around hers almost reverently. "It's nice to meet you, Beth Davenport."

Click HERE to purchase your copy and start reading today!

Strictly Professional

A Christmas Proposal

<u>Box Sets</u>

Finding Anna Boxed Set (Books 1-4)

Daniels Brothers Box Set (Books 1-4)

Boys In Blue: Everyday Heroes

ABOUT THE AUTHOR

Sherri picked up her first romance novel when she was twelve and immediately she was hooked. She would stay up reading long after everyone else in her house had gone to bed, needing to see the hero and heroine get their happily ever after. But Sherri never imagined becoming an author.

At the age of thirty, all that changed. After getting frustrated with the direction a television show was taking two of its characters, Sherri decided to try her hand at writing an alternative ending to give the characters the happy ending they deserved.

Since then, writing has become a creative outlet that allows her to explore a wide range of emotions, while having fun taking her characters through all the twists and turns she can create.

facebook.com/SherriHayesAuthor

amazon.com/Sherri-Hayes/e/B004MIO9O4?ref=sr_ntt_s-rch_lnk_1&sr=8-1

bookbub.com/authors/sherri-hayes